MW00983734

PENDRAGON

JOURNAL OF AN ADVENTURE THROUGH TIME AND SPACE

Book Three:
The Never War

Book Four:
The Reality Bug

PEⅡDRAGOⅡ

JOURNAL OF AN ADVENTURE THROUGH TIME AND SPACE

PENDRAGON

JOURNAL OF AN ADVENTURE THROUGH TIME AND SPACE

Book Three:
The Never War

Book Four:
The Reality Bug

By D. J. MacHale

Aladdin Paperbacks
New York London Toronto Sydney

This book is a work of fiction. Any references to historical events, real people, or real locales are used fictitiously. Other names, characters, places, and incidents are the product of the author's imagination, and any resemblance to actual events or locales or persons, living or dead, is entirely coincidental.

ALADDIN PAPERBACKS
An imprint of Simon & Schuster Children's Publishing Division
1230 Avenue of the Americas, New York, NY 10020
Pendragon: The Never War and *Pendragon: The Reality Bug*
copyright © 2003 by D. J. MacHale
These works were previously published
individually by Aladdin Paperbacks.
All rights reserved, including the right of reproduction in whole or in part in any form.
ALADDIN PAPERBACKS and colophon are registered trademarks of Simon & Schuster, Inc.
Designed by Debra Sfetsios
The text of this book was set in Apollo and Helvetica.
Manufactured in the United States of America
This Aladdin Paperbacks edition June 2005
2 4 6 8 10 9 7 5 3 1
ISBN-13: 978-1-4169-1225-5
ISBN-10: 1-4169-1225-8

PENDRAGON

JOURNAL OF AN ADVENTURE THROUGH TIME AND SPACE

Book Three:
The Never War

This is for my dad.

FIRST EARTH

That's where I am. First Earth. Veelox was a misdirection. Spader and I flumed to Veelox, but found the action wasn't there. It was here on First Earth.

Where is First Earth? The better question is, *when* is First Earth? I'm in New York City and it's 1937. March of 1937 to be exact. To be *really* exact, it's March 11 of 1937. I'm writing this on my birthday. Here's a weird thought: If I'm in 1937 and it's my birthday, did I still turn fifteen? Kind of freaky, no?

I'll begin this new journal by telling you I stumbled into the most bizarro, confusing, dangerous situation yet. But then again, haven't I said that before? Let me give you a little taste of what happened in only the first few minutes since I got here. . . .

Spader and I were nearly killed. Three times. We were also robbed and witnessed a gruesome murder. Happy birthday to me! The way things are going, I know what I want for my fifteenth birthday . . . the chance to have a sixteenth.

When Spader and I flumed in from Veelox, I had no idea of what "First Earth" meant. Since I'm from Second Earth, I could only guess that First Earth was sometime in the Earth's past. But how far past? For all I knew we were fluming back to a time when quigs were dinosaurs and we'd be on the run from hungry, yellow-eyed raptors.

I was totally relieved to find that when we landed at the gate, it was the exact same rocky room that I had been through many times before. Yes, we had arrived at the gate off the subway tunnel in the Bronx, New York. Phew. At least there were no T-rexes or Neanderthals waiting for us. That was the good news.

Bad news was that we weren't alone. As soon as the flume dropped us off, I saw two guys standing there, facing us. They wore old-fashioned gray suits, like Clark Kent wears in the old *Superman* show on TV Land. Actually, a better analogy is that these guys were dressed like the *bad guys* from that old show, because that's what they were. Bad guys. *Very* bad guys. They wore wide-brimmed hats that were pulled down low and had white handkerchiefs around their noses and mouths like banditos. There's only one word to describe these dudes.

Gangsters.

Their eyes looked wide and scared. No big surprise. They had just seen Spader and me drop out of nowhere in an explosion of light and music. They seemed totally stunned, which was good because there was one other detail I haven't mentioned. . . .

They were both holding machine guns that were aimed at the flume—and at us.

"Down!" I yelled at Spader.

The two of us jumped to opposite sides of the flume just as the gangsters started shooting. I crouched in a ball, totally unprotected as the deadly clatter from their rapid-fire guns echoed off the rocky walls. I thought for sure I'd get hit, but after a few seconds the shooting stopped, and I was still intact. I was afraid to move and even more afraid to look over and see if Spader was okay. The sharp explosions fell off to a distant echo that bounced around the cavelike room. My ears were ringing and the chemical smell of gunpowder burned my nose. I figured this was what it must be like to be in a war.

"Get up!" one of the gangsters ordered. "Hands in the air!"

I cautiously looked over to Spader and saw that he was okay. We stood slowly and raised our hands. The gangsters held their guns on us. I didn't know why. It wasn't like we had weapons of our own. The second gangster kept glancing nervously between the two of us. He looked almost as scared as we were. Almost.

"Th-They from Mars?" he asked his buddy nervously.

Under less terrifying circumstances, I would have laughed. It must have looked like we had just landed from outer space. Not only did we flash in through a storm of light, we were still dressed in our bright blue swimskins from Cloral. For a second I thought about pulling a huge bluff and chanting: "Drop your weapons or we will vaporize you with our mind-heat," or something equally sci-fi, but I didn't get the chance.

"Don't matter," barked the other gangster. He was definitely the one in charge, but I could tell from his voice that he was a little shaky too.

"We done our job," he added.

"S-So what about th-them?" the nervous gangster asked.

The guy in charge looked us over. I could almost hear the wheels turning in his brain. He didn't exactly seem like a rocket scientist, so they must have been very small wheels. I wondered if they hurt when they turned.

"You!" the guy barked at me. "Gimme that ring!"

I couldn't believe it. He wanted my Traveler ring! This was serious. You guys know how badly I need that ring. It shows me where the flumes are, and it's the only way I can get my journals to you. Without this ring, I'm lost.

"It's not worth anything," I said in a feeble attempt to talk him out of it.

"Don't matter," the gangster snapped back at me. "All I want is proof to show you two are real."

"Then take us with you, mates!" said Spader, trying to be friendly. "We're all the proof you need, in the flesh!"

"Those ain't my orders," he snarled.

"Really? What *are* your orders?" I asked.

"Just hand over the ring," the boss commanded. He raised his machine gun to prove he meant business. What could I do? I took off my ring and tossed it to him. He caught it and jammed it into his pocket.

"Let's step outside, nice and easy," the guy said.

This was good. It meant they weren't going to gun us down right that moment. Maybe there was a way out of this after all. The nervous gangster threw the wooden door open, then both stepped aside and motioned with their weapons for us to go through. I looked at Spader. Spader shrugged. We had to play along. With our hands up, we both stepped out of the gate and into the dark subway tunnel.

Everything was familiar, so I made a sharp right, knowing it was the way to the abandoned subway station.

But the gangster had other things in mind. "No, you don't," he ordered. "Keep walking."

We had to walk straight ahead, away from the door. Three steps later we stepped over the rail of the subway track. This was beginning to look bad again.

"Stop! Turn around."

Oh yeah, this was bad. We were both now standing on the train tracks.

"You move, you die," said the first gangster.

Yeah, right. We move, we die. If a train comes along, we *don't* move, we die. Not a lot of wiggle room here.

"Where are we, Pendragon?" whispered Spader.

His answer came in the form of a far off whistle. We both looked to our right and saw the headlight of a subway train rounding the bend, headed our way, on our track.

"What is that thing?" asked Spader nervously. Being from a territory that was covered entirely with water, he had never seen anything like a train before.

"That," I said, trying not to let my voice show the fear that was tearing at my gut, "is a pretty big tum-tigger."

"Hobey," said Spader in awe. "We just got here and we've already lost."

We had been on First Earth for all of two minutes, and we were staring death right in the eye.

Welcome home, Bobby Pendragon.

That's a taste of how our adventure on First Earth began. I don't want to get too far ahead because there was a whole lot that happened between the time I finished my last journal, and when we landed here. But I wanted to explain to you how I lost my ring. This is serious because as I write this journal to you, Mark and Courtney, I'm not really sure if you're ever going to read it. If I don't get that ring back, I'll never be able to send this to you. The only thing I can do is keep writing, hang on to the journals, and hope that I get the ring back soon.

Now, let me rewind to where I finished my last journal and get you guys back up to speed.

I spent my last few days on the territory of Cloral in a haze. We'd defeated Saint Dane, but I didn't feel much like celebrating. That's because Uncle Press was gone, and I kept replaying his last moments over and over in my head. Saint Dane had escaped through a flume and Spader tried to chase him. But a storm of bullets came back at him. Uncle Press realized what was happening, knocked Spader out of the way . . . and took the bullets himself.

He died in my arms. It was the absolute worst moment of my life. The only thing that kept me from totally losing it was that just before he died, he promised me we'd be together again. I know this sounds pretty loopy, but I believe him. If being a Traveler has taught me anything, it's that nothing is impossible. My eyes have been opened to so many new worlds and levels of existence that the idea of hooking up with Uncle Press again doesn't seem all that far-fetched.

Of course, I have no clue how it might happen. That's because I've only scratched the surface of knowing all there is to know about being a Traveler. I wish there were an instruction manual I could buy through Amazon.com that would spell out all the rules and regulations. Unfortunately, it's not that easy. I've got to learn things as I go along. And now I've got to do it without Uncle Press.

Welcome to my life as a Traveler, phase two.

In those last days on Cloral, I knew what my next move had to be, but I was putting it off because, well, I was scared. Things were different now. I was alone. It was a whole new ballgame and I wasn't sure if I was good enough to play in it.

When Saint Dane flumed out of Cloral, he was headed for a territory called Veelox. I knew I had to follow him, but the idea of going after him alone was about as appealing as setting my hair on fire. All things being equal, I think I'd rather have set my hair on fire. So I made a decision that I hope I don't regret.

I asked Vo Spader to go with me.

Don't get me wrong, Spader is a great guy. He's the Traveler from Cloral, after all. He saved my life more than once; he's an incredible athlete; he's about as brave as can be; and most importantly, he's my friend. So why should I be worried about asking him to come with me?

It's because his total, blind hatred of Saint Dane is dangerous. Saint Dane caused the death of his father and for that, Spader wants revenge. Big time. Hey, I don't blame him. But there were a few times on Cloral where Spader got so completely wrapped up in Saint Dane—hating that he nearly got us all killed. Truth be told, Spader's anger toward Saint Dane is one of the reasons Uncle Press is dead.

Since then, Spader promised me he would control himself, and his anger. I can only hope that when we come face-to-face with the demon again, and I guarantee we will, Spader won't do anything stupid. These were some of the conflicted thoughts that were banging around inside my head as I finished my last journal.

"Hobey-ho, Pendragon," Spader said as he strode into my apartment the morning of our departure.

Spader had almond-shaped eyes that looked sort of Asian. They turned up slightly and made him look as if he were always smiling. The truth was, most of the time he *was* smiling . . . when he wasn't obsessing over Saint Dane, that is. His long black hair was still wet, which meant he had been in the water. Spader spent a lot of time in the water, playing traffic cop with the boats and barges that came and went from Grallion. He loved his job, and his life there. At least he loved it before he found out he was a Traveler. Things had changed a little since then.

"It's time," I said.

"For what?" was his quick response.

"Cloral is safe. Uncle Press is gone. And I'm as ready as I'll ever be to go after Saint Dane."

Spader gave me a devilish smile. "Now you're talking, mate! I've been waiting to hear those words for weeks! What if the trail's gone cold?"

"I don't think that's possible," I answered. "Uncle Press always said that time between territories isn't relative."

Spader frowned. "You lost me."

I had to laugh. This didn't make a whole lot of sense to me either, but I had to trust Uncle Press.

"Look at it this way," I explained. "Saint Dane flumed to Veelox a few weeks ago, but since then he may have spent five years there. Or a minute."

"Now I'm totally lost," Spader said in frustration.

"Bottom line is, we're not too late," I said. "It doesn't matter when we go after him, because the flume will put us where we need to be, *when* we need to be there."

"O-kay," said Spader tentatively. "I'll trust you on that."

I'd already said good-bye to our friends on Grallion, and I'd sent my last journal to you. I had explained the importance of journals to Spader and he had already started his own. The person he chose to send them to on Cloral for safekeeping was Wu Yenza. She was the chief aquaneer and Spader's boss. He couldn't have picked a better person.

I took a last look around my apartment. Then we went down to the docks, loaded our air globes and water sleds onto a skimmer boat, and left Grallion for the flume. Spader was the expert, so he drove. As we shot across the water I looked back at the giant, floating farm habitat of Grallion, wondering if I'd ever see it again. I liked Cloral. There were times when I actually had fun on that territory. It gave me hope that being a Traveler didn't mean I always had to live in a state of fear and confusion.

Now the question was, what lay ahead of us? Pretty much a state of fear and confusion. Great. Here we go again.

The trip to the flume was cake. We anchored the skimmer near the reef, popped on the air globes that allowed us to breathe underwater, triggered the water sleds, and quickly sank below the surface. We didn't run into any shark quigs either. I think that once Saint Dane is finished with a territory, the quigs no longer patrol the gates. Still, I wasn't taking any chances. As we sped through the water being pulled by the sleds, I kept glancing back to make sure nothing nasty was sneaking up on us to try and get a nibble.

I didn't relax until we shot under the shelf of rock that led to the gate. Following the glow from my ring, we quickly found the wide circle of light that led up and into the cavern that held the flume. Moments later we were standing together in the cavern, staring up at the dark flume tunnel that was cut into the rock wall high over our heads.

This was it. The last few seconds of calm.

Spader looked at me and smiled. "My heart's thumpin'."

So was mine. We were standing at the starting line and the gun was about to go off. Spader loved adventure. Me? I'd just as soon be home watching toons. Knowing Spader was nervous made me feel like I wasn't such a weenie after all.

He added, "We're in for another natty-do, aren't we, mate?"

"Yeah," I answered. "Pretty much."

"No use in wasting time here then," he said, sounding a lot braver than I felt.

"Yeah," I said. "We're on the wrong territory."

I stood straight, looked up to the dark hole of the flume, and shouted, *"Veelox!"*

The tunnel sprang to life. Shafts of bright light shot from deep inside. The familiar jumble of musical notes could be heard faintly at first, but quickly grew louder. They were coming to get us.

Spader turned to me and smiled. "Hobey-ho, Pendragon."

"Hobey-ho, Spader," I answered. "Let's go get him."

A second later we were swept up by the light and sound and pulled into the flume.

Next stop . . . Veelox.

◎ SECOND EARTH ◎

Mark Dimond and Courtney Chetwynde huddled together in the vault of the National Bank of Stony Brook, reading Bobby's journal from First Earth. It was a journal unlike any of the others Bobby had sent.

First off, the pages weren't loose. They were bound nicely into a book with a deep red cover. And the pages weren't hand-written. They were typed . . . on an old-fashioned typewriter. They knew it was a typewriter because the letters weren't all perfectly lined up and there were a ton of mistakes. Besides, they didn't have computers or printers back in 1937. This new journal was definitely a far cry from the pieces of rolled up parchment paper Bobby had written his first journals on.

The other difference was that Bobby usually sent only one journal at a time. When he finished writing one he'd send it, through his Traveler ring, to Mark's ring. But this time, sitting in front of Mark and Courtney were four journals. After reading what happened with the gangsters on First Earth, Mark and Courtney knew why.

Bobby's ring had been stolen.

The mysterious manner in which the journals arrived was further proof of that. Earlier that day, Mark had gotten a strange phone call from a lady at the National Bank of Stony Brook. She asked for Mark and Courtney to meet her at the bank to discuss something about a Mr. Robert Pendragon. That was all Mark needed to hear. He and Courtney were at that bank in half an hour.

When they arrived, they discovered that Bobby had rented a safe-deposit box at the bank in 1937. Bobby had left explicit instructions that the bank should contact Mark Dimond on this very date—August 21, Mark's fifteenth birthday.

When Mark and Courtney opened up the safe-deposit box, they found the four journals. They had been lying in that box for over sixty years.

This whole episode was another bizarre twist in an already incredible situation. Bobby Pendragon had mysteriously left their hometown of Stony Brook, Connecticut, with his Uncle Press almost nine months before. Since then his family had disappeared, and the journals began showing up. The only people who knew the truth were his best friends, Mark and Courtney. Bobby trusted them to take care of his journals in case he might need them again someday.

But more important, it seemed to both Mark and Courtney that writing these journals helped keep Bobby sane. He was now smack in the middle of an incredible adventure that had nothing less than the future of everything at stake. Writing the journals seemed like a perfect way for Bobby to help keep his head on straight, while everything around him was so twisted. Both knew that one day Bobby's adventure would take him home. But until then, the only thing they could do to help him on his quest was to read his journals, try to understand what he was going through, and keep them safe.

"We're closing," snapped Ms. Jane Jansen, the bank manager, making Mark and Courtney jump.

Ms. Jane Jansen had only just met the two, but she didn't seem to like them. She didn't seem to like much of anything. Her face was in a permanent state of pucker, like she had a lemon in her pocket that she was constantly sucking on.

"Oh, sorry," said Mark, as if he had been caught doing something wrong. "We were reading. Can we come back tomorrow?"

"Tomorrow's Sunday," snapped Ms. Jane Jansen. "And this isn't a library. You children have spent far too much time here already."

Courtney didn't like Ms. Jane Jansen's attitude. And she definitely didn't like being called a child, especially by such a prune.

"So if we can't read here, what are we supposed to do?" asked Courtney politely, trying not to let her distaste for the woman show through.

"The content of that box belongs to you," Ms. Jane Jansen said. "Do whatever you want with it."

"You mean, we can take it all home?" asked Mark.

"I said, whatever you want," said Ms. Jane Jansen impatiently.

"Why didn't you say that in the first place?" asked Courtney. "Or do you always provide such lousy service?"

Mark winced. He hated it when Courtney clicked into wise-ass mode.

Ms. Jane Jansen's eyes popped open wide. "Miss Chetwynde, I have been an employee of the National Bank of Stony Brook for over twenty years and I have always provided thorough and professional service."

"I'll be sure to include that in our report to your president," Courtney said. "That's what this is all about, you know. To test how bank employees deal with unusual situations. So far, you haven't exactly rolled with the punches, now have you, Ms. Jane Jansen?"

Ms. Jane Jansen's eyes grew wide. She suddenly turned all friendly and polite. "Well, uh, if you have any complaints I'd be more than happy to personally ensure your complete satisfaction."

"There *is* something," Courtney said. "If you'd be so kind, would you return the empty drawer to our safe-deposit box? We'll be taking the contents with us."

Ms. Jane Jansen clenched her teeth. It wasn't her job to clean up after people. But she sucked it up.

"Of course," she said with a big, phony smile. "I'd be happy to."

Mark quickly scooped up the four journals and stashed them in his backpack. He wanted to get out of there before Courtney got them into trouble.

"Th-Thanks," he said with sincere courtesy. "We'll get out of your hair now." He went for the door, pulling Courtney along with him.

"Thanks for all your help, ma'am," said Courtney sweetly. "You really put the *ass* in *ass*-istance."

Mark yanked Courtney out of the vault, leaving Ms. Jane Jansen with a twisted smile that actually looked painful. A minute later they rushed out of the gray bank building onto Stony Brook Avenue. Courtney was all smiles. Mark was angry.

"Are you crazy?" he yelled. "What if she threw us out of there? We could have lost the journals!"

"No way," assured Courtney. "You heard her. They belong to us. Besides, she deserved it. She treated us like a couple of turds."

"Yeah, well, some things are more important than your bruised ego," Mark muttered.

"You're right, Mark," Courtney said sincerely. "I'm sorry."

Mark nodded, then looked at Courtney and smiled. "She *did* deserve it."

The two burst out laughing. Now that their bank adventure was behind them, their thoughts turned to the important issue. After waiting for months, they had another journal from Bobby! Better, they had *four* journals. In Mark's pack was an entire new adventure. They wouldn't have to wait impatiently for new journals to show up. They had a full story in their hands.

"I don't know about you," said Mark, "but once I start reading again, I'm not going to want to stop."

"Agreed," said Courtney.

"Here's what I'm thinking. It's getting late. How about if we wait till tomorrow?"

"You're kidding!" protested Courtney.

"I'm serious. Tomorrow's Sunday. I'll come over to your house real early, like eight A.M. We'll go down to your father's workshop and won't come out until we're finished."

Courtney gave this some thought. "You promise not to read anything tonight?" she asked.

"Promise," Mark said, crossing his heart.

"Okay, cool," she said. "I'll make some sandwiches. You bring chips. We'll make it a marathon."

"Excellent. I'll bring the Dew, too," Mark said with excitement.

"Whatever." Courtney didn't do the Dew.

"This is gonna be great!" Mark shouted.

The next day at 8 A.M. sharp, Courtney's doorbell rang. Courtney's dad opened the door to see Mark standing there with a loaded grocery bag.

"Morning, Mark," he said through sleepy eyes. "Going on a picnic?"

"Uh . . . no," answered Mark. "Courtney and I are working on a school project in your basement. It's gonna take all day so we need provisions."

"Really?" said Mr. Chetwynde. "It's August."

"Right," said Mark, thinking fast. "Summer school."

"Courtney doesn't go to summer school."

"I know," Mark said, mentally kicking himself for being such a lousy, uncreative liar. "I do."

Mr. Chetwynde looked at Mark. Mark smiled innocently.

Mr. Chetwynde shrugged and yawned. "Whatever, c'mon in." He stepped aside and Mark rushed in.

Mark knew exactly where to go. He and Courtney had used Mr. Chetwynde's basement workshop as a private place to read Bobby's journals many times before. Mr. Chetwynde had set up an entire workshop down there and never used it. He was a lousy do-it-yourself type guy. Mark and Courtney could be there all day, even on a Sunday, and never worry about anybody coming down.

Mark settled into the big, dusty couch as Courtney ran down the stairs. "Sandwiches are in the fridge," she announced. "Ready when we need 'em."

She sat next to Mark on the couch as he pulled the four red-leather journals from his backpack. He put them down reverently on the low table in front of them. The two sat there, staring at the precious stack. Neither made a move to pick one up.

"This is kind of weird," Mark finally said.

"Really," agreed Courtney. "I'm excited and afraid at the same time. I'm dying to know what happened to Bobby, but what if it's bad?"

The two fell silent, staring at the books.

"There's something else," added Mark thoughtfully. "This whole *First* Earth thing makes me nervous."

"Why?" Courtney asked.

"It's like Saint Dane is coming closer. To us."

"You don't know that," Courtney said quickly.

"No, but Second Earth is a territory like all the others. One day Saint Dane is going to come here, too. And when he does, we're going to be doing more than just reading about it."

"Unless Bobby and the Travelers stop him first, right?" Courtney asked hopefully.

Mark didn't answer. He looked at the journals thoughtfully, then reached for the top one. "Let's just read, okay?"

Courtney took a breath to calm down, then said, "Let's try something different this time. We'll read out loud to each other."

Mark was secretly relieved. He was a faster reader than Courtney and always had to wait for her to catch up. This was the perfect solution.

"Yeah, that sounds good," he said, and handed her the journal. "You first."

Courtney took the journal and cracked open the cover. "We left off where Bobby and Spader flumed to Veelox, right?" she asked.

"Right," answered Mark. He sank back into the couch, put a hand behind his head, got comfortable and said, "Go for it."

Courtney turned to the page where they had left off the day before, and began to read out loud.

"A second later we were swept up by the light and sound and pulled into the flume. Next stop . . . Veelox."

FIRST EARTH

Flying through an interstellar tunnel across time and space was never a normal experience, but making the trip with somebody along for the ride kicked it a couple of notches higher on the strange meter.

"I could get used to this!" declared Spader as he did somersaults and flips, looking like an astronaut pulling zero g's.

I had to hand it to the guy—he knew how to have fun. Me? I was more interested in kicking back and looking out at the stars beyond the crystal walls. Whatever. To each his own.

We had only been sailing for a few minutes when the flume dumped us off again. Spader had been flying headfirst and barely had time to spin around and land on his feet. Once the light from the flume was sucked back into the tunnel and the musical notes left us, we found ourselves standing in . . .

Nothing. Seriously. It was pitch-black. I couldn't see an inch in front of my face.

"Whoa, Veelox is dark," Spader declared.

"Yeah, no kidding. Let's wait a second for our eyes to adjust."

They didn't. We stood there for two minutes, but the

place stayed just as inky black as when we landed.

"Get behind me," Spader ordered protectively. "I'll walk with my hand out until I hit—"

"Stop right there!" a voice boomed at us.

Uh-oh. We weren't alone. This had never happened before. Was it Saint Dane? Could the quigs on Veelox talk? Was unseen danger hurtling toward us at this very second?

"Back up," I said softly to Spader.

I took hold of his arm and was about to pull him back into the flume and get the hell out of there, when a light suddenly appeared, hovering in the air over our heads.

"You seeing this, mate?" Spader asked, his voice sounding shaky.

"Yeah," I answered, just as shaky.

The light grew larger. It was all soft and watery at first, but then suddenly snapped into sharp focus to reveal . . .

A girl. Actually, not a full girl. A girl's *head*. No kidding. Just a head. It was big, too. It floated over us like a huge Macy's Thanksgiving Day Parade balloon.

"Who are you?" the head demanded.

Her voice was loud, as though amplified. The girl-head looked normal enough. She had long blond hair tied back in a ponytail. Her eyes were blue, and she wore small, wire-rimmed glasses with yellow-tinted lenses. I'd even say she was cute, for a monster head, that is. She didn't look danger-ous, but then again, a giant floating head didn't exactly look normal, either.

"I'm Bobby Pendragon," I said to the head, trying to sound head-friendly.

"And my name's Vo Spader," Spader added. "Who are you?"

"I'll ask the questions!" boomed the head.

I felt like I was standing before the great and powerful

Wizard of Oz. With any luck, there'd be some befuddled old man hiding behind a curtain pulling on levers to control the big thing.

"Where do you come from?" demanded the head.

"I'm from Cloral," answered Spader. "My mate here is from Second Earth. Do you have a body to go with that head?"

The head suddenly dipped down toward us. We both hit the floor. For a second I thought she was going to take a bite.

"I said I'll ask the questions!" she roared.

"Sorry, mate," yelled Spader. "No worries. I'm with you now."

The head floated back higher without taking a chomp. Spader and I exchanged worried looks.

"Why did you come here?" asked the giant blonde girl-head thing.

"Spader and I are Travelers," I said. "We followed someone here. His name is—"

"Saint Dane isn't here now," the head announced.

Whoa. The head was a couple of steps ahead of us . . . no pun intended.

"Uhh, sorry to disagree," Spader said. "But he definitely came here from Cloral."

The big head rolled her eyes like we were annoying her, and said, "I didn't say he was *never* here. I said he's not here *now*. Weren't you listening?"

Spader and I shot each other looks. This was getting even stranger. We were talking to a big, floating, *obnoxious* head.

"Watch," the head said impatiently, as if she were talking to a couple of naughty children. "This happened a few minutes ago."

The head then disappeared. Just like that. It faded out like a movie. I began to wonder if it had really been there or if it were some kind of projection. We were in the dark again, in more ways than one. But not for long.

Another light began to grow. At first I thought the head was coming back, but what appeared right in front of us was another image entirely. It looked like the mouth of the flume! It was like a 3-D movie projected in space. Very cool. That started to explain the giant head. My guess was these guys on Veelox had some hot technology going on.

Spader backed off. "What is this, Pendragon?" he asked nervously.

"It's okay," I assured him. "I think it's like a movie."

"Oh," Spader said. "What's a movie?"

The image of the flume then came to life. Bright light shone from the mouth and the musical notes told us that somebody was about to arrive. And then this strange movie took an interesting turn.

Saint Dane stepped out of the flume.

"Hobey!" shouted Spader in surprise.

"It's okay," I assured him. "It's just pictures."

Saint Dane stood in the mouth of the projected flume. This may have been a hologram movie, but it sure looked real. His long gray hair cascaded over the shoulders of his dark suit, and his piercing blue eyes cut through me as if he were actually standing there. Saint Dane even gave us a wave, as if he knew we were watching him.

Even though I'm still trying to understand where we fit into this whole Traveler picture, there are a few things I know all too well. Mostly they have to do with our mission and with the guy who was standing before us in a hologram—Saint Dane.

Halla is in danger because of him. Halla is everything—every territory, every person, every thing, and every *time* that ever existed. I know, it doesn't make total sense to me, either, but that's what I've been told. Saint Dane is a Traveler who wants to control Halla. In a word, he is evil. But simply calling him evil is like saying Tiger Woods is a good golfer. Saint Dane is the Tiger Woods of bad. He enjoys causing pain and suffering. I've seen what he's capable of. It isn't pretty. If he gets his way and somehow takes control of Halla, well, I don't even want to think about that.

The only thing standing between Saint Dane and his wicked plans are the other Travelers. That's us. Every territory is reaching a critical turning point. Saint Dane is doing his worst to influence these important events so that each territory will fall into chaos. If he succeeds, then all of Halla will fall to him.

We've got to make sure he doesn't succeed.

So far we are 2 and 0. Denduron and Cloral were wins. But it's going to be a long war.

As we stood staring at the hologram of Saint Dane, every fear I had about the guy came screaming back. He was one bad dude. I watched as his recorded image turned back toward the flume.

"First Earth," he commanded.

An instant later the light and music swept him up and carried him into the tunnel. The image then faded out and the flume projection was gone. We were back in the dark.

"Now do you understand?" the girl-head's voice boomed out of the darkness. "He was here. He left. End of story. Now go away."

"Who are you?" I called out to the girl-head. "Why should we believe that?"

Another hologram appeared before us. It was the same view of the flume as before. Again, the tunnel activated with light and music. Who was going to arrive this time? A second later Spader and I watched as . . .

Spader and I stepped out of the flume in the hologram!

"I've gone totally off my nut," Spader said in awe.

"Whoa, Veelox is dark," the projection of Spader declared.

"Yeah, no kidding," the projection of me said. "Let's wait a second for our eyes to adjust."

It was exactly what had happened a minute before.

"My name is Aja Killian," boomed the head voice as our holograms disappeared.

Spader and I spun around to see the big head had returned. It hovered over us like a blond cloud.

"I'm the Traveler from Veelox," she said. "I've got the flume monitored and I record everything that happens. That's why I know Saint Dane isn't here anymore. Any more questions?"

"Yes," I said. "Would you please stop with this giant-head thing and show yourself? If you're a Traveler, then we're all friends here."

I was feeling a little more bold now, and getting tired of staring up at this girl.

"I would," Aja answered. "But I'm nowhere near you."

Spader said, "So you're telling us that Saint Dane flumed in here for a second, then flumed right back out again?"

"I'm not telling you," she said curtly. "I just *showed* you. Don't you believe what you see?"

Spader looked at me and asked softly, "Why did he leave so fast?"

"Because he's wasting his time here," Aja answered quickly. "Veelox is totally under control."

I laughed and said, "Yeah, that's what I thought about Cloral, until people started turning up dead."

"Look," the Aja-head scolded. "Nobody comes or goes through the flume without my knowing. He's not here. So go chase him to First Earth where you can be more useful."

Spader and I shared looks. "I guess she told *you*!" he said with a raised eyebrow.

I looked back up at the Aja-head and said, "If you think he's dumb enough to be controlled by your little home movies, then you're not as smart as you think you are."

That seemed to strike a chord. The big head floated down closer to us and stared me right in the eye. It took all I could do not to back off.

"And what makes *you* the expert on all things Saint Dane?" she asked with disdain.

"I'm not," I answered. "But I've battled him twice and both times been lucky enough to win. How about you?"

Aja-head blinked. I don't think she liked being challenged. She floated back up higher.

"If you take him on alone, you'll lose," added Spader. "He won't get spooked by a big floating head . . . like us."

"I'll try to remember that," she said sarcastically.

Aja Killian was the Traveler from Veelox, and she thought she was smarter than Saint Dane. That was dangerous. I knew we'd be back on Veelox sooner or later. I just hoped that when that time came, we wouldn't have to fight both Saint Dane *and* Aja Killian.

"Go to First Earth," Aja-head scolded. "Have fun, play your little games. Don't worry about Veelox."

With that, the giant head disappeared. Spader and I were once again alone.

"Fun?" Spader said. "I can think of a lot of things to call the tum-tigger we're headed into. Fun isn't one of them."

"Should we believe her?" I asked.

"I'm not sure we have a whole lot of choice," Spader answered. "Looks like Saint Dane came here to throw us off, and the big-head girl caught him."

"Then we're on the wrong territory, again." I said.

"He went to First Earth," Spader said. "That anything like Second Earth?"

"I think we're about to find out."

The two of us then stepped into the mouth of the flume.

First Earth.

Being from Second Earth I couldn't help but think I would be going home. At least that was what I hoped. I didn't know that we were about to flume into the laps of two murderous gangsters who were waiting for us with machine guns.

Yes, the real fun was about to begin.

FIRST EARTH

"You're lucky," Mr. Nasty Gangster chuckled. "It'll be quick. You won't feel a thing."

"How would *you* know?" asked Spader nervously.

The two gangsters held their machine guns on us, keeping us from moving off the subway track. To our right, a subway train was barreling along, headed our way.

This was not a happy homecoming.

"Trust me," the gangster answered. "There won't be enough of you left to feel nothin'."

How's *that* for a grim thought?

"We were just supposed to scare 'em," the nervous gangster said. "Not splatter 'em." The guy looked like he was having second thoughts. I liked this guy. At least I liked him better than the guy who wanted us dead.

"They'll be scared all right," the nasty gangster chuckled. "Just before they catch the train."

Or the train catches us.

"But—" the nervous guy protested.

"Hey, we're on our own now," Nasty shot back. "I'm calling the plays."

The track beneath our feet was now shaking from the imminent arrival of the death train. The headlight was shining on us. The horn shrieked. The trainman must have seen us, but it was too late to stop. The express was coming through whether we were on the track or not.

Believe it or not, in spite of what Mr. Nasty thought, I wasn't scared. That's because I knew how we were going to escape. It was going to be pretty simple. The tricky part would be timing.

"I think we should move, mate," Spader whispered to me. "This could be a messy-do."

"Wait," I said.

"Bye-bye, boys!" shouted the gangster over the screaming horn.

The train was nearly on us.

"Uh, Pendragon?" Spader whined.

"Now!" I shouted.

I grabbed Spader's arm and we both jumped back, off the track. Instantly the train flashed by in front of us. What did those two idiot gangsters think? We were going to stand there and get slammed?

"Run!" I yelled.

The speeding train was now between us and the gangsters. We had a short window of protection. Using the train as a shield, Spader followed me toward the abandoned subway station. With any luck, the train would have enough cars to give us time to get there. It was about forty yards from the gate to the old platform. Not a long run, but it was tricky because we had to do it on another track that ran parallel to the one the train was on. One misstep and we'd go down with twisted ankles.

I shot a quick glance back over my shoulder to see how

long the train was. Luckily there was still a bunch of cars to come. Our luck was holding. I figured we'd hit the station right about the time the train passed us. Then we could jump up on the platform and book out of there. I took another glance back and saw that the last car was almost on us.

"Stay with me!" I shouted back to Spader.

A second later the train whipped by us. I put on the brakes, ready to leap across the track and climb up onto the platform of the abandoned station. But what I saw in the next instant jolted me to a standstill. The two of us stood across from the abandoned station platform to see . . .

It wasn't abandoned anymore!

I couldn't believe it. Everything up until now was exactly as I remembered it: the flume, the gate, the tracks, even the location of the platform. Everything was the same, except for the station. The place was lit up and busy with people. The token booth was open and selling fares to passengers flooding down the stairs; the grimy, broken tiles on the walls looked new and clean; and there was a busy newsstand selling papers to eager customers. How could this be?

"Now's not the time to stop, mate," warned Spader.

He was right. We leaped over the track and hoisted ourselves up onto the platform. People stared at us in shock. I guess they weren't used to seeing people scramble across active tracks, especially not when a train had just blasted through. Spader stood up, winked at an older woman who was watching us, and said with a charming smile, "No worries, mum. Routine inspection. Everything checks out spiff." The woman stared back in total confusion.

An idea hit me and I pushed my way through the passengers toward the newsstand. There was a stack of newspapers right in front. If I was right, the paper would tell me everything I needed to know. I picked it up, stared at the front page, and my whole body went numb.

"What's the trouble?" Spader asked as he came up behind me.

"It's 1937," I said, barely believing my own words. "First Earth is in 1937."

"Right," he said, trying to understand. "What does that mean?"

"It means this is my home territory, but in a time more than half a century before I was born."

The date on the newspaper was March 10, 1937. I couldn't believe what I was seeing, but there it was in good old black and white.

"You gonna buy that paper, mac?" growled the news vendor. "This ain't a lendin' library."

The guy was a pudgy, gruff-looking munchkin who hadn't shaved in a few days. He wore a wool cap with a visor and chewed on a stubby cigar that looked like a rotten stick. It didn't smell much better than it looked. I slowly put the paper down and took a look around the station. Now it made sense. The station was open because it wasn't abandoned *yet*.

I now registered what the people were wearing. It looked like an old-time movie with men wearing suits and hats and women all wearing dresses. I didn't see a pair of jeans or sneakers in the place.

We really were in the past.

"Howdy, Buck Rogers!" came a voice from behind us. "Bring any spare change from outer space?"

We both turned to see a tall, gray-haired African American man in a long, woolen coat walking toward us. Buck Rogers? Oh, right. Spader and I were still wearing the swim clothes from Cloral. We must have stuck out like orange on black.

"Sorry," I answered the man. "I'll catch you next time."

"That's all right," he said with a chuckle. "Give my regards to Ming the Merciless."

Suddenly the sound of machine-gun fire shattered the station.

There were screams of panic as everybody ducked down. I couldn't believe it. Were the gangsters shooting up the place? Spader and I ducked down and looked to the far side of the platform where the shooting came from. Standing there were the two gunmen, still wearing white handkerchiefs over their faces. The nasty guy in charge had fired his machine gun into the ceiling. The weapon was still smoking.

"Everybody freeze!" he shouted. "We're lookin' for a couple of wise guys dressed like spacemen."

That was us. There was no way we could blend into this crowd. I looked around, hoping a cop was on duty. If there was, he was just as scared of these nimrods as everybody else, because he wasn't stepping forward. We were on our own.

The gangsters started walking slowly through the station, scanning the crowd. People were crouched down all around us, afraid to move. I caught the eye of a woman who looked at us with fear. She knew we were the guys they were looking for. But she didn't say anything. Maybe she was afraid of getting caught in the crossfire. Spader and I glanced around, desperate to find an escape route.

"Here! Over here!" somebody yelled. It was the news vendor guy. I looked up and was shocked to see he was leaning out of his newsstand, pointing us out to the gangsters. Nice guy.

Spader and I had no choice but to stand up. Everybody else stayed on the ground. If the gangsters wanted to open fire, they'd have a clear shot at us. I think the term was "sitting ducks." Or maybe it was more like "standing ducks."

The gangsters turned to us and raised their machine guns. "What is all the ruckus here?"

It was the African American guy who had called me Buck Rogers. He stepped between Spader and me and put his arms around our shoulders. "You think shootin' up these spacemen will get rid of 'em?" he declared. "No sir-ee! I seen this in the movin' pictures! You shoot 'em up and they'll just start duplicatin'! That what you want? Bunch of little blue spacemen running around?"

"Get outta the way, old man," snarled the nasty gangster. "Unless you want to blast off with 'em."

"Now there's an idea!" said the man.

Just then, another subway train entered the station. But rather than speed through, this one slowed down to a stop.

"I always wanted to see what was goin' on up there in outer space!" the old guy cackled. "Maybe now's my big chance!"

The head gangster smiled and brought his machine gun up higher, ready to fire. The second gangster kept glancing nervously between us and his partner. "Suit yourself, old man," said the nasty gangster.

"Oh, I don't think you want to go doin' that," said the old man with such certainty that it actually made the nasty gangster hesitate.

"Look around," he continued. "All these fine people are watching."

The nervous gangster was already looking at all the people whose eyes were fixed on them. Now the nasty gangster took a quick look too. He was having second thoughts.

The subway train came to a stop, the doors opened, and people flooded out onto the platform. A few saw what was going on and quickly jumped out of the way. Others ducked back inside the subway car. The old guy kept his hands on our shoulders and led us over toward the train. As we walked, he kept talking.

"Every one of these good people are witnesses. This isn't some lonely back alley. You can't hide in the shadows. Your dirty work is on display for everybody to see, and remember."

The old guy definitely had the gangsters thinking. Now even the nasty guy looked unsteady. In the meantime, we were moving closer to the open subway door. All I could do was hope it wouldn't close before we got there.

"I believe you two are smart gentlemen," our friend continued. "You understand what I'm telling you."

I didn't think the gangsters understood anything. I thought the old gent was confusing them. But that was okay. If it gave us time to escape, I didn't care what was going through the minds of these bad guys. The old man turned us around so we were still facing the gangsters. Our backs were now to the open subway door. He kept us moving though. He gently pulled us backward and onto the subway train. A few seconds later the three of us stood inside the car. Now I prayed for the doors to shut.

"I am so proud of you gentlemen," said the old man to the gangsters with a smile. "You are two upstanding individuals."

Everyone waited for something to happen. The gangsters stood with their mouths open. Every single person in the station was afraid to move. Spader, the old guy, and I stood just inside the open subway door.

Time stood still.

Then a bell rang on the subway train and the doors started to close. That woke the gangsters up. They both jumped for the train. They were a ways behind us, so they leaped onto the train through the set of doors farther back on our car. At that instant, the old man shoved Spader and me forward. We all jumped off the train and back onto the platform at the exact moment the doors closed behind us . . . with the gangsters trapped on board!

A second later the train began to pull out of the station. The three of us watched as the subway car slid past, along with the two gangsters. The nasty gangster grabbed at the door, angrily trying to pull it open. But it was too late. Next stop for them . . . someplace else. The old guy smiled and gave him a wave as they disappeared into the tunnel ahead. All around us, people started to move again. They all seemed a little shocked, but none more than Spader and I.

"That was incredible!" Spader shouted. "You had them stupefied."

"You saved our lives," I said. "I don't know how to thank you."

The friendly smile dropped off the old man's face. In an instant he went from a warm, charming grandpa to a serious man on a mission.

"Follow me," he said sternly, and walked off.

Spader and I didn't move. "Should we?" Spader asked me.

A second later people started to gather around us. They were moving in like we were two escaped animals from the zoo. We had caused a pretty big disturbance, and they wanted to know why. This was not a good place to be.

"Absolutely," I answered, and ran to follow the old man.

The guy may have been old, but he was quick. He was already halfway up the stairs to the street. Spader and I barreled through the turnstile and ran after him. I was in such a hurry to catch up that I didn't stop to think about what we would see outside. But when we got to the top of the stairs, reality hit me square in the face.

We had arrived in a different time.

This was the same section of the Bronx where Uncle Press first brought me to begin this adventure . . . over sixty years from now. But as much as it was sort of familiar, it was also way different. I recognized many of the buildings. Even in my time there were no modern steel-and-glass structures in this neighborhood, so a lot of these same buildings would be around sixty years from now. The only real difference was that in 1937, they looked clean and new.

The big, obvious difference that jumped out at me was the cars. They were all so old. But they *weren't* old. Here in 1937 they were the latest models. Very strange. Traffic was just as hectic here as in my time, and the street was jammed with ancient vehicles. There was an odd smell, too. It was kind of like chemicals. It took me a while to realize that this was long before people worried about clean air and car emissions and unleaded gasoline and all those things that are supposed to keep pollution down. These cars were all spewing old-fashioned, full-leaded, full-stink emissions. It reeked.

Another thing that caught my eye was the billboards. They were everywhere, advertising things I never heard of. There was one showing a lady with a big smile who brightened her teeth not with toothpaste, but with tooth powder. Another had a guy looking all sorts of happy because he gassed up his car with "Esso" gasoline. Still another showed a group of quintuplets, all girls, who were advertising a soap made with olive oil. Gross. Wasn't that like washing with spaghetti sauce? I knew this was Earth, but it sure felt like a different planet.

Spader stood right by my side, looking dazed. This all must have been strange to him, too. But in a very different way.

"You two going to stand there all day?"

We looked to see the old African American guy standing by a yellow cab, holding the back door open for us.

"Look," I said. "Thanks for bailing us out and all, but we're not gonna get in that cab with—"

"Vincent Van Dyke is my name," he said with a smile. "My friends call me Gunny."

"O-kay, Gunny. Like I was saying, we got things to do so—"

"I know you do," Gunny said. "I know all about it."

"Oh, yeah?" Spader asked. "What do you know?"

Gunny chuckled and said, "I know that if you want to start looking for Saint Dane, you might need my help."

It was like the whole world had stopped again. Did he really say what I thought he said? I turned to Spader. He looked as shocked as I felt.

"Yeah," Spader said. "I heard it too."

The old guy didn't move. He stood with his hand on the open cab door and a smile on his face.

"Who are you?" I asked.

"Like I said, my friends call me Gunny. And I'm pretty sure we're all gonna be good friends, seeing as I'm the Traveler from First Earth."

He held up his hand to show us that he was wearing the familiar silver ring with the dark gray stone in the middle.

Our visit to First Earth was getting more interesting by the second.

FIRST EARTH

"Fifty-ninth and Park, my good man," Gunny said to the cabbie as we got into the car.

It was a big, old-fashioned cab with lots of room in back. I think I have to stop calling things "old-fashioned," though. This was First Earth. This was 1937. This was the past, but it was today. Totally whacked.

The cabbie pulled into traffic and headed toward Manhattan. Along the way I kept looking out the window to see the differences between First and Second Earth. The odd thing was, it really wasn't as different as you might think. I wasn't exactly an expert on history and all things New York, but from the view of a kid from Connecticut who had only been to the city a few times, I was surprised to see how similar things were.

Like I wrote before, the most obvious difference for me was the cars. I'd seen old cars before, but always in some black-and-white movie or picture. When I was a little kid, I thought the whole world was black-and-white in the "olden" days. But I'm here to tell you, things were definitely not black-and-white in 1937. The sky was just as blue, the sun was just as yellow and the grass in the parks was just as green as on Second Earth. But the cars were mostly black. Some were cream colored and a few gray, but black was definitely the most popular color. They rode a little rough, too. The three of us bounced around in the back of that cab every time we hit a pothole. Yeah, they had potholes in 1937 too.

As much as I wanted to check out the wonders of the past, the guy sitting in front of me was more important. He said he was the Traveler from First Earth. I had no reason to doubt him, especially since he wore the ring. But still, he didn't fit the profile of all the other Travelers. First off, he was old. I couldn't tell exactly *how* old, but he had to be up there. Maybe sixty? All the other Travelers were young. Uncle Press was older. So was Osa. But not *this* old. Besides, they were gone. They had passed the torch on to a younger generation of Travelers. Did that mean Gunny's days were numbered too? I decided not to ask him. That wouldn't have been cool.

He seemed like an okay guy. It was incredible the way he had controlled the gangsters and helped us escape. He had a soothing voice that made you feel like everything was all right. As I had learned, Travelers have the ability to be very persuasive. It's like a hypnosis thing. I've tried it myself. It works, sometimes. I'm still not very good at it.

"You two sure do believe in making a dramatic entrance," Gunny said with a chuckle. "My heart's still pounding."

Wow. If he was scared back in that station, he sure didn't show it. Add that to the list. The guy was cool under pressure.

"We didn't expect a welcoming committee," I said. "But we're sure glad you were there."

Gunny nodded thoughtfully. "I'm guessing you're Pendragon," he said, then looked to Spader. "Which one are you?"

"Vo Spader, mate," answered Spader proudly. "Aquaneer supreme from the territory of Cloral."

"I like that!" Gunny laughed. "I have no idea what an aquaneer supreme is, but it sure sounds fine!"

"What's your story?" I asked, still not sure how far we could trust this guy.

"I could bore you for hours with my story."

"Go for it," I said.

"Start by telling us where the name Gunny came from," Spader said.

"The army," Gunny answered. "It's sort of a joke. I signed up back in seventeen to fight in the Great War. Not sure why they called it that, but who am I to say? Trouble was, I couldn't bring myself to fire a gun. I tried, mind you. I really did. But it was the strangest thing. I'd pick up a rifle, point it, but couldn't bring myself to pull the trigger. Didn't matter how much they hollered at me, I couldn't do it. That's when I got the nickname. Spent the rest of the war cooking and cleaning pots."

"Did you know you were a Traveler back then?" asked Spader.

"Nope. Found out two years ago," Gunny said. "I've lived most of a life thinking things were one way. Come to find out it wasn't that way at all. I can't say I'm too happy about it, but I guess I don't have a choice, do I?"

No, he didn't. Neither did we. Welcome to Travelerhood. I glanced quickly up at the cabbie, wondering what he would think of this conversation. My guess was New York cabbies had seen and heard far stranger stories than this.

"How'd you find out?" I asked.

"I work at this hotel," Gunny explained. "Near twenty years now. Started scrubbing pots, now I'm a bell captain. One day this fella showed up. Nice enough gentleman. Soon as I showed him to his room, he started telling me things. Things about me he never could have known."

"Like what?" asked Spader.

"He knew about my family; about where I was raised down in Virginia; about things I said and did forty years before that I near forgot myself. I have to tell you I was a little scared of this fella. But he calmed me down and said everything was going to be fine. He said it was time I knew about my true calling."

"So he laid the whole Traveler gig on you right there?" I asked.

"Not exactly. He asked me to take a trip with him. Uptown. If I had known just how far uptown he meant, I'm not so sure I would have gone with him."

"I guess he took you to the flume," I said.

"That's right. Before I knew it, I was flying through space. I was lucky my poor old heart didn't give out right then and there. We landed at a place called Ta Da or some such thing."

"Zadaa?" I asked.

"That was it. Zadaa. It was this beautiful city in the desert, with a river running under the ground."

Spader and I shared looks. We had been there too. It was Loor's home territory.

Gunny continued, "And he introduced me to the most beautiful lady I had ever seen."

"Osa," I said.

"That was her!" Gunny stopped talking for a second. I could tell his mind was back on Zadaa, with Osa. She was Loor's mother and like Gunny said, an amazingly beautiful woman. Gunny came back to the present and said, "She's the one who told me all about being a Traveler and how it was up to us to stop this Saint Dane fella from causing trouble. I wanted to know why I was chosen, but both of 'em said I'd find out in due time."

"Sounds familiar," I said.

"It was too much for my brain to take in all at once. I'm still not sure I understand it all, even now. The gentleman took me on a few more trips, just to show me more of what was out there. I never thought I'd ever see such wondrous sights. Then he brought me back home. I asked him what I was supposed to do, and he said I didn't have to do anything except wait and keep my eyes open. That was two years ago. After a time I began thinking I dreamed the whole thing. I kept my eyes open, but there was nothing to see. That is, until today."

"The guy who took you to Zadaa," I asked. "What was his name?"

"Went by the name of Tilton. Press Tilton. I suppose you know him."

"He was my uncle," I answered.

"Your uncle!" exclaimed Gunny with a smile. "Now that explains a few things. He told me all about you. Said you'd be showing up someday. He talked about you like you were the upside of buttered bread. Now it makes sense!"

"Upside of buttered bread?" said Spader, giving me a sideways look.

"Hold on," Gunny said. "You said he *was* your uncle?"

"Yeah," I answered quietly. "Uncle Press is dead. I hate to tell you this, but Osa is too."

The smile dropped from Gunny's face. He looked down, letting this information work through his head. "I am truly sorry to hear that," he finally said. "He was a good person. I can say the same for Osa. The world is worse off without them."

"Thanks, but there's more you gotta know," I said.

"I'm not so sure I want to," Gunny shot back. For the first time since we'd met, he looked nervous.

"Those gangsters back at the subway station," I began. "They're the ones who killed Uncle Press."

"No!" exclaimed Gunny. "Press came back?"

"No. We were at a flume in another territory. Saint Dane took off, but before we could chase him, bullets came back at us through the flume."

I could feel Spader grow tense next to me. This was a tough memory for him.

"Uncle Press was killed by those bullets," I continued. "Saint Dane had his hand in it. I'm sure of that. He's the only one who could have activated the flume to send those bullets through."

Gunny looked away. The expression on his face grew dark. He needed to get his mind around this. After several seconds he finally spoke.

"I guess that means it's starting," he said softly.

"What?" asked Spader. "What's starting?"

Gunny was anxious. His mind was racing to places I didn't think he wanted to go. "I hear things, you know?" he said nervously. "Being at the hotel and all, I see and hear it all. Maybe that's why I was chosen for this Traveler business."

"What did you hear?" I asked.

"Those gunmen at the subway station, they are a couple of bad apples. I heard rumors that there was going to be a hit. Somebody was going to get killed, you know? I hear things like that all the time. Usually it's just rumors. But the thing that made me take notice this time was the place it was supposed to happen. It was that subway station. The one with the flume thing. I was hoping it was just a coincidence, but I had to see for myself. That's why I was up there today."

"And then we showed up," I said.

"Yeah," said Gunny. "And a Traveler died. I'm afraid that can only mean one thing."

"Yeah," Spader said to Gunny. "Looks like your days of watching and waiting are over."

"Whatever Saint Dane's plan is for First Earth," I said, "it's on."

The car came to a stop and the cabbie slid the glass partition back that separated the front seat from the back. "Fifty-ninth and Park," he announced.

I wondered how much of our conversation he'd heard. It didn't matter. It wouldn't have made any sense to him.

"Where are we?" asked Spader.

"This is my home," said Gunny. "The Manhattan Tower Hotel. They all come through here sooner or later—movie stars, politicians, captains of industry. And gangsters."

"Gangsters?" I said with surprise.

"Yes," answered Gunny. "After what I've seen and heard today, I've got a feeling they're the reason we've all been gathered together."

"Welcome home," I said to myself and stepped out of the cab.

FIRST EARTH

Gunny paid the cab fare as Spader and I gazed up at the Manhattan Tower Hotel. It was a real swankadelic place. It was thirty stories high and definitely the tallest building in the neighborhood. The front entrance was set back from busy Park Avenue to make room for an elaborate garden in front. There were trees and fountains and everything. It must have been a full-time job for a team to take care of, because even though it was March and kind of chilly, the garden was green and packed with colorful flowers. It was a dense, colorful jungle in the middle of a gray city.

The building itself stood out from the others because of its color. Every other building was some shade of cement. But the Manhattan Tower Hotel had a touch of pink to it. I'm not talking pukey-bright, Pepto-Bismol pink; it was softer than that. It made the place look warm and inviting. I couldn't remember if this hotel was still around on Second Earth. But then again, like I said, I'm not an expert on New York history.

"Let's try something," Gunny said as he joined us on the sidewalk. He took off his long woolen coat to reveal he was wearing his bell captain uniform underneath.

"Hobey!" exclaimed Spader when he got a glimpse. "What a spiffer!"

Gunny had made an amazing transformation. The dark woolen coat he had been wearing made him look like everybody else on the street, but the outfit underneath was spectacular. The jacket was a deep, dark red with shiny brass buttons that went all the way up to the collar. The collar stood straight up and had two lines of golden trim running all the way around his neck. On each cuff of his sleeves were four golden bars. On his left breast was a fancy logo with the letters *MTH* for Manhattan Tower Hotel. On the other breast was a name tag that read "Vincent Van Dyke, Captain." The pants were black, with a gold bar running down the outside of each leg. To finish it off, his shoes were shined to within an inch of their lives. The whole package had a military feel, like he was ready for a parade.

Gunny stood up straight and proud as we admired the uniform. He was a big guy, I'm guessing at least six foot four. But in his uniform, he looked seven feet tall. I think he knew it too. He had a little smile on his face. That was cool.

"Be honest, Gunny," Spader said. "You were kiddin' us before. You're really a royal prince, right?"

Gunny laughed. "Don't I wish," he said. "Come here, Pendragon." Gunny held up his woolen coat for me to put on. "Can't have you guys walking through my hotel looking like Martians," he added.

The coat was about a dozen sizes too big. The sleeves were so long you couldn't see my hands and the bottom dragged on the sidewalk.

"Now I look like a Martian wearing my father's coat," I complained.

Gunny took off the coat and put it on Spader. It looked a

little better on him. At least the bottom only skimmed the ground.

"It'll do," Gunny said. He then turned to me and winked. "We'll take our chances with you looking like a spaceman, shorty."

"Gimme a break, I'm only fourteen!" I said defensively, but I knew he was just giving me a hard time. I was beginning to like Gunny Van Dyke.

Before we could head into the hotel, a big limousine pulled up to the curb near us. I didn't think anything of it, but Gunny got tense.

"Stay right here," he said to us under his breath.

The two front doors to the limousine opened at the same time and four guys in suits jumped out. It all happened so fast it was almost funny. All I could think of were clowns jumping out of a car at the circus. I wondered how many other guys in suits were packed inside. One of the suits hurried to the back door and opened it up. The others stood around, scanning the sidewalk like Secret Service agents. A second later a guy pulled himself out of the back of the limo.

I knew instantly that this was "the man."

He wore a suit like the others, but that's where the similarity ended, because he was big. I'm talking massive. Everything about this dude was huge. His hands, his head, his feet, his body. He wasn't fat. He was just big. His suit was light gray, and I could see he had a big gem stuck in his dark blue tie. I'd bet anything it was a diamond. His hat was the same color as his suit, with a dark blue band around it. A perfectly folded handkerchief that was the same color as his tie poked up from his breast pocket. He had a couple of rings on his fingers that looked pretty expensive too.

This guy seemed like someone who pretty much got whatever he wanted. He stood up, adjusted his suit so everything looked just right, then turned toward the hotel. The other guys gathered around him, forming a protective shield. As they walked, they kept scanning the sidewalk for any threats.

No question. They were bodyguards.

"Who is this guy?" I asked. "Some foreign president?"

"I wish," answered Gunny under his breath. "Most foreign presidents aren't killers."

Uh-oh. Not a good answer.

The guy caught sight of Gunny and broke out in a big smile. "Gunny, my friend!" he bellowed. He changed direction and headed right for us. That meant all of his bodyguards had to adjust and follow. It was like a big cargo ship had suddenly changed direction and all the little tugboats around it had to hurry to keep up.

Gunny tried to look casual. Spader and I didn't move.

"You working the street now, Gunny?" the guy asked with a big smile.

"No sir, Mr. Rose," answered Gunny politely. "Just taking a break. Wanted a breath of fresh air."

"Good man," the big guy exclaimed. He reached into his pocket and pressed a dollar bill into Gunny's hand. "Don't work too hard now, understand?" he said, and gave Gunny a friendly cuff on the shoulder.

"Only when I'm working for you, Mr. Rose," Gunny replied.

The guy let out a laugh that was bigger than necessary. But that was okay. If he was a killer, then I wanted him to be in a good mood. It seemed like he thought Gunny was okay. That was good too. But then he looked down at me and stopped laughing.

Uh-oh. Was I in trouble? What should I do? I had this image of King Kong—gazing down on all those poor natives who were running around—getting ready to choose one to pick up and swallow.

"Howdy there, Buck Rogers," he said. "Little late for Halloween."

I wasn't sure of how to react, so I pretended he had made a really funny joke and forced out a laugh. It was the right move because the guy laughed with me. He grabbed my hand and stuck something in it.

"No offense, pardner, just making a joke," he said. "You look real cute." He then walked toward the hotel with his boys scrambling to follow. I looked down at my hand to see he had given me a dollar bill too.

"The spaceman comments are getting old," I said.

"Who was that guy?" Spader asked Gunny.

"Name's Maximilian Rose. He's a businessman who lives in the penthouse here at the Manhattan Tower. He's got more businesses than Heinz got pickles."

"And? . . . " I asked.

Gunny took a quick look around to see if anyone was listening. He continued in a whisper, "And he's about as crooked as a rattlesnake in an accordion factory."

I looked at Spader. Spader shrugged. "Who's Heinz and what's an accordion?"

Gunny continued, "What I'm saying is he didn't make all his money being an honest businessman. He puts up a respectable front, but he is a very bad individual. Trust me on that."

"Those gangsters in the subway," I said. "Do they work for Rose?"

"No, they're from a whole 'nother gang downtown."

"Is there anyone in this town who *isn't* a gangster?" Spader asked.

"I know three for sure," said Gunny. "You, me, and Pendragon."

"Swell," said Spader sarcastically. "It's your basic tum-tigger."

"Tum-what?" asked Gunny.

"Let's just go inside, all right?" I said. Hearing these guys confuse each other was getting almost as old as the spaceman comments.

A few moments later, a doorman wearing a uniform similar to Gunny's held open a heavy, glass door for us and we stepped into the lobby of the Manhattan Tower Hotel. The place was even more spectacular inside than out. It gave me the feeling that I was in some huge, rich-guy mansion. The ceiling of the lobby soared up three stories and was decorated with stained glass scenes of a beautiful green forest. The sun shone down through the glass and sprayed colored specks of light all over the room like a kaleidoscope.

We walked on thick, oriental carpets under giant crystal chandeliers that looked as if they'd come from a European castle. Several sitting areas had red-leather furniture where people sat chatting or reading newspapers. Nobody spoke above a whisper. It was like being in church, or a library. It was pretty obvious that you had to have bucks to stay here. This was no cheaply hotel like the one my parents took me to at Niagara Falls. That place was skuzzy and smelled like b.o. Here you could eat off the floor. Not that you'd want to. Everyone I saw looked as if they had just stepped out of an old-fashioned department-store window. All the men wore suits and hats. The women had on dresses.

There were only two people in the whole room who looked

totally out of place—me and Spader. I was feeling pretty stupid wearing a bright blue suit with shoes to match. Spader didn't look much better in Gunny's big coat.

"We're out of our league here," I whispered to Gunny.

"Nonsense," Gunny replied. "You'll fit right in."

Yeah, right. If we were circus people here to juggle for the good folks.

"Come with me," Gunny said, and walked off.

We followed him, staying close, hoping nobody would notice us. Gunny walked through the lobby like he owned the place. He had a slow, smooth walk that said, "This is my house and I'm proud of it." Several people nodded and smiled at him as they passed. Gunny knew everybody's name and had a little something personal to say to each of them.

"Afternoon, Mr. Galvao, see you again next month. Hello, Mrs. Tavey. I see you've been to our beauty salon. Very lovely. Mr. Prevett, your luggage has all been sent ahead, just as you requested." The guy was good. He knew every guest by name. No wonder he was a captain.

We made it across the lobby and up to a bank of shiny, brass elevators. Gunny hit the button.

"Where are we going?" asked Spader.

Gunny glanced around casually to make sure nobody could hear him. "They're doing a big renovation up on the sixth floor," he said softly. "Nobody will know if we have a couple of spacemen staying there."

That sounded pretty cool to me. We were going to be staying in the swankiest hotel in New York, with a whole floor to ourselves. Not bad. The elevator door slid open and Gunny motioned for us to enter.

There was a guy inside. He was a little dude, about my size, with wire-rimmed glasses, who wore the same uniform as

Gunny. The only difference was he only had two gold stripes on his sleeves and wore a round cap with a flat top.

"Going up!" he announced professionally.

"Sixth floor, please, Dewey," said Gunny.

"Yes sir, Mr. Van Dyke," he said with a squeaky voice. "Sixth floor."

The little guy was the elevator operator. He slid the elevator doors closed, pushed the handle, and the elevator immediately started . . . down. "Oops, sorry," he said. He pushed the handle and the elevator jolted to a stop. He struggled with it and the elevator shook. He finally found the right gear and we started to go up. Phew. The operator gave us a sheepish look of apology. I didn't get his problem. Up, down, start, stop. Not a whole lot of options. I had the strong suspicion that this guy might be a nimrod.

"This is Dewey Todd," said Gunny. "His father built this hotel."

That explained a lot.

Dewey looked up at Gunny with a scowl. "I asked you not to tell people that, Gunny. I don't want people treating me different. I want to make it in the hotel business on my own."

"Well, you've almost got the elevator part, mate," said Spader, trying to hold back a smile. "That's a good start."

Dewey smiled proudly. He didn't get the cut.

"Sixth floor!" he announced, and slid the door open. We all made sure the elevator was safely stopped and everything was cool before stepping out.

"Enjoy the costume party," Dewey said. "Those are great circus outfits!"

"We're spacemen," I corrected.

"Oh, sorry." He closed the elevator doors and we were alone.

"He really is a fine boy," Gunny said, chuckling. "Just a little confused sometimes."

"I know the feeling," I said.

The sixth-floor hallway was definitely being worked on. The walls were bare and there were painting tarps spread out all over the place. As Gunny led us down the corridor he explained, "This was the first floor they finished when the hotel was new, so it's the first they're going to modernize."

Modernize. What a joke. They were trying to make this floor look like 1937. Not exactly "modern" by my standards. We reached the end of the corridor and turned left into another long corridor. Gunny walked up to room 615 and used a key to open it up.

"Welcome home, gentlemen," he said.

The room was huge. Actually, it was a couple of rooms. I think they call this a suite. I could imagine that when the work was finished, this was going to be a pretty fancy place. But right now, while they were doing the renovation, it was being used as a storage area for chairs and sofas.

"You sure this is okay, Gunny?" I asked.

"Absolutely," he answered with confidence. "It breaks about eighteen different hotel rules, but I've been here long enough to pull the right strings. Just don't go ordering room service."

There were a bunch of sofas lined up in a column along one wall. They were up on their arms and reached almost to the ceiling. All we had to do was bring two down and we'd have a comfortable place to sleep. There were big cushy chairs, along with a bunch of stacked tables. There was only one thing missing.

"Where's the TV?" I asked.

Gunny gave me a curious look. "The what?"

Duh. TV wasn't invented yet. "Never mind," I said, feeling like an idiot. "How about a radio?"

"I'm sure there's one around here someplace," answered Gunny. "Are you two hungry?"

"Absolutely," I answered.

"I could go for a kooloo fish and some sniggers," said Spader.

Gunny gave him the same curious look he gave me when I asked about the TV. "I'll see what I can find," he said. "You two make yourselves at home. I'm going to get you some clothes. Is there anything else you might need?"

"Something to write on," I said. "We've got to keep up with our journals."

"Right," answered Gunny. "I'll be back."

Gunny ambled out of the room, leaving Spader and me alone. I walked to the far side of the room, where fancy doors led to a balcony. I opened them and stepped outside. It was close to sunset. From our sixth-floor landing, I got a pretty good view south and west, where the sun was headed down.

"Is this where you grew up?" asked Spader. He was standing right behind me. I hadn't heard him coming.

"No, about thirty miles from here," I answered. "And more than half a century in the future. How weird is that?"

It really was. This was home, but not really. I had an idea that maybe I should try to find my grandparents. They were around in 1937. But then I remembered that my family had disappeared. Did that mean our whole family history disappeared along with them? I had to stop thinking about it. It was making me homesick.

"It's a scary-do," Spader said while gazing out at the city. "I've never seen anything so busy."

"You'll get used to it," I assured him.

"I suppose so," Spader added. "But I'm thinking about Saint Dane. There's a lot of natty-do that monster could get into in a big city like this. How are we going to find him?"

Good question. Saint Dane loose in New York City was a scary thought. "Something tells me he'll find us," I said. "I'm going to take a shower."

The bathroom was almost as big as the living room. This was definitely a suite for hotshot guests. The whole room was covered with white tiles. The bathtub was huge and stood on feet. There was a giant silver showerhead that sprayed enough water to wash a horse. I cranked up the shower, got it good and hot, and stood underneath the spray to let it massage my head.

As I stood there trying to get brain dead, an odd thought hit me: I wasn't going to school anymore.

I know. Weird thing to think about all of a sudden. Maybe it was because I was sort of home. Part of me was psyched. School was important and all, but it wasn't exactly something I looked forward to. On the other hand, school *was* important. It was where you learned stuff. What your parents didn't teach you, school did. As I stood in that shower, I actually started to get nervous. All my friends were going to pass me by. They were learning things that I wasn't.

Then I thought of all the places I'd been that day. Hmmm. Maybe I was getting a pretty intense education after all. I wasn't going to Stony Brook Junior High anymore; I was a full-time student at Traveler U. Maybe that was all the education I was going to need. After batting these ideas back and forth in my head, I came to one solid conclusion:

All this thinking was ruining my shower.

I stood there for another ten minutes, then found a stack of thick white towels, dried off, and left the bathroom to Spader.

A few minutes later I was in the living room, settled into a cushy chair with my feet up while Spader washed away his own thoughts. I was so dog tired, my eyes started to close. It was the first time since we got here that I could let the air out, and it felt great.

Then an urgent knock came at the door.

My eyes shot open instantly. I wasn't asleep anymore. I wasn't even tired. So much for letting the air out.

Spader poked his head out of the bathroom. He shot me a questioning look that said, "What do we do?"

I had no idea. We were busted. It looked like our stay at the hotel was going to be a short one.

FIRST EARTH

This looked bad. How could we ever explain who we were and why we were hanging out on a closed floor of the hotel? In bathrobes. I didn't want to get Gunny in trouble, but I didn't want to get arrested, either.

I snuck quietly over to the door, desperately trying to think up a story that would get us off the hook. None came. I peered through the peephole to get a look at who we would have to deal with and saw . . .

"Room service!" announced Gunny with a big smile.

Phew. Talk about relief. I opened the door and Gunny came in wheeling a big cart that was loaded with those silver domes they put over plates to keep them hot.

"Feeling better?" he asked.

"I am now," I answered. "We gotta get a secret knock or something so we know it's you."

"Secret knock. I like that," Gunny said with a sparkling smile. "Like G-men."

"Like what?" asked Spader as he walked in with a towel around his waist.

"Can we eat now?" I asked.

"All in good time, gentlemen," Gunny said. "We've got business first."

The cart was draped with a white tablecloth that went down to the floor. Gunny reached underneath and pulled out two brown packages. "Try these on for size," he said, and tossed one to each of us. We tore them open to find our First Earth clothes, courtesy of one of the shops here in the hotel. We each had a pair of wool pants with jackets. My pants were light gray with a darker gray jacket. Spader's were a light brown with a matching jacket. We each had plain white shirts.

"What do I do with these?" Spader asked as he held up a pair of long, white boxer shorts.

Gunny laughed. "Don't they wear underwear where you come from?"

"Sure," answered Spader. "But I could make a sail out of these. They'll get all twisted up."

I put mine on and they came down to my knees. But you know what? I didn't care. It felt good to wear regular cotton underwear again, even if I looked like some kind of grandpa. We also had white T-shirts, black socks, and dark leather shoes. The pants had suspenders, too. That was kind of cool. I'd never worn suspenders before. And everything fit perfectly. Gunny was a good judge. After we both got dressed, Gunny looked us over and smiled.

"Now you look like you belong," he said proudly.

"Can we eat now?" I asked.

"Patience, shorty, patience." Gunny reached under the cart and pulled out a stack of white paper and a small typewriter. "You can use this to type your journals," he said. "It's faster than writing."

"What is that thing?" asked Spader.

"I'll teach you," I said. I had only typed on a computer keyboard before, but figured I could learn how to do it the old-fashioned way. "Now can we eat?" I begged. The smell of the food was making me salivate.

"One more thing," said Gunny. "Since you boys are going to be coming and going around here, I figured out a way you can fit right in." He reached back under the cart and pulled out two uniforms like the one Dewey, the elevator guy, wore. "You're going to work here as bellhops."

"What's a bellhop?" asked Spader.

Gunny explained. "You greet guests, help them with their luggage, and run errands around the hotel. It's easy work, and you'll have a terrific boss."

"Who?" Spader asked.

"Me."

"This all sounds good but, can we *please* eat now?" I asked in desperation.

"Have a seat, gentlemen," Gunny said. "It's chow time."

We both sat down while Gunny wheeled the cart in front of us. "I wasn't exactly sure of what to order," he teased. "But after some deep thought, I believe I came up with the perfect menu." With a flourish, Gunny lifted up two of the silver domes.

What I saw made me so happy I wanted to cry.

Since I left home I had eaten some very strange food. It wasn't bad, just different. On Denduron I had lots of vegetables and an occasional rabbit. On Cloral I ate a ton of fish and all sorts of weirdball fruits and vegetables from the underwater farms. On Zadaa, Loor had made us some good crunchy bread along with spicy vegetables. All of the food I had was good, but nothing compared to what was sitting before us right now.

We each had our own big, juicy cheeseburger and pile of golden French fries . . . direct from heaven. Gunny reached under the cart and pulled out a champagne bucket loaded with ice and bottles of Coke.

"What do you think?" he asked.

"I think you're a genius," I said quickly.

Spader wasn't enthused. "What is that stuff?" he asked nervously.

"Cheeseburger, French fries, Coke—food of the gods, my friend," I said. I lifted up my burger, took a delicious whiff, closed my eyes, and wolfed into it. Oh, yeah, I was home.

Spader lifted up a fry, looking at it curiously. "What exactly is a french before it's fried?" he asked.

"White vegetable, cut in strips, fried in grease," I answered. "Stop talking. I'm trying to focus."

We didn't say another word for the rest of the meal. Spader ate reluctantly, but didn't seem to hate it. I put ketchup on our fries and salted them up real good. Man, they were excellent. The whole while Gunny stood over us, smiling. He was like a proud chef who enjoyed the way his food was being appreciated.

Then, for dessert, Gunny lifted two more silver covers to reveal . . . banana splits. Yes! He even had a couple glasses of milk to wash it all down. It was all so incredibly excellent. It had been a very long day, but this dinner made it all worthwhile. I wanted it to last forever, but my stomach was screaming for me to stop. I was totally stuffed and absolutely happy.

"Now don't go expecting this kind of service again," Gunny cautioned. "This is special because you just arrived. After this you eat in the kitchen with the rest of the staff."

"Gunny," I said. "You have no idea how perfect this is."

"Oh, I got a pretty good idea," he said with a smile.

"But it's better than you think," I added. "Tomorrow's my birthday and this is the best present ever."

"Then happy birthday, shorty," Gunny said, beaming. "Many happy returns."

"Happy birthday, mate," said Spader. "Wish I could raise a pint of sniggers."

"Yeah, but this'll do me just fine," I said, holding up a bottle of Coke.

Gunny took the now empty cart and put it by the door. He then came back into the living room and sat down with us. As much as I wanted to kick back, burp, and pretend life was good, that wasn't meant to be. We were here for a reason, and it wasn't to gork out stuffed on burgers.

"This is all new to me," Gunny said. "Chasing Saint Dane, I mean. What do we do?"

It was time to get down to some *real* business. The party was over.

"All the territories are reaching a turning point," I said, holding back a burp. "We've got to figure out what that turning point is here on First Earth, and what Saint Dane is doing to push it the wrong way."

"This should be snappy-do, Pendragon," Spader announced. "You're from this territory. I mean, you're from the *future* of this territory. Think of something big that happened in 1937 that Saint Dane might be messing around with."

The pressure was on. I wasn't very good at history. It all seemed so boring, memorizing dates and places and speeches made by guys I didn't care about. But even though I was historically challenged, it didn't take me very long to come up with an idea. To be honest, it was a no-brainer.

"You've got something, don't you, mate?" Spader asked with a sly smile.

I did, but I wished I didn't. The more I thought about it, the more freaked I got. This was bad. This was *really* bad. My heart started to pump faster and my palms got sweaty.

"What is it?" asked Gunny.

"There *is* something," I began. "I don't remember all the dates. But there is definitely something big about to go down."

"So tell us, mate!" exclaimed Spader.

"The war you were in, Gunny," I said. "The Great War? That became known as World War One."

Gunny's eyes grew very wide. "Are you saying there's going to be a World War Two?" he asked in shock.

I nodded.

Gunny looked down and shook his head sadly. "And they said it was the war to end all wars."

"They were wrong," I said.

"When did it happen?" asked Spader. "Who was fighting?"

I suddenly wished I hadn't slept through Mr. Varady's world history class.

"I don't know all the facts," I said. "There was this Hitler dude from Germany who tried to take over Europe. And Japan tried to take over Asia."

"That's *two* wars," Spader said.

"I think that's why they call it a *world* war," I shot back. "They fought against Russia and the United States and England and China and France and oh, *man*! This is huge! Millions of people died. Millions. It changed the world!"

Spader said, "So maybe we should go over to Germany and talk to this Hitler fella."

I laughed at that. "You don't get it," I said. "We can't just go over to Berlin, knock on Adolf Hitler's door and say, 'Excuse me, Mr. Hitler, you don't know us, but we'd really like you to reconsider this Holocaust thing. Okey dokey?'"

"Why not?" asked Spader innocently.

"Trust me. We're talking about leaders of huge nations ruling millions of people. This is so far out of our league, it's not even funny."

"So when does it all happen?" he asked.

I had to stand up and pace, hoping it would rattle loose some factoids I might have picked up somewhere.

"I don't know the dates. But it wasn't all of a sudden. There was a buildup. The wheels were definitely turning by 1937 but I don't think it got to be a full-blown war until almost 1940. Guys, this sounds *exactly* like something Saint Dane would stick his nose into, and we are *way* over our heads."

Gunny had been listening quietly. It must have been tough for him to hear that the world was about to be turned upside down again. Finally he said, "Don't be so sure about that."

"Are you crazy?" I shouted back at him.

"Think about it," Gunny argued innocently. "We know the war is coming, and we know Saint Dane is here to cause trouble. It all sort of fits. Our job might be to stop this war from happening."

"That's impossible!" I shouted. "There's no way the three of us could stop something so big."

"Maybe," Gunny said thoughtfully. "Or maybe we're thinking about it the wrong way."

"Gunny," I said patiently. "It's a *world war.* Airplanes. Guns. Bombs. Soldiers. Millions of soldiers. We're two kids with big underwear and a tall guy in a fancy suit. I don't mean to sound negative, but I'm thinking Saint Dane may have picked a winner here."

Gunny nodded thoughtfully. "I hear you. There's no way in heaven we could stop something like that once it got going.

But the thing is, what if it's only a little thing that gets it going in the first place?"

"Explain that, please, mate," said Spader.

"I'm saying that you never know what leads to what. There might be a little old something that happens that seems like nothing at first, but it might lead to something else, and that leads to something else, and so on and so on until you find yourself in the middle of a big old war."

"But—"

"Don't 'but' me so quick, shorty," Gunny interrupted. "Think about it first."

"Okay," I said, forcing myself to stop hyperventilating. "You're thinking there might be something small about to happen, that's going to start a chain reaction that will lead to World War Two . . . and we have a shot at stopping it?" I asked.

"Maybe."

"You're dreaming!" I shouted.

"I might be, at that," Gunny said. "But I know we're here for a reason. I also know that Saint Dane is here, somewhere. From what I've heard, he doesn't show up just to sightsee."

"He's right, mate," exclaimed Spader. "What if Saint Dane is here to make sure something happens that leads to the big war? Or what if he's trying to make the war into something bigger than it was going to be already? Hobey, if we find out what it is, we could make sure it doesn't happen."

I wanted to believe it was possible. I really did. But it just seemed too incredible. The idea that we could do something to stop the worst war in history was a total fantasy.

"If you're right," I said, "and I'm not saying you are, then it would have to have something to do with the gangsters Saint Dane sent to the flume to kill Uncle Press."

"Now you're thinking!" Gunny exclaimed. "If we find a

connection between those thugs and what's brewing overseas, I'm guessing it'll lead us straight to Saint Dane."

The three of us looked at each other. Was that it? Was our mission to figure out how Saint Dane was using some gangsters in New York to cause World War II?

"It sounds crazy," I said. "But one thing is for sure: Whatever Saint Dane is doing here, it's definitely got something to do with these mob guys. I don't know if it will have anything to do with the war, but it's where we gotta start."

"Right," Spader said. "With the gangster-wogglies."

Gunny stood up and straightened his suit. "That's where I come in. I've got friends in a lot of places; not all of them are good. I can ask some questions to get us started."

I had no idea where any of this would lead, but I felt confident that we were starting in the right place. Where it would take us was anybody's guess.

"Get some rest," Gunny said. "I'll come get you in the morning when it's time for work. Be ready early."

Gunny took the cart and wheeled it toward the door. "Oh, one more thing. Before work, we'll stop by the barbershop in the lobby. We can't have you two working here looking like ladies."

I hated to admit it, but Gunny was right. My hair was getting long and shaggy. Spader's black hair was almost to his shoulders. These were definitely *not* 1937 cuts.

"What's a barbershop?" Spader asked.

"G'night, gentlemen," Gunny said. "Sleep tight." He opened the door, then turned back to us and said, "How's this?" He rapped twice on the door, then once, then three times.

"The perfect secret knock," I said.

"I always wanted to be a G-man," Gunny said with a smile. He closed the door and we were alone.

"What's a G-man?" Spader asked again.

"It's not important," I answered.

"Then tell me about this World War Two. Is it really the natty-do you're saying?"

"Worse," I answered solemnly. "I don't know the words to describe how bad it was. If there's a chance we could stop it, it would be beyond incredible."

Spader stood up and smiled. "Right then! I have a sudden urge to pee. Not that I'm nervous mind you. I'm just . . . scared to death." He went for the bathroom, leaving me alone with my thoughts.

The ideas we were throwing around were too huge to comprehend. Was it possible that we might find the trigger here in New York that would start a chain reaction to prevent World War Two? A horror like that war was right up Saint Dane's alley. Of course, that meant Saint Dane would be doing his best to make sure we wouldn't find that trigger. That would be the challenge. Same old, same old.

Then three knocks came at the door.

I got up to let Gunny back in, figuring he had forgotten to tell us something. I hoped it was about breakfast. I was stuffed, but the thought of bacon and eggs was a sweet one.

"I can't believe you forgot the secret knock already," I called out as I headed for the door. "You'd make a lousy G-man."

I opened the door and instantly got shoved back into the room. I fell down on my butt, hard. At first I didn't get why Gunny would have done that. When I got my wits back and looked up, I had my answer.

It wasn't Gunny.

Standing over me were the two gangsters from the subway station. The nasty one had a black revolver pointed right at my nose.

"Ain't no G-man around to help you now," he snarled.

FIRST EARTH

I was on my butt, looking up at two guys who only a few hours before had tried to kill me. They didn't even bother covering their faces with handkerchiefs this time. They were a couple of gnarly-looking dudes too. The nasty one was, well, nasty looking. He had a pudgy face and dark, wild eyes. He was one of those guys who had to shave every hour or he'd have a Fred Flintstone thing going on.

The other guy, the tense one, looked a little less tense than before. I'm sure that was because he didn't have an audience now. He had thin features and a sharp, beaklike nose. He still didn't look all too happy about what was going on though. I glanced into his eyes and thought I caught a hint of sympathy. But not enough to call off his bulldog partner. The nasty guy held his pistol on me. It was an old-style revolver with a long barrel. It wasn't high-tech, but I'm sure it could get the job done.

"How did you find us?" I asked while crawling backward.

"We got eyes everywhere," said the nasty one, with a touch of cockiness. "You can run, but you can't hide."

"Why are you after us?" I asked.

"I got nothing against you," Nasty said. "But my associate is another story."

His associate. Who was that? Saint Dane? I wanted to keep these guys talking. Maybe I could use my Traveler hypnosis on him. But that would be tough, seeing as I was too scared to think straight, let alone concentrate enough to use mind powers I wasn't even sure I knew how to use in the first place.

"You have the wrong guy," I said with desperation, though I knew he probably had the exact right guy.

The gangster bent down and stuck the muzzle of the gun in my face. "Winn Farrow don't make mistakes like that."

Winn Farrow. Who was Winn Farrow?

More important, why did he want us killed? It was then that I saw something move out of the corner of my eye. It was Spader. He was behind the gangsters. I tried not to look at him because that would give him away.

"I . . . I don't know any Winn Farrow," I said.

Spader cautiously moved behind one of the sofas that was standing on end.

"I'm not here to argue with you, sonny boy, I'm here to tell you how it's gonna be. Don't go sticking your nose where it don't belong," he said. "If somebody gets in Winn Farrow's way, he won't be there for long, if you catch my drift."

The sofa behind the gangsters started to move. Spader was going to topple it over on them. I had to use every ounce of willpower to keep the gangsters' eyes on me.

"Okay, I hear you. Can I ask you a question though?"

"What?"

"Can I have my ring back?"

The question caught the gangsters off guard. They both looked at me as if I were nuts. Here they were putting on this big strong-arm intimidation show, and all I cared about was my ring. It confused them. Good. It was the perfect time for Spader to make his move. But it didn't exactly work out that way.

Instead, the nasty gangster got this evil gleam in his eye and said, "The hell with orders. I'm gonna end this right here."

Uh-oh. He pulled the hammer back on his revolver. I willed Spader to hurry.

He did.

With a giant shove, the sofa came toppling over. The big couch first nailed the nervous guy, then continued down to take out Mr. Nasty. The gangsters didn't know what hit them. I had barely enough time to roll out of the way before the two thugs hit the floor in a pile of gangster and sofa. I sprang to my feet and dove over the pile toward Spader.

"What took you so long?" I shouted at him.

"It was heavy!"

"C'mon!" I bolted out of the room with Spader right behind me. Those gangsters were going to be back on their feet in seconds, and I didn't want to be anywhere close when that happened. We ran down the hall, turned right, and blasted for the elevators. I hit the button and looked to see that the needle pointed to "1." Bad news. I looked over the second elevator. That needle pointed to "30." Worse news. We were on 6. Not even close.

"C'mon, c'mon!" I coaxed the elevators while furiously hitting the button . . . not that it would do any good.

"Who's Winn Farrow?" Spader asked. "Is it Saint Dane?"

"I don't know. Maybe," I answered breathlessly. "But those guys were only supposed to give us a warning and they decided to kill us."

"You can't trust anybody," said Spader.

"Hey!"

We both looked to our right and saw the gangsters rounding the far corner, headed our way. We had to keep running. Spader and I jammed it down the corridor. Our only hope was to find a stairwell, or at least another corridor. Luckily it was a long hall and we were too far away from the gangsters for them to take a shot at us.

When we got to the end of the corridor, we found a door that probably led to a stairway, but it was blocked by furniture and painting supplies. If we tried to dig through that mess, the gangsters would have us.

"This way," ordered Spader.

We turned right and sprinted down the next corridor. This hallway ran parallel with the corridor where our room was, on the far side of the hotel. It was pretty long too, so we could stay out of bullet range. But we couldn't keep running in circles. We had to find an escape route.

Halfway down the corridor, I saw it. An exit sign. Without stopping to think, I took a right into that door. I was hoping to find a stairway, but no luck. It was a service corridor. We were now running parallel to the hallway with the elevators.

"Maybe we can loop around back to the elevators," I said. "If we're lucky we'll catch one closer this time."

"Hobey-ho," Spader said.

We ran to the far end of the service corridor and stopped. I slowly opened the door to peek out. No bad guys anywhere. So far so good. We quickly ran out, turned right, and sprinted back along the corridor toward our room. We had come full circle.

But this was scary. For all we knew, one of the gangsters could have doubled back and would soon be rounding the corner in front of us. We passed our room and had only a few yards to go before hitting the elevator corridor again, when we heard footsteps coming toward us. Oops. At least one of the gangsters decided to circle back. He would be on us in seconds!

We were done. I froze in panic.

Spader didn't. He grabbed my shirt and pulled me into the last room of the corridor before the turn. There wasn't a second to spare. I caught a glimpse of the gangster coming around the corner.

The two of us dove to the inside of the door. All we could do was hope the gangster wouldn't peek in. A few seconds later we heard footsteps run by. I looked to Spader. He winked at me. We waited a few more seconds, then slowly took a peek outside to see the gangster running full throttle down the corridor, away from us. Excellent.

Now we had to move fast. We booked out of the room and back toward the elevators. We made the right turn again and saw an empty corridor. We also saw one of the elevator doors opening up! We took off on a dead run.

"Going down?" a voice called from inside the elevator.

We were too far away for him to see us. We kept on running, and I saw the elevator door starting to close. At this point it didn't matter if the gangster heard us or not, so I shouted out, "Dewey!"

Too late. The elevator door slid shut. We missed it. A second later the nasty gangster appeared at the far end of the corridor. I guess it *did* matter if he heard us. We were now staring right down the pike at worst case scenario.

That's when the elevator door opened up again! Dewey heard me after all.

"What are you guys doing?" he asked.

We both dove into the open car before the door was all the way open. "Close it! Close the door!" I shouted.

Dewey was totally confused. Both Spader and I started pushing the door closed ourselves. "Hey! That's *my* job!" Dewey whined.

We ignored him and almost had the door shut when the nasty gangster arrived. He got his fingers in the door and tried to pry it open.

"Down, Dewey!" I shouted. "Not that way." I looked up. "*That* way." I looked down.

"But there's another passenger out there!" Dewey complained. That's when the nasty gangster showed his revolver. Dewey got the message. He leaped at the door and helped us close it.

"Get us out of here!" I yelled.

Dewey grabbed the control lever and surprisingly enough, we started down. Dewey was better under pressure than I would have guessed. But he looked wild-eyed and scared.

"Who was that?" he screamed. "He had a pistol!"

"Where's Gunny?" Spader demanded, ignoring Dewey's question.

"I just saw him in the lobby, headed outside. What's going on?"

"Nothing Gunny can't handle," I said. "Forget about what you saw."

"But I gotta tell my father about this," Dewey complained.

"Don't do that!" I shouted. I think I scared the little guy because he backed up against the side of the elevator. I got my head back together and said calmly, "It was just a joke. Like a prank, you know?"

"But, but that guy had a gun," Dewey whimpered.

"Gun?" I faked a laugh. "That wasn't a real gun. That

was . . . that was . . . a costume. For the costume party. You know the clothes we had on before? Those were costumes too. You thought it was a real gun?"

I faked another laugh, looking sideways at Spader. Spader got the idea and he faked a laugh too.

"Yeah," Spader said. "It was a toy."

Dewey wasn't sure we were telling the truth, but I think it was easier for him to accept it than to think there were guys running around his father's hotel flashing guns. That was good. If Dewey called the police, they'd have to question us, and I'm not so sure they'd like the answers we had to give. No, it was better this way. But we had to find Gunny and let him know what was going on. Finally we got to the lobby, and Dewey opened the door.

"Thanks, Dewey. We'll let you know when the next costume party is, okay?" I said.

"Great, thanks!"

Dewey was a simple kind of dude.

We ran from the elevator and went looking for Gunny. We hurried to the front doors of the hotel and booked outside. Night had fallen and the garden was lit up like Christmas, with lights hidden among the greenery.

"There!" shouted Spader, pointing to the sidewalk in front.

Gunny was there talking to a man. We ran down the front stairs of the hotel, through the garden and out onto the street. Gunny saw us. He shook the hand of the man and the guy walked off just as we ran up to him. We were both out of breath and excited.

"What's wrong?" he said, sounding a little angry. "I told you boys to stay put."

"We had visitors," I said.

"The guys from the flume," Spader panted. "They came looking for us."

I didn't like the look on Gunny's face. It was a cross between shock and fear. Bad combination.

"Who is Winn Farrow?" I asked.

For a second I thought Gunny was going to faint. He actually looked unsteady on his feet. Whoever Winn Farrow was, his name made a strong guy like Gunny very scared. This was getting worse by the second.

"I can't believe he sent people here," Gunny said. "That's crossing a very dangerous line."

"Why? Who is he?" I asked.

Gunny looked down at us and was about to answer when we heard a scream.

It was a horrifying, tortured scream that came from far away. Actually, it didn't come from far away, it came from far *up*. The three of us spun quickly to look up at the hotel. What we saw made my knees go weak.

Somebody had jumped out of a window!

The whole building was lit up by floodlights, so the dark figure was easy to see, though I wished I couldn't. The fall took only a few seconds, but those few seconds will stay with me forever. It was horrible. The figure screamed all the way down. Luckily for us, the tall trees in front of the hotel blocked us from seeing the final second. We stood there frozen, then Gunny broke and ran for the building. Spader and I followed right behind him. I didn't want to see what had happened, but I was sure I needed to. Chances were this had something to do with the gangsters and this Winn Farrow dude.

The victim had fallen onto the roof of a car and pretty much caved in the whole thing. There was no way anybody could survive that. I couldn't bring myself to look closer. Neither could Spader. We stood several feet away, while Gunny did the tough thing and walked over to investigate.

While we waited for him, Spader saw something and nudged me. I looked and saw someone standing on the steps of the hotel. It was one of the gangsters. The nervous one. He looked at us like he wanted to say something, but decided not to and ran off. The question was, where was the other guy?

Gunny walked back to us and said softly, "It's him. The ugly one from the subway. He's dead."

That answered my question. Spader and I shared disbelieving looks.

"I guess that means he won't be trying to kill us anymore," Spader said, sounding numb.

This was unbelievable. When I first saw the falling body, I thought somebody had made a suicide jump. Now that I knew it was Mr. Nasty Gangster, nothing made sense anymore. Why would he jump? He had other things on his mind, like hunting for us so he could gun us down.

I stared up at Gunny. He looked sick.

"You gotta tell us what you're thinking, Gunny," I said.

Gunny glanced back at the body. People were starting to gather and stare.

"I'm afraid we're going to have our own war pretty soon," Gunny said. "Right here in our backyard. It may not be as big as the one brewing over in Europe, but it's going to be ugly just the same."

I heard a police siren scream in the distance. It was a far-off, sorrowful wail that was headed our way.

The show was definitely on.

◆   ◆   ◆

I'm going to end this journal here, Mark and Courtney. I wish I had my ring so I could send these pages to you. Hopefully, it'll turn up soon. But until it does, I'll keep these pages safe and keep writing. I'm beginning to get the hang of this typewriter.

I hope this journal finds you well, and that your lives are much simpler than mine.

It's March 11. It's my birthday. Do I still turn fifteen, even though it's 1937?

END OF JOURNAL #9

FIRST EARTH

I'm getting ready to launch to another territory.

It's been nearly two months since I finished my last journal, and I can't tell you how worried I am. I don't want to leave here. At least not now.

But I think we found the turning point.

Gunny was right. I think that if we can change the outcome of this one event, there's a really good chance we can stop World War II. Is that incredible or what? The idea of saving the lives of millions of people is almost too good to be true. Gunny was right. The turning point isn't as big as a war between tribes like on Denduron, or the poisoning of an entire territory, like on Cloral. It's actually one single event. One big, stupid, spectacular event.

But it's going to be hard to stop it from happening. Dangerous, too. Big surprise, right?

Since I wrote you guys last, we have crossed paths with some truly foul characters. It's getting hard to tell the good guys from the bad guys. If we have any hope of stopping this event, we've got to go up against these guys again, and I can't guarantee we'll win.

That's why I'm fluming to another territory. We need some information and there's no way we can get it here. But I'm nervous about leaving because I don't want to miss anything. I'm typing this to you guys on the night of May 5. Tomorrow is the day everything is going to hit the fan. That much we know for sure. We absolutely, positively have to be back in time and leaving now means we'll be cutting it really close. I'm counting on the fact that the flumes always send us Travelers where we need to be, *when* we need to be there. It wouldn't be cool to get back late.

But I think it's a risk worth taking because, like I said before, we need all the help we can get.

The last time I wrote to you it was my birthday, March 11. Spader and I have been here for almost two months. So much has happened since I last wrote that I hope I can remember it all.

When Mr. Nasty Gangster took that header off the Manhattan Tower Hotel, it was truly disturbing. Seeing a man fall to his death is about as horrible and gruesome as it gets. But as bad as that was, it also left us with a mystery. How did he fall? *Why* did he fall? He had been chasing us around on the sixth floor. I couldn't imagine he took a wrong turn and suddenly said, "Oops, this door leads to . . . air! Let's go!" No way.

I also couldn't imagine that he jumped deliberately. Not that I know anything about suicide, but this guy was busy doing other things, like trying to murder Spader and me. Why would he suddenly stop in the middle of the chase and say, "I can't believe I lost those guys. I'm such a lousy gangster, I think I'll just end it all." That didn't make sense either.

The only possible explanation was that he was murdered.

That leads to the bigger question. Who did it? It wasn't his partner, Mr. Nervous Gangster. Spader and I saw him leaving the hotel only a few seconds after Mr. Nasty took the dive. That meant somebody else was guilty. There was somebody else in the hotel who was part of all this, and I could make a pretty good guess as to who it might be.

Yeah, you guessed it too. Saint Dane.

He had to be here somewhere, looking like somebody else. Still, why would Saint Dane murder a guy who was trying to murder us? I guess the bottom line was, we had a ton of questions and not a whole lot of answers. There was only one person who could shed any light on this, and that was Gunny. It was time for him to tell us what he knew about these gangsters.

After Mr. Nasty took the fall, Gunny told Spader and me to go back up to our room. He had to talk to the police and let them know what he saw. Of course he didn't want Spader or me talking to them. They might ask tough questions like: "And where do you live, sonny boy?" or "Give us the name of your parents so we can call them." That would have been tricky. So Spader and I went quietly back up to our room and waited for Gunny.

Once we hit the room though, we weren't quiet anymore. Spader was all worked up.

"He's here. I can smell him," he said while pacing.

"Who?"

"Saint Dane. He's in this building."

"We don't know that."

"C'mon, mate!" Spader exclaimed. "You know he's got to have his slimy hands in this. He sent those gunmen to the flume to kill Press, then he sent 'em after us. How else would those wogglies know we were here?"

"Then how come one of 'em is dead?"

"I'm still working on that; give me some time."

Spader's hatred for Saint Dane was starting to bubble up again. That was bad. We had to keep our eyes on the ball, and that meant not letting our emotions take over.

"Spader," I said cautiously. "You know you've gotta be cool about this, right?"

"Yeah, yeah," he assured me. "Cool as a cooger fish, that's me. Don't worry, Pendragon. I made you a promise. I won't go back on you."

"I believe you," I said. I really, *really* hoped I was right.

That's when the door opened and Gunny walked in. I thought he looked a little older than he had earlier. He was the kind of guy who wanted everything to be just so. Having gangsters plunge to a gruesome death from his hotel wasn't part of his perfect picture.

"I've seen a lot of things happen at this hotel," he said with a shaky voice. "But this beats 'em all."

"Be patient," I cautioned him. "We're just getting started."

Spader said, "What's all this talk about a natty-do around here?"

"A what?" asked Gunny, once again confused by an expression of Spader's.

"You said there was going to be a war here at the hotel," I jumped in. "What's up with that?"

Gunny sat down in one of the easy chairs and let out a tired breath. Spader and I sat across from him on the same couch Spader had toppled over on the gangsters.

"You ever hear of a thing called Prohibition?" he asked.

"Yeah," I said. "Isn't that when the government out-lawed booze?"

"Exactly," said Gunny. "No wine, no beer, no whiskey, no

nothin'. From 1920 until they gave up on it in 1933. It was all against the law, unless you knew where to go. Most people knew where to go."

"Speakeasies, right?" I asked.

"Speak easy?" asked Spader. "I'm losing you two."

"A lot of people got rich during Prohibition," Gunny continued. "Some did it making booze—they called it bootlegging. Others sold it in secret clubs called speakeasies; still others shipped it here, there, and everywhere right under the noses of the police. It was all very illegal. It made a lot of gangsters rich and put a lot of others behind bars. Put a lot of them six feet under dirt, too."

"What's that got to do with us?" I asked.

"There was a gang," Gunny continued. "Operated on the Upper East Side here. They had it all covered—bootlegging, shipping, even ran a couple of speakeasies. Made a lot of money for the two bosses. One of 'em was a gentleman named Maximilian Rose."

"The big guy with the fancy suit we met outside?" I asked.

"One and the same," answered Gunny.

"Who was the other boss?" asked Spader.

"Fellow named Winn Farrow."

Spader and I shot each other a look. "That's who those gangsters were working for!" I shouted. "Farrow and Rose are partners?"

"They *were* partners," Gunny answered. "Long time ago. As I heard it, Rose was the smart one. He knew Prohibition wouldn't last forever, so he started investing his money into other businesses. Some legal, some not. He got his fingers into all kinds of criminal activities like gambling and smuggling and even art theft. When Prohibition ended, he didn't miss a beat. Just kept going on making money."

"What about Farrow?" asked Spader.

"He was just as crooked, but not as smart. He didn't have the same style as Rose. Let's say he was rough around the edges."

"So he was a dumb thug," I said.

"Pretty much," agreed Gunny. "He spent his money fast as he made it. When Prohibition went away, he had nothing to show for it. Rose didn't have any use for him, so they split up. Way I heard it, Farrow didn't like that much. Now the two are what you might call enemies."

"What's Farrow doing now?" I asked.

"He's got his own gang that operates out of an old meat-packing plant downtown. They're a bad bunch. They'll slit your throat just to get your wallet. It's pretty much all they're good at."

"So while Max Rose is hanging out in a fancy penthouse uptown," I said, "his old partner, Winn Farrow, is struggling to get by downtown."

"That about sums it up," Gunny said. "And that's why I'm getting nervous. If Winn Farrow is sending his goons up here to make trouble, and they start falling out of windows, we might find ourselves in the middle of a gang war. People die in gang wars. We may have just seen the first."

"It's worse than that," I added. "Saint Dane has gotta be in this equation somewhere."

"Take it another step, mates," Spader jumped in. "What do these two gangs have to do with setting off this tum-tigger you call World War Two?"

"There's one thing we can say for certain," I added. "Whatever Saint Dane's got in mind for First Earth, I think we're sitting right in the middle of it."

"So what do we do?" asked Spader. "Just sit around waiting for more wogglies to show up with guns, looking for us?"

"I have an idea," said Gunny. "You two have jobs now. Once people get to know you, you can come and go as you please. You might even get closer to Max Rose and his boys. He's got a whole penthouse up there, with people coming and going all the time. There's a lot you can learn just by doing your job in a place like this."

"Sounds like a plan," I said. "Tomorrow we go to work."

And that's how we began our careers as bellhops at the Manhattan Tower Hotel. Our goal was to learn as much about Max Rose and his gangster buddies as we could. We were going undercover. No problem, right?

Yeah, right.

Early the next morning Spader and I put on our spiffy uniforms and reported to Gunny in the lobby of the hotel. Our first duty was to get haircuts. Gunny brought us to the hotel barbershop where Spader and I sat side by side in big, padded leather chairs that spun around. I knew we were in trouble when the barbers didn't start with scissors. They went right for the electric sheers. Gulp. With Gunny behind us smiling, Spader and I got buzzed. We didn't end up with Marine cuts or anything drastic like that, but our hair ended up so short, it wasn't even worth brushing.

The barbers put some kind of goop in our hair that smelled like lemons. It gave us both a slicked-back kind of look that may have been perfect for 1937, but felt greasy and awful. Mental note to self: Wash hair often.

Now that we were all cleaned up and presentable, we went to work. Gunny was right. The job wasn't all that hard. We had to meet guests when they arrived at the hotel and bring their luggage up to their rooms. When they checked out, we'd pick up their luggage and bring it down to the lobby. It was pretty much a no-brainer. The main thing was to be polite and not break anything.

We ate our meals in the big, noisy kitchen with the other bellhops and soon became accepted as regular staff people. That was key because it meant we could pretty much go wherever we wanted in the hotel. Nobody questioned us. The only tricky thing was going back to our room. We didn't want Dewey to start wondering why we always got off on the sixth floor. So at the end of our shift we always climbed the stairs instead of taking the elevator. What a pain.

I could tell you guys more about what it was like to be a bellhop, but that's not the important part of the story. What mattered was figuring out the connection between the gangsters and Saint Dane. That meant we had to watch Maximilian Rose. Easier said than done. He always had these gorilla-look-alike bodyguards surrounding him and we couldn't let them catch us spying on their boss. They might take us out into the alley and rub us out, or whatever it was the old-time gangsters did to people they didn't like. So we had to be careful. Luckily there were three of us, so we could take turns and hopefully not be too obvious.

Rose lived in the penthouse on the thirtieth floor of the hotel. He didn't leave very often. That's because he had a lot of enemies and liked to stay where it was safe. He had tons of visitors though. I guess that's how he did his business. People would come to him. Dewey told me stories about the odd assortment of goons he brought up to the thirtieth floor. What a strange and scary way to live.

Since Rose didn't go out much, we didn't see him much. Mostly all we could do was check out his visitors to try and figure out what he might be up to. But I'm no detective, and it's not like these guys were walking around with big signs saying "Friend of Saint Dane" or anything. They all looked like average guys. Okay, they looked like average *gangster* guys, but you get the idea.

That is, except for one man. His name was Mr. Zell. I knew this because whenever he showed up, he had to pick up the lobby phone and call the penthouse to announce that he was there. Mr. Zell had a style that stood out from Rose's other visitors. His hair was blond and shiny and greased straight back. He always wore these perfect, gray suits that looked real expensive, like they were made for him. His eyes were sharp and always darting around, checking out the room. But he wasn't nervous. Just the opposite. He was real confident. I think he looked around because he always wanted to know exactly what was going on and who was watching him. The word would be "observant." I had to be extra careful not to be observed by Mr. Zell.

But there was one other big thing that made Mr. Zell stand out.

He had an accent. A German accent.

Ordinarily I wouldn't think twice about something like that, but I was in the middle of something that was definitely *not* ordinary. In a few years the United States would be at war with a whole bunch of guys with the same kind of accent. They weren't our enemies yet, but they would be. And since we figured that World War II was probably the turning point for the territory of First Earth, having a German guy hanging out with Mr. Rose definitely caught my attention.

I couldn't help but wonder if hiding beneath that slick, buttoned-up, German-accented appearance . . . was Saint Dane. Of course, I looked at *everyone* as a potential Saint Dane, but this guy jumped to the top of my list. It was making me nuts trying to figure out how to find out what he was doing with Max Rose.

Then one day I got my shot. It was a quiet afternoon and I was hanging in the lobby trying to look busy, when Mr. Zell strode in. I pretended to be polishing a table near the telephone he always used to call the penthouse. I was getting to be a pretty good detective.

Bobby Pendragon, Undercover Traveler.

"Penthouse, please," Zell said into the phone. He listened, then said, "Good morning, this is Ludwig Zell. Yes, I will be staying for lunch today. Thank you." He hung up and walked to the elevators.

Score! He was staying for lunch. That meant they would order room service. One of the other jobs the bellhops had was to deliver room service. This was my chance. I hurried through the lobby, trying not to look like I was hurrying through the lobby, and found Gunny at the bell captain station, reading a newspaper.

"Zell is here," I said quietly. "They're ordering room service."

Without a word, Gunny dropped the paper and headed for the kitchen. He knew what I was thinking. Normally, one of the more experienced bellhops would take the order up to Mr. Rose. It was a sweet gig because the gangster boss always gave good tips. I didn't care about the tip. I wanted to be in the same room with Max Rose and Ludwig Zell. When we got into the kitchen, the head waiter was already on the phone, taking the order. When he hung up, Gunny told him to give the order to me. The head waiter gave me a dirty look that said: "Why should *he* get special treatment?" But he couldn't argue. Gunny was the boss.

I was on.

While we waited for the food to be prepared, Gunny took me aside. "Be careful," he said. "Listen, but don't be obvious about it. If they think you're spying, you'll end up taking a walk off the balcony like that gangster from the subway."

"Don't worry," I answered. I'm not sure why I said that. *I* sure as heck was worrying; why shouldn't Gunny?

"These are bad people, Pendragon," Gunny warned.

"I know. I got it," I assured him. He was making me more nervous than I was already.

Ten minutes later the order was ready. It was spread out on a big cart that was covered with a sharp white tablecloth. There must have been two dozen plates covered with shiny steel lids. I wondered how many people were having lunch because there was enough food here to feed the Pittsburgh Steelers. Gunny gave me a wink of encouragement and I pushed the cart for the elevators.

"Going up!" Dewey announced as he slid open the elevator door.

I pushed the cart in and said: "Thirty, please."

Dewey's eyes grew wide as he closed the door. "You're taking that to Mr. Rose?" he asked with awe. "Whatever you do, don't look anybody in the eye."

"Why not?" I asked.

"I once made the mistake of looking at one of those thugs," Dewey said. "The goon picked me up and shoved me in the laundry chute. Headfirst! It was horrible."

I almost laughed, but that would have been rude. The idea of somebody jamming this geeky little guy into the chute was pretty funny. "How far did you fall?" I asked.

"I didn't," Dewey said. "I stuck my arms and legs out and held on to the sides until he was gone. Then I climbed out. But I could have been killed."

"Thanks for the advice," I said. "I'll be careful." As funny as the image was, Dewey's warning was valid. Max Rose and his pals were not nice guys. If they would jam somebody down a laundry chute for just looking at them, I didn't want to think what they might do if they caught me spying on them. I had to push that thought out of my head or I would have chickened out. Not that I had a choice, because a few seconds later we arrived at the thirtieth floor. The curtain was about to go up.

Dewey pulled the door open and said, "Good luck."

I gave him a weak smile and wheeled the cart outside. I had barely gotten out of the elevator when Dewey slammed the door shut behind me. I guess he didn't want to be sent on another laundry run.

I was met by two thick-looking dudes who stared at me like I was toe jam. One guy made a motion for me to step away from the cart. I took a few steps back, not sure of what was about to happen. As it turned out, this was a security check. While one guy examined the cart, the other guy examined *me*. I guess he was making sure I didn't have a gun or anything. The guy pawed me over pretty good. I felt like a melon being checked for ripeness. But I didn't complain. I didn't want to end up in the laundry chute. After this totally rude once-over, both guys stepped back and motioned for me to pass.

I wanted to complain about the rough treatment, but remembered Dewey's warning and put my head down and shut up. After all, I was on a mission.

Bobby Pendragon, Undercover Traveler.

The door to the penthouse was at the end of the corridor. I wheeled the cart up and was about to knock when I saw that there was a button for a doorbell. Pretty fancy. I pressed it and heard soft chimes ringing inside. A second later the door opened, and I came face-to-face with another tough-looking dude.

"Room service," I announced cheerily. I probably didn't have to say that, since I was wheeling a cart loaded with food, but this guy didn't look like a brain surgeon. I didn't want to take any chances. He motioned for me to come in. I wheeled the cart in and kept my eyes down.

"Wait here," the guy grunted, and walked off. That's when I looked up and got my first glimpse of the penthouse suite. Man, this place was fancy! It looked like I had stepped into some kind of European drawing room. Not that I had ever been in a European drawing room, but I had been in those fancy period rooms in the Metropolitan Museum of Art. I'm not exactly sure why they were called drawing rooms either. It's not like they were doing any drawing.

The furniture was way fancy and kind of fragile looking. On the ceiling was an elaborate painting of some chubby babies with wings, flying around in the clouds, blowing trumpets. Not exactly my taste in art, but I guessed some people thought it was elegant. The room I stood in was a central entrance hall. Corridors spread in three different directions to the rest of the penthouse. As I stood there gazing at the fancy surroundings, one thought came to mind: There must be a lot of money in being a gangster.

Then I heard a gruff voice bellow from somewhere else, "This is what's gonna happen. . . ."

It was Maximilian Rose. He sounded angry. That was bad.

"If he says he needs two weeks, give him one," Rose said angrily. "If he asks for one week, give him three days. If he doesn't like it, I'll have somebody pay him a visit and convince him to like it, understand?" This was followed by the *slam* of a telephone.

A second later a door opened, and Max Rose stepped out. I tried not to look right at the guy, but it was hard not to. He was like a giant storm cloud—big and loud and angry. Though it was afternoon, he was wearing pajamas, a bathrobe, and slippers. It was a fancy robe, all red and shiny, like silk. I caught a quick glimpse into the room behind him. It was an office with a desk loaded with papers. This guy did business in his pajamas. Nice life.

When he stepped through the door, the first thing he saw was me. Before I knew it, we had made eye contact. Gulp. Hello, laundry.

"Hey, Buck Rogers!" he shouted with a smile. He wasn't angry anymore. Phew. "Didn't think I'd remember, did ya?"

I didn't. He had only seen me for a few seconds a couple of weeks ago. Note to self: This guy was observant and had a good memory. Be careful.

"Hello, Mr. Rose," I said politely. "Ready for lunch?"

"I'm starving," he said. "Follow me."

I wheeled the cart across to the far side of the foyer and into a room that was even fancier than the entryway. It was a huge, totally swanky living room. The couches were big and cushy, the tables were intricately carved, and there were tons of giant oil paintings with thick gold frames. But the big deal in this room was the view. One whole wall had nothing but floor-to-ceiling windows that looked out over Manhattan. It was pretty cool.

Again, all I could think was that gangsters sure made a lot of money.

"Set it out there, Buck," he ordered, pointing to a large, dark table.

Buck. Right. That was me. "How many should I set up for, Mr. Rose?"

"How many?" He looked at me like I had just asked him how many arms he had. "There's two of us. How many did you think?"

I then noticed that Ludwig Zell was sitting in an easy chair near the door. The guy looked at me with cold eyes that made me shiver. Was it Saint Dane? If so, he wasn't tipping his hand.

"Yes sir, Mr. Rose," I said. I didn't want to point out that he had more food here than they served to the whole school for lunch at Stony Brook Junior High. Then again, at Stony Brook they didn't serve steaks and lobsters and salads made with vegetables carved into flower shapes. I kept my mouth shut and set the table.

"So, Ludwig," Rose said to the German. "I wanted to make this meal special, like a celebration, you know?"

The German stood up and walked to Rose. "You are too thoughtful, Mr. Rose. This is the beginning of a relationship that will be long and fruitful for both of us. And our people."

This was better than I could have hoped for. I was listening in on these two guys doing business. I didn't want to finish setting out lunch too quickly so I could hear as much as possible, but I didn't want to make it look like I was, well, doing exactly that. This was tricky.

"You know, Ludwig, I've gone out on a limb for you," Rose said. "I've already started to deliver and haven't seen a dime from those people of yours."

"I understand, my friend," answered Zell. "And we appreciate your trust. Now that we have determined the most efficient means of payment, you won't have to work on faith much longer."

"Yeah, but how *much* longer?" asked Rose.

"Your first payment will be arriving May sixth, as promised," answered Zell. "You have my word, and the word of my party."

This was incredible. I was getting all sorts of stuff. Max Rose was doing some kind of work for this Zell guy. But what party was he talking about?

"Hey, spaceman!" barked Rose. "You done or what?"

"Yes sir, Mr. Rose," I said, and stood at attention.

Max Rose walked toward me, digging into the pocket of his bathrobe. Uh-oh. Did I hear too much? Did he have a gun? Was I about to get filled full of lead?

No. He pulled out some dollar bills and jammed them into my hand. It was my tip.

"Now blast off," he said.

"Thank you, sir. Enjoy your lunch," I said, and beat it for the door. I had already gotten more information than I could have hoped for. So while Rose and Zell sat down for their stupid-huge lunch, I closed the door and made a beeline for the front door. I couldn't wait to tell Spader and Gunny what I had learned.

I was halfway to the door when I saw something that made me stop. It was the door to Max Rose's office.

It was open and the office was empty.

I knew instantly that I was faced with a huge opportunity. Sitting on that desk could have been more information about the business that Rose and Zell were in. All I had to do was duck in, take a quick look, and get out. Of course, I could also get caught, and rather than leaving through the front door, I could be exiting the penthouse through a window. Next stop: pavement. I had to make a decision, fast. Every second counted.

I did it. After a quick look around to make sure none of

Rose's goons were close, I shot into the office. It was crazy, but I had to.

As soon as I got inside, I closed the door. If somebody happened to walk by, it would be better if they didn't see a sweaty bellboy flipping through Max Rose's personal papers. That would hurt. Once the door was closed, I turned my attention to the desk. I wanted to be in and out fast, so I moved quickly behind the desk and looked down at the mass of papers.

I had no idea what to look for. It was just a bunch of business papers, contracts, and lists of figures like an accountant would use. My heart sank. Saint Dane's plan on First Earth could have been sitting right in front of me and I wouldn't know it.

I was about to give up and run out when something caught my eye. It couldn't have stood out more from the rest of the pages if it had a flashing red light on it. First off, it looked nothing like any of the other pages. It was a single sheet with a bold logo on top. That alone would have made my eye go to it, but there was one other thing. It was the logo itself. It was something I had seen before, many times. I'd seen it in movies and in books and on TV. But seeing it now, this way, made my stomach do a flip. I knew what this logo represented. And this wasn't a movie.

It was a swastika, the crooked cross that was the symbol of the Nazi party. It was surrounded by a wreath, upon which an angry eagle was perched with its wings spread wide. As I already told you, I'm no expert on World War II history, but I knew for sure that this was a letter from Germany and the Nazi party. The big question was, what was it doing on Max Rose's desk? I did my best to calm down and read the letter. It was short and straight to the point.

April 9, 1937

Dear Mr. Rose:

This letter is to confirm our agreement that the initial payments due to you for services rendered will be arriving in the U.S. via LZ-129 on May 6 of this year and will be available to you immediately. Form and amount of payment is as previously agreed upon. I trust this will be satisfactory and look forward to a long and successful partnership.

Sincerely,

Ludwig Zell

Now I knew what party Ludwig Zell was talking about. The Nazi Party. I couldn't take my eyes off the paper. It was an actual letter from the Nazis to Max Rose, proof they were doing business together. The frustrating thing was that it didn't say what kind of business. All it said was that payment was going to be made on May 6 and it was coming via LZ-129 . . . whatever *that* was.

LZ. Ludwig Zell? Were there 129 Ludwig Zells? Whatever it was, it proved that my suspicions about him were correct. He was not only a German dude, he was working for the big bad guys over in Europe. He was a Nazi.

But the most important thing was that I had found hard evidence of a connection between the Nazis in Germany and these gangsters in New York. Suddenly Gunny's far-fetched theory wasn't looking so far-fetched. Up until then we only suspected that the turning point on First Earth was about World War II. This piece of paper confirmed it. We already knew there was a link between Saint Dane and the gangsters. Now we had a link between the gangsters and the Nazis. Connect the dots. We were getting closer.

There was no way I could take this paper out of here, so I

committed it to memory. No problem. It was short enough that I could remember the most important facts: LZ-129; May 6; payment from the Nazis to Max Rose. Got it.

Now I had to bolt out of there. I snuck back to the door and put my ear to it, listening for sounds of anyone hanging around outside. I didn't hear a thing, so I grabbed the door-knob and gently gave it a turn. What happened next was so impossible, my mind wouldn't accept it at first.

The door was locked. I turned harder, but that didn't make it any less locked. My heart started to race. Maybe it was just stuck. I gave it a jiggle and a twist and a push. But no amount of jiggling or twisting or pushing helped. Nope, the door was locked all right . . . and I was on the wrong side. I looked to see if there was a locking lever that I could flip. There wasn't. There was only an old-fashioned keyhole. But seeing as I didn't have an old-fashioned key, that wasn't any help.

I wanted to scream. How could I have been so dumb as to pull the door closed without checking it first? This was totally my fault. I had snatched defeat from the jaws of victory. It would only be a matter of time before I was discovered, and then any hope of untangling the mystery of May 6 and LZ-129 would die right along with me.

Bobby Pendragon, *Dead* Undercover Traveler.

FIRST EARTH

Things couldn't be worse. I was locked in the private office of a vicious mobster who was going to eat me for dessert. Max Rose had a lot of goons on the payroll. One of them was bound to come by any second. I had to think fast and figure out some other way out of there.

I spun around and scanned the office. Yes! There was another door behind his desk. Why hadn't I seen that before? I ran for it and twisted the knob. It was locked.

Ahhhh! What was it with this guy and locked doors? You'd think he was a crook or something. I had to come up with a Plan B. Fast. Uncle Press always had a Plan B. I really wished he were there to give it to me, because I was coming up empty.

Then I saw the telephone. Of course! Max Rose had slammed down this very phone a few minutes ago. How could I forget? I could call Gunny for help. I wasn't exactly sure of what Gunny could do, but right now, this was my only hope. So I dove for the old (okay, new for 1937) black phone, yanked the receiver off the cradle, and dialed. It was a rotary dial thing, and my hands were shaking as I stuck my finger in the "9" hole. Number 99 was the bell captain's desk. Dialing 9-9 would bring Gunny to me, and hopefully Gunny would bring me to safety. I dialed the first nine and winced as it made a loud, raspy sound like a saw cutting through wood. But I couldn't stop now.

I was just about to dial the second nine when I heard something. It was a quiet sound, but it might just as well have been a nuclear explosion, because I was sure it was going to be just as bad for me.

Someone was opening the door behind the desk.

It was too late to run and there was no place to hide. I was busted. As scared as I was, I made sure *not* to dial the second nine. I didn't want them to know I was calling Gunny. No sense in getting us *all* killed. So I slowly returned the receiver to its cradle and waited for a gun muzzle to be jammed into my back.

"I don't think you're supposed to be in here," came a voice from behind me.

Yeah, right. You think?

But the sound of this voice gave me a flicker of hope. For one, it was the voice of a woman. She didn't sound angry, either. Maybe I could talk my way out of this. After all, I had the Traveler power of persuasion, right? Without turning around I said, "I just brought lunch up to Mr. Rose. The hotel wanted to make it special, but somebody forgot to put champagne on the cart. It was supposed to be a gift, on the house. So I came in here to call down for somebody to bring it up and the door locked behind me."

It was a total bluff, but all I could think of. Would she buy it? Or would she scream for Rose's goons to come in here and toss me out the window? The next few seconds felt like a lifetime.

Finally she said, "Here, take this."

Uh-oh. Was it a bullet?

"Turn around," she said with a laugh. "I won't bite."

I slowly turned around to see who I was dealing with.

Wow. Standing in the doorway was a beautiful woman who looked like some kind of old-time movie star. She was dressed in a long, ivory nightgown that looked as slick as silk. It wasn't embarrassing or anything because she had a silky robe over it. Her hair was dark and done in a perfect do. She wore perfect makeup, too. This wasn't somebody who had just fallen out of bed. She looked ready for a photo shoot. I couldn't tell how old she was, not with all the elegant makeup and all, but I'm guessing she was in her twenties. She had a little smile that told me she knew exactly how scared I was.

Once I got over the shock of seeing her, I saw something else that made my heart leap. She was holding out an old-fashioned brass key on a ring.

"I don't know why he makes all the doors lock that way," she said softly. "Maybe to catch people who go into places they shouldn't." She said this with a smile, like she was needling me. I think she liked to see me squirm. Good for her, because I was definitely squirming. I reached out and took the key.

"Thanks," I said. "It was a big mistake. I never should have come in here."

I went back to the main door and used the key to unlock it. When I opened the door, I was relieved to see that nobody villainous was lurking around in the entryway. I was beginning to think I had a chance of getting out of here alive. Quickly I returned the key to the woman, saying, "I'm very embarrassed."

"Don't worry about it," said the woman. "I'll never tell." She put her finger to her lips to emphasize her promise to "shush." It all seemed kind of flirty. Oh yeah, this was going to work out. I gave her a sincerely grateful smile, then turned for the door and freedom.

"Hey!" she shouted after me. I froze. I was seconds away from a clean escape. What had gone wrong? I turned back to her sheepishly.

"What about the champagne? Aren't you going to make that call?"

Oops. I hadn't followed through with the bluff. I was such a bad liar. Was this going to bite me in the butt? I had to think fast, again. "Uh . . . I really shouldn't be in here," I said. "I'll go downstairs and bring it back up myself."

"Good idea," she said. "You're a smart kid." With that, she left through the door behind the desk..

Ding Dong! The doorbell rang. In a few seconds one of Rose's thugs would appear to answer it, and I was still in the office! I quickly dashed out and across the entryway toward the front door.

"Hey, you still here?" somebody bellowed. It was the guy who first opened the door for me when I arrived.

"Just leaving," I said. The thug pushed past me and opened the door. Standing outside was Gunny, with a bottle of champagne chilling in a bucket of ice.

"For Mr. Rose," he said. "Compliments of the Manhattan Tower Hotel."

I glanced back over my shoulder and saw that the movie-star lady was watching from the corridor. It was perfect. Gunny had cemented my bluff without even knowing it. I was home free.

The thug took the champagne, then pushed me out the door and closed it behind us. Gunny and I made brief eye contact, but didn't say a word. We walked quickly past the two security guards in the corridor, stopped at the elevator, and rang for Dewey. The elevator arrived seconds later and we rode silently down to the lobby. Dewey looked at me the whole way down, dying to know what had happened. But he wasn't going to ask with Gunny there, and I sure as heck wasn't going to tell him anything. When we got to the lobby, Gunny and I stepped out of the elevator and kept walking until Dewey was out of earshot.

Finally Gunny said under his breath, "You were up there too long, shorty. I was getting nervous. I had to make up an excuse to go up."

"It was perfect," I added. "And totally worth it. Wait'll you hear." The two of us parted and went about our business for the rest of the day as if nothing scary had happened.

That night Spader, Gunny, and I met in our room, and I told them everything that had happened in Max Rose's penthouse.

"So these Nazi wogglies," Spader said, "they're pretty nasty characters?"

"Yes," was my simple answer.

"As bad as the gangster boys around here?" he asked.

"Worse," I answered. "These guys aren't just criminals. The Nazis are about taking over the whole territory and murdering millions of people along the way."

"So they're like, Saint Dane—bad," was Spader's conclusion.

"Yeah, they're Saint Dane—bad," I agreed.

"So then, what are they planning together?" Spader asked with frustration.

"That is the big question, isn't it?" Gunny said.

What was Saint Dane trying to do here? Aside from the murderous mission of two gangsters at the flume in the subway, the demon hadn't made his presence known.

"The Nazis are going to pay Max Rose for his services on May sixth," I said while pacing. "I think if we figure out what Max Rose is doing for the Nazis, we'll know what Saint Dane's plan is."

"And what is Ludwig Zell-one-twenty-nine?" asked Spader. "Sounds like some kind of code."

"We don't know if it's Ludwig Zell-one-twenty-nine," I said. "Only L-Z-one-two-nine."

I looked to Gunny, but Gunny only shrugged. LZ-129 might be the key to this whole thing, or mean absolutely nothing.

"I'll keep snooping around," said Gunny.

We ended the meeting by saying we had to keep a closer eye on Max Rose and his band of merry men. We decided to read every newspaper we could get, every day, to see if there was any mention of LZ-129 or Ludwig Zell. You never knew. For the first time since I had gotten to First Earth, I had the feeling that we were on our way to figuring out what Saint Dane had in mind to disrupt this territory.

I was absolutely, totally wrong.

What *really* happened after that meeting was nothing. I'm serious, absolutely nothing. The trail went stone freakin' cold. Max Rose never left the penthouse. Ludwig Zell didn't come by the hotel again. We didn't have any trouble with Winn Farrow and his gang of killers. We read every newspaper from New York, New Jersey, and Connecticut, but didn't find a single reference to Ludwig Zell or LZ-129. Remember, this was long before the Internet. It's not like we could sign on to a search engine, input "Ludwig Zell, evil Nazi mobster plan" and get a complete history of the guy and what he was up to.

This was *way* frustrating.

Gunny even went to some government offices to look for

any documents that showed the kinds of businesses Max Rose was involved in. Good idea, except for one thing. This was 1937. An African American guy walking into government offices looking for information wasn't exactly common. This was long before the civil rights movement. Guys like Jackie Robinson, Martin Luther King Jr., Colin Powell, Clarence Thomas from the Supreme Court, and Nelson Mandela hadn't broken down any barriers yet. They didn't even have very many black movie stars like Will Smith or Eddie Murphy.

So Gunny pretty much walked into a bunch of brick walls.

It would have been a totally depressing situation, if Spader and I hadn't tried to have a little fun along the way. He showed me a good time on his home territory of Cloral, so I wanted to do the same for him on First Earth.

I took him to see a lot of movies. He had never seen anything like a movie before, and it was fun to watch his reaction. He was freaked at first, kind of like when we saw the holograms on Veelox. But after a while he got with the program. The admission price was only twenty-five cents. Can you believe it? I took him to see lots of Marx Brothers movies, my favorite being *A Night at the Opera*. We saw some Westerns with a guy named Tom Mix, and even saw the original *King Kong*. It was fun to see these movies on a big screen instead of television.

We toured all over New York. I took him to the top of the Empire State Building, which was cool because we had just seen King Kong climb the thing. We went to the Statue of Liberty and Grand Central Station and even took a subway out to Coney Island to ride the rides and eat hot dogs.

I think my favorite day was when we went up to the Bronx. No, not to the flume. We went to a Yankees game. I couldn't believe it, but I saw both Lou Gehrig and Joe

DiMaggio play! How cool is *that*? Spader didn't understand the game and it was hard to explain, but it didn't matter. I was in hog heaven.

And speaking of heaven, we also played a lot of basketball.

When it comes to athletic stuff, I have to admit that Spader is better than I am in everything. He's a little older and bigger, which helps. (At least, that's what I tell myself.) But when it comes to basketball, well, that's my game.

At the risk of sounding crude, I kicked his ass. We set up a hoop in an alley behind the hotel and snuck out every chance we got. Gunny found us a crusty old leather ball. The rim was all bent and rusty with no net, but it didn't matter. I recruited some of the other bellhops, and we played two on two. We even got Dewey to play, but he was worse than Spader. Poor guy.

Our games were like minivacations away from Traveler worries. They put my mind back to a time and place when things were a whole lot easier, and the biggest concern I had was whether or not Courtney liked me as much as I liked her. (Yes, Courtney, I used to think about that a lot. I admit it.)

Though our adventures exploring First Earth were excellent, there was always the big old sword of worry hanging over our heads. The longer we went without finding out anything about Max Rose and the Nazis, the more anxious I became. May 6 was drawing closer. It was beginning to look as if nothing would happen until then.

I was wrong. On May 3, things started getting interesting again.

The day started out normally, except that the hotel was expecting a celebrity guest. Her name was Nancy Olsen, but everybody knew her as "Jinx." She was a pilot who flew for the Coast Guard. They didn't have many women pilots back then, and Jinx was a real hotshot. She was touring around the country doing public relations. I guess the idea was to get women interested in signing up for military service. In 1937 women didn't normally do things like fly for the Coast Guard, so Jinx Olsen was unique.

Her tour brought her to New York, where she was going to stay at the hotel for a week while making appearances and giving speeches. There was even a big party planned for her in the ballroom on the twenty-ninth floor of the hotel. It was going to be a big doo-dah with a band and celebrities and politicians and the works. Spader and I had already been asked to be waiters for the party because there were going to be over two hundred guests, and they needed all the help they could get.

When Jinx Olsen arrived at the hotel, I could tell instantly why she was chosen to be the poster girl for the Coast Guard. She was tall and pretty and oozed confidence. Most of the women I had seen on First Earth wore dresses— but not Jinx. She had on khakis and a worn, brown leather jacket. But she didn't look like a guy. No way. She had these dazzling green eyes and a big smile that absolutely lit up the room. When she first strode into the hotel lobby with her duffel bag over her shoulder, the first word that jumped into my head was "adventurer."

The hotel manager, a chubby guy named Mr. Caplesmith, was right there to greet her. "Welcome, Miss Olsen," he said. "We are so honored to have you stay with us."

Jinx stopped short, stared the guy square in the eyes and asked, "Why?"

Mr. Caplesmith got a little flustered and said, "Well, because you're such a famous, uh, pilot person." He had no clue about what made Jinx Olsen tick, and Jinx Olsen knew it.

"Let's be honest," she said. "You're happy to see me because Uncle Sam is paying you to put on a big old party tomorrow night, right?"

Mr. Caplesmith was embarrassed, but he knew better than to lie to her. "Well, you could say that," he said sheepishly.

Jinx smiled and gave him a friendly punch on the arm. "No problem. Just so we all know the score. Where's my room?"

Mr. Caplesmith tried hard not to grab his arm in pain. He looked around and saw me.

"Bell boy!" he ordered.

I ran up and stood at attention. Mr. Caplesmith liked that.

"Please take Miss Olsen up to room fifteen-fifteen." He gave me the room key.

I reached for Jinx's bag, but she didn't give it up. "I can handle it, chief," she said with a smile. "Just show me the way."

"Yes ma'am," I said, and made for the elevator. Jinx followed right after me. I glanced back quickly and saw Mr. Caplesmith massaging his sore arm. It was hard not to laugh. Jinx Olsen was the coolest person I had met since starting work at this hotel, aside from Gunny of course.

"You've got a pretty exciting job," I said. "Making rescues with the Coast Guard and all."

"Yeah, real exciting," she said. It didn't sound like she meant it.

"It's not?" I asked.

"It would be if they actually let me do it once in a while. It's not easy getting the call, being a woman and all." We arrived at the elevator and Dewey started us on our way up. He even got the controls right the first time. He must have been practicing.

"That's not fair," I said to Jinx. "If you've got the chops, you should be flying the missions."

"You know how many times I've told them that?" Jinx said. "But they'd rather trot me out on these public relations tours where I won't get scratched. Heck, I'm a better flier than most of the boys in my squad, but because I'm a woman, well, I don't get the chance."

"Do you know Amelia Earhart?" Dewey asked.

"I've met her," answered Jinx. "Now *that* gal is a flier!"

"Amelia Earhart?" I asked. "Isn't that the woman pilot who disappeared when she was trying to fly around the world?"

Dewey and Jinx looked at me like I was from Pluto.

"You must be mistaken," Jinx said. "She's leaving on her round-the-world trip the end of this month."

Oops. First Earth. I was talking about something that hadn't happened yet. I wasn't wrong though. I remembered seeing a TV show about Amelia Earhart. She never made it. I didn't have the heart to tell them. On the other hand, they never would have believed me because I was talking about the future. Luckily, we had arrived on the fifteenth floor.

"We're here," I announced, and hurried out of the elevator before I had to talk any more about Amelia Earhart. I opened up room 1515 for Jinx and told her that if she needed anything, she should call Gunny, the bell captain, and he'd make sure one of us took care of her. She thanked me and gave me a twenty-five-cent tip. Not exactly a lot of cash, but it would pay for another Marx Brothers movie.

"You know something?" I said. "You may be having a tough time, but someday soon there will be a lot of women fliers. People are going to realize they're just as good as the guys. Things will change. I guarantee it."

This made Jinx smile. She came across as pretty tough, but

I'll bet that was because she had to survive in a macho man's job. But in that brief moment, her guard came down, and I saw beyond the bold front to the real person.

"What's your name, chief?" she asked.

"Bobby Pendragon."

"I'm Jinx, Bobby. Thanks for the kind words. I'll remember them." She winked at me and we shook hands.

I liked Jinx Olsen. Her confidence and cockiness reminded me a lot of Spader. I hoped she was going to get the chance to prove herself someday.

The party in her honor was the following night, and it was a real fancy deal. The ballroom on the twenty-ninth floor was all decked out with red, white, and blue decorations. There must have been a thousand colorful balloons floating up on the ceiling. The men wore tuxedos and the women were in long, formal gowns. I recognized some old-time movie stars, but didn't know their names. There was one guy I definitely recognized though—it was Lou Gehrig. Even out of his Yankees uniform, I knew who he was.

There was a big orchestra playing for people to dance. The musicians all wore white jackets and looked like they had stepped out of an Abbott and Costello movie. I even recognized some of the music they were playing. Like I always said, if you want to learn about classical music, watch old Bugs Bunny cartoons. If you want to learn about old-time swing music, watch Abbott and Costello movies. Who says TV isn't educational?

There was a long table set up on one side of the room for the dignitaries. That's where Jinx sat, right in the middle. She was wearing a dress but looked totally uncomfortable in it. I felt sorry for her. This was the price she had to pay for being allowed to fly. She had to be a goodwill ambassador and put on a happy face for the world. I guarantee she hated it.

The rest of the room was full of tables where people ate and drank. This was where Spader and I did our thing. A whole bunch of other waiters were brought in for the party, and we all wore these short white jackets, black pants, and white gloves. It was pretty cake work. We were each assigned to a table and had to shuttle back and forth to the kitchen, bringing out the food. Basically all I had to do was make sure I didn't spill anything.

The reason I'm telling you guys so much about this party isn't because it was such a gala, fun affair. Bo-ring. It's because of one particular table of guests. Sitting prominently, right near the long head table, was Max Rose and his crew. I couldn't believe it. Here was a swanky party put on by the U.S. government and sitting front and center was a known gangster. My guess was he was there because he was the most important guest of the hotel. I guess when you're the best customer, you get privileges . . . even if you're a mobster.

Gunny made sure that Spader and I were assigned to Max Rose's table. We both hovered around him and his guests, taking care of their every little whim. But what we were really doing was listening to everything being said, hoping to catch some clue as to what LZ-129 was, or what was going to happen on May 6.

"Buck Rogers!" shouted Rose when he saw me. "My favorite spaceman. They got you working as a waiter, too?"

"Yes sir, Mr. Rose," I said. "Nothing but the best for you."

He laughed. I think he liked it when somebody was a little bit cocky. Especially if they complimented him. "Keep the wine coming, Buck," he said. "I'll make it worth your while."

"Yes, sir!" I said. This was good. I planned on being right by his side every chance I got. All the seats were taken by various thugs I had seen coming in and out of the hotel. Unfortunately Ludwig Zell wasn't one of them. But the chair next to Rose was empty. I hoped that it was reserved for our Nazi friend. I had just popped a bottle of champagne and was pouring it for Rose, when the guest who was assigned to the empty chair finally showed up. It wasn't Zell.

"Sorry I'm late, Maxie," came a woman's voice. "It took me forever to find the perfect gown to wear."

I looked up and nearly dropped the champagne bottle. It was the movie star–looking woman who caught me in Max Rose's office.

She looked at me and winked. My heart stopped. I was afraid she'd say something about what had happened in the office. That would be death. My death. She picked up her champagne glass and held it out for me to fill.

"Such a handsome young waiter," she said. "Have we ever met?"

Was she kidding? Did she remember me or was she just pulling my chain?

"I don't think so, ma'am," I lied.

"You must be right," she said. "I'd never forget a handsome young man like you." She gave me a small smile and a wink. She knew *exactly* who I was. She was just messing with me again. I was starting to sweat, so I got away from there fast. This was going to be an interesting night.

Right after dinner there was a bunch of speeches that all sounded alike. A lot of politicians talked about the important role that women were going to play in the military and the Coast Guard and blah, blah, blah. The final speech was given by Jinx herself. I'm sorry to say, her speech wasn't so hot either. She did her best to deliver it like she cared, but I could tell she hated every minute of it.

After the speeches the band kicked in again for people to dance. That's when I got my next surprise. The bandleader stepped up to the microphone and announced in a silky smooth voice, "Ladies and gentlemen, please welcome to the microphone our featured vocalist for this evening, the lovely Esther Amaden."

I looked around to see who the lovely lady was, and who should stand up but Max Rose's girlfriend! Yeow! No wonder she looked so great. She was a professional singer. She was good, too. Not that I'm a big fan of that music, but she had a great voice and looked terrific under the spotlight. She sang a couple of songs that sounded sorta familiar. The people at the party must have known all of them because they each got big applause when she started to sing.

In all, it was a very elegant evening . . . and totally frustrating. After a long night the party was about to wind down, and I hadn't heard a single nugget of useful information from anybody at Rose's table. As far as our mission was concerned, the night was going to be a total bust.

At least, that's what I thought. Truth was, things were about to change dramatically.

There were a lot of waiters working the party. I knew all the bellhops, but didn't know any of the new waiters who'd come on just for the night. There was no reason to. All I was interested in was Max Rose and his table. But as I stood there listening to Esther Amaden sing, I saw something that got me interested in something besides Max Rose real quick.

I was standing near the kitchen door, watching the show. The band was glowing under a warm, blue light. A mirrored ball on the ceiling was spinning and shooting out little white sparkles of light that looked like fireflies. They washed over the band, the dancers, and the tables. Esther looked beautiful in the center of it all in a white spotlight.

I don't know what made me look away when I did, but it was a good thing. What I saw rocked me into Defcon 10. It was one of the new waiters. I think I noticed him because he was walking slowly, with his back to the wall. If there was one thing the waiters weren't doing that night, it was walking slowly. It was way too busy for that. But this guy was just sort of creeping along.

He was holding a big serving tray with a silver dome over it. That wouldn't have been weird . . . two hours before. But now we were done with the food. What was he doing with a serving tray? To make things even more interesting, he was headed toward the table with Max Rose. I took a few steps to get a better look at him, and when I did, my jaw dropped.

I knew this guy! It was Mr. Nervous, the gangster from the subway!

The music was loud. The party was in full swing. People were dancing like crazy.

Nobody saw this guy stalking closer to Max Rose. A moment later he reached under the dome of the serving tray and pulled out a gun. Winn Farrow's men may have been laying low for a long time, but tonight they were back in action. Tonight they were going after Max Rose.

And I was the only one who knew it.

FIRST EARTH

The assassin drew closer to Max Rose.

About a million thoughts clicked through my head rapid fire. Max Rose was a criminal, a killer. A guy in that line of work is bound to have something ugly come down on him sooner or later. That was his business. But Rose and his gang were somehow connected to the Nazis. If he died, our only hope of discovering what they were up to, and what Saint Dane was up to, would die along with him. The future of First Earth depended on what Max Rose knew . . . and that was *my* business.

It took me all of two seconds to realize I had to save Max Rose. But how? If I shouted a warning, the nervous gangster would start shooting and that would be the ballgame. No, I had to act.

Spader walked out of the kitchen at that exact moment. I grabbed him and pointed him toward the stalking gangster. "He's going after Max Rose. We gotta stop him," I said, trying to sound like I was more in control of my emotions than I really was.

Spader didn't question me. He didn't debate or hesitate. As

soon as he saw the situation and knew I wanted it stopped, he clicked into "go" mode.

"I'll take out the wogglie, you go for Rose," he ordered with total authority. A half second later he was pushing through the crowd, headed after the gangster.

The show was on and I had to move. I started running for Max Rose's table. The shortest line was straight through the crowded dance floor. I tried to skirt the swinging dancers, but that was impossible and slowing me down. There was no way I'd make it in time by being polite. I figured everybody's evening was about to be ruined in a few seconds anyway, so why worry? I put my head down and started pumping my legs like a fullback. I blasted through a few unsuspecting bodies, and I'm embarrassed to say that a few of them were ladies. But it didn't matter. I had to make it into the end zone and I would not be denied.

A few seconds later the final dancer between me and Rose's table spun out of the way, and I had a clear shot at my target. Max Rose was sitting on the far side of the big, round table, laughing and puffing on a fat cigar. A quick glance to my left showed me that the gangster with the gun was getting closer. Spader was fighting his way through the crowd to get to the guy, but he was going to be too late. The assassin was only a few steps away from his date with Max.

I looked back to Max Rose and saw there was a whole bunch of table and glassware and even a flowered center-piece between me and him. I had to make a snap decision. My blood was already boiling from my frenzied run across the dance floor, so the choice I made wasn't a tough one. I kicked it into another gear, ran for the table, and launched myself over the top. It all happened so fast that the goons sitting at the table didn't have time to react. I slid across the tabletop, pulling the tablecloth and everything else along with me.

Max Rose saw me coming and his eyes grew wide with surprise. The bodyguard sitting next to Rose went for his gun. But he was too late because just as he pulled the gun from under his jacket, Max Rose got slammed with a wave of tableware, flowers, and Bobby Pendragon, Undercover Traveler.

Rose had begun to stand up and that may have saved his life, because he was a little off balance. The force of me hitting him knocked him straight back. If he had been firmly planted in his chair, I probably would have bounced off him and he would have still been a target. But as it was, we both went over and he landed backward on the floor. He let out a huge grunt as I landed right on top of him. I told you, he was a big guy, and I swear I think I bounced off him like I'd hit a trampoline. The only thing missing was the sound of a timpani drum going *boing!*

It was at that exact instant that I heard a gunshot. I winced, thinking that the bodyguard had shot at me. But it wasn't the guard who fired the shot. As we fell, his gun had clattered down on the floor right next to my head. I must have knocked it away from him in my wild slide across the table. I quickly grabbed it. No way I wanted the bodyguard to pick it up and use it on me.

So where did the shot come from? I looked up to see Mr. Nervous Gangster standing near us, pointing his smoking gun. The look of surprise on his face was almost funny. He must have had Max Rose right in his sights, only to have me come flying through to knock his target away. He fired. He missed. Luckily he didn't hit anybody behind us either.

A second later Spader leaped out of the crowd and knocked the gun out of the assassin's grip. The guy was in shock. He had been a second away from success, only to have his whole plan explode before his eyes.

"Shoot him!" ordered Rose.

It took me a second to realize who he was talking to. It was me! I was sitting on top of him with the bodyguard's gun in my hand. Max Rose wanted me to shoot his would-be assassin. I had never even shot a gun before, let alone one that was aimed at somebody.

"Do it, Buck, shoot him!" shouted Rose.

I was stunned and confused. I turned the gun toward the nervous gangster because that's what I was ordered to do. The guy looked back at me and our eyes locked.

In those eyes I saw something I had never seen before and never wanted to see again. I had his life in my hands. He knew it. It was up to me whether he would live or die. That was a power I didn't want, under any circumstances. It was a frightening moment. This gangster was my enemy. He tried to kill us down in the subway. Worse, he was one of the assassins who killed Uncle Press. Nobody deserved my revenge more than this guy.

But in spite of all that, there was no way I could take his life. That wasn't something I had in me.

So I dropped the gun.

Instantly the gangster ran. You would think with so many people standing around, somebody would have stopped him. But all those fancy folks in tuxedos and gowns were in a state of shock. By the time somebody got their head together enough to shout "Stop him!" the gunman had already ducked out of a service door and was gone.

I looked around and saw nothing but stunned faces. The band had stopped playing and people were now slowly circling us to see what had happened. It was eerie. Nobody said a word; they just stared. I realized I was still sitting on Max Rose's stomach. I looked down to see he was staring up at me with razor-sharp eyes.

"I told you to shoot him," he said flatly.

I was too stunned to say anything.

"Did you hear me, Buck? I told you to shoot him!"

This was a crucial moment. Not only for my own survival, but for the future of our mission on First Earth. I felt like the whole ballgame was right here, right now. I couldn't screw it up.

"Yeah, so what?" I said, trying to sound cocky.

It was a bold move. Max Rose stared right into my brain. I didn't look away. My adrenaline was still spiked way too high to back off now.

"Wasn't it enough that I saved your skin?" I asked. "I'm not hearing any thank-yous."

A moment passed. I felt the hot stares of Rose's bodyguards on me as they waited for Rose to tell them what to do.

After a painfully long few seconds, Max Rose . . . smiled. "Thank you, Buck," he said. "Now would you please get off my stomach?"

Things got pretty hectic after that. People were either scared and jumping over each other to get to the elevator, or pressing in on us to see what had happened. The band started playing again. I guess they were trying to calm everybody down. Isn't that what the band did while the Titanic was sinking? I was getting shoved around by the mass of people. All I wanted to do was get out of there, but it was impossible to move. I thought I was gonna get crushed.

Finally a strong hand grabbed my arm. I looked up to see who it belonged to, and was totally relieved to see Gunny.

"Time to go," he said calmly.

He had my arm in one hand and Spader's in the other. He quickly pushed the two of us through the crowd and back into the kitchen and away from the hubbub. But we didn't stop there. He wanted us out of that place as fast as possible, before anybody could talk to us. Again, once the police showed up there would be a lot of questions asked. The less they knew about us, the better, so it was a good thing we got out of there while it was still a madhouse.

A few minutes later, after a quick ride down on the service elevator, we were safely tucked back into our sixth floor suite, as if nothing had happened.

"Don't come out of here," ordered Gunny. "And don't come to work tomorrow. I want things to calm down first."

"No problem," I said.

"We hear you, mate," added Spader.

Then Gunny smiled nervously. "You were right, Pendragon. We *are* just getting started."

"All in a day's work, Gunny, my friend," said Spader with a touch of his usual cockiness.

Gunny then left and we were alone. My heart slowly stopped sprinting. Spader and I looked at each other. Neither of us knew what to say. Finally we both burst out laughing.

"Hobey, Pendragon!" shouted Spader. "That was amazing!"

"You were great!" I shouted. "You didn't even stop to think before taking off after that guy!"

"Good thing," Spader said. "I probably would have run the other way if I gave it any thought. That was a natty-do, all right!"

"Yeah, yeah, it was," I said.

The two of us fell into chairs, feeling proud of ourselves. We sat there for a while, enjoying the moment, enjoying the victory.

It wouldn't last.

Spader took a final deep breath, blew it out and said, "It's back on, isn't it?"

I knew exactly what he meant. "Yeah," I said. "No more basketball."

As I drifted off to sleep that night, it was with the realization that after weeks of sitting around and spinning our wheels, the curtain was finally about to go up on this show. The scary thing was, we still had no idea what to expect.

I really missed Uncle Press.

The next morning we were woken up by a knock on the door. I figured it was Gunny, but when I looked through the peephole I was surprised to see Dewey.

"I know you're in there, Pendragon," he said. "I know everything that happens in this hotel."

Busted. I had no choice but to open the door. Spader came up from behind me. "What do you want, Dewey?" he asked.

"Did you two really think I didn't know you were living here?" he asked. "How stupid do you think I am?"

Spader and I shared a look. We didn't want to answer that.

"Look at this," he said, and handed us a newspaper. The headline blared: NEAR MISS AT THE TOWER! It was an article about the shooting the previous night. And there was a picture. It was a shot of Max Rose, flat on his back, with me sitting on his stomach. I had no idea somebody had taken that picture. Luckily you couldn't see my face. As far as this big news story went, Spader and I were mysterious waiters who disappeared right after the shooting, along with the would-be assassin.

"Yeah, that was pretty exciting," I said. "I wonder who those two hero waiters were?"

Dewey gave me a sour look. "That answers my question. You must think I'm an idiot."

Suddenly the newspaper was grabbed out of my hand.

"Morning boys," said Jinx Olsen with a smile. "Some party last night!" She then turned to Dewey and touched his cheek. "Thanks, Dewey. You're a peach." Dewey turned all sorts of red. Jinx then pushed past us and into the room.

I wasn't sure of what to do, so I closed the door in Dewey's face.

"Hey!" he protested. Too late.

Jinx strode into the suite, checking out the place. "Nice digs," she said. "Must be tough paying for this on a bellboy's salary."

Spader said, "Yeah, but there's two of us."

"Ahhh!" said Jinx with a knowing smile. "*Two* bellboy salaries. That must make all the difference." She was being sarcastic.

"What can we do for you, Miss Olsen?" I asked.

"It's Jinx," she said. "Sorry to barge in like this. I just wanted to tell you what a great thing it was you did last night. It was the highlight of my night. No, it was the highlight of my year."

I wasn't sure of what to say. Should we admit it was us? She knew me and obviously saw the whole thing. What was the use of lying?

"We'd just as soon you didn't tell anybody it was us," I said.

"And modest, too," said Jinx with a big smile. "You guys are the perfect heroes. You should be wearing white hats."

"What does that mean?" asked Spader.

"Tell you what," Jinx said. "I want to do something for you boys, seeing as you won't take any credit for being heroes. I want to give you a reward myself."

"You don't have to do that," I said.

"I know," said Jinx as she strode to the door. "But I want to. Get dressed. We're going for a ride. Dress warm." She then blew out of the apartment as quickly as she entered. Spader and I stood there, a little stunned.

"She wants to take us for a ride," Spader finally said.

"But Gunny told us not to leave until things calmed down."

Spader started pulling on his pants. "Pendragon, a beautiful girl just asked us to go on an adventure with her. You can stay here if you'd like, but as for me, I'd like to know what kind of ride she wants to give us."

I'd seen Spader like this before. There was nothing I could say that would talk him out of this. If there was a chance for adventure, then he was going to take it, no matter how irresponsible it might be. I had the choice of staying there by myself, or going along to make sure he didn't get into trouble. To be honest, I liked Jinx and I was kind of interested in what she had in mind too. It took me a solid three seconds to reach for my clothes and start getting dressed myself.

Whatever it was she had planned for us, there was no way I wanted to miss it.

FIRST EARTH

Five minutes later we were downstairs and climbing into a taxicab with the lady flier. I wasn't totally irresponsible though. I told Gunny we were going out with Jinx. He didn't like the fact that we were leaving, but then thought it might be a good idea for us to be away from the hotel for a while. Since the night before, the place was crawling with reporters trying to find the mysterious waiters who saved the life of the notorious Max Rose. Getting away from that circus was probably a smart thing to do.

As we rode in the taxi, Jinx wouldn't tell us where we were headed. She said it was a surprise, but guaranteed we'd like it. To be honest, the thought flashed through my head that she might have been sent by Saint Dane, or even worse, she might actually *be* Saint Dane. But nothing about her set my radar off. I was pretty sure she was exactly who she said she was: Jinx Olsen, an incredible flier for the Coast Guard.

The taxicab took us over to the West Side of Manhattan and the Hudson River. That's when we saw what Jinx had in store for us. When she said she was going to take us for a ride, she really meant it. There, tied up at the end of a pier, bobbing on the water, was Jinx's airplane. Or maybe I should call it a seaplane.

It was a wacky-looking contraption, not at all like the sleek planes of Second Earth. The silver ship floated gently on the swells, looking as if it wanted to be in the air instead of pretending to be a boat. It was a biplane, which meant it had two sets of wings, one on top of the other. Between the two wings was a big, single engine. But rather than the propeller being in front, it faced backward. Weird. There were two cockpits, one behind the other, ahead of the wings. They weren't closed in, either. When you flew in this plane, you were going to feel it in your face, and probably in your stomach, too. Painted on the silver fuselage, just under the front cockpit, was the crossed-anchor emblem of the U.S. Coast Guard.

"That's my baby," she said. "The V-one-fifty-seven Schreck/Viking. She may not look like much, but she's a sweetie in the air."

She jumped aboard and began her preflight check. I was psyched.

Spader pulled me aside so Jinx couldn't hear and said, "Odd looking speeder, that one."

"It's not a speeder," I said. "It's an airplane."

"A what?"

"An airplane. A seaplane, actually. We're going to take off on the water and fly up in the air."

For the first time since I'd known him, Spader looked totally dumbfounded. His mouth actually hung open. No kidding. Wide open. I might as well have said we were going to drink every drop of water in the Hudson. That's how alien a concept flying was to him.

"We're going to fly? Up there? In the air? Like a bird? In that thing?" he asked.

"Yup," I answered.

"That's unnatural!" he exclaimed.

"No more unnatural than putting a clear dome over your head and breathing underwater, but you do that on Cloral every day."

"Yes, but that's simple," he said. "Flying is . . . is . . . impossible."

"Want to bet?" I asked.

Jinx handed us each a brown canvas sack with straps that looked like an old-fashioned backpack. I knew what it was, but I was a little nervous about explaining it to Spader.

"Can't go up without a chute," Jinx said while putting on one of her own. "Just a precaution, like wearing a life vest on a boat." She then demonstrated how to put on the parachute. Uncle Press had taken me skydiving a few times, so I was familiar with the whole deal. Even though this parachute pack was ancient, the principals were the same. I buckled in the way Jinx showed us. Spader did too. He didn't ask what it was for, until we were all buckled up and Jinx did a safety check.

"Looks good," she said.

"What is this for?" Spader finally asked. I looked to Jinx. I didn't want to be the one to break the news.

"It's a parachute, of course," Jinx said as if she couldn't believe he didn't know. "If you fall out, pull on this metal ring. But try not to fall out."

She winked and headed for the plane.

Spader looked at me with a sick expression, "If I fall out, pull this ring?" he repeated. "What happens then? I sprout wings and fly?"

I laughed and said, "Sort of. Don't worry about it. You won't need it."

I pushed him toward the plane, and we boarded. Jinx was at the controls in the forward cockpit. I sat in the back with Spader. It was cramped, especially with the bulky parachute packs, but I didn't care. Jinx gave us each some leather flight caps and floppy goggles to wear. It was a good thing she had warned us to dress warmly. If we were going to be flying around in an open cockpit, it was going to get chilly.

"Buckle in!" Jinx commanded. Spader and I both found some cheesy leather seatbelts and strapped ourselves in. Good idea. Remember, the cockpits were wide open. We didn't want to have to use the parachutes.

"Ready?" she shouted from up front.

"Hobey-ho, let's go!" I shouted.

Spader just grunted. I think he was already nauseous.

Jinx turned over the engine, and with a throaty roar, the giant propeller behind our heads began to turn. Man, it was noisy. I'm not talking about loud. I'm talking about teeth-rattling, bone-jarring, makes-your-stomach-throb-and-your-ears-hurt noisy. At least the leather caps helped to cut some of the noise. I wished I had my CD Walkman.

The whole plane rattled from the force of the engine. I had been in a lot of airplanes—mostly big jetliner-type planes. But Uncle Press had taken me in a few smaller planes. Remember, he was a pilot. So between the flying lessons and the skydiving lessons, I was pretty comfortable in the air. But this plane was rickety. It may have been new in 1937, but by my standards it was only a couple of steps ahead of Wilbur and Orville–time. Still, I trusted Jinx. She was a national poster girl for the Coast Guard, right? She knew what she was doing. At least that's what I told myself.

Spader was another matter. He was scared to death. He had never experienced anything close to this. He sat next to me as stiff as a tree. I could almost feel his heart thumping in his chest. But believe it or not, I knew he wanted to be here. He may have been scared, but he was always up for an adventure.

I had never taken off in a seaplane before. It was a bumpy experience. The water on the Hudson was calm, but even on a calm day there was some chop. So when Jinx turned the plane into the wind and gunned the throttle, we were treated to nearly thirty seconds of bouncing, bumping, and rocking as the plane accelerated over the swells. Then, just when I thought my brain was going to break loose inside my skull, Jinx pulled back on the yoke and we rose into the air. The ride became instantly smooth as we lifted up from the river and headed for the sky.

What followed was an hour that I will remember for the rest of my life.

Jinx treated us to an aerial tour of New York City. We flew up the Hudson and over the newly built George Washington Bridge. We rounded the northernmost tip of Manhattan and got a bird's-eye view of Yankee Stadium. We flew down the East River, watching the barges slowly make their way from the ocean to Long Island Sound. We flew over the Brooklyn Bridge and into New York Harbor, where we were treated to a close-up view of the Statue of Liberty . . . at eye level. Jinx circled the statue four times, then turned back toward Manhattan. We flew north over the island until we got to the Empire State Building, where we did another four turns around.

Somewhere between the Brooklyn Bridge and the Statue of Liberty, Spader began to relax. Up until then he had been clutching the side of the cockpit so hard I thought he'd bend the metal. But gradually he loosened up and enjoyed the tour as much as I did.

"What a great plane!" I shouted to Jinx over the roar of the engine.

"Isn't she?" Jinx shouted back. "We've been all over the country together."

"Isn't it hard to always find water to take off and land?" I asked.

"Don't need it!" she shot back. "She's got wheels for a runway. I can fly this sweetheart wherever the wind takes me. Or the Coast Guard sends me."

The trip ended with a perfect landing on the Hudson, where Jinx guided us expertly back to the pier. She killed the engine and we were treated to something unbelievably fantastic—silence. Once the plane was safely secured, the three of us stood together on the pier.

"Jinx," I said. "I don't know what else to say but 'thank you.'"

"Double for me," added Spader. "I never would have believed it was possible for people to fly."

"You're kidding!" said Jinx with surprise. "Where do you live, under a rock?"

"No," answered Spader. "Under the water most of the time, but I'm not sure what that's got to do with it."

I figured I'd better step in and change the direction of this conversation. "We'll never forget this, Jinx," I said.

Jinx looked at her plane. I thought I sensed a bit of sadness in her. "I love to fly," she said. "Hard to believe it's all going to end."

"What do you mean?" I asked.

"I just got word this morning. After this tour, I'm grounded."

"What? Why?"

"I think the brass is afraid something might happen to me," she said with a hint of anger. "I agreed to do all this public relations stuff so they'd let me fly. Now I've become so famous, they're worried if something happens to me it'll look bad for everybody. Stupid thing is, they're probably right. If I crashed, they wouldn't let another woman in the cockpit for thirty years. Here I thought I was paving the way for women fliers, and all I did was take myself out of the sky."

Neither Spader nor I knew what to say. Jinx then put on her big, trademark smile. "But until they yank me outta the cockpit, I'm going up whenever I get the chance. So thanks, you two, for giving me the excuse to go on this little jaunt."

We all climbed in a cab and headed back to the hotel. Jinx was her old self again, telling us stories about how she learned to fly, and how she once crash-landed in a pasture in Maine and had to dodge a herd of moose. I really liked her and felt bad that soon she would no longer be able to do the thing she enjoyed so much. I really hoped she would find another way to get back into the air.

When we got back to the Manhattan Tower Hotel, Spader and I thanked Jinx again and left her at the front curb. We didn't want to run into any reporters so we ducked into a side entrance. We made it through the kitchen and the dining room and were just about to climb the service stairs to our room, when somebody grabbed both of us by the back of the neck. It was one of Max Rose's bodyguards.

"I've been looking all over for you two," he growled. "Mr. Rose would like a word with you."

Uh-oh. Was this good news or bad news? Was this going to be another chance to learn about Max Rose and his evil plot with the Nazis? Or was he ticked about me not following his order to shoot the gangster and planning to make us both pay the price? The truth was, it didn't matter because we didn't have any choice. We were going to have an audience with Max Rose, whether we liked it or not.

FIRST EARTH

Max Rose's bodyguard kept a firm hold on both of our jackets and marched us to the elevator like two kittens being carried by the neck. I can't speak for Spader, but my feet barely skimmed the ground. Dewey rode us up to the penthouse without a word. He didn't look at any of us. I knew he was thinking about the laundry chute. We hit the thirtieth floor and the bodyguard carried us toward the penthouse. Finally I couldn't take it anymore and pulled away.

"Enough, all right!" I shouted. "We're not going anywhere."

The guy looked at me with fire in his eyes. He didn't like being told what to do, especially by a punk bellhop. For a second I thought he was going to punch my lights out, but he held back. I would have bet anything it was because Max Rose wanted us alive and in one piece. This was good. I started to feel like we weren't being led toward a gangland execution. At least not today, anyway.

We followed the thug into the penthouse and right to the living room where I had set up lunch for Mr. Rose and Ludwig Zell. Max Rose was there waiting for us. He stood behind a bar, dressed in another silky bathrobe, only this one was deep purple. The bodyguard stood at the door with his arms folded. If we had to make a run for it, we'd have to get through him first. That pretty much meant we weren't going to be making a run for it.

"There you are, Buck!" he said with a warm smile. "And we got your sidekick, too. What's your name? Flash Gordon?"

"Vo Spader," answered Spader.

"Vo?" said Max with surprise. "What kind of name is that?"

"What kind of name is Rose?" asked Spader. "Isn't that some kind of flower?"

I winced. I didn't think it was a good idea to match wisecracks with a mobster. Max Rose stared at Spader for a moment, then smiled. "You've got brass, just like your buddy," he said. "I like that, Flash."

Spader gave me a sideways "Who is Flash?" look. But I ignored him.

Rose fixed himself a drink. He poured some amber liquid into a crystal glass, then gave it a squirt of bubbly water that he shot out of a bottle with a trigger. I'd seen those babies before. The Three Stooges used them all the time. I never knew people used them for anything other than water fights though.

The door on the far side of the room opened and in walked Esther Amaden. Actually, "walked" isn't the right word. She slinked in like a cat. She was wearing another long nightgown with a violet-colored shimmery robe over it. Didn't these people ever get dressed?

"You know my associate, Miss Amaden, right?"

"My friends call me Harlow," she said as she draped herself on a couch. "You saved Maxie's life. I think that makes you a friend."

"That's why I wanted to see you boys," said Rose as he lowered his huge frame into an easy chair. "Harlow's right. I think you've got more guts than most of the knuckleheads who work for me." He gestured at the bodyguard by the door. The big goon looked down, embarrassed.

"So I brought you up here to say a proper thank-you," continued Rose. "And to give you a reward." This was looking good. Max Rose felt as if he owed us something. We had to be smart about this.

"We don't want any reward," I said. "We did what we had to do."

"That's a good little spaceman, but I'm telling you, you deserve it."

"Don't disappoint him," Harlow said. "He isn't always so generous."

"You boys name it," Rose said after gulping down some of his drink. "Within reason, of course. What is it you want? Money? You can't be making all that much dough working at this hotel. Or a car? I can get you any ride you want. What is it you little Martians would like?"

This was our chance. It wasn't about money or cars or any kind of reward. This was about Max Rose feeling as if he owed us something. If we were going to find out more about him and about his connection with the Nazis and Saint Dane, this was the time to do it. I had to come up with something fast.

"What do you think, Pendragon?" Spader asked. I could tell by the look on his face that we were thinking the same way. He saw the opportunity here too. The question was, how to handle it?

A thought blasted into my head. It was a dangerous thing to do, but I couldn't think of anything better in a nanosecond. So my mouth started working before my brain could catch up.

"I'll tell you what we want," I said, trying to sound confident. "We want a piece of the action."

Max Rose spit his drink halfway across the room. I swear, he did this huge, wet spit-take. Most of his drink was now on the carpet.

"You want *what*?" he shouted.

"Yeah," said Spader, sounding pretty nervous. "What exactly is it we want?"

I had gotten myself into this. It was time to start making it work or we'd never leave this room. Max Rose stood up and went to the bar to fix himself another drink.

"We hear things, you know," I said, trying to sound cocky but not disrespectful. "Can't help it, working in a place like this."

"Yeah? What is it you hear?" said Rose. He was annoyed. I was going to have to talk our way out of this . . . or into it. Either way, I had to talk fast.

"We hear you're in for a pretty big score, maybe in a couple of days."

Max Rose shot me a look, going from annoyed to angry. I was pushing too hard.

"I'm not saying we want a part of that or anything," I assured him. "We don't deserve nothing like that. I'm just saying we want to be part of your operation. You know, like maybe help you out with whatever it is you got going on."

Max Rose poured his drink and squirted more fizzy water. I could tell he was thinking about what I had said. The question was, *what* was he thinking? The answer would probably mean the difference between life and death for Spader and me.

"What did you hear about this score I got coming up?" he asked.

I shrugged. I had to keep up the tough-guy act or he'd eat

me alive. "Not much," I said. "Just that there's some big pay-off coming in for something you did, and that there might be more where that came from. A lot more."

I didn't want him to know we knew about Ludwig Zell and his connection with the Nazis. That would put us dangerously close to the category of knowing too much. Rose looked at me. I felt like he was deciding whether to keep up the conversation or grab his gun and shoot me. I really hoped he was feeling talkative.

"That's all you know?" he asked.

"That's it," I said. "But you're the smartest, best-connected guy we've ever met. It would be an honor to work for you." I figured throwing in a little butter couldn't hurt.

"So that's it," Max Rose said. "You want a job."

"That's it," I answered confidently.

"Why should I trust you two?" he asked. "You're nothing but snot-nosed kids."

"With respect, mate," said Spader. "We're snot-nosed kids who saved your life."

Max glanced over to Harlow. Harlow raised an eyebrow. "They've got more smarts than any of the clods you got on the payroll now," she said. "Maybe you should give 'em a small job to start. You know, as a test."

Rose looked at Harlow with a mischievous little gleam. "You got something in mind?" he asked her.

Harlow stood up and slinked over to us. She walked around us, sizing us up like a cat plays with a mouse. Of course, right after a cat does that it usually kills and eats the mouse.

"Why don't you send these boys down to see Farrow," she said slyly.

"What for?" Rose asked.

"To give him a message," was the answer. "Have them tell Farrow to lay off. You'll give him a pass for sending his hitman up here, but only if he lays low for a couple of days. Let him know that if he doesn't back off, you'll come down on him, hard. If he listens, you won't have to worry about him until after your score comes in."

"And if he doesn't listen?" Rose asked.

"Then you'll know you've got to take care of business," Harlow answered. "*His* business."

Wow. Harlow may have been beautiful and talented, but she had some cold blood running through her. She liked playing dangerous games. Trouble is, I didn't. There was no way I wanted to go meet this Winn Farrow dude. From what everybody said, he was a psycho and more dangerous than Max Rose.

"I don't get it," I said, trying not to sound chicken. "I thought we proved ourselves last night?"

"Yeah, maybe," answered Rose. "But you turned yellow, Buck. You didn't shoot when I told you to. If somebody's gonna work for me, I gotta know they got the guts to do what I tell 'em, when I tell 'em, no matter how ugly it is."

Harlow walked behind Rose and played with his hair while he spoke.

"I got enemies," he said. "Hard to believe since I'm such a sweet guy, but it's true. That gunman last night, I know him. He works for a competitor of mine."

"We know. Winn Farrow," I said. "Your old partner."

Rose looked up at Harlow. "I told you these boys were smart," she said.

"Yeah, Winn Farrow," said Rose. "I have no beef with the man. He's got his business, I got mine. But lately he's been getting a little, I don't know, jealous. You're right. I got a big score coming in. I don't want Farrow doing anything to mess that up. So here's what I want you to do. Go see my old friend and tell him to back off. That's it. Just tell him to back off. Tell him I'm mad, and by all rights I should hit him back for what he did. Hard. But for old times' sake, I won't. But if he doesn't mind his own business, then I'll come down there and put a hurt on him like he's never seen before."

"That's it?" asked Spader. "All you want us to do is deliver that message?"

"That's it," answered Rose. "Do that for me, and you're in."

"He'll kill us," was all I could say.

Rose laughed. "I figure one of two things will happen. Either you boys make it back in one piece and I'll know I won't have any problems from Farrow, or you'll come back in a bunch of little pieces, and I'll have a war on my hands." He then broke into a grin that can only be described as evil. "So, how bad do you two still want a piece of my action?"

Gulp. I knew the answer to that. We were going to have to accept Rose's offer. But that meant we would have to meet Winn Farrow and his gang of cutthroats. These were the guys who tried to kill Max Rose. These were the guys who tried to kill us. These were the guys who Saint Dane had taken to the flume and used to kill Uncle Press. As suicidal as this mission was, we had to go.

At least we were getting closer to the truth. I had no doubt in my mind that when we met Winn Farrow and his gang, we'd find Saint Dane. I just hoped we'd stay alive long enough to do something about it.

FIRST EARTH

"**Y**ou're going to what?" shouted Gunny with horror.

"We're going to deliver a message from Max Rose to Winn Farrow," I said.

Spader added, "And that's going to get us in good with Rose so we can find out about the natty-do he's cooking up with the Nazi wogglies. It's perfect."

"It's *not* perfect," Gunny said nervously as he paced the floor of our hotel room. "First off, you're not delivering a message, you're delivering a warning. Winn Farrow doesn't take kindly to warnings."

"But we're just the messengers," I said.

"That's even worse, shorty," Gunny shot back. "He tried to kill Max Rose. Do you think he'd bat an eye over bumping off two messenger kids? No, sir. You boys can't do this."

"I hear what you're saying, Gunny," I said. "But May sixth is tomorrow! We're running out of time."

"This is what we do," Spader added. "It's what being a Traveler is all about."

Gunny stopped pacing and looked at the two of us. Like it or not, what Spader said was true. This was what we were there for. To chicken out and hide wasn't an option. I wished it *were* an option, but it wasn't.

"Then I'm going with you," Gunny announced.

"You can't," I said. "If something happens to us, you're the only one who knows what's going on."

"He's right, mate," Spader said. "You'd have to push on without us."

This was the last thing Gunny wanted to hear.

"That doesn't make me feel any better," Gunny said softly.

It didn't do much for me, either, but it was the truth. "It's not going to come to that," I said with more confidence than I actually felt. "We're going to go down there, give him the message, and get out."

"And what happens if you run into Saint Dane?" Gunny asked.

"I'm counting on it," said Spader with conviction.

I didn't like the way Spader said that. The simple mention of Saint Dane's name always cast a dark shadow over his normally bright personality. Our best hope of pulling this off was to keep our heads on straight and be smart. If Spader lost it and went after Saint Dane, well, then Gunny would probably end up being on his own after all. I couldn't let that happen, mostly because I didn't want to end up on the front page of the newspaper under the headline TWO BELLBOYS RUBBED OUT IN GRISLY MOB SLAYING.

"I'm not going to argue with you anymore," Gunny finally said, sounding tired. "You boys have had more experience with this Traveler business than I have. But I know about Winn Farrow and how he operates. I promise you, the man isn't right."

"We know," I said. "We'll be careful."

I really, really hoped that "careful" was going to cut it.

◆   ◆   ◆

Twenty minutes later we were in a taxicab, headed down-town to meet the infamous Winn Farrow.

I have to admit, I was having second thoughts. What if Winn Farrow was as nutzoid-vicious as everybody said? He might start shooting before we even got in the door. The more I thought about it, the more I worried that we had gotten a little bit too cocky.

Spader must have sensed my tension because he gave me a friendly shove.

"It's gonna be fine, mate," he said, actually sounding oddly cheery. "We're the good guys. We can't lose."

I wished that were true.

"Besides," he added, "nothing's gonna happen to you so long as I'm around."

"How do you figure that?" I asked.

Spader didn't answer right away. I think he was trying to find the right words. When he next spoke, it was with a serious tone I hadn't often heard from him. I'd seen him blind with rage at Saint Dane. I'd also seen him devastated by the death of his father and the disappearance of his mother. But this was different. This was a thoughtful, sincere side of Spader that I hadn't known existed.

"I may not know much about being a Traveler," he said. "But from what I've seen, the key to this whole thing is you, Pendragon."

That took me by surprise. "We're all in this together," I said quickly.

"True, but you're the one keeping us together. I think we're all playing our parts, but I've got no doubt, the most important piece to this natty puzzle is you, mate. If anything happens to you, I'm afraid the show would be over. I won't let that happen."

I didn't know how to react. Though I was slowly starting to accept the fact that I was a Traveler, I wasn't ready to take on the responsibility of being some kind of ringleader. It was tough enough just trying to figure out why I was chosen to be a Traveler in the first place. I didn't want to be in charge, no way. The thought of it actually made me a little nauseous.

"I appreciate it, Spader," I said to him. "And I'll be watching your back too."

"I know that, mate," he said.

I wanted this conversation to end. It was freaking me out more than I was freaked out already. Anyhow, the time for talk was over because the cab had screeched to a stop. I looked out the window and saw we were two blocks away from where we told the cab driver to take us.

"We're not there yet," I said to him. "We need to go another two blocks west."

The cabbie turned around and said, "Maybe *you* gotta go two more blocks, but I sure don't. Ain't safe for cabs to go over there. They see us comin', they think it's Christmas. I been robbed too many times to go in there again. So whether you like it or not, this is as far as I go."

He meant it too. I didn't bother trying to talk him out of it. We got out of the car and paid him. The cabbie then hit the gas and did a quick U-turn with his wheels squealing. He gunned it out of there like he didn't even like being *close* to Winn Farrow territory. We watched him for a second as he made his escape, driving right through a red light.

It didn't help our confidence any.

"Maybe we should rethink this," Spader said.

"I'm tired of thinking," I said. "C'mon."

We started walking west. As I'm sure you've figured out by now, this was a bad section of town. Gunny told us it was the meat-packing district. Historically this was an area of Manhattan where all the slaughterhouses were. It was made up of big, rambling brick buildings where livestock were killed, cleaned, packed, and shipped. A grisly business by anybody's standards. Luckily for us, they didn't do the slaughtering here anymore. The main business was processing and shipping meat. It was a place most people avoided. Can you blame them? It wasn't exactly a fun spot for a Sunday picnic. I guess that's why so many criminals made their homes down here. It was the kind of place that even the cops avoided.

Yet here we were, Spader and I, walking right down the street like we belonged there. Believe me, we didn't. The further west we walked, the more I felt the hot stares of people's eyes on us. This was the kind of neighborhood where everybody knew everybody else. A stranger stood out like a brilliant light bulb in a dark cave. People watched us from doorways and windows and from passing cars. A few people even whistled. It was their way of taunting us, knowing that we were headed for deep trouble.

"I feel like we just arrived at a party we weren't invited to," Spader said nervously.

"Or like it's feeding time at the zoo . . . and we're a couple of pork chops."

Our destination was an old packing plant that was built onto a pier over the Hudson River. Max Rose told us exactly where it was. It was the place where Winn Farrow and his gang spent most of their time, when they weren't out slitting people's throats, that is.

After walking for a very tense five minutes, we found ourselves in front of a big brick building with the words WILD BOAR MEATS painted in two-foot-high faded white letters over the green, garage-style door.

"This is it," said Spader. "What do we do, knock?"

The answer came quickly. Somebody had walked up behind us. I turned to see that it was more than one somebody. There were five guys, all wearing greasy clothes and worn caps. Their sleeves were rolled up to reveal huge, Johnny Bravo–style arms. I also saw that their hands and arms were stained with dark-brown blotches. I'm guessing these guys worked in the meat-packing plant, which meant those brown stains were actually, gross me out, dried blood.

None of them looked happy to see us. They all had scowls that told me they didn't like strangers and would probably make us pay for invading their turf. Looking at their hands again, I really hoped that those blood stains came from working in the packing plant and not from pummeling bozos like us who wandered into their neighborhood.

"Do you guys work here?" I asked, trying to sound like I wasn't about to pee in my pants.

They didn't answer. Their expressions got darker.

"We're looking for Winn Farrow," Spader said.

Those were the magic words. But it was bad magic, because as soon as they heard the name "Winn Farrow," they circled us, cutting off any hope we had of escape.

"We've got to see Farrow," I said. "We got a message for him."

The thugs started to tighten the circle. Spader and I went back to back. We didn't stand a chance in a fight against these brutes. I could see them clenching their fists, which made the knotty muscles in their forearms flex. Now that they were in close, I could smell them too. Didn't these guys know about deodorant? It was getting real ugly, real fast.

"It's a message from Max Rose," I said in desperation.

The thugs stopped. I actually saw hesitation in their

focused, killers' eyes. We were seconds away from adding to the stains on their hands, but hearing Max Rose's name made them freeze. Better, they looked scared. Up until that moment we had only heard about what a tough guy Max Rose was. Seeing these thugs turn all Jell-O at the sound of his name confirmed it. Max Rose wasn't somebody you messed with.

Suddenly the garage door of the building flew up and four more guys stepped out. These guys were just as vicious looking as the smelly guys surrounding us, except they wore gangster-looking suits. They also had shotguns. I suddenly felt safer with the guys who only worked with their fists. One of the new thugs—I'll call him Shotgun—motioned toward us. Instantly the smelly thugs frisked us up and down, looking for guns. Of course they came up empty.

"We have a message from Max Rose to Winn Farrow," I said. "We don't want any trouble."

Shotgun looked back at the other thugs and laughed. The smelly thugs laughed with him. "You don't want any trouble?" Shotgun laughed. "Well, golly gee-whiz, we wouldn't want you to get into any trouble!"

The thugs laughed even harder. Great. Not only were our lives in danger, we had to be insulted, too.

Shotgun then barked, "Inside!" He motioned toward the garage door with his gun. Spader and I walked inside. The shotgun boys followed close behind us, but the smelly thugs stayed outside. I wasn't going to miss them.

Inside we saw what was once a busy slaughterhouse. Luckily for us, it wasn't in operation anymore. It was a big, open warehouse room that stretched up for three or four stories. There was a track running on either side of the ceiling with ugly metal hooks hanging down. My guess was this was where they strung up the cattle when they did the yucky stuff. There were cement troughs in the floor that I'm sure caught most of the yuk. At the end of the track were long rows of wooden tables where all the slicing and dicing happened. Yuk. It's impossible to overuse the word "yuk" when it comes to this place. I like hamburgers as much as the next guy, but I never wanted to see where they came from.

"What is this place?" asked Spader.

"You don't want to know," I answered.

"Pipe down!" shouted Shotgun. They marched us through this big room to the back of the building, where there was a large, open metal door on the back wall. "In there," ordered Shotgun.

I was starting to get nervous. Okay, I was already plenty nervous, but now I was getting close to that hairy edge of panic. I had a fleeting thought that we were being marched to a quiet back room where these guys would start blasting away.

"Max Rose sent us," I said again. "We want to see Winn Farrow."

I was cut off when Shotgun poked me in the gut with his gun, pushing me into the next room. Spader shot forward and grabbed the gun, but the other thugs jumped him and threw him in the room after me.

The next room was almost as big as the first. There was a big stack of wooden crates full of I don't know what. There were also hundreds of metal hooks that were evenly spaced along the walls and ceiling. A flight of metal stairs led up to a catwalk that ringed the walls over our heads. I'm guessing they stored the sides of beef high and low in here. There were only two doors—the one we came through and another off the catwalk above us. There were no windows.

"Tie their hands," ordered Shotgun. One of the other

thugs pulled out a length of rope and immediately started tying our hands together.

"If Max Rose finds out you wouldn't let us talk to Winn Farrow, there's going to be trouble," I said, trying not to sound too pathetic and desperate.

"Really?" said Shotgun without a trace of concern. "And how's he gonna find out?"

"Oh, he'll find out," was all I could think of saying. Great comeback. I'm not a good bluffer. The thug finished tying our hands so Spader and I were now roped together at the wrists.

"I'm saying this for the last time—" I said.

"You got that right," came a voice from the door we had just come through. "You're doing a lot of things for the last time."

Spader and I shot a look at the door to see a man standing there. I knew instantly that this had to be the one and only Winn Farrow.

It's not that he looked like the tough gangster we were expecting or anything. It was more the way the other guys reacted to him. They all backed off like they were afraid to be in his way.

To be honest, Farrow didn't look all that intimidating. He was a short guy. I'm guessing no more than five feet. No joke. He looked more like a gangster doll, than a gangster. Of course, I wasn't about to tell him that. He had on a suit that was probably nice at one time, but now looked kind of shabby. The material was faded and the elbows were worn through.

That pretty much described all of Winn Farrow's gang. Even though they wore suits, they all looked ragged. Where Max Rose's gang was all spiffed out with expensive, handmade clothes, Farrow's gang looked like they'd been wearing these same outfits for a long time. I guess that's the difference between being a successful uptown gangster and a hungry downtown crook. This was definitely the B team of gangsters.

Farrow entered, followed by two more of his gang. When Farrow walked, he took quick, short strides. He had to. His legs were so short that if he wanted to cover any ground quickly, he had to walk really fast. It was kind of funny looking, like a cartoon. But I wasn't laughing. Oh no. That would have been suicidal.

The men with the shotguns backed off as Farrow moved past them. He stopped in front of us and stood with his legs apart, firmly planted. For a second I thought he was going to put his fists on his hips and shout, "Hi yo, I'm Peter Pan!" Though he may have looked like an elf, his eyes had an insane gleam. I didn't doubt that he was capable of all sorts of mayhem. He was no Peter Pan. After looking us over, he spat on the ground, barely missing my foot.

"So you're the two brats who have been givin' me headaches," he snarled. "I should plug you right here."

"Max Rose wouldn't like that," I said, trying to pull that bluff again.

It was the wrong move. Saying "Max Rose" in front of this guy was like waving a red cape in front of a bull. His eyes lost focus, then rolled back slightly into his head. It was totally creepy. His gang didn't like it any more than I did. They all took a step back, as if expecting him to blow up or something.

A moment later his eyes snapped back into focus. But in my opinion he had just gone another notch higher on the crazy meter.

"You think I care what that rat thinks?" he snarled. "Max Rose is garbage!" He turned to his men. As if on cue, they all chimed in with: "Yeah! Garbage! Rat! Yeah!" Farrow held up his hand and his men instantly shut up. I think they had done this before. It looked rehearsed. Farrow then turned to us and got in close.

"You say he's got a message for me?"

I glanced to Spader, which wasn't hard seeing as we were only about six inches apart. He nodded, giving me encouragement. I had to choose my words carefully. I didn't want to say the wrong thing and set this evil munchkin off. Trouble was, how could I possibly deliver the message I had to deliver without sending him off the deep end?

This plan was now officially stupid. But we were in it now so we had to keep going.

"Yes," I said calmly. "He wants you to know that he's not mad you tried to bump him off. He's willing to forget it ever happened."

"Well," Farrow said with a smile. "Ain't that gentlemanly of him."

So far so good. "But," I added.

"But?" Farrow echoed.

"Yes, there's a but. He'd like you to back off. That's it. He's just asking, very politely, I might add, if you would kindly back off." I hoped I hadn't softened it so much that I sounded like an idiot.

"Oh? Is that all?" asked Farrow. "And what, may I ask, will happen if I *don't* back off?"

We had come to the hard part.

"Well," I went on, clearing my throat. "He said, and I quote, that if you don't mind your own business, he'll come down here and put a hurt on you like you've never seen before."

I winced. That was it. That was the threat. All that was left now was to see how Farrow would react.

At first he didn't. He just kept looking at me like he was

trying to understand what I had said. Then, after a few seconds, Winn Farrow started to laugh. I swear, he burst out laughing. All of his men started to laugh with him, but that didn't mean anything. They only did what Farrow did.

"He's going to come down here and put a hurt on me?" he laughed out. "Who is he kidding? That rat has already hurt me worse than if he put a bullet in my skull." His laughter was slowing down. It was being replaced by anger. "He's the reason I'm in this dump in the first place! We were partners. We ran this town. But he got too full of himself and turned on me. Now he's up there in his castle eating steak and drinking champagne while I'm down here scrambling for crumbs. He's gonna put the hurt on me? He can't hurt me any more if he tried."

He then walked right up to me and stuck his nose in my face. I could smell his sour breath. The guy had been drinking. I guarantee it wasn't expensive whiskey with a shot of Three Stooges fizzy water.

"But I'll let you in on a little secret," he seethed. "I'm gonna get him back where it hurts the most." He turned away from me and made a motion to one of his goons standing at the door.

Spader and I exchanged looks again. What did *that* mean?

The goon walked up to Farrow and handed him something. Farrow then spun back to us with a big smile. He held what looked like a rocket on a stick. No kidding, a rocket. It was red and about a foot long. One end had a pointed nose, the other had fins. Sticking out from between the fins was a wire that had to be a fuse.

Farrow waved the rocket thing under our noses. "I ain't gonna hit him," he said playfully. "I ain't gonna hit any of them saps who work for him neither. You know what I'm going to do? I'm gonna put the mighty Max Rose out of business with this little beauty."

"What is it?" Spader asked.

Farrow pretended to play with the rocket, making it fly up and down like a kid with a toy airplane.

"Oh, just a little toy I got from some friends over in Chinatown. I think this one'll do just fine, but I'm not sure yet. I'd like you boys to help me decide."

"Decide what?" I asked. "What are you gonna do with it?"

"It's very simple," he answered, sounding as if he were talking to a child. "We're going to play a little game. It's called, How many sparklies will it take to light up old Maxie Rose? One? Two? Or maybe even three? That's what we're going to see."

I was beginning to think Winn Farrow was a nutburger.

He turned to his goons and made a motion. Quickly the guy who had tied us up came forward with another length of rope. He tied one end around our wrists and threw the other up and around a meat hook over our heads. This was bad. We were going to be strung up like sides of beef.

"I've got a better idea," I said, trying to think fast. "Why don't we go back to Max and tell him he's the one who's got to back off. Yeah, that's it! I'll tell him you've got a nasty trick up your sleeve and if he doesn't let you back in the gang, you'll use it."

"Yeah," added Spader. "You could be living up in the penthouse yourself!"

Farrow looked at us with dead eyes. All the creepy, happy game stuff was over. "All I want," he seethed, "is to see that scum suffer like I did. I want him to crawl down here and beg me to take *him* in. That's what I want. That's what I'm gonna get."

With a nod, the thug yanked on the rope. First our arms were pulled over our heads, then we were hoisted up into the air with our feet dangling several feet over the floor. Farrow walked over to us and held out the rocket.

"Now, let's see how many of these I'm going to need, okay?" He then turned and hurried out on those short little legs. It wasn't funny anymore.

"What are you going to do?" I yelled with a shaky voice.

"If I told you, it wouldn't be a surprise!" he called back over his shoulder.

Yeah, nutburger. He left through the door, followed by the two guards and the goons with the shotguns. Spader and I were left alone, hanging from the meat hook.

"Now what?" Spader asked.

"We gotta get loose," I said while struggling to get my hands free.

We went to work on the ropes, but it was painful. Our weight made the rough rope dig into our wrists.

Spader glanced toward the door and said, "Hey, what are they doing out there?"

I turned to look and I think my heart stopped. I now understood what kind of game Farrow was planning. The group of gangsters were gathered together about halfway back, in the large slaughterhouse room where we first had entered. The black stick that was attached to Farrow's rocket was now nailed into a wooden crate. The crate was on its side and the rocket was aimed through the door . . .

At us.

"What is that thing?" Spader asked.

I didn't tell him. He was going to find out soon enough.

"Work faster!" I ordered. "We gotta get outta here!" I worked on the ropes, but had to glance back to the other room. Farrow took a cigar from his jacket and plugged it into his mouth. He pulled out a match and struck it against the crate. He then took his sweet time about lighting his cigar.

This was torture. I looked at the ropes to see we were working them loose, but it was going to be too late.

Farrow finished lighting his cigar, then touched the still flaming match to the fuse on the back of the red rocket. Instantly the fuse sparked to life like a Fourth of July sparkler. In seconds the rocket would ignite.

"Pendragon? What is that?" Spader demanded to know. "What's going to happen?" Fear had crept into his voice.

"Keep working on the ropes," I said.

A few seconds later . . .

Ignition.

"Cover your eyes!" I shouted.

Spader turned his head to the wall, but I had to watch. The rocket shot from its makeshift launch pad, flew across the slaughterhouse and sailed right through the center of the open door into the room where we were hanging. Bull's-eye. I turned away at the last instant, ready to get hit.

But the rocket missed us. Instead it blasted into the pile of wooden crates. A few more feet to the right and we would have been torched. We were spared, but not for long. This wasn't your ordinary firework. This was meant to do damage. It must have been loaded with some kind of flammable stuff because it exploded and sent a wave of fire over the crates. In seconds the pile was engulfed with flames.

Spader and I stared at the growing fire with fear and awe. It was growing impossibly fast. I could already feel the heat.

"There's my answer!" shouted Farrow over the roaring flames.

Spader and I turned to see he was standing in the doorway.

"One of those babies is all I'm going to need," he said while puffing on his cigar like a proud papa. "Now, boys," he said, "let's see how fast this dump burns to the ground. Thanks for playing!"

With a laugh, he spun around and strolled out of the room. The door was slammed behind him and I could hear the sound of a heavy lock being thrown. A quick glance at the fire told me that this room would soon be an inferno. All Spader and I could do was dangle there helplessly. Winn Farrow had proven to be as crazy and evil as predicted. Max Rose was going to get his answer. Farrow was not going to back off. The proof would be our deaths.

That's when I heard a voice.

Given that the heat from the fire was already roasting us, I didn't think it was possible, but when I heard that voice, I got a cold chill.

"Hello, Pendragon," the voice said calmly. "Enjoying your visit to First Earth?"

Spader and I both shot a look to where the voice was coming from, to see a man standing on the catwalk over our heads. It was one of the gangsters who had followed Winn Farrow into the room earlier. At least he *looked* like a gangster. His voice told me otherwise. This was a guy from another place and time who finally decided to reveal himself.

"You certainly took your time finding me," he said with a cocky smile. "I was beginning to think you had lost interest."

Saint Dane had dropped by to watch us cook.

FIRST EARTH

The fire spread quickly. It had already engulfed the stack of wooden crates and was creeping across the floor toward us, leaving black, burned wood in its path.

"And hello to you too, Spader," Saint Dane said. "Having second thoughts about teaming up with young Pendragon?"

I looked at Spader and saw the hatred in his eyes. "Forget him," I said softly. "We've got to get loose."

Spader nodded. But while we continued to work on the ropes, Saint Dane worked on us.

"Such a simple territory you come from, Pendragon," he said. "The people are so easy to influence. It's pathetic, really. It's all about money here. Getting it, keeping it, using it for power. Their greed will prove to be their own downfall."

The fire had reached the wall and was starting to climb.

"Winn Farrow and his disgusting little band of ruffians have quite the spectacular plan to bring down Max Rose," Saint Dane said. "Farrow's a feisty little toad, but I admire him. I couldn't have devised a more interesting scenario myself."

I couldn't take it anymore and shouted, "What is it? What are they going to do?"

Saint Dane laughed. "You should have paid more attention in history class, Pendragon. All the clues are there for you. Perhaps you're finding life a bit more difficult without the aid of your dear, departed uncle."

I didn't take the bait. Saint Dane was trying to mess with our minds and I wasn't going to let him. The fire was now climbing the wall near us. I guess I don't have to point this out, but I was scared.

"I'll leave you boys now," Saint Dane said. "I need to help prepare for the big day tomorrow. Too bad you're going to miss it. It's going to be a sizzling-good time."

Saint Dane started for the door, then stopped and looked down to us one last time. "Oh, one more thing," he said. "As I'm sure you guessed, I brought those two gunmen down to the flume and had them fire their crude weapons back to Cloral. I meant it as a warning to you. I had no idea Press would be foolish enough to be standing there. Such a shame. But from the looks of things, you'll be joining him soon. Give him my best, won't you?"

With that, Saint Dane turned and left through the door on the catwalk.

My suspicions had been confirmed. Saint Dane had used those gangsters to kill Uncle Press. It crushed me to think about it. But I had to fight my emotions and stay focused, or we were going to die.

Spader was another matter. I saw a look in his eyes that actually frightened me. Saint Dane's words had touched the dark, raw nerve that he tried so hard to protect. He was ready to explode with anger and hatred.

"Don't go there, Spader," I cautioned. "That's what he wants. Stay focused."

My warning did no good. Spader blew. He frantically

pulled on the rope with a fury like I couldn't believe. He thrashed our hands back and forth so violently I had to lean away or he would have smacked me in the face. When I leaned back, I saw that the fire had crept across the wall over our heads and had reached the rope. The rope was on fire! Spader let out a final ghastly shout of anger and jerked the rope with such ferocity that it broke! The two of us tumbled to the floor and fell together in a heap.

As much as I hated to see Spader lose control, I liked that Saint Dane's needling had backfired. Spader's anger had helped set us free, with a little help from a burning rope. But we weren't safe yet.

"Spader!" I shouted, and yanked his hands to force him to look at me. "You gotta focus or we're gonna die."

"He's a demon, Pendragon. We've got to stop him."

"We will, but first we gotta get outta here." I tried to keep my voice level to calm him down. "Stay with me, all right?"

Slowly, I saw the ferocity leave his eyes. He was back in control. "Yeah, yeah, right," he said, and refocused his attention on saving our skins.

We were off the hook but still tied at the wrists. Spader stretched one way, I pulled the other, and a few seconds later I was able to yank one of my hands free. After that it was easy to untie the rest.

We were loose, but trapped in the middle of an inferno. The flames now covered the walls and licked at the ceiling. If the fire didn't get us, a collapsed ceiling would. I glanced around, desperate to find a way out. It looked hopeless. There was nothing but fire raging all around us.

That's when I saw something strange.

Smoke swirled near the center of the room like a small tornado. The dark funnel moved up toward the ceiling, then shifted direction toward its destination—the door off the cat-walk. My eyes followed the smoke and I realized that Saint Dane must not have closed the door all the way, because the twisting cloud of smoke was being sucked outside.

"There!" I shouted. "He left the door open!"

Without waiting for Spader, I ran for the metal stairs that led up to the catwalk. Spader was right after me. The fire had been raging for several minutes now. The heat was unbearable and the metal stairs were burning hot. I felt incredible heat through the soles of my shoes and had to force myself not to use the handrail. That would have fried my hands for sure. Because heat rises, with each step the temperature grew more intense. The smoke was getting bad too. It was tough to breathe. We had to move right through the swirling smoke that was being sucked out the door.

Finally we got up to the catwalk, and I ran for the door. I prayed I was right about it being open and kicked it. The door flew open. Yes! I turned to see Spader was right there with me. We ducked through the door and all I could hope was that it would lead outside.

It didn't. We found ourselves in a long, narrow corridor. Choking smoke filled the narrow, dark space and made it impossible to know which way to go.

"Right or left?" I yelled.

"My eyes are burning, mate. Doesn't matter. Just move!"

I took a chance and turned right and immediately saw good news and bad news. Good news was that in spite of the dark smoke, there was something to guide us forward. The wooden floorboards were so old that there were spaces between them. Through those spaces I could see fire below. It lit up the floor and kept us from running into the walls. But that was bad news too. If there was fire below an old wood floor, it meant the floor was going to burn. All the more reason to get out of there fast. I grabbed Spader's hand and ran. I could only hope that we'd get to the end of the corridor and out before the whole floor caught fire.

We didn't make it. After running about ten steps, I heard a loud *crack!* It was the only warning we had that the floor was collapsing beneath us. A second later we both crashed through in a shower of sparks, smoke, and burning wood. The next few seconds were a blur. I'll try to describe it as best as I can, but it happened so fast, I'm not sure I remember it all.

When we fell through the floor, I lost my grip on Spader's hand. Fire was everywhere. I remember thinking that I was falling into the center of an inferno and that I was gonna roast. But the fire had been burning below for some time and the next floor down was already weak. When I landed, those boards gave way too, and I crashed through again. It was a miracle I didn't break any bones.

The next thing I knew, I was underwater. The slaughterhouse had been built on a pier jutting out over the Hudson River. In a matter of seconds I went from fearing I was going to burn to death, to fearing I was going to drown. Somewhere in my fall I slammed my head pretty hard and couldn't focus. I remember flaming chunks of stuff falling into the water all around me. There was a maze of pilings that must've held up the pier. Every way I turned I seemed to either hit one, or knock into burning debris from the firestorm above. I gulped water. I couldn't breathe. I was exhausted and losing consciousness fast. My head kept going underwater and I was losing the strength to keep pushing myself back up.

Then things got *really* bad. I heard a loud, screeching sound from above. That could only mean one thing. The building was breaking up. The pier was going to collapse on our heads. I had just about given up any hope of getting out of there alive, when I felt a strong grip on my arm.

"Hold your breath!" Spader ordered.

I barely had time to gulp in some air before Spader pulled me under. I totally gave myself over to him and relaxed. While holding on to me with one hand, he swam with a strength that I couldn't believe. No, who am I kidding? Sure I could believe it. Spader was part dolphin. If he wasn't hurt, a swim like this was a piece of cake. I really hoped he wasn't hurt, for both our sakes.

I didn't know how long I could hold my breath, but I knew we were safer under the water than on the surface because I heard the sounds of the building above us collapsing. We had to keep moving and get out from under the structure if we had any hope of surviving. I don't know how long we were below the water. It couldn't have been more than a few seconds because I don't think I could have lasted more than that.

When we finally broke the surface, the first thing I remember seeing was the sun. The next thing I saw was Spader's smiling face as he tread water next to me, looking as relaxed as if he were floating in a kiddie pool.

"Took a little knock there, did you, mate?"

I touched my forehead and felt the lump that was already forming. "I'm a little out of it," I admitted.

"No worries," he said. "On your back, I'll tow you in."

I didn't argue. This was no time to be macho. I gladly let Spader pull me to shore. It only took a minute until we made it to a small, wooden dock. Spader dragged me up onto the platform like a wet doll. We made it. We were alive.

The two of us lay there, trying to get our wind back. After breathing in disgusting smoke for the last ten minutes, the air actually tasted sweet. I closed my eyes and focused on clearing my lungs. I was in pretty rough shape. Besides the slam on the head, I had cuts and burns all over my body. My clothes had protected me some, but they were now less like clothes and more like rags.

Spader spoke first. "It's a horror, mate; it truly is."

I opened my eyes and saw that he was staring at the burning slaughterhouse. The place was nothing more than a giant, twisted, flaming wreck. Black smoke billowed up and drifted out over the Hudson. I wondered why the fire department hadn't shown up yet. My guess was they were afraid to come down to this neck of the woods.

"Farrow said this was a test," Spader said through gasping breaths. "If this was just the test, what are they planning to do for real?"

That was the big question. What was their target? Saint Dane said we had all the clues, but I couldn't put them together.

I saw that Spader was in just as bad shape as I was. His clothes were shredded and burned, and his arms were covered with scratches. "You okay?" I asked.

"I will be just as soon as we finish off Saint Dane," he said angrily.

"You trust me, don't you, Spader?" I asked.

"Of course, mate," he said quickly.

"Then, please, remember that the next time you get all bent out of shape and want to go after Saint Dane," I said. "He's gotta be stopped, but we have to be smart about it."

"Right," Spader said in response. "Smart. Let's be smart now and get out of here."

I felt like he was blowing me off, but now was not the time to argue. We were still stuck in the badlands. As beaten up as we were, we had to move.

The river was about six feet below street level. At the end of the dock was a wooden ladder. I climbed up first and carefully poked my head up and over to see what was going on.

My heart sank.

We were about fifty yards upriver from the wrecked slaughterhouse. Between me and the burning building was nothing but a big empty lot . . . and a group of gangsters. They were all standing there: Winn Farrow, his tattered thugs, the big-armed muscle boys, and of course, Saint Dane. They all stood with their backs to me, no more than thirty yards away, watching their handiwork. If we tried to make a run for it, they'd see us for sure.

But worse than that, parked only a few yards to our right were the gangster's cars. When they went for those cars, they'd find us. We were trapped with no place to hide. In a few seconds we'd be right back where we started.

FIRST EARTH

"What do you see, mate?" Spader asked.

I looked down at him and put my finger to my lips to "shush" him. The last thing we needed was for one of these goons to hear us. If we were going to get out of there, we had to do it before they got tired of watching the burning building. As soon as they went for their cars, they'd see us. The only thing we could do was run. I was pretty sure they'd see us if we ran, but at least we'd have a chance. So I looked around for the best escape route.

Parked about twenty yards from us was a derelict truck with WILD BOAR MEATS painted on its side. It was halfway between us and the street beyond. I thought that if we could run to the truck without being seen, we'd have a shot at making it all the way past the bad guys to the street. From there we could disappear into the city. The crucial move would be from here to the truck. It wasn't going to be easy because we would have to run across the wide open, empty lot. If somebody happened to look back while we were running, well, good night.

I climbed back down and told Spader my plan.

"Right," Spader said. "Me first."

Before I could argue, Spader scrambled up the narrow ladder. He peered over the top, looked back to me, winked, and was gone. I quickly climbed the ladder to watch.

Spader crouched low and ran fast. I held my breath. He was totally exposed. But none of Farrow's goons saw him. He made it to the truck and pumped his hand in the air in victory. Yes! He then peeked over the hood of the truck at the gangsters. They had no idea what was going on behind them. Spader then motioned for me to follow. Gulp. My turn. I bolted over the top and ran.

I wasn't as lucky as Spader. I had only gone a few feet when one of the thugs turned and saw me. It was as simple and stupid as that.

"Hey!" he shouted. Instantly all the gangsters turned and saw me. I made it to the truck and crouched next to Spader. The last thing I saw before ducking down was Winn Farrow angrily grabbing a shotgun from one of his men.

"I guess this was a bad plan," I said.

Bang! Farrow fired the shotgun. The window over our heads shattered, and bits of glass rained down on us. The other gangsters followed his lead. They all started firing at the truck. *Boom! Boom! Boom!* The truck was pounded with rounds of shot. The whole thing rocked each time it was hit. We were protected, but for how long?

"Maybe we should have hid underneath the dock until they left," Spader said.

"*Now* you think of that?" I shouted over the booming shotguns.

"Sorry," he said.

We then heard the sound of a car horn blasting and the

screech of rubber wheels on the road. The gangsters stopped shooting, so Spader and I took the chance to peek out and see what was going on.

I hoped to see a police car screaming to our rescue, but instead saw a black car flying off the street, out of control, headed right for the group of gangsters! The thugs scattered like bowling pins as the car nearly plowed into them. The wild car didn't stop. With its horn blaring, it skidded past the fleeing gangsters and blasted right toward us. The gangsters got themselves back together and now took aim at the careening car. They unleashed their shotguns, this time shattering the car's back window.

But the demon car kept coming.

We had no idea what to do. Was this crazy person going to slam into the truck? We couldn't run or the gangsters would start shooting at us. All we could do was watch and get ready to dive out of the way. The driver accelerated right for our hiding place, then spun the wheel at the last second, barely missing the truck. The car skidded sideways, then the wheels got traction and the vehicle charged forward. A second later it wheeled around to our side of the truck and slowed down. Who was this crazy driver?

"Get in!" shouted Gunny from the driver's seat.

Spader and I didn't hesitate. We both ran for the car and dove into the backseat. Gunny never stopped. He only slowed down long enough for us to get in.

"Go!" I shouted before we got the door closed.

Gunny punched the gas, the wheels spit gravel, and Spader and I were thrown back in the seat. But we weren't safe yet. Two more explosions sounded, and the doors of the car were slammed with shot.

"Stay down!" Gunny commanded. He didn't need to. Spader and I were already down on the floor with all the shattered glass from the rear window. Three more shots were fired, but this time, only one hit the car. We were moving quickly out of range. Gunny bumped over a curb, skidded into a turn, and sped us away from the ugly scene. A few seconds later Spader and I got the guts up to peek out of the back window.

Through the shattered glass we saw the burning slaughterhouse falling away in the distance. We had made it. We were safe, thanks to Gunny.

Spader and I both let out a huge yelp of joy. "Gunny, yeah!" "Hobey-ho!" "You saved us!"

Gunny turned back to us. His eyes were wide with fear. He may have just coolly executed an incredibly daring rescue, but it scared him half to death. "I don't want to do anything like that ever, ever again," he said with a shaky voice. "My heart is trying to bust out of my chest."

"Slow down," I said. "We made it."

Gunny took his foot off the gas and slowed the car to a normal speed. I saw that his hands were shaking at the wheel. "This is gonna cost me my job, you know," he said nervously.

"Why, mate?" asked Spader.

"This car belongs to the hotel manager, Mr. Caplesmith. What's he gonna say when he sees I got it all shot up?"

I'm embarrassed to say that Spader and I both laughed. We didn't mean to, but it was just so . . . funny. What was a shot-up car compared to what we had just been through?

Gunny said, "I don't see anything funny about it at all!"

"I'm sorry, Gunny," I said. "You're right. It's not funny."

Spader added, "Thanks for being there, mate. We owe you."

"You owe me a new car is what you owe me," Gunny said. He then laughed too. He was starting to relax. He looked at us through the rearview mirror and winced. "You two all right? You look like you touched toes with the devil himself."

"That's exactly what happened," Spader said.

"We found Saint Dane," I said. "Or should I say, he found us."

Gunny gripped the wheel tighter. "He have something to do with burning that slaughterhouse?"

"In a way," I answered. "Winn Farrow is the one who lit the match though."

"He burned his own place down?" Gunny asked, confused.

"He's planning something," I said. "They've got these fireworks that explode in a ball of fire, and he's going to use them on Max Rose."

"It's all about revenge," Spader added.

An idea hit me. "The hotel!" I exclaimed. "The Manhattan Tower. If he shot one of those rockets up to the penthouse, it would be all over for Rose."

"That's it!" Spader shot back. "It must be. He's going to torch the hotel. He could do it with one of those fire nasties, easy."

"We should evacuate the building," I said, getting excited. "And tell the police. They can protect the place and—"

"It's not the hotel he's after," Gunny said calmly.

Spader and I both fell silent. "How do you know that?" I asked.

"Because I found out about LZ-one-twenty-nine," Gunny answered with no emotion.

Spader and I were both stunned speechless. Gunny had just casually announced that he had found the critical piece to the puzzle. I had almost forgotten about it. The mysterious LZ-129. We both looked at him. Gunny stared ahead, focused on the road. Finally I couldn't take it anymore.

"So? Are you going to tell us?" I asked.

"What was it that letter said, Pendragon?" Gunny asked me. "You know, the one with the Nazi symbol on it."

I thought back to the letter from Ludwig Zell to Max Rose that I had committed to memory. "It said that payment would be coming to Max Rose on May sixth via LZ-one-twenty-nine," I answered.

Gunny nodded and said, "Whatever Max Rose did for the Nazis, he's going to get his payment tomorrow, and it's coming by LZ-one-twenty-nine. If Winn Farrow really wanted to hurt Max Rose, he could stop him from getting that payment."

"That's what Farrow said," exclaimed Spader. "He was going to hit Rose where it hurts the most."

"So what is LZ-one-twenty-nine?" I asked, getting impatient.

"I saw it in the newspaper today," he answered soberly. "I can't believe I didn't figure it out before. LZ-one-twenty-nine stands for Luft Zeppelin-one-twenty-nine."

"What's a Luft Zeppelin?" Spader asked.

The truth suddenly hit me.

I felt sick. Saint Dane was right. I should have paid better attention in history class. I had the answer staring me in the face all along, but couldn't put it together. It was a famous event in American history. There were movies made about it. There were books written and TV shows made. It was a tragedy as famous as the sinking of the *Titanic* or the destruction of the space shuttle *Challenger*.

"What's he talking about, Pendragon?" asked Spader. "Do you know?"

"Yeah," I answered softly. "I think I do. And it makes a whole bunch of sense."

Gunny reached to the seat next to him where he had a newspaper. "Luft Zeppelin-one-twenty-nine left Germany last week. Tomorrow morning it's going to arrive at the naval air station in Lakehurst, New Jersey."

He threw the paper to us and it landed in my lap. There on the front page was a big picture of Luft Zeppelin-129. It was a giant silver blimp. Only it went by another name that was way better known. That name was written on the silver nose of the air ship.

It was called the *Hindenburg*.

"I'm guessing that Max Rose's payment is aboard that airship, direct from Germany," said Gunny. "I believe that's Winn Farrow's target."

Spader picked up the paper and stared at the picture of the giant airship with the Nazi swastikas painted on its tail.

"This thing flies too?" Spader asked. "It doesn't look like Jinx's airplane."

"It's a big balloon," Gunny answered. "Lighter than air. They've been flying them across the ocean for a few years now. They say it's the wave of the future."

"It's not the wave of the future," I said quietly.

"What do you mean, Pendragon?" Gunny asked. "This is your history. Did you ever hear of the *Hindenburg*?"

I took a breath and swallowed. "Yeah, I heard about it," I answered. "When the *Hindenburg* arrived in New Jersey, it blew up. The balloon burned and the passenger compartment crashed. A lot of people died and the ship was totally destroyed by fire. I don't think they ever figured out how it happened."

The three of us sat in silence for a good long time. Finally Spader said the one thing that was on all our minds.

"Well," he said. "I think we know how the *Hindenburg* is gonna blow up."

"Yeah," I added. "What we don't know is if we can stop it."

FIRST EARTH

We rode the rest of the way back to the Manhattan Tower Hotel in silence. I think we were all trying to get our minds around the fact that there was going to be a disaster the next day. Winn Farrow was going to light the fuse that would lead to one of the most infamous catastrophes in history. He was going to blow up the airship *Hindenburg*.

There wasn't all that much I knew about the crash. The basic event was one of those things that everybody knew about because it was such a big deal. I'd seen pictures of the *Hindenburg* in flames. I'd seen scratchy news footage of people jumping from the passenger compartment, desperately trying to escape. There was also a famous radio broadcast where some news guy was announcing the arrival of the ship, and then had to keep his head together to describe the horror of the fiery crash.

It was a famous moment in history; it was going to happen the next day. Question was, what were we going to do about it?

When we got back to the hotel, Gunny stayed in the car. "You boys go up to your room," he said. "I've got a friend who can fix this car up like new. No sense in having Caplesmith on my back. We've got bigger fish to fry." He hit the gas and peeled out, leaving us alone on the sidewalk.

"Why are we going to fry big fish?" Spader asked.

"It's just an expression," I said.

"Too bad," he said. "I'm hungry."

We entered the building through the kitchen and grabbed some fruit. Turned out I was pretty hungry too. The next trick was to get back to our room without being seen by any of Max Rose's goon squad. The plan was to dodge them.

We got halfway through the kitchen when we walked straight into the same thug who nailed us the last time. Didn't he ever go home?

"Well, lookee here," he said. "You two boys look like you been through the war. You smell like it too."

"Back off, bozo," I said, trying to act all tough. "We gotta go change and—"

The goon grabbed us by the arms and marched us toward the elevators. I guess I didn't act tough enough. Next thing we knew, we were being shoved into the living room of the penthouse. So much for our plan of dodging Max Rose.

"And don't touch nothing," the goon ordered. "You two are disgusting."

The guy left, giving us a short window to figure out what we would say to Max Rose.

"We gotta tell him," Spader said instantly. "Everything."

"Yeah, right," I shot back. "We'll tell him how I'm from the future and that's how I know the *Hindenburg* is going to explode tomorrow. Perfect."

"Well, you can't say *that*," Spader countered.

"Duh."

"But if we tell him Winn Farrow is going to blow up the

zeppelin, Rose could send his thugs to stop him. They could do the job for us!"

I had to think about that. Spader might be right. If our mission was to stop Farrow and Saint Dane from blowing up the *Hindenburg,* we could use all the help we could get, even if it was from a gang of thugs. This could be a real easy solution. But for some reason, the idea of telling Max Rose what was going to happen made me uneasy.

"You might be right," I finally answered. "But let's not tell him anything yet. Not until we've worked this through."

"We don't have time, Pendragon!" Spader argued. "The sooner we tell him, the better chance he'll have of stopping Saint Dane."

"You mean stopping Farrow," I said.

"Whatever. Hobey, mate, we gotta tell him!"

"No, we don't. Not yet. Don't say anything, all right?"

Before Spader could answer, the door opened on the far side of the room and Max Rose entered with Harlow. Both were dressed in silky pajamas. Big surprise. When he saw us, Max Rose's face lit up with a big smile.

"Buck! Flash! You're not dead!" he bellowed.

Obviously.

Harlow got close to us, took a sniff, and wrinkled her nose. "You boys been playing with fire?"

"No, but Winn Farrow has," Spader said quickly.

I shot Spader a look, willing him to keep quiet.

Rose and Harlow plopped down on the couch, waiting to hear our report. "I'd ask you to sit down, boys, but to be honest, you stink," Rose said.

"No problem," I said. "How 'bout if we get changed and washed up before telling you what happened?"

"Do I look like a patient man?" Rose asked. "Tell me now."

Spader looked at me, expecting me to start talking because that's what I always did. But as I stood there in front of Rose, I didn't know what to say. I was in total brain lock. Nothing was coming.

Rose added, "I guess since you two aren't dead, my old friend Winn is going to respect my request to mind his own business, am I right?"

I needed to come up with a story that would give us time to figure out the best way to handle the news. But I was coming up empty. A second later it didn't matter anymore.

"Winn Farrow is going to blow up the *Hindenburg*," Spader blurted out.

I closed my eyes. There it was. *Bang*. Spader had just set something in motion that was now officially out of our hands.

Max Rose jumped to his feet in surprise. "He's going to . . . ?"

He couldn't finish the sentence. He started to pace nervously. Believe it or not, he not only seemed surprised, he looked scared. That was the last thing I expected. Max Rose was a guy who didn't even blink while staring into an assassin's gun. But now, after hearing that the *Hindenburg* might go down in flames, he was on the hairy edge of cracking. He stormed over to his bar and poured himself a drink. This time he didn't shoot any Three Stooges fizzy water into it either. He wanted it strong.

"How?" he demanded to know.

I didn't answer. This was Spader's show now.

"He's got these rocket nasties," Spader said. "He's going to shoot one at the airship and blow it up."

"You think it'll work?" Rose asked.

"Take a look at us, mate," Spader said. "He shot one of

those bad boys into his slaughterhouse, with us inside. There's nothing left of the place."

Rose gulped down his drink and wiped his mouth with the sleeve of his expensive bathrobe. His hand was shaking. Harlow stood up and slinked over to him.

"Don't worry, Maxie," she said calmly. "Farrow's too dumb to pull off something like that."

Rose was starting to sweat. "Yeah?" he barked at her. "And what if he gets lucky? Do you know how much I got riding on that big balloon?"

I took a chance and asked, "What is it that's coming in?"

I don't think Rose would have answered if he weren't so upset.

"Payment," he shot back at me. "I've done a lot of work for those Germans. I've shipped them equipment and tools and scrap metal and a whole lot of other things. It's cost me millions. I went out on a very long limb for those Nazi creeps. I'm in debt to a lot of people. The kind of people you don't want to be in debt to. If I don't get that payment . . ." He didn't finish the sentence. Whatever it was, it would be ugly. Oh yeah, Max Rose was scared.

"Why don't the Nazis just write you a check or something?" I asked.

"It ain't that easy," Rose answered. "This isn't the kind of transaction you want traced. By anybody. We had to be creative. There's cash on that balloon. Lots of it. They're also sending me bonds and a load of diamonds. Flawless diamonds. I've even got a couple of paintings coming in that were done by some famous dead guys. They're worth millions! That's the way they wanted to pay me and I agreed. They're sending it all in on that blimp so it'll be easier to get through customs. I *knew* it was a rotten idea."

Now I knew what Winn Farrow meant when he said he was going to hit Max Rose where it hurt the most. If Farrow destroyed the *Hindenburg,* it would be the end of Max Rose's business. Worse, going by how scared Rose looked, I'd say it would be the end of Max Rose himself.

"It's okay, Maxie," Harlow said soothingly. "You'll figure something out."

Rose took another drink to calm himself. "You boys did good," he said softly. "I won't forget that. Now get out of here. I need time to think."

Time to think. Yeah, tell me about it. I needed a little of that too. I wished I had more time to think before I let Spader give away the show to Max Rose. Now a chain reaction had started that we had no control over, all because I didn't have enough time to think.

I think I had better start learning how to think faster.

FIRST EARTH

Spader and I backed out of the room and quickly left Max Rose's penthouse. We took the stairs down to the sixth floor to avoid Dewey. We didn't want to explain the way we looked to him or anybody else. As soon as we got inside our room and closed the door, Spader let out a happy shout.

"Hobey, yes!" he yelled. "Rose is going to send his thugs to stop Farrow. We did it. The *Hindenburg* is safe."

I stared at Spader, my anger slowly building. "I asked you not to tell him about Farrow's plan."

"I know, mate, but I had to. That was our chance. You weren't talking so I had to take it."

"And what if it was the wrong move?" I asked, trying not to boil over. "This isn't just about two gangsters who hate each other. We've got a whole territory to worry about."

"C'mon, Pendragon," Spader cajoled. "You know it was the right thing to do. We outsmarted Saint Dane. Again. We won!"

"Man, I hope you're right."

I needed to be alone to think, so I left Spader and headed for the bathroom. I got rid of my burned clothes and stood in the warm shower to clean off the dried blood. The cuts and bruises were nothing that wouldn't heal quickly. We were both very lucky.

As I stood in that shower, I wracked my brain for answers. Not just about the *Hindenburg,* but about Spader. He was driven by his need for revenge. Fine, I wanted to put Saint Dane out of business too. But though Spader and I were on the same side, we had different ideas on how to fight the war. I was afraid this would show up to bite us in the butt someday. Today was that day. Our butts had been bitten.

Still, I didn't want this to be an ego thing. I didn't want to be angry at him just because he didn't listen to me. Who am I? I don't know everything. Maybe he had done the right thing. Maybe the reason we were on First Earth was to do exactly what he had done. By uncovering Farrow's plot to destroy the *Hindenburg* and telling Max Rose about it, we might have saved the airship.

But that led me to the most troubling thought of all. As horrible as the destruction of the *Hindenburg* was going to be, we didn't know what it had to do with Saint Dane's overall plan. Saint Dane's goal was to find the turning point of a territory and push it the wrong way. The question was, what did the *Hindenburg* have to do with the turning point of First Earth? It was a German ship, but did it have anything to do with the coming war? Would saving the *Hindenburg* stop the war from happening?

There were too many unanswered questions for me to think our mission here on First Earth was over.

When I got out of the shower, Gunny was there. Spader had already told him how he felt sure Rose's gang would save the *Hindenburg.* Gunny wanted to be happy, but he had this confused look that told me he wasn't any more convinced than I was. It was time to put everything out there in plain language.

"Here's what we know for sure," I began. "Max Rose has been working for the Nazis. They owe him a bunch of money. He needs the payment, bad, and it's coming in on the *Hindenburg*. Cash, diamonds, bonds, paintings, and who knows what else. It's all flying in over the ocean right now. Winn Farrow, Rose's enemy, knows how important the payment is to Rose, so he's going to blow the *Hindenburg* out of the sky."

"That's an extreme thing to do, just to get revenge," Gunny said.

"Farrow's an extreme guy," Spader shot back. "But now Max Rose knows what he's up to, and he'll stop him from destroying the ship. The *Hindenburg* will be saved! Sniggers for everyone!"

"Maybe," I cautioned.

"He'll do it," Spader said with confidence. "You saw how scared Rose was. He'll do everything he can to stop Farrow."

"But this isn't just about two gangsters who hate each other," I said, trying not to let frustration creep into my voice. "This is about the turning point on First Earth. We haven't figured out why Saint Dane has his hand in any of this."

"Sure we have," Spader said, acting all sorts of cocky. "It's all about the big natty-do war that's coming, right? Isn't that the kind of thing Saint Dane is all about?"

"Yeah, but what's that got to do with the *Hindenburg*?" I asked.

"Maybe everything," Spader shot back. "It's like Gunny said. One little event leads to another and another. I think Saint Dane wants to make sure the war is going to happen, and somehow blowing up that airship will do that. So if we stop them from wrecking that ship, we'll stop the war and Saint Dane loses."

"Maybe Spader's right," Gunny said. "If we can stop the war by saving the *Hindenburg*, it would be like beating Saint Dane."

Spader looked at me with a proud smile.

"Yeah, maybe," I said. "I just wish we could be sure."

"C'mon, Pendragon! How can we lose?" Spader pleaded. "Even if it doesn't stop the war, we'd still be saving the people on the *Hindenburg*. Like you always say, this is a no-brainer."

Spader was making a really strong case, but something was keeping me from buying it a hundred percent. "I just wish we had more to go on," I complained.

We all fell silent for a moment, then Gunny said softly, "I think I know where we can find out more."

"Really? Where?" I asked quickly, grabbing at the lifeline.

"We're Travelers," he said with a matter-of-fact tone. "We can take the flume into the future of this very territory and look back on how things happened."

My heart sank. As much as I loved the idea of going home to Second Earth, I knew it would be a waste.

"It wouldn't help," I said with disappointment. "Sure, we could go to Second Earth and do some research about the *Hindenburg* and World War Two, but that wouldn't tell us anything. We need to figure out what would happen if the *Hindenburg doesn't* blow up."

"Who said anything about going to *Second* Earth?" Gunny said with a mischievous smile.

At first I didn't know what he meant. If we were going to look into the future of Earth, then of course we would go to Second Earth. That is, unless . . .

"Are you saying what I think you're saying?" I asked, barely able to contain my excitement.

"What's he saying?" Spader asked.

Gunny said, "I'm talking about taking a trip to *Third* Earth, of course."

"There's a Third Earth?" I asked, trying not to sound like a giddy geek. "Have you been there? When is it?"

"Yes," he answered with a smile. "I've been there. The year, I believe, is 5010, give or take a year or two."

I had to sit down. The idea of seeing what Earth was like three *thousand* years in the future was making my head swim.

"I am all over this," I said. "But seriously, why would going to Third Earth help us any more than going to Second Earth?"

"I told you, I've been there," he answered. "I went with your uncle Press when he first told me about being a Traveler. It was like something out of a book of fantasies. They have libraries there. But not like the ones we know. There aren't any books or papers or anything you can touch. All this information is kept on little tiny specs of nothing, no bigger than a grain of sand. They had the entire New York City public library on just one of those little things. Imagine that."

Gunny was talking about some kind of computer. At home when you got a computer, it was already outdated. That's how fast advances were being made. I couldn't imagine how far things had gotten in three thousand years.

Gunny continued, "It seemed like they had every little bit of information about everything that ever happened on those little bits of things. I'm guessing if we went there and spoke to Patrick—"

"Patrick?" Spader asked.

"The Traveler from Third Earth. Nice fella. Smart, too. I'm thinking Patrick might be able to tap into all that information and maybe give us a little more idea of what we're dealing with here."

The man was incredible. How many times had Gunny bailed us out already? I'd lost count.

"I think that's a great idea!" I shouted. "Let's go right now."

I couldn't sit still. I had forgotten how bruised and banged up I was and started getting dressed for the trip. But then, in the next second, the air was totally sucked out of my balloon.

"I'm not going," declared Spader.

"What do you mean? We're all going!" I said.

"Not me," Spader said. "There's too much at stake here to go fluming off. We might come back too late."

"It won't be a problem," I said. "Time between the territories isn't the same, remember? We could be gone for a year, but then flume back here an hour from now."

"It's too big a risk, mate," Spader said with conviction. "That airship is due early tomorrow morning. I want to be here when it shows up, just in case Max Rose doesn't take care of Winn Farrow. You're right, mate. We can't rely on Max Rose to do our job. If he fails, it'll be up to us to save the *Hindenburg*." He looked at Gunny and asked, "How far is this Lakehurst place?"

"About eighty miles, give or take," Gunny answered. "It'll take the better part of four hours to drive there. Longer on the bus."

"See?" Spader said. "It's going to take a while to get there. I don't want to risk being late."

"Spader," I said. "I'm telling you, we'll be back in time."

"Sorry, mate," he said stubbornly. "Can't take the chance."

We were slipping into dangerous territory. We were a team. I had to get Spader back with the program.

"Remember what you told me in that cab?" I asked. "You said we were all important, but I was the one who was going to hold us all together. Well, that's what I'm doing now. I'm holding us together. The only chance we've got of beating Saint Dane is if we stay together. You've risked your life to save me, Spader. I need you to be there for me again."

Spader thought about this for a moment. Was I finally getting through to him?

"If you're right," he said, "there won't be a problem. You'll get to Third Earth and back in plenty of time. We'll hook up and take on Saint Dane and his gangster wogglies like you were never gone. But if you don't make it back in time, then somebody's got to be here to make sure they don't blow up that ship. That's why I'm staying."

I didn't know what else to say. He had made up his mind, and to be honest, I wasn't completely sure he was wrong.

Spader then walked up to me and said, "Go to Third Earth. Find out what you can. It might be a big help. But let me stay here and take care of things in case something goes wrong."

I knew Gunny and I would be back in time, but that wasn't the point. What bothered me was that Spader was pulling away from me. He was always a guy who wanted action. Right now he had Saint Dane in his sights and didn't want to let him get away, even if it meant going against what I thought was best.

"Have it your way," I finally said. "We'll meet back here and then we'll all go to Lakehurst. Together."

"Now you're talking!" Spader said, then left us and went into the bathroom to clean himself up.

I didn't want to look at Gunny. I felt as if I had messed up and the team was falling apart.

"When he's got his mind set on something," Gunny said softly, "I don't think it's possible to change it."

"Saint Dane is strong and smart, and he's got way more

power than any one of us," I said. "The only chance we have to beat him is by staying together."

"We'll be back in plenty of time."

"Yeah, probably. But I'm afraid Spader is on his own mission now."

Gunny fell silent. He knew I was right.

I wanted to leave right away, but Gunny said I should get some rest. It had been a busy day and I was beat up pretty badly. Suddenly the idea of a little sleep sounded really good. He left the room, saying he'd be back in a few hours, ready to head uptown.

I lay down on the couch and closed my eyes, ready for sleep. But it didn't come. Even though I was dog tired and needed to recharge my batteries, my mind was working in too many directions to let me nod off. So I got up, hit the typewriter, and finished this journal.

I'm excited and scared at the same time. I can't believe I'm going to see Earth in 5010. How cool is that? I wish this were a trip about fun and discovery, but it isn't. I've got a very bad feeling about the way things are unfolding here on First Earth.

If there's one thing I've learned about dealing with Saint Dane, it's that just when you think you've got things figured out, he changes the rules. He did it on Denduron. He did it on Cloral. Question is, will he do it again here on First Earth?

That's what I hoped to find out on our trip to Third Earth.

I know this is going to sound totally bizarre, but the next time I write to you guys, I will have seen the future. I can only hope that it's a happy one.

END OF JOURNAL #10

THIRD EARTH

This may be the most important journal I've written to you guys.

I'm back on First Earth now. I wrote most of this journal on Third Earth, but I'm adding this little bit to the beginning because I want you to know right away how valuable these pages might end up being. I know, you treat all my journals like they're important, but this one might be the topper. Handle it like gold.

Gunny and I are on a subway train headed back to the Manhattan Tower Hotel. We've returned from Third Earth and we're running out of time. We've got to hook up with Spader and get to New Jersey before the *Hindenburg* arrives. But it's critical that I write down what we discovered on Third Earth because, just as I feared, Saint Dane has changed the rules. No, that's not exactly right. He didn't change the rules. We weren't smart enough to figure out what the rules were. But now we know and I can't begin to tell you how scared I am.

What we found on Third Earth was beyond horrible.

I hope you're reading this, Mark and Courtney. I know I've written that before, but I mean it now more than ever. Because if we fail today, history will be turned upside down, and there's a very good chance you two will never be born. I'm serious. You will not exist. Neither will most anything else as we know it. I don't mean to scare you. In fact, if you're reading this it means we've won. But if you're not reading this, then the journal I'm writing now may be the only record that Mark Dimond and Courtney Chetwynde of Stony Brook, Connecticut, ever existed.

That would be tragic, but only the beginning of the horror to come if we don't stop Saint Dane.

Most of this journal has already been written. I've tried to include every little detail, because in many ways, I'm recording history.

After finishing Journal #10, I put it safely in the desk where I was keeping Journal #9. Gunny planned on taking the journals to have them bound and covered, but not right away.

We first had to take our trip into the future.

Once the pages were put safely away, I closed my eyes and tried to get some sleep. Spader was already conked out. Just as well. I was getting tired of worrying about what he would do next and warning him to be careful. I hoped I could count on him in the future, but right now I didn't want to talk to him.

The plans were set. Gunny and I would flume to Third Earth, and Spader would wait here in case we didn't get back in time. As nervous as I was, I think I caught a few z's. Man, I needed it. But it couldn't have been for long, because before I knew it, Gunny was gently shaking me awake.

"Ready to see the future?" he asked with a smile.

"Absolutely," I answered, wide awake.

The idea of jumping three thousand years into the future had me totally jazzed. Though I wished we were doing it for less intense reasons. Gunny and I took the subway to the

Bronx. We changed trains twice and found ourselves back at the familiar station that I had been through so many times before. It was still kind of strange to see it open for business though. When I thought of this place, my mind always went to the first time I came down here with Uncle Press on Second Earth, when the place was abandoned. Was that a million years ago? It sure felt like it.

With so many people hanging around, it was a tricky thing to sneak down onto the tracks to get to the gate. We didn't want people going all nuts and calling the police because two lunatics had jumped down onto the subway tracks. But Gunny had done this before. We walked to the far end of the platform and waited for the next train to show up. When the train came in, the doors opened, passengers got out, passengers got on, the doors closed, and the train began to roll out of the station. This was the perfect time for us to move because the station was then pretty empty. As soon as the train cleared the platform, we jumped down onto the tracks and ran for the gate.

Nobody saw us. Nobody yelled. Success.

"After you," Gunny said, pointing to the wide mouth of the flume. We had decided to flume separately. Gunny was too big of a guy to flume tandem with and neither of us felt like knocking heads while rocketing across time and space. Besides, I liked fluming solo. It gave me time to think.

"Is there anything I should be ready for?" I asked. "I mean, is there anything on the other end I've got to watch out for?"

"There's plenty to watch out for," Gunny said. "But nothing you have to worry about."

I then stepped up to the mouth of the flume. I have to admit, I had goose bumps. This wasn't an ordinary flume ride—if any flume ride can be described as ordinary, that is.

No, this was more like stepping into a time machine. Next stop: three thousand years from now.

"Third Earth!" I called out.

The flume growled to life. The sparkling light could be seen far in the distance, headed this way. Along with it came the familiar jumble of musical notes that would lift me up and take me into the future of my own territory. I was thrilled, nervous, and terrified all at the same time. Then again, that pretty much defined my life as a Traveler.

"Enjoy the ride!" Gunny shouted.

An instant later I felt the tingling of energy, a slight tug, and I was pulled into the flume.

The ride was uneventful, or at least as uneventful as rocketing through a tunnel headed to a different time and territory can be. It felt good to be alone with my thoughts for a while, and I tried to imagine what Earth might be like in the year 5010. Would it be all Jetson-like and modern? Or did the human race evolve back into monkeys, like in *Planet of the Apes*? I didn't worry too much about the ape thing. Gunny would have filled me in on that little nugget of information.

I don't know how long the trip took. Actually, now that I think of it, it took around three thousand years. Time sure flies when you're having flume. Of course, it only felt like a few minutes. I felt a slight pressure on my chest, then seconds later I found myself standing in a surprising spot.

I was back at the mouth of the same flume, inside the same gate, looking at the same rocky room I had just left.

Huh? Did I make a mistake? Did I say "First Earth" instead of "Third"? Did I somehow make a U-turn somewhere in flumeworld? That's when I heard the musical notes sneaking up behind me. Gunny was incoming. I jumped to the side as he landed in a flash of sparkling light.

"Uhhh, did we make a mistake?" I asked. "We're back on First Earth."

"Nope, everything's fine," Gunny said.

He walked over to the side of the cavern where a pile of clothes lay. I hadn't seen them when I first landed. I was too busy being confused. "Only looks like First Earth," he said as he sorted through the clothes.

Hearing that made me relax a little. We weren't going to step into some bizarro new world. But I have to admit, I was a little disappointed, too. I kind of wanted to step into a bizarro new world.

"I have no idea how these show up," Gunny said as he looked through the clothes.

I joined him and looked through the clothes for myself. "Uncle Press told me it's the acolytes."

"Acolytes?" exclaimed Gunny. "What's an acolyte?"

"I'm not sure. I've never met one. But Uncle Press once told me they're people from the territories who help the Travelers. Beyond that, I haven't got a clue."

I was glad to see the clothes weren't all weird and futuristic. I picked out a pair of normal-looking khaki pants and a navy blue turtleneck. There were even regular old socks and boxers, too! The shoes were the most futuristic thing there. They didn't even look like shoes. They were more like big, white doughnuts. That is, until you slipped them on your feet. As soon as your foot was in, they molded to you and made a perfect fit, kind of like the air globes on Cloral. One size fits all. Cool.

Gunny put on a regular old white shirt with buttons, and a pair of black pants. He chose a black pair of doughnut shoes. White shoes weren't his style. He also put on a black jacket that finished off the look nicely. He then reached into the pocket of his jacket and took out a small, silver square that was about the size of a baseball card.

"What's that?" I asked.

"Some kind of telephone thing," he answered.

"Telephone?"

"Uh-huh. It's how we get in touch with Patrick. Don't ask me how it works—it's all magic to me." He pressed a button on the card and a red light on top blinked twice. It then blinked green and went out. "He knows we're here," Gunny announced. "He'll come get us."

"Cool. Can we, uh, take a look around?"

Gunny smiled. He knew I was dying to see what the future looked like. "That's what we're here for," he said. "C'mon." He led me to the wooden door that was the gate.

Before he opened it, I asked, "Any problems with quigs?"

"Quigs? You mean those yellow-eyed dog things? Nah. If they know you're not scared of them, they don't bother you."

That wasn't what I wanted to hear. I *was* scared of those yellow-eyed dog things. I hoped Gunny gave off enough brave vibes to counter my fear vibes. Gunny then pulled the door open and we stepped out of familiar territory. I expected to see the subway tunnel of First and Second Earth. But that's not what was waiting.

It was a subway tunnel all right, but nothing like the one I was used to. First off, it was bright. White light came from long tubes than ran along the ceiling. The walls were white and shiny and totally clean. This was nothing like the subways I was used to. Along the floor were two silver rails about ten feet apart. I guessed the subway train of the future was a monorail, like at Disney World.

The tunnel stretched far off in each direction. I could see ahead to the lights of the station. It was still there. I wondered if it had reopened since being abandoned in my time of Second Earth.

We then both heard a loud *click* and turned quickly to see the gate had closed behind us. If I hadn't known better, I'd say the door had disappeared, because it was absolutely flush with the wall. You had to look really close to see the outline. Weird. The inside of the gate was the familiar, wooden door. But the outside was shiny white like the rest of the tunnel. There was only one clue that it was even there. Carved into the wall was the familiar star symbol that marked all the gates.

"We best get moving," Gunny said. "Don't want to get caught by a train."

I ran ahead of Gunny because I was so excited. When I got to the platform, I quickly jumped up, then helped Gunny when he caught up with me. I turned around and got my first look at a subway station, Third Earth–style.

What I saw blew me away.

The station was there, all right, and it was definitely open for business. It wasn't very crowded. Only a handful of people wandered about, waiting for their trains. They all looked pretty normal, too. People hadn't changed at all in three thousand years.

But the subway station sure had. I walked a few yards away from the track and was hit with an incredible sight. Standing at a railing, I looked down onto a massive, underground mall. It must have gone down fifty floors below train level! Imagine the biggest mall you've ever seen, then multiply it by like forty times, and you'd have this place. And it was all underground! We were on the very top and could see down to multiple levels that had tons of shops and restaurants, and even a whole section that looked like private entrances. They must have been apartments or something.

People moved around on every level. Some walked, but many rode these odd two-wheel scooters that silently and quickly moved them along. Looking all the way down to the bottom, I saw a humongous pool. It was practically an indoor lake, where people swam and played ball. It was even big enough for people to paddle kayaks around.

This was an enormous, underground city in the Bronx. Or should I say *under* the Bronx.

Gunny had walked up behind me but didn't say anything at first. I think he wanted me to get over the shock.

Finally he asked, "What do you think?"

"Amazing is a good word," I said in awe.

"The way I heard it," Gunny explained, "they were running out of space, so they decided to move into the only unexplored area left on Earth."

"Underground," I said.

"That's right," Gunny said. "From what Patrick tells me, this is nothing. There's whole cities like this all over the world."

I watched as people went about their business, like this was normal or something. I guess to them it *was* normal but . . . wow. I also saw all sorts of people of every race. This wasn't a segregated neighborhood. Maybe people had finally learned how to get along with one another.

"It gets better," Gunny said.

He led me to the escalator that would take us up to the surface. As we walked, I saw a subway train pull into the station. Gone was the clash of wheels on metal and the screech of brakes. The train slid smoothly into the station with a quiet hum. Very cool. Very Disney.

We hopped on the escalator and I had to stop myself from running up faster. I was dying to get my first look at the outside world of Third Earth.

As we rode up Gunny said, "I guess people got smart somewhere along the line. It stopped being about building more and bigger. People began to understand they had to respect what they had or it wouldn't be around for the future."

"So what did they do?" I asked.

"Look," Gunny said.

We had reached the top of the escalator where I was expecting to step out into the middle of the normal, busy Bronx. Well, we were in the Bronx, all right, but it was far from normal.

The first thing I saw was grass. Lots of it. It looked like a park! There was a vast lake where people were fishing under the shade of leafy-green trees. The terrain wasn't flat, either. There were hills and rocky rises and even a footbridge over a stream that fed the lake. The sky was clear blue on this amazing, sunny day. I even smelled something familiar. It smelled like—

"Pine trees," Gunny said. "That's what you're smelling."

He had read my mind. The green subway kiosk was built on the edge of a dense grove of pine trees. It was a far different smell from the chemical fume–odor of First Earth.

There were a few odd buildings scattered around that looked like a jumble of boxes stacked on top of one another. They must have been apartment buildings because I saw people out on their balconies, talking and reading and playing and basically hanging out.

There were streets, but rather than the normal grid pattern of a city, these roads gently curved around the natural terrain. There was traffic, but the cars were small, and must have been powered by electricity because the only noise they made was a gentle hum. Many people rode bikes or walked or zipped along on those two-wheel jobs I had seen underground. I also saw a lot of small, dark green shelters scattered around. We had just stepped out from under one of them. My guess was that these shelters marked the entrances to the incredible underground complex below.

"The first time I came here," Gunny said, "I just stood and stared like you're doing right now. Then I got this wonderful, warm feeling."

"Why's that?" I asked.

"Because I realized it may have taken a few thousand years, but we finally got it right."

"It's incredible," I said. "Why didn't you tell us?"

"I figured we had more important things to handle back on First Earth," Gunny answered. "The future would always be here. It's the present we have to worry about."

I then heard a friendly voice call to us. "Looks like we've got a couple of tourists in town!"

A small car slid up behind us that wasn't much bigger than a golf cart. It was much sleeker than a golf cart, though, with a front end that came to a narrow point and had regular-size wheels. It was a silver vehicle, with no top and four seats facing forward.

Behind the wheel was a guy who looked to be in his twenties. He had long brown hair, bright eyes, and a big smile. He was dressed like a normal guy from Second Earth, with jeans and a dark green, short-sleeved shirt.

"Afternoon, Patrick," Gunny said. "Thanks for coming to fetch us so quickly."

Patrick jumped out of the car and gave Gunny a warm hug. "Good to see you, Gunny. Where's the wild man?"

Gunny motioned to me and said, "This is his nephew, Bobby Pendragon."

Patrick shook my hand with a firm grip. "Pendragon! Press

told me you'd be showing up someday. I'm glad to meet you."

"Me too," I said.

"So? Where is he?" Patrick asked.

Gunny gave me a look. The answer had to come from me.

"Press is dead," I said softly. I didn't know how else to say it.

I saw the genuine look of pain on Patrick's face. The three of us stood there silently for a moment, out of respect.

"I'm sorry, Bobby," Patrick finally said. "Your uncle was like a brother to me. I'm going to miss him."

I nodded. Wherever Uncle Press went, no matter how many lives he touched, he always made friends. With everybody but Saint Dane, that is.

"Just before he died," I said, "he told me it was the way it was supposed to be. I have a tough time buying into that."

"I know," Patrick said softly. "But Press believed it. And sure as we're standing here right now, I can't remember a time when he was wrong about anything."

I nodded.

"We need your help, Patrick," Gunny said, getting to business. "I thought you could take us to that library place."

"Absolutely. Hop in."

Since this was my first visit to Third Earth, Gunny got in back and I sat next to Patrick. My new Traveler friend hit the accelerator and we zipped ahead.

"Have you ever been to the New York Public Library in Manhattan?" he asked me.

"I've been by it," I answered. "The place with the big stone lions in front, right? Is it still there?"

"Yes. But, well, things have changed a little."

"Yeah, no kidding," I interrupted.

Patrick laughed. "I've been to First and Second Earth. I hear you," he said. "But there are still many links to the past. There's a strong sentiment that history should be respected and honored. You'll see what I mean."

Saying that things had changed was the understatement of all time. New York City, as I remembered it, was gone.

This was once an area where every square inch was cemented over or built on. It was clogged with traffic and people and noise and air pollution. I'm not saying it was a bad place, but it was definitely a busy place. What New York had become in the year 5010 was very different.

We drove our silent car along a winding road through the country. Trees lined the nearly empty roadway. Off to either side were beautiful, green, rolling hills. Every so often I saw another of those odd, boxy buildings where people lived, but besides that you would think we were driving through Vermont. There were even a few farms with rows of lush fruit trees. When we passed one, I got the definite smell of apples.

"Where is everybody?" I asked.

"I'll give you the short version," Patrick said. "By the mid-twenty-first century, we were running out of natural resources. Pollution was worse than ever and overpopulation was beyond serious. Governments had to start getting smart or it would have been disaster. From then on, Earth functioned as one planet, as opposed to a group of countries with different agendas."

"So they went underground?" I asked.

"That was one solution. It began with manufacturing and energy. There are power plants close to the center of the planet."

"Unbelievable," was all I could say.

"It took more than a thousand years, but by the year 4000, every commercial enterprise was moved underground. From factories to the Gap stores."

"You still have the Gap?" I asked.

"I think that sweater you're wearing came from there."

I took a closer look at the sweater. It didn't look much different than what I could have gotten on Second Earth. Good old Gap. Gotta love 'em.

"The only businesses that stay above ground are farms and some solar power facilities," Patrick explained. "Most of the big power sources are out West in areas that are unpopulated."

"Makes sense," I said.

"Then people began relocating underground as well. There are vast housing complexes just below the surface, all interconnected by a train system."

"Isn't that a little claustrophobic?" I said.

"Not as bad as it was on the surface. We were running out of space. That's what prompted the other move. We not only went down, we went up."

"Up?"

"Space colonies. It started with Space Station Alpha at the turn of the twenty-first century. A few larger orbiting space platforms soon followed. From there we could jump out farther. The next step was the moon. There were colonies of a thousand people each, living on the moon by the year 3000. Mars was next, followed by Venus and two of the moons of Jupiter. By last count there are one hundred and fifty-five million people living off-planet. Combine that with the fact that people finally started getting smart about family planning, and we finally achieved zero population growth."

This was a future that could only be imagined by science fiction writers in my time.

"Are there colonies under the sea as well?" I asked.

"Oh yeah, that too," answered Patrick. "But that's not significant. Maybe only a few million people are in underwater habitats."

"A few million? Not significant? Amazing."

"I'll tell you what was amazing," Patrick said. "Once man began to pull back from the surface, nature began to take charge again. Pollution was reduced. The air and water gradually cleaned up. Forests reemerged, starting with the rain forests in South America. In a lot of ways it was like the world took a giant step backward."

"But what happened to all the stuff? I mean, most of the buildings and roads are gone. Where did everything go?"

"It was all slowly dismantled. It was like a giant recycling project. Much of the material from the surface was retooled and used below to create the underground cities. There were billions of tons of material that couldn't be re-used, like road surfaces. Not to mention all the material that had to be dug out to create the cities below. Most of that was broken down and used to create new terrain. The rolling hills you're looking at were made from the streets and buildings of New York that were demolished. The whole idea was to heal the surface and preserve our resources for the future."

"But some people still live on the surface?" I asked.

"Oh, yeah. There are still cities all over the world. My guess is that it's about half and half, surface dwellers and below grounders. But the below grounders spend a lot of time on the surface, too. People still take vacations to the ocean, or the mountains to ski, and pretty much do most of the things they did on Second Earth. If you want, we can go to a Yankees game."

"There's still a Yankee Stadium?"

"Of course," Patrick answered with a smile. "There are some things that shouldn't be changed."

"It's like . . . perfect," was all I could say.

Patrick laughed. "No, nothing's perfect. But it's better than the direction man was headed."

We rode the rest of the way to the library in silence. Of course I had a million more questions, but I wanted to stop thinking so much and take in the surroundings. Gunny was right. It was a good feeling. It took a while, but it seemed as if mankind had finally figured out the right way to get by.

We sped along the roadway, headed for Manhattan. The closer we got to the island, the more I realized what Patrick meant about preserving the past. Though most of the terrain had been returned to its natural state, there were still a lot of structures on the surface, like the bridges over the rivers that circled Manhattan.

And the Empire State Building was still there. But it now had a shiny, steel surface that made it look like high-tech Empire State. I wasn't sure if it was the exact same building from my time, but it was definitely a huge reminder of the past. Very cool. In general, Manhattan was a little more built up than the Bronx. There were more streets and a lot more of those boxy apartment buildings, and it felt more like a city. Still, it was all very relaxed and civilized.

But something was wrong.

As I saw more of this reborn world, I began to get an uneasy feeling. I couldn't put it into words just then because I wasn't sure what it was, but I was feeling strangely unsettled. I didn't say anything, but a nervous vibe was definitely tickling the back of my brain.

"This is it," Patrick announced as he stopped the vehicle in front of the library.

I was happy to see that the two big stone lions I remembered from Second Earth were still there. The wide cement stairs leading up to the library were the same too. But the building itself was a very different place. I remembered a big, imposing structure, with arches and columns that looked like something you'd see in ancient Rome. But that building was long gone. In its place was a small, modern structure that wasn't much bigger than the library in Stony Brook.

"This is it?" I asked with surprise. "It's kind of . . . small."

Patrick laughed and said, "We haven't used traditional books in about two thousand years. It's amazing how much room they took up. Believe me, you won't be disappointed."

He got out of the car and hurried up the stairs. Gunny leaned over to me and said, "I told you, it's all about those little specks of things. That's where they keep all the information. It's magic."

"Gunny," I said. "I'm kind of nervous."

"About what we're going to find here?"

"Yeah, and about what we've already seen."

We both took a look around at the quiet neighborhood. Some kids were playing kickball on the grass across the street. People rode by the library on their bicycles. A group of musicians played some classical music on the library steps. They all looked relaxed and as happy as could be, not like the frenzied New Yorkers I knew from First and Second Earth.

Gunny took this all in and then said, "This is why I brought you here. You needed to see this. It raises a whole lot of questions, doesn't it?"

"Yeah," I said. "Let's go find some of the answers."

THIRD EARTH

This was like no library I had ever seen because, well, there were no books. Actually, I take that back. There was one book, but it was in the lobby of the building, encased in a heavy glass box like a museum exhibit. I figured this was a book that was here to remind people of the past and the way things used to be. As I walked over to it, I wondered what would be the one book chosen to take this place of honor. Was it a dictionary? A Bible? Maybe the complete works of Shakespeare or some famous poet.

"*Green Eggs and Ham*?" Gunny said with surprise. "What kind of doctor writes about green eggs and ham?"

"Dr. Seuss," I answered with a big smile on my face. "It's my favorite book of all time."

Patrick joined us and said, "We took a vote. It was pretty much *everybody's* favorite. Landslide victory. I'm partial to *Horton Hears a Who,* but this is okay too."

The people of Third Earth still had a sense of humor.

Patrick led us through the large, marble-floored lobby where several people sat in comfortable chairs, reading from flat computer screens. Since space was a problem, this was a good way to go. Still, I loved to read and couldn't imagine not being able to hold a book and turn the pages.

There were several long corridors leading off from the lobby. Patrick led us down one that was lined with doors on either side. Some were open and I could see people inside. I glanced into one room and saw something that made me stop short. Three people were seated around a silver platform that was raised about a foot in the air. Standing in the center of the platform, speaking to them, was Abraham Lincoln! I swear. He was right there. Honest Abe.

" . . . and that government of the people, by the people, for the people, shall not perish from the earth," Abe declared.

"Th-That's Abraham Lincoln!" I said to nobody in particular.

"Yup, Gettysburg Address. Want to listen in?" Patrick asked.

"That's some guy dressed up like Abe, right?"

At that instant Abraham Lincoln disappeared. Zap. Just like that, he faded out and the platform was empty. I shot a quick, questioning look to Patrick. He put an arm around my shoulder and led me farther down the hall.

"Think of how the caveman felt the first time he saw fire," he chuckled. "It probably wasn't much different than you're feeling right now."

"That was no fire, and I'm no caveman," I said in shock. "What *was* that?"

"I'll show you," Patrick said, and led us into one of the rooms off the corridor. This room was pretty much like the one with Abe Lincoln's ghost, but bigger. There were six simple chairs circling a silver platform that was about eight feet across.

"I'm a teacher," Patrick explained. "So I have access to this super deluxe room."

I looked at Gunny. "Have you seen this before?"

"Yeah," Gunny said with a smile. "Like I said, it's magic."

"Take a seat," Patrick said. We did and he closed the door behind us so we had privacy. "The concept is simple. Every bit of information that exists has been stored in the data banks. It's not much different from the computers you have on Second Earth, but about twelve billion times more powerful." He took the center seat, pressed a glowing white button on the armrest, and said in a loud, clear voice: "Computer. New search."

A pleasant woman's voice spoke back to him, saying, "Welcome. How can I help you?"

Whoa. *Star Trek* or what? The lights dimmed automatically, and our attention was shifted to the round stage in front of us.

Patrick touched the button on his armrest and said, "Computer. Lincoln, Abraham. United States president." Instantly the image of Abraham Lincoln appeared on the platform in front of us. But it wasn't just an image, it looked like he was actually standing there in the flesh.

"Oh, man!" I said. "It's a hologram."

"Exactly," said Patrick. He then touched the button again and said, "Gettysburg Address."

Instantly Abe began to speak. "Fourscore and seven years ago our fathers brought forth—"

"Clear," Patrick said, and Abe disappeared.

"How cool is *that*?" I exclaimed. It reminded me of the holograms that Aja Killian showed us on Veelox.

"That was an easy one," Patrick said. "Abraham Lincoln is a common entry."

"Then let's get a little uncommon," Gunny said. "We're here to learn about the *Hindenburg*. Ever hear of it?"

"Are you kidding?" Patrick said, scoffing. "I thought this was going to be tough." He hit the button and said, "*Hindenburg,* zeppelin, early twentieth century."

Before us, floating over the platform, was a familiar sight. The silver airship appeared and hovered in the air, in miniature form, of course.

"Interior views," Patrick commanded.

The full zeppelin disappeared and we were shown a bunch of different views of the passenger cabin of the *Hindenburg.* I can't tell you how cool this was. It was like tearing open a seam in time and peeking back into another era. The *Hindenburg* was a fancy airship. I guess they designed it like an ocean liner. There were staterooms and a dining room, and a long deck where you could stroll around and look down on the world from behind the safety and comfort of glass.

"It was a luxury liner," Patrick said. "Designed to ferry people across Europe and over the ocean in style."

"We're interested in the crash," Gunny said quietly.

"I figured that," Patrick said. He then pressed the white button and said, "Computer. *Hindenburg* disaster."

The full blimp reappeared. Then a second later fire flashed on its right side, near the tail. The fire spread so quickly it was like watching a movie that had been sped up. The tail dipped as flames spread over the silver skin of the balloon. The image was so realistic, I expected to feel the heat. The zeppelin hit the ground, tail first. Then the nose started coming down. I could even see people scrambling out of the gondola underneath and running for safety. It was horrifying, and fascinating.

Finally the entire balloon was engulfed in flames. The skeleton of the structure was revealed as the outer skin burned away. Then, horribly, the frame collapsed into a pile of burning metal. The image stopped moving, like a freeze-frame in a movie.

The computer voice then said, "Zeppelin LZ-one-two-nine. *Hindenburg*. Crashed on first transatlantic flight of 1937. Origin of flight: Frankfurt, Germany. Destination: Lakehurst Naval Air Station, New Jersey, USA. Date of incident: May sixth. Time of incident: 7:25 P.M. Duration of incident: thirty-seven seconds. Passengers and crew aboard: ninety-seven. Dead: thirty-six."

"Thirty-six people died," I said in awe. "And it only took thirty-seven seconds. Unbelievable."

Maybe not so unbelievable. I remembered how quickly the flames spread in that slaughterhouse when Winn Farrow's rocket exploded.

"It landed at 7:25 P.M.?" asked Gunny. "I thought it was supposed to come in the morning?"

Patrick said, "Computer. Reason for delayed arrival."

The computer said, "High winds. Storms. *Hindenburg* delayed until storm subsided."

"Spader will be happy to hear that," Gunny said. "We've got twelve more hours to work with."

Patrick turned to Gunny and asked, "What are you looking for?"

"We want to know what caused the crash," Gunny said. He glanced at me. We thought we knew the answer to that, but it was as good a place to start as any.

Patrick hit the button and said, "Computer. Cause of *Hindenburg* crash."

The pleasant computer voice said, "Several theories. One: Zeppelin filled with flammable hydrogen gas. Possible cause of ignition, residual static electricity from earlier thunderstorm. Two: Shell of balloon covered with volatile aluminum powder.

Potential ignition cause, same static electricity. Three: Lightning strike. Final theory: Sabotage."

"Sabotage?" I asked.

Patrick said, "Computer. More on sabotage."

The computer said, "Potential for explosive device having been placed on board by crew member. Never proven."

"State most likely scenario," Patrick ordered the computer.

The computer answered, "No likely scenario. Cause of disaster unproven."

The still frame of the burned zeppelin then disappeared.

"It's one of the great mysteries of all time," Patrick said. "Why did the *Hindenburg* burn? Even with all our technology, we don't know for sure."

Gunny and I glanced at each other. We knew.

"So this computer has information stored on all people?" I asked. "Not just famous presidents?"

"Every single bit of information that exists is at your disposal."

I thought for a second, an idea slowly forming. "Can I try?" I asked.

Patrick stood up and gave me the chair. "Have fun," he said.

I sat down in the chair, feeling like I had a whole bunch of power at my fingertips. I touched the button and said, "Computer. Rose, Maximilian."

The computer answered, "Over eight hundred thousand entries. More specifics, please."

Patrick chuckled. "The computer cross-references everything in its databases. Give it more to go on."

Okay. I hit the button again and said, "Computer. Rose, Maximilian. United States. 1937. Manhattan Tower Hotel. Criminal."

Bingo. Who should appear on the platform in front of us but Max Rose. He was even wearing one of his familiar silk bathrobes.

"Friend of yours?" Patrick asked.

"Sort of," I answered, then hit the button again. "Computer. Rose, Maximilian. May sixth, 1937."

The computer said, "Maximilian Rose, killed in automobile accident on May sixth, 1937."

Huh? I shot a look to Gunny. Gunny sat up straight. Things were getting interesting. I then said, "Computer. When and where?"

The computer answered, "Six fifty P.M. Intersection of Toms River Road and Route five-twenty-seven, Lakehurst, New Jersey, USA."

"He must have been on his way to meet the *Hindenburg*," Gunny said.

I hit the button again and said, "New Search." The image of Max Rose disappeared.

"Computer. Farrow, Winn. New York. 1937. Criminal."

Bang. There he was. Winn Farrow, right in front of us. I was beginning to think this computer was as good as Patrick said.

"Computer. Farrow, Winn. May sixth, 1937," I said.

The computer answered, "Received speeding ticket from New Jersey State Police. Four twenty-five P.M."

"That's it for May sixth?" I asked.

The computer answered, "He was driving twelve miles over the speed limit."

"There's gotta be more than that," I said in frustration. "Let me try something." I hit the button again and said, "Computer. Amaden, Esther. New York. 1937."

The image of Winn Farrow disappeared. There was a

second of silence. Nothing appeared on the platform.

The computer said, "No data."

That was weird. I gave it more to go on. "Computer. Add nickname, Harlow. Manhattan Tower Hotel. Singer. Friend of Rose, Maximilian."

A moment, and then, "No data."

"Does this machine ever make mistakes?" asked Gunny.

Patrick answered, "Well, no. Someone named Esther Amaden never existed or the computer would have a record of her."

"What if she changed her name?" Gunny asked.

"The computer would know that. Guaranteed. Who was she?"

Uh-oh. A bad thought hit me and I started getting a sick feeling in the pit of my stomach.

"Computer," I said weakly. "Van Dyke, Vincent. Nickname, Gunny. Manhattan Tower Hotel. New York. 1937."

There was a pause, and then the computer answered, "No data."

Now I started to sweat. Things were happening fast. "Computer. Tilton, Press. Stony Brook, Connecticut. Early twenty-first century. Uncle to Pendragon, Robert. Sister to Pendragon, Kathleen."

A pause, and then, "No data."

Patrick said, "We're Travelers, Pendragon. There wouldn't be any records."

This was getting more horrifying by the second. I was learning something new about being a Traveler. As far as the world was concerned, we didn't exist. That's why my house on Second Earth was gone. That's why my family disappeared.

"Computer! Pendragon, Robert. Nickname, Bobby. Stony Brook, Connecticut."

There was another pause, and then, "No data."

"Don't do this to yourself, Bobby," Gunny said softly.

I was freaking out, but not for the reason Gunny thought. In some ways, I think I knew something like this had to be true. Yeah, it was horrifying to know we had no history. But as frightening as that was, it wasn't what was making my brain explode.

I couldn't sit down anymore. My heart raced. I jumped up, hit the button again and shouted, "Computer! Amaden, Esther. Nickname, Harlow. Girlfriend to Rose, Maximilian. New York. 1937."

The computer paused for several seconds and then said calmly, "No data."

"Uh-oh," Gunny said. He now realized where I was going with this.

"Yeah, uh-oh," I shot back. "Travelers don't have records because Travelers don't have histories. *All* Travelers, not just the good ones."

"Do you think—"

"Yeah, I do. Esther Amaden is Saint Dane. He's been playing the game from both sides from the very beginning."

THIRD EARTH

"He's been playing with us," I said. "He's got Max Rose listening on one side, Winn Farrow listening on the other, and we're the monkeys in the middle."

"You mean to tell me that pretty lady singer is Saint Dane in disguise? That's hard to believe," Gunny said.

"But it's true," I shot back. "He can change himself into anyone. Trust me, I've seen it."

I paced the library room, trying to rethink everything that had happened since I arrived on First Earth. It was a whole different ballgame now that I knew Saint Dane was pulling all the strings. What was he up to?

Patrick said, "Tell me what's going on, maybe I can help."

"We've been thinking the turning point on First Earth is the *Hindenburg*," I explained. "But Saint Dane's plans have to be bigger than the crash of a single ship. World War Two is coming on fast and we thought that if we could prevent the *Hindenburg* from going down, it might somehow stop the war from happening. But we can't know for sure. The tough part is that since Saint Dane is playing both sides of the game, we don't really know what he wants to happen. Does he want the *Hindenburg* to crash or not?"

Gunny added, "We know what happens after the ship goes down. What we don't know is what will happen if that big airship *doesn't* go down."

We all fell silent for a second. That was the problem, exactly. Would saving the *Hindenburg* be a good thing or a bad thing? There was no way to find that answer.

At least, that's what we thought.

"Well, I could help you figure that out," Patrick said casually, like it was no big deal.

"You can? How?" I asked in disbelief.

"I know it's hard for you guys to understand," he began. "But the capacity of our data systems is incredible. What we've been doing here with Abe Lincoln and the *Hindenburg* doesn't even scratch the surface."

"Yeah, it's all pretty cool," I said. "But you can't predict the future."

Patrick smiled and said, "Well, in a way, we can."

Gunny and I looked at each other in surprise. Who was this guy kidding? No computer, I don't care how great it is, can do that.

"Look at it this way," Patrick said. "It's like math. Two plus two equals four. But if you change a two to a three, it doesn't equal four anymore. It equals five."

"And that's how you can predict the future?" I asked. I was losing faith in Patrick, fast.

"Stay with me," he said. "Now imagine a really complex mathematical equation with thousands or even millions of numbers. Same thing. If you change even one number, the whole equation changes, right?"

"Yeah, I guess," I said. "But what's that got to do with predicting the future?"

"Okay," Patrick continued. "Think of all the events that ever happened in the past as numbers in an equation. If you changed even one of those events, it would change all the events that followed. The whole equation would have to be recalculated."

"But numbers are real," I said.

"So is the past," Patrick countered. "As real as any number. I can't predict what will happen tomorrow, but I can definitely predict how changes in the past would play out in the past."

"That's impossible!" I shouted. "That computer would have to know everything about everybody and everything they ever did to make that kind of prediction."

"That's what I've been telling you!" Patrick said with excitement. "That's exactly the kind of data we've got. We can take events from the past and change one of the factors. The computer will cross-reference billions of other factors and calculate the likely new scenario, just like a math equation. It's called variable technology."

He was losing me. And if he was losing me, I knew Gunny was long gone.

"Okay, here's an example of a simple one I did. 1969. Super Bowl Three. The New York Jets beat the Baltimore Colts, sixteen to seven. I brought up all the information I had about that game, the players, the weather conditions, the coaches, everything. I even knew what each of the players had for breakfast. Then I changed one thing. I input that Joe Namath, the Jets' star quarterback, went down with an injury in the first quarter. The final score the computer predicted was very different from sixteen-seven Jets."

"What happened?" I asked. "The Colts kicked butt, right?"

"Well, no," Patrick said. "The Jets actually won the game twenty-four-zip. Weird, no?"

"Predicting a football game is one thing," I said. "Figuring out the course of history is a slightly bigger deal."

"Trust me, Pendragon," Patrick said. "Think of all the things you've seen on Third Earth. If I told you about all this three thousand years ago, would you believe it could happen?"

"Well, yeah, maybe," I said.

"Then believe this too," he said with total confidence. "A big event like the crash of the *Hindenburg* is bound to change things. I can't guarantee that I can predict exactly what will happen if it doesn't crash, but I know I can come up with the big picture."

I looked to Gunny. He was a guy who couldn't even imagine Nintendo, let alone the kinds of things Patrick was talking about. Still, I needed another opinion.

"What do you think?" I asked.

Gunny gave a very wise answer. "As far as I'm concerned, most everything here is impossible. Yet here it is, real as can be. I'm inclined to give Patrick the benefit of the doubt. If he says he can do this, who are we to say he can't?"

That was a pretty good argument. Besides, if Patrick really could do this, we'd have the answers we so desperately needed.

"Okay," I said. "Give it a shot."

Patrick let out a big smile. He was psyched for the challenge. He ran to a cabinet where he pulled out two pads of blue paper and two pens. "I need you two to write down everything you can think of that has to do with the situation. Names, dates, events, locations . . . I mean *everything*. No bit of information is too small."

"I thought the computer does that?" I asked.

"We need to give it as many cross-references as possible," Patrick answered. "The more guidance we give it, the more accurate the result will be."

I looked at the pen he handed me, and chuckled, "You guys still use pens and paper?"

"Not usually," answered Patrick. "But it would take too long to show you how to interface with the computer."

Good point. For the next half hour, we wrote down everything we could think of about the mystery. I made sure to get everything down that I knew about Max Rose and Winn Farrow. They were the key figures here. It was because of their relationship that the *Hindenburg* was in danger. When we finished, we each presented Patrick with many pages of data.

"Now what?" I asked.

"Go outside and relax. It'll take me a while to input all this and start the process. I'll find you as soon as I come up with something."

That was that. Gunny and I left Patrick alone to do his thing. We walked back out to the lobby, where I was hit with the smell of food. I hadn't realized it until that moment, but I was starving. I really hoped there was a cafeteria around and this wasn't some virtual smell coming from somebody using the computer to look up "pizza."

We found a small counter selling simple foods like cookies and drinks. It didn't matter to me. They could have been selling brussel sprouts and I would have bought a bundle. That's how starved I was. Gunny was too. We each picked out a handful of cookies and some juice.

"Uh-oh," Gunny said. "All I've got is First Earth money."

I shrugged and said, "Give it a shot."

Gunny handed the counter guy a First Earth twenty-dollar bill. He looked at it strangely and said, "I'm not really sure what that is, but you don't have to pay for food when you're using the library."

Wow. Free food. That surprised me almost as much as seeing the underground city. Life here on Third Earth was pretty sweet.

Gunny and I took our food outside to the front steps of the library and sat down to eat. We didn't say much at first. We were too busy enjoying the taste of fifty-first century chocolate chip cookies. They tasted the same as the twenty-first century variety. Luckily time hadn't changed everything.

While we ate, I had a chance to think. I wrote before that I had a nervous feeling, but didn't know why. It wasn't until now, as we sat on the steps of the library, that the reason became clear. It had been staring me in the face since we arrived on Third Earth, but I couldn't bring it into focus. Now, as we sat there on that beautiful warm day, I finally got my mind around it. It was totally obvious, too. Maybe that's why I didn't get it at first. It was too simple. But the more I reasoned it through, the more sense it made.

And I didn't like it. My appetite was suddenly gone. I put the last cookie down uneaten.

"What's the trouble, shorty?" Gunny asked.

"It doesn't matter what Patrick comes up with," I said.

"Excuse me?" Gunny replied. "I think it matters a whole lot."

"But it doesn't. I already know what we have to do."

"Really?"

"You know it too, Gunny," I said. "I think we're both hoping that Patrick comes up with something that tells us we're wrong, but he won't."

Gunny stopped eating his cookie and looked out over the scene in front of us. What had once been a busy, congested city was now beautiful countryside. We could see a few modern housing units scattered around, but mostly it was clean, green country full of people enjoying a beautiful, sunny day. In the distance I could see the unpolluted East River. The air smelled fresh. There was no violence. It was perfect. From what Patrick told us, the rest of Third Earth was the same way.

Perfect.

I looked into Gunny's eyes. He was troubled. We were on the same page.

"Doesn't look like a territory that Saint Dane pushed into chaos, does it?" Gunny said.

Exactly. The wreck of the *Hindenburg* was a horrible disaster and classic Saint Dane. We even hoped that by saving it, we might be able to stop World War II. But the truth was, Earth had evolved into a truly wonderful place in spite of the fact that the *Hindenburg* blew up.

"We won't make things better by changing history, will we?" Gunny said.

"No."

Reality was closing in fast. Our mission was about to be turned upside down. If we wanted Earth to evolve into the wonderful territory we were now looking at, we had to make sure history played out the way it was supposed to.

That meant only one thing. Winn Farrow had to succeed. The *Hindenburg* had to go down.

"Saint Dane *wants* us to change history," I said with finality. "That's what this has been about. That's the turning point. If we change history, this is a world that may never be."

Suddenly the whole challenge seemed too huge. I'm embarrassed to say this, but I snapped.

"I hate this!" I screamed, jumping up.

"What's the trouble?" Gunny asked with sympathy.

"The trouble is I don't want to do this anymore. It's not fair. Why are we the ones responsible for saving the territories?"

"Because we're Travelers," Gunny answered.

"Yeah, well, I don't want to be a Traveler. I didn't ask for this. I didn't volunteer. How did I get chosen? How did *you* get chosen? Don't you wonder about that?"

Gunny said softly, "Everyday."

"And it doesn't bother you?"

Gunny took some time to think about this. "To be honest, I think that if I had the choice, I'd still be sitting here with you right now. But it's different for me. I lived a long life before finding out my true calling. I can understand why you're troubled."

"Yeah, you got that right!" I said. "I'm fifteen years old. I had to leave home when I was fourteen. Nobody my age should see the things I've seen. I'm supposed to be playing ball and sweating over tests and zits and hoping girls like me—not making sure thirty-six people die in a horrible accident. I don't want that responsibility!"

The stakes had suddenly gotten very big, very fast, and it scared me to death. I knew I wasn't smart enough, or strong enough to have that kind of responsibility. I wanted somebody else to do the job. I wanted Uncle Press to be there. Or Osa, or even Loor. I didn't want to have to make these kinds of decisions. I wanted to go home. I wanted to see my mom and dad again.

I wanted my old life back.

I was half a second away from going back to the flume and launching myself home to Second Earth for good, when I heard a voice call to us.

"I'm finished."

It was Patrick. He walked down the last few steps to join us. I hope I can do a good job of describing the way he looked. He was shaken. I swear, it was like all the color had left his face. I know this sounds weird, but he looked ten years older than when we last saw him. He didn't even stand up tall, he was kind of hunched over, like there was a tremendous weight on his shoulders.

"Come inside and see what I found," he said softly.

"What is it?" Gunny asked while standing up.

"You're going to have to see for yourself, because you won't believe me otherwise."

"I'm guessing you don't have good news," I said.

Patrick managed a sad smile. "No, no good news, except to say you were right. You found the turning point on First Earth, all right. It's the *Hindenburg*. And you hit the mother lode. It's not just the turning point for First Earth. What happens on May sixth, 1937, is going to affect First, Second, and Third Earth as well."

"Is it as bad as all that?" Gunny asked.

Patrick's only answer was an ironic chuckle. He then turned and walked up the stairs back to the library.

Gunny and I stood there, stunned. I wanted to run home now more than ever. I felt sure that whatever was waiting for us in that library, it would be gruesome. I was truly at a crossroads. I knew how important this was, but I had to convince myself not to run for my life.

"You want to know why we're the ones responsible?" Gunny asked.

I looked up into a pair of wise eyes that had seen far more than mine.

"Because there's nobody else," he said. With that, he slowly walked up the stairs after Patrick.

I stood alone, trying to keep from crying. What Gunny had said was simple, and it was the truth.

I closed my eyes, took a deep breath, and ran up the stairs after them.

THIRD EARTH

"You've got to get back to make sure the *Hindenburg* is destroyed," Patrick said. Though his voice was quivering with fear, he couldn't have been any more clear. "If you don't, everything is going to change."

"I'm guessing it won't be for the better," Gunny said.

"Not even close," Patrick answered.

"Do we want to see this?" I asked.

"No," was Patrick's answer. "But you have to."

We were back in the small library room. Patrick motioned for us to take seats. Gunny sat, but I was too nervous. When I get anxious like that, it's hard for me to sit still.

"Here's the deal," Patrick began. "Remember I talked about mathematical equations and if you changed one number, the whole equation would be altered?"

"Yeah," I answered tentatively.

"Well, it's true, but it also depends on what number you decide to change," Patrick explained. "You might change one number and the overall difference would be small. Or you might change a number that has a much bigger impact."

"What about the *Hindenburg*?" Gunny asked. "How big a change could that make?"

Patrick had to sit down. It was like the weight of what he was about to say was making it hard for him to stay on his feet.

"Saint Dane hit the jackpot," he said. "He found a single event in history that if changed, would turn the future inside out. If he succeeds, he'll push all three territories into chaos."

That was exactly what I didn't want to hear. "How can one change do so much?" I asked.

"That's what I've got to show you," Patrick answered. He hit the white button on his chair and called out, "Computer. *Hindenburg* Variation. Item number one."

Instantly the image of Max Rose appeared before us.

"It's all about this guy Maximilian Rose," Patrick began. "He started doing business with the Nazis in 1935."

"We know that," I said. "He said he was shipping them tools and scrap metal."

"That's not all he was shipping them," Patrick said. "Computer. Item number two."

Appearing before us was a group of men. None of them looked familiar. They were all white guys with short haircuts and wearing suits. They looked like a bunch of dorks.

"Who are they?" Gunny asked.

"Spies," Patrick answered quickly.

"Spies?" I asked. "You mean like James Bond?"

"Industrial spies," said Patrick. "The kind of guys who sell secrets about companies and manufacturing plans and designs. These are all Americans who worked for Max Rose. Some of them did it for the money, others were forced into it by Rose's thugs. Every one of them had valuable secrets the Nazis would have loved to get hold of."

"And Max Rose was selling them these secrets?" Gunny asked.

"Yes. That is, until May sixth, 1937. Computer. Item three."

The gang of spies disappeared and was replaced by an image of a wrecked car. Whatever had happened to this vehicle, it was ugly, because it was a step above scrap metal. I guarantee, nobody could walk away from a wreck like that.

"May sixth, six fifty P.M.," Patrick explained. "Intersection of Toms River Road and Route five-twenty-seven . . . Max Rose is killed in a collision with a state trooper. But that alone wouldn't have stopped his spy business. He had lieutenants who would have picked up right where he left off. Except for one thing. Item four."

The car wreck disappeared and we then saw the familiar image of the *Hindenburg* on fire.

"When the *Hindenburg* went down," Patrick explained, "a huge payment from the Nazis to Max Rose went down with it. Records show there was a shipment on board with four million American dollars, bonds, jewels, and artwork. All gone in thirty-seven seconds."

"Bad for Rose," Gunny said.

"Worse than bad. Losing that money destroyed Rose's organization," Patrick said. "Payments couldn't be made. Ties were severed. Some of the spies sank back into deep cover, never to be heard from again. Others got arrested. Bottom line is the crash of the *Hindenburg* put Rose's spies out of business."

"Okay," I said. "Now we know what happened. What did your computer figure out would happen if the *Hindenburg* didn't crash?"

Patrick hesitated, then stood up and paced.

"I input one single change," he finally said. "I input the variable that the *Hindenburg* arrived safely." Patrick took a deep breath, then continued. "It took the computer twenty minutes to calculate all the changes. Pendragon, that's like saying a computer from Second Earth took a lifetime to calculate pi. That's how extensive the changes were. Every resource, every data bank, every bit of memory was called into play. It knocked everybody else in the library offline. I've never seen anything like it."

"So? Show us," I said.

Patrick sat back down in his chair. He hit the button and said weakly, "Item five."

A man appeared. A lone man with salt-and-pepper-colored hair. He was short, with wire-rimmed glasses and a gray suit. He didn't look familiar at all.

"This is Dani Schmidt," Patrick said nervously, "a physicist working for the Nazis. He never played a big part in history, because he was a failure. The project he devoted the final years of his life to was never finished. He was executed by the Nazis in 1944. His only crime was failure. But that was under the old scenario. If the *Hindenburg* had survived, his life would have taken a different turn. Item six."

The image of Dani Schmidt disappeared, and was replaced by a large, gray piece of equipment that looked like a fat torpedo.

"When the *Hindenburg* arrived safely, the payment was made to keep Max Rose's spy operation in business. More information was stolen from the U.S. and fed to the Nazis. They in turn gave it to Dani Schmidt. It was scientific data they never would have gotten if the *Hindenburg* had crashed."

"So what is that thing?" I asked, pointing to the gray torpedo.

"That was the project Dani Schmidt was working on," Patrick said. "With the scientific information stolen from the

"It's not," Patrick said. "This was always the Nazis' plan. But they never developed a working bomb, so it was never carried out. With the help of the information stolen from the United States by Max Rose's spy network, Dani Schmidt was able to complete his work. There's very little guesswork here. If the *Hindenburg* arrives safely, Germany will be the first to develop an atomic bomb. And they will use it."

"What will happen from there?" Gunny said softly. He looked like he was in shock. "I don't want to see it, just tell me."

"Most of the northeast United States will be devastated by the two blasts. They'll have to deal with radiation for years. Pendragon, your home of Stony Brook, Connecticut, will no longer exist. Earthquakes set off by the blast in New York will see to that."

Now I had to sit down. I wasn't nervous anymore. I was sick.

"Bottom line is, the Germans will win the war," Patrick said. "Adolf Hitler's evil vision will spread throughout the world, just as he planned. As you can imagine, from that point on, the world will take a much different course. Let me show you one last thing. Item fifty-six."

On the platform we saw another overhead view. This was of New York City. The only reason I knew it was New York was because I saw a chunk of building that looked like the Empire State Building. But it wasn't a tall, majestic building anymore. It was only the top few floors. The building must have tumbled when the bomb fell and now only the top few floors were left. We saw several more views of the destroyed city. There were people waiting in line for food. Children slept in the streets, cold and hungry. Tents were set up where the roads had been. Thousands upon thousands of people lived in the rubble like rats.

United States, he was able to put the final pieces of his proje together." Patrick then took a deep breath. "Item seven."

The image of the torpedo was replaced by an image tha looked very familiar. It was a bird's-eye view of Washington D.C. I could see the Capitol, the Washington Monument, anc the Lincoln Memorial.

"May twenty-fourth, 1944," Patrick said with a shaky voice. "The Germans were on the run. The Allies would invade Europe in two weeks. The war would only last another year or so. But on that date, Dani Schmidt's project was brought into play."

We then saw an image that made my knees buckle. There before us, looking as real as if we were watching it from an airplane, we saw Washington, D.C. hit by an atomic bomb. The city was vaporized. The familiar, horrific mushroom cloud rose up over the shattered capital like an evil tombstone.

"That was at ten o'clock in the morning," Patrick said. "There was more to come. Item eight."

The rubble of Washington, D.C. was replaced by a view of Manhattan Island.

Gunny breathed out, "Oh, no."

Boom. New York got slammed too.

"That bomb landed north of Manhattan at ten fifteen. Item nine."

The mushroom cloud over New York was replaced by an aerial view of London. *Boom*. London was history.

"Ten twenty-five. The Nazis sent out long-range bombers with the world's first atomic bombs."

"Shut it off!" I yelled.

"Clear," Patrick said softly, and the destruction of London was gone.

"How can this machine know that?" I demanded. "It's just a guess."

"Was this right after the bomb fell?" I asked.

Patrick answered. "This is a view of New York City on Third Earth, over three thousand years later. Today."

I then saw something that made me want to cry. Lying on its side, along what was once the busy street of Fifth Avenue, was a green structure that was being used for makeshift housing. It must have covered ten city blocks. Holes were cut in the sides for people to crawl in and out of. The image was stunning, and horrible, because lying there, broken and destroyed among the rubble of once proud buildings, was the Statue of Liberty.

"I'll say it again," Patrick said quietly. "Saint Dane hit the jackpot. He found the perfect moment in time that he could manipulate and send three territories into oblivion. Clear."

The images disappeared. Good thing. I couldn't take it anymore. The three of us sat there in silence. We had just seen doomsday. It's hard to know what to say after that.

"Could there be a mistake?" Gunny asked.

"Specific details may change," Patrick answered. "But the basic situation would be the same. If Max Rose continues to operate his spy network, the Germans will develop the atom bomb first, and they will drop it on England and the United States."

I had heard enough. We already figured that saving the *Hindenburg* would be a mistake. Seeing how great Third Earth was told us that. But now, seeing the horror show Patrick had just presented slammed the point home to me about as hard as possible. Any doubts I had about what I wanted to do were gone.

I stood up and said, "We're on the wrong territory."

Gunny stood up. "Yes, we are," he said with purpose.

"I'm coming," Patrick announced. "I want to help."

Gunny looked at me. I wasn't sure if Patrick coming along was a good idea or not.

"I don't think so, Patrick," Gunny said. "We've got to hit the ground running once we get back. We wouldn't have time to teach you all you'd need to know about First Earth. No offense, but you might end up being more trouble than help."

Gunny was right. Patrick wouldn't know simple things, like how to get across a busy street. We couldn't afford to be slowed down by anything, even a friend.

"I understand," Patrick said, looking disappointed.

"Besides," Gunny said. "You did your part. Now it's our turn." Gunny then turned to me and said, "You ready for this, shorty?"

How could I answer that question? How could anyone be ready for what we had to do? I know why Gunny asked me though. A few minutes before, I was out of control. I wanted my life back. Though I knew stopping Saint Dane from destroying the territories and taking control of Halla was important, it felt like a fantasy. I was tired of living in a fantasy. But after seeing what Saint Dane had in mind for the three Earth territories, the fantasy had suddenly become real. Now he was hitting me where I lived. So how did I answer a huge question like that?

"Absolutely."

Gunny smiled. Next stop, First Earth.

Before hitting the flume, I sat in the library and wrote most of this journal. I didn't want to wait until we got back, because if something happens to me, well, let's just say I wanted to make sure this journal was written. I trusted that the flumes would get us back in time.

Patrick drove us back up to the Bronx and the green shelter that would lead us down to the subway.

"We'll see you again," Gunny said with certainty. "And it will be here on Third Earth. *This* Third Earth."

Patrick nodded. He didn't seem as confident as Gunny. He then turned to me and said, "Pendragon, your uncle told me that if I ever doubted myself, or our mission, that I should put my faith in you. Should I put my faith in you?"

Whoa. Uncle Press said that about me? Patrick was looking for some kind of guarantee that everything was going to be okay. I wished I could give it to him.

"I'm not sure why he'd say that," I answered truthfully. "But I do know one thing. You might as well put your faith in us, because there's nobody else."

On that solemn note, the three of us parted.

A second before we went underground, I took one last look at Third Earth. I really hoped it wouldn't be the last time I saw it like this. Gunny and I then hurried down the escalator, across the platform, down onto the tracks, and back to the gate that led to the flume. There we quickly traded our Third Earth clothes for our First Earth clothes. We didn't even talk. We were both focused on getting back as quickly as possible.

"First Earth!" I shouted at the mouth of the flume. A second later I kissed Third Earth good-bye and shot my way back to 1937.

A few minutes later we found ourselves surrounded by all the familiar sensations of First Earth—the smells, the noise, the people, the energy. It was a rude change from the quiet serenity of Third Earth. But I have to admit, I didn't mind it. It felt like going home.

Once Gunny and I got back to the subway platform, we

waited for the first train downtown and jumped on board. There weren't many subway stops in the Bronx that were underground, so we shortly emerged into rainy daylight. As much as I thought Third Earth was a perfect place, I was glad to see the buildings of old-fashioned New York again. Still Gunny and I didn't speak. We knew what we had to do.

We had returned early in the morning on May 6, 1937. We weren't too late. Our first goal was to get back to the Manhattan Tower Hotel, find Spader, and tell him what we had discovered on Third Earth. From there, we'd decide on a plan to make sure Winn Farrow destroyed the *Hindenburg*. That was a weird feeling. We had to help make sure that a killer succeeded in murdering thirty-six people. But I couldn't think of it like that. It was too horrific. I had to keep telling myself that we were making sure that history played out the way it was supposed to, and that Saint Dane wouldn't change things. That was our mission. That was why we were on First Earth.

As we rode on the subway, I kept my head down finishing this journal. Like I told you up front, this may be the most important journal I've written yet. If we fail, and Saint Dane prevents the *Hindenburg* from burning, the world will change, and this document will be the only proof of the way things were meant to be.

There's one last thing that happened that I should write down. It didn't really affect anything, but it's worth writing about anyway.

The subway car rumbled toward the bridge that would take us across the East River into Manhattan. But I wasn't watching. I was too busy writing. That's when Gunny nudged me. He didn't say a word; all he did was point out the window of the subway car, up toward the skyline of Manhattan. I didn't know what he wanted me to see at first, but a few seconds later I caught sight of it—and it made me catch my breath.

It was just coming into view, high above the tallest buildings. It floated there like a quiet, majestic bird, lazily surveying the ground below. It was Luft Zeppelin-129. The *Hindenburg*. It had arrived in America. I watched the ship in open-mouthed awe. It was way bigger than I had imagined. I also couldn't help but focus on the bold logos on its tail. There were two giant black swastikas on a red and white background, the symbol of the Nazi Party. Seeing them gave me a shiver.

People pressed against the subway windows to get a look at the impressive blimp. They waved, as if expecting the crew and passengers high above to see them. Cars honked their horns, people cheered, other cars pulled over to the side of the street so their passengers could get out and watch. It was like a joyous celebration. People gazed at the airship in awe. To them it was a mighty symbol of the future.

Gunny and I knew differently. The future of the zeppelin was going to be a short one. It had to be.

We're almost at our stop, so I'll end my journal here. It's a horrible feeling. If we fail, this will be the last time I'll be writing to you two, Mark and Courtney. I feel like I want to say good-bye. But I can't think that way. I've got to get it in my head that in a few hours, the majestic zeppelin we just saw floating over Manhattan has to crash to the ground in a flaming ball of fire.

That's our mission. Our future, *your* future depends on it.

END OF JOURNAL #11

FIRST EARTH

As I look back on this last, incredible year, I feel like I've gone through two huge, personal turning points.

The first was the moment I was pulled into a flume for the very first time. That was when I realized the rules of the universe weren't exactly what I thought they were. Ever since then I've had to struggle to keep my head above water in the scary seas of Travelerworld.

The second turning point came in that library on Third Earth. Up until then, the idea of an entire territory falling into chaos didn't really mean anything to me. It was all just theory. But when I saw the images of what Saint Dane had planned for the Earth territories . . . man. It was like everything suddenly came into focus. Saint Dane had to be stopped, now and forever. End of discussion.

Before that moment, I knew it in my brain. Now, I feel it in my heart.

The only people who have a chance of ending his evil campaign are the Travelers. It would be nice if we were a race of invincible superheroes with powers far beyond those of mortal men, but we're not. A stranger group you couldn't find, but only because we're all so normal. It's scary to think that the only force trying to prevent Saint Dane from destroying Halla is a group of regular-old people.

More frightening is knowing I'm one of them.

When I saw those horrifying images of Saint Dane's Earth, something changed in me. It's hard to put this into words, because I'm not sure I understand it myself. Call it anger. Call it outrage. Call it fear. Definitely call it fear. But seeing the evil depths of Saint Dane's vision locked me in. I know I'm in it now, for good. I don't know if my being on this quest is right or wrong or someplace in between. All I know is, I'm here now, and that can't be changed. It's up to me and my fellow Travelers to stop Saint Dane. We're the ones on the spot. I accept that now. I don't like it, but I accept it.

I'm writing all this to you so you'll know where my head is, but also to explain some of the things I did over the past few days. To put it right out there, I messed up. Bad. And the thing is, I'm not so sure that if I had to do it all over again, I wouldn't do the exact same *wrong* thing again. That's what has me so upset right now. Saint Dane must be defeated. Part of that responsibility is mine. But after what happened with the *Hindenburg,* I don't know if I'm up to the job.

The true events that happened on May 6, 1937, will never be reported in any newspaper. They will not be part of recorded history. They will live only in my journals and the journals of my fellow Travelers.

This is what happened.

It was a gray, cold May day. The sky was full of roiling clouds, rain showers, and occasional cracks of thunder and lightning. The *Hindenburg* was supposed to arrive in New Jersey early in the morning, but bad weather forced it to circle the New York area for most of the day. History was playing out the way it was supposed to. So far.

The whole atmosphere had an ominous feel to it. I don't know if that was because of the weather or because I knew what was going to happen. Either way, there was tension in the air.

Gunny and I got back to the Manhattan Tower Hotel as quickly as we could.

But as soon as we got back to our room on the sixth floor, things began to unravel. Spader was gone. He'd left a note for us.

Pendragon and Gunny,

I'm writing this on the morning of May 6. When you two didn't return in time, I thought for sure we had failed. But I heard on the radio-talk-thing that the Hindenburg has been delayed. I'm sorry, mates, I can't wait for you any longer. I'm going to New Jersey on my own. I found out how to take a bus, so that's what I'll do. I promise, I'll do all that I can to save that airship from being destroyed.

Hobey-ho,

Spader

"He's on his way to New Jersey," I shouted to Gunny. "I *knew* we should have stayed together!" I threw the note down in anger.

"It's early," Gunny said reassuringly. "We've got all day to figure something out."

"Yeah, but do you know what this means? Max Rose knows about Winn Farrow's plan. Spader told him, remember? History has already been changed. Strike one. Now Spader's on his own. He's going after Winn Farrow to stop him too. Strike two. Now we've got to stop Max Rose *and* Spader."

"There's a lot that can happen before strike three," Gunny said calmly. "I think the first thing we should do is go see Max Rose."

"Why?" I asked.

"He trusts you. Maybe we can find out how he plans on stopping Winn Farrow."

Okay, that made sense. At least one of us was thinking clearly. It sure wasn't me.

"We'll find out what we can," Gunny continued. "Then we'll take Caplesmith's car and drive down to New Jersey. We might even beat Spader there."

I nodded. This sounded like a plan.

"You all right now?" Gunny asked.

"Yeah, I'm cool," I answered. My heart rate was dropping back down from three hundred beats a minute.

"A wise person once said that the only way we've got a chance here is if we keep our heads screwed on straight and work it through, together."

I looked at Gunny and smiled. "I said that."

"Was that you, shorty?" Gunny asked in fake surprise. "I knew I heard it somewhere."

"Okay, I hear you," I said. "My act is officially back together."

We took the elevator up to the thirtieth floor to see Max Rose. I had no idea what we'd say to him, but it was the obvious place to start. We'd have to wing it once we got there. When we hit the elevator, Dewey looked all sorts of confused.

"What's goin' on?" he asked.

"What do you mean?" Gunny asked him.

"Men have been coming and going from the penthouse all day," Dewey said. "Is Max Rose moving out?"

Gunny and I shared glances. Whatever Max Rose's plan

was to stop Winn Farrow, it was under way. The elevator arrived and Gunny and I jumped out. As usual, Dewey closed the door quickly. It was like he thought the floor was haunted or something.

As soon as we entered the hallway, we knew something was wrong. That's because the two thugs who worked security were gone. There was nobody around to protect Max Rose. Gunny and I ran for the door to the penthouse. We stopped, caught our breath so it wouldn't seem like we were as excited as we were, and rang the doorbell. No answer. We rang again. Nobody came to the door. Gunny then noticed that the door wasn't even closed. He gave it a push with his finger and the door creaked open.

"Hello?" Gunny called. "Bell Captain!"

No response. We took a chance and went inside. Nothing looked out of the ordinary, except that nobody was around.

"Hello?" Gunny called again. Still no answer.

"Do you smell that?" I asked.

Gunny took a whiff. "Smoke," he said.

We both looked around quickly and Gunny spotted it first. Smoke was creeping out from under the door to Max Rose's office. We ran for the door and I threw it open. Instantly billows of smoke blew out. The room was on fire.

"I'll get the hose," Gunny shouted, and ran back into the corridor. A few seconds later he came back into the penthouse pulling a heavy fire hose. "Go turn it on!" he ordered me.

"Don't close that door," I yelled. "It locks automatically."

I ran back to the hallway, following the hose to the source. I quickly cranked the handle and the limp hose jumped to life. I sprinted back into the penthouse in time to see Gunny expertly killing the fire. Billows of smoke and steam blew out from the room as he doused the flames. Seconds later it was over.

"Okay," he announced. "Turn it off."

I ran into the corridor and turned off the water, then returned to the office to check out the damage. What a mess. It looked like the inside of a barbeque grill. It didn't smell so great either. Luckily all the damage was contained in the one room. A few minutes more, though, and it would have spread.

"This was deliberate," Gunny said. He kicked at a few garbage pails that were full of ashes and water. "Burning evidence is my guess."

I saw that the file cabinets were open and empty. The desk drawers were empty too. Max Rose was covering his tracks. Every bit of paper in this room was now a charred memory. There was nothing left that might connect him with his network of spies, or with the Nazis.

"I guess this means everybody's gone," I said.

"Probably," Gunny said. "We should do a quick check though."

We left the wet, smoldering mess and searched the penthouse for signs of life. We checked bedrooms, sitting rooms, the kitchen, and the dining room. Not only were there no people, all the drawers had been emptied too. Max Rose had definitely pulled up stakes and moved out. We knew where he was going, too. He had a date with a zeppelin.

The final stop on our search was the grand living room where I had set out lunch for Rose and the Nazi, Ludwig Zell. Nobody was in there, either.

Gunny said, "We're wasting our time here. I'll get Caplesmith's car so we can get down to—"

We then heard a sound that made the hair go up on the back of my neck. It was the steady sound of somebody clapping.

There was someone in the penthouse after all. Gunny and I looked at each other, then slowly turned toward the door. Standing there looking as beautiful as ever was Esther Amaden. Her friends called her Harlow. Her enemies called her Saint Dane. She was clapping in mock approval.

"Congratulations, boys," the bogus woman purred. "I'm guessing you finally solved the riddle."

"At least have the guts to show yourself," I said defiantly.

The beautiful woman closed the door behind her. Gunny shot me a curious look. It was hard for him to believe that this movie-star-gorgeous woman could be the demon Traveler who was about to turn three territories into rubble. But I knew better. I'd seen it before.

"Whatever you'd like, Pendragon," she said with a smile.

Esther Amaden then went through the transformation that I had seen too many times. Her body became fluid as she left behind the image of the beautiful big-band singer. Her body grew taller until it was near seven feet. Her rosy complexion turned the pasty white color of a corpse. Her short dark hair grew out into a long, gray mane. Her silky bathrobe turned black and changed shape into a black suit that, as I've written before, looked vaguely Asian. The final step was always the toughest to watch. It was the eyes. Harlow's soft, dreamy brown eyes turned razor sharp. They took on the icy blue fire of our nemesis—Saint Dane.

I sensed Gunny's surprise and fear. He took a step back. This was the first time he'd witnessed this transformation. It was also the first time he was seeing Saint Dane in his true form.

"Better?" Saint Dane hissed through a twisted smile. "We really don't spend enough time together, Pendragon, do we?"

It took every bit of willpower I had not to scream.

FIRST EARTH

"I'm disappointed in you, Pendragon," Saint Dane said. "I've left so many clues for you like breadcrumbs in the forest, and it's still taken you all this time to uncover my little plot. Time is growing short. Are you losing interest?"

Saint Dane walked casually around the room with his hands clasped behind his back. Gunny and I kept our distance. It was like being trapped in a room with a wild animal. You never knew what this guy was going to do.

"I suppose the loss of your uncle's sage guidance has made it all the more difficult for you to keep up with me."

Oh, man. This guy loved to hit where it hurt the most.

He then added, "I must admit, you surprised me on both Denduron and Cloral."

"Why's that?" I asked.

"You were a force to be reckoned with. For that, I bow to you. And I must apologize for my own foolishness. It was a mistake to ask you to join me on my quest."

"You got that right," I said quickly. "No way I'll ever join you."

Saint Dane stopped walking and smiled. He was enjoying this.

I wasn't.

"You misunderstand," he said. "My only mistake was asking you too early. It gave you the impression that I was somehow . . . vulnerable." He chuckled. "I assure you, I am not. That's why I chose to play out this latest game on the Earth territories. *Your* home territories. I wanted to demonstrate how easy it is for me to make you dance like a toy puppet. *My* toy puppet. In spite of what you may think due to our past encounters, I am in total control."

"You aren't in control," Gunny said with authority. "Not anymore."

Saint Dane let out a deep, bellowing laugh. I hated that.

"Such an amusing old man," Saint Dane chuckled.

"Old enough to know how to handle the likes of you," Gunny shot back.

"Oooh," Saint Dane bellowed in mock fear. "Forgive me if I don't feel threatened by an old man who doesn't possess the courage to fire a weapon."

"You think you're bothering me," Gunny said without missing a beat. "But you're not."

"Stick around, Gunny," Saint Dane snapped back at him. "By the time we're done, I promise, you will be very, very bothered."

Saint Dane walked to the glass doors that led to the balcony. He threw them open, letting in a chilly wind. He stood with his back to us, looking out over the gray city.

"You see, Pendragon, my victory here on First Earth means much more than the toppling of three territories. What makes this all so wonderfully special is, you're the one who is doing it for me."

That was a strange comment. I didn't like it, one bit.

"We know what's going on, Saint Dane," I said. "We know what will happen if the *Hindenburg* doesn't crash. We went to Third Earth."

Saint Dane spun back to us and exclaimed, "Well, of course you went to Third Earth! I was counting on it. I *wanted* you to know what would happen."

That wasn't the reaction I expected. Gunny and I shot each other a quick look.

Saint Dane chuckled and said, "You still don't understand, do you? I've been leading you and your band of merry men around like trained dogs. Everything that's happened, every turn, every surprise, I've orchestrated. You knew to follow me to First Earth because of the bullets that killed your uncle. But to be sure, I first went to Veelox. That annoying Traveler girl thought she was being so clever by recording my arrival. I couldn't have been any clearer in telegraphing my ultimate destination if I had painted a sign on my back."

I thought back to the hologram that Aja Killian showed us of Saint Dane arriving at the flume on Veelox, then making a show of calling out "First Earth!" before leaving again. Now that I think of it, it *was* pretty obvious.

"Once you were here, my only challenge was to make sure you discovered Winn Farrow's plot to destroy the *Hindenburg*. I knew that once you learned of his plan, you'd do everything possible to prevent that ship from blowing up. The idea of innocent lives being lost is just too horrible a concept for your righteous mind to accept."

As Saint Dane spoke, I thought back to the events that led us to crossing paths with Winn Farrow.

"The gangsters in the subway?" I asked.

"I brought them to the flume to put you on the trail of

Winn Farrow," he answered. "Killing Press was a bonus."

I forced myself not to let that throw me.

"But they tried to kill us. Twice."

"They were supposed to warn you to stay away from Winn Farrow, which I knew would send you running to him like rats to garbage. Killing you was their idea. Idiots. That's why I had to dispose of one of them. Or should I say, Harlow had to."

"The gangster who fell from the hotel was pushed by Harlow? I mean, by you?" Gunny asked in surprise.

Saint Dane answered with a proud bow. Now we knew how Mr. Nasty Gangster died. It was Saint Dane.

"I couldn't let him kill you," he said. "Not before my drama played out. You might say I was your guardian angel, Pendragon."

"In the slaughterhouse," I said, remembering. "You left the door open so we could escape."

"Again, guilty," he said, gloating.

He then took a step back, and transformed. His body grew watery and in a few seconds he became . . . Ludwig Zell.

"You were Zell, too?" I shouted in surprise.

"Not until recently," Zell/Saint Dane said. "Once Max Rose learned of the plot to destroy the *Hindenburg,* I knew he would warn Herr Zell."

Zell/Saint Dane walked over to a closet door.

"I couldn't have our Nazi friend sending the zeppelin back to Germany, so I had to intervene."

Zell/Saint Dane opened the door and a body rolled out. It was Ludwig Zell. The *real* Ludwig Zell. He was pretty dead. No matter how many times I see dead guys, I can't get used to it.

"Poor Ludwig was in the wrong place at the wrong time. Max Rose thought he was giving his Nazi cohort the bad news, but he was actually telling me."

The truth was rushing at me way too fast. I was getting dizzy.

"But why?" I asked. "If Ludwig Zell warned Germany, the *Hindenburg* would be saved. That's what you want, isn't it? What difference would it make *how* it was saved?"

Zell/Saint Dane's attitude grew dark. He took a step toward me, and as he did, he transformed back into his evil-looking self. His horrid eyes locked on mine and he spoke through clenched teeth.

"Because this is about *you*, Pendragon!" he seethed. "I don't care what happens to that airship. I don't care what happens to these pathetic Earth territories. I don't care who wins their silly war or what they do with this useless world afterward."

"You don't?" I said, totally confused.

"In a few short hours the course of your world will be changed forever. The Earth territories will fall into chaos. And who will be to blame? You! If you hadn't come here to stop me, history would have played out the way it was intended. But you couldn't stay away. You put yourself into the equation and because of that, three territories will collapse. Your *home* will collapse."

I stared into Saint Dane's fierce eyes. I'm not sure which I was more afraid of: him or the horror to come. Everything he said was true. If Spader and I hadn't chased him to First Earth, the *Hindenburg* would be destined to crash, the way it was supposed to. But now, because of my meddling, there was a good chance the *Hindenburg* would be saved and the Earth territories doomed. This whole adventure was to prove how easily Saint Dane could manipulate us. Manipulate *me*. The amazing thing was, he was willing to destroy three territories to do it.

Saint Dane then said, "How does it feel, knowing this was all for you?"

The two of us held eye contact. In that one, horrible moment, things became all too clear. I knew where the struggle between Saint Dane and the Travelers was headed. Someday, somehow, somewhere, it was going to come down to Saint Dane . . .

And me. That's why he was doing his best to prove himself to me. What a sickening thought. The only thing that kept me from losing it was knowing that the ultimate day of reckoning wasn't today. No, this was far from over.

"I'll tell you how it makes me feel," I answered with a very small voice. "I feel that as long as you're trying to impress me, I can beat you."

There was a frozen moment.

"You think you understand me?" he said. "You think you have the strength to bring me down? Talk to me again in a few hours, after you've gone to Second Earth to see the scorched world where your friends used to live. Everything you've ever loved will no longer exist, Pendragon. Your home will be turned into a charred pit of death . . . and it will be your fault."

"We still have time," I said. "We can still make sure the *Hindenburg* crashes."

An odd thing happened then. Saint Dane smiled. It wasn't like the sly, knowing smiles he usually threw at me. This was a genuine, wide, Cheshire-cat grin. The guy was actually happy. Being that it was Saint Dane, a sincere smile seemed all the more grotesque. It was totally creepy.

"Yes," he said. "You still have time. Please, make the most of it."

He backed away from me and walked over to the door. He turned the knob and gave a look of mock surprise. "Oh, no, it's locked." he announced. "Max Rose is so paranoid. He's made all of these doors self-locking. But you already knew that, didn't you?"

He then reached into his pocket and pulled out an old-fashioned brass key. He waved it at us, taunting us.

"But no fear," he said. "I've got the key." Saint Dane walked out on the balcony. "Do you think you can stop it, Pendragon?" he asked. "If I let you out of here, do you think you can stop Spader? And Rose? Could you let the *Hindenburg* crash?"

"We can try," I said.

"Of course you can," Saint Dane said as he backed toward the edge of the balcony. "And I want you to. I want you to come close. I want you to feel as if you've beaten me one more time, because that's when victory is the sweetest . . . when your opponent feels as if he actually has a chance to win, just before it all comes crashing down."

He looked out over the city and said, "I think I'll return to Veelox and see what trouble I can stir up. That little girl Traveler is even more sure of herself than you, Pendragon. She's in for a big surprise." He was at the edge of the balcony now.

"Good-bye, my friends. Enjoy your afternoon." Saint Dane gave an exaggerated bow, and in one graceful move, jumped up and off the balcony!

Gunny and I gave each other a quick, unbelieving glance, then ran for the railing. Just as we were about to look over the side, a huge, black raven rose up from below. I swear, it was the biggest crow I had ever seen in my life. It was more like the size of an eagle. The bird rose as if riding on thermals. Then with one quick snap of its wings, it turned and sailed off. But the instant before it left, I saw that it was holding something in its curved beak. It was only a quick flash, but I was certain I had seen it.

It was an old-fashioned brass key.

"You don't think—?" Gunny asked.

"I don't know," I answered. "I don't care. We've got to get outta here."

I ran back into the apartment and over to the door. I tried the knob to make sure it was locked. It was. I took a quick look around and saw another door. I ran to that one. Yeah, it was locked too. Those two doors were the only way out of this room.

"We'll have to break 'em down!" I announced.

I was all set to put my shoulder to the door and start bashing away, when Gunny warned, "Don't!"

"We have to!" I shouted.

"We'll never break those doors down," Gunny said. "Max Rose had them reinforced with steel. This was his fortress. You couldn't knock them down with a battering ram."

I quickly scanned the living room, looking for another way out . . . and saw the telephone. I grabbed it, only to find it was dead.

"He cut the phone lines," I announced. I then looked at my watch. It was almost noon. "Gunny, we're running out of time."

The *Hindenburg* was going to arrive in nine hours.

FIRST EARTH

"This is your hotel!" I shouted. "How do we get out of here? There must be some kind of emergency way to let people know we're in here."

Gunny looked around the fancy living room, then shook his head. "Not if the telephone's out."

This was insane. The world was about to collapse and we were locked in a dumb hotel room.

"I got it!" I shouted. "We can start a fire. It'll set off the smoke detectors."

Gunny gave me a strange look. "What's a smoke detector?"

Oh yeah. 1937. I looked around the room, then ran out on the balcony. Looking over the edge, I hoped to see Saint Dane's smashed body lying on the pavement below. It wasn't. I don't know why, but I wasn't surprised. I thought about that big raven. How weird was that? But I couldn't obsess about it. We had to get out of there.

I looked down to see if there was a ledge we could crawl out on. But the closest foothold was thirty floors down. On the sidewalk. I looked up, thinking we might be able to climb onto the roof. No go. It was out of reach. We really were trapped.

I have to admit, I even stood there for a second and tried to change myself into a raven. What the heck? If Saint Dane was a Traveler and he could do it, maybe I could too.

I couldn't. But just the fact that I tried showed how desperate I was.

I ran back into the room to see that Gunny had come up with a brilliant plan. A dangerous plan, but a brilliant one. He was pulling down the drapes that hung on either side of the balcony doors. With his pocketknife he cut a small tear on one end to get started, then ripped off a long strip of fabric. I knew instantly what he wanted to do. We were going to make a lifeline.

"You keep cutting strips," he ordered. "I'll tie the knots."

I set to work with his knife, tearing off long strips of fabric. Gunny expertly knotted the ends together.

"There's another balcony below us, about thirty feet down," Gunny explained. He then pulled on the fabric, testing its strength. "I'll tie one end onto the railing up here, then lower myself down."

This was a plan. As good as any. But as I cut the pieces of fabric, I knew there was only one thing wrong with it.

"This is gonna work, Gunny," I said. "But you're too heavy. This won't hold you."

"It'll have to," Gunny said quickly. "Because I'm not sending you over the side."

We continued working for a few minutes, until Gunny had fashioned a rope that looked plenty long enough. I tugged on it. It was strong, but still had a little play. Gunny was six foot four and probably weighed 220 pounds. I was five foot five and weighed half that much.

"Gunny, if you go, this'll tear," I said.

Gunny tested the rope himself. I could tell by his

expression he didn't think it would hold his weight either.

"I'm light," I added. "It'll hold me."

I didn't wait for his response. I started tying one end around my chest and under my arms. I had to do it fast, not because I thought Gunny would stop me, but because I was afraid I'd chicken out if I thought too much about it. We were thirty floors up. My mind flashed on the horrible sight of Mr. Nasty Gangster falling through the air.

Note to self: Stop thinking.

"No, Pendragon, I can't let you—"

"We don't have a whole lot of choices," I interrupted. "Either I go, or we hang out here until the housekeeping staff finds us tomorrow morning."

Gunny looked at the floor. If there were any other way around this, he would have taken it. But he knew I was right.

"Let's do it," I said, and carried the makeshift rope out on the balcony.

Gunny tied the loose end securely around the balcony railing. He knew what he was doing. Maybe it was his army training. I trusted that his knots would hold. It was the drape material I wasn't so sure about.

"You're in control," he instructed. "Grab on to the rope near the railing, face the building, keep your feet against the wall and walk backwards. Let the rope move through your hands as you go down. I'll handle the slack."

"I've done this," I said. "It's sort of like rappelling."

Uncle Press had taught me how to rock climb. It seemed like things kept popping up that Uncle Press had prepared me for. I always thought he took me on those great adventures because he was a fun uncle. I had no idea he was training me for life as a Traveler. Because we had gone on a rock-climbing trip when I was twelve, I knew how to rappel down the side of a sheer rock face. The only difference here was, I wasn't secured by a solid climber's rope. I was trusting my life to a raggy piece of drapery. Gulp.

I sat up on the railing and swung my legs over. I made sure not to look down. I didn't need to see how far I would fall if things went south, so to speak. So while pretending I was only a few feet up in the air, I carefully turned around. I stood with my toes on the balcony, holding on to the rail, looking back at Gunny. It all seemed so natural, except that he was standing on the safe side of the railing and my butt was dangling over midtown Manhattan.

"Can of corn," he said reassuringly. But his eyes gave him away. He was scared. Probably not as much as I was, though.

Gunny then threaded the slack rope through the railing and pulled my end tight. As I lowered myself down, he would play out my end of the rope, keeping pressure off the railing knot. It was like being double-secured. At least, that's what I told myself.

I tested the strength of the cloth rope, nodded, and stepped down off the balcony. With my feet firmly planted on the wall, I began to walk down backward.

I flashed on the old *Batman* TV show where those guys used to walk up the sides of buildings with their Bat ropes. That was idiotic. But not as idiotic as what I was doing now. I held the cloth rope tightly, and slowly slid my hands down it as I moved. The only tricky part came when I got to one of Gunny's knots. They were too big to slip through my clenched hands, so I had to let go with one hand at a time and cross over below it. That was scary.

I could hear the cloth rope straining under my weight. Obviously, this material wasn't made to hold so much weight, because I kept hearing tiny little tearing sounds. They were faint, but they might as well have been exploding cherry bombs. If enough of those little tears got together, they'd make one big rip and, well, look out below.

Just to make me even more nervous, I looked up to see that Gunny didn't have enough drape left to hold on to. I wasn't double-secured anymore.

The whole trip only took a couple of minutes, though it felt like I was dangling from that building for a week. Finally I slid my right foot down another few inches and felt air. I had made it to the ceiling of the balcony below! I couldn't see the balcony because it was cut *in* to the building, but I knew it was there. My foot told me so. I was almost home.

That's when the bad news came.

No, the rope didn't break. It wasn't that bad. But it was close. I had another six feet to go before my feet would touch the railing of the balcony below, when I realized the worst: I had run out of rope. We made it too short! I dangled there, twenty-nine stories high over pavement, with the wind blowing and drops of rain beginning to fall . . . with nowhere to go.

"It's too short!" I called up to Gunny. "I can't go any lower."

Gunny winced. "You sure?"

"Uh, yeah." It didn't take a genius to figure this one out.

"You're going to have to climb back up," Gunny called down.

This was a disaster. We blew it. How could we have made such a simple mistake? I had to climb back up and figure out a Plan B. But as soon as I reached my hand farther up the rope, I felt it tear again. It wasn't a little tear either. I must have jolted down an inch. The rope was going to go! If I tried to climb back up, I wouldn't make it very far. I was trapped. There was no place to go but down. Way down.

I then realized that I had one chance. It was horrifying to

think of, but it was the only way. Without stopping to second guess, I grabbed higher up on the rope with one hand and pulled up to take some of my weight off the rope. I then began to untie the knot that secured the rope around my chest.

"Pendragon, what are you doing?" Gunny shouted in horror.

"I need more rope," I called back. "This'll give me another couple of feet."

It was a totally scary maneuver. If I could untie the knot, I could use the extra length of rope that was wrapped around my chest to lower myself down a few more feet. Hopefully that would get me low enough to touch my feet to the railing and swing into the balcony.

Yeah, hopefully. It could also be suicide.

I had to pull myself up with one hand, and untie the knot with the other. To make things worse, if that's possible, the knot was now squeezed into a tiny, tight ball because my whole weight had been pulling on it.

And it started to rain.

The fabric was getting wet and slick. This was insane.

So with one hand I pulled myself up; with the other hand I worked on the knot. It was really hard. After a few minutes my arm started to scream with pain from the stress. I wasn't sure which was going to give out first, my arm or the rope. But I couldn't rest. If I put my weight back on the rope, the knot would pull tight and I'd have to start over.

This was quickly looking like a very bad idea.

After a few agonizing minutes, I managed to loosen up the knot. The next step was the scary one. My right arm was shot. I had to reach up and grab the rope with my left arm to give it a rest. I couldn't let my full weight back on the rope now. The knot was too loose. If I let go, the only thing that would break my fall was the pavement.

With a couple of quick tugs, I pulled the knot entirely free, then grabbed the rope with both hands. I was now hanging by my hands. My really tired hands. I then slipped down a few inches at a time, letting the slick rope slide through my hands. The pain was incredible. I was so tired.

I checked to see how much of the rope was left and saw about a foot until the end. This was going to be close. Then, with only a few inches of rope left, I felt the railing with my toe. I was there!

But I wasn't safe yet. My arms were straight up over my head and I was still staring at building. I was so freakin' close, but still not low enough to swing in. I was going to have to put my full weight on the rail, let go of the rope, and duck under the ceiling. Sounds easy, right? It wasn't. It was totally awkward. Making it worse, the narrow rail was slick with rain.

I eased myself down until my feet were resting on the rail. Man, it felt great to be on something solid again. There wasn't much more than an inch of rope left, but that was okay. For the first time, I thought I was going to make it. I gingerly let go of the rope, putting all my weight on my feet. I then started to crouch down to duck under the ceiling and jump onto the balcony when . . .

My feet slipped.

It all went so fast that I'm not exactly sure what happened. Luckily, when my feet went off the rail, they slipped toward the balcony side, not toward air. That saved my life. But when I fell, I was so close to the rail that my head thumped against the hard, slick metal.

Our escape plan had worked, but we weren't any closer to getting out of there, because that head slam knocked me straight into dreamland.

I found myself lying on a beach. It was the Point in Stony Brook. Best beach in the world. At least it was the best beach in Stony Brook. Mark, how many times did we ride our bikes there to hang out for hours, watching the girls? I can still picture that pink bikini Courtney got last summer. Courtney, hot suit. Yeah, I was lying in the sand at the Point, listening to the waves, kicking back, hanging.

When I opened my eyes I expected to see you, Mark. Or Courtney, or any of the other kids from class, kicking it right along with me. Instead, I saw Dewey.

His eyes were as big as baseballs as he stared down at me.

"Pendragon!" he shouted, all nervous. "Are you alive?"

I wasn't sure. But dead people didn't get headaches, so I figured I was still among the living. I slowly sat up and looked around. All thoughts of the beach at Stony Brook and Courtney's pink bikini were long gone. Oh, well. Dewey's face pretty much ended that. Instead, I saw that I was lying on the floor of the ballroom on the twenty-ninth floor of the hotel. It was the same ballroom where we saved Max Rose's life. It was empty now, except for Dewey and me.

"I was gonna call a doctor, but Gunny told me not to," Dewey whined. "You want me to get one?"

"No," I said quickly. I probably needed one, but now wasn't the time. "I'm fine. Where's Gunny?"

"Downstairs. He told me to wait with you till he got back. Did you really climb down that drapery?"

It all came back to me—Saint Dane, being locked in the penthouse, Ludwig Zell, the trip down the rope, the fall. I really wished I were on that beach in Stony Brook.

"One of the cooks found you lying here," Dewey said. "But you were out cold. He saw the rope hanging down and found Gunny upstairs. Pendragon, there's a dead body up there! Who is that? How did you two get locked in the penthouse?"

"Long story," I said. Then another thought hit me. "What time is it?"

Dewey looked at his watch and said, "Almost three o'clock."

Yeow. If I wasn't awake before, I was now. I had been out for hours! The *Hindenburg* was going to arrive in four hours and we were still in Manhattan!

"I gotta get outta here," I said as I tried to get up. But the pain shot through my head like a bolt of lightning. It pushed me right back down to the floor.

"Don't move," Dewey said. "I'll get you some water." He ran off, leaving me alone.

This was bad. Very bad. Where was Gunny? I forced myself to sit up, then pulled myself into a chair. I had to get my act together and down to New Jersey, or everything would be lost. The *Hindenburg* was going to land at 7:25. Gunny said it was a four-hour drive down to Lakehurst. Even if we left at that very minute, we still wouldn't get down there until almost seven o'clock. That wouldn't leave much time to figure a way to stop Spader and Max Rose.

"We're in trouble," came a voice from behind me. It was Gunny. He jogged across the ballroom toward me.

"I've been out for hours, Gunny! Why didn't you wake me up?"

"Because I was trying to find us a ride down to New Jersey," was his answer.

Good answer.

"I didn't find one," he added.

Ooh, bad answer.

"What do you mean? What about Caplesmith's car?"

"I went to the fella who's been fixing it. It's in pieces all over the garage floor. He said it would take him half a day to put it back together."

"Then we'll take the bus. Gunny, we gotta get down there."

"That's not good," Gunny answered. "The last bus going down that way today left at noon."

"What about a train?" I asked.

"Still no good. Earliest we could get down there would be tomorrow morning."

"This is incredible!" I shouted, jumping up. Bad move. Another bolt of pain shot through my head. It didn't stop my tirade though. "Three territories are going to crumble because we can't get a ride?"

"I'm sorry, Pendragon," Gunny said. "Unless you know some way of flying down there, we're out of luck."

I stopped short. My bruised brain raced. Gunny had said the magic word. Flying.

"C'mon," I said, and ran for the elevator. Gunny was right behind me. We blew right past Dewey, who was headed toward us with a glass of water.

"Where you going?" he asked.

I grabbed him by the arm and pulled him along. After all, he ran the elevator.

Five minutes later we were standing in front of room 1515. I knocked and closed my eyes. I had no idea if she was still staying at the hotel, but this was our last hope. After a few agonizing seconds, the door opened and we stood facing Jinx Olsen.

"Pendragon! Gunny! Here to say good-bye?" she exclaimed. "Come on in." She walked back into her room, where I saw all of her clothes spread out on the bed. She was packing up her duffel bag.

"You're leaving?" I asked.

"Just got the word," she said. "This is it. End of the line. I am officially off active duty." She said this like it was cheery news, but I knew it was eating her up. "I'm headed home to Maine. And you know what? I'm taking the train. Why not? Something different, right?"

Jinx continued to pack. I looked at Gunny. He gave me a nod of encouragement. I wasn't exactly sure what to say, but I had to think of something fast.

"Jinx," I began. "We need a favor."

"Whatever I can do, boys," she answered.

"Can you fly us somewhere?"

Jinx stopped packing. She looked at me, as if it were a strange request, then sat down on the edge of the bed.

"I told you, Pendragon, I'm grounded. No more joy rides."

"This isn't a joy ride," I said. I tried to be as convincing as possible. "We need to get down to Lakehurst, New Jersey."

"Lakehurst?" she said. "That's where the dirigibles come in. The *Hindenburg* is due today."

"Exactly," I said.

"What's so important? You want to be there with all the other lookey-loos to see her float in? To be honest, I think those blimps are a lot of hot air. Get it? Hot air."

I got it. I wasn't laughing.

"That's not it," I said seriously. "I don't really know how to say this. It's a long story and there's no way you'd believe it. But what I'm going to tell you is the absolute truth. If we don't get down there right away, I mean now, something horrible is going to happen that I can't even begin to describe."

"Really?" she said with surprise and a touch of curiosity. "What is it?"

"I can't tell you. I know that sounds stupid, but it's the truth. I'll tell you this much, though, we're asking you to fly the most important mission taken by any pilot, man or woman, ever. I'm not exaggerating."

"He's telling you the truth, ma'am," Gunny added.

It was now up to Jinx. I want to say that it was my brilliant powers of persuasion that convinced her to take us. I want to say that I was smart enough to know she wanted to do something important with her flying and not just be a sideshow. I even want to say I used my Traveler mind powers to convince her. I want to say all those things, but none of them would be true.

"To be honest, Pendragon," she said, "you didn't have to tell me all that other stuff. I was ready to go the second you asked me if I'd fly you somewhere."

I had to smile. Could Jinx be any cooler? "You aren't worried about the Coast Guard?" I asked.

"Nah," she scoffed. "What are they going to do? Ground me? If I've gotta go, I'm goin' out with a bang!"

It was nearly an hour later when we found ourselves strapped into Jinx's V-157 Schreck/Viking, ready for takeoff. I was in the front cockpit next to Jinx because Gunny was a much bigger guy than Spader. He needed the rear cockpit all to himself. The monster engine pounded away as we bounced over the swells of the Hudson River. The weather was still nasty, so the water was pretty choppy. My aching head throbbed each time we hit a swell. I was miserable, but had to gut it out. My bigger worry was that if the weather got any worse than this, I didn't think we'd be able to take off. I looked to the sky and saw that there were still thunderstorms dancing around.

"Can you fly in this weather?" I shouted to Jinx over the roar of the engine.

Jinx gave a quick look around, then said, "What weather?"

That was good enough for me. It was now almost 4:30 P.M. The flight was going to take about an hour and a half, getting us to Lakehurst around 6:00 P.M. The *Hindenburg* was going to land at 7:25 P.M. Not much time to find Spader and Max Rose and figure out a way to stop them. We were cutting it very close.

I looked back at Gunny and shouted, "You ready?"

Gunny was doubled over in the back, puking. He looked up, smiled, and gave me a thumbs up. It was going to be a long flight. Jinx gunned the throttle, the plane bounced over the swells, and after a gut-rumbling thirty seconds, we were airborne.

Just as I feared, the flight was ugly. The little plane was constantly buffeted by gusts of wind and downdrafts. Jinx tried to fly at different altitudes, searching for smooth air, but nothing helped.

Most of the time, we were flying blind. The gray, angry clouds were thick and low. Every time we entered one, I gritted my teeth and held my breath. If there were another plane coming from the other direction, we'd be history. But this was 1937. There wasn't as much air traffic back then, so we were fairly safe. At least that's what I kept telling myself.

A few times I looked back to check on Gunny. The poor guy was having a rough time. His face looked green, but he still gave me a brave thumbs up. At one point I wondered if Gunny thought the thumbs up meant "I'm going to puke again," because that's pretty much all he was doing.

They didn't have radio beacons or radar back in those days. All Jinx had to navigate was a compass, her eyes, and a great sense of direction. As it turned out, she had been down to Lakehurst before, so she knew what landmarks to follow. I think back on that flight and I realize that Jinx's cockiness was deserved. She really was a great pilot. It was too bad nobody recognized her for it.

There was one whopper of a hairy moment that still makes my palms sweaty when I think back on it. We had been flying for almost two hours. That was bad. The flight was taking way longer than Jinx figured. It was because of the weather. We were fighting head winds the whole way. I was getting more anxious by the second.

We then entered a huge cloud bank. This was the darkest, longest one we had been in yet. I kept looking ahead, praying to see light on the far side that would mean we were about to break out. But it wasn't coming. This cloud was huge. No sooner did we enter than we were pelted with more rain. Remember, we were in open cockpits. When it rained, we got wet. We had to keep wiping off our goggles or we would have been totally blinded. I kept reaching forward to wipe off the glass shield in front of Jinx so she could see better. Total waste of time. Visibility was pretty much zero.

I had just finished wiping off the windshield and sat back in my seat, when I saw something that made me stop breathing. There in front of us, only a few yards ahead, was a sight so unbelievable I thought I was imagining it. But I wasn't. It was a giant, floating, black swastika on a white circle, surrounded by a red field.

"Look out!" I shouted.

Jinx banked the plane hard to the right. The engine

groaned, the g force built up so hard that I was crushed back into the seat. I think our wings went vertical. I shut my eyes, ready for the collision, but it never came. Jinx had dodged it. It wasn't until a second later that I realized what we had nearly hit.

It was the tail of the *Hindenburg*.

It had crossed right in front of us. We didn't see it because of the cloud, and we didn't hear it because our own engine drowned out its engines. I swear, we couldn't have missed it by more than a few inches.

Jinx looked at me and smiled. "That was exciting."

Exciting. Okay, that was one word for it. I looked back at Gunny . . . and he wasn't there! My first thought was that he had fallen out. But a second later he sat up and looked at me with watery eyes. He had been doubled over, losing it once again. He couldn't even give me the thumbs up this time. The poor guy wouldn't be the same until his feet were back on solid ground.

"Does that mean we're getting close to the field?" I shouted to Jinx.

"We've still got a few minutes," Jinx shouted back.

That's when we finally blasted out of the cloud bank. I looked down to the ground and saw something that made me sit up straight. It was a long, silver bus moving along the narrow highway. This was a pretty empty section of New Jersey. There wasn't a whole lot of traffic down here. I motioned for Gunny to look down.

"Could that be the bus Spader is on?" I shouted.

Gunny looked, then nodded and gave the thumbs up. Either this was the bus, or he had to puke again. I figured it was the bus. It was a huge stroke of luck. If we could get to Spader, we could stop him from going after Winn Farrow.

Then all we would have to worry about was Max Rose. I quickly turned to Jinx.

"You gotta put us down," I shouted.

"What?" she shouted back. "Why?"

"We've got to get to that bus!" I shouted over the roar of the engine.

Jinx looked down at the ground. She banked the plane right, then left, so she could get a view of the landscape.

"Can't do it, Pendragon," she shouted back. "There's no place to put down."

"Are you sure?" I asked.

"I'm sorry. I would if I could," was her answer. "I won't be able to land until we get to the air station."

That would be too late. I needed to get to Spader now, before he had the chance to mess with Winn Farrow's plans. Stopping him was going to be half the battle. This could very well be the critical moment of the mission. I didn't want to blow it. There had to be a way.

A few seconds later, it came to me. I once again remembered an adventure I had with Uncle Press. Like I wrote before, I now understood that he was preparing me for my life as a Traveler. I learned a lot of skills through him, and I was about to put another one to use. The idea scared me to death, but I knew I could do it. I had to.

"Fly ahead of the bus," I yelled to Jinx.

Jinx didn't question. She gunned the throttle and shot forward. I glanced over at the plane's altimeter to see we were flying at three thousand feet. I then asked her, "Are these parachutes okay?"

She gave me a sideways look and said, "Of course. I packed 'em myself. Don't worry, you won't have to use it."

That's where she was wrong.

"Thanks, Jinx. Make sure Gunny gets to the airfield," I said.

Jinx gave me a strange look. She had no idea what I was talking about. I turned back to Gunny and shouted, "I'll see you at the airfield."

Gunny gave me a strange look. He didn't know what I was talking about either. How could he? There was no way either of them would think in a million years that I was about to do what I was about to do. I glanced at the altimeter and saw we were still at three thousand feet. That was plenty high enough to make a safe jump. At least that's what the book said. Before I had the chance to convince myself I was being an idiot, I clicked out of my seat buckle and turned to Jinx.

"Thanks for the ride, Jinx," I said.

"What are you doing?" she shouted back, stunned.

I showed her. With one quick move I launched myself up and out of the cockpit. A second later I was freefalling through the clouds, really hoping that Jinx was as good at packing parachutes as she was at flying airplanes.

FIRST EARTH

Before today I'd jumped out of a plane exactly three times. Each time I had other, experienced divers with me and always used a static line. That was a line on my ripcord that stayed attached to the plane. After falling for only a few seconds, the static line automatically pulled the ripcord and the parachute came out. I think they do that with new divers to make sure they don't freak and forget to pull the cord. Yeah, right, like there's any chance of *that* happening.

Now, jumping out of Jinx's plane, I was totally on my own. I thought back to all the instruction I'd had. I was taught proper body position and how to sight objects on the ground and all those things that had to do with good form. But as I plummeted away from that plane, all thoughts about good form went right out of my head. All I wanted to do was get down alive.

A second after I left the cockpit, I yanked on that ripcord as if my life depended on it, because, well, it did. I was three thousand feet in the air and dropping fast. This was dangerously low, but if the chute opened the way it was supposed to I'd be fine. I'm happy to report that no sooner did I pull that cord than I felt the familiar tug of the chute and shroud lines being quickly pulled out. Lucky for me, Jinx knew how to pack a parachute. Phew.

Two seconds later I was floating lazily under a beautiful, round white canopy. I looked up to see that the chute was fully open and all the lines were clear. Believe it or not, that's when I got scared. When I decided to jump from the plane, I bolted so fast I didn't give myself time to think about what an idiotic move it was. Now I found myself floating through a thunderstorm. Judging from the bright shots of lightning that were tearing through the sky around me, I'd be lucky to get down to the ground without being flash fried. It wasn't like I could do anything about it though. I had to take deep breaths and force myself to calm down.

I looked up at the chute again and saw Jinx's plane flying on toward the airfield. I also caught another glimpse of the *Hindenburg*. A cloud parted and the giant, silver nose poked its way out. I knew from the history lesson we got on Third Earth that the zeppelin was circling the airfield, waiting for the weather to clear so it could land. Man, that thing was huge! Jinx's plane looked like an ant next to a football. It was awesome. The scary thing was, I was on a mission to make sure it would crash and burn. Worse, if I were successful, thirty-six people would die. This was about as horrible a situation as I could imagine. The only way I could keep going was to bring back the images of the horror that would follow if the *Hindenburg* didn't crash. I had to look away from the zeppelin.

The ground was coming up fast. The key was to straighten up and relax. If all went well, landing was pretty much the same as jumping off a three-foot ladder. If all *didn't* go well, I'd break both my legs and the show would be over. I grabbed the shroud lines, kept my head down, straightened my body perpendicular to the ground, and bent my knees. Soft knees . . . soft knees . . . that was my mantra. Soft knees absorbed the shock. Stiff knees didn't. I hit the ground with both feet and rolled. It wasn't the most graceful landing, but nothing broke. That's a win in my book.

But I wasn't out of danger yet. The parachute then became my enemy. If a gust of wind filled it while I was still attached, it would easily drag me along on an uncontrollable bumpfest. But instinct took over and I quickly released the buckles that held me in the harness. At that exact moment, the wind did kick up. The parachute snapped open as it filled with air and the harness was ripped off my body. If I had waited a second more, I would have been yanked along, out of control. Now the parachute simply flew away from me. I didn't bother chasing after it. I stood and watched it fly away like a giant jellyfish with its tendrils dragging behind. I would owe the U.S. Coast Guard a new parachute.

What a rush! I had leaped out of a plane at three thousand feet and lived to tell the tale. But the truth was, it didn't matter. This wasn't about the jump. This was about getting to Spader. I had to force myself to get my head back together and plan my next move.

I was standing on a lonely road in the middle of nowhere. There was scrubby grass on either side of the road, broken up by a few lonely trees. It was probably farmland for grazing cows. Now what?

I then heard a sound. I didn't know what it was at first, because for the past few hours I had been hearing nothing but the roar of Jinx's engine and the shrill whistle of wind. This new sound was loud, harsh, and getting louder. Whatever it was, it was coming closer. I looked one way up the road and saw nothing. I turned around and saw it.

It was a silver bus, blowing its horn, headed my way. Yes! Jinx had put me exactly where I needed to be. Suddenly my insane jump from the airplane didn't seem so crazy. I had gotten ahead of Spader and we'd soon be back together.

I started waving my arms like crazy. Either this bus was going to stop, or splat me like a bug on a windshield. The sound of gushing air told me that the bus driver was putting on the brakes. I guess he didn't want to scrape me off his windshield. So far so good. The bus rolled to a stop in front of me and I ran to the door as it opened.

"Howdy, Lindbergh," the driver said. "Lose your aeroplane?"

Lindbergh? Aeroplane? Oh, right. I was still wearing the leather flight cap and goggles. What a doofus. I quickly pulled them off and asked, "Okay if I ride to the next stop?"

"Sure enough, Wilbur," he said. "Welcome aboard."

I climbed onto the bus as the driver closed the door behind me. He hit the gas and we were under way. The bus was packed with people. My guess was that they were all coming down to see the *Hindenburg* arrive. There was an excited vibe in the bus, like they were on an adventure. They were ready for the thrill of seeing the big airship.

I walked down the aisle, looking into every seat, expecting to find Spader. But when I reached the back of the bus, I hadn't seen him. I turned back toward the front, double-checking each and every passenger. Could I have missed him? No way. But I got back to the front and still no Spader. It was time to get nervous again.

"Excuse me," I said to the driver. "Did this bus come from New York City?"

"All the way," he said.

"A friend of mine was supposed to be on this bus, but I don't see him."

"Who's your friend?" he laughed. "Orville?"

Orville. Wilbur. Lindbergh. Ha ha, this guy was a real comedian.

"His name is Spader. He's taller than I am and has black hair. His eyes are kind of Asian looking. Did he get on the bus in New York?"

"Look, Ace," the driver said, "I don't remember every Joe who rides my bus. Who do I look like? Sherlock Holmes?"

"No, but, this guy's different looking," I said, pressing the issue. This was 1937. I didn't think there were many Asian-looking people riding New Jersey buses.

"Look," he said impatiently, "if I saw him, I'd tell you. But I didn't, so I can't. All right?"

That was it. Spader wasn't on the bus. But that didn't make sense. If this was the bus from New York, then why wasn't he on it? I fell down into an empty seat, beaten. My death dive from Jinx's airplane was a waste of time and adrenaline. I had no idea what to do next. Worse, I was alone. Gunny was still flying through the storm. All I could do was ride to Lakehurst with the other tourists and figure out something once I got there. I glanced at my watch. It was 6:30. The *Hindenburg* would arrive in less than an hour. Things were looking bleak.

A few minutes later the bus pulled into a gas station. The driver stopped at the pumps, then stood up and spoke to the passengers. "It's another ten minutes to the airfield, folks," he announced. "I need to gas up. It won't take long, so don't go wandering off." The guy then left the bus to fill up.

This was torture. I needed to get to the airfield as soon as possible. Every minute was critical. But I didn't know where I was going or how to get there, so I had to wait it out here with the tourists. I listened in to some of their conversations. They were all talking about the *Hindenburg*. They chatted about how it was such an amazing ship and seeing it was like getting a glimpse into the future. Man, this was freaky. If they had any idea of how horrible that future was going to be, they wouldn't be so happy.

I couldn't stand hearing this anymore, so I tuned out. That's when I glanced out the window and saw something that made me sit bolt upright in surprise.

A black car was on the other side of the pumps from the bus. Sitting in the driver's seat was the goon who worked security for Max Rose! He was the guy who kept grabbing Spader and me in the kitchen of the hotel and bringing us upstairs.

Then, walking out of the gas station, I saw Max Rose himself. I couldn't believe it. These were the guys I was chasing and here they were, right in front of me! I was back in business. I jumped up and ran out of the bus, nearly knocking over the driver who was trying to get back on.

"Mr. Rose!" I shouted. Max looked up, but didn't break out in his usual confident smile. No, he was on his own mission now. He had to stop Winn Farrow from blowing up his criminal empire.

"Buck! I was wondering where you were," he said. "Flash didn't think you'd make it."

Flash? That meant Spader. But when did he talk to Spader?

"Hobey-ho, Pendragon," came a familiar voice.

I spun around to see Spader climbing out of the backseat of the gangster's car! That's why he wasn't on the bus. He had hitched a ride with Max Rose.

A second before, I had thought all was lost. Now I was

standing right in front of the very people I came down here to stop. I still didn't have any idea what to do, but at least I was back in the game.

I ran to Spader, grabbed his arm, and pulled him away from the car. This would be tricky. He was here to help Max Rose and his goons. I had to let him know that things had changed. Drastically.

"Hey, where you going?" Max Rose shouted.

"Be right back!" I shouted. I pulled Spader far enough away so we couldn't be heard.

"What are you doing, mate?" Spader asked. "Don't make him mad. He's on our side, remember?"

"No, he's not," I whispered back. "Don't ask questions; just listen. We've gotta let Winn Farrow blow up the ship."

"What?"

"Max Rose has a spy network that's working with the Nazis. If the ship lands safely, those spies are gonna help Germany build a terrible weapon and win the war. If that happens, three territories are going down."

Spader looked confused. I didn't blame him. It was a lot to swallow.

"I don't understand," he said. "How do you know that?"

"We saw it all on Third Earth. Look, it'll take too long to explain, but believe me, it's true. We have to make sure history plays out the way it's supposed to. Winn Farrow *must* blow up the *Hindenburg.*"

"We're leaving!" shouted Max Rose. His car was all gassed up and they were ready to roll. We had to go with them.

"You gotta believe me, Spader," I said.

I then pulled Spader back toward the car. It was strange. I had never seen Spader act like this. Normally he would charge right out front, leading the way into whatever adventure lay ahead. But now, he seemed lost. I guess I couldn't blame him. I had just hit him with some pretty confusing news. Everything he thought to be true had just been turned inside out. Hey, I knew the feeling. I could only hope that he'd get his mind around it fast, so we could come up with a plan.

But all we could do just then was get in the car with Max Rose, stay close to him, and be ready to move when the chance came. *If* the chance came.

Spader and I got in the backseat with Max Rose. Two of Rose's big thugs were in front. It was three on two. I hoped it wouldn't come down to a fight between us, because we'd get pounded. The driver hit the gas and we were on the way to our date with a zeppelin.

"I owe you boys," Max Rose said while wiping nervous sweat from his forehead with an expensive silk handkerchief. "Help me stop that rat Farrow, and I'll take care of you. The deal I've got brewing is bigger than you can imagine."

I could imagine it, all right. The deal he had going was to send the U.S. down the tubes by selling atomic secrets to the Nazis. There was a rat in this equation, but it wasn't Winn Farrow.

"We know how they're getting close to the *Hindenburg*," Rose continued. "They have uniforms and badges like the ground crew wears. Nobody will look twice at 'em."

"How'd you find that out?" I asked.

One of the thugs up front said, "We convinced one of Farrow's boys to come clean." The two laughed, like they were all sorts of proud for having squeezed that information out of him.

My guess was the guy who "came clean" was probably Saint Dane. He wanted Rose to know exactly what Farrow was up to. As always, he was pulling the strings, making us dance.

"I know every one of those boys," Rose continued. "I'll point 'em out, then we take 'em down." He patted the gun that was hidden under his jacket. That was Rose's plan. He was going to find Farrow's men and shoot them. Simple as that. *Bang bang*. Not exactly a complicated Mission Impossible–style caper.

"How are we going to get inside the airfield?" I asked. "We don't have uniforms."

Rose pulled out a wad of cash. "We'll get in," he said. "We're just some innocent tourists who want to see the big ship come in, and we're willing to pay to get a good view. Money talks. Always has, always will."

I stared out the window. Forty minutes to go. As I sat in that car, speeding toward destiny, I had no idea how this would play out.

Then something caught my eye. It was a street sign that showed we were traveling on Toms River Road. We then passed another sign. The intersection for Route 527 was coming up. That was weird. I had never been here before, but it seemed familiar. How could that be?

The car charged forward, headed for the four-way intersection. That's when it hit me. I definitely knew this place. I'd heard about it in the library on Third Earth. History showed that Max Rose died in a car crash, 6:50 P.M. on May 6. Intersection of Toms River Road and Route 527. I glanced at my watch. It was 6:50. Spader and I were in the very same car, charging toward a gruesome date with an innocent motorcycle cop.

We were only a few yards from the intersection now. I quickly glanced to the left and saw it. The motorcycle cop was speeding toward the same intersection. We were seconds away from getting T-boned into oblivion.

There wasn't time to warn the driver. I dove for the front seat and grabbed the wheel.

"Look out!" I yelled and pulled the wheel hard.

We skidded into the intersection, but were moving so fast that the car started to go over. The motorcycle cop hit us, but barely. He only grazed us from behind. If I hadn't pulled the wheel, he'd have slammed us square on, and we'd be dead. The next few seconds were a blur. The car flipped. I don't know how many times. All I could do was cover my head and close my eyes. We were all bounced around like we were in a washing machine. It was a jumble of arms and legs and screams. The sounds were hideous as metal crunched and squealed on the pavement.

Finally the car stopped moving and all was still.

I slowly opened my eyes, not sure if I was dead or alive. Amazingly, the car had ended up back on its wheels and the engine was still running. This was nothing like the wreck the computer had shown me. We had dodged a fat bullet. I was on the floor, wedged between the seat and Spader.

"Spader?" I called out tentatively.

Spader slowly opened his eyes and focused on me. "You all right?" he asked.

"I think so. You?"

Spader squirmed and flexed his arms to see if everything worked. "All in one piece," he answered.

I looked around the car and saw that the driver was now in the passenger seat. He was dazed, but alive. Nobody else was in the car. Max Rose and the other thug must have been thrown out when we flipped.

Spader and I struggled to sit up. He kicked the door open and we had our way out. Carefully we crawled from the battered car. It wasn't until later that I realized how many bruises

I had. At the time I was too shocked to feel them. Besides, my head still hurt from getting conked back at the hotel. That hurt worse than anything else. I was a mess.

We stood up on shaky legs and checked out the accident scene. The motorcycle was on its side behind the car. The cop was next to it. I went to him quickly and saw that he was unconscious, but alive. Phew. The second thug was already on his feet. He staggered around like he was drunk, but it looked like he was going to be okay too. Finally we saw Max Rose on the side of the road. The big guy was struggling to sit up. It was hard to believe, but we all lived through the spectacular wreck.

I was amazed and grateful. But then a thought hit me. Max Rose was supposed to die in this accident. But now, because I had taken the wheel, Max was thrown from the car and he survived. I had changed history. Again. Now Max Rose was still able to stop Winn Farrow. If I hadn't acted, he would probably be dead now and the Earth territories would be safe. By saving Max, I may have sealed Earth's doom.

Did I mention how bad my head hurt?

"Buck!" called Max.

Spader and I went to him. He was alive, but in bad shape. He had a big gash on his forehead and had trouble focusing his eyes. "You gotta stop him, boys," he said. "You gotta stop Farrow. I'm counting on you."

Yeah, right. No chance. That's exactly what we *wouldn't* do. Max then laid back down on the ground. He was out of it. I may have changed history by saving his life, but there was no way he could do anything about saving the *Hindenburg* now. Maybe all wasn't lost after all.

That's when I heard the sound of an engine starting.

Spader and I spun to see that the second thug had gotten his act back together and picked up the cop's motorcycle. He was in the saddle, ready to roll. The sound I heard was him kicking over the bike's engine.

"I got it covered, boss," he shouted to Max. "I'll stop him."

Uh-oh. Rose's gang wasn't out of commission yet. I didn't know what to do. Should I rush the guy and try to tackle him? Should I jump in front of his motorcycle? I had seconds to act, but I didn't. That's when something happened that is going to haunt me for a long time.

Spader ran for the bike.

"I'm coming with you!" he shouted as he jumped on the back.

What was he doing? All I could get out was a confused "Spader?"

"Sorry, mate," Spader said. "We've got to save the people on that ship."

"No!" I shouted. I tried to grab him, but the thug gunned the engine and they lurched forward, just out of my reach.

"I won't let Saint Dane win," Spader shouted as they sped away from me.

There it was. The moment I had feared for months. Spader's hatred for Saint Dane had come roaring back. He was going to avenge the death of his father, no matter what the cost. Spader had promised me he could control his emotions, but he was wrong. Or he lied. It didn't matter which. The fact was, he didn't believe me about what we had found on Third Earth. Maybe I hadn't explained it well enough. Or maybe it was too much for him to understand. Whatever. All he saw was that Saint Dane was about to cause a horrific crash and people would die. He was so blinded by hatred he couldn't believe he was doing exactly what our enemy wanted him to do.

I realized all this as I stood on the road, alone, with no way to follow him or stop him. I glanced at my watch. It was 7:00. In twenty-five minutes the first domino would fall in Saint Dane's plan to destroy Halla.

It would be the end of the Earth territories, now and forever.

FIRST EARTH

There was only one way I could get to the airfield. I had to take the car.

I had driven a grand total of once. I was thirteen years old, my mother was in the passenger seat and we were in an empty parking lot with all sorts of room for error. That experience didn't exactly qualify me for the Indy 500. But hey, I had already jumped out of an airplane in the middle of a thunderstorm, rappelled down the side of a hotel, and lived through a horrendous, flipping wreck. How much worse could driving a car be?

A quick glance around the accident scene told me nobody was going to stop me. Max Rose was lying on the side of the road, unconscious. So was the motorcycle cop. The only guy I had to deal with was the thug who was still in the car, slumped in the passenger seat. Out cold. No way I was taking him along for the ride.

This was the same guy who had grabbed Spader and me and dragged us around the hotel like we were bags of trash. I didn't mind returning the favor, so I grabbed his jacket and pulled. The guy barely moved. He was twice my size and totally limp. It was like trying to maneuver a huge bag of bowling balls.

I guess my adrenaline kicked in because on my second try I was able to drag him out headfirst. His shoulders hit the ground with a dull thud. Sorry, dude. I then dug my legs in and dragged the rest of his bulk out of the seat. I didn't have to feel bad for the guy, he was totally out of it. I made sure to drag his deadweight far enough away from the car so that if something wacky happened with me behind the wheel, I wouldn't run the poor guy over.

I then jumped into the driver's seat and instantly realized I was in trouble.

This was an old-time car. It didn't have an automatic transmission. It had a stick shift on the steering column and a clutch pedal on the floor that I was going to have to learn how to use real fast. My father's car had a stick shift, so at least I knew the basics. I used to sit in his car in the garage with the engine off, pretending to drive. He hated that. He thought I was wearing out the clutch or something. But it was a good thing I had done it because now I knew how to shift. Sort of. The trick was to push the clutch pedal all the way to the floor, put the car in gear, then gently lift the pedal back up while stepping on the gas. If it was done smoothly, the car would move. If it wasn't, the car would stall out. It was a touchy-feely thing. I didn't have the touch or the feel. This was going to be interesting.

The engine was still running, so at least I didn't have to worry about starting it up. I moved the seat as far forward as possible so I could reach the pedals. I put my foot down on the clutch, moved the gear lever up to what I thought was first gear, then gently released the clutch while pressing on the gas.

The car began to roll forward. This was going to work! On the first try, no less. I grabbed the wheel, looked forward, and stepped on the gas.

The car bucked twice and stalled. Man! Not only did I not know how to drive, now I had to figure out how to start the car. I had to force myself not to panic.

There was a key in the dashboard, but when I turned it, nothing happened. For a second I thought the car was officially dead. After all, it had just been through a pretty hairy crash. Still, maybe I was doing something wrong. There weren't a whole lot of control knobs on the dashboard. Remember, this was long before the age of CD players, air-conditioning, and cruise control. I saw one knob that worked the headlights and another that turned on the windshield wipers. That was pretty much it.

Then I spotted a small, silver button below the dashboard. I had never seen a button like this on a car, but then again, I had never been in a car made in 1937 either. What did I have to lose? Unless it operated an ejection seat, it wouldn't hurt to press it. So I did . . . and the engine groaned to life. Yes! I had found the starter button.

The car bucked forward and stalled again. That's because I still had it in gear. What a dope. I jammed my foot down on the clutch pedal to disengage the gears, then hit the silver button again. After a few coughing backfires, the engine rumbled back to life. Excellent. Now I had to move. Four times I tried to get rolling in first gear, four times it stalled out. I was wasting precious time and getting ready to abandon ship and start running.

I decided to give it one more try. This time I gave it lots of gas. When I felt the car start to shake and stall again, I gave it even more gas. I thought the car was going to rattle into pieces, but a second later the ride smoothed out and I was moving. I had done it.

But getting the car to move was only the first step. Now I had to drive. This is where it got scary. I was so focused on getting the car moving, I didn't look at where I was going. As soon as I remembered to look up, I saw Max Rose standing right in front of the car! He had somehow gotten his huge bulk vertical and was now staggering toward me. I yanked the wheel hard and barely missed him. But now I was in the dirt on the side of the road. I didn't dare step on the brakes because I didn't want to stall out and have to go through that whole start-up ordeal again. So I kept my foot down on the gas and desperately cranked on the wheel, trying to get back on the road. After bouncing around and nearly missing a couple of rocks, a tree, and a stop sign, I finally got the tires back on pavement.

I was on my way.

As I pointed the car down the road and focused on keeping it straight, I heard the far-off sound of a siren headed my way. I didn't want to be stopped by a cop. No way. I had to get far away from the accident scene, so I gritted my teeth and put the pedal to the metal.

It was a good thing there wasn't much traffic out there in the boonies because I was all over the road. The steering wheel was huge and turning it was hard. Every little adjustment was an effort. Man, you had to be strong back in those days just to drive! It took me a few minutes, but I kind of got the hang of it. I even changed gears when the engine started to rev really fast. I didn't exactly feel ready to take my driver's license test, but at least I was on my way.

This whole adventure wasted ten minutes. It was 7:10. Fifteen minutes left. But at least I was headed toward the airfield.

Now that I knew I was going to get there, my thoughts turned to what I would do once I arrived. Truth was, I had no idea. Spader and the gangster were going to try to stop Winn Farrow. I had to stop them from stopping him. But how? One step at a time. First I had to get there in one piece. After that, I'd have to wing it.

I pressed the car on even faster. The speed scared me, but I couldn't be late. That point was driven home hard when I rounded a bend in the road, cleared a few trees, and saw a spectacular sight before me. I was driving along a rise that gave me a perfect view of my destination.

It was the airfield. Because I was still a mile or so away, I had a wide-angle view of the scene. The weather had cleared, and though the sun had already slipped below the horizon, the sky was still light enough to give me a pretty good look at the place. It wasn't huge by modern-day standards. It was a lonely airport in the middle of nowhere. There were a few runways that crisscrossed each other, and I saw several planes parked wing to wing. There were a few airplane hangars, but one stood out from the rest. It was giant. I mean *really* enormous. There was only one massive door, which told me this was the hangar where they kept the zeppelins. Aside from that colossal hangar, there was nothing all that unique about this place, except for one other very obvious thing:

The *Hindenburg* had arrived.

I glanced at my watch. It was 7:15. I had ten minutes before Winn Farrow would shoot his rocket to destroy the blimp. But it looked like the *Hindenburg* was already lining itself up for the final approach. There was a big crowd gathered, with floodlights blasting skyward, lighting up the silver-skinned zeppelin as if it were daytime. I'm guessing that the airship was still about a half mile from the landing point.

But with something that big, a half mile wasn't very far at all. It was an awesome and frightening sight.

The ship was traveling from my right to left. It was a scene that looked all too familiar. All the pictures of the burning ship I had ever seen were taken with its nose pointing to the left. The crowd was all gathered to one side—the ship's left side. That's where all the pictures were taken from. Having seen those pictures, I knew exactly where I needed to be. Winn Farrow must be somewhere on the ship's far side. The right side. It was the only place he could be and not be seen by the gathered crowd. The question was, would I get there in time to stop Spader?

As I drove closer to the airfield, I passed the same bus I thought Spader had taken. It was pulled over to the side of the road and all the passengers were out, watching the arrival of the airship. I wasn't sure why they had stopped here, this far away. A few seconds later I had my answer.

As I drove closer to the airfield I saw that a high, chain-link fence surrounded the place. There was a security check set up at the gated entrance, and guys in Navy uniforms were checking people's identification before letting them drive in. That meant they were only letting in authorized personnel.

And I was about as unauthorized as you could get.

There was no way I was going to drive through the front gate and past that security team. I'd probably get arrested for driving without a license, anyway. And arrested for car theft. So before I reached the gate, I turned the wheel and stayed on the road that ran parallel to the fence.

As I cruised past the gate, a few of the Navy guards looked up at me. I sat up extra straight, trying to look like an adult. I'm happy to report that nobody came after me.

But now what? I followed the road that led around the

perimeter of the field, hoping to find another entrance that wasn't being watched as closely. Time was running out. I was beginning to think that I was going to have to go back to the main entrance, gun the car, and blast my way through. What other choice would I have?

Then, halfway around to the far side of the airfield, I found another way in. It was a smaller gate and there were no Navy guys doing security. Yes! I cranked the steering wheel and turned the car into the gate. As I passed through, I saw why this entrance wasn't being guarded.

Two Navy guards were lying in the grass, bound and gagged. Somebody who didn't belong there had jumped them and gotten inside. Was it Winn Farrow and his gang? Or was it Spader and Max Rose's pal? Or both? It didn't matter. I was in the right place. I didn't stop to untie the guards. They were on their own.

It was getting darker. I thought about putting on my head-lights, but I didn't want anybody to see me coming. One glance ahead showed me that the *Hindenburg*'s nose was now pointed to my right. I had made it all the way around to the far side, exactly where I needed to be. Somewhere around here, Winn Farrow was camped out and ready to light the fuse on his deadly rocket. Somewhere around here too, was Spader. I glanced at my watch. It was 7:20. Going by history, only a few minutes were left before all hell would break loose. That meant whatever was going to happen, it was going to happen soon.

That's when I heard a gunshot.

FIRST EARTH

The shot came from somewhere ahead of me, toward the incoming *Hindenburg*. I stepped on the gas and headed that way. I soon saw a cluster of small wooden huts. They were probably storage sheds. But more than that, they looked like the perfect place where somebody could hide and set up a rocket. I gunned it for those buildings, not really sure what I would find when I got there, or what I would do.

That's when I saw the motorcycle Spader and the gangster had taken off on. They were here, all right. I pulled the car up to the motorcycle and slammed on the brakes. Instantly the car bucked and stalled again. I didn't care. It had gotten me here.

Then I heard another shot. It was coming from around the corner of the small building closest to me. I jumped out of the car and cautiously made my way forward.

The *Hindenburg* was now almost directly overhead. The loud drone of its multiple engines filled the air. Since the flood-lights were all on the far side, this side of the ship was thrown into shadow. It felt like a huge, ominous cloud was settling in.

When I rounded the corner of the building, my heart leaped. Right in front of me, crouched down behind some wooden crates for protection, were Spader and the gangster. The two were peering out at another wooden building about twenty yards farther ahead.

I knew Farrow must have been hiding there.

I then heard another shot. A nanosecond later something hit directly over my head, and a splinter of wood was torn away from the wall. I ducked, then took a closer look. The bullet had embedded itself right over my head. Now I knew why Spader and the gangster were hiding. Someone was shooting at them. I crouched down low and ran to join them.

"Spader!" I called out with a loud whisper.

Spader turned toward me quickly. So did the gangster. The thug had a gun and pointed it right at my nose.

"Pendragon!" Spader shouted with surprise. He pushed the barrel of the gun away from me. The gangster saw it was me and quickly turned his attention back to his enemies.

"Farrow's right over there!" Spader said quickly. His eyes were wide with excitement. "There's two of 'em."

"There's only one," the gangster corrected. "I already plugged one. Farrow's alone."

Oh, great. There was already blood spilled.

"It's a tum-tigger, mate," Spader said breathlessly. "He's going to fire the rocket any second."

"Not if I can help it," the gangster declared.

He then did something I couldn't believe. He jumped up from behind his protection and made a kamikaze run toward Farrow. Man, this guy was dedicated. He was making a suicide run to protect Max Rose and his criminal empire. This guy should get the gangster of the month award.

Though he was being very brave, he was also incredibly stupid. There was a twenty-yard stretch of open grass between our hiding place and Winn Farrow. The charging gangster had no protection. He only made it a few steps when three shots were fired. The gangster spun and went down hard.

"No!" Spader shouted, and made a move to jump from behind the crates and do the same thing himself. But I grabbed him.

"You can't!" I shouted.

"He's going to blow up the ship!" he shouted back. "Saint Dane is going to win!"

"No!" I said while holding him back. "This is exactly what Saint Dane wants. He wants us to stop Winn Farrow. Didn't you hear me before?"

"That doesn't make sense!" Spader shot back. "How could you know that?"

I looked Spader right in the eye. There was no way I could quickly explain to him all that we had seen on Third Earth. There was only one way I could convince him. I spoke calmly and directly. I didn't want to let emotions get in the way.

"Do you trust me?" I asked.

"You know I do," Spader answered.

"Then believe me. Our job is to make sure the ship blows up. I know it's horrible, but it's the truth. We've been through a lot together, Spader. You know me; you know what it means to be a Traveler. You've got to put your faith in me."

Spader and I held eye contact. I tried to will him into believing me. I could tell he was wrestling with feelings of trust in me, and what his brain told him was reality.

It kills me to say this, but his brain won. He pushed me away so quickly I didn't have time to brace myself, and I fell back on my butt.

"Sorry, mate," he said. "I can't let this happen."

"Spader, don't!" I shouted.

It was too late. He jumped over the wooden crates, headed for Winn Farrow.

I cringed, ready to hear the gunshots that would hit him like they hit the gangster. But they didn't. I scrambled to my feet, gazed over the crates and saw an incredible sight.

Spader wasn't running. He was standing stock-still in the clearing between the wooden crates and the small hut. He had stopped because Gunny was blocking his way. Gunny had picked up the pistol from the fallen gangster blocking his way and now stood between Spader and Winn Farrow.

Overhead the *Hindenburg* was floating closer to the ground. Guide lines were thrown out from the zeppelin and workers scrambled to grab them and control the huge ship.

"I'm sorry," Gunny said calmly. "I can't let you pass."

I couldn't believe it had come to this. One Traveler was holding a gun on another Traveler.

Spader glanced up at the airship. He knew he didn't have any time left. He looked at Gunny and said, "You won't shoot me, Gunny. You can't."

Gunny flinched. Spader was right. There was no way Gunny would shoot him. It was a bluff. Gunny slowly lowered the pistol.

"The ship has to be destroyed," Gunny said.

Spader wasn't listening. He ran forward, determined to get to Winn Farrow. Gunny bent his knees and tried to grab him, but Spader was too strong. He hit the older man like a fullback and knocked him flat on his back. Now there was nothing to stop him. I expected Farrow to shoot him, but no shots came. He was either out of bullets or focused on his rocket.

I jumped out from behind the crates and sprinted after Spader.

"Spader! Stop!" I shouted. But he couldn't hear me over

the roar of the *Hindenburg*'s engines. It wouldn't have mattered anyway. He was on a mission, and no amount of yelling from me would stop him.

When I got to the building, I saw that Spader had nailed Farrow the same way he hit Gunny. He had barreled into Farrow and knocked the crazy little guy to the ground. Now the two of them wrestled in the dirt.

I saw something else. On the ground, a few feet from them, was Farrow's rocket. It was nailed into a board that acted as a makeshift launch pad. Its nose was pointed up at the incoming zeppelin, and the fuse was lit. The deadly rocket was poised and ready to bring the airship down.

The fight between Farrow and Spader was one-sided. Farrow was small, but he was a battler. Spader wasn't. The gangster was too much for him, and the fight only lasted a few seconds. Farrow quickly had Spader pinned to the ground with an arm twisted behind his back. There was no way Spader could get to the rocket now.

My friend arched his neck and saw me standing there. The pained, desperate look on his face made me cringe.

"Pendragon!" he cried. "Don't let those people die!" His voice cracked with emotion. Tears welled in his eyes. In his mind, we were about to let thirty-six people die. He didn't understand the bigger picture.

And at that moment, neither did I.

The reality of what was about to happen hit me like a punch in the gut. What was happening? I suddenly had the lives of thirty-six people in my hands. All I had to do was lean down, move the rocket, and they would be saved. It would be so easy. Farrow wouldn't be able to stop me because he was tangled up with Spader.

"Nothing you can do about it now!" Farrow laughed.

"Max Rose is gonna go down in flames, just like this ship!"

"Please, mate!" Spader begged me, in tears. "They're all going to die!"

I looked up at the ship. The lights were on in the gondola. That's where the people were. The people whose lives would soon be filled with terror. I looked down at the rocket. The fuse was nearly burnt, but I still had time. All I had to do was kick it out of the way. Simple as that. One move from me and the ship would arrive to the cheers of all the spectators. The newspapers would carry a very different, triumphant story and thirty-six people would still be alive.

It was at that moment I realized I couldn't let them die.

The concept of history changing so that the Nazis would develop the atomic bomb and win the war seemed impossible at that moment. But those people up in that airship were very real. They were about to die, and I could save them. So I bent down and reached out to move the rocket.

"Pendragon," came a soft, calm voice.

I turned to see Gunny standing behind me. He was as calm as if standing in the lobby of his beloved hotel greeting guests. He looked at me with his warm, knowing eyes and said the one thing that made sense. It was a phrase I had heard many times before. It was supposed to help explain our lives and the lives of all Travelers. It was supposed to give the feeling that all was well with Halla, and we were on the side of right. It was supposed to explain our sorrow and loss. I heard it when my uncle died, when Osa died, and when my family disappeared. It always seemed to come at the worst possible times.

Gunny said softly, "This is the way it was meant to be."

I held his gaze for a second. He smiled. I looked back at the rocket. A million thoughts flashed through my head. But one thought rose above all the others.

I couldn't let those people die. I didn't have it in me.

"I'm sorry, Gunny," I said. "I can't do it."

I took a step toward the rocket, prepared to kick it away. I'd worry about the consequences later. I was a second away from saving the *Hindenburg* when I felt Gunny's arms wrap around me in a firm bear hug.

"Then let me do it," he said softly.

He was stopping me from kicking the rocket! I struggled to get away. All day I had been desperate to get here to make sure history played out the way it was supposed to. Now I was desperate to save that ship and those people.

"Gunny, let go!" I pleaded. But Gunny held firm.

"No!" screamed Spader in anguish.

An instant later the fuse hit the powder, and the rocket flamed to life. It blasted off its wooden launch pad and streaked into the sky, headed toward a very big target.

FIR8T EARTH

How do you describe a nightmare?

A nightmare is an exercise of the mind. It digs up your deepest fears and throws them in your face with only one purpose—to terrify. You can't control a nightmare. The ghastly images come at you like a raging storm. The best you can do is ride it out and hope it will end. And it does end. When you wake up, you know that as real as the frightening experience may have seemed, it existed only in your mind.

The next few minutes could best be described as a nightmare. The only difference being, it wasn't happening in my mind.

We watched as the missile shot toward the dark shadow that was the *Hindenburg*. For the few seconds it took to streak upward, it was like time stood still. I wanted to grab those few seconds and hold on to them, because once they were gone, the horror would begin.

The rocket hit the blimp in front of the tail section. Start the clock. In thirty-seven seconds it would be over.

Gunny said softly, "We should go." His voice cracked. He was shaken as badly as I was.

Winn Farrow had already released Spader. The four of us quickly backed away to get out from under harm's way. We knew what was coming. It was going to be ugly. As we moved back, I kept my eyes on the airship.

The fire spread impossibly fast. First the burning material from the exploded rocket sprayed over a large section of the zeppelin. Then the coating of the balloon caught fire. The flames spread quickly over the skin of the airship, gobbling up the soft, silver covering. In seconds the skeletal frame of the ship was exposed. Then it began to fall, tail first. Once the tail sank, the flames spread up toward the nose, fueled by the burning hydrogen gas that was now being released.

I saw both of the swastikas on the tail crumble into the ground and burst into flames. It was a symbolic moment and the one small victory I took from this calamity.

People scattered, running for their lives. The ground crew dropped their lines and fled in terror. It was all they could do.

Then the passenger gondola under the burning zeppelin hit the ground. Instantly people inside smashed out the windows and jumped to safety. Amazingly, a few people walked down the access stairs and simply stepped off. They were the lucky ones. As soon as their feet hit the ground, they ran for their lives, as bits of burning material fell around them like fiery rain. These people would survive. But there were many people still trapped inside who wouldn't be so lucky.

I had seen all this before, in the computer library on Third Earth. But now I was seeing it for real. Close-up. I felt the heat. I saw the shocked, terrorized faces. I heard the screams. But the most horrible feeling of all was that we could have stopped it from happening . . . and didn't.

I then saw something that was hard to believe. While all the people were fleeing from the disaster, there was one person who actually ran toward it. At first I thought it might be a brave rescue worker who was going to valiantly try to pull people from the dying ship. But as he got closer, I saw who it really was.

It was Max Rose. I had no idea how he got there. Maybe it was the police who picked him up from the scene of the crash, or maybe some of his gang found him on the side of the road. It didn't matter. He was now running crazily toward the doomed gondola. We'll never know what was going through his mind, but I can guess. He was going to try and save his money. As insane as that was, it was the only possible explanation. His mind must have snapped. Or maybe he knew his world was going to crumble anyway, so why not make one last ditch effort to save it?

Nobody tried to stop him. Everything was happening too fast, and there was only one thing on anyone's mind: survival. Max Rose actually made it all the way to the gondola and climbed aboard. It was the last time he was ever seen. In a way, history had returned to normal. Max Rose was destined to die on May 6, 1937. The only difference was that it wouldn't be in a car crash. It was in the burning wreckage of the *Hindenburg*.

A second later the huge, flaming airship collapsed. The framework that was still in the shape of a zeppelin crumpled in on itself. A storm of sparks flew into the air, and the once majestic airship was reduced to nothing more than a giant heap of burning embers.

Thirty-seven seconds.

As I stood there feeling the heat from the massive fire, I saw something that actually gave me a chill. It was a bird. A large, black bird. It soared over the flames like a shadow, made a sharp turn, and shot over our heads. Then with one quick snap of its wings, it flew off into the night. Was it Saint Dane? Had he been there to witness his latest failure?

I didn't think so. I thought he was there to mock me. The Travelers had won, yes. We had insured that history would play out the way it was supposed to. The Earth territories were safe. But did Saint Dane truly care? Or like he said, was this about me?

The truth came clear to me in that one, horrible moment. Everything that had happened, all of Saint Dane's manipulations, were about putting me here, in this exact spot. When the critical moment arrived, I didn't have the strength to stop the rocket. He knew I wouldn't be able to do it. He knew. He wanted to see me fail.

The Travelers may have won the battle here on First Earth, but Saint Dane has won the war. He proved that I was no match for him.

Winn Farrow laughed. He actually laughed. The guy really was a psycho. To cause this kind of disaster just to get revenge on one person is nothing short of lunacy.

"Payback," he said with glee. "Sweet."

"You animal!" Spader shouted, and lunged at the guy. But Gunny caught him and held him back.

"Let it go," Gunny said. "He's none of our concern."

"Yeah," Farrow laughed. "None of your concern." He looked at Gunny and gave him an oily smile. "Thanks, pal," he said. "Couldn't have done it without you."

Gunny winced as though he had been hit. My heart went out to him. He did what he knew was right. He did what I couldn't do. But this poor man who couldn't bring himself to fire a gun had just allowed the destruction of the *Hindenburg*.

No matter how right it was, he was going to have to live with that for the rest of his life.

Farrow then turned and ran into the darkness. I didn't care where.

Spader stepped right up to Gunny and looked him in the eye. His face was twisted with anguish. "You stopped him," he cried. "Pendragon was going to save the ship and you stopped him. Those people are dead because of you! You let Saint Dane win."

Gunny couldn't speak. I thought I saw him shivering.

"He did the right thing," I said.

Spader pulled away from Gunny and shot me an angry look. "Why? Because someone told you it would change history? I don't believe it. How could you know that?"

I didn't answer. Now wasn't the time. Gunny said with a weak voice, "We've got to get out of here."

"I've got a car," I offered.

"No," Gunny said. "Come with me." He hurried off. Spader and I stood there a moment longer, looking at the flaming wreckage.

"Hobey, I hope you're right," he finally said, and followed Gunny.

The airfield was in chaos. Fire trucks raced toward the scene. People were running every which way, trying to help the survivors. Some of the victims were rushed into cars that screamed off, headed for the nearest hospital. Others were loaded into ambulances. There was so much frantic activity that nobody noticed three guys walking calmly away from the action, headed toward the runways.

The flames from the *Hindenburg* lit the airfield up like daytime. I wasn't sure where Gunny was leading us and I didn't care. I didn't want to think anymore. Finally I looked ahead and saw a welcome sight. Sitting on the end of the runway, lit by the flames, was Jinx Olsen's odd little seaplane. After all that happened, I'd forgotten about Jinx.

She came running from the direction of the crash. Her eyes were wild and scared. I'd have been surprised if they weren't.

"Was this it?" she asked with a touch of desperation. "Was this why you had to come here? Were you trying to prevent this?"

We all shared looks. All but Spader. He stared at the ground. I didn't know what to say. Thankfully, Gunny took charge.

"We heard some things," he said. "We thought we could help."

"But we were too late," Jinx said. "It's horrible."

"Yes," Gunny said. "It's horrible." He then walked up to Jinx and looked her right in the eye. He spoke to her in a calm, assured voice. "No one will ever know what happened here. You thought you could help, but there was nothing you could do. There was nothing anyone could do. Remember that."

It was weird. Jinx stared up at Gunny with glassy eyes. All the tension seemed to leave her body. It was like Gunny was hypnotizing her. He was using his Traveler skills to put her mind to rest. I wished he could have done the same for me.

"Right," she said slowly. "There was nothing I could do."

"We should get back," Gunny said to her.

"Yes," Jinx said. "Let's go back."

The four of us got into the plane—Jinx and I in the front cockpit, Spader and Gunny in back. I doubt if anyone took notice of our small plane as we lifted off on the far side of the airfield. Every single person on the ground was focused on the burning zeppelin. As we rose up and away from the destruction, I realized we were leaving behind one of the great mysteries of all time. People would always wonder what really caused the *Hindenburg* to catch fire and crash. Nobody would know of the role two rival gangster mobs from New York had in bringing the massive airship down, or of the part played by Travelers from different territories.

That was the way it was meant to be.

The flight back was uneventful. Thankfully the weather had cleared and it was a smooth trip. Nobody spoke. We were all alone with our thoughts. We landed on the Hudson and got the airplane back to the dock without a problem. The four of us then rode together in a cab back to the Manhattan Tower Hotel. I don't think anyone said more than two words for the whole trip. When we were dropped on the sidewalk in front of the hotel, there was an awkward moment. Spader left us and went inside without saying a word. Gunny and I stood with Jinx. I had no idea how we would leave this with her.

Again, Gunny took charge. "You are a very special person," he said to Jinx. "I'm proud to have known you."

"I hope you get to fly again someday," I added.

"Oh, I will," she said with a wink. "Bet on it."

We all exchanged hugs, then Jinx started inside. But she stopped and turned back to us with a concerned look. "This trip we just took," she said. "Why do I have the feeling there was more to it than there seems?"

"There isn't," Gunny answered. "It was just a trip."

That seemed to satisfy Jinx. She nodded and went inside. In all the accounts of what happened to the *Hindenburg,* there was never any mention of Jinx Olsen having been at the airfield. I can only believe that whatever thoughts Gunny planted in her head, or took away, he made sure that Jinx never said a word to anyone about our flight. It was too bad. All Jinx ever wanted to do was fly and make a difference. She would never know that on that chilly night, she had done exactly that.

Gunny and I stood alone on the sidewalk. Nobody else was around. As I stood there, I really didn't know what to think. Was this an incredible victory over Saint Dane? It sure didn't feel like it. I had to keep reminding myself that if we hadn't been there, things would have been worse. Much worse. But that was something I knew in my head. My heart felt otherwise.

Reality for me was, I had failed. There's no other way of putting it. When it was all on the line, I blew it. If it hadn't been for Gunny, Saint Dane would have won. The Earth territories would have been doomed, and it would have been my fault. And that makes me question my worth as a Traveler. I couldn't help but think of Uncle Press. He had faith in me. He told everyone to trust me. By failing with the *Hindenburg,* I had let him down. What was I supposed to do from here?

"I'm sorry, Gunny," I said softly.

"For what?"

"For putting this on your shoulders."

Gunny looked up at his beloved hotel. The lights reflected in his brown eyes.

"Never in my lifetime did I ever imagine the things we've seen. But now that my eyes are opening up to what life is really about, I have to tell you, I honestly do believe what I said before. This is the way it is supposed to be. Our job is to make sure of it. You didn't put anything on my shoulders, Bobby."

"But I did the wrong thing."

Gunny looked at me. I saw the kindness in his eyes. No, I

felt the kindness. "Maybe. Or maybe today was my day. Maybe the whole reason I'm part of this is to do what I did. You've got a long road ahead, Pendragon. I believe your day is still to come."

We went inside and said good night. I was dog tired and all I wanted to do was fall into bed. When I got to the room, Spader was sitting on the couch, waiting for me. I didn't want to have to deal with him. Not now. But Spader wanted to talk.

"I'm scared, mate," he said. "Everything's been turned inside out. How could Gunny let those people die?"

I didn't say anything at first. I was angry and confused and a little bit scared myself. We had reached a turning point of our own, Spader and me. As great a team as we were, when it came to crunch time, Spader hadn't trusted me. I still needed to convince him that we had done the right thing.

"Tomorrow," I finally said. "Tomorrow I'll show you everything."

That was it. I left him and went to bed. The last thought I had before nodding off was that I hoped I wouldn't have any dreams. Or nightmares.

The next day Spader and I took a trip. We went to the one and only place where he would get the answers he needed. We went to Third Earth.

The trip to the Bronx and the flight through the flume were nothing special to write about. It was amazing to think that something as wild as fluming to a different time and territory didn't seem special anymore. But the truth was, I was getting used to it. We arrived at the gate on Third Earth and changed into the clothes of the territory without saying a word to each other. Hidden in the pile of clothing was the same communicator Gunny had used to contact Patrick, the

Traveler. I hit the button, knowing Patrick would soon be there to pick us up.

I have to admit, I was nervous about what we would find on Third Earth. Had history played out the way it was supposed to? By allowing the *Hindenburg* to be destroyed, had we kept the territories on track? Or did we change something else that might have allowed Max Rose's gang to continue their spy operations?

The moment we stepped out of the gate, I had my answer. The subway was exactly as I remembered it. So was the massive underground mall. When we took the escalator up to the surface I saw the rolling, green hills of the Bronx. What a huge relief.

I'm sure you can imagine the wonder Spader felt as we walked through the territory. He looked every bit as stunned and impressed as I was when Gunny and I first came here. He started to ask me questions, but all I said was, "Ask Patrick." I didn't feel like being a tour guide. Not today.

It didn't take long for Patrick to arrive at the green kiosk that led from the subway. He pulled his small car up to us and gave me an expectant look.

"It's done," I said.

Patrick exhaled with relief.

"Let's celebrate!" he shouted.

Spader and I both got into the car without saying a word. Neither of us were in the mood to celebrate.

"Take us to the library," I said flatly.

Patrick knew something was wrong. He didn't press though. We drove the same route into Manhattan as last time. I asked Patrick to explain to Spader how the Earth territories had come this far. Patrick gave him pretty much the same story he had given me. This was good. I wanted Spader to know just how special a place Third Earth was.

At the library Patrick gave Spader a quick lesson on their computer system and its amazing capacity for information storage. He gave another quick demo, this time bringing up a holographic image of the Beatles singing a song called "She Loves You." Not exactly my kind of music, but it was pretty cool to see four famous guys standing there singing.

As you might imagine, Spader was blown away. It was then time to see what we came for.

I asked Patrick to explain the *Hindenburg* Variation. Patrick first showed Spader history the way it actually happened, with the *Hindenburg* being destroyed. The only thing that had changed from the last time I saw this was that there was no information about Max Rose being killed in a car accident on Toms River Road. This time it showed that Max Rose had mysteriously disappeared on May 6, never to be seen again. Of course, we knew what had really happened. Max Rose died in the wreckage of the *Hindenburg*. History would never know that.

Patrick then took Spader through the alternate scenario, step by step, showing him what would have happened if the *Hindenburg* had arrived safely. He showed Spader Rose's spy network, and the atomic bomb the German scientist Dani Schmidt would create to help the Nazis win the war. He also showed Spader frightening scenes of Third Earth the way it would have existed if the *Hindenburg* had arrived safely.

This is a strange thing to admit, but seeing these horrifying images actually made me feel better, because I knew this was a future that would never be. I would never feel good about the fact that the *Hindenburg* crashed, but any doubts about Gunny having done the right thing were now gone. All we did was keep history on track.

This was the way it was meant to be.

Spader didn't say much during the demonstration. It was a lot to understand. The two of us walked out of the library and sat down on the steps where Gunny and I had sat earlier. It was only yesterday. A lifetime ago.

"I'm sorry, mate," Spader said. "I don't know how else to say it. But look at it through my eyes. I hadn't seen all that stuff back there. I didn't know the same things you did. Hobey, if I had seen what was going to happen if we saved the *Hindenburg,* I never would have done the things I did."

"If we had stayed together," I said. "You *would* have seen all that."

Spader fell silent. I think he was beginning to realize just how badly he had screwed up.

"You're my mate, Pendragon," he answered. "Mates forgive each other."

I didn't say anything at first. In some ways, dealing with Saint Dane was easier than this. With Saint Dane there was good and there was bad. Not a lot of room in between. But this was different. Spader was my mate. He was a Traveler. We were on the same side. That's what made saying what I had to say so tough.

"I want you to go home, Spader," I said.

"What?" he shouted in surprise.

"Go back to Cloral, to Grallion," I continued. "Get back to being an aquaneer."

"But I'm a Traveler now," he protested. "My place is with you."

"Your place is to help the Travelers protect the territories," I corrected. "Until we can trust each other, you can't do that."

"But I *do* trust you, Pendragon," he said sincerely.

I took a breath and said, "But I can't trust *you.*"

Spader looked shocked. No big surprise, these were strong words.

"This isn't about you," I continued. "This isn't about getting revenge on Saint Dane. It's about saving the territories and protecting Halla. I don't think you get that. Until you do, you're better off at home."

There it was. I had laid it flat out. Spader was a good guy. A great guy. But he didn't get it. I didn't pretend to have all the answers, but there were some things I knew for sure. One of them was that the Travelers had to support each other. It was the only chance we had against Saint Dane's evil. Spader had shown that he didn't have that faith. More than once. Together we could stand up to Saint Dane. Scattered, we were lost. Gunny's selfless act at the critical moment was proof of that. I felt so strongly about it that I was willing to turn my back on a guy who had become my best friend. At least my best Traveler friend, anyway.

Spader looked down. I knew he hated hearing this. But I needed him to understand. He was a Traveler. Someday he would play a role again, and when that day came, I wanted him to be ready. His reaction to what I said would be critical to the future of the Travelers, our battle with Saint Dane, and his part in all of it.

"Let's go back to the flume," was all he said. Then he stood up and walked off.

Nothing was resolved.

As Patrick drove us back uptown to the subway in the Bronx, I could only hope that Spader was trying to understand. I didn't push. I didn't want to sound like some kind of parent. Spader had to work this through for himself.

Patrick dropped us off at the green kiosk, and after saying our good-byes, Spader and I made our way back down to the gate and the flume. Still, nothing was said. I worried that Spader would take off on his own without a word. I couldn't let that happen. We had to settle this.

When we got inside the gate, Spader stepped up to the black mouth of the flume. If he had called out a territory, I would have pulled him away.

But he didn't. He turned his back to the flume and faced me. We stood there for a second, then finally he said softly, "I'm with you, mate."

"Are you?" I asked.

"I said it to you before," he continued. "However this natty-do is going to play out, I believe it's you who will bring us through. If you want me to go home, then it's back to Cloral for me."

I was relieved and saddened at the same time. This meant we were officially going our own ways.

"Spader, you're like my brother," I said.

"I feel the same about you, Pendragon," he said with a small smile. "That's why I'm listening to what you say. It's true, I've been wanting to crush Saint Dane since my father died. I've tried to put it out of my head, but it's always there. I've got to find some way to deal with that, and if it means going home and taking time to think things through, that's what I'll do."

Spader then added, "I want you to promise me one thing though."

"What's that?"

"When you find yourself in a tum-tigger, and I know you will, come get me."

That was what I wanted to hear. Spader was the Traveler from Cloral. His spirit and talent had gotten us through in times when I was ready to give up. However this war with

Saint Dane was going to play out, Spader would have to take on a major role.

"Bet on it," I said.

That was what *he* wanted to hear. The two of us hugged. I didn't want to let him go. I didn't want to be on my own again. Especially now, when I was doubting my own worthiness as a Traveler. For a brief second I thought it would be better to deal with Spader's unpredictability than to let him go. But I had to be strong.

He held me at arm's length and said, "I'll be ready."

I nodded. Spader then backed away and glanced into the tunnel.

"Safe trip," I said.

Spader faced the infinite black hole and shouted, "Cloral!"

The craggy tunnel rumbled to life. The far-off light appeared from deep inside, growing closer. The familiar musical notes were on their way. The bright light quickly grew intense. Spader turned to me and smiled.

"Hobey-ho, Pendragon."

"Hobey-ho, Spader."

A second later he was gone.

I don't think I ever felt so lonely. Well, maybe once before. When I stood on the empty lot where my house on Second Earth used to be.

My whole life I was used to having people guide me toward the right answers. First it was my parents. Teachers were there too. So were my friends like you, Mark and Courtney. Of course Uncle Press played a huge part. I didn't always like being told what to do, but it was good to know somebody was always looking out for me.

Now I felt like I was on a highwire without a net. If I was going to get to the other side, the only one who would get me there was me. I had two choices. I could stand here and feel sorry for myself, or move forward.

I turned away from the now quiet flume and changed back into my First Earth clothes. Before doing anything else, I had to get back and let Gunny know what had happened.

"First Earth!" I shouted into the flume.

I then closed my eyes, looking forward to the few minutes of a flume ride when I wouldn't have to worry about anything.

FIRST EARTH

When I walked through the front doors of the Manhattan Tower Hotel, Gunny was the first person I saw. He was at his Bell Captain post, dressed in his spiffy uniform, acting as if nothing had happened. The lobby was buzzing with people, all reading special-edition newspapers that had accounts of the *Hindenburg* disaster. It seemed like everybody had their own theory as to what had caused the explosion and crash.

None of them were right, of course.

Gunny and I took the elevator up to my room on the sixth floor so we could talk in private.

"Everything's cool," I said to Gunny as we entered the room. "Third Earth is exactly the way we left it."

Gunny let out a relieved breath. "Where's Spader?"

"Back home on Cloral," I said. "He needs some time to get his head around what happened."

"Does he understand?" Gunny asked.

"About the *Hindenburg,* yeah," I answered. "The big question is, can we count on him in the future?"

"And?"

"I don't know," I answered honestly. "I hope so."

I sat down on the couch, sinking into the soft cushions. I was suddenly very tired. I think I could have fallen asleep for a week. The tension was finally gone. We had been in overdrive for a long time, and now that we were done, I was ready to crash. But my mind wouldn't let me.

"Gunny, I'm scared," I said.

"About what? Saint Dane?"

"I'm scared about what we had to do to stop him," I said. I spoke slowly, trying to put my thoughts into words. "Letting the *Hindenburg* blow up was . . ."

I couldn't think of a big enough word to describe how horrible it was.

"I hear you," Gunny said.

"And I'm scared of what might happen the next time Saint Dane tries to test me," I added. "What if I don't have somebody like you around to cover my back? Gunny, he didn't care about what happened to the Earth territories. This was about proving he could control us. Control *me*! You know what that means? It means he won. I was going to kick over that rocket."

"But you didn't."

"Only because you were there. Saint Dane proved his point. Gunny, I can't do this."

Gunny sat back in his chair, nodding slowly. When he finally spoke it was with a calm, sure voice that I wanted so badly to believe in.

"None of us asked for this job," he began. "I'd just as soon live out my days here at the hotel, never knowing anybody named Saint Dane or people called Travelers. But that's not the way things turned out."

"Yeah, tell me about it."

"But there's one thing I think about that gives me a little peace of mind. Maybe it'll help you, too."

"Go for it," I said. "I'll take anything."

"Ever since your uncle told me I was a Traveler, I've been wondering why I'd been chosen. Still do. Why us? We're nothing special, just regular folks. But the more I think about it, the more I've got to believe there's something bigger at play here. I think we've each been chosen for a reason. Like last night. I truly believe I was at the *Hindenburg* to do what I did. This may sound silly, but thinking that way gives me a little hope that maybe we just might be the right ones to be doing this after all."

"So, if we were chosen, who did the choosing?"

"Exactly! That's the big question. Who is it that has the kind of vision it takes to see how things should be, and play chess with a guy like Saint Dane? I haven't got a clue. But whoever it is, he wants Saint Dane to fail. That means he's a good guy. And I like the idea of a powerful good guy being on our side." Gunny smiled and said, "Maybe your back is covered a little bit more than you think."

Could it be? Could there be some grand plan at work? Was there a guy out there who wanted to stop Saint Dane and chose us to be his soldiers? If there was, I'd sure like to know. Maybe I wouldn't feel so alone anymore.

"You're a smart guy, Gunny," I said.

"I'm nothing of the sort," he said back to me. "I've just been around a while. I plan on being around a good while longer, too."

I rolled over, closed my eyes, and went to sleep. Right there on the couch. It was the first good night's rest I'd had in a long time.

The next few days were spent finishing this journal and saying good-bye. I tried to see Jinx, but she had already checked out of the hotel. Maybe it was a good thing. I wasn't sure what I'd say if she started asking about the *Hindenburg.* Wherever she was, whatever the future held for her, I silently wished her luck.

I said good-bye to my friends on the hotel staff. Dewey Todd was all sorts of excited because his father had just built another hotel out in Hollywood, and he was leaving New York to run the place. Can you believe it? Dewey was going to get his own hotel. I hoped he had learned more about running a hotel than he had about running the elevator. He wished me well and said if I was ever out in Hollywood to look him up.

As soon as I finish this last journal from First Earth, I'm going to give it to Gunny to have them bound. I wish I could send them to you through my ring, but I'm afraid it's gone for good. There's no way I'm going looking for it. I've had my fill of gangsters.

Tomorrow I'm going to take the train out to Stony Brook and put the journals in a safe-deposit box at the National Bank. This way, when the calendar comes around, you'll be able to pick them up. After that, I don't know what I'll do with my journals.

The next question is, where do I go from here? The logical answer would be to Veelox. Saint Dane said he was headed there. But was that to lure me into another trap? Even if it were, do I have any choice?

I began this journal by telling you guys I had reached my own turning point. Part of that was because I had seen the kind of destruction Saint Dane was trying to cause on the Earth territories. You don't see something frightening like that and shrug it off. If I didn't fully realize it before, I do now.

But maybe more important was the moment when I watched the fuse burning on the rocket that was about to destroy the *Hindenburg*. In that moment I knew what I was supposed to do, but I didn't do it.

When it comes right down to it, was my mistake any different than what I accused Spader of? I let my emotions control me, just as Spader did. As I'm writing this journal, I'm admitting that I have very real doubts about myself as a Traveler. Saint Dane put me at that rocket to prove a point. He knew I wouldn't be able to let the *Hindenburg* crash, which means he knew how to control me.

I can't let that happen again. The stakes are way too high. I know that, now more than ever. If there's anything good that came from my failure on First Earth, it's that I have now totally given myself over to being a Traveler.

One way or another, I'm in it to the end.

As I've written so many times before, I hope you guys are reading this. I have no idea when I'll be able to write again, or from what territory. All I can say is, check the safe-deposit box at the bank every so often to see if there are any new deliveries. I won't stop writing. I can't. Writing these journals has kept me sane. It makes me feel as if you guys are here with me. So until the next time, have fun, be safe, and think about me every once in a while.

Your friend,
Bobby

END OF JOURNAL #12

◉ SECOND EARTH ◉

. . . Your friend, Bobby.

Courtney lowered the final journal and looked at Mark. They had been taking turns reading aloud to each other for the last five hours in Courtney's father's basement workshop. They ate turkey sandwiches and chips and carrots. Mark drank Dew, Courtney stuck with water. They only took breaks for the bathroom. It had been a marathon, and now it was over.

Courtney slammed the journal down on the table in front of them. "I'm totally freaked out," she announced.

"Yeah, m-me too," Mark said, relieved that Courtney admitted it first. "If Gunny hadn't let the *Hindenburg* blow up—"

"We wouldn't be talking about it," Courtney concluded.

"Exactly," Mark said. "No New York, no Stony Brook, no . . . us."

"I'm afraid to look outside," Courtney said. "What if the world has changed?"

"It hasn't," Mark said with authority. "The Travelers made sure of that."

"This is getting serious, Mark" Courtney said with rising panic. "I mean, this is too close to home."

The two stared at the closed journals, letting the thought hang there. Finally Mark said, "Maybe not."

"What do you mean?" Courtney shot back with surprise. "You're the one who said Saint Dane was going to show up here sooner or later, right?"

"Yeah, I did," Mark answered. "I've been worried the battle was going to land on Second Earth from the very beginning."

"And it almost did!" Courtney exclaimed.

"But you know," Mark continued thoughtfully. "After reading this last journal, I'm thinking there's a chance we might be off the hook."

"Seriously?"

"Think about it. If Saint Dane's plan with the *Hindenburg* would have destroyed all three Earth territories, maybe he won't come here after all. I mean, maybe he already took his shot."

Courtney gave a hopeful look to Mark. "You're thinking there might not be a turning point here on Second Earth?" she asked.

"No," he replied. "I'm thinking the turning point for Second and Third Earth might have been the destruction of the *Hindenburg.* Kind of like three-for-one. There's a chance we may have dodged a pretty huge bullet."

Courtney thought about this for a moment, then said, "That would be incredible! But, how will we know for sure?"

Mark answered, "That's the thing. We won't."

The two let this hang for a moment. Courtney studied Mark for a second and then said, "You seem kind of disappointed."

"Me? No, what are you kidding? I'm totally relieved. I just hope I'm right."

Mark put the journals into his backpack. "I think we should keep all the journals in the safe-deposit box at the bank from now on. It's way safer than the desk in my attic."

"Cool," Courtney said. "I'll come by your house tomorrow morning. Eight o'clock. We'll take all the journals in together."

When he got home Mark went to his bedroom and reread some of Bobby's adventure. He was looking for clues that might prove his theory about Second Earth. The more he read, the more he felt certain that Second Earth was safe.

And it bothered him.

Courtney had read Mark right. He *was* disappointed. It wasn't that he wanted there to be trouble on Second Earth; it was more that he was feeling left out. Bobby had a new life now. It didn't help when Bobby referred to Spader as his best friend. That stung. He and Bobby had been inseparable since they were toddlers. Now they were growing about as far apart as possible.

Though he never admitted it to Courtney, Mark had fantasized about the day when Saint Dane would make his move on Second Earth. It meant Bobby would come home, and they could all work together to outwit the demon. Now it looked like that chance would never come. If Saint Dane didn't target Second Earth, Bobby would have no reason to come home.

Mark went to sleep that night feeling as if his one shot at adventure had passed him by.

First thing the next morning Courtney arrived at Mark's house, and they loaded all twelve of Bobby's journals into his backpack. It made them nervous to move them, but they felt sure it was worth it. The vault at the National Bank of Stony Brook was way safer than the wooden desk in Mark's attic.

As they walked to the bank Mark made a decision. He had to tell Courtney how he felt. The two had made a pact to tell each other everything about anything that had to do with Bobby and the journals. When Mark lied to her about Andy Mitchell discovering them, it had led to a total mess. After that Mark promised that he would share everything.

So on the way to the bank, Mark admitted to Courtney that he hoped Saint Dane would still come to Second Earth, so they could join forces with Bobby and battle the evil demon together.

He knew she'd understand.

"Are you crazy?" she shouted back at him.

She didn't understand. Not even a little bit.

"This isn't a game, Mark. It's easy to read those journals while we're eating carrots all comfy on the couch, but getting involved is a whole 'nother ballgame."

"I know that—" Mark said.

"It's like watching reality shows on TV," Courtney went on. "People do crazy stuff like jumping across buildings or living on an island with no food or eating bugs, and it doesn't seem all that hard. But that's because we can turn off the TV, and go to bed, and know breakfast will be on the table in the morning. If Saint Dane shows up here, we can't turn off the TV and go to bed."

"I understand—"

"Do you?" Courtney was getting worked up. "Really? I'll tell you what I think. I think you sound like Spader."

"How's th-that?" Mark shot back, tweaked by the comment.

"Spader is more worried about Spader than about protecting Halla," Courtney reasoned. "That's why Bobby told him to go home. If you're hoping Saint Dane shows up here so you can have an adventure with Bobby, then you're thinking more about you than you are about Second Earth."

"Jeez, all right," Mark shot back. "I get it. It's not like I can do anything about it, anyway. I'm not gonna call Saint Dane up and invite him over for lunch."

The two looked at each other, and laughed. The image of Mark calling up Saint Dane was pretty ridiculous.

"Sorry, Mark," Courtney said with a smile. "I didn't mean to go up on you like that. I'm just scared, is all."

"I am too," Mark said. "But I wanted to let you know how I felt. We promised to do that, right?"

"Yeah, I'm an idiot. I'm sorry," she said. "I get it. It's tough reading about all this stuff and not being able to do anything about it. It's like being on the bench during a big game."

Mark shrugged. He knew exactly what she meant. He'd never been anyplace *but* the bench during big games. It looked like he was going to have to ride the pines during this one too.

They arrived at the bank just as the doors were being unlocked. Courtney went in first through the revolving door. Just as Mark was about to follow, he stopped. He wasn't exactly sure why, but he had an odd feeling. Was somebody watching them?

He glanced around the Ave to see several stores were opening up for the day. Some shop owners were using squeegees on their windows, others were unfurling the colorful awnings that hung over the entrances. There was a policeman standing in the center of the intersection, directing traffic. Nothing out of the ordinary. Mark had no idea why he had the strange feeling, so with a shrug, he entered the bank.

Mark and Courtney marched right up to the desk of Ms. Jane Jansen. The pinched woman was already hunched over her computer keyboard, looking busy . . .

Playing solitaire.

"Working hard?" Courtney asked.

Ms. Jane Jansen was totally embarrassed and closed out her game. When she saw who it was, her face grew even more pinched. Mark thought if she squeezed her cheeks any tighter, her whole face would get sucked in through her mouth.

"Can I help you, children?" she asked through gritted teeth.

"We'd like to get into our safe-deposit box," Mark said politely.

"But if you're busy," Courtney said sarcastically, "we can wait."

"I don't suppose you remembered to bring your key?" Ms. Jane Jansen asked.

Mark reached to the chain around his neck and pulled it out from under his shirt. There were now two keys on the chain. One was to the desk in his attic, the other to the safe-deposit box.

"Surprise!" Courtney said.

"Follow me," Ms. Jane Jansen said as she pulled away from her desk. She looked totally bothered by the interruption.

Mark and Courtney knew the routine. Ms. Jane Jansen led them through the big, round vault door, into the inner vault, and right up to the wall of doors that protected the safe-deposit boxes.

"Would you like me to open it for you?" she asked with a snippy attitude, as if it were the last thing she wanted to do.

"Nah, we can handle it," Courtney said. "Go back to your game."

Ms. Jane Jansen wanted to say something back, but thought better of it. After all, they were clients. Instead, she scowled at them and left.

"I love her," Courtney laughed.

While Courtney opened the door, Mark unloaded all twelve journals from his backpack and placed them into the big steel box. There was plenty of room left over for any new journals that might show up. He then slid the drawer closed, shut the door, and Courtney locked it. The key then went right back to the chain around Mark's neck. The journals were now as safe as they could possibly be.

On their way out of the bank, they didn't bother stopping to say good-bye to Ms. Jane Jansen. They didn't want to disturb her game again. They left the vault, walked through the lobby, and were almost to the front door when—

"Children! One moment please!" It was Ms. Jane Jansen. She hurried up to them, her heels clicking on the marble floor. Her cheeks were rosy and her eyes flared.

"I want you two to understand something," she said angrily. "You may be clients of this bank, but that does not entitle you to messenger service."

Mark and Courtney looked at each other. They had no idea what she was talking about. "Translation, please," Courtney asked.

Ms. Jane Jansen held up a brown paper bag, about the size of a grocery bag, with wet stain marks on the bottom.

"When you two went inside the vault, someone came in and asked that I give this to you," she explained. "This is not appropriate, this is not a service the bank provides, and whatever is in this bag smells."

Courtney took the bag with curiosity.

"Who was it?" Mark asked.

"I have no idea and I didn't ask," Ms. Jane Jansen replied. "As I said, I am not a messenger."

Courtney cautiously unfolded the top of the brown bag and looked inside. What she saw were three white containers, along with a Dew and two cans of ice teas. She showed the bag to Mark. He looked inside and was just as confused as Courtney. There was also a folded piece of paper inside. Mark pulled it out and read aloud, "Never too early in the morning for Garden Poultry fries. Meet me in the pocket park." Mark looked to Courtney and added, "It's signed 'B.'"

Could it be?

"Do we understand each other?" Ms. Jane Jansen asked.

Courtney reached into the bag, pulled out one box of fries and handed it to the cranky bank lady.

"Absolutely," Courtney said. "Here, have a party."

Courtney and Mark ran out of the bank, leaving Ms. Jane Jansen holding a greasy box of French fries. She was just about to toss it in the garbage, when the oily-delicious smell finally got through to her. She took a deep whiff, looked around to make sure nobody was watching, then turned back to her desk with the greasy treat.

Mark and Courtney blasted out of the bank and ran down the Ave, headed for the pocket park. The Ave cut straight through the middle of downtown Stony Brook. It was loaded with small shops, restaurants, and bookstores. It was definitely the biggest kid hangout in town, but since it was so early, no kids were awake and around.

The pocket park halfway down the Ave was a familiar meeting place. At one time there had been a building where the park stood. Now it was an empty space between two other buildings that had been landscaped with grass, trees, and benches.

Courtney arrived first and looked into the park.

The place was nearly empty. There was only one person there, and it wasn't the person they wanted to find. Mark finally caught up to Courtney and saw the guy. His shoulders sagged. It wasn't Bobby. This guy was older and taller than Bobby. He had really short, spiky, blond hair and wore thin wraparound sunglasses. He looked like a hip-hop skateboard kid from New York, not Bobby Pendragon from Stony Brook. Courtney and Mark walked cautiously up to him.

"Did you send us this?" Courtney asked while holding up the greasy bag.

The guy was slouched down with both elbows on the back of the bench. When he spoke, he didn't even look at them. He was being very cool.

"I guess that answers my question," he said.

"Wh-What question?" Mark asked.

"The question of whether or not anybody would recognize me around here," he answered.

The guy then pulled down his sunglasses to reveal his eyes. He looked right at Mark and Courtney and broke into a huge grin. "Read any good journals lately?"

Oh yeah, it was Bobby.

◉ SECOND EARTH ◉

Mark and Courtney were totally stunned. Bobby jumped to his feet and the three of them clung to each other in a three-way hug. Nobody said anything. No words could add to the feeling. Finally Bobby pulled back.

"We gotta be cool," he chuckled. "The last thing we want is to have people checking me out."

"I swear I didn't recognize you," Courtney said with excitement. "You're . . . older."

"Yeah, well, you guys are too," Bobby said. He gave Courtney an extra look up and down. "Like, a *lot* older." Courtney wasn't sure if she should slug him in the arm, or blush. She did both.

"Ow!" Bobby shouted. He then smiled and said, "Man, it's been almost a year since I've seen you guys. Happy Birthday, Mark."

"Thanks, man," Mark said. "This is a pretty amazing present."

"What's with the blond hair?" Courtney asked.

"I had 'em do this at the hotel beauty shop before I left First Earth. They thought I was nuts. It's not exactly a 1937 look. But I didn't want anybody recognizing me here."

Mark said, "I've got a million questions."

"Let's go someplace else," Bobby suggested. "This is a little public."

The three of them walked farther down the Ave toward Long Island Sound and a big, woodsy town park. There they could lose themselves in the trees and not be bothered. The three friends found a secluded spot in the shade and sat down to a picnic.

"Man, I miss these," Bobby said as he chomped another mouthful of fries. "Best fries in the world. *Any* world."

Courtney and Mark weren't interested in eating. They had Bobby, right here in front of them. There was too much to say to waste time chewing.

"How did you know we'd be at the bank?" Mark asked.

"I figured if you got my journals on your birthday, last Saturday, then this morning would be the earliest you could get back here to check them into the safe-deposit box."

"Smart," Mark said, impressed.

"Lucky guess," Bobby said modestly.

"Why did you come home?" Courtney asked. "You wrote you were going to Veelox."

Bobby didn't answer right away. It seemed to Mark and Courtney that the answer troubled him.

"That was the plan," Bobby answered thoughtfully. "But at the last minute, I couldn't."

"Did Saint Dane turn up somewhere else?" Courtney asked.

"No," Bobby said. "I just thought that, well, to be honest, I need a break."

"I don't blame you," Courtney said.

Bobby continued, "But it's more than that. I'm afraid the more I learn about being a Traveler, the more I forget about being Bobby Pendragon. I feel like I'm changing. I guess that has to happen, but I can't say I'm happy about it."

The three looked at each other. It was true. Time does that. Bobby's memory of Mark and Courtney was absolutely solid, but the two kids sitting in front of him didn't quite fit that memory.

"I guess I needed a reality check," Bobby said. "I didn't want to forget who I am, or where I come from. I thought maybe I could hang out here for a few days, just to chill. You guys know everything that's been going on with me. I want to know what's been happening with you. Is it okay if we hang out for a while?"

"Okay?" Courtney shouted. "It'll be great!"

"But risky," Mark added. "There's still a big search going on for you and your family."

Bobby laughed. "Yeah, I figured. But if you guys didn't recognize me, I don't think anybody else will."

"Aren't your parents in Florida this week?" Courtney asked Mark.

"Yeah," he answered tentatively.

"They leave you alone?" Bobby asked with a smile.

"Hey, I'm fifteen," Mark answered defensively. "They trust me." Then under his breath he said, "And my aunt lives two blocks away."

"Then it's perfect," Courtney declared. "Bobby can stay with you!"

Bobby looked at Mark. "Is it okay?"

Mark thought for a bit, then broke out in a big smile. "Are you crazy?" he shouted. "I'm psyched!"

For the next week Bobby did his best to put any thoughts about being a Traveler out of his head. For these few special days he was going to pretend that he was simply Bobby Pendragon.

Most of their time was spent at Mark's house. Courtney would come over, and the three would sit for hours talking about everything. They filled Bobby in on what bands were hot and who dropped off the face of the earth. They rented movies, and listened to music, and watched bad TV, and gossiped about who was going out with who at school.

Courtney told Bobby all about the softball championship she had been part of, and Mark gave him a demonstration of the killer battle robot that won him first prize in the state science fair. Mark told Bobby about his dreams to one day go to engineering school and maybe get into the space program.

They even went to the town library to do some research. Bobby wanted to know what had become of Jinx Olsen and Winn Farrow. The Second Earth library had about one zillionth the information that the library had on Third Earth, but it was enough. They discovered that Winn Farrow didn't live long enough to enjoy his victory over Max Rose. He was killed during a bank robbery in June of 1937. The secret of who really brought down the *Hindenburg* died along with him.

The news about Jinx Olsen was much better. Bobby was thrilled to learn that when World War II broke out, Jinx joined the Army Air Corps, pretending to be a man! She flew several bombing missions over Germany and received the Distinguished Flying Cross for heroism in flight. Jinx had lived her dream, and then retired to Maine, where she got married and had three kids.

And they ate. Pizza, spaghetti, Chinese food, ice cream, burgers, burgers, and burgers. At least once a day they got fried chicken and fries from Garden Poultry.

They went swimming at the Point, where Courtney was sure to wear the pink bikini Bobby mentioned in his journal. Bobby appreciated that. He also noticed that Courtney filled it out a little better than the last time he'd seen her wear it, but didn't say anything. That wouldn't have been cool. They also watched

Courtney pitch a two-hitter fast-pitch softball game. She hoped to go to a big college to play softball and soccer. Her true love was soccer though. She had dreams of getting on the national team.

When they traveled around, they took pains to make sure Bobby wouldn't be seen and recognized. There was only one close call. The three of them were riding bikes toward the beach and were stopped at a light when Lieutenant Hirsch, the guy who was handling the Pendragon missing persons investigation, pulled up in a car right next to them.

Mark's heart nearly stopped. Courtney was cool though. She smiled and waved. Bobby didn't know who the guy was, so he didn't know enough to be nervous. When the light changed, Hirsch drove on without a second look. It wouldn't have mattered anyway. Bobby didn't look the same anymore.

The three friends packed a year of fun and friendship into one week. In all, they probably didn't sleep more than three hours a night. There was only one rule: Nobody was allowed to talk about anything to do with being a Traveler. No exceptions. There were a couple times when Mark touched on the subject, and Bobby pretended not to have heard him. Mark got the hint. Nothing more was said. They all pretended like there was nothing more important going on than deciding what DVD they should rent, or if the Yankees would whup up on the Red Sox again. It was exactly what Bobby needed. It re-charged his batteries and made him feel human.

But after several days, Bobby began to grow restless. It's not that he wasn't having fun—he absolutely was—but he knew it couldn't last forever. The change started when he reached the point where he was totally relaxed. That's when his mind started to turn the other way. As much as he tried to forget about it, he always knew that Saint Dane was out there somewhere, plotting a world of grief.

Mark began to sense this in Bobby. It took a day or so for Bobby to relax and get back to his old, fun self. But then Mark noticed Bobby wasn't talking as much. It seemed like there were times when his mind was a million miles away. Mark didn't dare to ask him about it. He was afraid Bobby would close up again, or worse, it would somehow break the magic spell that had given them this great week together. Mark didn't want it to end, though he knew it would have to.

Then one night, while the two of them were trying to fall asleep in Mark's bedroom, Mark took the chance and brought up the taboo subject.

"Bobby?" he asked tentatively. "I want to become an acolyte."

This caught Bobby off guard. "Whoa," he said. "Where did *that* come from?"

Bobby didn't cut him off this time. It encouraged Mark to keep going.

"You know, the acolytes," he said. "The people who help the Travelers. They live in the territories and bring the clothes to the flumes and help you get around and—"

"Yeah, I know who they are," Bobby interrupted. "But I don't know anything about them. I never met one."

"But they're out there," Mark insisted.

"Yeah, I guess so," Bobby said with absolutely no enthusiasm. Reality had returned. Bobby knew he couldn't ignore it anymore. Vacation was over. Time to put the game face back on. He took a deep breath, hesitated one last moment, then clicked back into Traveler mode.

"Why, Mark?" he asked. "What makes you want to be an acolyte?"

"A lot of reasons," Mark answered. "I want to help. It's hard sitting around doing nothing when there's some guy out there trying to bring down the universe and hurt your best friend. Reading your journals has changed things."

Bobby nodded. He understood where Mark was coming from. "Funny thing," he said thoughtfully. "In a couple of days you and Courtney are going to start Davis Gregory High, and all I really want is to forget about being a Traveler and go with you."

"But you can't," Mark said.

"No, I can't."

"There's another reason," Mark added. He took a pause before saying this, because he knew it was a tough subject. "I won't let you down. Not the way Spader did."

Bobby winced. "Spader didn't let me down," he said sharply. "He just lost sight of what was important."

Mark realized he had touched a raw nerve. "I know that," he said quickly, doing damage control. "I just want you to know that I'd always be there to cover your back. No matter what."

"How does Courtney feel about it?" Bobby asked.

"We haven't exactly talked about it," Mark answered. "But I guarantee, if we got the chance, she'd jump right in. You know Courtney."

Bobby chuckled. Yeah, he knew Courtney. "Tell you what," Bobby said. "I'll find out what I can. If there's a chance for you guys to do something, I'll let you know."

That was good enough for Mark. He now had hope that he might join Bobby on his mission after all. He had trouble falling asleep that night because his mind was so alive with the possibilities.

Bobby had trouble getting to sleep too, but for a very different reason. He knew his time here on Second Earth was over. He needed to be somewhere else, doing what he was destined to do. Tomorrow he would say good-bye to his friends one more time and jump back into the game. That's what rolled through his brain while he tried to get to sleep. But it wasn't easy nodding off to dreamland while one thought kept pushing all others away . . .

Where is Saint Dane? What is he up to? And when I find him, will I be strong enough to beat him?

◉ SECOND EARTH ◉

Courtney arrived at Mark's house early the next morning, all set for another day at the beach. She had made a bunch of salami sandwiches and wore the famous pink bikini under her shorts and T-shirt. There were only two days left of summer vacation, two days before they would begin Davis Gregory High. She knew that once they began this new school, life would change again. Not only would they be leaving the familiar comfort of junior high, but Bobby would be gone. There was no way around that one. These last few days felt like the end of an era. She wanted to make the most of them.

But that wasn't meant to be.

She knew it the second she stepped into Mark's house. The atmosphere had changed. Every time she had come over before, the guys would be playing Nintendo, or watching a game on TV, or cranking up music. Today the house was quiet. Bobby and Mark sat in the living room, talking. The air was heavy. It felt to her like a pregame locker room where everyone had the butterflies.

"You're leaving today, aren't you?" she asked Bobby.

Bobby nodded.

Courtney plopped down on the couch next to him. "That's it then," she said. "The next time we hear from you, it'll be in some journal?"

"Probably," was Bobby's answer.

There was an awkward silence. They knew that as soon as Bobby walked out the door, their lives would all officially change. It had been a great week, but it was over.

That's when the telephone rang.

"Probably my parents," Mark said, and answered the phone. "Hello?"

A deep voice came through from the caller. "Hello. Is this Mark Dimond?"

"Yeah." Mark didn't recognize the voice. "Who's this?"

"You don't know me, Mark," said the voice. "My name is Vincent Van Dyke."

"Gunny?" shouted Mark in surprise.

Bobby jumped to his feet and grabbed the phone away from Mark. "Gunny?"

"Howdy there, shorty. Enjoying your vacation?"

"What's wrong? Where are you? Are you okay?"

"Whoa, whoa, slow down," Gunny said with a laugh. "Everything's fine. I'm here on Second Earth."

"Yeah, I figured. But where? What are you doing here?"

"I need to see you, Bobby, right away," Gunny said. "Is there someplace we can meet? I can come to you, no problem."

Bobby looked at Mark and Courtney and said, "Gunny wants to meet me. Can he come here?"

"No way," Mark said. "My parents are due back soon."

Bobby looked at Courtney, but she shook her head. "Mom's

home. I don't think I could explain this to her."

Bobby thought fast, then an idea came to him. "Where are you, Gunny?"

"New York City."

"Then here's an address. It's in my hometown of Stony Brook. It's Two Linden Place."

Mark and Courtney looked at each other. They knew exactly where 2 Linden Place was. They had been avoiding it all week. It was the address where Bobby grew up. Now it was an empty lot. It had been empty ever since everything that had to do with Bobby Pendragon had mysteriously disappeared.

"I'll find it," Gunny said. "Meet me there in an hour."

"You sure everything's okay?" Bobby asked.

"See you there," Gunny said, and hung up.

"You sure that's a good idea?" Courtney asked. "I mean, isn't it gonna be tough for you to go back there?"

Bobby shrugged. "I can't pretend like things haven't happened."

Two Linden Place was only a short walk from Mark's house, so they had some time to kill before meeting Gunny. They didn't want Courtney's salami sandwiches to go to waste, so they sat at Mark's kitchen table and scarfed them down. They did their best to talk about anything other than what was really on their minds. But it was all just blah, blah. Their minds were elsewhere.

Finally Bobby stood up, saying, "Time to go."

Mark and Courtney weren't sure what to do. Was this it? Was it time to say good-bye?

Mark said, "Make sure you tell us what Gunny had to say in your next journal."

"Why?" Bobby asked. "You're coming with me."

Mark's heart swelled.

"You sure?" Courtney asked.

"Absolutely," Bobby answered. "I've got no secrets from you guys."

The three left the house and walked through the quiet suburban neighborhood toward 2 Linden Place. The last time they had done this, Bobby was expecting to be reunited with his family after his adventure on Denduron. It was a gut-wrenching moment when Bobby first realized his house, and his life, were gone. Everyone knew that going back again would be tough.

It only took them five minutes to get there. Nobody said a word as Bobby stood in front of the empty lot. Grass and weeds had taken over since the last time they were there, making the empty space look all the more forlorn. Bobby started to walk onto the lot, but stopped himself and stayed on the sidewalk. Mark and Courtney shared a look. They saw a tear in Bobby's eye.

A car horn sounded a short hello, and the three turned to see a long, black limousine pull up to the curb. The three exchanged curious looks. This was the last thing any of them expected. But when a back door opened, sure enough, out stepped Gunny Van Dyke. He wore a plain, dark suit and tie that could have been in style any time since 1937.

"Morning, folks," Gunny said with a big grin as he strode over to meet them.

Bobby began to introduce his friends, saying, "Gunny, this is—"

"I know who they are," Gunny interrupted with a warm smile. "Courtney Chetwynde and Mark Dimond. It is a pleasure to make your acquaintance."

They all shook hands.

"You're my hero," Courtney said in awe.

"I am?" Gunny asked with surprise.

"Hey, anybody who saves Earth from annihilation is a hero in my book."

Gunny laughed.

"Is it okay that we're here?" Mark asked. "I mean, you guys have business and all."

"No, it's good you're here," Gunny assured them. "This involves you too."

Mark and Courtney exchanged glances. That was weird. What could Gunny have to say that would involve the two of them?

"What's up? You win the lottery?" Bobby asked, pointing at the limo.

"Don't I wish," Gunny chuckled. "Back on First Earth, shortly after you left the hotel, a fella came by looking for you. Said he had something important to tell you and wanted to give you something. I told him you were gone, but that I could get it to you."

"Who was it?" Bobby asked.

"Don't go jumping ahead, shorty," Gunny chastised. "Let me tell the story. Anyhow, he wouldn't give up. Said he wanted to talk to you himself. When he finally told me what it was all about, I understood why he wanted to see you so bad. I told him I wasn't sure if you'd ever be back and promised to give you the package as soon as I saw you."

"So what is it?" Bobby asked.

"Hang on. So I went to the flume to come looking for you. But when I arrived here on Second Earth, I got an idea. I wondered if the guy who wanted to see you so bad back in 1937 was still around. I did a little snooping and sure enough, he was still alive and living in New York."

"You're kidding? How old is he?" Bobby asked.

"Must be in his nineties, near as I can tell," answered Gunny. "I looked him up and introduced myself."

"Didn't he wonder why you hadn't aged a single day since

the last time he saw you?" asked Courtney.

"He thinks it was my granddad who worked at the hotel back then," Gunny answered. "I told him Granddad never again saw the bellhop called Pendragon, but he never forgot. I said how he handed the package down to his son, and then to me, and I finally tracked down the grandson of that bellhop. That would be you, Bobby."

"And he believed you?" Bobby asked.

"Why wouldn't he? It made sense. A lot more sense than the truth," Gunny added with a chuckle.

"So who is the guy?" Bobby asked.

"Ask him yourself," Gunny said, and motioned toward the limo. "That's his car."

"He's here now?" Bobby said in surprise.

"Go on," Gunny directed. "Talk to him. Just remember, you're not you. You're your grandson."

"Uh . . . yeah," Bobby said, and walked tentatively toward the car.

A driver wearing a black suit jumped from the front seat, ran around back, and opened the rear door. He reached inside and helped his passenger get out. Bobby saw that the guy getting out of the back was indeed very old. He looked a hundred if he looked a day. He was wearing a cream-colored suit and a bright yellow tie. Whoever this guy was, between the limo and the nice clothes, he had some bucks. The driver gave him a cane to lean on. But once he was out of the car, he didn't want any more help. This guy may have been old, but he still had some life in him.

Once he was firmly on the sidewalk, he looked over at Bobby. When their eyes met, the old man actually stood up straighter. Bobby could tell this was a proud man who didn't care much for being trapped in an old body. Bobby didn't recognize him, but then again, he didn't expect to. Yet, as they looked into each other's eyes, Bobby felt something strangely familiar.

"What's your name, son?" the old man asked in a raspy, yet strong voice.

Bobby glanced to Gunny, who nodded encouragement. "Bobby Pendragon," he answered.

"Just like your grandfather," the old man said. "My name is Peter Nelson, though I don't suppose that means anything to you."

"You came a long way to see me, Mr. Nelson," Bobby said with respect. "Do you have something to tell me about, uh, my grandfather?"

Nelson looked away for a moment. He was spinning the memory wheels to get back to 1937. "I've been very successful, young Pendragon," he began. "With business, with family, and with life in general. But I didn't start out that way. In my youth I did some things I wasn't proud of. Things I'm too ashamed to speak about even now. But those were different times, and I was able to put it behind me. I have one person to thank for that . . . your grandfather."

Bobby had no idea what this guy was talking about. He tried to remember something he might have done on First Earth to help somebody out, but came up empty.

"You see," the old man continued, "your grandfather saved my life."

Now Bobby was really confused.

"I was headed down a very dark path," the man said. "Your grandfather gave me a second chance."

"Excuse me," Bobby interrupted. "My grandfather told me a lot of stories, but he never told me about saving anybody's life."

"I'm not surprised," the man responded. "I think that's the kind of person he was. But he saved my life, all right, sure as I'm standing here before you."

"How?" Bobby asked. This was making him crazy.

Mr. Nelson thought for a second, then said, "I don't know how much I should be telling you, but I guess it's all water under the bridge now. Your grandfather saved *two* lives that day. One was mine, the other was a very powerful man named Max Rose. You see, I tried to kill Max Rose, but your grandfather stopped me. Then Max Rose ordered your grandfather to shoot me, but he didn't. He had my life in his hands and gave it right back to me. I ran off and never looked back. Coming that close to dying, well, it changed my life. I have your grandfather to thank."

It all came flooding back to Bobby. He took a closer look at the old man, and now recognized the thin nose and sharp eyes. Could it be? Yes, it was Mr. Nervous Gangster. He was a million years older, but it was definitely him. This was the guy who attacked Spader and him in the subway and tracked them down to the hotel. As Bobby stood there, the memory of looking into this guy's frightened eyes returned as clearly as if it had happened yesterday. He had held a gun on the gangster while Max Rose ordered him to shoot. He remembered the feel of the pistol and knowing he was close to taking a life. But Bobby dropped the gun and the gangster ran.

Now the guy was here, thanking him, sort of. The old man raised his hand to shake Bobby's, saying, "I wanted to thank him personally, but it didn't work out that way. Thanking you is the closest I'm going to get."

Bobby didn't take the guy's hand.

"I remember now," Bobby said to him. "I mean, I remember the story from my grandfather. Can I ask you a question?"

"Of course," the old man said while dropping his hand.

"My grandfather told me about the first time he saw you. It was in a cave off a subway station in the Bronx."

Nelson dropped his head. "I've tried to forget that," he said.

"Yeah, well, try to remember," Bobby said sharply. "What were you doing there?"

The old guy squinted, trying to bring back the memories. "What I remember doesn't make a whole lot of sense. There were three of us. Me and my partner, Tony, and a third guy. A strange fella. Real persuasive, if I remember. He wasn't part of the gang very long."

Bobby figured this must have been Saint Dane.

"This guy brought us to that cave with the tunnel," Nelson continued. "He walked up to the tunnel and said something. What was it? Oh, right. I think it was Clorox . . . you know, like the bleach."

Bobby knew exactly what was said. It was Saint Dane, all right, and he had said "*Cloral.*"

"Then the damnedest thing happened. The tunnel started lighting up like the Fourth of July. The guy told Tony to take his tommygun and shoot into the tunnel. Tony was a wild guy. He didn't have to be convinced to shoot his gun at anything, so he shot right into the lights. A second later, the lights went out. None of it made any sense."

It made sense to Bobby though. Those were the bullets that were fired through the flume and killed Uncle Press.

Nelson continued. "Then the guy took off. He told us to stay there for a while and if anybody came through that tunnel, to scare 'em and tell 'em to stay away from Winn Farrow. Does that answer your question?"

"Almost," Bobby said. "So you're telling me it was your partner who fired the gun into the tunnel? It wasn't you?" Bobby asked.

"Not a chance," he said adamantly. "I remember that very clear. I didn't see the point. Tony fired the gun."

Bobby took a breath, then held out his hand and said, "Then

on behalf of my grandfather, I'll accept your thanks."

The old man shook Bobby's hand. It was a shake that was as strong and sure as if he were twenty years old. Bobby saw the joy in his eyes because in some small way, he was able to thank the man who saved his life. Of course, the guy would never know that he was actually shaking the hand of the real guy, not his grandson.

"Thank you," Nelson said. "Thank you so much."

He let go of Bobby's hand and started back for the car, when he remembered something.

"Oh, one more thing," he said. He reached into his jacket pocket and took out a small package, wrapped in brown paper. "This is something I wanted to give to your grandfather as a small token of my gratitude. I'm sorry I never got it to him, but I hope you will appreciate it."

"Thanks. I'm sure I will," Bobby said graciously.

Nelson handed the package to Bobby, then looked at Gunny. "Mr. Van Dyke," Nelson called. "Do you need a lift back into the city?"

"I do, Mr. Nelson," Gunny answered. "Can I have a few moments?"

"Take all the time you need," answered Nelson, and walked back to his car, where his driver helped him get inside.

Bobby walked back to the others. They'd heard the whole conversation.

"Unbelievable!" Mark said.

"What did he give you?" Courtney asked.

Bobby looked to Gunny. Gunny had a big smile on his face. "Open it," he said.

Bobby shrugged and tore at the brown paper. "It doesn't look very old," he said.

"It isn't," Gunny said. "I only got it yesterday."

Bobby laughed. Of course. Yesterday Gunny was back in 1937. Bobby pulled off all the brown paper to reveal a small, square black box. He looked at Gunny. Gunny winked. Bobby opened it and . . .

"Oh, man!" Mark yelled with surprise.

Courtney laughed.

Gunny said, "Now you know why I came all the way here to get you this."

Bobby couldn't believe his eyes. Sitting in the box was his ring—his Traveler ring.

"He told me he got it back from his partner after the guy took the fall from the tower," Gunny explained. "He figured getting it back to you was the least he could do, seeing as you saved his life and all."

"Excellent," Courtney said. "We're back in business."

Now Bobby could send his journals back to Mark and Courtney the old-fashioned way. Bobby couldn't stop smiling. In some ways, things had come full circle. He took the ring out of the box and slipped it on his finger. As soon as he did, the ring began to twitch. Bobby held his hand out quickly.

"What's the matter?" Mark asked.

"It . . . it's activating," Bobby said.

"Really? You mean there's a gate around here?" Courtney asked.

The answer came quickly. The gray stone in the ring began to glow, then sparkle. A second later a single beam of light shot from the ring, projecting an image in front of them. There, floating in the air before them, was a girl. Actually, it was a girl's head. She had blond hair pulled back in a ponytail and wore small, yellow-tinted glasses.

"Whoa," said Courtney.

"Yeah, whoa," added Mark.

"Aja Killian," whispered Bobby in shock.

"Who?" Gunny asked.

"The Traveler from Veelox."

"Where have you been?" demanded Aja's image. "I've been trying to contact you for ages!"

"Long story," Bobby answered.

"I don't want to hear it, Pendragon." Aja shot back. "You'd better get back to Veelox."

"Why?" Bobby asked.

"I'm not saying I made a mistake," Aja's head explained. "This may be a total false alarm, but—"

"Just say it!" demanded Bobby.

"All right!" Aja snapped. "Saint Dane may have slipped through my security system. He is here on Veelox."

Bobby smiled and said, "You're telling me your perfect security system isn't all that perfect?"

"Are you coming or not?" Aja snapped angrily.

"On my way," Bobby answered.

"Don't take your time," Aja said snottily. Her image shot back into Bobby's ring and everything went back to normal.

"Well," said Courtney. "That was . . . strange."

"I guess I'm going to Veelox," Bobby said. Then looked to Gunny and asked, "Want to come?"

"Wouldn't miss it," Gunny answered with a smile. "We'll have Mr. Nelson drop us off in the Bronx."

Bobby turned to face Mark and Courtney. "This has been the best week of my life," Bobby said sincerely.

Courtney then walked up to Bobby and before he realized what was happening, she grabbed him and planted a serious kiss on him. Bobby didn't mind. Once the shock was over, he wrapped his arms around Courtney and held her close.

Kissing Courtney was even better than he remembered.

Mark and Gunny turned away, totally embarrassed. "So?" Gunny asked Mark. "How 'bout them Yankees?"

Courtney and Bobby finally unlocked lips. Bobby's eyes were a little watery, but Courtney's gaze was razor sharp.

"Let's not wait another year before the next one, okay?" she said.

"Uh . . . sure. Sounds good," Bobby said, trying to keep his knees from buckling.

Mark and Courtney each gave Gunny a hug, and the two Travelers started for the limo.

"Remember what we talked about, okay?" Mark called to Bobby.

"I will," Bobby said.

As he and Gunny walked toward the car, Gunny asked, "How are you feeling, shorty? I mean . . . where is your head, you know, with things?"

Bobby didn't answer right away. He wanted to make sure he used the right words.

"I feel like Saint Dane got the better of me on First Earth," Bobby said. "And I'm not gonna let it happen again."

Gunny chuckled.

"What's so funny?" Bobby asked.

Gunny broke out in a big smile and said, "Shorty, you're starting to sound just like your uncle."

Bobby smiled too. Then he and Gunny got into the back of the big car. Bobby opened the window so he could get one last look at his friends. As the car pulled away from the curb he put his arm out and waved to them.

Mark and Courtney watched as the black limo picked up speed along the quiet street, with Bobby's arm still out, waving.

"What was it you guys talked about?" Courtney asked.

"All sorts of things," Mark said with a sly smile. "But I'll tell you one thing, I'll bet we're going to see Bobby Pendragon again, a lot sooner than you think."

They looked back up at the departing limousine in time to see Bobby pull his arm back inside. The car turned onto the main road and disappeared.

to be continued

PENDRAGON

JOURNAL OF AN ADVENTURE THROUGH TIME AND SPACE

Book Four:
The Reality Bug

*This is for my sister, Patricia,
the true artist of the family.*

◎ SECOND EARTH ◎

Bobby Pendragon slipped the heavy ring onto his finger, where it belonged. But no sooner was it back in place when surprisingly, it began to twitch.

"What's the matter?" Mark Dimond asked.

"It . . . it's activating," Bobby said with surprise.

"Really? You mean there's a gate around here?" Courtney Chetwynde asked.

The gray stone in the center of the ring began to glow, then sparkle. A second later a sharp beam of light shot from its center. With a flash, the light blossomed into an image that hovered in front of the group.

Mark and Courtney took a surprised step backward. Gunny Van Dyke stepped protectively in front of them. But Bobby held his ground. Of the four of them standing on the empty lot at 2 Linden Place, Second Earth, Bobby was the only one who had seen this particular phenomenon before.

Floating before them was the image of a girl. Actually, it was a girl's head. Just a head. It was bigger than life, but definitely a girl. She had blond hair pulled back in a ponytail and wore small, yellow-tinted glasses.

"Whoa," said Courtney in awe.

"Yeah, whoa," added Mark.

"Aja Killian," whispered Bobby.

"Who?" Gunny asked.

"The Traveler from Veelox."

"Where have you been?" the floating head demanded angrily. "I've been trying to contact you for ages!"

"Long story," Bobby answered.

"I don't want to hear it, Pendragon," Aja's head shot back. "You'd better get back to Veelox."

"Why?" Bobby asked.

Aja-head hesitated. She looked nervous. Or at least as nervous as a 3-D floating head could look. "I'm not saying I made a mistake," she explained with a touch of embarrassment. "This may be a total false alarm, but—"

"Just say it!" Bobby shouted.

"All right!" Aja snapped. "Saint Dane may have slipped through my security system. He is here on Veelox."

Bobby smiled and asked teasingly, "You're telling me your perfect security system isn't all that perfect?"

"Are you coming or not?" Aja demanded. She didn't like being challenged.

"On my way," Bobby answered.

"Don't take your time," Aja said snottily. Then the image vanished. The beam of light shot back into the ring and all was normal.

"Well," said Courtney with a sigh. "That was . . . strange."

"I guess I'm going to Veelox," Bobby said. Then looked to Gunny and asked, "Want to come?"

"Wouldn't miss it," Gunny answered with a smile.

Bobby turned to face Mark and Courtney. "This has been

the best week of my life," he said sincerely.

The three friends had just spent an excellent week together, forgetting for a short while that Bobby Pendragon was a Traveler who shot across the universe, protecting Halla from an evil demon. Mark was nearly in tears. Courtney wasn't far behind. She walked up to Bobby and before he realized what was happening, she grabbed him and planted a serious kiss on his lips. Bobby didn't fight it. Once the shock was over, he wrapped his arms around Courtney and held her close.

Mark and Gunny turned away.

"So?" Gunny asked Mark. "How 'bout them Yankees?"

When Courtney and Bobby finally unlocked lips, Bobby's eyes were a little watery. But Courtney's gaze was razor sharp.

"Let's not wait another year before the next one, okay?" she said.

"Uh . . . sure. Sounds good," Bobby replied, trying to keep his knees from buckling.

Mark looked at Bobby, his best friend, and said, "Remember what we talked about, okay?"

"I promise," Bobby answered sincerely.

Bobby and Gunny walked toward the street and the limousine that was waiting to take them to the Bronx, and the flume.

"How are you feeling, shorty?" Gunny asked. "I mean . . . where is your head you know, with things?"

"I feel like Saint Dane got the better of me on First Earth," he answered thoughtfully. He then locked eyes with Gunny and said with total confidence, "And I'm not gonna let it happen again."

Gunny chuckled.

"What's so funny?" Bobby asked.

"Shorty, you're starting to sound just like your uncle Press."

Bobby smiled. He liked that. The two got into the back of the big car, the driver gunned the engine, and they were on their way.

Mark and Courtney watched as the black limo picked up speed with Bobby's hand still out the window, waving good-bye.

"What was it you guys talked about?" Courtney asked Mark.

"All sorts of things," he said with a sly smile. "But I'll tell you one thing: I'll bet we're going to see Bobby Pendragon again, a lot sooner than you think."

They took a last look at the departing limousine and saw Bobby pull his arm back inside. The car turned onto the main road and disappeared.

◉ SECOND EARTH ◉

Mark Dimond was ready for an adventure.

He had spent the first fifteen years of his life on the sidelines, watching everybody else have all the fun. It was getting old. He was tired of being wallpaper, tired of being the brunt of geek jokes, and *really* tired of wishing he was somebody else. Anybody else. But even Mark had to admit that it was going to be tough pulling himself out of the deep hole of dorkdom he had been digging since birth.

When he was a baby, his parents barely let him out of the house because he was allergic to everything but air. In three years of Little League he got on base only once, because he was hit by a pitch that broke his glasses. Girls scared him, but that wasn't much of a problem because most girls never looked at him twice anyway. They weren't interested in a guy who constantly gnawed on carrots (to improve his vision), sat in the first row of class (because he had every correct answer, always), and had a stringy mop of hair that always looked like it should have been washed yesterday.

No, Mark hadn't exactly been living large. But now that he

was fifteen, he was determined to make a change. He was ready to seize the day and kick start a new life filled with adventure and excitement. Why?

Because he had a best buddy named Bobby Pendragon.

They had been friends since kindergarten, though most people thought they were as different as east and west. Bobby was athletic and funny and people loved to be around him. Mark was quiet and tripped a lot. But that was just surface stuff.

Mark and Bobby liked the same things, and not always the normal things that other kids thought were cool. They loved old Abbott and Costello movies, '80s music, Thai food, and James Bond novels (not the movies, the original novels). They laughed at the same jokes. They started a band, but Bobby could barely play the guitar and Mark only had an ancient set of bongos. Neither could sing. They were terrible. They had a blast.

They liked to fish in the small river that wound its way through their little town of Stony Brook, Connecticut. It didn't matter that they hardly ever caught anything. It was all about getting away for hours to just hang. Like most guys, they talked about girls and sports, and about what teachers they wanted vaporized. But they also talked about ideas, about traveling and seeing different places, and about the future.

Each always seemed to know when the other needed encouragement, or a kick in the butt. For Bobby, Mark was the only guy he knew who thought outside the box. For Mark, Bobby was his lifeline to the rest of the world. Both knew that no matter what twists their lives took, they would always be best friends.

What they *hadn't* known was that during the winter of their fifteenth year, Bobby and his entire family would mysteriously disappear. A huge investigation by the local police turned up nothing. Literally. It was like the Pendragons had been magically erased from existence.

But Mark knew the truth.

He wasn't sure what had happened to the rest of the Pendragon family, but he knew where Bobby had gone. He had left with his uncle, Press, to become a Traveler. Bobby Pendragon and his uncle had flown through a portal called a flume that took them to strange, distant territories where they joined with other Travelers to do battle against a demon named Saint Dane. In the year and a half since Bobby had left home, he helped prevent a medieval territory called Denduron from blowing itself up, halted the spread of a poison that would have wiped out the entire population of a water territory called Cloral, and traveled back in time to stop Nazi Germany from developing the world's first atomic bomb.

What was Mark doing while Bobby was defending humanity? Watching a lot of SpongeBob SquarePants. Yes, Mark was desperately ready for an adventure. He needed an adventure.

He was about to get one.

"Courtney!" Mark shouted.

Courtney Chetwynde had just stepped off the school bus that brought her to the first day of classes at Davis Gregory High School. Courtney hated the bus, but school was too far from home to bike, and her parents wouldn't let her ride in cars with the older kids yet. Courtney was the only other person who knew the truth about Bobby Pendragon. But unlike Mark, Bobby and Courtney had started out as rivals—athletic rivals. Courtney had done her best to beat Bobby's butt at everything. It had been her way of covering up that she had an incredible crush on him.

Now not a day went by where she didn't think back to the night a year and a half ago when she finally admitted to Bobby that she liked him. That moment got better when Bobby told her that he liked her, too. It got *seriously* better when the two of them kissed. But it all went south when Bobby's uncle Press showed up to break the magic and whisk him away on the back of a motorcycle to begin his life as a Traveler. If Courtney had one wish, it would be that she could wind back the clock to that night and stop Bobby from riding off with his uncle.

As she stepped off the hated school bus, Courtney saw Mark scurry up to meet her.

"Anything?" she asked hopefully.

"Nope," Mark answered.

He knew she was asking if another journal had arrived from Bobby. It hadn't.

These two made an odd couple. Courtney was beautiful, popular, confidant, and athletic. Mark . . . wasn't. If it weren't for their connection with Bobby, they never would have been on each other's radar screens.

"First day of high school," Mark said. "Nervous?"

"No," she answered truthfully. Courtney didn't get nervous.

They were starting the tenth grade, which was the first year of Davis Gregory High. Last year they were on the top of the pyramid at Stony Brook Junior High. Now they would have to start over again at the bottom of the school food chain.

As the two walked toward school, Mark had to hurry to keep up with Courtney's long strides. "Courtney, there's s-something I want to talk to you about."

"Whoa, you're stuttering," Courtney said seriously. "What's the matter?"

"N-Nothing," Mark assured her. "I just need to talk to you is all."

"About, you know, journals and stuff?" she asked while glancing around to make sure nobody heard her.

"Sort of. Can we talk after school?"

"I've got soccer practice."

"I'll come watch. We'll talk after."

"You sure everything's okay?"

"Yeah. Good luck today!"

The two then separated and began the first day of their high school careers.

Courtney pretty much hung with her regular friends, though she made sure to check out any new kids. In English class she found herself staring at a cute guy named Frank. It felt a little weird, like she was cheating on Bobby. But Bobby had written in his journals about how fantastic the Traveler girl named Loor was. Courtney thought that if Bobby could like a girl from a far-off territory called Zadaa, then why couldn't she like a guy from two desks over in a class called English?

Mark stepped into high school with expectations of starting a new life. Three junior highs emptied into Davis Gregory, which meant at least two-thirds of these kids didn't know the dorky truth about him. The Etch-A-Sketch of his life had been turned over and given a healthy shake.

Unfortunately, by the end of last period, Mark had gotten lost six times, showed up late for every class, made a girl in chemistry gag because his sneakers smelled like an experiment gone sour, and got laughed out of the cafeteria when he made the mistake of sitting down to eat lunch next to an all-county wrestling jock. As punishment for invading his space, the guy made Mark stand up on the table and sing "Wally the Green-nosed Tuna" to the tune of "Rudolph the Red-nosed Reindeer."

It was junior high hell all over again, only with bigger kids.

While Mark was discovering the horrible truth that his life of humiliation was going to continue, Courtney was learning that things for her were going to be very different. Courtney was tall and pretty with long, light brown hair, deep gray eyes and a nice smile. She had lots of friends, too. Except when it came to sports. In sports, Courtney had no friends. She hated to lose and had the goods to back it up. It didn't matter what sport, either.

Baseball, track, basketball, even judo. She had absolute confidence in herself. In fact, she had gotten so used to winning that she was looking forward to high school because she desperately wanted more competition.

She got it.

"Chetwynde! Get your shoes on the right feet!" the soccer coach yelled at her.

Courtney's fall sport was soccer. She had played center forward on the junior high team and led the town in scoring. She fully expected to step onto the high school varsity field and dominate like always.

She didn't. Courtney realized she was in trouble during the very first drill. It was a dribbling drill. Courtney brought the ball forward with a confidant smile, ready to give these high school girls a taste of Hurricane Courtney. She ducked right, moved left . . . and the defender stole the ball.

Whoa.

When it was her turn to play defense, the girls put moves on her and dribbled past like she wasn't even there. One girl made such a hot move that Courtney got her feet crossed and fell on her butt—prompting the comment about her shoes being on the wrong feet.

All afternoon Courtney was one step behind. These high school girls were good. Really good. They shot no-look passes, stole the ball from her, and basically made her look like she was a little kid playing with grown-ups. One girl stole the ball, flipped it up with her foot, bounced it off her knee, and slammed a header downfield. She then looked to Courtney and said, "Welcome to the big time, superstar." When it came time for sprints, Courtney was nearly last every run. That was unheard of. Nobody beat Courtney Chetwynde. Ever! What had happened?

The truth was, nothing had happened. Courtney was always

big for her age. It was one of the reasons she had been so good at sports. But between the ninth and tenth grades, the other girls caught up. Girls who had been too small to compete with Courtney were suddenly eye to eye with her. It wasn't that Courtney had suddenly gotten bad, it was that everybody else had grown up and gotten better. Much better. For Courtney it was an absolute, total nightmare. But she wouldn't let it show. No way.

On the sidelines Mark sat under a tree, watching practice. He couldn't believe what he was seeing. Everybody had bad days, but seeing Courtney struggle like this was disturbing. There were some things in life that were absolute. He knew that pi times the radius squared gave you the area of a circle; he knew that water was made up of two parts hydrogen and one part oxygen; and he knew that if you challenged Courtney Chetwynde, you would lose.

The last one of Mark's all-time truisms was now being proved wrong. It was the perfect way to end a totally crappy day.

"Looks like she ain't so tough after all," came a familiar voice from behind Mark.

Mark looked up quickly to see that the horror of this day wasn't yet complete. Standing over him was Andy Mitchell. The guy snorted back a lougie and spit, barely missing Mark's hand. Mark spun out of the way, but Mitchell flicked his cigarette butt in the other direction and Mark nearly rolled into it. Mark had to pop to his feet or risk getting gobbed on.

"What'sa matter, Dimond?" Mitchell laughed. "Twitchy?"

"What do you want?" Mark grumbled.

"Hey, don't get all testy with me," Mitchell shot back. "I'm just out here having a smoke. Seeing Chetwynde getting whupped up on was a bonus." Mitchell wheezed out a laugh through yellowed, smoke-stained teeth.

"Go away," was all Mark managed to squeak out. He turned and walked off, but Mitchell followed.

"I didn't forget, Dimond," Mitchell snarled. "About them journals. Pendragon is out there somewhere. You know it and I know it and I know you know I know it."

Truth be told, there was a third person who knew about what happened to Bobby Pendragon. It was Andy Mitchell. Mitchell had seen one of Bobby's journals and blackmailed Mark into showing him the rest.

Mark turned to Mitchell, standing toe to toe with him. "All I know is, you're an idiot. And I'm not afraid of you anymore!"

Mark and Andy held each other's gaze. Mark had had enough of this bully and would almost welcome a fight. Almost. Mark wasn't a fighter. If Mitchell called his bluff and took a swing, things would get real ugly, real fast. For Mark.

"Hey, Mitchell," Courtney said.

She stood behind Mitchell with her gear bag in one hand and her cleats in the other. She looked tired and dirty and not in the mood to be messed with. "What are you doing in high school? I thought you'd be out stealing cars by now."

Andy ducked away from her. He didn't mess with Courtney, no matter how bad she looked playing soccer.

"Real funny, Chetwynde," Mitchell sneered. "You two think you're being all smart, but I know."

"What do you know?" Courtney asked.

Mark said, "He knows we know he knows . . . or something like that. You know?"

Mark and Courtney chuckled. They knew Mitchell wasn't a threat to them anymore. He wasn't smart enough for that.

"Yeah, you laugh," he sneered. "But I read those journals. You gonna laugh when that Saint Dane dude comes here looking for them?"

With that, Mitchell snorted back another good one, then turned and hurried away.

Mark and Courtney weren't chuckling anymore. They silently watched Mitchell jog off. Then Courtney said, "Well, today pretty much . . . sucked."

The two walked to catch the late bus home. Normally Courtney would sit in the back of the bus with the cool kids and Mark would sit up front with the not-cool kids. Not today. There were a couple of girls in back who had just taken Courtney apart on the soccer field. They were sitting with some guys from the football team, laughing and flirting. Courtney wasn't welcome. She had to sit in the front of the bus with Mark. It was the final indignity.

"You want to tell me about your day?" Courtney asked.

"No," answered Mark. "You?"

"No."

They rode in silence, both wondering if the rest of high school was going to be as painful as the first few hours. Finally Courtney asked, "What did you want to talk to me about?"

Mark glanced around to make sure nobody was listening. He kept his voice low, just in case. "I've been thinking," he began. "Remember what I said before? In spite of what Mitchell just said, I think we dodged a bullet. When the Travelers stopped Saint Dane on First Earth, I think they saved all three Earth territories. Remember?"

"Yeah, I remember," Courtney said, then added with growing annoyance, "and I remember you saying how disappointed you were because you wanted Saint Dane to come here so you could help Bobby fight him. And I remember saying that you were totally crazy. Do *you* remember that part, Markie boy?"

Mark nodded.

"Good," Courtney said. "Then stop thinking so much."

"But still," Mark added. "I want to be able to help Bobby."

"We *are* helping him," Courtney corrected. "We're holding his journals."

"But that's like almost nothing," Mark countered. "I want to *really* help him."

"We *can't,* Mark."

Mark gave her a sly smile. "Don't be so sure."

Courtney gave Mark a long, probing look. "*Now* what are you thinking?"

"I want to become an acolyte. I want us *both* to become acolytes."

"Aco-whats?"

"You know, acolytes. Bobby wrote about them. The people from the territories who help the Travelers. They put supplies by the flumes for the Travelers. They're the ones who kept Press's motorcycle, and had his car ready when he got back. It's totally safe, but really important."

"Safe?" Courtney shot back. "You think going to that abandoned subway in the Bronx and getting past those quig-dogs is safe?"

"Maybe there's another flume here on Second Earth," Mark added hopefully. "They have more than one flume on other territories, why not here?"

"And what if it's in Alaska?" Courtney lobbed back. "You want to move to Alaska?"

"After the day I had, absolutely."

"You don't mean that."

The two rode in silence for a few more stops. A couple of the soccer girls got off and made a point of ignoring Courtney. Courtney didn't care. Her mind was back on the journals, and Bobby.

"I know you care, Mark," Courtney said softly. "I do too. But even if I thought this acolyte thing was a good idea, how would we do it?"

Mark sat up straight, encouraged that Courtney was at least considering it.

"I don't know, but when Bobby was home I talked to him about it—"

"You already asked Bobby?" Courtney interrupted. "Without talking to me first?"

"All I did was ask him to look into it," Mark said. "He didn't know any more about acolytes than he wrote, but he promised to try and find out. What do you think?"

"I think I gotta think about it. And I think this is my stop." Courtney stood.

"Promise me that?" Mark asked. "You'll think about it?"

"Yeah," Courtney answered. "But I gotta know more."

"Absolutely," Mark said.

Courtney swung down the bus stairs and out the door. Mark felt better than he had all day. He felt sure that if Bobby got them information about the acolytes, Courtney would join up with him. It was a great feeling to know he might actually have a shot at helping Bobby in a real way.

As Mark lay in bed that night he couldn't stop his mind from imagining the possibilities. If they became acolytes, could they actually fly through the flumes? That would be awesome! He imagined himself on Cloral, speeding underwater with Bobby. He could see himself racing a sled down the snowy slopes of Denduron, dodging the charging quig-bears. He even saw himself on Zadaa, battling through the capture the flag game alongside Loor.

Mark had to force himself to think of something else for fear he'd never get to sleep. He turned his mind to math problems. He thought of lying on the beach at the Point. He imagined looking up at puffy clouds on a warm summer's day. He pretended his ring was twitching and another journal from Bobby was about to show up.

Mark sat bolt upright in bed. That wasn't his imagination. Mark's ring *was* twitching. He looked at his hand. The stone in the heavy silver ring was dissolving from dark gray into crystal clear. That meant only one thing. . . .

Mark wouldn't be getting to sleep anytime soon.

He threw his feet over the side of his bed, yanked off the ring, and placed it on the rug. The small circle became larger, revealing a dark hole where the floor should have been. Mark knew this was the conduit to another territory. He heard the jumble of sweet musical notes that sounded far away at first, but quickly grew louder. Sparkling light then blasted out of the hole, lighting up his room like a thousand fireflies. Mark had to shield his eyes from the brilliant show.

Then, as always, the event abruptly stopped. The lights went out and the music was gone. Mark peeked through his fingers to see that the ring had returned to normal. As always, the mysterious ring had made a delivery.

Lying on the rug was Bobby's latest journal.

But this was unlike anything Bobby had sent before. In fact, it didn't even look like a journal. It was a small, shiny silver device that was roughly the size and shape of a credit card. Mark curiously picked it up and saw three square buttons on it. One was deep green, another was bright orange, the third was black. The thing didn't weigh much more than a credit card either. There was a piece of paper stuck to the device. It was a short note, written in Bobby's handwriting.

It read: GREEN—PLAY. BLACK—STOP. ORANGE—REWIND.

It seemed to Mark like CD player instructions, but this tiny little card didn't look like any media player he had ever seen. But if Bobby sent it, who was he to argue? So he touched the green button.

Instantly a narrow beam of light shot from one end of the card. Mark dropped the device in surprise. The silver card hit the floor and the beam swept across the room. Mark jumped over his bed and crouched down on the far side for protection. Was it a laser? Was he going to get sliced? A second later the beam grew until it projected a holographic image in the middle of the bedroom. Mark had to blink, then rub his eyes, then look again, because standing in front of him was Bobby Pendragon. The image looked as real as if his friend were standing there in the flesh. The only thing that reminded him it was a hologram was the beam of light that came from the device on the floor.

"Hiya, Mark. Hey, Courtney," Bobby's image said as clear as can be.

Mark fell back on his butt, stunned.

"Greetings from the territory of Veelox. What you're seeing and hearing right now, is my journal number thirteen. Pretty cool, aye?"

VEELOX

Hiya, Mark. Hey, Courtney. Greetings from the territory of
Veelox. What you're seeing and hearing right now is my journal number thirteen. Pretty cool, aye? I'll bet it beats having
to read my lousy handwriting. Heck, it beats having to write
everything down, too. I'm loving this. But this projector thing
is a toy compared to the science fiction stuff they've got going
on here. It's totally incredible.

Just to tease you a little, imagine the most amazing video
game you ever played. You know, great graphics, realistic
sound, 3-D environments, excellent challenges, the whole
deal. Now, imagine that game being about twelve billion times
better. That's what they've got on Veelox. I'm not exaggerating. There's no way I could give you a quick description
beyond that. You'll have to learn about it the way I did, a little
at a time. Be patient. It's worth it.

But before we dive into the wonders of Veelox, I want to
tell you what happened after I left you guys on Second Earth.
Borrowing one of Spader's phrases, I found myself in the
middle of a tum-tigger.

Again.

Gunny and I were given a limo ride to the Bronx by the old gangster, Peter Nelson. We were headed for the abandoned subway station and the flume to the territories. Our ultimate destination was Veelox. Where Saint Dane goes, we go.

Unfortunately.

As we rode toward the Bronx, my head was in a strange place. It was because of what happened on First Earth. Simply put, I failed. On First Earth Saint Dane tried to prove I wasn't worthy of being a Traveler, and that's exactly what happened. It all came down to the moment when the airship *Hindenburg* was about to be destroyed. As horrible as that was, the *Hindenburg* was *supposed* to be destroyed. If history was changed, it would have been Armageddon for Earth. As I stood over the rocket that was about to shoot into the air and blow it up, I knew I had the future of all three Earth territories in my hands.

And I choked. In that horrible moment, I couldn't bear to let the innocent people in that zeppelin die. So I made a move to kick over the rocket, save the *Hindenburg*, save those people, and send the Earth territories spiraling toward doomsday.

But Gunny held me back. He stopped me from making the worst mistake possible. The rocket took off and the *Hindenburg* exploded. Gunny saved the Earth territories. That was the way it was meant to be.

Though the Travelers had beaten Saint Dane, Saint Dane had beaten *me*. Call it what you want: a moment of truth, a test, whatever. But I blew it. From that moment on I questioned whether or not I was up to this job. Heck, I've questioned it from day one, but my screwup on First Earth totally rocked me. I think Saint Dane expected me to shrivel up and crawl into a hole, never to bother him again in his quest to rule Halla. Believe me, I thought about it.

But that wasn't going to happen.

My screwup on First Earth had the opposite effect. It got me mad. I wanted to prove to that monster I'm not the loser he thinks I am. Or maybe what I really wanted to do, was prove it to myself. Whatever. Bottom line was, for the first time since I left home to become a Traveler, I felt like I wanted the job. Seriously. I wanted to live up to the trust Uncle Press had in me. Saint Dane's plan had backfired. Rather than making me go away, he fired me up. If he thinks I'm too weak for the job, that's cool. That means he won't see me coming.

And I am definitely coming.

After the limo dropped us off at the abandoned subway station, Gunny and I stood on the sidewalk, enjoying our last few moments of Second Earth sunlight. Gunny's a great guy and I'm proud to call him my friend. There's a lot of great things I can say about him, but probably the most important is that he was strong enough to take the heat for me on First Earth.

But at that moment, standing on a Bronx sidewalk, he didn't seem to be in any hurry to go Saint Dane hunting. He was a tall, African-American guy, about 6'4", who looked pretty happy being there with his eyes closed and the sun on his face.

"What're you thinking?" I asked the Traveler from First Earth.

Gunny opened his eyes and glanced around at the busy city intersection. It must have looked strange to him. After all, he was from 1937.

"Tell me, shorty," he said. "Do you think the day will ever come when we can all go home and get back to normal?"

I had been asking myself that same question from the minute I first left home with Uncle Press.

"Don't know," I answered truthfully. "But then again,

I'm not so sure I know what normal is anymore."

I led him down the garbage-strewn stairs of the closed station. It was a familiar route. The entrance was boarded over with wooden planks that were plastered with flyers and advertisements. But I knew the way in. Two of the boards were loose and a quick tug revealed our entrance.

The empty station looked the exact same as it had the first night Uncle Press brought me here. It was a long forgotten piece of New York history—forgotten by everyone but us, that is. A subway train rumbled through, kicking up pieces of crusty paper full of yesterday's news. Once it passed we quickly jumped down onto the track and made our way along the oil-stained wall toward the wooden door with the star symbol. A few seconds later we entered the rocky cavern that would be our last stop on Second Earth. The first leg of our trip had been cake. Now things would get interesting. The two of us stood there for a moment, silently gazing into the long, dark roadway to the territories . . . the flume.

"Tell me about this Veelox place," Gunny said.

"Not much to tell," I answered. "I was only there for a few minutes and never left the flume."

"That floating-head girl?" he asked. "You sure she's a Traveler?"

"So she says," I answered.

Gunny shook his head in wonder. "Heads floating in space," he said philosophically. "What next?"

"I think we're about to find out," I answered.

He gave me a small smile, then stepped into the mouth of the flume. *"Veelox!"* he shouted and the flume came to life. The rock walls cracked and groaned as if they were stretching out the kinks after a long sleep. Deep in the tunnel a faint light appeared that would soon come to sweep Gunny away. Along with it came the faint jumble of sweet musical notes that always accompanied the spectacular light show.

Gunny turned to me. I saw a hint of tension in his eyes. "Did I ever tell you I'm not a big fan of this fluming business?"

I laughed. "Gunny, there's plenty of stuff out there to be scared about. The flume isn't one of 'em."

As the light grew closer, the dark rock of the tunnel began its transformation into clear crystal.

"I'll hold you to that," Gunny said. The light flashed nuclear, music echoed throughout the space, and Gunny was gone. I dropped my hand in time to see the light disappear into the depths of the tunnel. The flume had returned to normal, waiting for its next passenger. Me.

"Veelox!" I shouted, and the process began again.

As the light and music came for me, I closed my eyes, waiting for the first tug that would signal the beginning of my trip.

Here we go again.

The flume ride to Veelox wasn't different than any other. I crossed my arms, kicked back, and enjoyed the sensation of shooting through the crystal tunnel. I gazed out through the clear walls at the star field beyond, trying to pick out a constellation, but none looked familiar. I still didn't know exactly what happened when a Traveler went through a flume. I was beginning to understand that it wasn't like moving through the regular old three dimensions of space that we're used to. You know: up, down, forward, back. I believe a flume trip sent you through a fourth dimension, which was time. That's why the Travelers are able to show up where they need to be, *when* they need to be there.

Uncle Press explained to me about Halla. It was everything . . . all times, all places, all people, and all things that ever were. And they all still existed. If that were true, then

maybe there was a fifth and even a sixth dimension, and the flumes were interdimensional highways between them. Something like that would make sense, or the universe would be getting pretty crowded.

Did I say that made sense? Who am I kidding? Does *any* of this make sense? There was only one thing I knew for sure: All this thinking about multiple dimensions was ruining my cool flume ride. I had to lighten up.

Too late. The jumble of notes grew more furious, which signaled I was nearing Veelox. A few seconds later gravity kicked in and I was gently set down. The first thing I saw was Gunny's back. He stood at the mouth of the flume a few feet in front of me. The second thing I saw was . . .

Saint Dane.

Whoa.

"Hello, Pendragon," the demon said with an oily smile. "Welcome to Veelox."

VEELOX

8aint Dane stood facing us in the dark room.

His sharp blue eyes cut through the gloom like cold fire. He was in his normal form, standing seven feet tall with long gray hair that fell over his shoulders. To say I was shocked to see him doesn't cover it.

"I'm surprised, Pendragon," Saint Dane continued. "After your embarrassment on First Earth, I thought you would have given up your foolish pursuit."

I couldn't talk. I was in total brainlock.

"No matter," he continued. "My work here is complete. Veelox is on the verge of crumbling. I must say, I didn't expect Veelox to be the first territory to fall, but in the end it won't matter, since all of Halla will ultimately meet the same fate."

"Veelox is about to crumble?" Gunny asked, stunned.

"I don't believe you," I said, finally kick starting my brain.

Saint Dane smiled from one corner of his mouth and said, "You say that as if I should care. Now, please, step aside. I have business elsewhere."

"You're not leaving," I announced defiantly.

Gunny gave me a quick, nervous look. That was a pretty bold threat, especially since I had no idea of how to back it up.

"What are you going to do?" Saint Dane chuckled. "Hold me here?"

"If we have to," I said, trying not to let my voice crack. I meant it too. If Saint Dane ran for the flume, I was ready to tackle him. We had to know what happened on Veelox.

"Isn't that a little unimaginative?" Saint Dane said. But the words didn't come from his mouth. They came from our right. Huh? Gunny and I both turned quickly to see . . .

Another Saint Dane was standing there. There were two of them! "Certainly you can be more creative than that," the second Saint Dane said.

"Or maybe you've reached your limit for resourcefulness," came another voice.

Uh-oh. Gunny and I spun to our left to see a *third* Saint Dane.

"Press would be so disappointed in you."

We turned to see yet another Saint Dane behind us, standing in the mouth of the flume. "They're not real, Gunny. They're holograms," I said. "Like movies."

"Correct!" Saint Dane announced. The *fifth* Saint Dane. We were now standing in a circle of Saint Danes. There were twenty of them, all the exact duplicates of one another. They started to move together, circling us.

"The question is," they all said in unison, "which one of us is real?" They let out a chilling laugh. "What to do? What to do?" they sang together.

Gunny and I stood back to back, trying to spot any sign that would tell us which was the original. It was impossible.

They were perfect clones. Then, in one unified voice, they all shouted, *"Eelong!"*

Uh-oh. The flume came to life. If we were going to do something, it would have to be fast. Gunny made the first move. He jumped forward and wrapped his arms around the closest Saint Dane. But all he got for his trouble was an armload of air.

The Saint Danes laughed. This was fun for him. Or them, or whatever.

Light from the flume lit up the room and the musical notes were nearly on us. Gunny lunged at another Saint Dane, but his arms swept through the hologram like it wasn't even there. Because it wasn't. In seconds Saint Dane would escape to another territory and we'd be left to pick up the pieces. As scared as I was, I lunged at one of the Saint Danes. . . .

And wrapped my arms around the demon Traveler. The real one. I had guessed right. First try. Lucky me.

It's hard to describe the feeling. Yes, I was petrified, but I guess that's obvious. What I remember most is that Saint Dane felt cold. It was like hugging a block of ice. With my chin stuck in his chest, I looked up into his eyes. For an instant I was afraid the blood in my veins would freeze solid. Maybe it did, because I couldn't move. When he opened his mouth to speak, his breath smelled like something had crawled in there and died.

"Does this mean you're coming with me?" he asked with a wicked sneer.

That threw me. I felt as if holding on to him wasn't going to stop him, but instead make me his prisoner. The thought was so gruesome, I automatically let go. Bad move, because Saint Dane instantly bolted for the flume. Gunny lunged at him, but the demon was too fast. He leaped into the flume at the exact instant the light came to take him. All that was left was the echoing sound of his laughter as he flumed away.

Saint Dane was gone.

So were the holograms. Gunny and I were left alone in the big empty room, staring at a dark flume.

"I'm going after him," Gunny announced.

"No!" I shouted. "We've got to figure out what he did here on Veelox."

"He's going to start in on a new territory, Pendragon," Gunny declared. "What's done here is done."

"We don't know that for sure," I countered. "Just because he said it, doesn't mean it's true. He's not exactly an honest guy."

We were at a crossroads. What was the best thing to do? Stay here and do damage control, or stop Saint Dane from digging into a new territory called Eelong?

"You've been here before," Gunny said. "You know the Traveler. What's her name?"

"Aja Killian."

"Right. The floating head. I think you should find her. She'll know what Saint Dane has been up to."

"What about you?"

"I'll follow him to Eelong and see what we're up against there. Then I'll be back."

"I don't like splitting up," I said. "Remember what happened on First Earth when Spader took off on his own? That was nearly a disaster."

"I know," Gunny reassured me. "But this is different. Spader had his own ideas. You and I are working *together*."

I didn't want him to go, but if we had the chance of heading off Saint Dane before he could get started on Eelong, we had to take it.

"Promise me you'll bolt if something wacky happens," I demanded.

Gunny laughed. "Shorty, seems to me like everything is pretty wacky."

"You know what I mean."

"Course I do. Don't you go worrying; I'll be fine," Gunny said.

The two of us hugged, then Gunny pushed me back and asked, "What was the name of that territory again?"

"It sounded like 'Eelong,'" I answered.

Gunny stepped into the mouth of the flume, stood up straight, and faced the tunnel. *"Eelong!"*

On cue, the flume sprang to life. The moment before he was taken away in the shower of light and music, he smiled at me and said, "What is it that Spader always says?"

"Hobey-ho, Gunny."

"Hobey-ho, Pendragon. See you soon."

I hoped so. An instant later he was gone and I was alone. I stood there, trying to collect my thoughts. The idea of Gunny being lost to me was horrible. I was a fraction of a second away from jumping in the flume and going after him, when I heard a familiar voice.

"What took you so long?"

I spun quickly to see a giant face. It was Aja Killian. The hologram-head was back. I looked up at the bizarre image and said, "You called. I'm here. Now what?"

The head vanished. A second later I heard a faint sound from across the room. I looked to see a door opening, by itself. Light spilled in from whatever lay beyond.

It was time to meet Aja Killian and get my first look at the territory of Veelox.

VEELOX

I found myself in a long, narrow tunnel that stretched far off in two directions. Light came from overhead bulbs, but it was pretty dim because every other bulb was burned out or smashed.

Slam!

The gate shut behind me. It was a plain, metal door that practically disappeared because it was the same gray color as the cement walls around it. The only thing that told me it was there was the star symbol that marked it as a gate. I hoped I wouldn't have to find it again in a hurry.

I saw that I was standing on tracks. Uh-oh. Another subway. My adrenaline spiked. Was I going to have to run from a speeding train? A closer look showed me there was no danger. Big chunks of the track were missing and a thin coat of brown rust covered the silver steel. There hadn't been a train through here in a very long time.

"Walk to your right," Aja's voice boomed from nowhere. "You'll find a ladder."

"Where are you?" I shouted. I was getting tired of all this mystery. "Why don't you just show yourself?"

"Find the ladder, Pendragon," Aja's voice commanded.

Fine. Whether I liked it or not, the mystery was going to continue. As I walked through the tunnel, I wondered if the people on Veelox were giants. If Aja's projection was life-size, then I was in for a whole *Gulliver's Travels* adventure. That wouldn't be fun.

I came to a metal ladder that disappeared up into a dark opening in the ceiling. I was about to climb up, when a thought hit me. I was still wearing the flannel shirt and jeans you loaned me on Second Earth, Mark. We weren't supposed to mix things from other territories, including clothes. But there hadn't been any Veelox clothes at the flume. What was I supposed to do? I actually had a quick thought that since I had only seen Aja's head, maybe the people on Veelox didn't wear clothes at all. How's *that* for an image? Big, floating, naked giants. Sheesh. No way I was taking my clothes off.

The ladder led up through a round shaft that wasn't much wider than my shoulders. A few more steps up the ladder and I hit the ceiling. I tested it with a push. It moved. This was it, my portal into Veelox. With a quick breath to calm myself, I pushed the heavy hatch up and climbed through to get my first look at this new territory.

I'm not sure what I expected to see, but this wasn't it.

First off, I was relieved. Since Saint Dane had said he had already done his dirty work here, I was nervous about finding a territory that was on fire, or laid waste, or had people running around screaming in panic. But there was none of that. What I did see was totally strange, if only because it wasn't strange at all.

Veelox looked like Second Earth. I found myself standing on a city street that could have been a neighborhood from home. The hatch I had just climbed through was a manhole in the street. The buildings were city-style brownstones. There were sidewalks and trees and even streetlights. If I didn't know any better I'd say I had pulled a U-turn in the flume and landed back on Second Earth.

Still, as familiar as this place was, something felt off. I looked around, trying to figure out why I was getting such a strange vibe. It took me all of three seconds to understand.

The place was deserted.

Not just empty, I'm talking desolate. No people, no cars, no music, no nothing. The only sound was the whisper of wind as it blew through the buildings and rustled the trees. It was totally eerie. The place was . . . dead. That was the word. Dead. Veelox was a ghost territory.

Great. Giant, naked, floating *ghosts*. Could this get any stranger?

"Over here!"

I spun to see a welcome sight. Standing on a street corner not far away was Aja Killian. The real deal. I was relieved to see she had a body to go with the head. Better still, she was normal size. Still better, she was wearing clothes. Phew.

I jogged over to her. Aja was shorter than I was, and I'm guessing a little bit older. She wore a dark blue jumpsuit that fit her pretty well. She was kinda cute, with big blue eyes behind those yellow-tinted glasses. The only thing non–Second Earth about her was a gizmo she had strapped to her right forearm. It was a wide, silver bracelet with lots of buttons that looked like a high-tech calculator.

And she was cute, too. Did I say that?

"Hi," I said, being all sorts of charming.

I held out my hand to shake. She didn't take it. Aja snapped angrily, "What took you so long to get here?"

Whoa. Where did *that* come from? I had been here for a

grand total of ten seconds and she was already giving me grief. Not a good start.

"What are you talking about?" I asked.

"I've been trying to contact you about Saint Dane, but you haven't been responding," she scolded. "I was ready to give up on you when—"

"Whoa. Hang on," I interrupted. "I didn't get your message because my ring was stolen. The second I got it back, your message came through and here I am."

She couldn't argue with the logic but still wanted to fight. So she changed her tack.

"How could you let your ring get stolen?" she demanded to know. "Do you know how important these rings are? If you're not—"

"*Stop!*" I yelled. "I got here as soon as I could. Let it go at that, all right?"

"Fine," Aja said, sounding snotty. "But everything's fine now, so you can flume off with that Gunny person and worry about some other territory. Good-bye." She turned and walked away.

My head was spinning. What just happened here? Was she blowing me off?

"Time out," I said while running after her. "Did you hear what Saint Dane said?"

"Of course. I have the flume monitored, remember? I know everything that happens down there."

"Good, then you know he said Veelox was ready to crumble."

"He was wrong," Aja said without looking at me.

"Explain, please."

Aja came to an abrupt stop and I nearly ran into her. "Technically he's right," she explained. "Veelox *is* ready to crumble. But it hasn't yet, and it won't. I made sure of that."

"So what was he up to?" I asked. "Is there some kind of battle going to happen? Are there armies going to march on one another? Who's fighting here?"

Aja shook her head like she pitied me for being totally pathetic. "No, Pendragon. There is no big war. There are no guns or bombs. Nothing is going to explode, which I'm sure is disappointing to you."

I let that comment slide. "So then what's the conflict? What's the turning point on Veelox?"

Aja stepped up to me and touched my forehead. "The turning point is in the head of every single person on Veelox. There are no good guys or bad guys here. This is a war that is being fought in people's minds, not on any battlefield."

"I have no idea what you're talking about," I admitted.

Aja smiled. I think she liked feeling superior.

"It doesn't matter. Everything is under control. I contacted you because that's what I was supposed to do, but you aren't needed here, Pendragon. Veelox is safe. Go away."

She turned and walked off again. I wanted to believe her. One less territory to worry about was, well, one less territory to worry about. But I couldn't just take her word for it. So I ran after her again.

"What do you mean, you were *supposed* to contact me?" I asked.

"Because you're the lead Traveler," she said, throwing me a look of disdain. "Hard to believe."

Yikes. New twist. Lead Traveler? Nobody told me that. "Uh . . . who said I was the lead Traveler?"

"Everyone," she answered.

"Everyone who?"

"The Traveler from Denduron, for one. Alder was his

name. Did you really blow up an entire castle?"

"Yes. Alder told you I was the lead Traveler?"

"I first heard it from Press Tilton. Now *that* guy I could see being the lead Traveler. Do you know him?"

"Yeah," I answered. "Press was my uncle. He's dead."

Aja stopped walking. It was kind of harsh to give her that news so abruptly, but at least I had gotten her to stop being annoying for a few seconds. "I . . . I'm sorry, Pendragon," she said with sincere sympathy. "I didn't know."

I didn't want to have to battle this crazy Traveler girl. So at the risk of getting insulted again, I decided to put it all on the table. "I'll be honest with you, Aja," I began. "Up until you just said it, I had no idea I was a lead Traveler. I don't even know what that means. But whether it's true or not, I'm not your enemy. So cut me a little slack, all right?"

I looked her in the eye, trying to will her into trusting me. I wasn't sure if Traveler mind persuasion worked on other Travelers, but I was willing to give it a try.

"Come with me," she finally said, and walked off.

Phew. That was a start. The two of us walked along the center line of the empty street. The block reminded me of those big movie sets I saw on the tour of Universal Studios. Everything looked normal, but totally without life.

"Where is everybody?" I asked tentatively.

"Most everyone is in Lifelight," she answered.

"Lie flight?"

"No, Lifelight."

"Sorry," I said. "I don't know what that means."

Aja stopped walking and touched her silver bracelet to my head. I felt a short, warm buzz, then she pulled it away.

"What was that?" I asked nervously.

Aja then pointed her hand, hit a few buttons, and said, "Look."

I looked to where she was pointing and saw something that made me want to laugh and cry at the same time. It was Marley, my golden retriever. She stood facing me, wagging her tail so hard her whole backside wiggled. She had a goofy grin on her face and wore the green collar I got her for Christmas two years before. This wasn't just any golden, this was *my* golden.

"Marley?" I called out tentatively.

Marley wagged her tail harder and ran to me. She was all set to jump and I was ready to catch her, but the second her front paws left the ground, she disappeared. Poof. Gone. All I caught was air. After a frozen moment, I looked to Aja and squeaked out a stunned, "How did you do that?"

"Lifelight," she answered. "It pulled that from your memory."

"Huh?" was all I could get out.

Aja smiled. She was back in charge again. "Veelox is the perfect territory, Pendragon, because we can live any existence we choose."

I was sinking deeper into the land of confusion. "Now I'm totally lost," I said.

"Imagine the perfect place," she continued. "It could be anywhere you want and populated with the people you choose. Like that dog. That's Lifelight. People here can live a life tailored specifically for them."

"So Lifelight sends people all over the territory and sets them up in whatever perfect life they want?" I asked.

"No," she answered. "I said people live any life they choose. They don't go anywhere."

"Still not getting it," I complained.

Aja motioned for me to follow her. She took a few more steps, rounded a corner and pointed to a sight that actually took my breath away. No kidding. For a second I couldn't breathe. That's how awesome it was.

Sitting in the center of the city, maybe a mile away from us, was a huge, four-sided pyramid. It dwarfed the buildings around it, looking as if a massive, alien spacecraft had set down in the center of town. The shiny black walls reflected the sun toward us, making the immense structure seem more like a shadow than a building.

"You're telling me everybody from this city is in that pyramid?"

"Not everybody. Most."

"Why?"

Aja shook her head like I was a lousy student, then walked to the side of the road. Parked near a lamppost was a strange, two-seater pedal car. The seats were side by side and it had three wheels, like a tricycle. Aja climbed on to the left seat and said, "I could tell you, or I could show you. Which would be easier?"

Man, this girl really thought I was a dimwit. But I didn't want to argue anymore, so I took the right seat. Aja kicked off and the two of us pedaled toward the monster pyramid.

"Is Lifelight some kind of virtual reality game?" I asked.

"It's no game," Aja scoffed.

"But it's all just holograms, right? Like my dog, and your big floating head."

"Don't pass judgment until you know what you're talking about."

Fair enough. I decided to see what Lifelight was about

before asking any more questions. The two of us rode in silence and I took the chance to check out more of this forlorn, deserted city. We passed grocery stores and clothing shops and office fronts. All very normal, but empty. Looking closer, I saw that the buildings were run down. Signs were turning yellow, garbage was collecting in corners, windows were thick with grit. It was like the people had just . . . walked away.

I saw lots of signs for something called "gloid." There was NEW GLOID and TASTE SENSATION GLOID and even GLOID PLUS. It was one of the few words that my Traveler brain didn't translate into English, so I assumed it was something unique to Veelox. Another unique word I kept seeing was "Rubic." Street signs pointed to RUBIC CENTRAL. Stores used the word too, as in RUBIC LAUNDRY. I even saw a sign that said: BEST GLOID IN RUBIC. That one put me over the edge. I had to ask.

"What is Rubic?"

"That's the name of the city," she said. "Rubic City."

"And what's gloid?"

"That one I'll have to show you," she answered.

As much as this place looked like Second Earth, these subtle differences reminded me that I was nowhere near Second Earth. That's when I remembered something else.

"My clothes!" I blurted out. "I need Veelox clothes."

Aja looked me over. "Nobody will notice," she said calmly.

If she wasn't worrying, then maybe I shouldn't either. Besides, there were more important things to worry about. Looming up before us was the Lifelight pyramid. Man, it was massive! I'm guessing that it had to be fifty stories high. The shiny black surface made it seem even more imposing because it was such a contrast to the lighter-colored buildings that surrounded it.

"I'm off duty, so I can give you a tour," she said.

"You work here?"

"Yes, I'm a phader."

"Huh?"

"Don't think too hard. I'll show you what that means."

I was beyond caring about Aja's intellectual digs. I was way more interested in this strange pyramid. We headed toward a revolving door that looked tiny at the base of this massive building. As we rode closer I finally saw some of the other people of Veelox. They were walking around the pyramid, wearing coveralls like Aja's. Some were blue, others were red. That was it. Blue and red. Not a whole lot of fashion going on here.

"The people in red are vedders," she explained. "No way I'd want their job."

"What do they do?" I asked.

"You'll see."

Aja guided our bike right up to the revolving door and hopped off. "Open your mind, Pendragon. Don't judge until you've experienced it."

"Experienced what?"

"Lifelight, of course. I'm going to take you on the most amazing trip you could possibly imagine." With that, she turned and entered the pyramid.

I had been on plenty of amazing trips lately. She would have to go a long way to top any of them. To be honest, I wasn't so sure I wanted her to try. But there was one thing I was dead sure of: If I wanted to figure out what Saint Dane had been up to on Veelox, the answer would be inside this pyramid.

So with one last quick glance around at the world outside, I stepped into the dark pyramid and a world called "Lifelight."

VEELOX

Forget everything I said about Veelox being like Second Earth.

Stepping into that pyramid was like entering a different world. Inside the revolving door we walked through a narrow tunnel that was lit by long tubes of purple neon light. As soon as we stepped inside, the hair stood up on my arms. It was like the room was charged with electricity.

"Sterilization," Aja explained.

Sterilization? That sounded like something the veterinarian did to your dog when you didn't want it to have puppies. Gulp.

"It's totally safe," she assured me. "The process kills any foreign microbes that might foul the grid."

"Sure, wouldn't want to foul the grid." Whatever *that* meant.

At the end of the corridor, we walked our newly sterilized selves through another revolving door that led to a quiet, dimly lit room. There was a long counter, behind which were four people wearing red coveralls. "Vedders" is what Aja called them. She led me up to a guy I guessed to be about my age. He had coal black hair parted in the middle that went right down to his shoulders. There was definitely a Goth vibe going on, but I doubted they called it that on Veelox.

"Hello," the vedder said to Aja flatly.

"This is my friend's first time; I wanted to walk him through."

The vedder snapped a look at me like I had two heads. "You've never jumped before?"

"Uh . . . not that I can remember," I said, then held out my hand to shake. "My name's Pendragon."

The Goth vedder stared at me blankly. He didn't care what my name was. He didn't shake my hand, either. Creep.

"Yes, well, welcome to Lifelight," he said, sounding totally bored. He reminded me of somebody who had worked at McDonald's selling burgers for too long. He finally reached out to take my hand, but rather than shaking it, he flipped it over and jabbed a tiny needle into my pinkie.

"Ow!" I quickly pulled back and sucked on my stinging finger. "What was that for?"

"You need a bio workup," Aja explained.

I had already been sterilized, dissed, and stabbed. So far there wasn't much to like about Lifelight. The vedder put the needle into a computer-looking thing that I assumed was doing the bio-whatever analysis on the blood he had just stolen from me. While we waited for him to finish, I glanced around the room. It reminded me of the ticket counter at an airport. It was all very modern. There were no signs, but on the wall behind the counter was a big oil portrait of a kid. He looked to be about ten years old, with short, blond hair and a blue jumpsuit like Aja's. He was a serious-looking little dude, too. He seemed to be staring right at me.

"Who's that?" I asked.

that there were around two hundred of these high-tech rigs.

There was one phader in each, wearing the signature blue jumpsuit and sitting in the coolest looking chair I had ever seen. It was black, with a high back, and wings near the head that spread out to either side. The arms of the chair were wide, with a silver control panel on each side where the phader could touch the myriad of buttons that worked . . . whatever.

In front of each phader was a wall of computer screens. A quick count told me that each phader was looking at around thirty screens. Here's the strange part (as if everything up until now *wasn't* strange): Each of the computer monitors was showing a different movie. Multiply the thirty movies playing in each cubicle by two hundred cubicles and that's like six thousand movies, all playing at the same time. I figured this might be some kind of satellite TV operation that beamed shows all over Veelox.

I couldn't have been more wrong.

"This is where I work," Aja explained. "It's called the 'core.' The phaders troubleshoot the hardware, upgrade when necessary, and monitor the jumps to make sure everyone is okay."

"And what do the vedders do?"

"They take care of the jumpers physically. That's why they took your blood. They make sure the jumpers are safe and healthy."

"What are the movies they're watching?" I asked.

"Those are the *jumps*," Aja answered, trying not to sound too impatient.

I looked through the glass at one of the banks of monitors and saw that the action on the screens wasn't continuous. Every few seconds each screen changed to another bit of action, like turning the channels on a TV. I focused on one

The vedder shot me a look as if I had suddenly s[p]
a third head to go with my other two.

"You're funny," Aja said, covering for me. She then
at the vedder and said, "He's always making dumb jok[es]

The vedder wasn't laughing. "Give me your hand, [p]

"Not if you're gonna poke me again," I protested.

Goth boy gave Aja an impatient look.

"Hold up your hand, Pendragon," she commanded.

Reluctantly I held up my hand again, prepared fo[r]
pain. But the vedder quickly snapped a silver bracelet a[round]
my wrist. It looked more like a high-tech device than je[welry.]
It was smaller than Aja's, about two inches wide, with
square buttons that were flush to the surface.

"Enjoy your jump," the vedder said, though I was b[etting]
he didn't care one way or the other.

I smiled at the guy anyway, then followed Aja tow[ard a]
door at the far end of the room. "Who was the kid in the [pic-]
ture?" I whispered.

"Dr. Zetlin, the person who invented Lifelight."

"A kid invented all of this?" I asked, unbelieving.

"A very smart kid," was her answer.

"Yeah, no kidding."

Aja then pushed open a door, and we continued in [a]
long corridor that can be best described as mission control
times about a thousand. The walls were made of glass. Thro[ugh]
them I saw a series of high-tech workstations that looked [like]
they each had enough electronic muscle to launch about a [mil-]
lion space shuttles. Each station was its own separate, enclo[sed]
cubicle. I guessed that there were around fifty of these wo[rk]
stations on either side of the corridor. Then there was a wh[ole]
nother row of workstations above them. So a rough guess v[as]

screen to see a hot sailboat gliding through tropical waters. The image then changed to the point of view of a skier flying down a snowy mountain, expertly dodging through trees. On the screen next to that I saw what looked like a stadium full of people watching a game that was like soccer, but played with a big orange ball the size of a monster pumpkin. That screen then changed to the quiet scene of a cozy fireplace and an older woman drinking tea.

"People come here to watch movies?" I asked.

Aja chuckled. "Something like that. Come on."

She led me down the long corridor of cubicles. I glanced into the different workstations that made up the core to get an idea of what kind of movie I'd choose when it came my turn. I figured I'd want to watch a movie about basketball. I hadn't played in a long time and missed it. I hoped they knew what basketball was on Veelox.

When we reached the end of the corridor, Aja said, "Are you ready for this?"

"Uh, yeah. I guess." I had no idea if I was ready or not because I didn't know what to expect.

Aja shook her head again, amused by my innocence . . . or stupidity. We pushed through the next revolving door, and what I saw beyond proved only one thing . . .

I wasn't ready for it.

We stepped into the central chamber of the pyramid. Everything up to this point had been pregame. This was the main event. I took a step inside, looked up, and my knees buckled from seeing the sheer size of the place. The pyramid was pretty much hollow so I could see all the way up to the point. In the center of the structure was a tube that ran from the floor right up to the uppermost tip. Off this central tube were hundreds of walkways that spread out like spokes of a wheel in different directions and levels. They attached to the inside walls of the pyramid, which had hundreds of levels, with walkways ringing all the way around.

Aja didn't say anything at first. I guess she wanted me to get my mind around it all. She shouldn't have bothered. There was no way I could get my mind around any of this.

"You asked me before where everybody was," she finally said. She then pointed up to the walls of the pyramid.

"You're telling me everybody from Veelox is up there, right now?"

"No," she said. "But most everybody from Rubic City is. There are at least eight hundred more of these Lifelight pyramids all over Veelox."

The idea was staggering. "So, everybody's in here watching movies?" I asked.

Aja lifted her arm to look at her wide, silver bracelet. She touched a few buttons while staring intently at the high-tech device.

"What are you doing?" I asked.

"Looking for a vacant station," she answered, and started walking. Like an obedient puppy, I followed. She led me to the center of the pyramid, which was not a short walk. Along the way we passed several phaders and vedders who were ferrying equipment or supplies of some sort. Nobody said much to anyone else. To me, they all seemed a little depressed. Maybe not as bad as the miners of Denduron, but these guys weren't exactly whistling while they worked, either. We got into an elevator and quickly rose up the central tube.

When Aja stopped and opened the door, my palms instantly went wet. We were seriously high up in the air. Worse, the guardrails on the walkways were only about knee-high. Aja stepped out. I didn't.

"It's safe, Pendragon," she said. "Look straight ahead and follow me." She walked out on one of the bridges that led to the far wall of the pyramid. "Don't look down."

Yeah, right. That's the first thing I did. Yikes. We were about halfway up the pyramid, but that was plenty high. It felt like I was standing on a rickety Lego structure. I could only hope these walkways were sturdier than they looked. I didn't want to be on that bridge any longer than I had to, so a few seconds later I caught right up with Aja and blew past her. I made it to the far end and the balcony that ran the length of one side of the pyramid.

Aja gave me a disapproving look. "Are you sure you're the lead Traveler?" she asked.

"No. Where are we going?"

Aja checked her high-tech bracelet once more, then walked along the balcony. I followed, hugging the wall to stay as far away from the edge as possible. There were doors every few feet. If you figured this was only one side of one level of the pyramid, there must have been hundreds of thousands of doors just like it. Each door had a small round, white light next to it. Most were lit. Aja stopped at a door marked 124-70. The light over the door was out so I guessed that meant nobody was home. Aja touched the door and it instantly slid back into the wall like we were about to step onto the bridge of the starship *Enterprise*.

The room inside was pretty bland. It reminded me of a doctor's exam room because it looked simple and sterile. There was no furniture or anything, just a round, silver disk on the back wall about three feet wide. Next to it on the wall was a square silver panel that looked like a bigger version of the control bracelet Aja wore. On the panel were several rows of flat, silver buttons, none of which were marked. Above the rows of buttons was a narrow black section that I guessed was some kind of computer screen that gave readouts of . . . whatever. Aja went right to this silver panel and began hitting buttons. The narrow computer screen flashed with green numbers.

"This pyramid is operating at about eighty-seven percent capacity," she explained.

She touched one button and, with a slight hum, the round silver disk slid sideways into the wall to reveal a circular tube that stretched back into the wall space for about seven feet. Another touch of a button and a white table slowly emerged from the tube.

"Lie down," Aja ordered.

Yeah, right. If she thought I was going to lie on that table and get sucked back into this sci-fi-looking tube without an explanation, she was dreaming.

"Tell me what's going to happen first."

"Don't you trust me?" she asked with a sly smile.

"It's not that I don't trust you," I said quickly. "It's just that this is all . . . I mean, I've never seen . . . I don't understand . . . uh, no, I don't trust you."

"Even though I'm a Traveler?"

"Look," I said. "I don't know why you have an ick against me, but if you want me to trust you, you gotta start acting a little more human."

It bugged me that Aja had such disdain for me. I had no idea why. Yeah, she was a Traveler, but I didn't see her out there fighting quigs or getting shot at or jumping out of airplanes or doing any of the scary things I'd had to do. What made her so special?

"Sorry," she said. "Lifelight is such a normal part of life that it's hard for me to understand how someone doesn't know all about it."

"Fine. Start explaining or I'm not lying down on that thing."

"It's totally safe," Aja began. "Nothing happens to you physically. It's all about expanding your mind into areas of your own choosing. You lie on the table, the table slides back into the tube and I close the round disk. To be honest, some people get a little nervous because it's dark and the space is closed. But the sensation doesn't last long. I promise."

"Then what do I do? Lie there and watch a movie?"

"You focus your thoughts. Think about a place you'd like to be. Or a person you'd want to see. That's all it takes."

"And it reads my mind? Like when my dog appeared?"

"Exactly."

It seemed impossible, but Marley sure as heck looked real. It may have been a holographic illusion, but it was a good one.

"What if something goes wrong? Like if I get claustrophobia or something?"

"You won't," she assured me. "But if it makes you feel better, the vedders and phaders monitor all the jumps from the core. If something goes wrong, they'll stop the event. Believe me, they know what they're doing."

I lifted my arm and touched the silver bracelet on my wrist with the three buttons. "What's this for?"

"It's your ultimate control over the jump. If you want to talk to your phader, push the left button. If you want to end the jump, push the right button."

"And the middle button?"

"That's for advanced jumpers. Don't push it."

Oh man, that was like saying: "Don't look down." Now all I wanted to do was push that middle button. "How long will I be in there?" I asked.

"I'm going to time your jump to last only a few minutes.

The point is to show you what Lifelight is all about. After that, I'll be able to explain why Saint Dane doesn't pose a threat to Veelox."

We had come full circle. That's exactly why I was here. This was all about figuring out what the turning point of Veelox was, and how Saint Dane had tipped the territory toward chaos. I was beginning to understand why Aja wanted me to see this for myself. Hopefully after I completed my jump, or whatever they called it, I would be up to speed and could focus on the main problem. Saint Dane.

"Now lie down," Aja instructed. "Feet first."

With a shrug, I laid down on the table. It was soft and molded to my body. Very comfy. I guess it would have to be if people were lying down for long periods of time.

"Try to relax," Aja said in a surprisingly soothing voice. "Fold your arms over your chest. I'm going to retract the table and slide you inside. Be sure to breathe. If it helps, close your eyes. Then I'm going to close the front panel and the tube will go completely dark. It's okay. That's supposed to happen. Your job is to focus your thoughts."

My heart rate started to climb. Should I trust this girl? Or was she sending me into some high-tech atom smasher that would pulverize me into pocket lint? But she was a Traveler. I had to believe she knew what she was doing.

"Ready?" she asked.

"Yes," I lied.

With a slight shift and a soft hum, the table began retracting into the tube, bringing me along with it. Gulp. I wanted to yell: "Time out!" but that would only prolong the torture. I had to suck it up. A few seconds later I looked up and saw the top of the tube pass by my face as I slid inside. I didn't close my eyes. Maybe I should have, but I wanted to see what was happening. I lay there in this tight, round tunnel, staring up at the top, which was only a few inches above my nose. I never had a problem with claustrophobia, but if there ever was a time to get it, it was now.

"You okay?" Aja asked.

"Fine," I lied again. I had one question. It wasn't sophisticated. It wasn't smart and maybe it proved I was a weenie. But I had to ask it. "Aja?" I asked, trying not to let my voice quiver. "Is this going to hurt?"

Aja leaned down until she was just behind my head. When she spoke, it was the first time I sensed that there was actually a human being with feelings behind those yellow-tinted glasses.

"Pendragon," she said, "it's going to be the most fun you've ever had."

With that, the round panel hummed and began to close behind me. Seconds later the last of the light from the chamber room was cut off and I was in total darkness.

☉ SECOND EARTH ☉

It was an act that required a huge amount of willpower.

Mark reached down to the floor and touched the black button on the small silver projector. Instantly Bobby's hologram disappeared. It killed Mark to stop it, especially at such a crucial moment. Bobby's image was about to reveal the mystery of Lifelight. But that's exactly why he had to stop it.

Courtney wasn't there.

Mark felt like he had already cheated on their pact by watching so much of the journal without her. But the hologram thing was so incredible, Mark couldn't wait. In fact, he had been so captivated by the 3-D image that it took a while before he even realized what he was doing. Rule #1 was that they would always read Bobby's journals together. He had just broken it. Sort of. He would have to explain to Courtney how he was so surprised by Bobby's image that it took him a while to get his head back together. He didn't deliberately choose to watch the journal without her. It just happened. She would understand.

No, she won't. She's going to be totally ticked off, Mark thought.

He started getting sweaty. He had betrayed Courtney's trust once before by not telling her that Andy Mitchell found out about the journals. Now he had done it again. Courtney was going to be mad and Mark knew she had every right to be.

He took the small, silver projection device and put it in his bedside drawer. He then crawled back into bed and tried to relax. He had trouble getting to sleep before the journal arrived. Now it was impossible. He was dying to know what happened to Bobby in Lifelight. The answers were in the drawer only inches from his head. Talk about torture!

In his mind he replayed all that Bobby had recorded. It was an incredible device. Not only did it look as if Bobby were standing in the room talking right to him, Bobby was able to act out the events he was describing. He played the different parts, changing his voice to mimic the different characters and using hand gestures for emphasis. Bobby knew how to tell a story, too. His written journals were great, but seeing him tell the story aloud was awesome. Mark couldn't wait to hear more.

He ended up staring at the ceiling for the rest of the night.

When morning finally came, Mark tucked the silver device safely into a small zipper pocket of his backpack and took it to school. His hope was that as soon as Courtney saw it, her curiosity would overpower her anger. Neither of them shared any classes, so Mark didn't see her all day. The best thing he could do was meet her after soccer practice again. He hoped she would have a better practice than the day before. He didn't want her in an ugly mood.

Mark's second day of high school wasn't as painful as the first. That was because he mostly kept to himself. It wasn't hard. His body may have been at Davis Gregory High, but his mind was on Veelox. The day went by without any major incident, until the end of last period. He barely listened to his chemistry teacher because he was spending so much time staring at the clock, willing the hands to move faster. The instant the final bell rang, he quickly packed up and was the first one out the door.

"Excuse me? Mark Dimond?"

Mark spun around and saw a teacher calling to him from down the hall. His name was Mr. Pike, the physics teacher. Everybody knew who he was because he was one of the younger, cool teachers. His hair was kind of long and he wore jeans and a cotton sweater. To Mark he looked more like an artist than a science teacher.

"Yeah?" Mark answered tentatively.

"I've been looking forward to meeting you," the teacher said, holding out his hand to shake. "My name's David Pike. I teach physics."

"Y-Yeah, I know who y-you are." Mark wasn't used to grownups introducing themselves by their first names. Especially not teachers.

"How do you like Davis Gregory so far?" Mr. Pike asked.

"Uh . . . fine, I guess." Mark didn't understand where this was going. "You were looking forward to meeting *me*? Mark Dimond?"

"Absolutely." Mr. Pike laughed. "I saw your battling robot at the county science fair. I was impressed, but when it took the state prize, I knew I had a star coming to school."

Mark had built a battling robot as a science project that literally destroyed the competition. It had a hook that trapped its prey, a shovel that flipped its victim over, and then a buzzsaw that went in for the kill. Mark never lost. He had thoughts about going on one of those TV shows to test his baby against the big boys, but after the state prize he decided it was better to go out on top, and intact. So he retired his killer robot and forgot all about it. Until now.

"Your design was light-years ahead of the other students," Pike continued. "I was thrilled when I heard you were coming to Davis Gregory."

Mark wasn't used to getting compliments. "It wasn't all that hard," he said with his eyes down.

"You're being modest," Pike said. "Have you thought about joining Sci-Clops?"

Mark couldn't believe it. Sci-Clops was a science club that was made up of the brainiest students at school. It was legendary. At least with the science-geek crowd. Having Sci-Clops on your record was an incredible plus if you wanted to go to a top engineering school after high school. There were even a few former Sci-Clops students who got into MIT.

"Are y-you serious?" Mark asked. "You mean, *the* Sci-Clops?"

Pike laughed. "Sure, how many are there?"

Mark's face turned red with embarrassment. Pike put a reassuring hand on his shoulder. "Think about it," he said. "We'd love to have you."

Mr. Pike left Mark standing there speechless. It took a while for him to put his brain back into gear and say, "Y-Yeah. Sure I'll join!"

But it was too late. Pike was already gone.

Mark was stunned. It wasn't just because he had been given the chance to join a club that he never considered himself good enough for, it was more that somebody had actually recognized him for having done something well. As he stood in that hallway, he sensed an alien feeling growing inside. It was pride. He still wasn't sure if he was good enough to join Sci-Clops. Confidence was still something he had to work on. But it made him feel great that at least one person, besides his mother, thought he had something special going on. Mark's second day of high school was definitely turning out better than the first.

Except he still had to face Courtney. The thought made his stomach turn, so instead of going directly to the practice field, he ran after Mr. Pike.

Courtney, on the other hand, was *not* having a great day. She had tried to shake off the horrible practice of the day before and arrived at school ready to regain her rightful place as the girl who set the standards by which everyone else was judged.

She failed.

Word had spread how Courtney the Unbeatable had suddenly become Courtney the Diminished. Friends gave her sympathy and wanted to know what went wrong. Girls and guys she had intimidated for years wanted to know if it was true. Had Courtney lost it? Some kids were devastated at the thought that their hero could have feet of clay. Others simply wouldn't believe it. Many quietly enjoyed seeing someone so mighty get knocked down a few pegs.

Courtney did her best not to show how upset she was. People always envied her. Now that envy had turned to pity. That was the worst. As the day wore on, she kept smiling and telling people she was fine and simply had an off day. But inside, the fire was burning. She couldn't wait for the end of school so she could blast onto that soccer field and put some serious hurt on the nonbelievers.

A crowd had gathered around the field. More kids showed up for this practice than Courtney had heard showed up to watch the games. She was used to having an audience when she performed, but not like this. They were there to bear witness. They wanted proof that all was right with the world, or that it was the end of an era.

From the moment she stepped onto the field, Courtney played angry. It was the worst thing she could have done. It meant she tried too hard and allowed the other girls to hang her out to dry. They dribbled around her; they wouldn't pass to her; they stole the ball from her. During sprints, they left her in the dust.

Courtney looked really bad. The harder she tried, the worse it got. Her confidence was shattered. As she ran down the sidelines she'd see the faces of kids she had dominated in years past. Some looked disappointed. Others stunned. Still others had smug smiles that said: "Payback is sweet." She tried not to look into anyone's eyes, friend or foe. They all hurt the same.

The crowd didn't hang around long. They saw all they needed early on. The rest was like staring at a car wreck long after the dust settled. But the worst indignity was yet to come. When practice was mercifully over, Courtney ran toward the school locker room.

"Courtney! Hang on!" It was the coach, Ms. Horkey. She jogged up to Courtney and the two walked toward the school together. "Tough day," Ms. Horkey said with sympathy.

Courtney could only shrug.

"Look," Horkey said. "I know this is hard for you. I've watched you play since you were barely old enough to kick a ball. I know how good you are. Don't get discouraged."

"I won't," Courtney said, feeling totally discouraged.

Then Horkey dropped the bomb. "I think it would do you a world of good to start playing with the junior varsity team."

Courtney stopped short. "You're cutting me?" she said, barely able to say the words.

"No," Horkey assured her. "But you need to work on fundamentals. It's not a horrible thing. It's rare for a sophomore to be on varsity anyway."

"There are two other sophomores on varsity," Courtney pointed out. "Look, Ms. Horkey. I just had a slow start."

"I know. But look at the big picture. You're not up to the level of the varsity players. If you stayed here, you'd be working to keep up, rather than getting better. On the JV level you'll be more competitive. Then next year you can—"

"Next year! I'd have to wait a whole year to get back on the team?"

"You're still on the team, Courtney. You're just playing at a level that's better for you."

"On the loser level, you mean," Courtney snapped at her.

"No," the coach corrected. "On the level that is going to help you improve. You're not a quitter, Courtney. You're going to get better, but you're going to have to work at it. Maybe you're not used to that."

Courtney wanted to scream. But the truth was, the coach was right. Courtney had never had to work all that hard to be good. Maybe she didn't know how to.

"It's really for the best," Horkey concluded.

"Yeah, sure," Courtney said under her breath. Horkey then jogged ahead toward the school.

Courtney wanted to run home. She didn't want to go into that locker room and get changed with all those girls who looked at her like a loser. She wasn't a loser. But at that moment, she sure felt like one.

"Courtney!" Mark yelled as he ran up to her. "The most amazing thing happened! I got asked to join Sci-Clops!"

"Cyclops? Like the monster with one eye?"

"No," Mark laughed. "Sci-Clops with an s-c-i like in science. It's only the most respected science club in the state. Is that incredible or what?"

"Yeah, that's great, Mark," Courtney said, not sounding as if she meant it. She continued walking toward the school.

"Uh-oh. Bad practice again?"

"I just got cut."

"What!"

"Not really. I've been demoted to JV."

Mark didn't know what to say. This was alien territory. He wasn't used to boosting Courtney's confidence.

"You know you're better than that," Mark said sincerely.

"Am I?" she said softly.

Courtney had never admitted defeat before. Mark glanced around quickly to make sure he was the only one who heard it. "Don't say that," he chastised. "You just had a slow start." Then a thought hit him and he added, "Besides, I've got more good news."

He waited for her to react. A few moments went by, then Courtney looked at him and actually smiled.

"Are you serious?" she asked cautiously.

"It showed up last night," Mark answered with a big smile. "I've got a confession to make, though. I think you'll understand why it happened when you see the journal, but I already saw the beginning part."

Courtney stopped walking and stared at Mark. Mark didn't let the moment hang. He had to explain himself, fast.

"I didn't mean to, but it's not a regular journal. It's a hologram."

"Say what?"

"Bobby recorded the journal like a 3-D movie. I was so surprised that I didn't turn it off right away. But I only heard the beginning. I stopped it before he got to anything really important. I didn't want to hear it without you."

That was the truth, mostly. Mark could only hope that Courtney would understand. A long moment went by. Mark wasn't sure if Courtney was going to forgive him or kick him in the head.

After an eternity, Courtney said, "It's cool. I get it. Can you come over tonight?"

"Right after dinner," he said, totally relieved.

Courtney then continued on, jogging into the school. Mark

nearly leaped into the air. This was an incredible day. Sci-Clops, then Courtney's forgiveness. As he jogged around the school building to catch the late bus, Mark was elated. Things were turning out perfectly.

But still, he felt a little strange. He wasn't used to taking the upper hand when it came to Courtney. He thought she would have at least made him feel a little guilty for what he had done. But she forgave him and let it go at that. It was like they had reached a new level in their friendship.

Mark wasn't entirely sure he liked it.

A few hours later Mark and Courtney sat together on the big, dusty old couch in Courtney's basement. They usually read Bobby's journals there because it was a workshop full of rusty tools that Courtney's father never used. She called it the "Tool Museum." It was a perfectly private place for them to read and discuss the journals. Being private was even more important this time, because they weren't going to be reading, they would be listening and watching.

"How does it work?" Courtney asked. She was all showered and feeling a little bit better. Time and a good dinner will do that. A new journal from Bobby didn't hurt either.

Mark was in the same clothes he wore at school. He hadn't eaten dinner. He was too excited. He reached into his pack and took out the small, silver device that contained Bobby's journal.

"It's like a CD player," Mark explained. "I'll rewind to the beginning." He touched the orange button. There was no sound or feeling of movement.

"How much did you see?" Courtney asked.

"Just a little," Mark fibbed. He figured since they would both see it from the beginning, he could get away with stretching the truth.

"Is he okay?" Courtney asked.

"Seems so," Mark answered. "But you can see for yourself." Mark put the silver device down on the table in front of the couch and pressed the green button. Instantly the beam of light shot out and projected Bobby's life-size image in space.

"Hiya, Mark. Hey, Courtney," Bobby's image began.

"Wow!" shouted Courtney. "It's like the hologram with the floating head."

Mark let out a relieved breath. Up until that moment he wasn't sure if the device had actually rewound all the way. Now he was totally off the hook with Courtney. He didn't mind that he was going to have to rehear Bobby's story from the beginning. All that mattered was that they were under way.

Together this time.

And they were about to learn about Lifelight.

VEELOX

"Bobby! It's getting-up time!" came a familiar, singsong voice.

I was still asleep. It was one of those perfect moments when no matter what position you roll into, it's more comfortable than the last. No, I didn't care what time it was, I was staying in bed.

"Big day today!" came the pleasant voice again.

I was too comfortable to care. I rolled over, determined to continue the bliss. But then I felt a huge weight land on me. I knew what was coming next. Any chance of staying in bed would soon dissolve because . . .

A slippery, sandy tongue started burrowing into my ear. I don't know what was so tasty about my ear, but it was the spot that Marley would lick when she wanted me to get up.

"All right, all right!" I laughed and pushed my golden retriever away. I think she liked the whole ear-licking-while-I-was-trying-to-sleep thing because it was one of the few times she had complete control over me. That, and of course when I walked her and had to pick up her poop. She pretty much called the shots then, too.

A second later another weight landed on the bed. I knew

what this was too. It was my little sister, Shannon.

"Breakfast is ready," she informed me. "You have to eat or you won't be strong enough to play."

Shannon thought she pretty much knew everything about everything, and for an eight-year-old she wasn't far from wrong. She was cute, too, with long dark brown hair that she always tied into two ponytails. She had these big brown eyes and a broad smile that lit up the room. People always told Mom that Shannon should be a model, but Mom wasn't hot on the idea. I think she was afraid Shannon was already growing up too fast.

"Eat soon so you can digest," she continued. "I don't want to see you barfing on the court." With that last little nugget of wisdom, she jumped off the bed and ran out of my bedroom. Marley bounded off the bed and scampered after her.

The smell of bacon found my nose. That was the last bit of convincing I needed. I loved bacon and we didn't get it that often because Mom thought it was too fatty or something. But every so often when there was a special occasion, she would give in. I guess today's basketball game counted as a big occasion. Fine with me. I threw my legs over the bed and stood up, now fully awake. I was wearing boxers, but pulled on a pair of sweats because sitting at the breakfast table in my underwear wasn't cool. I then picked a T-shirt off the floor, sniffed it to make sure it wasn't rank, and pulled it over my head. It was going to be a good day. Big breakfast, basketball game, maybe Courtney would come to watch and . . .

What the hell?

Reality struck. My knees went weak and I actually fell back down onto the bed. What was happening? I looked around my bedroom and it looked as familiar as always. My desk, my computer, my trophies, my stack of CDs, my New York Jets posters, even my clothes strewn on the floor. This was my bedroom. At home. In Stony Brook.

On . . . Second . . . Freakin' . . . Earth!

Nothing was out of the ordinary but *everything* was out of the ordinary. How could this be happening? I started to hyperventilate. Nothing made sense, even though it made perfect sense. Could everything that had happened since the night I left home with Uncle Press have been a dream? Denduron, Cloral, the *Hindenburg,* Saint Dane . . . everything. Had it all been a nightmare? I glanced at my window, half expecting Professor Marvel from *The Wizard of Oz* to poke his head in to see if I was okay.

"C'mon, Bobby, breakfast is getting cold!" came a voice from outside my room. It was my father. What was happening? I had faced a lot of scary situations since I became a Traveler, but on the strange scale, this was at the top. It took every ounce of courage I had to get my legs moving. I had to find out what was going on.

I cautiously left my room. The upstairs hallway had all the same pictures, the same rug, the same doors, the same everything. I half walked, half floated down the stairs, through the living room, past the dining room and straight into the kitchen. When I poked my head in, I saw a scene that was totally normal and totally impossible at the same time.

The table was set for breakfast. Mom was scooping scrambled eggs from a pan; Dad was sitting in his normal spot, pouring orange juice for everyone; Shannon sat at her place, politely waiting for everyone to sit so she could begin; and Marley sat on the floor at Shannon's side, waiting with equal patience for somebody to drop food on the floor.

I stood in the doorway, staring. Part of me wanted to dive into that kitchen, throw my arms around everybody and cry like a baby. Another part of me wanted to turn and run.

Finally Mom saw me and said, "Eat. You can't be late."

I didn't know what else to do, so I drifted over to the table and sat down at my place. It was the place by the window where I had eaten since I was old enough to sit up. It was the place I never thought I'd take again, since my house and family and everything I had ever known had disappeared.

But now they were back.

I must have looked as stunned as I felt, because my father said, "You all right, Bobby?"

I wasn't sure how to answer him, because I wasn't. "To be honest, Dad, I'm a little confused."

"About what, sweetheart?" Mom asked innocently.

I chose my words carefully, knowing just how ridiculous they would sound. "Has anything . . . odd happened?"

Dad asked, "Like what?"

Shannon chimed in. "We're having bacon for breakfast. That's odd."

"What are you talking about?" Mom asked while taking her place at the table. I sat looking at my family. The three of them looked back at me over their plates of bacon and eggs, waiting for me to say something. Marley poked her brown rubbery nose up from below the table and looked at me too, though I think she was more interested in sniffing out the bacon. I didn't say anything. Instead, I picked up a piece of bacon and took a bite. It was as delicious as any bacon I'd ever had. Done just the way I liked it too. Not too crispy. I didn't know why that surprised me, but it did.

Finally I dropped the bacon on my plate and stood up. "I . . . I'm not hungry. I better get dressed." I left the table, headed for the door to the dining room.

"But you have to eat something before the game!" Mom called after me.

"I'll get something later," I yelled back.

I was going mental. If my parents had said: "Well, Bobby, you were in a coma for the last year and a half," I would have understood. That would have meant that everything about the territories had been a dream. But they didn't. They acted as if nothing out of the ordinary had happened at all.

There was only one possible explanation. It must have been a dream. A really long, detailed, incredible dream that happened all in one night. Isn't that how it worked with Scrooge from *A Christmas Carol*? I read somewhere that dreams may seem long, but they really only last a few seconds. I figured that must have been what happened to me. As I walked back toward the stairs, I began to accept that possibility. A few moments crept by where I actually started to relax. I was home. The nightmare was over. Everything was going to be normal.

That warm, fuzzy feeling didn't last long.

I walked by a mirror and saw my reflection. What I saw wasn't the image of the guy who had kissed Courtney, then got on the back of Uncle Press's motorcycle bound for the flume. No way. This guy was older. About a year and a half older, to be exact. Everything in this house was the exact same as I remembered it . . . except for me. In that instant, my dream theory came crashing down. There was no way I could have slept for one night and dreamed up the whole adventure, because I wasn't the same guy anymore. No, the answer wasn't as simple as that.

It was then that a single word came to my mind. I didn't know what it meant at first, but it definitely felt like it was the key to unlocking this mystery.

The word was . . . Lifelight.

No sooner did I remember that word, than I felt something on my wrist. I looked down and saw I was wearing a wide, silver bracelet with three buttons. It surprised me at first because it wasn't there a second ago. But still, it seemed familiar. What was I told? If I needed to talk with someone, push the left button. Well, I couldn't imagine a bigger need to speak with someone than right now, so I pressed the button on the far left. The button glowed white for a moment and gave off a soft, quick hum.

"Not bad, Pendragon," came a voice from the top of the stairs. "You put it together faster than most."

I spun around and looked up the stairs to see someone sitting on the top step. It was the one thing that was out of place in this house. Besides me, that is. She was a pretty girl with a blond ponytail, blue eyes, and yellow-tinted glasses. I stared at her for a few seconds, confused. It was like having an answer on the tip of your tongue, but you couldn't quite get it out.

"Breathe, Pendragon," she said. "It'll come back."

"Aja . . . ," I said.

Aja smiled and clapped. "Very good. There's always a little disorientation at first, especially if you've never jumped before."

I looked around the house. My house. It seemed so real, but it wasn't. It was an illusion. An incredible, wonderful, heart-wrenching illusion. It was all coming back. I wasn't home. I was lying in a dark tube in a giant pyramid on the territory of Veelox, and this was all happening in my head.

"I know what you're thinking," Aja said. "You've seen a little of what Lifelight can do and you're pretty impressed." She walked down the stairs and came right up to me. "But you've just had a taste. The only limits to Lifelight are the limits you put on it yourself." She touched her finger to my forehead. "It's all up there, waiting to come out."

"There's more?" I asked.

Aja laughed. "Pendragon, you're just getting started."

VEELOX

I walked around my living room in a daze. Or should I say, I walked around the *illusion* of my living room. The dazed part was real, though. No illusion there. I ran my hand along the back of my couch and felt the soft, cotton fabric. I turned the switch on a table lamp, and the light came on. I picked up a frame that held a picture of me holding a newborn Shannon the day she came home from the hospital. Everything looked and felt totally normal, and *real*.

"You shouldn't be surprised," Aja said. "Everything is going to be right because it's coming out of your head."

"But I can *feel* things," I said. "And I tasted bacon. How is that possible?"

"You know how it should taste, so that's what it tasted like. Simple as that."

Simple as that? Who was she kidding? This was the furthest thing from simple I could imagine. I had about ten miles of questions. "What if I hurt myself?" I asked, my mind racing with possibilities. "Do I really get injured?"

"No. You'll feel the pain if you get injured, and you'll stay that way until the jump is complete, but you're not really here.

You're in the Lifelight pyramid. Nothing physical happens to you; it's all in your head."

"So I can't, like, die or anything?"

"If you die, the jump is over."

I looked at the silver wrist bracelet that had magically appeared when I began to remember Lifelight.

"Why didn't I see this at first?" I asked, holding my arm up.

"The goal of jumping is to completely immerse yourself in the experience," she answered. "Having that control band on your wrist would be a constant reminder that none of this is real. You'll only see it when you need to."

"Really? It's like my mind tells the band when to appear?"

"Exactly. Your mind controls everything."

"So I could, like, wish for a pizza to appear? Or for a swimming pool to be in the garage? Or for a spaceship to land on the front lawn and take me to Mars?"

Aja laughed. That was a surprise. For a change she didn't sound annoyed. I think she liked showing off what Lifelight could do. "Sure, but only if those kinds of things would normally happen. Lifelight was designed to create a perfect experience. A *realistic* experience. You can't suddenly sprout wings and fly away. Your mind wouldn't let you because you know that can't really happen. You're governed by the rules of reality. But the thing is, it's a *perfect* reality."

She reached over to me and lightly touched the middle button on my wrist controller. *Dingdong*. The front doorbell rang. Mom hurried out of the kitchen to get it.

"You expecting somebody?" she asked me on her way to the door.

I shrugged. I was expecting nothing . . . and anything. When she opened the door, I saw that standing outside was a pizza delivery guy from Domino's Pizza.

"Large pepperoni, extra cheese," the guy announced.

Mom gave me a look. "No wonder you didn't want breakfast." She paid the guy and took the pizza. "Do you have any idea how disgusting it is to eat this so early in the morning?"

"Uh, yeah," I answered, dumbfounded.

Mom then smiled and said, "Fine, you can have this because it's game day, but do not give any to Shannon or Marley, or your father. And eat it in the kitchen."

She disappeared back into the kitchen along with the pizza. She hadn't even said anything about Aja.

"Lifelight read my mind," I said to nobody in particular.

"That's what I've been telling you," Aja said.

"Why did you press the button? What did it do?"

"This starts getting a little advanced," she explained. "When you started the jump, I told you to think about a place you'd like to be. Lifelight read those thoughts and created this house and your family. That's the basic jump. That middle button is only used if you want to vary it. Let's say your family wanted to go on a picnic, but it was raining. All you'd have to do is touch the button and the storm would clear. Or let's say you wanted an old friend to be part of the jump. Think about the person, touch the button, and they'll show up."

"So it's like controlling the experience?"

"That's exactly what it is. But it's also a safety feature. When you first enter a jump, Lifelight creates the environment you're thinking of. Once you're in, Lifelight only reacts to what is actually happening. The trouble is, you can't control every idea that pops into your head. You might suddenly get a thought about being on a boat. But Lifelight won't do anything with that unless you push the button. If not for that button, there would be too much input coming from your brain and the jump would be a mess."

"So I could think about climbing a mountain right now—"

"And nothing would happen unless you pushed that button. Then a friend of yours might show up to tell you he's going on a trip to the mountains and ask you to join him."

"That is so cool!" I said.

"That's one way of putting it," Aja replied.

"So then, where are you?" I asked. "I mean, Lifelight isn't reading your thoughts, is it?"

"I'm your phader for the jump. Remember the core we passed through on our way into the pyramid? I'm sitting in one of those control cubicles, watching your jump."

"Those video monitors!" I exclaimed. "They're showing you what the jumpers are experiencing."

"Exactly. The phaders monitor the jumps to make sure everything goes well. To be honest, it's a boring job. Things rarely go wrong. But every so often a jumper needs some help or his wrist controller needs replacing or some minor problem arises and we get sent into their jump. But the thing is, we can't become part of a jump unless the jumper presses the left button. That's why I was able to show up when I did. If you hadn't pressed that button, I wouldn't be able to join you."

"So can you control the jump now too?" I asked.

"No, I'm only a visitor."

"Bobby? Are you going to eat this pizza before it congeals?" asked Mom. She stood in the doorway of the living room.

"Uh, yeah. As soon as I finish talking to my friend here." I had no idea how to explain Aja.

Mom gave me a strange look. "You want to run that by me again?" she asked.

"She can't see me," Aja said with a chuckle. "I'm not part of this jump."

How weird was that? Aja was like a ghost. There were a lot of rules to this bizarro experience.

"Never mind," I called to Mom. "I'll be right there."

Mom did a double-take, then left again.

"So what do I do now?" I asked.

"Anything you want. I think you have some kind of game to go to?"

"Yes! The basketball game! I can play ball?"

"If you want."

"Oh, man, this is great! How long does this go on?"

"Don't worry about it. Have fun. When you get back, we'll talk about the big picture."

"C'mon Bobby!" shouted Shannon impatiently. She stood at the door to the living room with her hands on her hips, looking irritated with me for holding up the show.

I looked to her and said, "Coming!" I then looked back to Aja, but she was gone. Just like that. My silver control bracelet was gone too. At least I couldn't see it anymore. I had a moment where I wasn't sure what to do, but then decided if I was going to learn all about Lifelight, I had to go along with the program. And heck, if it meant playing a little roundball, that wouldn't be so bad. So I decided to give myself over to the experience and ran into the kitchen and tucked into the most delicious pizza I had ever eaten. But better than that was being together with my family. Shannon told me all about a play she was in at school, Dad talked about a newspaper article he was having trouble finding the inspiration to write, and Mom announced she was up for a promotion at the library. It was all so . . . excellent. I was home. The only sour note was that I couldn't tell them anything about me. My guess was that would have thrown a monkey wrench into the whole illusion, so I kept quiet. Then again, nobody asked me anything either.

After breakfast we all piled into the SUV and headed for my basketball game. I had played some pick-up hoops with Spader on First Earth—when we went there together in pursuit of Saint Dane—but that wasn't the same as putting on a uniform and playing five-on-five in a gym. The last time I played organized ball was for Stony Brook Junior High. If I hadn't left home I would be going to Davis Gregory High right now. Question was, where would my mind take us? Junior high, or high school?

Dad drove us to Davis Gregory High. I had been there before and even played a city final in their gym, so I knew the place. I left my family and went right to the locker room, not entirely sure of what I'd find. For a moment it felt like one of those dreams where you've got to take a test, but suddenly realize you never went to any of the classes. But I didn't panic. After all, Lifelight was supposed to deliver a perfect experience, right?

It did. When I stepped into the room, I was thrilled to see all my teammates from junior high. But they weren't getting dressed in the yellow jerseys of the Stony Brook Wildcats. They were putting on the crimson jerseys of the Davis Gregory Cardinals. I had always dreamed about playing for the Cardinals. My dream was about to come true. Sort of.

The guys all greeted me, but didn't act like anything was out of the ordinary. I wanted to grab them all and hug them and tell them how psyched I was to be back, but I played it cool. For some reason I knew which locker was mine. Hanging up inside was a Cardinal jersey with my number: 15. Any doubt I had about being in the right place went away when I picked up that jersey, turned it around, and saw the stitched lettering over my number. It read: PENDRAGON.

As I look back and analyze what happened, I can figure

out why Lifelight did what it did. But at the time, I was totally taken up with the illusion. Even though I knew what was going on, it didn't matter. I'm not sure if it was Lifelight doing it to me, or it was my own brain guiding things, but it was like I had forgotten that I was lying in a vast pyramid and mind tripping through a computer. As far as I knew, I was really there.

And the game was awesome. The stands were full, and rocking like it was a championship. The band pounded out a war rhythm. The cheerleaders fired up the home side. Our opponents were the crosstown rival Black Knights of Easthill High. Our starting five were the same as back in junior high: me, Jimmy Jag, Crutch, Petey Boy, and Joe Zip. Man, I missed those guys. Coach Darula was on the bench looking confident, the same as always. As we came out of the locker room and headed for the court, I got that old familiar feeling in my stomach. The butterflies. They always started dancing right before tip-off. It meant I was ready to play.

And man, did I play.

From the opening tip-off, I was on fire. Being a point guard, I was used to shooting and scoring, but what happened in that game was nothing short of phenomenal. Everything clicked. We played together like a dream team. Most every shot I took found nothing but the bottom of the net. I didn't gun the ball, though. Oh no. I dished it around. I shot no-look passes to Joe Zip, who laid it in. I alley-ooped a few to Crutch, who could leap high enough to jam it home. I stole the ball a bunch of times and generally ran the offense like a pro. It was a dream game. Yeah, that's *exactly* what it was.

We didn't win by a hundred points either. The game was close, which made it that much more exciting. With only a few seconds left to go, we were actually down by two points.

Jimmy Jag passed me a give-and-go, I drove the lane, and as I went in for the lay-up, I got hammered by their center. Yeah, you guessed it. Two points down, seconds on the clock, and I was on the foul line. It doesn't get any sweeter than that. I stood at the line with my hands on my hips, totally exhausted and sweating. It was awesome.

I looked around at the crowd. Everyone was on their feet, cheering for me. The ref bounced me the ball. I dribbled once, bent my knees, lined up my shot and . . . swish. All net. The crowd went nuts. I took another second to soak it all in before my next shot. I gazed around at all the excited faces. Some I recognized, others were people I had never seen before. But they were all cheering for me.

Then I saw something that made a great moment even greater. Sitting on the bleachers behind our bench was my family. Mom, Dad, and Shannon. But that's not all. Sitting behind them was you, Mark. Next to you was Courtney. You were all waving and cheering. It was the best moment I could imagine.

The ref bounced me the ball; the crowd grew silent; I put up the shot and . . . oh yeah, it was good. The buzzer sounded. We were going to overtime. I jogged over to our bench while looking up at you guys. You were going nuts. I couldn't have imagined a better scenario. Come to think of it, from what I learned about Lifelight, it was the *exact* scenario I imagined.

The team manager threw me a towel and I sat down on the bench to catch my breath. I wiped the sweat from my face and did my best not to smile too broadly. That's when I heard a voice I didn't want to hear.

"Having fun?" asked the intruder.

I looked up and saw Aja sitting next to me on the bench. It actually took me a second, again, to remember who she was.

But I did, and I didn't like it. I didn't want her there, no way. Not then. She was going to ruin it.

Aja looked around at the screaming crowd and added, "Wow, you really like to get the old adrenaline pumping, don't you?"

"Yeah, so?" I shot back. "It's my fantasy. I can do what I want, right?"

"Absolutely," Aja continued. "Only one problem. Your jump's over."

"What?" I shouted. "It can't be over, we're going into OT!"

"Sorry," Aja shrugged. "I told you, the jump was timed."

"Give me twenty more minutes," I begged.

"Sorry. Besides, it's good to end like this," Aja said. "It's the perfect demonstration."

"There's nothing perfect about ending this now," I complained. I then noticed that the silver band had returned to my wrist. The button on the right was blinking red. I didn't like the looks of that.

Aja picked up another towel and threw it at me. "Wipe your face. You're all sweaty," she ordered.

I caught the towel and wiped my face. But when I dropped it, I realized with horror that I had gone blind. At least that's what it seemed like because the gym had gone black. Worse, I had gone deaf, too. A moment before, the place was rocking with the sound of hundreds of frenzied fans. Now it was like somebody had pulled the plug on the TV. Everything had gone dark and silent. I was totally disoriented, until I heard a voice. It was a calm, familiar voice that brought me back to reality.

"Relax, Pendragon," Aja said. "Nothing is wrong. You're coming out of the jump."

I then realized the truth. I wasn't deaf or blind. I was lying in a dark, silent tube.

"Just lie still for a few minutes," Aja said. "I'll be right there to bring you out."

I was filled with all sorts of emotions. First off, I was angry. Lifelight had just given me the most incredible gift I could imagine, only to snatch it right back. But I was also still high from the excitement of the game. I wasn't physically tired because I hadn't actually done anything. But the emotions were still there. I could remember the thrill of sinking those foul shots. But most of all, I felt sad. I had been given a small taste of being back with my family. It all seemed so real, and it made me miss them even more.

I heard a slight hum as light entered the tube. The silver disk behind my head was sliding into the wall. It was now official. I hadn't moved an inch since I was first sealed in. I had "jumped" into a computer simulation. I felt a slight movement and the table slid out of the tube. The first thing I saw was Aja. She stood at the control panel looking down at me.

"How do you feel?" she asked.

"Like I need another twenty minutes in there, thank you very much."

"I'm glad it ended that way, because it only helps illustrate the point I need to make."

"What point?"

Before she could answer, an alarm sounded. At least I thought it was an alarm. It was a loud, persistent horn that sliced through the quiet pyramid. Aja quickly glanced at her wrist band.

"What is it?" I asked.

"Medical call," she said, suddenly sounding all official. "It's in this sector."

Without another word of explanation, she bolted for the door. I was still a little dazed after coming out of my jump, but

I wanted to know what was going on, so I threw my legs over the side of the table and stood up. I was a little wobbly at first, but a second later I was running after Aja.

I blasted out the door and almost lost my balance again when I was hit with the sight of the interior of this vast pyramid. Man, talk about a rude awakening. I had to shake off my disorientation, fast. I looked both ways and saw Aja sprinting along the balcony. I sucked it up and ran after her.

Up ahead, a red light was blinking outside one of the cubicle doors. It didn't take a genius to know that was where the alarm was coming from. Just before Aja got to the door, I saw a red-suited vedder running up from the other direction.

"Where is this jumper's phader?" Aja demanded.

"I don't know," the vedder answered.

They both entered the cubicle with the flashing red light. I ran up and peered into the open door to see what was happening. Aja was at the control panel, quickly pushing buttons. A second later, the alarm stopped blaring.

"It came out of nowhere," the vedder said nervously. "There weren't any signs."

"Did the jumper try to abort?" Aja asked.

"No! His vitals just suddenly spiked."

A second later the silver disk in the wall slid open and the table emerged with the jumper lying there. The vedder immediately attended to the person. The jumper was a man maybe around my father's age. He didn't seem to be in any kind of trouble. It looked like he was sleeping peacefully. The vedder had a device that resembled a Game Boy. He put it to the jumper's chest, then checked the readings. A second later he took it away and shook his head.

"Too late," he said sadly.

"Too late?" I asked, entering the room. "What do you mean, 'too late'?"

"What do you think he means, Pendragon?" Aja said quietly. "He's dead."

Whoa. Left field. I hadn't expected that. "I thought this was supposed to be safe!" I said, feeling numb.

"It is," Aja shot back. "But sometimes . . . things happen."

The vedder started for the door.

"Where are you going?" Aja asked. "You've got to fill out a report!"

"Not me," the vedder said haughtily. "My shift's over. I'm jumping. The next shift can handle it."

The guy left. What a tool. Someone just died on his watch, and all he cared about was jumping into his own fantasy.

"Aja, what happened?" I asked.

Aja looked shaken. She tried to collect her thoughts. "I don't know. We'll have to look at the records of his jump. There are thousands of people in the pyramid. Sometimes they die of natural causes. But . . ."

"But what?"

"But it's starting to happen more often," was her sober answer.

I didn't like the sound of that.

"You've seen Lifelight at its best, Pendragon," she continued. "It's a wonderful tool that has brought joy to the people of Veelox. But it's got a downside, too. That's what you've got to see next."

I'm going to end this journal here, guys. While Aja did a postmortem on the dead jumper, she put me in a room by myself with this incredible recording device. I wanted to be part of their investigation, but Aja didn't know how to explain who I was. Still, I'm curious to know what they come up with. Once they're finished, Aja is going to take me to her home. Then tomorrow she's going to show me more of Rubic City.

But the truth is, I'm not here to sightsee. I'm not here to learn about the wonders of Lifelight or tour the city or take a trip into my own fantasies. I'm here to find out what evil Saint Dane has brought to this territory. After seeing what happened with the jumper, I have the sick feeling that I just got my first taste of it.

So I'll sign off now. This is the end of my Journal #13. By the time I record #14, I should have more answers. Good-bye, guys. I miss you.

END OF JOURNAL #13

☻ SECOND EARTH ☻

After a quick good-bye wave, Bobby's image disappeared in a flicker, leaving Mark and Courtney staring into the empty space of her father's workshop. Neither could say anything. They had been watching Bobby's story unfold before them, spoken by Bobby himself. It was like he had been standing in front of them, in the flesh.

"Well," Courtney said after several silent seconds. "That was . . . *different*."

"I can't imagine something like Lifelight being real," Mark said thoughtfully. He reached forward and picked up the silver, credit card–size projector. He turned it over in his hand, inspecting it. "Then again, I can't imagine something like this, either, so what the heck do I know?"

"Do you think Saint Dane sabotaged Lifelight?" Courtney asked.

"That's my guess," Mark answered. "But I'll bet it's not as simple as that. Man, what I wouldn't give to try it out."

"What would you do?"

"A million things," Mark answered quickly. "I'd ride a horse.

I've always wanted to do that. I'd fly an airplane, and play in a rock band, and run the New York marathon."

"But you can do all that for real," said Courtney.

Mark shrugged. It didn't feel to him as if any of those things were within his reach. "What would *you* do?" he asked Courtney.

Without hesitation Courtney said, "I'd put some major whup-ass on that soccer team."

Mark said, "Same thing, you can do that for real."

Like Mark, Courtney shrugged. Her confidence was so low, the idea of putting major whup-ass on anybody seemed like a fantasy. Mark then looked back at the silver hologram projector. A thought came to him, and he frowned.

"What?" Courtney asked.

"This is wrong," Mark answered. "Bobby shouldn't have sent this to us."

"Why not? It beats having to read the journals."

"But he's not supposed to mix things from other territories," Mark answered while fingering the device nervously. "It's totally against the rules."

"We'll put it in the safe-deposit box at the bank," Courtney offered. "Nobody will ever see it."

"Good idea. I'll go first thing after school tomorrow," Mark said. "Man, why didn't Bobby think of this?"

"Maybe they don't use paper on Veelox. It might have been the only way he could send a journal."

"Still," Mark said. "It might cause—"

Mark's ring started to twitch. He stopped talking and held his hand up.

"You're kidding?" Courtney said with surprise. "That was fast!"

Mark stared at the ring quizzically. "It feels different" was all he could say.

He quickly took off the ring and put it on the table. Courtney stood next to him and the two gazed at it. Normally when one of Bobby's journals was arriving, the gray stone in the center of the ring would turn crystal clear. The band would then grow and the journal would arrive in a flash of light and music. But that wasn't happening this time. The large gray stone didn't change. But something else did.

Engraved in the silver band and circling the stone was a series of odd characters. Each symbol was unique, with no apparent pattern. When Mark first got the ring he did a search on the Internet, thinking he could decipher them. But he came up empty. After tons of research there was only one thing he knew for sure: The symbols had no relation to any language or culture on Earth.

Now one of those symbols was starting to glow. It was as if there were a light inside the ring, shining out through the engraving. The glowing symbol was nothing more than a squiggle with a straight line passing through it. Mark and Courtney watched, dumbfounded, as the ring finally began to grow.

"Something's coming in," Mark gasped. "I think."

The ring didn't grow as large as usual. But they heard the familiar jumble of sweet notes that accompanied every trip. The light from the symbol then flashed across the room, momentarily blinding Mark and Courtney. A second later they looked back at the ring. As always, the event was over quickly. The ring had returned to normal. No more light, no more sound, nothing unusual . . .

Except for what the ring had deposited. It wasn't a journal. It was an envelope. A regular old white, Second Earth–style envelope.

"What is it?" Courtney asked.

"It's an envelope," answered Mark.

Courtney rolled her eyes. "Duh. Why did Bobby send us an envelope?"

Mark cautiously leaned over and picked up the piece of mail. He turned it over, examining it. There was nothing weird about it. It was sealed, with no writing on the outside. Courtney gave Mark a nod of encouragement and he carefully opened it, trying not to rip it more than he had to. Inside was a piece of plain white paper.

"I don't think this is from Bobby," Mark announced.

Courtney looked at the page. There was handwriting on it, and it was definitely not Bobby's. Bobby wrote in a kind of classic script. This note was written with block letters. It was actually jittery looking, as if the person who wrote it didn't have a sure hand. The note was simple. It was an address.

"'Four twenty-nine Amsterdam Place. Apartment Five-A. New York City,'" Mark read aloud. "You know anybody who lives there?"

"No," Courtney answered. "Why would Bobby send us an address? With no explanation?"

Mark suddenly looked up, as if he were hit with an idea.

"What?" asked Courtney.

"Could it be?" he asked, half to himself, half to Courtney.

"Could it be what?" Courtney asked, growing impatient.

Mark looked at the address again, then back at the ring. "Could this be about the acolytes?"

Courtney deflated. This wasn't the answer she wanted to hear. "Are you still on that kick?" She plopped back down onto the couch.

Mark was gaining energy. "I asked Bobby to find out about the acolytes. Maybe this is his way of pointing us in the right direction!"

"I don't want to hear about it," Courtney said sharply.

"You promised you'd think about it," Mark shot back at her.

"I did. I decided I don't want to hear about it."

"But this could be our chance to help Bobby, for real!"

"Mark, I've got enough stuff to worry about."

Mark didn't back down. "Like what?" he asked sarcastically. *"Soccer?"*

It was like Mark had flashed a red cape in front of an angry bull. Courtney jumped to her feet. "Yes, soccer!"

In the past Mark would have backed off when faced with Courtney's rage. But not this time. He stood his ground. "How can you care about stupid sports when there's so much more important stuff going on?"

"It's important to me!" Courtney defended herself.

"But it's just a game!" Mark countered.

"It's not! Can't you see that? I've never failed, Mark. Never. You just can't relate!"

Mark stiffened. "Why? Because I'm used to failure?"

Courtney forced herself to calm down and speak with more control. "I'm sorry, I didn't mean that." She sat back down on the soft couch and took a deep breath. "It's not just about soccer," she continued. "Everybody's got a role. You know? An identity. I liked mine. I liked how people looked up to me. But after what's been going on the past few days, I'm beginning to think I might not be the person I thought I was."

"Courtney," Mark said with sympathy. "It's just a *game.*"

"Yeah, maybe," Courtney said. "But who knows what might turn up tomorrow? It's the first time I've doubted myself. Ever."

Mark thought for a moment, then picked up the silver hologram projector and the envelope with the address, and put them in his backpack.

"I'm sorry, Courtney," Mark said. "I hear what you're saying about roles and stuff. I always thought mine was to be the lamewad who everybody made fun of. But I'm beginning to think I'm better than that. You might not be the person you thought you were either, and maybe that's not such a bad thing. Maybe it means you've got more important things to do."

Courtney gave Mark a quick look; then Mark headed for the stairs. "Tomorrow's Friday," he said. "I'll put this stuff in the safe-deposit box at the bank. On Saturday I'm going to the address on this paper. I hope you come with me, but I'll understand if you don't."

Mark left her alone in the basement.

The next day in school Mark and Courtney had no contact. Mark met with Mr. Pike about Sci-Clops and was given a schedule of meetings for the rest of the semester. He tried to be enthused about it, but it was hard to focus. All he could think about was being on the verge of a much bigger adventure.

When school was over, Mark went to the National Bank of Stony Brook on the Ave. The pruny Ms. Jane Jansen brought him into the vault where he deposited the projector that held Bobby's Journal #13 in the same safe box where he was keeping Journals #1–12. He didn't put the mysterious slip of paper with the New York address in the box though. He needed that.

As for Courtney, she'd made the tough decision and took the demotion to play for the junior varsity. Her plan was to prove herself so superior that Coach Horkey would have no choice but to bring her right back up to the varsity.

Things didn't work out that way. It was clear from Friday's practice that she was one of the better girls on the team, but definitely not the best. She didn't let it get to her though. She wouldn't go so far as to accept her fate, but forced herself to try and make the best of it. At least for the time being.

The next day, Saturday, Mark got up early and told his parents he was going to take the train into New York City to go to a science museum. He was old enough to do that on his own now. Taking the train into the city was easy. The station was at the bottom of Stony Brook Avenue, a short distance from Mark's house. He checked the schedule and planned on catching the 8:05 local that would get him into Grand Central Station around 9 A.M. He figured that would leave him plenty of time to go to the address on the note and be back home before dinner.

He was hoping to get a call from Courtney, but that call didn't come, and he wasn't going to beg. So he found himself early Saturday morning standing on the train platform, alone, ready to begin the next chapter in the adventure that had begun so long ago when Bobby first left home.

The train pulled into the station and the doors opened quietly. During the week this train would be packed with commuters headed in to work. But on Saturday not many people took the train, so Mark pretty much had the car to himself. He picked a seat directly in the middle because he knew it was the smoothest ride. He threw his backpack in the overhead rack, then plunked down into the seat.

"What's the matter?" came a voice from the seat behind him. "Don't want to sit with me?"

Mark spun in surprise to see . . .

Courtney.

"I called your house," she said. "Just missed you. Your mom told me you were catching this train. I got on one stop back."

"You sure about this?" he asked cautiously.

"No, but who else is going to watch your back?" she answered with a smile.

Mark broke out in a huge grin and moved into the seat next to her. For the time being, they were a team again. As the train took them into the city, they talked about everything except the mysterious note. It wasn't that they were avoiding the subject, it was more that they had no idea what to expect on Amsterdam Place.

They arrived in Grand Central Station and went right to the subway. Courtney knew that Amsterdam Place was on the upper East Side of Manhattan, so a quick scan of the subway map showed them the trains they had to take. The ride took twenty minutes, with only one change. Soon enough they found themselves emerging from the underground station on Amsterdam Place. Mark double-checked the building number, 429, and they walked two more blocks north.

Finally they found themselves standing in front of an old, brick apartment building. It looked like a pretty nice neighborhood, with a view of the East River. There was a park across from the address with little kids running around and a bunch of guys playing touch football. Since it was September, the leaves were just beginning to show autumn colors. But the air was warm and the sky was the kind of deep blue that only showed up in the fall. The whole scene was about as normal and safe as could be.

Except that Mark and Courtney now had to find out what was waiting for them in apartment 5A. With a quick look at each other, they climbed the cement stairs that led to the entrance. The double door looked like it had about five hundred coats of black paint on it. Mark grabbed the brass handle and pulled it open, letting Courtney go in first. Inside was another set of doors, but these were locked. The only way to get in was to be buzzed in by a tenant. On the right wall was a gray metal panel that listed all of the occupants of the building. Mark and Courtney eagerly checked for 5A.

"'Dorney,'" Mark said, reading the typed name. "Nothing weird about that."

"What did you think it was going to say?" asked Courtney. "Acolyte Headquarters?"

In spite of his nervousness, Mark laughed. The two stood staring at the name. Next to it was a black button. Neither was quick to push it.

"What are we going to say?" Mark asked.

"How about: 'Hi! We're here to interview for the acolyte position.'"

Mark gave Courtney a smirk. Before he could change his mind, he pushed the button. They waited. Nothing happened.

"Maybe they're out doing acolyte stuff," Courtney offered.

Mark hit the button again. Still nothing. Mark then said, "I guess we should come back—"

"What?" came a man's gruff voice from a speaker near the names.

Mark and Courtney shot each other a look. Courtney got her head together first and said, "Uh, Mr. Dorney?"

"Who is it?" the gruff voice demanded.

"Uh, my name's Courtney. I'm here with my friend Mark. We were wondering if—"

"Go away!" the man barked, and the speaker went dead.

"Now what?" Courtney asked.

Mark hit the button again.

"Whatever you're selling, I don't want any!" the voice growled at them.

"We're not selling anything," Mark said politely. "We're here to talk to you about . . . uh . . . Bobby Pendragon."

No response. Mark and Courtney exchanged looks again. Mark reached forward to hit the button one more time, but was jolted by the harsh sound of a buzzer.

"What's that?" Mark said nervously.

Courtney glanced at the door, then pushed it open.

"He just buzzed us in," she answered. Courtney stood in the doorway, holding the door open. "Last chance," she said.

"Don't say that," Mark threw back. "I might change my mind."

He took a quick breath, then turned and walked quickly past Courtney, through the door. Courtney followed, letting the door close behind them.

Next stop, apartment 5A.

☻ SECOND EARTH ☻
(CONTINUED)

The creaky elevator took them up to the fifth floor. Mark and Courtney anxiously watched the numbers above the door light up as they ascended.

"What if it's Saint Dane?" Courtney blurted out nervously. "He could be, like, luring us in."

"I thought about that," Mark responded, almost as nervously. "But why would he bother with us? We're just a couple of kids."

"Yeah," said Courtney. "Two kids he could use to get even with Bobby."

Mark shot Courtney a look. He hadn't thought of that. The elevator clunked to a stop and the doors slid open. Should they keep going?

"If he wanted to get us," Mark said, trying to sound confident, "he wouldn't have to go through so much trouble."

Courtney nodded and stepped out of the elevator. Mark was right behind her. The hallway was carpeted and pleasant looking. There were windows on either end that glowed with warm, autumn light. Under each was a table with a pretty flower arrangement. They were probably fake, but still made the place look homey. It wasn't a fancy place, but it wasn't run down either. There looked to be around a dozen apartment doors spaced evenly on either side of the corridor. All were painted glossy black like the front door. Each had a brass knocker with the apartment number engraved on a metal plate. Mark walked right and Courtney looked left in search of 5A. The "A" apartment was right next to the elevator.

"Go? No go?" Courtney asked.

Mark's answer was to reach for the brass knocker. He rapped twice. Not too hard as to sound insistent, but strong enough not to appear wussie. They heard the sound of footsteps inside shuffling toward the door. The person stopped, probably to peer out at Mark and Courtney through the peephole. Both of them sensed this, so they stood up straight, trying to look sincere. A moment later the door was unlatched and pulled open a crack. Just a crack. Mark and Courtney looked to each other as if to say: Now what? Courtney stepped forward and cautiously pushed the door open.

The first thing they saw was the back of a man shuffling away from them—an old guy, wearing a plaid shirt and khaki pants. His hair was gray and clipped short.

"Close the door," he called without turning around.

Mark and Courtney stepped inside the apartment and closed the door. But not all the way. With a silent look, Courtney showed Mark that she was leaving the door open a hair, just in case they needed to make a quick getaway.

"Come on!" the man shouted at them impatiently. "You got this far, don't be shy now."

Mark and Courtney walked cautiously after the man, staying close to each other for support, ready to bolt at the first hint of danger.

The apartment was normal enough. It looked exactly like the

kind of apartment one would expect an old man to live in. The furniture was old, but in good shape. There were oil paintings of landscapes on the walls and framed photos of smiling people on polished mahogany tables. There wasn't a single modern touch to the whole place.

Two things stood out though. First was the books. There were thousands of them. In bookcases, on tables, in stacks that reached the ceiling. Whoever this guy was, he liked to read. The other thing was the plants. The apartment was like a green-house. There were dozens of potted plants, as well as viney tendrils, that traveled along the walls and across the bookcases every which way, with no beginning or end.

The apartment in general looked very clean, even with all the plants. This wasn't some slobby old guy who couldn't take care of himself. So far, Mark and Courtney learned that the guy was neat, he read a lot, and had a green thumb. None of that helped to solve the bigger mystery of who he was though.

"Sit down," the old guy said while pointing to an overstuffed couch. He then shuffled over to an easy chair and slowly settled into it. Courtney and Mark didn't take their eyes off him. As he sat, he had to hold on to the arm for support, as if his legs weren't strong enough to do it on their own. The guy wasn't frail, but he wasn't going to run a marathon either. Mark and Courtney did as they were told and sat next to each other on the couch. Both thought it had the vague smell of mothballs. Neither mentioned it.

Now that they were facing each other, they saw that the old man wore small, wire-rim glasses. His short gray hair was almost military in style. He sat with incredibly great posture, which made both Mark and Courtney sit up straight as well. He stared at them with a steady gaze, as if sizing them up. The guy may have been old, but he looked sharp.

Mark got the ball rolling. "I'm M-Mark Dimond."

"And I'm Courtney Chetwynde."

A long moment went by. The man kept staring at them. Finally he asked, "Why do you care?"

Mark and Courtney exchanged confused looks.

"About what?" Courtney asked.

"You're here, aren't you?" the man said. "Why do you care?"

Mark said, "W-We got your address—"

"I know that," snapped the old man. "You wouldn't be here if you hadn't. What I want to know is, why?"

There was no nonsense about this guy. He didn't care about being polite or pleasant or anything else that would have put a visitor at ease.

"We're here because we want to help our friend, Bobby Pendragon," Mark said.

"Good," said the man quickly. "Why?"

"He's our friend," Courtney chimed in. "Isn't that enough?"

"Depends," answered the man.

"On what?" Courtney shot back.

"On whether or not you're willing to die for him."

Whoa. The tension in the room had just jumped a few dozen notches. The old man didn't even blink. Mark and Courtney didn't know how to respond.

And then Mark's ring began to twitch.

He quickly looked at his hand. Courtney saw it too. The gray stone was beginning to change color. Mark shot his other hand over the ring to hide it.

Too late.

"Take it off!" ordered the old man.

Mark looked at him, his panic rising.

"I said take it off! Put it on the table."

Mark didn't have a choice because the ring had already

begun to grow. He pulled it off his finger and placed it on the coffee table in front of them. Bright light blasted from the stone, dazzling the apartment. The ring quickly grew until it was the size of a frisbee, revealing the dark hole inside. Then came the musical notes. After a final blast of light and music, the ring returned to normal.

Mark and Courtney looked to the table to see what the ring had delivered. Sitting there was another small, silver hologram projector. Bobby had just sent his next journal. It was a totally awkward moment. Mark grabbed his ring, swiped up the journal, and stood up.

"This was a mistake," he said nervously. "We're outta here."

Mark turned for the door. Courtney didn't know what else to do, so she followed him.

"Stop right there!" the old man demanded as he struggled to his feet.

Mark turned and faced him head-on. "L-Look, mister," Mark said with passion. "We came here for answers, and all we're getting are questions. Well, you know what? I don't trust you. Why should I? If you think we're going to sit here and get grilled and threatened, then you'd better give us a good reason why, or we're gone."

Courtney gave Mark a quick look, as if surprised he had that in him. She looked back to the old man and added, "Yeah!"

The old man held their gaze, then slowly nodded. He turned away from them and walked over to a cabinet that was built into the wall.

"My name is Tom Dorney," he said firmly. "I've lived in this apartment for near fifty years. I'm not married. Never was. I have two sisters and three nephews." Dorney took a key ring out of his pocket and unlocked the cabinet door. He swung it wide to reveal several metal boxes, each about two-foot square.

"I served in the military for twenty years," he continued. "Saw action in World War Two. South Pacific." He pulled one of the boxes out of the cabinet and carried it over to the coffee table. It looked heavy, but neither Mark nor Courtney made a move to help. He didn't look like he wanted or needed any.

"These boxes are fireproof," he explained. "This whole place could burn to the ground and nothing would happen to what's inside." Dorney took another key from the ring and unlocked the box. He gave one more look to Mark and Courtney, as if debating whether or not to open it.

He then said, "And I'm an acolyte. You want proof of that?"

Mark and Courtney nodded dumbly.

Dorney lifted the lid on the box to reveal it was full of papers. Some were in folders, others were rolled up scrolls that were tied with twine. Mark and Courtney stared down at them in wonder.

Mark said, "Are those? . . ."

"They're the journals of a Traveler," Dorney answered.

"Which Traveler?" Courtney asked.

"They were written by my best friend, Press Tilton."

Dorney then raised his hand to show he wore a ring just like Mark's. "I brought you two here because I'm getting old, and need help. Now, my question still stands. Why do you care? If I don't get the right answer, you can walk right back out that door. I don't care what that Pendragon kid thinks about you."

VEELOX

Hey, guys. Getting used to watching me like this yet?

It's weird, after Lifelight, the idea of recording myself as a hologram seems pretty low tech. Lifelight is an incredible invention . . . that's also incredibly dangerous. The thing is, I'm afraid Saint Dane knows that, and we may not be able to stop him from taking advantage of it. I'm serious. We may already be too late to save Veelox. But I'm not ready to give up yet. Aja and I have come up with a plan. To pull it off I'm going to have to jump back into Lifelight. To be honest, it scares the hell out of me because this time it won't be the wonderful, fantasy visit back home like before.

This jump is going to be hairy.

I know, I'll bet you're thinking: How hairy can it be if it's all taking place in my mind? Well, the mind is pretty powerful. So is imagination. Trust me. I've just seen what can happen when things go bad. It isn't pretty. I don't want to risk jumping again, but I don't see any way around it. I've got to go back in. I know what has to be done.

I think.

Let me tell you what brought me to the point of having

to make this insane trip back into Lifelight. . . .

After my first jump I was thinking Lifelight was pretty cool. Going home and spending time with my family and kicking some serious butt against Easthill High was excellent, even if it was just an illusion. I'm sure this is hard to understand, but while I was in Lifelight, I sort of forgot that it was fake. The experience was so real, my brain wanted to believe it actually was. Or at least my heart did. Does that make sense? It would if you had been there.

But then I left the jump and witnessed the death of a fellow jumper. That made it pretty clear that Lifelight wasn't without risks. When Aja found me after her debriefing, I began to learn what those risks were.

"I'll take you to my home," she declared as she hurried into the office where I was recording my journal. "We'll have something to eat and I'll continue your education."

Education. Wow-wee. Aja really liked showing me what a brain she was. Lucky me.

"What happened to that jumper?" I asked. "Why did he die?"

"It happens," she said quickly. "There are a lot of people in the pyramid."

"But you said it's happening more often."

"It was an accident, all right!" she snapped. "I told you, things are under control here."

Yikes. She was a raw nerve. Things didn't seem like they were under control at all. But it wouldn't help to argue. Without another word, Aja left the office. I guessed she expected me to follow, so I did.

We left the Lifelight pyramid and went back to the three-wheeled vehicle that had brought us here. We climbed aboard and started pedaling along the quiet street. There were a million questions I wanted to ask about Lifelight and how it worked and why she was so sure Saint Dane's plan was doomed to failure and, for that matter, what the heck Saint Dane's plan *was*. But I didn't think it was a good time to grill her. She looked pretty upset. As she pedaled the odd bicycle, she stared ahead with a vacant look that told me her mind was miles away.

I was faced with a real dilemma. From all I've described to you, it must be clear that Aja wasn't the easiest person to get along with. She had a quick temper that flashed nasty the instant someone challenged her. She was a proud person, and totally brainy. And she took every chance she could to prove it. That was the exact opposite of somebody like, say, Uncle Press. Uncle Press knew pretty much everything about everything, but never rubbed it in your face. I think that came from confidence. With Aja, I got the feeling that beneath it all, she wasn't totally sure of herself, which is why she was always trying to demonstrate her brilliance.

But she was the Traveler from Veelox and we had to get along. If she was right and Saint Dane's plan was already derailed, then everything was cool. We didn't have to be friends and I could be on my way. But after hearing from Saint Dane about how he had already won on Veelox, and learning how Lifelight might have some problems, I had some serious doubts. I was pretty sure Aja and I were going to have to learn how to work together, and it was up to me to make that happen.

"Did you grow up here?" I asked, trying to make small talk.
"Yes."
"In Rubic City?"
"Yes."
"When did you find out you were a Traveler?"
"Two years ago."
She wasn't exactly being talkative. But I kept trying.

"How old are you?"

"Eighteen."

"Wow, are all the phaders so young?"

"You want my life story, Pendragon?" she snapped suddenly. "Here it is. From the time I was a baby I was raised in a group home. I never knew my parents. To this day I don't know if I was taken from them or given up for training."

Whoa. Lots of baggage in that one little sentence. I wasn't sure which topic to go after first.

"Training?" I finally asked. I figured it was less emotional than the whole "raised in a group home" thing.

"The directors find gifted babies and train them to become phaders and vedders. From the time I was old enough to sit up, I was at a key panel learning how to write code. I was a full-time phader by the time I was twelve. Now I'm a senior group leader."

This was good. She was opening up. "Who are the directors?" I asked.

"They make all the decisions when it comes to Lifelight. But to answer your question, yes. All the phaders are young. The vedders, too. The directors want the sharpest minds possible at the controls. But it's more than that. As people grow older, they want to spend their time jumping, not monitoring. By the time a phader gets to be twenty-five, they pretty much take themselves offline."

"And do what?"

Aja didn't answer. Instead, she looked around. I took the cue and looked around too. What I saw was . . . a deserted city. Like I described before, it pretty much looked like any city on Second Earth, except there were no people. Garbage kicked around in the wind and collected in alleyways. Glass windows were so grimy there was no way to see through them. Vehicles were parked along the curb, but many sat tilted on flat tires. I had the feeling that at one time this was a busy place.

I was starting to understand the problem.

"They're all in Lifelight, aren't they?" I asked softly.

"Why would they live anywhere else when they can create the life of their dreams?" was Aja's sharp reply.

"Is it like this everywhere?" I asked. "I mean, other than Rubic City?"

"It's the whole territory, Pendragon," she said. "Reality on Veelox only exists to support the fantasy." She then looked right at me. "That's why Saint Dane thinks he's won. This territory is about to fall apart, and we have nobody to blame but ourselves."

It made all sorts of sense. If nobody wanted to live in reality, then of course the territory would crumble. It made me think of a guy we used to go to school with. Remember Eddie Ingalls? He got caught up in playing one of those online fantasy games. He'd stay in his room on the computer for hours. I don't think he even slept very much, especially on the weekends. He ended up spending so much brain time playing that game, he lost most of his friends because he never wanted to come out and do anything. Then he started messing up in school. I'm not sure what happened to him, but I think his parents had to send him away to some kind of special school to help him catch up with real life. Well, what happened to Eddie Ingalls is what was happening on Veelox . . . times about eight billion.

The idea staggered me. My pulse started to race. We had lost Veelox before we had the chance to save it!

"Then Saint Dane was right," I declared. "We're too late. He *has* won!"

"Relax," Aja said sternly. "I told you, I've got things under control."

"Control? I'm seeing a lot of things here. *Control* isn't one of them! This city is falling apart. How long until Lifelight itself crashes? That's what'll happen, you know. Is that why jumpers are dying? Is that the future of Veelox? Are all the jumpers going to die in the middle of their fantasies because nobody bothers to take care of reality? We've got to get them out of there! Maybe we can pull the plug and force them to wake up! It's the only way they can—"

"Stop!" Aja shouted, and slammed on the brakes. I rocked forward, nearly launching out the front. Aja stared at me with such anger that I thought my brain would melt.

"I am trying to teach you about what's happening here," she said sternly. "We can't just 'pull the plug' and tell everybody to go back to their normal lives, though I'm sure you wish it were that easy. Salvation here can be found in only one place: the imagination. If you can't understand that, you might as well flume out right now."

I had to calm down. Though common sense told me otherwise, I had to believe Aja knew what she was talking about. The technology on Veelox was totally alien to me. If she said things were under control, I had to give her the benefit of the doubt. At least for a while, anyway.

"I'm sorry," I said, forcing myself to chill. "I'd like to stay and learn more about Veelox."

Aja stared at me. I wasn't sure if she was going to throw me out or take my head off again. Or both. Luckily she did neither. She started to pedal again. We didn't say another word until we arrived at her home.

Aja lived in a beautiful building on a quiet, tree-lined street. Did I say "quiet"? Hah, everything here was quiet. Her building was three stories high and made of brick. It looked like a millionaire's home. Completing the picture, the street was lined with huge, leafy trees that gave the neighborhood an inviting, parklike feel.

"Do all the phaders live in places this nice?" I asked as we walked up the marble steps to the entrance.

"They live pretty much anywhere they want" was her reply. "Most of the homes are abandoned. This place belongs to one of the directors. The prime director, actually, Dr. Kree Sever."

"Nice of him to let you live here," I said.

"It's not a him, it's a her," Aja corrected me. "And Dr. Sever couldn't care less. She's been on a Lifelight jump for over a year."

A year. Unbelievable.

She opened the heavy door and we entered the mansion.

"I'll be right back," she said, and ran up the stairs to the second floor.

The mansion was beautiful inside, too. There was a large entryway with thick, ornate carpets. A stairway led up to the second floor with a fancy wooden banister that was polished and gleaming. A hallway led deeper into the house with rooms off to either side. A quick glance showed me that the rooms were big, with high ceilings. It stunned me to think that somebody who lived in such a beautiful place would abandon it to live in a fantasy world. But then again, maybe the mansion Dr. Sever had in her fantasy was twice as nice. Or maybe she had twelve mansions. If it was a fantasy, she could have whatever she wanted.

As I looked around, something felt a little bit off. It was because the place was totally clean. I mean, immaculate eat-off-the-floor clean. The wood was polished, the crystal cases of knickknacks sparkled, and there wasn't a speck of dust anywhere. Rubic City was a falling-down mess because nobody cared, but this place was spotless. I couldn't imagine Aja taking the time to be so neat. Who was taking care of the place?

My answer came right away.

"You must be Bobby Pendragon!" came a warm voice from deeper in the house.

I looked to see an older woman hurrying toward me. She was the perfect image of a way-cool grandmother. Her gray hair was long and tied back in a ponytail, much like Aja's. She wore a deep blue sweater, dark pants, and black boots . . . no granny–style dresses for this lady. She hurried up to me and held out her hand. I took it, not sure of how hard to shake. But her grip was solid. This lady may have been old, but she still had it going on.

"Oh, this is silly, give me a hug," she said.

Before I could react, she pulled me in and gave me a strong hug. I figured it would be quick, but she surprised me by squeezing tight and holding on. It was totally awkward. I wasn't sure if I should hug back or not. We hadn't even been introduced.

"I was so sorry to hear about Press," she said. "He was a wonderful man."

Okay, now I got it. She was being sympathetic about my uncle. I still felt awkward, but a little less so. She then held me at arm's length and said, "You are exactly as he described you."

The woman had kind eyes, with a hint of sadness.

"Thanks," I said. "Uncle Press was a great guy."

"We're all going to miss him." She then smiled and said, "Come. You're just in time for dinner."

Dinner. Excellent. I hadn't eaten since I had breakfast with you guys back on Second Earth. The fantasy pizza in Lifelight didn't count. The woman held my hand and led me toward the back of the house.

"You didn't tell me your name," I said.

The woman laughed warmly. "I am so rude. It's Evangeline. I'm Aja's aunt."

Whoa. That didn't compute.

"Aunt? I thought Aja didn't know her family."

"Well, I'm not her real aunt. Not by blood, anyway. I worked in the group home where Aja was raised. Still do. I love all the children, but there was something special about Aja. When it was time for her to leave, it was like losing a child of my own. So we decided to move in together and, here we are."

"Your house is beautiful," I said, figuring it was the kind of thing an older lady would like to hear.

"Thank you, but it's not really ours," she said in a whisper, as if it were a secret. "I don't think Dr. Sever is coming back anytime soon, but I make sure to keep the place tidy just in case. Are you hungry?"

"Starved."

"Perfect! Then you're in for a treat."

I was beginning to like Evangeline. First off, she was nice. She had a pleasant personality. She had a sense of humor. And she seemed to like me, too. In other words, she was nothing like Aja. We entered the big kitchen which had a table set for two. Evangeline busied herself setting a third spot for me. I was getting hungrier by the second.

"What's for dinner?" Aja said as she entered the room behind me. She had taken off her blue phader jumpsuit and now wore gray sweats and dark, sneakerlike shoes. If I didn't know any better I'd think she was a normal kid, instead of an obnoxious, brainy, Traveler geek.

"Your favorite," Evangeline answered. "Tricolor gloid."

Gloid. I remembered the signs in the shop windows advertising gloid. I hoped it was as good as the pizza from Lifelight.

It wasn't. Evangeline placed a small cup at each of the

place settings. Each was filled with something that looked, well, it looked tricolor. It was a thick liquid, like soup, divided into half-inch-wide stripes of bright green, orangy rust, and royal blue. It looked like finger paint.

Evangeline and Aja both sat down and grabbed spoons.

"Sit, Bobby," Evangeline said. "Enjoy!"

I reluctantly sat and looked down at my bowl. My appetite was suddenly gone. But Aja and Evangeline dug in like it was the tastiest treat in the territory. And for all I knew, it was. I watched as they dipped their spoons into the goo. It had the consistency of bird doo. Evangeline was delicate. She tasted one color at a time. Aja was less discriminating. She dug up all three at once.

"We don't often have tricolor gloid," Evangeline explained. "It's getting harder to come by."

I smiled like I was impressed. I wasn't.

"I don't mean to be rude," I said. "But I've never had gloid."

Aja and Evangeline exchanged glances. Oops. It was the wrong thing to say. Aja knew I wasn't from this territory so she would understand. But if gloid was such a big deal, how would I explain why I'd never had it? It was like admitting I didn't know who Dr. Zetlin, the inventor of Lifelight, was. My mind searched for excuses, but I didn't know enough about Veelox to come up with any.

"It's pretty much all we eat," Aja said. "It was developed for Lifelight by the vedders to feed the jumpers when they're in the pyramid for long periods. It gets absorbed through their skin."

I had wondered how people could survive in Lifelight for so long without eating. I was bracing myself for Evangeline to ask me why I didn't know about gloid when Aja said to her aunt, "I don't think they have gloid on Second Earth."

Whoa. Did Evangeline know about the territories and the

Travelers? I mean, she knew Uncle Press, but Uncle Press knew a lot of people from the territories. He never told them about being a Traveler, though. He always made up some story about being from another part of the territory. At least, that's what I thought.

Evangeline then said to me, "Press once told me about something you had called . . . 'Gatorade'? Is that anything like gloid?"

"Uh, not really," I said dumbly. "Gatorade is a drink for when you're exercising hard and . . . I'm sorry. I'm confused. You know about Second Earth?"

I figured I had nothing to lose at this point. After all, she was the one who brought it up.

"Of course, silly," she answered with a smile. "Why wouldn't I?"

Okay. I figured I might as well cut right to the chase. "Evangeline, are you a Traveler?" I asked.

Both Aja and Evangeline laughed.

"No, silly," Evangeline giggled. "Of course not."

Now I was totally confused. If she wasn't a Traveler, why did she know about Second Earth?

Evangeline reached to her neck and pulled out a silver necklace. Dangling on the end of the chain was something very familiar. It was a silver ring with a heavy, gray stone at its center.

"I'm not a Traveler," Evangeline said. "I'm an acolyte. Now please, eat your gloid."

VEELOX

Acolyte.

There was that name again. Uncle Press had told me they were people from the territories who helped the Travelers. But the only evidence I ever saw of them was when I'd flume into a territory and there would be clothes and stuff to change into. I had never met an acolyte . . . until now. I was pretty psyched because it felt like another piece of the Traveler puzzle was about to fall into place.

"Eat your gloid, Bobby," Evangeline said sweetly.

Man, I didn't even like the name. Gloid. It sounded like a body part, as in: "I'm afraid we have to operate and remove your gloid." Ick. But I couldn't be rude, so I picked up my spoon and cautiously took a scoop of the orange stripe. It was gooey, like pudding. I don't mind pudding, but the bright color was throwing me off. Still, Aja and Evangeline seemed to like it, so how bad could it be? I wanted to hold my nose to kill the taste, but that wouldn't have been cool. So I took a quick breath and put the spoon in my mouth.

It wasn't bad. It was sort of bitter, like nuts. I then tried the green color and discovered it was pretty good too, though totally different from the orange. The green was more like berries, sweet at first but with a tart aftertaste. With more confidence I dipped into the blue . . . and nearly puked. Blue was bad. I had to force myself not to spit it out. It was like a brussel sprout had gone south and got mixed in with kitty litter.

At that exact moment I looked up and saw Evangeline put a big spoonful of blue into her mouth. My stomach twisted. But I felt like I had to finish my cup o'gloid, so I used the Aja technique and mixed all three colors together. It was a good move. The orange and green mellowed out the foul blue and I was able to choke it all down.

When I finished, I was surprised to find I wasn't hungry anymore. It wasn't because the weird taste had shut off my appetite, either. I really felt satisfied, like I had just polished off a big meal. I had all sorts of energy, too. Whatever the stuff was, it definitely did the job. I still wished it had been a big old pepperoni pizza, but I wasn't complaining.

"That was . . . delicious," I lied. "You make great gloid."

"Thank you," Evangeline said with a chuckle. "Not everybody knows how to scoop gloid from a container like I do." She winked at me. Ah, it was a joke. The gloid probably came ready-made, like ice cream. Oh well, so much for being a brownnoser.

"Gloid is pretty much the only thing we eat anymore," Aja said. "There's hardly anybody left to grow real food."

"It's a shame," Evangeline said. She cleared the plates and Aja went to the sink to wash them.

"What can I do to help?" I asked.

"Nothing. We'll be done in a second," Evangeline said.

I was looking for an opening to ask Evangeline about the acolyte thing, but wasn't sure how to bring it up without sounding stupid.

"You have no idea what an acolyte is, do you?" Aja asked with a snotty edge.

Gee, thanks, Aja. Never missed an opportunity to point out something I didn't know. Just as well, it broke the ice.

"Uncle Press told me about them, but didn't go into a whole lot of detail," I answered. "I'd like to know more."

Evangeline wiped her hands on a towel and sat back down at her place at the table. Aja kept her back to us, washing the dinner dishes.

"Everyone needs a purpose," Evangeline said while looking me right in the eyes. "What better role could someone play than to support those who have a higher calling?"

"Higher calling?" I said.

"What else would you call it?" Evangeline said quickly. "The Travelers are concerned with the well-being of the territories. You can't get a much higher calling than that. I, for one, am comforted by the fact that you Travelers are out there. It makes me sleep easier at night."

Yikes. Evangeline was sleeping easier because I was keeping the territories safe? How wrong was *that*? I wondered if she knew about Saint Dane. I'll bet she wouldn't be getting so much sleep if she knew the wicked stuff he was up to.

"I have to admit, Evangeline, I'm a little shaky on the whole Traveler thing," I said. "Uncle Press wanted me to learn as I went along, but I don't think I've learned all that much."

Evangeline gave me a little smile. She then reached out and held my hand.

"What about Denduron?" she asked. "I heard you saved that territory from a horrible civil war."

Whoa. She knew about Denduron?

"It wasn't just me," I said quickly.

"And Cloral would have been ravaged by a plague if you

and the others hadn't intervened," she said.

"The people of Faar saved Cloral," I corrected her.

"And First Earth? Saint Dane was trying to change the destiny of three territories by saving that zeppelin and altering history."

I guess she knew about Saint Dane after all.

"You're making it sound more dramatic than it was," I cautioned.

"Am I?" she said quickly. "You've got quite a reputation, Bobby. I think you've learned a lot about being a Traveler."

"How do you know so much about what I've been doing?" I asked.

Evangeline glanced to Aja, who turned away. She looked annoyed again. What was her problem?

"The acolytes share information," she answered, holding up the ring on her chain. "Many of us keep the journals that the Travelers write. Aja asked me to keep hers. It was a great honor, but I wanted to do more. That's why I became an acolyte."

"Now that you mention it," I said, "I have some friends who want to become acolytes too. They're the ones I send my journals to."

"Can you trust them?" Aja asked.

I was getting sick of Aja always challenging me. I decided to zing her back. "If I didn't, I wouldn't be sending them my journals, would I?"

"I'm not talking about holding on to a bunch of papers for safekeeping, Pendragon," Aja countered. "I'm talking about being there, anytime of the day or night, no matter what the situation, whenever they get the call."

"They're my friends. I trust them," I said firmly. I didn't

like the way she was questioning you guys, or me.

"I'll take care of it, Bobby," Evangeline stepped in, trying to be the peacemaker. "Your friend will get the chance."

"Two friends," I corrected her. "Mark Dimond and Courtney Chetwynde."

"Can we deal with the real issue here?" Aja asked impatiently.

"And what is that, dear?" Evangeline asked.

"I'm trying to convince Pendragon that Veelox isn't in danger from Saint Dane and he's wasting my time by being here."

That was it. Aja had pushed me over the edge. I looked to Evangeline and said, "Sorry for this."

Evangeline nodded as if she knew exactly where my head was and said, "I understand."

I then turned to Aja and said angrily, "Let's cut through it, all right? You've been treating me like an idiot since I met you. I took it because I didn't know how your territory worked, but now I do, and I gotta tell you, I think Saint Dane was right. He's already won. Veelox is falling apart. You say you've got it under control? I don't see it. You better start giving me some real answers or I'm going to flume out of here and come back with a whole bunch of my friends who have the same higher calling as me and—"

"And what?" Aja shouted back. "Blow up the pyramids? Destroy Lifelight? Convince everybody how they're better off living in reality than in their fantasies? Is that what you'd come back and do?"

I was really ticked off, but the truth was, I had no idea what I would do. Still, I couldn't let her think I was winging this. No way. I forced myself to calm down, but not lose my edge.

"You have no idea of what Saint Dane is capable of," I said through clenched teeth. "Have you even gone to another territory?"

Aja faltered. "Well, no, I'm too busy here and—"

"Well, I have, and even after all the horrible things I've seen, I'm not sure I know the true depths of Saint Dane's evil. That's the difference between you and me. I worry about the things I *don't* know. If I were you, I'd start worrying a little more."

This seemed to tweak Aja. She turned away from me, reached into a pocket, and pulled something out.

"I don't care what happened on the other territories, Pendragon. You can't beat Saint Dane here with a fight. There are no bad guys to battle or zeppelins to destroy. But it's every bit as dangerous as anything you've faced before. That's because the real enemy here is *perfection*."

"I get that," I said. "The people have to be shown what's happening to the real world."

"They already know!" Aja shot back. "They don't care! They think they've created the perfect system that runs itself. But the truth is the phaders and vedders would rather jump than do their jobs. You saw that vedder today. Someone died and all he cared about was starting his own jump. You only got a taste of Lifelight, Pendragon. And you know what? You didn't want to come out, did you? What was it you wanted? Twenty more minutes? They *all* want twenty more minutes, twenty more hours, twenty more days, weeks, months! Most of them don't even realize it's a fantasy anymore. If I hadn't timed your jump, you'd still be in there."

I had to admit it. She was right.

"Okay, you convinced me," I said. "Lifelight is, like,

addicting. But my question stands. What makes you think you've got it under control?"

Aja threw the thing she had taken out of her pocket onto the table. It was a small, silver disk about the size of a quarter in a clear, plastic case. It looked like a tiny CD.

"I've been working on that for nearly a year," she said with pride.

Evangeline picked it up and handed it to me reverently. "It's all she thinks about," she said.

"Saint Dane was right in some ways," Aja said. "He's done here. If things continue the way they are, it would only be a matter of time before Veelox falls apart for good. Lifelight itself wouldn't be far behind. But I know how to save the territory."

"With this?" I asked, holding up the disk.

"With that," she answered with confidence.

"What is it?"

"I call it the Reality Bug," she said. "And tomorrow you're going to jump back into Lifelight and get a firsthand look at exactly how it works."

VEELO·X

I wasn't so sure I wanted to jump back into Lifelight, not after seeing that jumper die. On top of that, I was starting to get nervous about Gunny. He had followed Saint Dane to the territory of Eelong and was supposed to take a quick look around and come right back to Veelox. Since Aja had the gate monitored, I asked her to let me know the instant Gunny arrived. I couldn't help but wonder what he'd found on Eelong. My guess was it wasn't good, but then again I always assume the worst.

Trouble is, I'm usually right.

I decided the best thing I could do was stay focused on Veelox and trust that Gunny could take care of himself. I spent the night in a guest room of the mansion. It was real comfortable and I would have had a great sleep if it weren't for the fact that I couldn't turn my brain off. It was all jammed up with worries about Gunny and jumping back into Lifelight. I ended up tossing around most of the night, nervous about what the next day would bring.

In the morning, Evangeline made us a yummy breakfast of, what else, gloid. We weren't treated to the tricolor stuff this time. This batch was all orange. That was okay by me, as long as it wasn't blue. I was surprised again by how filling the little cup of goo was. I would have preferred a stack of pancakes with maple syrup, but the gloid did me just fine.

Aja had on her blue jumpsuit, ready for business. She gave me a jumpsuit of my own, only mine was dark green. She said jumpers wore green when they spent long periods of time inside Lifelight. I didn't want to hang out inside Lifelight any longer than necessary, but figured I should be wearing Veelox clothes anyway. So I traded in my jeans and flannel shirt for this new suit. Aja also gave me some lightweight, black boots. I kept my boxer shorts, though. Rules or no rules, I always keep the boxers.

When we were ready to leave, Evangeline gave me a big hug. This time I hugged back. I liked her. Besides, she had to be pretty special to put up with Aja.

"Be safe, Bobby," she said to me.

"Don't forget, Evangeline," I said. "I told my friends I'd find out about the acolytes for them."

"I promise," Evangeline assured me.

I gave her one last squeeze of thanks and followed Aja outside. Evangeline watched as we went down the marble steps to the street and the vehicle that would take us back to the Lifelight pyramid.

"Bye, Vange," Aja called to her aunt. "I'll be home when I get home."

The two of us boarded the three-wheeled vehicle and began pedaling back toward Lifelight.

"Tell me about the Reality Bug," I said.

"I'm going to give you a demonstration," she said back.

"I know. Humor me."

"It'll be easier to show you," she argued.

"I'm sure," I countered, letting a touch of impatience creep into my voice. "But it would help if I knew a little bit about what to expect."

Aja sighed. I got the feeling that she thought of me as an inferior intellect who couldn't put two thoughts together without drooling.

"It's a computer program," she reluctantly explained. "Lifelight is designed to take the jumper's thoughts and give them the perfect experience. The Reality Bug alters the program . . . slightly."

"How?"

"It attaches to the data stream, changes it, and makes the experience less than perfect."

"Really? How?"

"That's what I'm going to demonstrate," she snapped. "You'll have a lot less questions after I show you."

I didn't want to argue. This was her show. I figured I was going to get the answers I needed soon enough anyway. Doing it on her terms was going to be less painful. So I shut up and we rode the rest of the way to the pyramid in silence.

When we arrived, we followed the same route as before. We went through the long hallway of freaky purple sterilization, then to the airlinelike ticket counter where I was fitted with another silver bracelet with three buttons. They didn't take any blood this time, I'm glad to say. I was already in the system.

As I waited for my control bracelet, I looked at the portrait of the kid Aja called Dr. Zetlin. After having been in Lifelight, I had even more trouble understanding how a kid could have invented such an incredible device. But then again, didn't Beethoven write symphonies when he was, like, four? I guess you've either got it or you don't.

We left the bracelet counter and continued on through the core. This time Aja stopped at one of the control stations. A glass door opened and we stepped into the high-tech room. Sitting in the coolio chair was a skinny little phader who looked like he was around twelve. He was gazing up at the wall of monitors, scanning each, looking for signs of trouble on the jumps while slurping down some blue gloid. Ick.

"Hey, Alex, we're doing a dual. I need you to phade for us," Aja said.

The kid, Alex, didn't take his eyes away from the screens. I noticed that he had a wicked case of acne. I wondered which color gloid caused that.

"I'm off soon," he said with a high voice that sounded as if he were talking through his nose.

"But you're the best, Alex," Aja implored, sounding a little flirty. "I hate jumping with anybody else."

Alex gave a little smile. Aja had him. She knew how to manipulate the guy.

"You need a vedder?" he asked.

"Nah, this is gonna be short and sweet," Aja answered.

I liked that.

Alex then tore himself away from the screens and looked at us. He checked me out, then looked to Aja and gave a sly smile. "Careful what you do in there. I'll be watching."

"Do you have any idea how creepy that sounds?" Aja said to him coldly.

Alex instantly lost the smile and went back to watching the screens, embarrassed.

"Don't be long," he said while shoveling more blue gloid into his mouth. "When my shift's up, I'm jumping."

"Don't worry" was Aja's reply as she turned and left the control room. I followed right after her.

"He's a jerk," Aja explained. "But he's the best phader there is. Next to me, of course."

"So then why aren't you going to be the phader for my jump?" I asked.

"Because we're jumping together. Didn't you hear what I said?"

"Yeah, but I didn't know that was possible," I said with total surprise.

Aja didn't explain. Instead she entered another control room. This one was empty. Nobody sat in the control chair and all the screens were dark. She gave a quick glance back to the corridor to see if anyone was watching, then sat in the control chair and expertly hit a few buttons on the control pad that was built into the arm. Instantly a small section of the console in front of us sprang to life with indicator lights. Aja reached into the pocket of her jumpsuit and took out the tiny, silver computer disk she called the Reality Bug. After another quick glance outside, she stood up, went to the console, and inserted the disk into a slot in the board. She quickly sat back in the chair, hit a few more buttons, then ejected the disk and popped it back into her jumpsuit. Another few keystrokes and the console went dark. The whole event took a grand total of twenty seconds.

"It's loaded," she announced, and left the control room.

She either knew exactly what she was doing, or knew how to put on a good show.

"What did you just do?" I asked.

Aja shot me a quick look that had "Shut up, idiot" written all over it.

We entered the center of the pyramid and I was once again stunned by the enormous size of the place. We took the elevator up, made the scary walk across the bridge to the far side, and found an empty cubicle. This one was different than the others I had seen. It was bigger, with two silver disks on the wall rather than just one. Aja went right to the control panel and started to program our jump.

"How does this work?" I asked. "I mean, how can we jump together?"

"It's your jump," she explained while programming the panel. "Lifelight will take all of its cues from you. I'm just along for the ride."

"Can you control anything that happens?"

"No, I told you. It's your jump. We'll experience everything the same way, though. We'll be in this together."

With a few more keystrokes, the two silver disks on the wall slid open, and the two tables slowly ejected.

"There's something I don't get—"

"There's a *lot* you don't get," she interrupted.

I ignored the insult. "If people spend months and years in here, how do they eat? And go to the bathroom?"

Aja pointed inside the tube. "See those two pads?"

There were two black squares that were flush with the top of the white tube. "If there's going to be an extended jump, those pads drop down and the vedders attach them to the stomach of the jumper."

She showed me that there were two zippers on the front of our jumpsuits. They were about four inches long, the exact same length as the black pads.

"Attach? That sounds gruesome."

"It doesn't hurt," Aja assured. "They rest on the skin. One pad excretes a form of gloid that gets absorbed into the jumper's system. The other pad removes waste."

"So you eat and, well, do your, uh, *business* through those pads?" I said, totally disgusted.

"Business?"

"You know what I mean."

"The system bypasses the body's normal metabolic processes. It's all about breaking everything down into its base chemical structure so it can pass through the skin. I'm not exactly sure how that happens. It's not my field. But I do know this much: perfecting the feeding system was the last piece in the trouble puzzle. Once people could stay alive inside the tubes for long periods of time, they had no reason to come out."

The idea of lying in a dark tube, being fed through my skin by a pad that took away waste was kind of gross. I was glad our jump was going to be quick.

"Let's go," Aja said, and climbed onto one of the tables.

"What do I do?" I asked while climbing onto the other one.

"Same as last time. Think of a place you want to be, and that's where we'll go."

"But the Reality Bug is going to make it different?"

Aja chuckled. "Oh yeah."

I didn't like that. I wanted to know exactly how much different it was going to be, but I didn't get the chance to ask. A second later Aja hit a few buttons on her wrist controller and our tables slid into the tube.

"You know what you're doing, right?" was all I could get out before my head went inside.

Aja answered with a laugh. I hoped that meant yes. A second later I was all the way into the tube, and the door closed behind me.

I was in the dark again. In more ways than one. Where was Lifelight going to send me this time?

VEELOX

My body started to feel heavy, like I was being pushed into the table. I felt a little sleepy too. This was pretty much what happened the last time I was in here, so I wasn't worried. But my heart was starting to beat faster with anticipation.

I felt something dry and scratchy brush against my face. It didn't scare me or anything because even though I didn't know what it was, it somehow felt . . . right. I reached up to find out what it was, and discovered there was something covering my face. It felt like a towel. How did a towel end up on my face? I grabbed hold of it and pulled it away as . . .

The roar of the gymnasium crowd came flooding back like someone had just swung open a soundproof door. I pulled the towel away to find myself sitting on the bench between Petey Boy and Jimmy Jag. I was back at the basketball game at the exact same moment where I'd left it. Yes! It looked like I was going to get my extra twenty minutes after all.

It took a few seconds for me to get my head back into the situation. I glanced up at the scoreboard. It was all tied up at fifty-eight and we were headed for overtime. I had just sunk two free throws and the crowd was going ape. Coach

Darula came over and knelt down in front of us.

"We've been here before!" he shouted over the noise of the crowd. "Five minutes of OT. We've got the experience, we've got the conditioning, and now we've got them scared. All we have to do is keep our poise and the game is ours. Bring it in."

We all brought our hands together and Coach shouted, "One, two, three . . ."

We all answered with *"Win!"* then dropped our hands and jumped up to take the court. I was back up to speed, warmed up, and ready to go. Oddly, I even felt a little tired and sweaty, as if I had just played a full regulation game of basketball . . . which I had, in my fantasy. As we trotted out onto the court I heard a lone voice calling from the stands. Though it wasn't very loud, it cut right through the noisy crowd.

"Good luck."

I turned back and saw Aja sitting in the stands behind the bench, dressed like a high school kid with jeans and a sweatshirt. She was holding a red pennant that said "Cardinals" and waved it with absolutely no enthusiasm. She really stood out against the rest of the crowd that was going totally nuts.

There was something about the way she said "good luck" that gave me an uneasy feeling. There was more. I looked up into the stands where I remembered you guys, Mark and Courtney, were sitting. But you weren't there. Odd. Everything was the same as when I left the fantasy before, except that the two of you were gone. Another look told me my family wasn't there either. I figured this was the kind of thing Aja was talking about when she said the Reality Bug made the jumper's experience less than perfect.

As soon as I got to the center of the court for the tip-off, I noticed something else had changed. The players from Easthill High seemed bigger than before. It wasn't like they were suddenly giants or anything, but they definitely had more muscle and a few inches of height. They didn't look all that tired, either. I wasn't sure of what was going on, but there was one thing I felt certain about.

This was going to be a long overtime period.

The ref threw the ball up, it got tipped away from us, and the fun began. It was horrible. This was an entirely different game. I'm not sure if it was because these guys were suddenly better, or we had gotten a lot worse. Didn't matter. The result would have been the same.

They ate us for lunch.

Skill-wise, they dribbled around us, passed behind their backs, and alley-ooped for a bunch of slam dunks. Physically, they pushed us around like we were little kids. I'd dribble to the top of the key with my back to the basket, and the guy guarding me would put a hand on my back so I couldn't move. If I tried to pass, he'd swat the ball away and steal it for a fast break, followed by an easy layup on the other side of the court.

Three minutes into the overtime period and they had outscored us twelve to one. It was worse than embarrassing. The only reason we got a point was because I took a jump-shot and the center hammered the ball back into my face so hard that it bounced off my head and landed two rows deep in the stands.

To be honest, the rejection was clean. No foul. But the ref took pity and called it. Unlike the last time I stepped up to the foul line, the crowd had grown deathly silent. I didn't think it was possible to have so many people in one place make so little noise.

I sank the first free throw, which was our one point. But I missed the second. It was a costly miss in more ways than one.

The ball bounced off the rim and rebounded back toward me. I jumped for it. So did their big center. He grabbed the ball and came down hard . . . elbow first.

Yeow! He nailed me right in the nose. Man, I saw stars! I landed on my butt with the gym swirling around me. This might have been a fantasy, but that shot to the nose felt totally real. They had to stop the game and Coach Darula ran over to help me up. Blood was spurting from my nose like a lawn sprinkler. My head was spinning. I wasn't sure if I could make it back to the bench. Crutch and Joe Zip had to help me get there.

The crowd gave me a decent ovation. At least that proved they were still alive. Then, just before I sat down, I caught a glimpse of Aja. She had a big smile on her face like she was all sorts of happy that I had gotten nailed. All I could do was give her a dirty look. She shrugged. I sat down on the bench with my nose bleeding and my head swirling. I was done for the day.

But the day wasn't done with me.

Even though we were getting our butts kicked, Coach Darula was still coaching like crazy. He was running up and down the court, shouting encouragement, calling plays, crying foul when the other team got too rough (which was pretty much all the time). I had never seen him so excited. His face was all sorts of red. It worried me that he was overdoing it. As it turned out, I was right.

There were thirty seconds left in OT. We were down by fifteen with no hope of making a comeback. At this point our guys were only trying to survive. I had a moment of guilt, thinking that it was my fault they were getting beat up like this. I had to keep reminding myself that it was all a fantasy. But at that moment, it didn't feel like one. I know my aching nose felt all too real. Easthill had just scored, again, and Coach Darula wanted a time-out. He jumped up from the bench, shouting at the ref, making the T symbol with his hands . . . and that's when it happened. Coach Darula clutched his left arm, his face went blank, and he fell to his knees. I'm no doctor, but I was pretty sure of what was happening.

He was having a heart attack. The game was stopped. The referee ran over and laid him on his back. He then motioned for the timekeeper to get the paramedics. Seconds later two guys in uniform hurried over to the coach to take care of him. I didn't think it was possible, but the crowd was even more quiet than before. Within minutes Coach Darula was on a stretcher, being wheeled out as the crowd applauded nervously.

Nobody wanted to play after that. There was no point. Everybody just kind of wandered away in shock. Even the Easthill guys didn't celebrate their victory. It was all so very strange. I looked around for Aja, but she was gone too. Not knowing what else to do, I followed my team into the locker room and took a shower. My nose had finally stopped bleeding and the warm water felt good. I stood alone in the shower with my sore nose, washing the dried blood from my face and watching it swirl down the drain.

"Any questions?" came a familiar voice.

Aja stood in the entrance to the shower with her arms folded, looking smug. I quickly grabbed my towel and covered up. Sheesh, could this get any worse?

"I've got a ton of questions," I said while turning off the shower. "But first I want to know why my nose hurts so bad if this is all happening in my head?"

Aja chuckled. "You're not hurt, Pendragon. Not really. When we leave the jump, your nose will be fine."

"Good. Would you mind turning around so I can get dressed?"

Aja rolled her eyes and looked away. I went quickly back to my locker and changed into the clothes I had put there in my earlier fantasy. The locker room was empty now. The other guys were long gone. As I tied up my hiking books, Aja came over and sat down next to me on the bench.

"Lifelight took your thoughts and created a perfect fantasy," she explained. "The Reality Bug took those same thoughts and also found the flaws and fears. Rather than only pulling out the good, it also found the bad. Just like reality. Getting beaten like that was something you feared might happen. You probably even worried that one day your coach would overdo it and get sick. The Reality Bug found those fears and made them real."

"But what's the point?"

Aja stood up and paced. "Haven't you learned anything? The people of Veelox will never leave Lifelight on their own. The territory is crumbling because nobody wants to take care of real life. Reality is too much trouble. People have to work and repair their homes and grow food and have babies and deal with other people who might not agree with them, and basically do all the things that it takes to run a world. But in Lifelight they don't have to worry about any of that. That's why Saint Dane is winning. He's got fantasy on his side. But my Reality Bug is the ideal solution. It makes Lifelight less than perfect so people aren't staying in as long as they used to. It's forcing them to return to real life."

"So . . . you've already tried it with other jumpers?"

"A few. Every time they ended their jumps earlier than planned. It works, Pendragon. Once I've fully installed the bug, it will affect every jump in every pyramid on Veelox."

Aja sat down beside me. It was the first time she seemed happy.

"Don't you see?" she said. "The bug will make Lifelight more like reality, so it won't be as attractive anymore. And nobody will know why. I've buried the bug so deep that no one will ever find it."

I hated to admit it, but Aja's plan made a whole bunch of sense. Still, there was something that bothered me.

"I think it's great, Aja, I really do," I said, still trying to form my thoughts. "If everything works out the way you say it will, then you did it. You beat Saint Dane."

"Thank you!" she said with a big, dramatic breath, as if this were the one thing she had been waiting for me to say all along.

"But—"

"There's no buts," she jumped in.

"Maybe not, but you said the battle on Veelox was going to happen inside people's imaginations. I understand that now. But aren't imaginations hard to control? I mean, look at me. I got hammered. You said this came from my own fears. What if somebody fears something really big? I mean, the jumps could get dangerous."

"So what?" Aja shot back. "It's a fantasy. Nobody gets hurt. They're all lying safely inside the pyramid."

"So when we come out," I asked, "my nose won't hurt anymore?"

"Exactly!"

I wanted to believe her, but something else was bugging me, so to speak. The Reality Bug was nothing more than a really advanced computer virus. And computer viruses were scary. You never knew where they'd turn up or what damage they'd do. I once got a virus on my computer at home that trashed my hard drive. If a virus could wreck my little PC, I'd hate to think what it might do to a system as complex as Lifelight.

"Tell you what," Aja said. "I'll prove it to you. Let's do the final test. Right here, right now."

"Test?" I asked nervously.

"Your control bracelet," she said. "Remember the middle button?"

I lifted my arm to see that the silver band with the three buttons had reappeared. "The middle button alters the jump, right?"

"Exactly. Press the button. Let's see what happens."

"Are you crazy?" I shouted, jumping to my feet. "What if things go wacky?"

"I hope they do," Aja countered. "It'll be the only way I can prove to you that no matter how wrong a jump goes, all we have to do is end it and everything will be fine."

I shook my head and paced. This was getting scary.

"This is the final test, Pendragon. Pressing that button is the first thing the jumpers will do when their jumps go bad. They're all going to try and change their fantasy. Let's see what will happen when they do."

"What do *you* think will happen?" I asked.

"I don't know. It all depends on you."

Truth be told, I was scared to death of what might happen. What if a fire broke out? Or an earthquake hit? I didn't want to have to go through that kind of mayhem, even if it was just a fantasy. My nose hurt bad enough.

"C'mon, Pendragon," she cajoled. "You're the big brave Traveler who beat Saint Dane all those times. Be the hero again. Push the button. Let's prove the Reality Bug works once and for all."

"You promise we can end the jump right away? I mean, all I have to do is say 'Stop!' and you can make all of this go away?"

"You can end it yourself, remember?" she said, pointing to my control bracelet. "Just press the right button. That ends the jump. Everything should work exactly as normal, except the Reality Bug will alter the fantasy."

Aja seemed to have found the solution to the turning point on Veelox. If her Reality Bug worked, it would force people to live in the real world again. The Travelers would have beaten Saint Dane and set the territory back on the right path. If all that was left to do was test the middle button, we had to do it.

"You sure you know what you're doing?" I asked.

"You already asked me that," she answered impatiently. "Haven't I impressed you yet?"

Okay, she had. I took a deep breath, raised my arm, and put my finger over the middle button on the silver control bracelet.

"Ready?" I asked her.

"Always," she answered.

I pushed the button. It glowed red for a moment and then . . .

Nothing happened. The ground didn't shake, the roof didn't collapse. We stood there like a couple of dopes.

"Nothing changed," I said. "Maybe it didn't—"

Then it all hit the fan.

Aja lifted her arm with the large, silver control bracelet. "My controller," she said with surprise. "It's activating."

"What does that mean?"

A second later a beam of light shot out of the wrist controller and projected a holographic image. If the idea of the Reality Bug was to dig into my subconscious and pull out all my fears, it did a very good job. Because standing in front of us in that locker room was the one thing I feared most.

Saint Dane.

"Checkmate!" the demon laughed.

"Is this my fantasy?" I asked Aja, stunned.

"No!" Aja answered with a shaky voice. "Your jump isn't tied into my controller. This is real. It's a recording."

"Aja, you sweet thing," the image of Saint Dane said. "Did you really think I'd let you sabotage Lifelight? I worked too hard for too many years helping those programmers create Lifelight to allow you to destroy it with a simple computer virus."

Aja shot me a look. This wasn't my horror fantasy.

It was hers.

"Sweet, little Aja," Saint Dane's image said. "I've watched you from the day you were born. I made sure the directors picked you for the phader program; I saw you grow into an arrogant little Traveler; and I even helped you program your nasty little bug. I'm sure Pendragon has told you I'm always around. I'll bet you didn't believe him."

She didn't. But she was beginning to.

"You see, dear girl," Saint Dane continued, "you're my back-up plan. If Veelox didn't crumble from neglect, then I wanted to make sure your Reality Bug worked far better than you could imagine. And it will!"

Saint Dane laughed. It was chilling.

"Either way, I win," he continued. "Thank you so much for all your help, Aja. You've made destroying Veelox such a pleasure! Give my regards to young Pendragon."

The recorded image disappeared and Saint Dane was gone. Aja looked like she was about to faint. None of this made sense to her. Unfortunately it made a whole bunch of sense to me. Saint Dane knew exactly what was going on from the beginning. He was in total control. Just like always.

"He's lying," Aja said. "The Reality Bug won't fail."

"I think that's the problem," I said. "He's saying it's going to work better than you planned."

"How could he know that?"

"I've been telling you from the start, Aja!" I shouted. "That's what he does. He works people, pushing them toward answers they think they want, but it leads them to disaster. You don't see him coming until it's too late. You're smart, Aja. But you made a huge mistake. You thought you were smarter than Saint Dane."

Aja shot me a look full of hurt and anger. But it was the truth. Just when you think you've gotten the better of Saint Dane, he comes back to bite you in the butt. And right now, our butts were stinging.

"Aja? You in there?" came a voice from outside the locker room.

"Who is that?" I asked.

"It's Alex," Aja answered with surprise.

She ran for the locker room door. I was right after her. The door led to a short corridor that led to the gym. We stopped, still inside the locker room, when we saw that standing outside in the empty gym was Alex, our phader. We stood on either end of the short corridor, Aja and I in the locker room, Alex in the gym. He was nervously punching buttons on his wrist controller.

"Aja, what's going on?" he called to us.

"What do you mean?" Aja shot back.

"I'm losing control of the jumps," he whined. "A surge of data shot through the grid in my quadrant, and I traced the source to you!"

"What does that mean?" I asked.

"I'm not sure," Aja answered, trying to stay in control. "It could mean the Reality Bug has activated."

"I thought it was already activated?" I asked, rubbing my stinging nose.

"Not fully. I had it isolated to our jump," Aja answered. "But it's programmed to spread through the entire grid once I give the command."

"I think that command was just given," I said soberly. "Saint Dane took care of that."

"Reality Bug?" Alex called to us. "What is that?"

"End the jump," she ordered me. "We've got to get back to the core."

I quickly hit the jump-ending button on my control bracelet.

Nothing happened.

"Why are we still here?" I asked.

"I'll override you and end it myself," Aja said. She hit a few buttons on her wrist controller, and frowned.

"What's the matter?" I asked.

"It's not responding."

"Not responding?" I yelled. I hit the right button on my controller a dozen more times. It still didn't work. Aja's fingers sped over the silver buttons on her wrist controller, trying to find the right combination that would put her back in control. She didn't find it.

"Alex!" Aja yelled out to the phader, who was still standing on the opposite end of the corridor, working his wrist controller. "Get back to the core and jam a shutdown. Get us out of here!"

"Are you sure?" Alex called back. "What if—"

Grrrrrr.

The sound came from out in the gym, where Alex was.

"What was that?" Aja asked. She started to walk curiously toward the corridor that led to the gym, but I grabbed her arm to stop her.

"I don't know," I answered. But the truth was, it sounded familiar.

"Alex," I shouted, "is something out there?"

The phader looked around the gym and shrugged. "I don't see anything."

GRRRRRRRR . . .

There was something out there all right, and it was getting closer.

"We gotta get outta here, Aja," I insisted.

"I'm trying!" she said while pounding out buttons on her useless controller.

I then heard what sounded like a scraping sound, as if something sharp were being dragged over a hard surface. I *knew* that sound. It felt so familiar, yet I couldn't place it. What was it?

A second later it hit me. But it was impossible. Not here. Not on Veelox. Or on a fantasy version of Second Earth for that matter. Or wherever we were. There was only one other place where I had heard a sound like that. It was on a territory far from here. The sound brought back horrible memories from a place I would never forget.

Denduron.

"Hey!" shouted Alex with surprise.

Aja and I both looked up. We saw the phader framed in the doorway to the gym. He was now looking off to his right . . . and he looked scared.

"Who thought *this* thing up?" he asked with a shaky voice.

"What is it, Alex?" Aja asked.

Alex took two steps back, the fear showing in his eyes. "I'm gonna get back to the—"

He never finished his sentence, because a set of strong jaws closed around his throat. Aja screamed. I took a step back in surprise. The beast had appeared from nowhere. It leaped at Alex, knocking him down.

"How could that happen? I thought the phaders aren't really here?" I yelled, trying to keep my head together.

"They aren't!" Aja screamed. "This is our jump. He's not part of this."

"Yeah?" I cried. "Tell that to Alex . . . and the quig that just killed him."

At that moment the beast looked up from its victim and stared down the corridor at us. The sight of blood dripping from its teeth was all too familiar. It was a quig from Denduron. It was in my high school gym, in my fantasy . . .

And it had just set its sights on us.

VEELOX

A nightmare from my past had just sprung out of my brain and was standing in front of us. In the flesh.

Somehow Aja's Reality Bug had found it in my memory and brought it to life. It was impossible, yet here it was. The quig looked exactly as it had on Denduron. It was like a prehistoric bear with an oversize head that was mostly jaws. It had big sharp teeth on both top and bottom that jutted out like a wild boar's. Its body was covered with dirty-gray fur. Yellow spikes of bone ran down its spine. Its paws were huge and strong, with knife-sharp claws. But the thing I remember most about these quigs, like all the quigs from all the territories, were its eyes. They were yellow and angry and focused. . . .

On us.

This one was smaller than the ones I remembered, about the size of a grizzly bear. But that was bad news because it was small enough to move through doors. We were only a doorway and a short corridor away from being eaten. The quig stepped over Alex's lifeless body, stalking toward the locker room . . . and us. There was only one thing I could think of doing.

I closed the door on our end of the corridor.

Just in time too. A second later I heard the quig smash against the door with a sickening thud. I knew the beast wasn't smart enough to open a door latch, so I didn't worry about locking it. The only thing I could hope was that the door would hold if it tried to bash it down.

Aja was frozen in shock. Her eyes were wide and frightened.

"Where did that come from?" I demanded.

"F-From your mind," she stammered out. "I told you, it'll find things in your memory that you fear."

"But you said Lifelight can only use reality," I shot back.

"Isn't that thing real enough for you?"

As if in answer, the quig smashed against the door again.

"But those monsters don't exist on Second Earth. It's from a different territory. From Denduron."

"That's impossible!" Aja shouted. "Lifelight can't do that!"

The quig slammed into the door again, letting out a bellow of pain and anger.

"Well, it can now!"

The door began to splinter. A couple more hits like that and it would be on us.

"C'mon!" I grabbed Aja's hand and ran. I didn't know where to go, but we couldn't stay there. We found a door on the far side of the locker room and blasted through. The door led outside, but once we were out, we both froze in horror.

We were near the large, football practice field. But there were no players scrimmaging today. Instead, we were faced with more quigs! The grass was swarming with them. They were all sizes, too. Some were as big as the beasts that had fought in the Bedoowan stadium on Denduron, others were smaller than the one from the gym. A few quigs were battling each other, trying to tear into each other's necks. I knew where that would lead. These quigs were cannibals. If one went down, the others would pounce and chow.

"The door!" I shouted.

It was closing behind us. If it locked, we were history. Aja reacted quickly and threw her foot out, wedging her shoe into the doorway just before it closed. If she had missed, we would have been quig lunch and I guarantee we were tastier than blue gloid.

I glanced back at the herd of quigs to see a few of them were lifting up their heads. They had caught our scent. In a few seconds they'd zero in on us and the dinner bell would ring.

"Back inside!" I shouted, and pulled the door open. After we ducked back in, I made sure to pull the door all the way shut. It was a good thing too, because a handful of quigs had spotted us and they were beginning to charge.

"Is there another way out of here?" Aja asked in desperation.

"I—I think so."

We ran back through the locker room, past the door to the gym, just as . . . *crash*! The gym door smashed open and the quig stood there looking totally ticked off that he had to go through so much trouble to get lunch. Aja and I kept running through the locker room, headed for the door that connected it with the girls' locker room. The quig chased us, awkwardly smashing into lockers that gave off a hollow, metallic thunder each time the monster slammed into one.

The door to the girls' locker room didn't have a latch, but it opened toward us. That was a huge break. There was no way the quig could pull a door open. We shot through and into a mirror-image locker room on the other side. We were safe, but for how long?

"Get us outta this!" I screamed at Aja.

"This isn't as bad as it seems, Pendragon," she answered.

"You're kidding, right?"

"No, this is a fantasy. Even if we got attacked and killed by one of those beasts, we'd just wake up inside the Lifelight pyramid."

"No," I said. "This isn't how it's supposed to work! You said it's impossible for those quigs to be here, but they are. And our control bracelets should work, but they don't. And Alex shouldn't be lying dead out there in the gym because he wasn't part of this jump, but he looks pretty dead to me. There are too many impossible things happening for me to risk letting one of those monsters eat us back to reality!"

"But—"

"You heard Saint Dane. He *knew* what you were trying to do with the Reality Bug. He messed with your program. Who knows what it's capable of now? We've got to get out of here alive and figure out what happened."

Aja nodded. I was making sense to her, for a change.

"I have no idea how to get us out," I added. "It's up to you."

I could tell the wheels were spinning in Aja's head, trying to figure a way to escape from the jump. Finally she said, "Our controllers were somehow taken offline. Whatever Saint Dane did, it happened when you pushed the reset button."

"Right, no more pushing the reset button," I agreed.

"But Alex's controller is tied into the general grid. It's on a different string."

"Can you use it to end our jump?" I asked.

"Absolutely," she answered with authority. "If it still works."

I knew what had to be done. We had to go back into the gym, get to Alex's body, and get his wrist controller. No problem, right? Yeah, sure. We quickly found the door that led from this locker room back into the gym. Aja and I cautiously opened it a crack and peered out.

The big gym was eerily empty. Not long ago it had been full of screaming basketball fans. Now the only person left in the gym was Alex, and he wasn't doing any screaming. Not anymore. Question was, where was the quig?

"You sure this is the only way out of the jump?" I asked Aja in a whisper.

"No, but it's the only way I can think of."

"Then we've gotta take the chance," I said. "Wait here."

I started into the gym, but Aja grabbed my arm.

"Where are you going?"

"To get the controller, where do you think?"

"You don't know how to get it off his arm."

Good point. We had to go together. Aja and I then shared eye contact in a way that hadn't happened up until this point. Though we were both Travelers, our relationship had been a battle from the get-go. But now we were about to step into danger. The look between us said it all. We were in this together, like it or not. I gave her a quick nod, and the two of us stepped into the gym.

The distance to Alex was only about twenty yards, but it might as well have been a mile. If the quig caught us in the middle of the gym, there was nowhere for us to run. We started out by walking slowly, but I think we both realized the faster we did this the better, because with each step we picked up the pace.

Alex's body was lying right in front of the open doorway to the boys' locker room. The quig was probably still in there. I had my eyes fixed on the door, waiting for it to spring out. Neither of us said anything for fear of alerting the monster.

As we got closer to the body, I realized I didn't want to see what horror the quig had done to the poor guy. Fantasy or not, this was all too real. But there was no chickening out. Not now. We were only a few feet from the body and I felt as if we were going to pull this off.

I was wrong.

The quig sprang from the doorway, exactly as I feared. Without thinking, I grabbed Aja and pulled her underneath the bleachers. It was the only place to go. Because of the basketball game, the bleachers were extended out into the gym. The move saved our lives, for the moment.

The quig swiped at me with its massive paw just as I ducked under a metal rail. The monster's hand smashed the rail, but one claw caught the back of my arm, slicing open the fabric of my jumpsuit. The stinging pain told me it had sliced through a part of my arm, too. But no matter how bad it hurt, I wasn't about to stop now.

"Keep moving!" I shouted at Aja.

A complex steel framework held up the bleachers. The two of us crawled through the labyrinth, moving up and over and around and under, desperate to get away from the quig. I glanced back to see the quig was still coming. It was having a lot more trouble getting through the tangle of steel than we were. But that didn't stop it. This thing was tearing the bleachers apart to get at us.

That's when I got a brilliant idea.

"Get to the far side, hurry!" I shouted at Aja.

If my idea was going to work, we had to get out from under here as soon as possible. I kept pushing Aja from behind, forcing her to snake through the metal rails. Finally we made it to the far side and out from under.

"Which way?" she shouted.

"Stay right there!" I commanded.

Aja looked at me like I was crazy. But I didn't have time to explain. Aja may have known computers, but I was a gym rat. Before I became a Traveler, I had spent every moment I could in gyms. I knew how they worked. I ran to a small silver box on the wall, flipped up the safety cover, and pressed the red control button inside.

Instantly the bleachers began to retract, with the quig trapped underneath.

"Brilliant!" Aja exclaimed.

It was the first nice thing she said to me. The two of us stood there, both hoping the quig would get crunched in the tangle of steel that was closing around it. All we needed was a minute to get the controller.

We didn't get it.

With a horrifying roar, the quig crashed out from under the retracting bleachers, pulling pieces of steel frame along with it. Turned out my brilliant idea, wasn't so brilliant. There was nothing we could do but run for our lives. We sprinted across the gym, maddeningly close to Alex's controller. But there wasn't time to get it. We ran out of the gym and down the corridor that led to the rest of the school.

I always felt like there was something spooky about an empty school building. I'm not sure why. Maybe it's because I was used to schools being busy and loud. A quiet school seemed wrong. Well, this school was definitely wrong. The fact that it was empty was the least of the reasons. Aja and I ran down the long, glass-walled corridor from the athletic wing into the student center that was the main hub of the school. It was a huge, airplane hangar–size room from which all the rest of the school wings could be accessed. Aja and I ran to the center of the big room so we would be able to get a complete 360 view around. If anything was going to enter the place looking for us, we'd see it in plenty of time to run the other way.

"There's gotta be another way to end the jump," I said, gulping for air.

Aja once again hit a series of buttons on her wrist controller, then grunted in frustration. "This can't be happening!" she shouted. "I have no control!"

There was no way around it. We had to figure a way to get past that quig, or at least distract it long enough to get Alex's controller.

"You know this place," Aja said. "Are there any weapons?"

"In a school? Yeah, right."

"Think, Pendragon! Is there anything we can *use* as a weapon?"

My first reaction was to say no, but that wasn't helpful. I had to give it some thought and be creative. Was there anything in this school we could use as a weapon to beat a quig? Uncle Press had killed some quigs with spears, but there was nothing like that here at Davis Gregory High. We had also blown up a quig using the explosive tak, but there was none of that stuff around. What else could we use?

That's when an idea started to form.

"These quigs," I asked. "Lifelight created them, but are they real? I mean, are they just like real quigs?"

"They're as real as you remember them," Aja explained. "Lifelight took them from your mind. It doesn't matter what real quigs are like, only what you remember about them. If you believe they can sing a song, they'll be able to sing."

"Then we need a dog whistle," I announced.

"A what?"

"Quigs are incredibly sensitive to high-pitched sound.

They go nuts when they hear it. If we can find some kind of whistle, we can keep that quig back long enough to get to Alex's controller.

"Perfect!" Aja exclaimed. "Where can we find a whistle?"

"I don't know," I admitted.

"Ugh!" Aja exclaimed in frustration. "Think! Is there anything we can use to make that kind of sound?"

We heard something that sounded like the rumble of thunder. I took a quick look around and saw movement outside the windows. I wanted to scream. The quigs outside had found us! They were peering in through the windows, staring at us, probably deciding the best way to attack. Suddenly I wished that I could find a *hundred* whistles.

A hundred whistles.

An idea was sneaking around the edges of my brain.

"Pendragon," Aja whispered. "We don't have much longer."

I had it. A hundred whistles. Plan B was starting to take shape.

"This way!" I shouted, grabbed Aja's hand and ran off. I led her through the student center to the wing housing the school offices. It's where the principal hung out and where the secretaries worked. If I was right, we'd find something there that would help us stop the quigs.

The office was dark and deserted. I made my way toward the long reception desk when suddenly . . . *crash!* A window blew out. Aja and I jumped in surprise and looked to see that a quig had smashed it and was now crawling in. *Crash! Crash!* Two more windows blew, followed by more squirming quigs. They knew exactly where we were. Either my idea was going to work, or Plan B was going to put us on the quig menu.

"What are we doing in here?" Aja asked. I could hear the growing terror in her voice.

"A hundred whistles," I answered while continuing on toward the reception desk. "We may not have a single whistle, but I might be able to come up with a hundred."

I was looking for the public address system. Every school had one for announcements and whatnot. I really hoped that Davis Gregory High was one of them. It was our last, best hope.

Crash! Crash! Two more windows shattered and glass rained down. The quigs were coming from all over. It was now or never. I found the PA system under the long reception desk. Now the trick was to figure out how to use it.

There was a power switch that I immediately threw. The lights on the machine blinked to life. There was a long row of buttons that I guessed operated the speakers throughout the school. I was about to turn every one on, when I saw a toggle switch marked "All speakers." Duh. I flipped it on.

The first quig had gotten inside and was now standing up. It would charge in seconds.

I cranked the volume knob to fifteen. If it had gone to twenty, I would have cranked it to twenty. I then grabbed the microphone. It was on a stand, with a trigger to turn it on. With a quick look at Aja, I hit the button and turned the microphone toward the amplifier.

They call it feedback. We've all heard it before, a thousand times. I'm not exactly sure what causes it, but it always seems to happen when the volume is turned up too high on something that is amplified. I think it has to do with an overload that the system can't handle and . . . to tell you the truth, I didn't care how it happened. I only cared that it happened now.

It did. The piercing sound screeched out from the speakers. It was horrible . . . and beautiful. The quigs began to bellow, just as they had on Denduron when I blew the dog whistle. It was perfect. They couldn't function. I quickly took some Scotch tape and wrapped it around the microphone to keep the button depressed, then leaned it against the amplifier. Unless it blew a fuse, we had our hundred whistles.

Aja grimaced in pain from the horrible sound, but still managed to smile.

"Can we go now?" she shouted.

The two of us ran out of the office, headed back toward the gym. The horrifying sound was piercing the entire school. As we ran, I looked outside and saw quigs fleeing in terror. Compared to a little old dog whistle, this feedback was monstrous.

Aja and I ran through the student center and down the long corridor back to the athletic wing. I had no doubt that the quig in the gym was in just as much agony as the rest of them. Now all we had to worry about was whether poor Alex's wrist controller would work.

We made it back to the gym and peered inside. Sure enough, our friend the quig was on its back, writhing in pain. With a quick look of relief to each other, Aja and I started into the gym.

And the screeching stopped.

Just like that. Maybe the amplifier blew. Maybe the power went out. Maybe, maybe, maybe. All that mattered was that our hundred whistles had fallen silent.

And the quig was back on its feet, ready to roll.

VEELOX

Aja and I froze. The quig didn't. It was back in control and madder than ever. It saw us and started to charge. All we could do was run.

That's when I saw it. I didn't know why I hadn't thought of this before, and didn't care. I saw it now, and we had nothing to lose by giving it a shot. So before we ran from the gym, I reached out next to the door and pulled the fire alarm.

Instantly the grating horn sound filled the gym, louder than the feedback from the PA system. Question was, would it be enough to bother the quig? Aja and I both turned to see . . .

The quig had fallen back down, clutching its head. We were back in business. Without stopping to think, Aja took off toward Alex. I was right after her. We dodged the squirming quig and made it to the body of the poor phader. I couldn't bring myself to look too closely at him. His body was still. Blood pooled on the gym floor. That's all I needed to know.

Aja quickly reached for his arm and pulled it toward her so she could have access to his elaborate wrist controller.

"Does it work?" I asked.

"We'll know in a second."

She expertly hit a few keys, and the strangest thing happened. I felt dizzy. It was like the whole gym started to spin. I wondered if all the sound of the feedback and the blaring fire alarm had finally gotten to my inner ear.

The next thing I knew it was pitch black. Was I back in the Lifelight pyramid? The odd thing was, I still heard the fire alarm blaring. But that didn't make sense. Either I was back or I wasn't. A second later I was bathed in light. The next thing I saw was my black boots. I was lying inside the Lifelight tube. I was back!

But why was I still hearing the alarm? The table slid out of the tube and I looked quickly to my left to see Aja was already jumping off her table.

"What's going on?" I asked.

"Come on!" she shouted.

We ran outside the cubicle into the center of the pyramid. One look around told me the problem. There were hundreds of lights flashing red outside the cubicles. Phaders and vedders were running around like crazy. The alarm sounding here had nothing to do with the fire alarm I had pulled in my fantasy. This was a full-out emergency . . . for real.

"We gotta get to the core!" Aja exclaimed, and ran for the elevator tube. We sprinted over a bridge, jumped in the tube, and flew down.

In the glass corridor of the core, things were frantic. There were alarms blaring and red warning lights flashing everywhere.

A phader grabbed Aja and yelled, "We've got hundreds of jumps going bad!"

"Contact the directors!" Aja shouted at the phader, and ran past him down the corridor. I kept up with her. As we ran by the control stations I saw that several of the screens showing jumps were flashing off and on. Phaders were in their control chairs, desperately hitting buttons on their arm controllers, but it didn't seem to be doing any good. A few seconds later I saw where Aja was heading. She threw open the door to Alex's control station.

"Alex! What happened?" she yelled.

Alex couldn't answer. He was sitting in his chair with blank eyes still staring at the screens.

Alex was dead. On his neck were bite marks. There was no mistake. The quig in my fantasy jump had somehow killed Alex out here in reality. Whatever the Reality Bug had done, it had turned Lifelight inside out. Right now, in cubicles all over the pyramid, all over Veelox, people were in mortal danger as they faced their worst nightmares in their own fantasies . . . for real.

"Shut it down," I said.

Aja continued to stare at Alex, unbelieving. She couldn't move.

"Aja, shut it down!" I shouted. "You gotta save those people!"

"This can't be happening," she said, stunned. "They're just *fantasies*!"

I grabbed Aja and forced her to look at me. "Not anymore they're not!" I shouted.

"But it's illusion!" Aja argued. "It's not real!"

"Is that real enough for you?" I asked, pointing at poor, dead Alex.

"There must be some other explanation," she argued.

"Yeah?" I shot back. "Then how do you explain this?" I let her go and turned my back to her, shoving out my arm. What I wanted her to see was proof positive that what was happening inside Lifelight was no fantasy. I showed her my arm. It was the arm that got sliced by the claw of the quig when we escaped under the bleachers. My jumpsuit was cut, with dried blood around the edges.

"That blood is real," I said. "It hurts, and so does my nose. My injuries didn't go away when we got back."

Aja stared at my arm as if her brain wouldn't let her accept what her eyes were seeing.

"Aja," I said softly. "It's not a fantasy anymore."

She looked at me with confusion. Her orderly world had just been blown apart. Then the door to the cubicle flew open and a phader ran in.

"Aja!" he shouted with terror. "It's happening all over Veelox. Lifelight has been totally corrupted."

Aja forced herself to think. She blinked once, then her eyes focused. "Did you contact the directors?" she asked.

"They're all jumping!" the phader answered. "Every one. We can't get to them!"

Aja looked to Alex's control board.

"Shut it down, Aja," I said again.

"I can't," she finally answered. "There's no such thing. People would die."

"But we have to do something!" I demanded.

Aja was thinking fast. I saw a spark in her eye. An idea. She turned back to the phader and said, "We've got to suspend the grid."

"What?" the phader shouted. "We can't!"

"Do you have a better idea?"

The phader didn't.

"Get your key!" Aja commanded him. She reached around her neck and pulled out a black-cord necklace from under her jumpsuit. Attached to it was a large, green card.

The phader hadn't budged.

"Move!" Aja commanded.

The phader was shocked back to reality. He hurried to the control panel while pulling out his own cord necklace. He had a green card on it, just like Aja's. The two stood at opposite ends of the complex array of controls.

"I hope you know what you're doing," the phader said softly.

Aja shot the guy a look. "Insert!"

They both took their green cards and inserted them into slots on either side of the control array. Aja then flipped about a dozen switches, the last of which was behind a clear, plastic cover. She lifted the cover to reveal a red toggle switch. The phader was working a duplicate set of switches, with the final being a similar red toggle switch.

Aja took a breath and said, "On my mark. Three, two, one . . . *suspend.*"

They both flipped the red switches.

Instantly all the monitors went blank. The thousands upon thousands of images that were being displayed had been replaced by the same single, flat color of green. The alarms all stopped as well, leaving everything eerily quiet.

I looked to the phader. He was crying.

"What happened?" I asked.

Aja stared ahead blankly. Her voice was calm and even. "We just suspended the grid."

"You mean, you shut it down?" I asked.

"No, the jumpers are still in Lifelight, but the jumps are frozen. Nothing will happen to them. All over Veelox. Millions of people are lying in the grid, waiting."

"For what?"

Aja then looked at me. Her eyes were red and frightened. "They're waiting for me to figure out what went wrong."

VEELOX

"How could you do that?"

"What happened?"

"This is impossible!"

Aja was in the center of a storm of phaders and vedders, all screaming at her, wanting to know why she suspended the grid. Whatever *that* meant. No sooner had the two switches been thrown, than the blue- and red-suited technicians came flooding into the control room, demanding answers. Most of the computer screens now showed live images of phaders and vedders from all over Veelox who were demanding to know what had happened. It wasn't until those faces started showing up on all those screens that I realized the full deal.

Aja hadn't only suspended Lifelight here in Rubic City, she had suspended the *entire territory*. At that moment millions upon millions of people all over Veelox were lying in suspended animation.

"Everybody, listen to me!" shouted Aja. Nobody did. They were too scared. I can't blame them. Their world was on the verge of crashing. Heck, if they weren't scared, they should be.

"Please, let me speak!" Aja begged. But the questions kept coming.

"My whole family is on a jump!"

"We've got to get back online and get them out!"

It was borderline chaos. All I could do was stay out of the way and hope that Aja could handle this. Finally she went to the control panel and with a look of pure determination, pressed a large green button. A screeching horn sounded that forced everyone, including me, to cover their ears. I saw that the technicians on the monitors were cringing as well.

After a few seconds Aja took her finger off the button and the horn fell silent. The phaders and vedders went silent too. They must have been afraid Aja would blast them again. Aja hit another switch and spoke into a microphone on the console. Her voice was amplified throughout the pyramid and heard by the technicians on the monitors.

"My name is Aja Killian," she said calmly. "I'm the senior phader on duty here in Rubic City. I'm the one who authorized the suspension of the grid."

Everyone started shouting again.

Aja jammed on the horn. Again, everybody quieted down. She released the button, but kept her finger close, ready to blast it again if anybody got out of hand.

"We had an emergency," she explained. "Jumpers were in trouble throughout Veelox."

I looked at the wall of monitors and saw several of the technicians nodding. For the first time I noticed how young they all looked. I scanned the monitors, searching for at least one gray-haired, wise scientist who would save the day. There weren't any.

"As best as I can tell," Aja continued, "the processing code has been corrupted."

People gasped. Whatever that meant, it must have been bad.

"How can that be?" a phader shouted, risking another blast from the horn. "That's never happened before!"

I looked to Aja. This had to be one of the toughest moments of her life. She knew *exactly* how it could be. Things had gone whacko because she had introduced a bug into the system. A Reality Bug. Worse, it was a bug that Saint Dane had somehow made even more powerful than it was supposed to be.

"But it *has* happened," Aja said firmly. "The jumpers are in danger. Suspending the grid was the only way to buy us time to solve the problem."

Everybody seemed to agree. Score one for Aja.

"With the grid suspended, the jumpers are totally safe," she continued. "I've been monitoring the situation and I believe I can ferret out the problem."

"We can't leave them inside like that," a vedder called out.

"We don't have any choice," Aja shot back. "If we go back online without solving the problem, we'll be back where we started and the jumpers will still be in danger."

I saw a lot of nervous heads nodding in agreement.

Aja then said, "Who is the senior vedder on duty?"

A guy stepped forward who looked like he wanted to be anywhere but here. "I just came on duty when the alarms started going off," the guy said softly.

I'll bet he wished he had overslept.

"How long are the jumpers safe with the grid suspended?" Aja asked.

"Theoretically, forever," the senior vedder answered. "But it's never been tried before, so who knows?"

"That's okay," Aja said confidently. "It won't take forever

to fix the problem. I'm going into the Alpha Core to start unraveling this."

"What do we do in the meantime?" the senior vedder asked.

"Nothing," Aja answered. "Just don't go far from the pyramid. When I crack this, everyone should be ready to go back online."

She then looked up at the faces on the monitors. "The same goes for all of you," Aja said to them through the microphone. "Let me work on the processing code. I'll keep you updated on my progress."

It was a great performance. Aja had shown total authority, and from the looks on everybody's faces, they believed she was going to solve the problem. The question was, did *Aja* believe she could solve the problem? I wanted to think so, but when she flipped the switch to turn off the microphone, I saw that her hand was shaking. Oh man. She was barely keeping it together.

She then glanced at me and we made eye contact. There was no mistake. She was scared. I hoped nobody else saw it. She then looked to the senior vedder and said softly, "You'll take care of Alex, right?"

The vedder nodded sadly.

Aja gave me a quick look and said, "Let's go."

She then walked away from the console, through the crowd of technicians, and out of the control room. I'm sure she felt the heat of everyone's eyes on her, searching for some sign of assurance that she would solve the problem.

I followed her to the far end of the glass corridor and up to a solid door marked ALPHA CORE—AUTHORIZED PERSONNEL ONLY. She took the same green card from around her neck and inserted it into a slot near the door handle. A metallic *click* signaled that the door was unlocked. Aja entered and I followed right behind her.

Inside was another control room that was a little different from the others. This one felt more important. Maybe it was because it was behind solid walls instead of glass. There was only one large monitor on the wall, and one control chair facing it. Beneath the monitor was a vast array of switches and knobs and lights, just like in the other control rooms. One arm of the control chair was extra long and held a silver keypad that looked way more complicated than the ones in the other control stations. I had no doubt that this was where we would have to undo the damage and save the territory.

Aja fell into the chair and started to cry.

Uh-oh. Not a good start. It must have taken every ounce of willpower she had to hold it together in front of the phaders and vedders, but now that we were alone, she lost it. I felt bad for her, but I was feeling worse for all those people who were stuck in the vacuum of Lifelight. Their only hope of getting out safely rested with Aja, and she wasn't looking all that capable of saving anybody. Finally she took off her glasses and rubbed her eyes.

"I didn't want you here on Veelox, Pendragon," she said. "Do you know why?"

"Uh . . . no" was my dumb but truthful answer.

"Because you're you," she said.

"What's *that* supposed to mean?"

"Give me a break," she said with tears forming again. "You're the lead Traveler. You swoop into a territory and take on Saint Dane like some kind of fearless savior. Denduron, Cloral, First Earth . . . every one a victory for the good guys. It's all so simple for you."

I wanted to laugh. I really did. Fearless? Savior? Me? Yeah, right. I didn't know what stories she had heard, but her information was definitely twisted.

"I'm not like you," she went on. "I'm not some big adventurer. What I am is smart. Smarter than you. That's not a boast; it's fact. My whole life I was trained to maximize my intellect. I lived with teachers and scientists. Evangeline was my only friend. It was a cold way to grow up. I hated it. Then one day your uncle showed up to tell me I was a Traveler. Suddenly it all made sense. I knew what I was meant to do. All the training and studying and loneliness I had to endure meant that I had the tools to protect Veelox. It was like I had suddenly come alive, because my life had purpose. I was all set to take on Saint Dane with the weapon I knew how to use best . . . my brain."

Aja stopped talking. I think she was trying to hold back tears. She swallowed and said, "The reason I didn't want you here, Pendragon, was I didn't want you to take that chance away from me."

I was slowly starting to get the picture. Finally. Aja had been cold toward me because she feared I would take away the one thing that gave her life meaning.

"But as it turns out," Aja continued, barely keeping her emotions down, "I not only failed to save Veelox, I made things worse. I didn't stop Saint Dane, I *helped* him!"

"We don't know that yet—"

"No?" she shouted, spinning the chair toward me. "I created the Reality Bug. It's my fault that millions of people are in danger. And that Alex is . . . I thought I was being so smart, and all along I was doing the worst possible thing."

"Aja, you have to understand," I said carefully. "Saint Dane may have had a bigger part in this than you know."

"No! I programmed it. I installed it. It was all me."

"I know that, but like I told you, Saint Dane is more devious than you can imagine. I'm not saying he was by your side helping you program the thing, but he probably put ideas in your head. It could have started years ago. He might have been a teacher who first planted the idea about how Lifelight would be better if it weren't so perfect. He could have been a phader who suggested it might be possible to alter the program, or a vedder who said it was impossible to be hurt while jumping. That's what he does, Aja. He plants ideas. He gets you thinking in directions that seem right, but are totally wrong."

Aja didn't turn her gaze from me. It was the first time she actually listened to what I had to say.

"And it probably wasn't just you," I added. "I'll bet he was doing the same thing with other phaders, and getting them to monkey with Lifelight so that when you installed the bug, it would blow up the way it did."

Aja let this information work its way through her brain. I wished she had done that when I first met her, but hey, no sense in looking back.

"There's something else," I said. "I don't know where you've been hearing these stories about me, but things didn't exactly happen the way you think they did. Yeah, we've been able to slam Saint Dane a couple of times, but it wasn't because I was a brave guy who charged in to kick butt and take names. Most of the time I was so scared I couldn't think straight."

"So how were you able to beat him?" she asked with a touch of confusion.

"Luck, as much as anything," I said. "To be honest, I blew it on First Earth. If I had been alone, there would have been a disaster worse than what we're looking at here. I'm still trying to figure how to live with that."

"But it all worked out," Aja said.

"That's because I wasn't alone. Gunny bailed me out. I don't think any one of us can stand up to Saint Dane alone, Aja. Working together is our only chance."

I hoped I was getting through to her. The future of Veelox depended on it, not to mention the rest of Halla.

I then added, "But what we've got here is a little bit different."

"How?" she asked, confused.

I walked over to the vast console and looked at the sea of buttons and switches.

"The Reality Bug was a brilliant idea. If Saint Dane hadn't stuck his nose in, it might have worked. But he did. We can't change that. We can only look forward. Our job is to save Veelox. But first we have to stop the Reality Bug. I have no idea how to do that. But you do. I can be here to bounce ideas off of, but only you can stop the bug. So when it comes right down to it, you *are* going to get the chance to save Veelox."

Up until that moment Aja looked like she was ready to crawl into a corner and shrivel up. But now the sparkle returned to her eyes. She sat up straight and put her yellow glasses back on. She stood up and faced me with the same confidence that I saw when she spoke with the technicians outside.

"Not a problem," she said. "All I have to do is tap into the grid and purge the bug from the processing code."

Whatever *that* meant.

"That won't solve the larger problem though," she added. "Once I'm done, Lifelight will go back to normal and Veelox will still be in trouble."

"One step at a time," I said.

Aja walked over to me and turned me around. I wasn't sure

why until I realized she was examining the cut on the back of my arm.

"Go see a vedder and get that taken care of," she said. She even sounded like she cared. A little.

"You sure you don't need me?" I asked.

Then . . . a miracle. She smiled. Was it possible? I'd like to take credit for getting her to lighten up, but the truth was that nearly causing the deaths of millions of people was probably earth-shattering enough to get anybody to see things differently . . . even an ego case like Aja. All I could do was smile back.

"It'll take me less time to purge the Reality Bug than it will for you to get your arm fixed," she said, then spun away from me and sat back down in the control chair. She pulled the control arm in front of her, ready to work. A few keystrokes later, the large monitor flashed to life. She had slipped into computer world, so I left her alone and went looking for some Bactine and Band-Aids.

The glass corridor of the core was empty and quiet. The technicians were gone and all the monitors at the control stations were showing the same blank green color. It was creepy seeing the place so dead, so I hurried to the end of the corridor to get out as fast as possible.

I stepped into the room with the long counter where I had been fitted with my silver bracelet for the jumps. It was empty too. I walked up to the counter and gazed at the portrait of young Dr. Zetlin, the inventor of Lifelight. He didn't look like a genius. He just looked like a regular kid.

"Hiya, Doc," I said. "This what you had in mind when you invented Lifelight?"

A voice then came from behind the counter. "Who are you talking to?"

For a second I thought it was the portrait, and it made me jump. But it turned out to be the Goth-looking vedder who had pricked my finger the day before.

"Uh, nobody," I answered, embarrassed. "Hey, you think you could take a look at my arm?"

The vedder rolled his eyes. "If I have to," he said, as if it were the last thing he wanted to do. I wasn't sure why he minded so much. It wasn't like he had anything else to do. I unzipped my jumpsuit to my waist and pulled my arm out.

"Where did everybody go?" I asked as he examined my cut.

"They're all up in the pyramid," he answered. "They're going to jump as soon as Aja gets Lifelight back online."

Unbelievable. Even during a crisis, all these guys could think about was jumping out of there.

"What about you?" I asked. "Don't you want to jump?"

"Not anymore, I don't," he said. "I'm beginning to think real life is safer than make-believe."

That was good to hear. Maybe there was hope for the territory after all.

"It's not a bad cut," he said. "Your jumpsuit got it worse than you did."

The vedder put an ointment on it and the stinging immediately went away. He then put a yellow pad over the cut and I was good to go.

"Thanks," I said.

"Don't worry," the guy said sincerely. "Aja is the best. If there's anybody I trust around here, it's her."

I nodded. I really hoped he was right.

There was nothing else to do, so I wandered back to the Alpha Core to see how Aja was doing. The door was unlocked, and I slipped in quietly, trying not to disturb her.

Aja was totally focused on her work. I glanced at the large

monitor to see that it was filled with several lines of computer code, each in a different color and each more complex than the last. Aja was furiously entering figures, and the data kept scrolling up with each new entry. She was good. My confidence rose.

"We've got a problem," Aja said flatly.

So much for my confidence.

"I thought you said it would be easy to purge the bug from Lifelight?"

"It would be, if I could get to it," she answered. As she talked, she kept inputting data. "The problem isn't the Reality Bug, it's the origin code."

"You lost me," I said.

"The system is programmed with security codes that make it difficult to get in," Aja explained while she worked. "It's to keep unauthorized people from monkeying with the grid. I know most of the codes because I'm a senior phader, but . . . but . . ." She slammed her fist down in frustration.

"But what?"

"When the Reality Bug infected the grid, it went so deep that the only way to reach it is to get past the final code, the origin code. And I don't know it!"

"Well, somebody's gotta know it, right?" I asked, trying to be helpful.

Aja jumped out of the chair and paced. "Only one person knows that code."

"So let's go get them!"

"That's not so easy. He hasn't been seen in three years."

"Three years? Who is it?"

"Dr. Zetlin," answered Aja.

"That kid in the painting? How come he's the only one with the code?"

"Oh, I don't know," Aja answered sarcastically, sounding like her old self. "Maybe because he *invented* Lifelight!"

Good answer.

"Besides," Aja continued, "he's not a kid anymore. He's got to be in his seventies by now."

"Fine. Let's find him, make him some warm milk, tell him the problem and get the freakin' code!"

"It's not that easy," Aja said.

"Why not?"

"Because Dr. Zetlin is in Lifelight, Pendragon."

Oh.

That was definitely a problem. A really big problem.

Aja looked up at the screen and said, "Without that code I can't purge the Reality Bug. And if I can't purge the bug then we can't put Lifelight back online."

"And if we can't do that, most everybody on Veelox is as good as dead," I concluded. I was getting the sick feeling that Saint Dane was right. The battle for Veelox was over and he had won.

"I don't suppose you've got a Plan B?" I asked.

I fully expected Aja to shout something like, "No, Pendragon! There is no Plan B, idiot!" Instead she looked down. The wheels were spinning in her head. That was good. She had a good head with good wheels.

"What are you thinking?" I asked.

"There is one possibility," she said reluctantly. "But it's too much to ask."

"Ask!" I shouted.

Aja sighed and said, "It's possible to jump into Lifelight and find Zetlin."

"But I thought the grid was in suspense?"

"Suspended," she corrected.

"Whatever."

"It is, but there's another way," Aja said.

She walked to the far side of the Alpha Core, where there was another door. She took out her green card and inserted it in a slot. Instantly the door slid open. I peered into the room beyond and was surprised to see a room similar to the jump cubicles in the pyramid. Only this one had three large silver disks on the wall.

"This is the original unit," she explained. "The alpha grid. It operates independently from the main grid. I could bring it back online by itself."

I gazed into the cubicle as the reality of what she was telling me slowly sank in. "Are you saying—"

"Yes. Dr. Zetlin is in there."

Whoa. The father of Lifelight was lying only a few feet away. It felt like I was peering into a tomb. But it was no time to pay respects.

"So fire up the alpha grid and pull the old guy out of there!" I said.

"I can't," Aja said. "He doesn't want to come out."

"So what!"

"It's the same problem," Aja said, trying to be patient. "He programmed the jump so nobody could end it. He doesn't even have a phader or vedder assigned to him. Without the origin code, I can't end his jump." She glanced into the cubicle and added, "But I can put somebody else in."

"You're telling me we could enter his jump, the way you were in my jump?"

"Well . . . sort of."

"Tell me everything, Aja. C'mon!" I suddenly understood the term "like pulling teeth." Sheesh.

"Yes, it's possible to enter his jump. The trick then is to

find Zetlin and convince him to give up the code."

"Then let's do it!"

"We can't! I mean, I can't. I mean . . . I can't go with you."

"Why not?"

"Because somebody has to stay out here and phade the jump or you might not get back out again. You'd have to go alone, Pendragon. That's why I said it's too much to ask."

Gulp. A few minutes ago I thought Aja was going to sit down at that control console and make everything okey-dokey. Now I was faced with the possibility of going back into that crazy fantasy world.

"Let me ask you something," I said. "If Zetlin's jump is on a different circuit—"

"Grid."

"Yeah, grid, whatever, stop correcting me. Since it's different, did the Reality Bug infect it?"

"I can't be absolutely sure," she said slowly. "But I would have to say . . . yes. The overall operating software is the same, and that's what I designed the bug to attack."

"So let me understand," I said. "The only way we can get rid of the Reality Bug is for me to jump into Dr. Zetlin's fantasy and get this code from him. But it might be a horror show if the bug is doing its thing?"

"Yes, that's about it."

Oh, man, no way I wanted to go. After what happened in my own fantasy with the quigs, the idea of jumping into some-body else's fantasy was truly horrible. Worse, I was going to have to do it alone.

"I don't want you to go, Pendragon," Aja said quietly. "It's too dangerous."

"Yeah, me neither. But what choice do I have?"

Aja shook her head. "What you said before makes sense.

We're stronger together. It's way too risky for you to jump in by yourself. I don't know what to do."

The reality of the situation was beginning to sink in. I was going to have to jump by myself.

That's when an idea hit me.

"There might be another way," I said. "What if I got somebody else to jump with me?"

"Who?" Aja asked quickly. "You can't ask one of those technicians out there. If they find out what's really going on, there'll be a riot."

"I'm not talking about one of them," I said. "I'm talking about another Traveler. Somebody who knows the bigger picture and how important this is. If anybody is going to jump with me, it has to be another Traveler."

Aja let the idea sink in, then nodded. "Sure. I could send you both in. Do you have somebody in mind?"

"Absolutely," I answered. "And I can't think of anybody I'd trust more to get us out of a gnarly situation . . . alive."

VEELOX

"If I thought there were a better way of doing this, I swear I wouldn't be here asking you to come along," I said.

This was tough. I was asking a friend and fellow Traveler to go on a dangerous mission. In some ways it was more dangerous than anything we had faced so far, because we were dealing with the unknown. When we were in my own jump, the Reality Bug searched my brain for things I was afraid of and came up with those vicious quigs. As scary as that was, at least I knew all about the quigs and could figure out a way to beat them. But once we were in Dr. Zetlin's jump, the dangers would be from *his* memory, and we wouldn't have a clue as to how to battle the nastiness that might come flying out of his genius brain.

"I could go myself," I said. "I will if I have to, but I think we have a better chance of pulling this off together."

I could have asked any of the Travelers to help me, except for Gunny because I still wasn't sure what happened to him on Eelong. But of all the Travelers, there was one I felt had a superior chance of helping me battle whatever boogeymen we found on the jump into Dr. Zetlin's fantasy world.

That was Loor.

"You have explained this Lifelight very well, Pendragon," she said. "Yet, it is hard for me to believe it is possible."

"Weren't you the one who told me that after all we've seen, we shouldn't think *anything* is impossible?"

Loor looked right into my eyes and gave a little smile. That didn't happen often. Loor wasn't the smiley type. But when she did, it made my heart melt. It wasn't until I saw her again, here on her home territory of Zadaa, that I realized how much I had missed her.

Aja had taken me back to the gate, where I flumed to Zadaa. I have to admit, part of me wanted to flume to Eelong to find Gunny, but I needed to find Loor. I could only hope that Gunny was okay.

I had been to Zadaa once before, with Spader, so I knew the way to Loor's home. I arrived at the gate on Zadaa and quickly changed into the white robe that was waiting for me. (Boxers stayed on, as usual.) I then made my way quickly through the labyrinth of underground tunnels that brought me out to the wide, subterranean river flowing under the city of Xhaxhu. Behind the waterfall that fed the river was a portal that I knew would lead me to the ramp up to the city. Everything was pretty much the same as I remembered it, except for a few disturbing changes.

Through the portal behind the waterfall was the giant gizmatron that controlled the flow of the underground rivers of Zadaa. It was a coolio-looking device with dozens of different-size pipes that ran floor to ceiling. In front of the pipes was a control platform with a series of levers and dials and switches they used to control the river water. Spader and I had watched a guy work this bad boy when we were there before. Well, when I entered the chamber this time, there was a guy working the controls again, but with one big difference.

"Stop right there!" a gruff voice shouted at me. "Where are you going?"

It was a big, beefy guard with a long, nasty-looking club that would do some serious damage if it made contact with any part of my body. In fact, three of these bad boys stood there, guarding the water controller. The people who lived underground were called Rokador. Loor told me that there was some tension between the Rokador tribe and the people who lived on the surface, the Batu. Whatever the tension was between these tribes, it must have gotten worse since I had been here. Before, the Rokador didn't need guards.

"I'm, uh, I'm going up to the city to, uh, get some supplies," I said, trying to sound like I wasn't making this up as I went along. Which I was. The Rokador were light skinned, like me, so they assumed I was one of them. Good thing. I didn't want to be a piñata.

"Do you want an escort?" the guard asked. That wasn't a bad idea. If I was safe down here with the Rokador, then it followed I might be in danger up with the Batu. But I had no idea how I would explain that I was going to visit Loor, who was a Batu.

"Thanks, but, no," I said.

"Be careful," the guard grumbled. "Return before sunset."

Now I was getting nervous. If things had gone south here on Zadaa, then it was going to be tricky finding Loor without getting hammered by some Batu guy who had an ick against the Rokador. The only thing I could do was try to be invisible. I hurried up the winding ramp that brought me into a building on the surface, and for the second time I saw the beautiful city of Xhaxhu.

If you remember, guys, I told you that it looked like ancient Egypt, with tall sandstone buildings. The streets were paved with stone and lined with palm trees. There were statues of all sizes, some towering as high as the buildings. It was a beautiful oasis in the middle of a vast, dry desert. Its water source was the river that ran below ground. Without that water, Xhaxhu would dry up and blow away like a forgotten sand castle. Knowing that, I saw something that made me nervous.

Running beside many of the streets were troughs that carried water throughout the city. At nearly every intersection was a fancy fountain that sprayed arcs of water in complex patterns. At least that's what I saw last time I was here. This time the troughs were nearly dry. Only a small trickle of water ran through them. The fountains weren't spraying water either. This was a really bad sign. If there was a problem with the water, the city was in trouble.

But that was something to worry about another day. Right now, I had to find Loor. It was a scary trip. The streets were alive with people, most of them Batu. As I described before, the Batu were dark-skinned warriors. They wore light, leather clothing that showed off their lean, muscular bodies. With my light skin and white robe, I stood out like a flashlight in the forest. I was getting some seriously bad vibes from these people. If looks could kill, I wouldn't have lasted two minutes. Seriously. I could feel pure hatred coming from them as soon as they laid eyes on me. It wasn't just the tough-looking dudes, either. The women were giving me the evil eye too. So were their kids. Heck, if a Batu dog walked by he probably would have peed on me. I put my head down and kept moving, hoping to make it to Loor's home in one piece.

Loor lived in a large, one-story building that was reserved for the military. She was a warrior in training, and was given a small apartment. I found it pretty easily, and was within a few yards of her place when my luck ran out.

Without warning, somebody grabbed the back of my robe and lifted me up like a doll. The guy spun me around and I came face-to-face with a giant Batu warrior. No, make that four giant Batu warriors. They all stared at me and none of them looked happy to see me.

"You have lost your way, little Rokador sheep," the guy snarled. "Are you looking to take back more of your precious water?"

"Uh, no, actually," I said, trying to be friendly, "I'm looking for—"

"Water!" he shouted. "Water is all you know, water is what you will have!"

The other Batu warriors cheered, egging him on.

"But my friend lives right—"

"Here is your precious water!" he shouted.

The Batu warrior dragged me over to a wall near the front of the building. I tried to break away, but the guy was too strong. It wouldn't have mattered anyway. If I broke loose, there were three other goons there to grab me. Behind the wall was the community bathroom. On one side of the enclosure was a trough of fresh running water for drinking and washing. On the other were holes in the ground with water running underneath for, yeah, you guessed it, going to the bathroom. It was basically an outhouse. Unfortunately we didn't stop at the fresh-water trough.

The warrior stopped at one of the open sewer holes, then stuck his nose in my face. "You love water so much," he seethed, "then have it."

The guy lifted me up and turned me upside down. The other warriors laughed and cheered.

"Hey, stop!" I yelled. "You're making a mistake."

I know, pretty lame, but I didn't know what else to say. The guy lowered me toward the open latrine hole. I was going into the sewer headfirst! I was in such a panic, I didn't even think to try and use my powers of Traveler persuasion on him. All I could think about was landing in smelly sludge. My head got closer to the hole. I did a quick calculation and unfortunately figured that it was plenty big enough for me to fit through. This was going to be gruesome. My head was only a few inches away from crossing the portal into the land of stench and disgust, when someone shouted out, "Put him down!"

I really, *really* hoped they were talking about me. Sure enough, the warrior flipped me over. I landed on my feet and looked up to see . . .

Loor.

I could have kissed her, but that would have been a major-bad move.

"I know this one," Loor said. "He gives me information on the Rokador. He must not be harmed."

The warriors grumbled in disappointment and shuffled off. Loor had spoiled their fun. Gee, too bad. Bullies. I hate bullies.

"Come with me, Rokador!" she barked at me. She then walked away quickly. I was all too happy to follow. Seconds later we were in her apartment.

"Nice friends you have," I said.

"They do not like the Rokador," Loor said with no emotion.

"Yeah, I got that. Thanks for saving me."

"No need to thank me. If they had finished what they started, I would have had to smell your stench in my home."

The two of us looked at each other, then I burst out laughing. Loor relaxed too.

"Man, I'm glad to see you, Loor," I said. I went over and hugged her. She didn't hug back. It wasn't that she didn't like me, it's just that Loor never showed affection. So as I hugged her, she only gave me a couple of friendly pats on the back. What can I say? That's Loor.

She started a fire and we settled into her woven chairs. I first told her all that had happened on First Earth and the *Hindenburg* disaster story. I left out the part about my chickening out at the last second. I didn't want Loor to know that.

Loor told me how tension between the Batu and the Rokador was worse than ever. She feared there would be a war. The Batu had strength, but the Rokador controlled the water. In her heart she knew this would be the turning point of Zadaa, but had no idea what to do about it.

I then told her about Veelox and Lifelight and the Reality Bug. Being a warrior from a territory that had no technology, it was hard for Loor to imagine the concept of a wristwatch, let alone something as amazing as Lifelight. Still, she listened and did her best to understand.

As I sat in that room with the dirt floor and the fire crackling in the fireplace, I couldn't take my eyes off her. The fire gave her dark skin a warm glow that looked as if she had stepped out of a painting. An amazing painting. And she's cut like an athlete. The leather outfit she wore showed off the long, strong muscles of her shoulders and arms. I've seen her battle guys nearly twice her size and kick butt. But more important than the physical stuff was that she had an incredibly clear way of seeing things. She didn't overthink things the way I sometimes do. Okay, the way I *always* do. With Loor there are only two ways: the right way and the wrong way. She wouldn't think twice about cutting down an enemy, or risking herself to save a friend.

That's why I was here. I needed Loor to cut down some enemies and risk herself for a friend. Me.

"I want to help, Pendragon," she said. "But I worry about what will happen here on Zadaa. I do not want to be somewhere else when trouble finally arrives."

"I get that," I said. "And when the time comes, I want to be here to help you. But the flumes will always put us where we need to be, *when* we need to be there. I don't understand it, but it's true. When the time comes that you're needed on Zadaa, you'll be here."

"And what if this Lifelight is as dangerous as you say, and we do not survive?"

Ooh. Good question.

"I don't know," was my only answer. "But I do know that millions of people are in trouble right now. If they die, Veelox will die along with them and Saint Dane will have his first victory. I can't let that happen."

Loor stoked the embers of the fire. In this light she looked like her mother, Osa, the woman who died saving my life. Loor was a little older than when we had our adventure on Denduron. So was I. Hard to believe this was possible, but she was even more beautiful. I was suddenly hit with the realization that I didn't want anything to happen to her. Not here, not on Veelox, and certainly not in the fantasy world of some wacky old scientist.

I was about to get up and walk out when she turned to me and said, "I want to return as soon as possible."

"No," I said quickly, and I stood up. "This was a bad idea. You don't need to be watching my back. Your place is here. I'm sorry. It was wrong of me to ask. I'm gonna go back and—"

"Pendragon!" she said firmly. "I am a Traveler. It is what we are meant to do."

She stood up and grabbed a nasty-looking sword that was leaning against the fireplace. She twirled it expertly, the sharp blade flashing with light from the fire. "What weapons will I use on Veelox?"

"We won't know until we jump into Lifelight."

Loor gave the sword one last swing, then put it back down. I knew she wanted to take it with her, but that was against the rules.

"What is it that Spader says?" she asked.

"Hobey-ho?" I answered with a smile.

"Yes. Hobey-ho, Pendragon. We belong on Veelox."

We were a team again.

We made it through the streets of Xhaxhu with no problem. Nobody was going to mess with me since I was with a Batu warrior. But we then had to go into the underground. Rokador territory.

"We have to get by some Rokador thugs," I warned. "They're guarding this machine that controls the water."

"Stay behind me," was all that Loor said. She wasn't worried.

We hurried down the ramp into the bowels of the underground. I thought that if we moved fast enough, nobody would notice us.

I was wrong.

Before I could stop her, Loor walked boldly into the room with the guards. It was a good move because she took them by surprise. I think the last thing they expected to see was a Batu warrior babe strolling into their secret subterranean chamber.

Before they had a chance to recover, Loor pounced. She took care of the first guy with a kick to the chest; the second guy fell to a leg sweep followed by a roundhouse kick that caught him on the side of the head; the final guard got the worst of it. He charged Loor from behind and grabbed her in a bear hug. Loor pumped her legs and drove the guy backward, through the room and out of the portal. She finished him off by flipping him over her back into the waterfall, sending him plummeting into the fast-moving river.

I looked up at the Rokador guy who was operating the water controls. He didn't stop working, but gave me a nervous glance.

"You should see her when she's *mad*!" I said to the scared guy.

I thought the poor dude was going to faint. I hurried out of the room, jumping over the bodies of the groaning guards, and joined Loor on the ledge behind the waterfall.

"Finished playing?" I asked.

She gave me a sly wink and we were off. A few minutes later we made it to the gate and hit the flume.

When we arrived on Veelox, I was glad to see that there were two sets of green coveralls waiting for us. Evangeline had been here. I made a mental note to ask her how the acolytes knew when to bring stuff to the flumes. We changed quickly and made our way along the derelict subway tracks and up the ladder to the manhole that brought us out onto the quiet street in Rubic City.

I was happy to see that Aja was waiting for us. She was at the wheel of a new vehicle. This one still used pedal power, but it had four seats rather than two.

"I didn't think it would take so long," was the first thing Aja said.

"Good to see you too, Aja," I shot back. "This is Loor. Loor, Aja."

Aja gave Loor an up and down once-over. She then said, "Is Loor a man's name or a woman's name?"

Ouch.

Loor answered, "It is the name of a legendary hero on Zadaa. A woman."

"Really?" Aja said. "What did she do that was so heroic?"

"She killed her enemies and ate them."

Aja's eyes opened in shock. She turned forward and clutched the wheel of the vehicle nervously. Loor looked at me and winked. She was kidding. Great. That's all I needed.

"Let's get to the pyramid," I said, and hopped in next to Aja. Loor climbed in back and we pedaled our way back to Lifelight.

On the way I filled Loor in on everything about Lifelight that I hadn't explained before. I wanted her as prepared as possible, because there were bound to be plenty of surprises along the way. I kept expecting Aja to correct my descriptions, but I think she was too scared to speak. Just as well.

After a few minutes of my lecture, Loor put her hand up to stop me.

"Am I going too fast?" I asked.

"You must understand, Pendragon," Loor said. "The things you describe are beyond my imagination. You talk of computers and codes like they are as normal as air and water."

Aja scoffed and rolled her eyes. I wanted to smack her.

"If Aja is as smart as you say she is, then I trust she will take care of us and get us to where we should be. I do not need to know all the details. My trust is with Aja."

I looked to Aja for her reaction. Aja looked to me and I saw the surprise on her face. She even let out a little smile.

"Thank you, Loor," Aja said. I think she meant it too.

"For what?" Loor asked.

"For trusting me . . . and for coming. We really need you."

We had reached an understanding. And we were under way.

This is where I'm going to end the journal, guys. While Aja prepped Lifelight for our dual jump into Zetlin's fantasy, I took the time to finish this. I'll send it to you with a reminder that you might be contacted by somebody named Evangeline. If you're serious about wanting to be acolytes, you're going to get the chance.

I have no idea what to expect when Loor and I make this trip back into Lifelight. Finding Dr. Zetlin will probably be the easy part. Finding his deepest fears is what I'm worried about. But having Loor with me gives me all sorts of confidence. It's great that we're together again.

Be safe and think about me every once in a while. I'll catch you on the other side.

END OF JOURNAL #14

◉ SECOND EARTH ◉

Bobby's image vanished.

Courtney and Mark kept staring at the empty space where the hologram used to be. Neither were sure of what to say or do next.

Then Dorney started to laugh. It started out as a chuckle, grew into a belly laugh, and finally changed into a wheezing, uncontrolled, coughing fit. Courtney jumped up and got a glass of water. Dorney took it gratefully and gulped it down.

"You all right?" Courtney asked as she sat back down next to Mark.

Dorney cleared his throat, took a deep breath. He was fine.

"What's so funny?" Mark asked.

"Just like his uncle, that one," Dorney said with a smile. "Always jumping out of one frying pan into another one that's even hotter."

Mark glanced at the metal boxes that held Press's journals. "Can we read some?" he asked.

The smile fell from Dorney's face. He glanced over at the journals, then back to Mark and Courtney. "Depends."

"On what?" asked Courtney.

"On whether or not I like what you have to tell me."

"We're here for Bobby," Mark exclaimed. "You heard what Bobby said to Evangeline."

"Evangeline?" he scoffed. "If the devil himself told that lady he was misunderstood, she'd invite him in for tea."

"You know her?" Courtney asked in shock.

"How do you think I knew to send you my address?"

"But she's from—"

"Veelox, yeah. So what?"

"But, you said you weren't a Traveler," Mark said.

"I'm not! Are you thick or something?"

Courtney and Mark were dumbfounded.

"I'm s-sorry if we're being dense," Mark said. "But I thought only Travelers could fly through the flumes. If you're not a Traveler, how could you know somebody from another territory?"

Dorney stared at them for a moment, as if debating about whether or not to answer. Finally he held up his hand—the hand with his Traveler ring.

"It's the rings," he said. "It's all about the rings."

Mark and Courtney sat there patiently, waiting for Dorney to explain. But he didn't. Instead he pushed himself out of the easy chair with a grunt and began moving the metal boxes with Press's journals in them back into the cabinet.

"I was a practical guy," Dorney finally said, sounding serious. "I always thought that everything had its place. B always came after A. Two always followed one. But then Press Tilton came into my life. He opened my eyes, so to speak, and I began to realize there was something else going on. Something bigger than me and my safe little life. I don't mind telling you, it scared me. All this business about fluming and territories that exist in different times—it's enough to make a fella want to lock his door and never poke his nose out again."

Mark and Courtney nodded. They knew how he felt.

"But what scares me even more," Dorney continued, "is that somebody out there is causing problems. Knowing Saint Dane is trying to make it all fall down has kept me from getting a good night's sleep in near ten years. Only thing that gives me a little piece of mind is knowing the Travelers are trying to stop him. That's why I'm an acolyte. I do what I can to help the good guys."

Dorney put the last of the metal boxes into the cabinet, then closed and locked it.

"Trouble is, I'm getting too old for this. Now that Press is gone, I'm not so sure I've got the energy. That brings me to you two. Pendragon seems to trust you. Question is, should I?"

"We told you!" Courtney shouted defensively. "Bobby is our friend and—"

Mark put a hand on her arm to quiet her down.

"You're right," Mark said calmly. "You don't know us. All we can say is that we're just as freaked out about Saint Dane as you are. Besides that, you've gotta trust that Bobby knows what he's talking about."

Dorney looked between the two of them. Finally he shrugged and said, "Don't matter anyway. It ain't my choice."

"What does that mean?" asked Courtney. "Whose choice is it?"

Dorney shuffled toward the front door. "Go home," he said.

Both Mark and Courtney jumped up in surprise.

"Mr. D-Dorney," Mark stuttered, "we came here because we wanted to learn about being acolytes. You can't throw us out."

Dorney opened the door and stood to the side. "I can do whatever I please," he said. "Truth is, you two ain't ready."

"But w-we are!" Mark protested.

"Not from what I'm hearing," Dorney countered. "When the

time is right, come on back. I'll help you then, not before."

Mark and Courtney looked at each other. They knew it was no use to argue. So Mark grabbed the silver hologram projector from the table and jammed it into his pack.

"How are we going to know when the time is right?" Courtney asked.

"Believe me." Dorney chuckled. "You'll know." He opened the door further, expecting them to leave.

"We'll be back," Mark said as they backed out the door. "Count on it."

"I hope so," Dorney said seriously. "I truly do."

He shut the door, leaving Mark and Courtney in an empty corridor.

"Well, that sucked," Courtney said. "We came all the way here and all he can say is we're not ready?"

Mark walked toward the elevator. Courtney hurried after him.

"We're not giving up so easy," she asked. "Are we?"

"We're not giving up at all," Mark said. "I think Dorney believes we can be acolytes, but the time isn't right."

"I think he's a crazy old coot who likes pulling our chain," Courtney said.

"Yeah, that too," Mark said. "But I'll bet you anything we'll be back here."

The two rode the elevator down and left the building. All the way back to Stony Brook, Mark and Courtney tried to analyze what Bobby had told them about Lifelight and the Reality Bug. Mark was fascinated with the idea of a computer that could read your thoughts and make them real. Courtney was too, but was more interested in talking about Loor. She thought Bobby made a bad choice. She thought he should have gotten Spader. Mark pointed out that Bobby wasn't a hundred percent sure he could rely on Spader. Courtney didn't care. She felt

Spader would have been the better choice.

Mark had a pretty good idea of what Courtney was *really* thinking. She was jealous. From what Bobby said in his last journal, it was obvious he had feelings for Loor. But Mark decided not to point that out. He didn't want to risk a punch in the head.

When the train brought them home, the two stood on the empty station platform at the bottom of Stony Brook Avenue.

"Now what?" Courtney asked.

"I don't know," Mark answered. Then added, "Does this mean you officially want to be an acolyte with me?"

Courtney had to think about that for a second. "It means I still want to find out what it means," she said. "I can't promise any more than that."

"Good enough," Mark said. "Maybe Bobby's next journal will tell us more."

Courtney nodded. "You'll tell me when—"

"Soon as it comes in," Mark assured her.

With a quick smile Courtney turned and headed for home. Mark stood there for a moment, twisting the ring on his finger. When Bobby was in the middle of an adventure the journals came pretty close together. Mark expected the next delivery to come through his ring at any moment.

It didn't.

Mark had to get his mind off Bobby and back into his own life. He busied himself at school and went to his first meeting of Sci-Clops. It was better than he could have imagined. Mr. Pike, or David as he insisted on being called, introduced him to the other members, all of whom were older than Mark. They were all working on different projects, like mixing unique metals to create a new lightweight alloy, and making a computer processor that responded to eye movement. It was heady stuff for Mark and he feared he was out of his league. But he quickly discovered they all spoke the same language. He had found a home.

Courtney focused on classes and soccer. She continued to practice with the JV team and did pretty well, but she always had one eye on the varsity squad that practiced on the other side of the field. More than anything she wanted to prove herself worthy of being back there.

Several days passed with no word from Bobby. Mark started to fear that something horrible had happened when he and Loor jumped back into Lifelight. But he forced himself not to worry. He had to keep reminding himself that time between the territories wasn't relative. Still, as days passed, Mark found himself thinking more and more about the trouble on Veelox.

Then, toward the end of the week, something finally happened.

There was no Sci-Clops meeting that afternoon, so Mark caught the early bus home after school. The bus stopped a few blocks from Mark's house and he always walked the direct route home. But today he took another route. He wasn't sure why; he just felt like walking. So he took the long way home.

Mark was pretty familiar with every other house in the neighborhood. Though a few were modern, most dated back a long time, some over a hundred years. All the yards were big, with huge leafy trees that shaded the grass. Fall was coming on fast now and many of the trees had already traded their green leaves for brilliant colors of orange and yellow. It was Mark's favorite time of year. Chilly but not yet wintry. The wind was brisk, the sky was blue, and he even loved the smell of burning leaves. It was the perfect afternoon to walk a roundabout route home and try not to think about territories and Travelers.

His vacation didn't last very long.

As he walked along the cracked sidewalk, kicking leaves,

Mark's ring began to twitch. He stopped short. Naturally his first thought was: "Bobby's next journal!" But when he looked at his ring, he saw that the large gray stone in the center wasn't making the change. It was the odd symbol that glowed brightly—the same symbol that foreshadowed the arrival of the note from Dorney. Maybe it was a message from the old man to say the time was right to learn about being an acolyte!

Mark ducked into the bushes near a tall cement wall. He didn't want anybody to see what was about to happen. He dropped his pack on the ground, then took the ring off and put it down next to the pack, waiting for it to start growing.

It didn't. The light continued to glow from the symbol, but the ring didn't change size. What was going on? Mark picked up the ring and put it back on his finger. The symbol glowed, but that was it. No change, no note, no nothing. Weird. With a shrug, Mark continued walking home. When he got to the next corner, he noticed that the glowing symbol had gone dark.

False alarm, he thought, and continued walking.

When he got halfway across the street, he realized he'd left his pack next to the cement wall. *Duh!* He did a quick about-face and jogged back to get it. But no sooner did he arrive at the pack than the ring twitched and the symbol began to glow again. Mark waited a few minutes to see if the ring would do anything more dramatic, but it didn't. He grabbed his pack, slung it over his shoulder, and hurried toward home. But when he reached the street, the symbol stopped glowing. Mark felt sure something was going on, but had no idea what it could be.

Then an idea struck him. He turned and slowly walked back toward the cement wall. Sure enough, as soon as he got close, the symbol grew bright again. Uh-oh. This was no false alarm. Something was happening, and it had to do with where he was.

Mark looked up at the cement wall to see where he was, and his heart sank.

"Oh great," he muttered.

He was standing in front of the Sherwood house. Everybody knew it. It was the biggest property in the neighborhood. The house was built in the early 1900s by some rich guy who'd made his fortune raising chickens and selling eggs, of all things. At one time there was a poultry farm on the property, but that was long gone. The house was still there, though. It was surrounded by the high cement wall that Mark was standing in front of now. It was actually more of a mansion than a house. The place was huge.

The thing was, nobody had lived there for years. Mark's mom told him that once old man Sherwood died, none of his kids wanted to run a chicken farm. But they couldn't agree on what to do with the property. So there it sat, a giant piece of land with a big old mansion on it, going to waste, falling apart.

Of course, all the kids in the neighborhood made up ghost stories about seeing shadows walking past windows and hearing strange sounds on Halloween. Bobby once made up a story about how the ghosts were actually chicken spirits looking for revenge. That was Mark's favorite. But he didn't believe in ghosts and didn't think for a minute that the place was really haunted. Still, he never went near the place by himself.

Until today.

The glowing symbol on his ring was telling him something, and he had the sick feeling that whatever it was, it was inside the Sherwood house. *Gulp.* Mark had a quick thought of putting this off until he could come back with Courtney, but his curiosity was stronger than his fear.

Halfway down the block was a big old set of black iron gates, but a heavy steel chain and padlock told him this wouldn't be the way in. He only had one choice. He had to go over the wall. So he walked alongside the high wall until he found a tree that was close enough to climb up and get over the top. As he stood looking up, he wasn't worried about ghosts or banshees or dead chickens running around with their heads chopped off. That was kid stuff. He was more worried about getting caught trespassing. The idea of calling his parents from jail was not a good one. Still, the insistent glowing of the symbol on his ring told him he had to keep going.

He pushed his hair out of his eyes and dug his sneakers into the tree. Moments later he was up and over the wall, landing in tall grass. So far so good. He looked at his ring to see the small symbol was glowing brighter. He was definitely on the right track.

He looked up at the house and could see why kids thought it was haunted. The place was ancient. The wind kicked up and the fall trees swayed back and forth, slashing against its walls. The yard was a mess too. A caretaker could be seen every month or so, cleaning up dead branches and making simple repairs, but that wasn't enough to make the place look lived in. No, this was a big, empty, lonely old haunted-looking house.

And Mark was on his way in.

The ground floor was surrounded by a wide porch. He imagined people sitting there in rocking chairs on a hot summer night, drinking iced tea and swapping chicken stories. But they were long gone. The only thing on the porch now was dead leaves. Mark walked up the five stone steps that led to the porch.

He thought he saw something move past a window inside the house. It was fast, and he wasn't completely sure he really saw it, but the hair went up on his arms just the same. He stopped at the top of the stairs, looking into the dark windows for any sign of movement. There was none.

He started walking toward the front door . . . and saw something again. It was a quick shadow moving past the window. For a second he actually thought it was a ghost. But there were no such things as ghosts. Then again, he never thought there were such things as Travelers, either. He looked around and decided the ghost was nothing more than the reflection of a tree branch waving in the wind. At least, that's what he told himself.

Mark walked cautiously up to the front door and tried the knob. It was locked.

"Great," he said to himself. "Now what?"

That's when he heard something inside the house. It was fleeting, but it sounded like something had run past, just inside the door.

"Heeeere, chickie, chickie, chickie!" Mark croaked nervously, though the idea of there still being chickens around was absurd. He looked at his ring. The symbol was glowing with a fierce intensity. He needed to know why.

He moved over to the big window next to the door and put his nose right against the glass to try and block as much of the outside light as possible. That helped a little, and he got a better view of the inside of the Sherwood house.

The place was empty. The only illumination inside came from windows farther back in the house, and they didn't do much to light the place up. Very creepy. There was no furniture, or pictures, or any sign of life—"

GRRRRRR!

A hideous, black animal face leaped out of the shadows inside. It stared Mark square in the eyes. Drool dripped from its white fangs as it snarled viciously, trying to bite through the glass and get a chunk of Mark-meat.

Mark yelped in surprise and fell backward, landing on his butt. He stared up at the window to see two more animals join the first. They were awful-looking black creatures that could have been dogs, but no dog Mark had ever seen looked as evil as these beasts. They were focused on him, with only a thin pane of glass holding them back.

Mark pushed himself along the floor of the porch to get away. The beasts barked and snarled. Mark's mind was reeling. What were dogs doing in there? Were they watchdogs? They definitely weren't ordinary dogs. They were vicious, uncontrollable demons, and they were out for blood. They were . . .

It suddenly hit him. It was something from Bobby's very first journal. What gave it away were the horrible, yellow eyes. There was no mistake.

"Quigs," Mark whispered to himself.

☻ SECOND EARTH ☻
(CONTINUED)

Smash!

The beasts threw themselves against the glass, desperate to attack Mark.

Mark knew the glass would be no match for these demons. He had to get out of there, fast. He jumped up and ran. He suddenly realized he had left his backpack on the porch, but the pounding on the window meant he wasn't going back for it. No way. Mark sprinted across the overgrown yard, heading for the wall and safety.

He now saw that he was in deep trouble. When he first arrived, he had been so worried about getting caught trespassing that he hadn't taken the time to figure out a way to climb back over the wall. Now he had another worry. He was worried about being trapped and eaten.

Crash!

The window shattered. The quigs were coming. Mark could hear them yelp and snarl as they tumbled over one another to get through the broken window.

He was still twenty yards from the nine-foot wall. He desperately scanned left and right, looking for a way to scale it. Without some kind of help, Mark didn't think he could make it over. He dared not look back, because he knew what he'd see. Every second counted. If the quigs got to him before he got to the wall, there wouldn't be enough of him left for anyone to find.

Mark saw nothing to help him climb.

The snarling quigs drew closer. In seconds they'd be on him. But Mark was focused. He had no plan, but had to think of one fast or in seconds he'd be dog food. He was almost at the wall, but didn't slow down. He thought to himself, "I'm gonna run right up the side!"

He hit the wall running and dug his sneaker into the crumbling cement. His toe caught. He launched off it and grabbed the top of the wall. Normally Mark couldn't even vault over the pommel horse in gym. But normally Mark wasn't jet powered by surging adrenaline. He heaved himself up by his arms, threw both his legs to one side, and flung his body up and over.

No sooner did he clear the top than all three quigs hit the other side of the wall, yelping and crying for having missed their prey. Mark sailed down and hit the ground, rolling away from the wall, lucky not to have broken an ankle. He jumped up and did a quick check to make sure all body parts were intact. They were. He stood there for a second, trying to catch his breath. He listened as the quigs snarled from the other side in frustration.

Mark smiled. He had made it. It was probably the most exciting moment of his life. He even dared to think that this adventure rivaled some of the stories that Bobby had told. He had met a pack of hungry quigs and lived to tell the story.

But his joy didn't last long. The glowing ring on his finger took it away. The truth was, the adventure wasn't over. Whatever was in that house, whatever was making his ring glow, he was going to have to come back and find it. Running away wasn't going to cut it. He was going to have to get past those quigs.

But next time, he was bringing Courtney.

Courtney knew this was her golden opportunity.

There was going to be a practice scrimmage between the varsity and the JV soccer teams. She had been practicing hard with the JV, swallowing her pride and improving her skills, waiting for the chance to prove herself worthy of being back on the varsity. This was her chance. She was going toe-to-toe with the very girls who had tarnished the golden reputation of the unbeatable Courtney Chetwynde. Revenge was not too strong a word to describe what was on Courtney's mind when she stepped onto that field. Her game face was on; her emotions were in check; she was ready.

So was the varsity. It seemed as if its entire game plan was about stopping Courtney. She was double-teamed all day and pretty much taken out of the action. Making things worse, with only a few minutes left to play, the JV team was losing 5-3. But truth be told, Courtney didn't care if they won or lost. All she wanted was to prove that she could compete. That wasn't happening.

Finally, with only seconds on the clock, she got her chance. She was playing forward and the ball was passed to her. She was being double-teamed and one of the defenders fell. Courtney used the player's body as interference and got past the second defender. It was now one-on-one between Courtney and the goalie. This was her moment . . . her chance to put a solid exclamation point on the game. She wanted this goal bad. She *needed* this goal. She dribbled the ball in quickly, deeked a kick that made the goalie move right, then drew back to fire the ball into the opposite corner of the net. It was perfect.

Almost.

Just as she was about to deliver the killer kick, the defender sprinted up from behind and took her out. It was a totally illegal move. The defender slid into Courtney's feet like a baseball runner sliding into second base. Instead of putting her foot into the ball, Courtney landed on her back. Hard. Whistles blew, a penalty was coming, but it didn't matter to Courtney. Her moment was lost.

She jumped to her feet, screaming, "What was *that*?"

Before the defender knew what was happening, Courtney gave her a wicked shove that sent her sprawling back onto the grass. She put her knee on the player's back so she couldn't get up. All her frustration finally came pouring out.

"I beat you and you know it!" she shouted.

A second later the other players descended and pulled the two girls apart. It was tough pulling Courtney away because she was so enraged. The defender got back to her feet and was ready to take Courtney on.

"Come on!" she taunted Courtney.

Courtney tried to lunge at the girl, but the other players held her back. Finally Coach Horkey ran in between the two girls and restored order.

"Enough!" she shouted. "Laura," she said to the defender. "Inside. All of you, locker room."

The fight was over. So was the scrimmage. The girls walked off, grumbling.

"Courtney," Coach Horkey said firmly. "Stay here."

As Laura, the defender, walked off, she looked over her shoulder and snarled, "Loser."

"Enough!" shouted Coach Horkey. Laura put her head down and kept walking. Courtney didn't budge. She was breathing hard, still fired up from the fight.

"She deserved it, Coach," Courtney pointed out. "It was a total cheap shot."

"It wasn't," Horkey countered. "She had a point to give and made the aggressive play."

"But don't you see? All they care about is shutting me down! It's been that way since day one!"

"I'll tell you what I see," Horkey said. "I see a girl who is faced with a challenge for the first time in her life. A *true* challenge. And she is losing. Courtney, you are a talented athlete. But it takes more than skill to be a winner. You know how to handle success, but not failure. Until you can do that, you won't help this team, or any other."

Courtney didn't say anything. As much as she hated to admit it, Horkey's words rang true.

"I'm suspending you for two weeks," Horkey added.

"What!"

"Players on my team don't fight. Especially with each other. Think about that and come back in two weeks." Horkey jogged off the field.

Courtney was left stunned. Not only was she demoted from varsity to JV, now she was kicked off JV! She stood in the middle of the field, covered with dirt, unable to accept this impossible turn of events. How could this have happened? How could she have fallen so far? In her heart she still believed she was as much of a competitor as ever, but reality was telling her otherwise.

Courtney walked off the field, but didn't go into the locker room. She didn't want to face the other girls. She knew the *old* Courtney would have walked right into that locker room and taken the heat. But then again, she'd never had to take any heat before. Not like this. Courtney began to wonder if there was ever such a thing as the old Courtney. Maybe this is who she always was . . . a gutless coward.

She walked past the locker room and made the commitment

to walk all the way home. It was going to be a long walk. But she wasn't about to take the late bus, either. All she wanted to do was crawl into bed. Since it was Friday, she wouldn't have to worry about facing anybody for a couple of days.

"Courtney!" a familiar voice shouted.

Courtney had rounded the school and was headed for the sidewalk when Mark came riding up on his bike. He was out of breath and excited.

"You're not going to believe it!" he exclaimed. "I was—" Mark focused on the fact that Courtney was still in her soccer uniform, totally dirty, still wearing her cleats, and walking away from school. "What's going on?"

"Don't ask" was all Courtney could get out. Mark got off his bike and walked alongside her.

"You're walking home?" he asked, confused.

"I'm really hurting, Mark," she said. "Can we talk about it some other time?"

"Yeah, sure." They walked in silence. Mark was dying to tell Courtney what had happened at the Sherwood house, but wasn't sure if she was in the mood to talk about anything. Still, she had to know.

"Can we talk about something else?" he asked tentatively.

"Whatever."

"Something happened today," Mark said. "I . . . I'm not sure exactly what it means, but I'm guessing it has something to do with the acolyte thing."

Courtney stopped short. A second before, she looked like the walking dead. Now a spark had returned to her eyes. Mark thought that whatever had happened at soccer, it had beaten her up pretty badly. But the fire still burned inside her. He knew Courtney too well to think otherwise.

"Another journal?" she asked.

"No," Mark answered. "Let's go for a ride."

Mark tried to ride Courtney on the handlebars of his bike. It didn't work. Courtney was too tall and Mark was too . . . Mark. So they switched places and Courtney gave Mark the ride. Along the way Mark told her everything that happened at the Sherwood house. Courtney didn't ask any questions. She just listened. By the time Mark had finished the story, they found themselves parked right back where the mystery began. They were in front of the locked iron gates of the spooky old house.

Mark held up his ring. The symbol was glowing again.

"What do you think?" Mark asked.

"I think we've got to find out what's inside that house," Courtney answered.

"Easier said than done," Mark replied. "You didn't see those dogs."

Courtney looked up at the sky and said, "It's gonna be dark soon. I say we come back tomorrow, with some help."

Courtney's idea of help was an obvious one. They waited until the next morning, then Mark came over to Courtney's house and they put a call into their friend on the Stony Brook police force, Captain Hirsch.

They had met Captain Hirsch when Bobby and his family first disappeared. Since then Hirsch had been working on the missing persons case. Of course, Mark and Courtney knew the truth about what had happened to Bobby, but decided not to tell, for fear of interfering with Bobby's mission as a Traveler. Still, they kept in touch with Hirsch. He was a good guy. Now, they hoped, he was going to help them get one step closer to unraveling the mystery of the acolytes.

Mark told Captain Hirsch about there being strange dogs running around the Sherwood property. He really built it up, saying how the dogs were vicious and wild. There was no way these dogs were somebody's pets. Of course, Mark left out the part about having been trespassing on the property. He also didn't mention that the dogs might be evil quig beasts who were guarding a secret inside the house. That wouldn't have been cool.

A half hour later Mark and Courtney met two uniformed police officers outside the front gate to the Sherwood house.

"Hi, guys," one of them said. "Remember me? Officer Wilson?"

"Sure we do!" Courtney said.

Officer Wilson had once given the two kids a ride to the police station. He was a good guy, too.

"This is Officer Matt." Everybody shook hands. "Tell us what you saw."

Mark again explained how there were three dogs inside. Big, vicious, slobbering dogs with sharp fangs. Mark wasn't exaggerating. He wanted to make sure the cops knew exactly what they were getting themselves into.

Officer Wilson had a key to the lock on the front gate. They explained to Mark and Courtney that the Sherwood family had given it to the police in case of an emergency. This definitely qualified. While Wilson unlocked the gate, Officer Matt opened the trunk of their squad car and pulled out two pieces of equipment. One was a long metal rod with a loop of cable on the end. It was a snare that animal control officers use to capture dogs. The other thing Officer Matt pulled out was a tranquilizer rifle. Mark knew that if one of these dogs got the chance, it would tear a person apart. He wasn't so sure that a tranquilizer dart would do anything to stop it either. Still, it was better than nothing.

"Don't bother with the snare," Mark advised. "You aren't going to want to catch one of these monsters."

Officer Matt chuckled, but kept the snare.

"We'd like to come with you," Courtney said.

The two cops shared looks. They didn't like the idea of putting the kids in danger.

"C'mon!" Courtney cajoled. "We'll stay behind you. And you've got guns and snares and stuff, right?"

Wilson shrugged. "Okay. Just stay close."

They followed the two cops onto the property. Wilson held the snare, Matt kept the tranquilizer gun pointed at the ground, but ready.

Mark made sure to close the iron gates behind them. He also took off his ring and put it in his pocket. He didn't want the cops to ask him why he had a ring that was shooting off light.

Officer Wilson whistled. "Here, boy! C'mon!" He whistled again.

Nothing happened.

The four walked up to the porch. Mark kept glancing behind them, making sure that one of the black dogs wasn't sneaking up quietly.

"Uh-oh, what's this?" Officer Matt said. He reached down and picked up the shredded remains of Mark's backpack. Oops. Mark had totally forgotten.

"That's mine," he said. "I dropped it outside. They must have dragged it in here." It was a small lie, but Mark didn't want to admit he had been trespassing. "Look," he added to change the subject. "That's where they broke through the window."

Wilson pointed out the shards of glass on the porch. "It was broken from inside," he deduced. "They must have cut themselves up pretty good."

"How did you know they broke through the window?" Officer Matt asked Mark. "You can't see it from the gate."

Oops. Mark had to think fast. "I heard the glass break and then saw them running around."

Were the police going to buy this story? Of course they were.

Mark wasn't the type to trespass on private property . . . or so they thought. Mark held up the remains of his backpack. The quigs had really chewed it up. He lost two textbooks, a library book, a chocolate bar, and all his carrots. Mark knew that chocolate wasn't good for dogs and hoped they choked on it.

"Let's check inside," Officer Wilson suggested.

Wilson had a key for the front door as well. When they all stepped inside, both Mark and Courtney had the same thought: *haunted house.* The place was huge, with high ceilings and a curved staircase that led to the second floor.

"Here, boy!" Wilson called out again, and whistled.

Again, no response. Mark looked to Courtney and shrugged. He really wanted to look at his ring, but didn't risk taking it out of his pocket. The policemen then led the kids on a tour of the house, checking each and every room. They first checked the ground floor, walking through the grand entryway, through the living room, the huge dining room and into the big kitchen. Besides the broken window, there was no sign of any dog.

They went down to the basement. It was a vast space with a cement floor. There were a few wooden doors that were closed. The officers opened them all. One room had nothing but empty, wooden racks. The wine cellar. Another room had a long wooden table that was scarred and stained. The workshop. Another room was nothing more than a large, cool space with wispy remnants that looked like dead weeds hanging from the ceiling. Mark had heard of places like this. Root cellar is what his grandmother used to call it. It was a cool, dry place for storing onions and potatoes and the like. It looked to be dug out of the earth, with one wall being nothing more than a vast chunk of the rock that the house had been built on top of.

It was all very interesting, but there were no dogs.

The caravan then went up to the second floor. There was one long corridor with empty bedrooms off either side. Each of the rooms was connected by an inner door, so that you could choose to travel from one end of the house to the other through the corridor, or by going from room to room. Again, no dogs.

The next stop was the third floor. This was a smaller floor than the others. There were two bedrooms on one side, and a large attic on the other with a high, pointed ceiling where you could see the rafters of the house. It was empty. No dogs and no sign that dogs had ever been there. Once they stepped into the attic, the last room of the house, the police officers relaxed.

"Whatever you saw, Mark," Wilson said, "they're gone now."

"Are you sure? I mean, maybe we should check the yard."

Wilson shrugged. "Sure, why not?"

They all went downstairs and out onto the porch. The four of them moved cautiously around the whole property. Mark had no idea it was so big. They saw some old wooden buildings that probably had something to do with the chicken farm. There were a lot of trees and an empty swimming pool and even a small golf green. At one time this was a busy place. Now it was forgotten and sad. The policemen even inspected every inch of the wall along the ground to see if an animal might have tunneled its way in or out. But there was no sign of anything like that.

"Any other ideas?" Officer Wilson asked. The cop respected Mark. If any other kid had given them this story, they probably wouldn't have believed a word.

"No," Mark answered. "Sorry."

Courtney glanced to Mark with a "You *sure* you saw dogs?" look. Mark could only shrug.

"Don't be sorry," Wilson said. "You did the right thing. Whatever was in here got away somehow, that's all."

They walked out through the front gate and Officer Matt locked it up. Officer Wilson returned the tranquilizer gun and the snare to the trunk of the police cruiser.

"If you see anything else, be sure to call, okay?" Wilson said.

"Okay," Mark answered.

The two cops got back into their cruiser and sped off, leaving Mark and Courtney alone in front of the house.

"I'm not lying, Courtney," Mark said.

"I didn't think you were."

"So then what happened to the quigs?" he said as he reached into his pocket and pulled out his ring. The strange symbol was glowing brightly.

"I don't know," answered Courtney. "But we saw pretty much every inch of that place and there was nothing strange that would make that ring glow."

"Then we missed it," Mark announced.

The two looked at each other. Each knew what the other was thinking.

"We gotta go back in," Mark said with finality.

"Yeah, I know. Where's the tree we gotta climb over?" Courtney asked.

● SECOND EARTH ●
(CONTINUED)

Mark led Courtney around to the side of the property and the tree that was their ladder. Courtney gave Mark a leg up, then Mark reached down and gave Courtney a helping hand. Seconds later the two of them jumped off the wall and landed back inside the property.

"Wait," Mark said. He looked back at the wall, scanning both left and right.

"What are you looking for?" Courtney asked.

"There!" Mark pointed to an old, wooden tool shed. "If we gotta get back over fast, head for that shed. We can climb up the side."

He wasn't going to make the same mistake twice. This time he wanted to be ready. Courtney nodded and headed for the house. Neither was nervous, since they had just done a thorough inspection and knew the quigs were gone.

"I say we start inside the house," Courtney said. "There are a lot of rooms we may have missed."

They climbed up onto the porch and stopped at the broken window.

"That's our door," Mark announced. He made a move to go in, but Courtney stopped him.

"Mark, I'm in," she said.

"What do you mean?"

"I mean I want to be an acolyte."

Mark couldn't help but smile. "You sure?"

"Yeah, it just took some time to get my head around it," Courtney said sincerely. "I think it's an important thing to do. And I don't want to let you down. Or Bobby."

Mark smiled. "I never thought you would," he said as he lifted one leg through the broken window.

Mark's confidence in her made Courtney feel better than she had in weeks. Maybe Mark was right. Maybe she had a more important role to play than sports superstar. She knew one thing for certain: She wanted the chance to find out. But there was no time to feel warm and fuzzy. They had work to do. So Courtney followed Mark inside.

The two of them stood in the grand entryway, once again taking it all in.

"Where to first?" Courtney asked.

Mark lifted his ring and saw that the symbol was still glowing brightly.

"Let's start in the attic and work our way—" Mark stopped talking. He had heard something. Courtney heard it too.

"What was that?" Courtney asked.

"Sounded like something scratching across wood."

"There it is again!" Courtney exclaimed. "It's outside, on the porch."

They both turned to the broken window they had just come through.

"It could be squirrels," Mark said hopefully.

More scratching. Whatever it was, it was moving quickly back and forth on the porch.

"Or birds," Courtney offered.

"Or . . . quigs."

Courtney laughed nervously. "Don't even joke—"

Smash! Smash! Smash!

Three windows shattered as black quig dogs came crashing into the house.

"C'mon!" Courtney grabbed Mark's hand and they ran up the stairs. The quigs were slightly dazed by the hammering their heads just took, and it gave Mark and Courtney enough time to make it to the top. But a second later the quigs had their wits back, sniffed the air, and charged up the stairs after them.

Mark and Courtney sprinted along the hallway, not sure where to go.

"The window at the end!" Mark shouted.

"We'll never make it," Courtney yelled, and pulled Mark into one of the empty bedrooms. They quickly closed the door. There were two other doors in the room. They were the doors that led to the adjoining bedrooms.

"Close those doors!" Courtney ordered.

They each ran to one of the doors and closed it.

"We're dead," Mark said.

Courtney ran for the window. She tried to lift it up, but it had been closed for years and wouldn't budge.

Mark then noticed something. "Look," he said, holding his hand up. His ring had stopped glowing.

"Not now, Mark. Wait here," she said, and ran to the other door that led to an adjoining room.

"Where are you going?"

Slam!

The quigs had found them. They were trying to batter down the door Mark had just closed. Mark leaned against it to keep them out. He could hear their angry growling.

"Get ready to open that door," Courtney ordered, and ran out of the room.

"What?" Mark screamed in shock. There was no way he was opening the door.

Courtney moved quickly and quietly through the next bedroom and poked her head out into the hallway. It was empty. She could hear the sound of the quigs slamming themselves against the door that Mark was holding shut.

"Hey!" she shouted. "Devil dogs! Suppertime! Come and get it!"

The banging stopped. Suddenly all three quigs came charging out of the far bedroom and into the hallway, headed for her.

"Psyche," she shouted, and ducked back into the bedroom. She then sprinted through the room and back into the bedroom where Mark was. She didn't close the door behind her either.

Mark yelled, "Close the door!"

"No!" Courtney shouted. "Open yours!"

Mark hesitated. He didn't know the quigs had left. But it was clear that Courtney wasn't stopping. If he didn't open the door, she'd run right into it. So he swallowed hard and pulled it open. It wasn't a second too soon, because Courtney blasted through at full throttle.

"Close it behind you!" she shouted.

Mark didn't know what she was doing, until he looked back and saw the three quigs flying toward him, through the bedroom. They had come through the door Courtney left open. Mark jumped out the door and pulled it closed as . . . *slam slam slam!* All three quigs hit the door. Now Mark and the quigs were on opposite sides from where they had been a few moments before. He still had no idea what Courtney was doing.

Courtney never stopped running. She turned into the hallway and sprinted along the same route the quigs had just taken after her. She knew that either her plan was going to work, or she was about to serve herself up for lunch. She ran into the third bedroom and ran toward the connecting door that led back to the second bedroom. Her plan was to lock them inside.

The quigs had figured it out. They stopped trying to beat down the door, and turned back for the door they had just entered through. But Courtney was too fast. She reached inside the room, grabbed the doorknob, said, "G'night kids!" and slammed the door closed, trapping the quigs in the bedroom. Again the quigs slammed at the door in a blood rage.

Mark poked his head into the room. "Can we go now?" he asked.

The two of them ran back along the hallway and hurried down the stairs. They were just about to exit through the broken window when Mark stopped.

"Look!" he exclaimed and held up his hand. His ring was glowing again. "Whatever it is, it's down here. Or down *there*," he said as he pointed at the door to the basement.

"Forget it! Those dogs are—"

Mark wasn't listening. He ran to the basement door and opened it. Sure enough, the symbol on his ring glowed even brighter.

"It's down there!"

"If the quigs get out, we'll be trapped," Courtney warned. Too late. Mark was already headed down the stairs. Courtney ran right after him. She made sure to close the door behind her this time, just in case.

The large basement didn't look any different than a few

minutes before, except for one thing: Mark's ring was blasting out light as if it were alive.

"This is it!" Mark declared.

"There's nothing here," Courtney exclaimed. "We looked behind every door!"

A horrifying sound came from above. It was the sound of the quigs running down the stairs from the second floor. They had gotten out of the bedroom. Mark and Courtney looked up in fear. Mark was about to say something, but Courtney held her hand over his mouth. She put her fingers to her lips for him to "Shhhh." They didn't move. They didn't make a sound. They thought that with any luck, the quigs wouldn't find them.

Slam!

No such luck. The quigs found them and were trying to batter down the door.

"We gotta find a way out," Courtney said with a shaky voice.

"No," Mark yelled back. "We gotta find out what's down here." Mark looked around. He went to the door that led to the wine cellar and threw it open.

Slam! Slam!

The quigs threw themselves at the basement door with a horrifying fury. They seemed even more out of control than before.

"They know we're close," Mark said. "They don't want us to find it."

Courtney saw something they hadn't noticed before. A raggy curtain was hanging on the wall, covering it from ceiling to floor. Courtney pushed it aside to find another door. She quickly pulled it open and shouted for joy. Daylight flooded into the basement.

"Yes! It's the way out! Mark, c'mon!"

Mark ignored her. He threw open the door to the workshop, but nothing was out of the ordinary.

"Mark, c'mon!" Courtney yelled.

Crunch!

The basement door was starting to splinter. A few more shots and it would come down . . . and so would the quigs.

"Mark!" Courtney cried.

Mark wasn't going to run. Not now. Not when they were so close. He was about to open the next door, the one that led to the root cellar, when he felt something strange. He looked down at his hand, then grimaced in pain.

"Ahhhh!"

Courtney ran to him. "What's the matter?"

CRASH!

The wooden basement door gave way and clattered down the stairs. The quigs were on their way.

"It's burning hot!" Mark yelled, and pulled off his ring.

Courtney turned to see the quigs had begun their final, fatal charge. "This is gonna hurt" was all she could say.

Mark threw the burning ring onto the floor. Instantly a high-pitched sound came from it. It wasn't a painful sound; it was more like a jumble of high musical notes that were all being played at the same time.

Courtney grabbed Mark. Mark grabbed Courtney. The two turned to face the charging quigs to see . . .

They had stopped. The three beastly dogs, their yellow eyes still intensely focused, had stopped. They twisted their heads as if the strange sound were irritating them. A second later the three dogs turned and ran back up the stairs, tails between their legs, whining in fear.

Mark and Courtney looked back down to the ring to see that it was moving. It wasn't growing though. It began to spin. It was slow at first, but picked up momentum until the ring was up on end, spinning so fast that it was nothing more than a blur. The high-pitched notes grew louder.

"Look!" Mark said, pointing at the door to the root cellar.

Courtney looked to see the door was starting to rattle on its hinges.

"Something's in there," Courtney said in shock.

"Maybe," Mark said. "Or m-maybe something's coming."

The rattling continued, then an intense light began to leak from around the edges of the door. Whatever was behind there, it was giving off a light so bright that Mark and Courtney had to squint, even though it was only coming from the crack around the edges. The strange sound from the ring grew even more intense. Now it was so loud it started to hurt. Mark and Courtney both had to cover their ears. The light from behind the door grew even brighter. The door shook furiously. Mark was ready for it to blow off its hinges.

It was then that the most incredible event of all occurred. As the ring continued to spin, a laser light shot from it, aimed at the wooden door. Mark and Courtney watched in awe as the intense white light hit the door at head level. Smoke rose from where the light hit the wood. The door was burning.

And then, like somebody pulled the plug on a lamp, everything stopped. Everything—the beam of light from the ring; the bright light from behind the door; the strange, piercing sound. And finally the ring itself stopped spinning. It rolled one last time, then came to a stop with a slight, metallic *ping*. It was over. All was back to normal.

All but one small thing.

"Oh, man," Courtney said in awe.

Mark saw that she was looking at the door to the root cellar. At first, Mark wasn't sure why she was so stunned, and then he saw it. It was on the door, right where the beam from the ring had hit it. There was no mistake. They had seen this once before and read about it many times over.

It was a star. The sign of a gate.

Mark reached down and picked up the ring. It was no longer glowing and was now cool enough to touch. It had done its job. Courtney walked over to the door and touched the blackened symbol.

"It's still hot," she said. She looked to Mark and asked, "Could it be?"

"Open the d-door," Mark said. "My hand's shaking."

Courtney reached down and grabbed the door handle. "My hand's shaking too," she said.

Mark put his hand over Courtney's and the two of them pulled the door open.

The room looked pretty much the same as it had when they searched it before. It was a large, empty space with a dirt floor and bits of dried weeds hanging from the beams of the ceiling. It was cool inside, just the way a subterranean root cellar should be. It was the exact same room that they had been in before, except for one small change. The rock that made up one whole wall of the cellar was gone.

Mark and Courtney stood together, staring, not breathing. Instead of a rock wall, they now looked into a craggy opening. It was unmistakable.

It was a flume.

Neither could speak. They both stood there, staring into the infinite tunnel. It was Mark who first broke the silence.

"D-Do you think m-maybe this means the time is right for us to be acolytes?"

Courtney stared into the tunnel a moment more, then started to laugh. "Yeah," she said through the laughter. "I'd say this is a pretty good sign."

Mark laughed too. The two laughed and hugged. Neither knew what the future held, but one thing was for certain: They were no longer just bystanders whose job it was to read Bobby's mail. They were in the game now. For real.

Mark's ring twitched.

"Uh-oh," he said, and held his hand up.

"Now what?" Courtney exclaimed. "I don't know if I can take any more fireworks."

But this event was safe and familiar. The center stone of the ring started to glow. Mark took it off and placed it down on the dirt floor. This time the ring grew, opening up the portal to the territories. The familiar musical notes grew louder, bringing with them a special delivery. The sparkling light filled the underground room. For Mark and Courtney, it was like being held in a warm embrace. The lights flashed one final time, the notes fell silent, and the ring was once again back to its normal size.

Lying next to it was the silver projector that held Bobby's next journal.

"Hobey-ho," whispered Mark.

VEELOX

We were good to go.

Loor and I stood facing the three silver disks in the wall of the alpha jump cubicle, wearing our dark green one-piece suits. Loor had been through the prep routine. Her blood had been scanned and she was fitted with a silver control bracelet. I got my own control bracelet too, but after what had happened during my last jump, I wasn't going to put a whole lot of faith in that thing.

Our safety was in the hands of Aja Killian. She had put the alpha grid that controlled Zetlin's jump back online. She would now monitor our jump into Zetlin's fantasy and yank us out if anything went wrong. At least, that was the plan. Once we were in Dr. Zetlin's jump, the Reality Bug might have plans of its own.

"Any questions?" Aja asked us. She stood at the door of the jump cubicle.

"No," Loor answered calmly.

What could Loor ask? This was a girl from a territory of primitive, tribal warriors. The idea of jumping into somebody else's fantasy was about as alien to her as, well, I seriously doubt if there's anything that comes close to being that alien.

Aja stepped back into the Alpha Core and sat in the big chair. She hit a few buttons on the silver control panel on the arm. Two of the three silver disks in the wall retracted, and the tables slowly slid out. These tubes were on either side of the center jump tube where Dr. Zetlin was lying. It was creepy to think there was a guy in there, and we were about to leap into his mind.

I hoped there was room for all of us.

"Lie down on the table," I instructed Loor. "Get comfortable."

She did. Loor trusted me. Man, I hoped she wasn't making a mistake. I walked out of the jump cubicle and went to Aja.

"Do you have any idea where we might find him?" I asked.

Aja frowned. "I'm sorry, Pendragon," she said. "It all depends on the fantasy he created."

She showed me a picture. It was the old-man version of the little kid in the oil painting outside. There was nothing unique about him. He just looked like a smart old man. He was bald and wore round little glasses. I memorized the face.

"So all I have to do is ask him for the origin code, right?" I asked.

"Yes. Tell him the main grid has been suspended because the processing code has been corrupted. Tell him we have to clean the string."

"Origin code, corrupted processing code, clean the string—got it."

"I doubt he'll give it up easily," Aja added. She leaned over my shoulder and glanced at Loor, who was now lying quietly on the table. "You may have to force him to end his jump."

"Let's find him first," I said.

"Right," she said.

There was something bothering me, and I had to say it. "Aja, if the Reality Bug is doing its thing, you might be in danger too. I mean, look what happened to Alex."

Aja shrugged and gave a cocky reply. "I'm not Alex."

Gotta love this girl. She wasn't short on confidence.

"Just be careful," I said, then turned and walked toward my jump tube.

"Pendragon," Aja called to me. I stopped at the door to the cubicle and looked back at her.

"I'm glad you're here," she said.

It was the nicest thing Aja Killian had ever said to me.

"We're gonna fix this, Aja," I said, trying to sound as confident as she was.

"We don't have a choice," she replied.

She was right. If we were to have any hope of rescuing Veelox from itself, and from Saint Dane, we had to purge the Reality Bug. I walked back to the jump tubes and looked down at Loor.

"What do I do, Pendragon?" she asked.

"Nothing," I answered. "Just relax. You'll slide inside, it'll be dark for a few seconds and then we'll be together in the jump." I called out to Aja, "Right?"

"Exactly," Aja called back. "I'll be watching it all on the monitor."

I hopped up onto my table and settled in. My heart started to beat faster. It was game time.

"Hobey-ho, let's go!" I called out.

Loor called out, "Aja? What should I be ready for?" I could sense the slight tension in her voice. Loor was the single most fearless person I had ever met. But this was scary, even for her.

Aja answered with one, simple word. "Everything."

Funny. That was exactly what I was *afraid* of.

Everything.

I was hit with a blinding flash of light and threw my hand up to cover my eyes. My first thought was that something had gone haywire and I was floating in limbo. But a second later I realized what had happened.

I was staring up at the sun.

I quickly looked down to see I was standing on hard-packed dirt. I didn't think there was a sun or dirt in limbo, so everything was cool. A few seconds later my eyes adjusted, and I got the first look at my surroundings. I was standing in the center of a rocky canyon. The walls rose steeply on either side of me. In the distance, the canyon made a few gentle turns, and emptied out into a green meadow. Beyond that in the far distance were snow-capped mountains. Not bad. Dr. Zetlin's fantasy took place on a warm, sunny day in the great outdoors.

"Where are we, Pendragon?" Loor asked.

Oh, right. Loor. I almost forgot. I spun around to see her standing behind me. I smiled and said, "Howdy there, buckaroo."

Loor gave me a strange look that said, "What the heck are you talking about?"

I didn't blame her, but I couldn't resist, because Loor was now dressed like a cowboy. Or cowgirl. Or cow-Traveler. Whatever. She had on blue jeans, a deep red shirt, and black cowboy boots. Her long black hair was tied back in a tight ponytail that reached down to the small of her back. Tied around her forehead was a rolled black bandana. She looked great.

I was pretty much dressed the same way: blue jeans, a deep green shirt, and the same kind of black boots. I even had a bandana around my neck. Dr. Zetlin's fantasy was something right out of the Old West, which raised a weird question. Was there an Old West on Veelox? I guess there had to be, because we were in it.

Loor knelt down and picked up a handful of dirt, then let it spill through her fingers.

"It is real," she said. "How can that be?"

"It's real because our minds are telling us it is," I answered. "Or Zetlin's mind is telling us it is."

Loor stood up and gazed around at the canyon. "This is what the man Zetlin is thinking?"

"Yeah," I said. "He must have wanted to be a cowboy when he grew up."

"What is a cowboy?" Loor asked.

Before I could answer, I heard a sound. It was a rumble, like far-off thunder.

"You hear that?" I asked.

The curious look on her face told me she did. We both stood there, listening, as the rumbling grew louder.

"It is coming from that direction," Loor said and pointed deeper into the canyon.

Behind us the canyon walls made a sharp turn. There was no way to know what lay beyond. But Loor was right. Whatever was making that sound was around the bend, and getting louder. That meant it was coming closer. I took a quick look in the other direction. The mouth of the canyon had to be at least a half mile away.

"Look," Loor said.

I looked back the other way to see a huge, brown cloud of dirt drifting out from around the bend in the canyon. What was coming? A storm? A rock slide? Godzilla? The thunder grew louder. The sound bounced off the walls of the canyon. Whatever was making that sound, it didn't seem happy. I took another quick look around to see if there was a place we could hide. But the rock walls to either side of us were steep and unforgiving. No way we could climb up. If we were in trouble, the only safe place would be out of this canyon . . . a half mile away.

I kept my eyes on the bend in the canyon, but started to back toward the mouth.

"I think we'd better get outta here," I said.

"If this is happening in Zetlin's head, are we in danger?" Loor asked.

"That depends," I answered.

"On what?"

"On what's coming around that corner."

A second later we had our answer. Charging around the bend of the canyon, running full throttle, was a herd of cattle. There must have been a thousand of them, headed right for us.

"Stampede!" I shouted. "Run!"

Loor and I turned and sprinted away from the charging mass of animals. I took a quick look back and saw that the swarm of beasts was packed nearly wall-to-wall in the canyon, all snorting and grunting with wild eyes. I'll bet the animals in front of the herd were just as scared as we were. If one of them went down, they'd be trampled by the others charging up from behind. No way they were going to stop. They were running for their lives. Just like us.

"What are they?" asked Loor breathlessly. "Do they eat meat?"

"No, but if they catch us there won't be anything left to eat anyway!"

There was no place to go for protection. We had to get out of that canyon. But it was too far away. No way could we outrun this charging herd. I looked back again and saw that they were catching up, fast. It was like racing against an avalanche and we were losing. I started to feel the prickle of grit on my neck from the cloud of dirt they were stirring up. In seconds we'd be roadkill. Or canyonkill.

"There!" shouted Loor.

She pointed to the canyon wall ahead of us, where I saw a single, brown vine that snaked down from somewhere above.

"Follow me!" Loor ordered, and ran for it.

There was only one vine. Even if it was strong enough, which I wasn't sure about, there was barely time for one of us to climb. The herd would be on us in seconds.

"Jump on my back!" Loor commanded.

What? Was she crazy?

"Now!" she demanded, and grabbed the vine.

I wasn't about to argue. I could feel the ground rumble with the thumping of oncoming hooves. Loor grabbed the vine and I grabbed Loor, wrapping my arms around her neck. She climbed, hand over hand, with her boots on the wall, walking up. I dangled from her neck, hoping she had the strength to do this and hoping the vine was strong enough to hold us both.

The cattle were on us. But we were high enough to be out of harm's way. They charged past as if we weren't even there. The mass of animals thundered by only inches below us. I could feel the heat coming up from their bodies. Or maybe it was my own sweat.

"You okay?" I asked Loor.

Loor gave a quick nod. No problem. I could feel the strength in her shoulders and arms. I shouldn't have doubted her. This was cake for her. Now all we had to worry about was whether the vine would hold until the herd was past.

The cattle kept coming. I couldn't believe how many there were. Finally, after what felt like a lifetime, the herd started to thin, so they weren't close to the canyon wall anymore.

And the vine snapped. Loor and I tumbled to the dirt. Luckily I broke Loor's fall. Lucky for her, that is. It wasn't so hot for me. She landed on me full force and knocked the wind out of my lungs. Ooof! It took me about a minute to catch my breath, but I didn't care. We had survived. I glanced up and saw a few straggling cattle trotting after the herd. The rumbling sound of hooves grew faint. I glanced to the end of the canyon and saw the herd spreading out over the green meadow.

"How do you feel?" Loor asked. She was sitting in the dirt, barely winded from the ordeal.

"I feel like a genius," I said.

"A genius?"

"We've only been here two minutes and you've already saved my butt. I knew it was the right move to bring you along. Thanks, Loor."

Loor stood up and helped me to my feet. We started to brush the dust off our clothes when we heard: "What in blazes are you two doing here?"

We looked up to see two cowboys on horseback trotting up to us. These guys were definitely out of the Old West, complete with cowboy hats, leather chaps, and coils of rope around the horns of their saddles.

Neither looked like Dr. Zetlin.

One cowboy asked, "Are you all right?"

"Yeah, we're fine," I answered.

"We checked the whole canyon before we drove the herd through," the other cowboy said. "Where did you two come from?"

"We must have wandered in right after you checked," I said. It was sort of the truth.

"You coulda gotten killed! What're you doing all the way up here?"

"We're looking for somebody," I answered.

"Up here? In the pass?" the first cowboy asked, totally confused.

"Yeah, well, we got lost," I said. "His name is Zetlin. Do you know him?"

The first cowboy looked at the other and asked, "That the name of the fella staying down in Old Glenville?"

"Could be," the second cowboy said with a shrug.

The first guy then looked at me and Loor and said, "There's a man living down in town who might be the one you're looking for. You been through there?"

"No," I said with growing excitement. "Could you point the way?"

"Sure," he answered. "Where are your horses?"

Loor and I looked at each other and shrugged.

"We lost 'em," I said. Wow, could I have given a more lame excuse?

"Lost your horses?" the second cowboy exclaimed. "How did you go and do that?"

"Long story," I said. "We can walk."

"It's too far," the first cowboy said. "We'll lend you horses."

"Really? That's great!"

"Climb on," the second guy said.

Loor and I each climbed on to the back of one of the

horses, behind the cowboys. A second later we were trotting out of the canyon. It wasn't exactly comfortable, but way better than walking.

When we reached the mouth of the canyon, I got a full view of the beautiful mountain pass. It was awesome. The dry, rocky canyon gave way to green, rolling meadows that stretched out as far as I could see. The mountains in the distance were immense. I had never seen the Rockies, but this was what I imagined they looked like. It was another example of Veelox looking like Second Earth. Or at least an example of Dr. Zetlin's fantasy looking like Second Earth. Whatever. It was great.

The two cowboys rode us over to a wagon where they had two more horses hitched. While they saddled up the fresh horses, they explained that they were bringing in the herd for the winter, and often stayed up in the mountains for weeks at a time. That's why they had four horses. If one got hurt, they didn't want to have to go back into town to get a replacement. They said that they were nearly done for the season, so they wouldn't mind lending us these two. They told us to leave them with the blacksmith in town. They'd be down in a few days to pick them up.

Man, these guys were pretty trusting. But then again, this was Dr. Zetlin's fantasy. Maybe he only put trustworthy people into his jumps.

I had ridden horses a couple of times, at summer camp. So I was comfortable enough to mount up and trot along. But I wasn't sure about Loor. Did she know how to ride? The answer came when Loor jumped up on her horse like a pro, tugged the reigns, and got her horse to spin in a circle one way, then the other. Show-off. I should have known.

"Follow the worn trail down out of the pass," the first cowboy explained. "It's pretty well traveled; you won't miss it. You should reach town before sunset."

"Thank you," Loor said.

"Yeah," I added. "You really saved us."

"Aw, heck," the second cowboy said. "It's the least we could do for nearly getting you killed back there."

After a few more thank-yous, Loor and I were on our way to town. It was an awesome ride. The slope was gentle, the air was warm, and the countryside was spectacular.

Loor didn't look half bad, either. Ever since I first met Loor, I had been trying to prove myself to her. She was an athlete and a warrior. I'd seen her battle guys twice her size and make them look bad. Next to her, I was a total weenie. But she wasn't all about muscle. Loor had a strong sense of right and wrong. She totally believed in the Travelers and our mission. Her mother died battling Saint Dane's evil, and I think that made her even more dedicated. But after all we'd been through, I didn't know how Loor felt about me. Yeah, she was on my side because we were both Travelers, and I know she respected me for some of the things I had done, but I think that's as far as it went. I thought of Loor as a good friend. I think she only thought of me as a teammate.

We had a long ride into Old Glenville, and there was a lot I wanted to talk to her about. I figured this was as good a time as any.

"When I was on First Earth," I said to her, "things didn't go too well."

"Saint Dane failed," she said. "That is all that matters."

"Did he?" I said. "We saved the territory, but no thanks to me."

"And how did that make you feel?" she asked.

"Like I never want to let him get the better of me again," I said. "And I won't."

Loor looked at me and said, "I know you, Pendragon. Your heart is in the right place, but you have been unsure of yourself, and of our mission."

I wanted to argue, but she was right.

"It sounds to me as if Saint Dane tried to take away your confidence, but instead made you more determined. If that is the case, he made a very bad mistake, for all he managed to do was bring you fully into the conflict. He will regret that."

In that single moment, things became incredibly clear. I had been struggling with my failure. But now, Loor made me believe that my weakness at that critical moment on First Earth might actually have been the best thing that could have happened. Any doubt I had up to that point about wanting to battle Saint Dane was taken away. Uncle Press always said that this conflict was about more than a single battle. Heck, even Saint Dane said that. By facing my own weakness, maybe I was now ready for the long haul.

"I missed you, Loor," I said. I wanted her to tell me she missed me, too.

She didn't. "I will always be there when you need me," she said. "As I know you will be for me. That is our destiny."

Okay, maybe not exactly a statement of undying friendship, but it was better than nothing. I guess.

We rode for a long time, mostly in silence. I was beginning to think those cowboys had pointed us in the wrong direction, when . . .

"Look!" Loor exclaimed, pointing ahead.

I looked to see the tops of buildings peeking up over some trees. This had to be Old Glenville.

"Last one there buys the sniggers," I exclaimed.

"The what?" Loor said.

Too late. I kicked my horse into action and galloped toward town. Loor probably could have beaten me, but I had gotten such a head start that there was no way she could catch up. A few minutes later, I rode straight down the center street of Old Glenville.

It was a ghost town. I pulled up my horse and Loor stopped right beside me. The two of us sat there in the middle of the dirt street, looking around at the empty town.

Old Glenville was something right out of an old-time Western movie. There were two-story wooden buildings down either side of the main street, with wooden sidewalks and hitching posts in front. I saw painted signs on the stores that identified them as: GENERAL STORE AND DRY GOODS; BARBER AND DENTIST; SHERIFF; TELEGRAPH OFFICE; and even one that said: CORONER. At the end of the street was a church with a tall steeple that dwarfed the rest of the buildings. It was the perfect little frontier town. The only thing missing was people.

"Here we go again," I said. "Just like Rubic City."

I kicked my horse into gear and we walked slowly down the center of the street. I listened for any sign of life, but there was none.

"I'm surprised there's no tumbleweed blowing through," I said.

"What is tumbleweed?" Loor asked.

As if on cue, a big piece of brown tumbleweed rolled past us. This was getting strange, in more ways than one. I guess I could believe that another territory was just like Earth, but this meant the territory of Veelox also had the same kind of history as Earth. This town of Old Glenville was exactly like a typical town from the Old West in America. Very strange.

"There," Loor said. She pointed to a barnlike building that was off the main road.

There was a hand-painted sign leaning against a fence that said: BLACKSMITH. This was where we were supposed to leave the horses. We rode over to the barn, but didn't find a soul. Even stranger, all the tools of the trade were lying around. There were hammers and nails and coal and all the stuff you'd think a blacksmith used. The barn even had a few horses in stalls, but they were the only sign of life. This town looked like it had been recently abandoned.

We tied the horses to a hitching post near the barn. I was about to suggest that we start on one end of town and work our way down the street, searching each and every building, when we heard something strange.

"Music," Loor said.

It was old-fashioned, honky-tonk piano music, which is the exact kind of music you'd expect to hear in a Western town.

"I'll bet you a dollar there's a saloon around here," I said.

"What is a saloon?" Loor asked.

"I'll show you."

Not that I had ever been in a saloon, but I had seen enough Western movies to know that's usually where the music was played. And since everything about this town smelled of the Old West, I had no doubt we'd find a saloon. So we took off walking back to the main street. The closer we got, the louder the music became. Sure enough, across the street I spotted a sign over a balcony that said in fancy gold letters: OLD GLENVILLE SALOON.

We walked across the dusty street like a couple of gunslingers headed toward the O.K. Corral. The music was definitely coming from the saloon. As we got closer I saw a set of swinging doors in front. Classic Western. We got as far as the wooden sidewalk and were about to step up, when the piano suddenly stopped.

Loor and I did too.

We then heard the sound of a chair scraping across the floor inside, as if someone were standing up. It was followed by the sound of footsteps walking across the floor, headed for the swinging doors, and us.

Loor and I didn't move. Whoever was inside, we were about to meet them. I really hoped it was Dr. Zetlin.

It wasn't.

When the swinging doors flew open, I saw something that made me question whether this was Dr. Zetlin's fantasy nightmare . . . or mine. Because standing in the door before us was Saint Dane.

He wore black from head to toe, like a gunfighter. On his hips were twin six-shooters. His gray mane of hair fell down to his shoulders, topped off with a black cowboy hat. The demon acted as if he were expecting us. He smiled a yellow-toothed grin, stared at us with those cold blue eyes, and said, "Looks like it's time to liven up this dead little town!"

VEELOX

"Howdy, Pendragon!" Saint Dane exclaimed jovially while leaning against the hitching post. "I see you brought along your violent little girlfriend. What a nice surprise!"

This didn't compute. How could Saint Dane be in Dr. Zetlin's fantasy? This wasn't like before where he was a prerecorded hologram. This was him. For real. Or should I say, in fantasy. My brain locked.

"You seem surprised!" he laughed. "This can't be possible, yet here I am. It seems as though Aja's Reality Bug has completely scrambled Lifelight."

Loor looked to me and said softly, "This is real, isn't it?"

"Real enough!" Saint Dane answered for me.

He pulled out one of his six-shooters, aimed it at the sky and pulled the trigger. The sharp crack sounded pretty real to me. A moment later four more cowboys with six-shooters appeared from the saloon. They moved quickly behind us, cutting off any chance we had of escape. These guys didn't look like the friendly cowpokes from the mountains either. The word that came to mind was, desperados.

"Since this is a fantasy," Saint Dane continued, "let's have some fun."

He stepped off the wooden walkway and strolled over to us with his thumb in his gun belt. He was enjoying this. We weren't.

"The man you're worried about?" he said. "I know where he is, and I'm going to give you the chance to rescue him."

I shot a look at Loor. This had just gotten interesting.

"Rescue?" I asked.

"About a mile south of town is a dam. It's an immense structure. Holds back an extremely large lake. Without that dam, this town would be underwater. On top of the dam is a small, stone hut. That's where you'll find him."

"That's it?" I asked. "Simple as that?"

Saint Dane laughed. "Pendragon, please, is it ever as simple as that?"

He pulled out a golden pocket watch and checked the time.

"Dynamite has been placed all over that dam, thanks to my associates here. In just about, oh, ten minutes, it's all going to explode and things around here are going to get very wet."

My adrenaline spiked.

"So you're giving us ten minutes to get to the hut and get him out? Is that what you're saying?"

"With one small complication. I'll give you a two minute head start. After that I'm sending my associates here, to stop you. Won't that be exciting?"

Saint Dane leaned down and looked me square in the eye, saying, "You didn't have the strength to succeed on First Earth. How will you handle this little challenge?"

Without thinking, I reached forward and quickly grabbed one of Saint Dane's guns from its holster.

"Nicely done, Quick Draw," he said, barely showing surprise. "Now what?"

I grabbed Loor's hand and started to run.

"Yahoo!" Saint Dane called after us.

If we had any chance of getting to that dam in ten minutes, we needed the horses.

"What is dynamite?" Loor asked as we ran.

"It's like tak," I answered. "It'll destroy the dam."

We made it to the blacksmith barn in a few seconds. I jammed the six-shooter into my belt and we started to untie the horses.

"Does it matter if this town is destroyed?" Loor asked. "It is not real."

"It's not the town," I answered quickly. "It's Zetlin. If something happens to him we'll never get the origin code and Lifelight will—"

Crack! Ping!

A bullet zinged off a metal bucket that was hanging near the barn door. It barely missed us.

"That wasn't two minutes!" I shouted.

Either the desperados didn't care, or they couldn't tell time, because I was answered with a series of gunshots.

"Inside!" Loor commanded.

We grabbed the bridles of the horses and ran them inside the barn. Loor quickly closed the big doors. We were safe, but trapped, and the clock was ticking.

"What do those noisemakers do?" Loor said while pointing to the gun I had jammed in my belt.

"It shoots out small pieces of metal. They're deadly. But it only fires six times and they have a lot more guns than we do. And to be honest, I've never even shot one before."

More shots were fired from outside, shattering a window, making the horses whinny in fear.

"We gotta get outta here," I said and ran to a door in the back of the barn. I opened it and was met with a gunshot that splintered wood just over my head. To use a cliché Western phrase, they had us surrounded. I ran back to Loor and shouted, "You're the soldier-in-training! What are we supposed to do?"

Loor wasn't panicking, I'm not surprised to say. She coolly looked around the barn, seeing what we had to use.

She then said calmly, "The animals. What did you call it before? Stampede?"

I could have kissed her. It was brilliant and insane. There were about a dozen horses in stalls, plus ours. If we could get them moving together out of the barn, we might be able to use them as shields. I was more than ready to give it a try.

"Get them together!" Loor commanded.

We ran to opposite sides of the barn, throwing open the stalls and yelling at the horses to get out. It was kind of scary. The horses were already nervous because of the gunshots. Having two crazy people running around waving their arms made them even more excited. This was dangerous. One quick horse kick to the head and it would all be over.

After a few frantic seconds, we had all the horses gathered together in the center of the barn. They were bumping into each other, kicking at the ground, and whinnying. They weren't happy about this at all.

"Go to the doors!" Loor yelled.

I ran to the big barn doors and grabbed the handles. Loor took our two horses with saddles and led them to the back of the pack.

"Are you ready?" she called out.

I was. So were the horses. They were starting to rear up and I was nearly stomped a couple of times.

"Let's go!" I shouted.

"Open the doors!"

I threw open both doors. Loor gave off a sharp whistle, and the herd of horses charged out of the barn.

I barely had enough time to jump to the side before getting trampled. Loor ran forward with our two horses. Without a second to think about how crazy this was, I jumped on mine and we charged out after the fleeing herd.

Outside, it was a chaos of wild horses and dust. The horses blasted into the open and ran together toward the main street. Loor and I pushed our horses forward to stay as close to the wild herd as possible. We both crouched low in the saddle, trying to offer smaller targets. I kept expecting to hear gunshots, but they didn't come. I guess there was enough confusion going on that the desperados didn't want to waste their ammunition. Good for the horses, good for us.

We were out, and we had our horses. Now it was a race. We had to get to that dam and find Zetlin before the whole thing blew up, or the desperados stopped us.

"Which way?" Loor yelled.

I figured we came into town from one direction, so the dam must be in the other. I gave my horse a quick kick in the butt, and we were off. We charged down the main street of Old Glenville, flew past the church, and blasted along the dirt road leading south. Side by side we galloped along the road like a couple of bandits on the run.

I soon realized there was something else to worry about. As much as I'd like to pretend otherwise, I'm not a very good rider. This was freaking scary! The horses were fast, which was good, but I barely knew what I was doing. If I fell off at the speed we were going, something would get broken. Probably my head. I grabbed the reins with one hand, and had a death grip on the saddle horn with the other. I didn't even look at Loor. She knew way more about riding than I did. I had no idea how much time had gone by, but every second counted. Slowing down was not an option.

"There it is!" Loor called to me.

Sure enough, looming up in the distance, tucked into a ravine, was a huge stone dam. Saint Dane said it was a mile out of town, but it was so big it looked much closer. I could even see the small, stone building on top, right in the middle.

Bang!

We weren't alone. I didn't turn around to look because I was afraid I'd lose my balance. But Loor did.

"They are coming," she announced.

"How many?" I asked.

"All of them. Saint Dane, too."

Swell.

More shots were fired. I kept expecting to feel the sting of a bullet, but they must have been too far back to be accurate. We had to keep it that way.

The road forked. It was clear that the right fork would take us to a trail that led up the side of the ravine, and to the top of the dam. Without a word we both steered our flying horses onto the right path. The trail quickly grew narrow as it rose up along the side of the steep ravine. But we still pushed the horses on. We couldn't risk being caught. Soon, we had risen up so high that there was a steep drop off to the left. I was in the lead. If my horse took one wrong step, adios.

The trail then entered a forest. Branches slapped at us from both sides, trying to knock us off. It was getting painful.

"We gotta slow down!" I said.

Loor and I both pulled on the reins and slowed to a trot. I could see through the trees up ahead that we were nearly at the top of the dam. There were only about a hundred yards to go.

"Give me the noisemaker," Loor ordered.

I looked back and was shocked to see that Loor was getting off her horse.

"What are you doing? We're almost there!" I shouted.

"Keep going," she said. "Find Zetlin and get him out. I will stop the others from following."

There was no way I was going to leave Loor here alone. "Loor, I won't—"

"You are wasting time, Pendragon!" she shouted at me. "We must save Zetlin! That is all that matters. Give me the noisemaker!"

It killed me, but I pulled the six-shooter out of my belt and tossed it to her. She looked at it curiously. My confidence wasn't high.

"Hold the handle, point the long end at the bad guys and pull the trigger," was the quickest instruction I could think of. "Hold it tight, it'll probably kick."

"Go!" she ordered.

I snapped the reins, kicked my horse, and galloped for the dam. I took one last look over my shoulder to see that Loor had pulled her horse into the trees. She was setting a trap. Man, what a brave girl. But then again, if the dam blew up, she wouldn't be on it. I would. I didn't know which was worse, facing the desperados, or standing on an exploding dam. Suddenly I wasn't feeling so bad for her anymore.

It was all about time now. I had no idea how soon the dam was going to blow. A few seconds later, I broke out of the trees on top of the ridge to see the huge lake that Saint Dane told us about. A quick look to my left showed me that I had made it to the top of the dam. The stone hut was about halfway across, which I'm guessing was about fifty yards away. Fifty very long yards. I figured I could cover the distance faster on horseback.

That's when I heard gunfire. The quick, sharp pops told

me that the desperados had caught up with Loor. I could only hope that she'd be safe, and keep them back long enough for me to get to Dr. Zetlin.

"Yah!" I slapped the horse's flank, and we charged out onto the dam. It was only about ten feet wide, with water on one side and a very long drop on the other. I hugged the water side.

Crack! Crack!

More gunshots, followed by splinters of stone kicking up around me. The desperados weren't gunning for Loor, they were shooting at me through the trees. I ducked down on the horse and begged it to run faster.

Ping! Crack!

A piece of flying stone stung my arm. They were getting better, but there was no way I would be stopped. Not when I was so close. We had played Saint Dane's evil game and nearly won. I made it to the stone hut and jumped off my horse. I tied it on the far side of the hut, making sure to use the building for protection against the shooting desperados.

A million thoughts flew through my head. What was my next move? I would get Dr. Zetlin out, get us both on the horse, and then go . . . where? If we went back the way we came, we'd land right in the laps of the desperados. But I couldn't abandon Loor! The only choice was to keep going to the far side of the dam. But then once the dam blew up, Loor would be trapped with the desperados.

It was a familiar, horrible feeling. I was faced with a choice. Which was more important? The future of Veelox, or the safety of my friend? It was the *Hindenburg* all over again. Was this what Saint Dane wanted to do all along? Did he want to put me in the same, horrible position just to see me fail again?

These thoughts took all of three seconds to flash through my head. I truly didn't know what to do. All I knew for sure was that I had to keep going. But when I threw the door of the hut open, I was rocked by a sight so incredible that it made all my other concerns seem trivial.

"Dr. Zetlin!" I shouted as I opened the door. "We've got to get off the dam or—"

When I saw the man inside the hut, I froze. It wasn't Dr. Zetlin. This wasn't playing out the way it was supposed to. But to be honest, Saint Dane hadn't lied, either. He told us that the man I was worried about was in this hut. And he was.

It was Gunny.

"Shorty!" he yelled when he saw me. "What in heck is going on?"

Gunny was tied to a chair with a long length of rope. Seeing him was such a shock, I couldn't function.

"Wha—how did you get here?" I stammered.

"Saint Dane sandbagged me! Get these ropes off!"

My brain clicked back into gear. I ran to Gunny and started working on the knots. I wasn't sure if I was happy to see him or totally freaked out.

"You're not gonna believe what's been going on," I said. "This isn't real. None of this is." I then stopped working and looked at him. "Wait, I don't get how you can be here. Did Saint Dane bring you into a Lifelight pyramid?"

Gunny was about to answer, when I felt a sharp rumbling. It felt like a short, quick earthquake. But it wasn't. Our ten minutes were up. More rumbling followed. The dynamite was exploding. There was no way we could get off in time. The dam was about to collapse, with Gunny and me still on it.

VEELOX

"What's happening?" Gunny asked. His eyes were wide with fear.

"The dam is exploding," I said. "Saint Dane loaded it with dynamite."

I caught a glimpse of my horse charging away. He had pulled free and was galloping off in terror. Smart horse. He knew what was about to happen.

"Get yourself outta here," Gunny ordered.

I wanted to argue. I wanted to be all sorts of brave and say: "We're getting out, together!" or something equally heroic. But the truth was, there wasn't time. The exploding dynamite was tearing the dam apart. The floor shook, the stone ceiling started to fall down around us. In a few seconds there would be no more dam and no more us.

"Run, Pendragon," Gunny implored.

It was too late. I knew there was only one possible way to get off this crumbling dam. I lifted my arm and pulled up my sleeve to reveal my silver control bracelet with the three square buttons. The button on the far right was supposed to end the jump. The last time it failed, but I couldn't think of anything else to do, so I pushed it, and prayed.

The stone hut shuddered. We were going down.

"Good-bye, shorty," Gunny said.

Everything went black.

I sat up fast and slammed my head.

"Ow!"

I was totally disoriented. My head hurt too. What had happened? A second later, the answer came. With a slight hum, the silver disk that enclosed the jump tube slid back and filled my little tunnel with light. I was back in the Lifelight pyramid! The table slid out, depositing me back in the jump cubicle off the Alpha Core. My bracelet had worked. I had ended the jump. I looked quickly to my left to see a welcome sight. Loor was sliding out of the other tube, safe.

"Pendragon! What happened?" she asked. "I was shooting the noisemaker at Saint Dane and suddenly the world went black."

She was breathing hard and her eyes were wild. I can honestly say it was the first time I saw Loor rattled. But who could blame her?

"I ended the jump," I said. "We're back. Are you all right?"

"I am confused, but not injured," she answered. "Did you find Zetlin?"

I looked to the tube between us to see it was still closed. Zetlin was still inside.

"No," I answered. "Something is whacked." I jumped off the table and ran out of the cubicle. "Aja?" I called. "What went wrong?"

But Aja wasn't there. Her control chair was empty. The large monitor was still showing images of our jump though. On screen, I saw a horrific sight. It was a view of the collapsing dam. The explosions had weakened the stone structure and tons of water from the lake came crashing through. The dam crumbled like wet sand. I saw the small stone hut on top fall into the chaos of crashing stone and water.

"Gunny," I said to myself.

The screen went blank. The jump was over.

"What went wrong?" Loor asked. She was standing behind me, watching the disaster. "Where is Aja?"

"I don't know," I answered.

I led Loor out of the Alpha Core in search of Aja. Where was she? Why had she left the controls in the middle of the jump? Of course, my mind rushed to all the worst possible answers. I feared she had somehow gone into the jump and gotten hurt. Stranger still, how had Gunny ended up in Zetlin's jump? Worse, if he was in the jump, did he go down with the crumbling dam? There were a ton of questions that needed answering. But first we had to find Aja.

We ran quickly through the core to see all was exactly as we had left it. The monitors were still showing green and there were no phaders or vedders around. There was no Aja, either. We left the glass corridor and hurried back to the counter where we had been fitted with our control bracelets. The Goth vedder was still there, looking as bored as ever.

"Have you seen Aja?" I demanded.

"She left a while ago," he answered. "She was in a big hurry, too. She said to tell you she had to get home."

"Home?" I shouted. "But the grid is still suspended!"

"Hey, don't ask me," the guy said. "I'm just a vedder."

This made no sense. What was so important at home that she would leave us alone in the jump? I looked to Loor, hoping she might have an answer, and saw she was staring at the oil portrait of the young Dr. Zetlin.

"We must find him," she said.

"Yeah, I know. But we can't do it without Aja. C'mon."

We started to leave when the vedder called to us. "Hey!"

We looked back at him and he pointed to his wrist. Right. We still had our jump bracelets on. Loor and I quickly unclasped the bracelets and put them on the counter.

"Thank you," the vedder said. "This is the way it was meant to be."

I shot the guy a surprised look. "Why did you say that?"

The Goth guy shrugged. "Just something to say," he answered, and smiled.

That was weird.

"Let's go," I said to Loor, and headed out.

I was confused and angry and frightened all at once. How could Aja abandon us? Loor and I jumped onto one of the three-wheel pedal vehicles and quickly made our way back toward the mansion that Aja made home.

"I am having trouble understanding what is happening, Pendragon," Loor said.

"Yeah, me too," I answered truthfully. "Nothing is making sense, but I guarantee that if Aja went home, it was for a good reason. Let's not sweat about it until we find her."

We pedaled the rest of the way in silence. The empty streets of Rubic City seemed even more chillingly quiet than before. This was a ghost town in the middle of a ghost territory, and we weren't doing much to change it.

We arrived at the mansion and ran up the marble stairs. I wanted to burst through the door, screaming for Aja, but that would have been rude. This was still Evangeline's house too. So I grabbed the door knocker and pounded it a few times. A few agonizing seconds later, the door opened and Evangeline was there. When she saw me, her face lit up with a bright smile.

"Pendragon! What a surprise!" she exclaimed. "And who is this?"

"This is my friend Loor," I answered. "She's a Traveler. Where is Aja?"

"Another Traveler?" Evangeline said. "How wonderful! You two are just in time for dinner."

She stepped back to let Loor and me inside.

"We need to find Aja, Evangeline," I said urgently.

"But surely you have time for some gloid," she said sweetly. "We're having your favorite. Blue. You like blue the best, don't you?"

Yeah, right.

"Where is Aja?" Loor demanded. She didn't care if she sounded rude.

"She's not here," Evangeline answered. "Please, come into the kitchen and eat."

She turned and walked down the hallway, headed for the kitchen.

"If she is not here," Loor said, "where else could she be?"

"I don't know," I answered.

We followed Evangeline through the house, toward the kitchen. No way I was going to get near any of that blue gloid, but we had to find Aja. I stepped up to the kitchen door, swung it open, and saw something that froze both Loor and me in our places. It was impossible, yet as real as can be.

Evangeline was scooping big ladles of blue gloid into white bowls. But that wasn't what shocked us.

"Sit down, you two," she said with warm hospitality. "Plenty of room."

Loor and I didn't move. That was because there were already two dinner guests seated at the table. As impossible as it was, sitting there, chowing down on huge spoonfuls of blue gloid, were the two cowpokes from the mountain ravine in Zetlin's fantasy.

"Howdy there, you two!" one of them said. "You come by to return our horses?"

"That's right nice of you to go out of your way!" the other one said. He then looked at Evangeline and said, "Ma'am, this chow sure is tasty."

"That's kind of you to say," Evangeline said, blushing.

What was going on?

Loor asked me, "Do you smell that?"

At first I thought she meant the gloid, but I took a whiff and realized it was something else. Something was burning.

"Evangeline, are you cooking something?" I asked.

Before she could answer, a door opened from the far side of the kitchen and another guest arrived.

"Gunny!" I shouted.

Yup. In walked Gunny Van Dyke, dressed in his bell captain uniform from the Manhattan Tower Hotel.

"Hey there, shorty!" he said. "I see you made it off that dam. You going to introduce me to your friend?"

I was numb. My brain wasn't computing any of this.

"This is . . . this is . . . Loor," I said numbly.

"Osa's daughter?" Gunny exclaimed. "I am very pleased to meet you."

Gunny reached across the table, holding out his hand to shake Loor's. Loor reached out, looking as dazed as I was.

And there was a gunshot.

The smile froze on Gunny's face. He pitched forward and fell face first onto the table. Gunny had been shot. Both cowpokes dove away from the table and hit the floor. Evangeline screamed and huddled behind a counter. I looked across the room to where the shot had come from.

Standing in the doorway was Saint Dane. He was still dressed in his black cowboy outfit and had a smoking six-shooter in his hand.

"You cheated, Pendragon," Saint Dane exclaimed. "There's no fun in a challenge if you cheat. Now you two will just have to pay the price."

From behind him, the desperados entered with guns drawn.

I was absolutely, totally frozen in shock. Things were happening so fast and seemed so impossible, I couldn't even begin to figure out what to do.

Luckily, Loor could.

She quickly grabbed the end of the kitchen table and flipped it up on end. Cutlery and gloid flew everywhere as the desperados opened fire. Bullets slammed into the table, shredding it. But Loor's quick thinking had protected us. At least for the time being.

"Outta here!" I shouted, and we ran for the door to the hallway.

More gunshots were fired as bullets ripped through the kitchen, barely missing us and instead slamming into the kitchen walls. The instant we ran out the door, we discovered where the bad smell had come from.

The mansion was on fire.

If that wasn't bad enough, the entire downstairs hallway was full of horses. I'm serious. It was like being in the frenzy of wild horses back in the blacksmith barn, times about a hundred because the animals were terrified by the fire that shot flames and smoke out of the rooms on either side of the hallway. Loor took the lead, pulling me behind her, pushing her way through the terrified mass of horses. She actually shoved some of the big animals out of our way. Good thing she was here. I probably would have been trampled.

We made our way back to the front door, but it was engulfed in flames. No way we were getting out that way.

"Upstairs!" I shouted.

We ran up the wide, carpeted stairway to the second floor. I figured that with any luck, we could make our way to the back of the house and get out of a window before being burned or shot or trampled.

"How could this happen?" Loor shouted as we ran up the stairs.

"You're asking me like I know?" I shouted back. "I'm just as freaked as you are!"

We got to the top of the stairs and ran down the hallway, headed for a window on the far end. We were just about to throw it open, when the window shattered. Loor and I both fell to the ground as bits of glass rained down on us. Saint Dane's desperados were outside, waiting for us.

We were trapped.

Another gunshot was heard that smashed a picture hanging right next to my head. We both spun toward the stairs to see a ghastly sight. Saint Dane was standing on the top stair, backed by the burning flames from down below. He was like a demonic shadow standing there, with two six-guns drawn.

"Time is running out, children," he chuckled. "What's your next move?"

I pushed Loor into a bedroom off the hallway and slammed the door shut. This wouldn't get us out, but at least it would buy us a few more seconds to think.

"How can this be?" Loor demanded to know.

My shock was wearing off now, and my brain was beginning to function. An idea was forming. It started when we first saw those cowpokes seated around Evangeline's table. With each new disaster, my theory became more real.

"There can only be one explanation for all this," I said. I then lifted my arm, and pulled back the sleeve of my jumpsuit to see . . . I was right.

I was still wearing a silver control bracelet. Loor lifted her arm to see she was still wearing one as well.

"But we removed these," she said, totally confused.

"We thought we did," I answered. "But that's because we didn't know the truth."

"And what is the truth?"

"We're still in the jump," I said. "This is still part of the fantasy."

Crack!

A bullet tore through the door. Saint Dane had come a-knocking. I pulled Loor across the room and we huddled down behind the bed.

"Why did we not see these before?" she asked.

"Because we thought we were out of the jump," I answered. "That's how it works, if you give yourself over to the fantasy, you won't see the bracelets. But as soon as I realized we were still in the jump, they appeared."

Crack! Crack!

Two more bullets splintered the wood of the door.

"Come out, come out, wherever you are!" came Saint Dane's singsong voice from the hallway.

"So then none of this is real?" Loor asked.

"Real enough," I said. "But it's time to get out."

I lifted my arm to look at the control bracelet and the three buttons. The one to the far right was supposed to end the jump, but obviously that didn't work. The one in the middle was supposed to change the jump, but the last time I tried using that, we almost got eaten by quigs. The button to the far left was my only choice, so I hit it.

The button glowed white for a moment, and then . . .

"It's about time!"

Loor and I looked up to see Aja standing there.

"I thought you'd never figure it out!"

"Aja, what happened?" I asked.

"You never went into Zetlin's jump," she answered. "It must have been the Reality Bug. I realized it the second I inserted you, but couldn't do anything about it until you realized it for yourself and called for me."

"Are you really here?" I asked.

"No," was the answer. "It's just my image. I'm still in the Alpha Core."

Suddenly a closet door blew open and flames licked out. The fire had reached the second floor. We were about to cook.

"Getting warm in there?" Saint Dane taunted from the hallway.

"Get us out of here!" I shouted to Aja.

"It's too risky," Aja answered.

"Risky?" I shouted back. "How can it get any riskier than this?"

"If I pull you out now, I may not be able to get you back in," she answered. "The Reality Bug is fighting to take over Zetlin's jump. I don't know how much longer I can keep it back, and we've still got to find Zetlin!"

"Aja," Loor said calmly. "If we do not get out of here, we will not live long enough to find anybody."

"I know," Aja said. "Pendragon, push the middle button."

"What?" I shouted. "The last time—"

"I know what happened the last time," Aja interrupted. "But while you were playing cowboy, I programmed a link."

"A link?" I asked.

Suddenly, with a crash, the door to the bedroom flew open and Saint Dane strode in.

"Time for the last roundup, buckaroos!" Saint Dane said. He raised his six-guns, ready to fire.

"Push the button, Pendragon!" Aja screamed.

I did.

Saint Dane let loose with both guns, blasting us. I heard the sharp cracks, I saw the fire come from the muzzles, but I didn't feel a thing, because a nanosecond later, everything went black.

VEELOX

I thought I was standing inside a giant colander. You know, one of those big silver bowls with all the holes in it for draining spaghetti. Everywhere I looked, I saw tiny, round dots. For a second I feared I was in some giant, fantasy kitchen, and a pile of boiling linguini was about to get dumped on me.

But that didn't make sense. Still, there were far too many of these holes to have been made by Saint Dane's six-shooter. So where was I?

I looked closer to see the dots weren't holes after all. They were little globes of water about the size of peas. There were millions, no, billions of them all frozen in space, everywhere. I lifted my hand and moved it slowly in front of my face. As I passed through the suspended drops of water, my hand got wet. Stranger still, my hand cleared a path through the drops. It was like what happens when you wipe a steamy window. Wherever I moved my hand, I cleared a trail.

"Where are we, Pendragon?" Loor was standing next to me, doing the exact same thing. She took a step forward, clearing a body-size path through the dots of water. As she moved, her green jumpsuit got wetter and wetter.

Yes, we were both still wearing our jumpsuits.

"I don't know." was my answer. I was tired of giving that answer. I looked around to get my bearings, but couldn't see much. It was like we were in a misty white cloud. The ground we stood on was pavement, but I couldn't see much more than a few feet in any direction.

"What is that?" Loor said, pointing at something.

I looked to see a faint, dark form not too far from us. It wasn't moving, and didn't seem to be a threat, so I cautiously walked toward it. It was strange feeling the water cling to my jumpsuit as I walked, making it wet. As I got closer to the dark form, it began to take shape. After one more step, the mist cleared enough for me to see what it was, and I caught my breath.

It was a man wearing a green jumpsuit, just like ours. He was a normal-looking guy about my father's age. There was nothing odd about him at all, except for the fact that he was frozen in place. Seriously, the guy didn't move at all. It looked like he was in the middle of taking a step while looking backward and beckoning with his hand when somebody hit the "pause" button on his life.

I looked to where he was gesturing, and saw two more people a few feet behind him. It was a woman holding the hand of a little girl. They seemed to be hurrying to catch up with the man, except that they were frozen too. It was like looking at a display in a wax museum. How seriously creepy can you get?

"What is wrong with them?" Loor asked.

An idea started to tickle at the back of my brain. I looked around at the billions of dots of suspended water all around us. Was it possible?

"I think it's rain," I declared. "All these drops of water. It's a rainstorm."

"How can that be?" Loor responded.

"I don't know," I said while passing my hand through the dots again. "But I think this Lifelight fantasy is somehow frozen in time."

I took a closer look at the stiff family. There was absolutely nothing wrong with them. Their eyes were clear, their skin was normal. Close-up they didn't look like wax-works; they seemed totally real. I even took a chance and touched the guy's hand.

"He's warm," I said. "This guy is stuck in time. So is the rain and the white mist. It's a storm. Everything just . . . stopped."

Loor walked a few steps past the woman and kid. She wanted to see more. So did I. I followed her and the two of us passed through more drops of water, beyond which the mist began to thin.

"Look!" Loor exclaimed.

Once we were out of the patch of fog, or mist, or whatever it was, we got a better view of our surroundings. We still couldn't see very far because the clearing only stretched for about a city block, but it was enough to get an idea of what this place was all about, and I have to say, it was like a surreal nightmare.

We were on a city street, but it wasn't like any city I had ever seen because the buildings were all jet black. They looked to be made from the same shiny material that covered the giant Lifelight pyramid in Rubic City.

The block was busy with people, though I guess "busy" isn't exactly the right word—they were all just as frozen as the family we had passed. There were people of different ages and races, all wearing green jumpsuits. The sidewalks were crowded too. Some people were in the middle of crossing the street; others rode in pedal vehicles like in Rubic City. But unlike Rubic City, this place was alive with people.

Did I say alive? It felt like we were standing inside a 3-D painting. "Alive" didn't really cover it.

We then heard a voice come from behind us. "This is incredible!"

Loor and I both jumped in surprise, then turned quickly to see Aja standing there. She was looking around with as much awe as we felt.

"So this is the fantasy of a genius," she said. "Not exactly paradise, is it?"

"Is this it?" I asked. "Is this Dr. Zetlin's fantasy jump?"

Aja checked her elaborate wrist controller. "Yes, I linked you in. Now the trick is to find him."

"What happened before?" Loor asked. "Where was that other place?"

"It was the Reality Bug," Aja explained. "I'm constantly fighting it. Every time I enter a string of commands, it tries to alter them. Instead of going into Dr. Zetlin's jump, Lifelight took its cues from you, Pendragon. Everything that happened was pulled out of your mind."

Loor gave me a confused look. This made no sense to her. Oddly enough, it did to me. All the things we ran into: the Old West, the stampede, Saint Dane, Gunny, everything. It all came out of my mind. It wasn't a fantasy out of the past of Veelox at all; it was a good old-fashioned Western from home.

"So, Saint Dane was not really chasing us?" Loor asked.

"Correct," Aja answered. "He was part of the fantasy."

"But now we're in Zetlin World, right?" I asked.

"Yes," Aja answered with confidence. "Sorry for the detour."

"Are you here with us, Aja?" Loor asked.

"No," Aja answered. "I'm still in the core."

Aja passed her hand through the drops of water, but her movement didn't clear a path the way ours did. This was only an image of Aja. Loor walked up to her curiously, and tried to touch her. Her hand passed right through. Loor backed away quickly. I guess touching a ghost spooked her, so to speak.

"It's okay," I assured Loor. "Everything's cool."

"Pendragon, I want to find Zetlin and leave here quickly," Loor said nervously.

"Yeah, me too. But I don't know where to start," I admitted.

"When Dr. Zetlin started his jump," Aja said, "he didn't want to be bothered. Ever. The last thing he wanted was to have people from Veelox entering his jump and disturbing him."

"Which is exactly what we're doing," I offered.

"Yes, but the guy is a genius," Aja continued. "He knew there might be an emergency where he needed to be contacted."

"I think this qualifies," I said.

Aja showed us a small, blue plastic box. It was about the size and shape of a floppy disk.

"Zetlin left one of these for every senior phader, in case of emergency," Aja explained. "Entering Zetlin's jump is difficult enough. Controlling it is a whole different challenge. These are the codes to do that."

"So, what happens when you use them?" I asked.

"I don't know," was Aja's quick reply. "Let's find out."

She held out the plastic case and snapped it open, revealing a thin silver square inside. Aja took out the square and examined it.

"Two sets of codes," she announced.

"I don't suppose either is the origin code?" I asked hopefully.

"I wish," she replied. "I'll try the first."

She lifted her wrist controller and input a series of commands as she referred to the silver square. It must have been a complex code, because it took her several seconds to enter it. Then, with one final keystroke . . .

It began to rain.

The once suspended drops fell from the sky, soaking us. Thunder rumbled in the distance.

"Look out!" somebody yelled.

Loor grabbed me and pulled me aside as a man driving a pedal vehicle sped by.

"Careful there, folks," the guy called with a friendly wave. "The street gets busy."

Yeah, no kidding. I looked down the block to see that the painting had reanimated. People splashed through puddles, rushing to get out of the rain. The lady and little girl caught up with the man. He took the girl by the hand and they hurried on their way. The white foggy mist was now moving too. It blew down the street, rolling quickly along with the storm.

"Fascinating!" was all Aja could say.

"Let's get off the street," I suggested, and the three of us ran to the sidewalk and under the protection of an overhang that covered the entrance to a building.

We stood there, watching Zetlin's fantasy city come alive.

"I don't get it," I said. "Here's a genius guy who could live in any kind of paradise he could think of, and he chooses a gray, rainy city with black buildings? He may be smart, but he doesn't have such a hot imagination."

I then stepped in front of a guy who was about to enter

the building we were using for shelter.

"Excuse me," I said. "Do you know Dr. Zetlin?"

The guy looked at me strangely, like I had three noses or something.

"What's the joke?" he asked.

I looked to Aja. She shrugged.

"No joke," I said. "Do you know where we can find Dr. Zetlin?"

The guy shook his head in confusion. "In the Barbican," he answered. "Where else would he be?"

"Barbican," I repeated. "Okay. Where's the Barbican?"

The guy shook his head again, like I was being an idiot. He sniffed and continued on into the building without answering.

"I guess everybody around here is supposed to know where he is," Aja said.

"Yeah, everybody but us," I said. "What's a Barbican?"

"Pendragon?" Loor said softly.

She stepped out onto the sidewalk, staring down the street with a dumbfounded expression.

"I do not know what a Barbican is, but if I were to wager, I would say that is it," she said in awe.

Aja and I turned to see what she was pointing at. What we saw was about as incredible a sight as I could imagine.

The rain had stopped. The storm was moving through quickly and the foggy mist was blowing away. We could now see a long way down the wide street. The buildings on either side were different sizes and styles, but all were made of the same, shiny black material. As the fog lifted, more people were revealed. They were all dressed in the same dark green jumpsuit style, going about their business. It was an incredibly drab city. But what we saw at the end of the street was anything but drab.

It was another black building. Actually, it was more like a

skyscraper. I'm guessing it must have been about eighty stories. It was way bigger than any of the other buildings on the street. But its size alone wasn't what made it stand out. The breathtaking thing about it was that this huge building was floating on its side!

Actually, it wasn't exactly floating. There was a massive, triangular brace that held it in the air. You know that big Gateway Arch thing in St. Louis on Second Earth? That's what this brace looked like. Imagine that big arch with a huge, horizontal building attached to the top. That's what we were faced with. It looked like a seesaw for a giant.

The three of us stood and stared at the impressive structure. Nobody knew what to say. It was Aja who moved first. Without a word, she began walking. It was like she was being drawn toward the bizarre building. I gave Loor a quick look and we followed. We walked along the sidewalk in a daze. I'd guess that by the time we got to it, we must have walked a mile.

As we stood under the monstrous structure, the clouds parted. Bright sun shone through and hit the side of the floating skyscraper, making its black skin sparkle.

Loor finally broke the silence, saying, "How are we to get inside?"

"Aja?" I said. "You said there were two codes?"

"Yes," she answered.

"Try the second one."

Aja shrugged, looked at the silver square, then input Zetlin's second code into her wrist controller. After hitting the final key, she said, "That's it."

Nothing happened. I glanced back at the street, afraid that the second code would refreeze the fantasy. But the drab people continued to move, going wherever they were going.

I said, "Try it again—"

And that's when it happened. At first we only heard the sound. It was a loud, grinding noise that hurt my ears. It sounded like giant pieces of metal were screeching against each other because, well, that's what it was.

"It is moving!" Loor exclaimed.

We all looked up at the black building to see it was beginning to rotate. Like a monstrous Ferris wheel, the massive building slowly began to turn on its axis. I looked to the ground under the giant brace to see the outline of a huge square.

"It's the footprint!" I shouted. "The building is righting itself!"

That's exactly what was happening. The building was slowly rotating to vertical. The only trouble was, we were standing inside the giant square.

"Back off!" I shouted.

All three of us hurried back out of the danger zone. The screeching and grinding continued as one end of the building dropped nearer to the ground. It was incredible that something that big could actually move like that. But then again, this was the fantasy of a genius. I guess in Zetlin's mind, it was possible.

The whole event took about a minute. With a final rush of air that sounded like the brakes on an eighteen-wheeler, times about a thousand, the base of the building settled onto the square on the ground. The ground shook with the deep rumble of an earthquake as the base touched down. We then looked up to see an eighty-story-tall skyscraper reaching vertically toward the sky. Its black skin sparkled with rainwater. There didn't seem to be a single window in the whole structure. But at the base, looking like a flea on a dog, was a single doorway.

"Man," I said. "This guy really makes it tough to pay a visit."

"That must be the way in," Loor said, pointing to the door. "Follow me."

"Wait," Aja said. "I should go back."

"Why?" I asked.

"It's the Reality Bug," she explained. "I have to keep putting up firewalls to keep it out of this jump. I need to be focused in the Alpha Core to do that."

"What if we need you?" I asked.

"Believe me, Pendragon, you need me in the Alpha Core a lot more than you do here. If the Reality Bug gets into the alpha grid—"

"I get it," I interrupted.

Aja looked to the ground. Something was troubling her.

"What's the matter?" I asked.

"I . . . I'm sorry, Pendragon," she said softly. "I hate that I've put you and Loor in this position."

"We're here because we're Travelers, Aja," I said. "Don't be sorry. Just keep that freakin' Reality Bug away from us, okay?"

Aja nodded. She then reached out toward me. I think she wanted me to take her hand. I looked into her eyes and actually thought I saw compassion. Did Aja really care about me? A little while ago she hated that I had ever set foot on Veelox because she feared I would steal her thunder. What a difference a few death-defying escapes can make.

"I believe," Aja said, "this is truly the way it was meant to be."

I reached out toward her, but my hand passed right through hers. After all, she was only an image of herself.

"Good luck to you both," she said sincerely. "I'll be watching."

She then disappeared in a ripple of light.

I stood there with my hand in the air, looking stupid.

"I believe she likes you," Loor said.

I quickly put my hand in my pocket. How embarrassing was that? I really didn't want Loor to think Aja and I had a "thing," because we didn't.

"Will you include that in your journal to Courtney Chetwynde?" she asked.

I couldn't believe it. Loor was teasing me. "There's nothing going on," I assured her, though I think I said it with such force that she didn't believe me.

"Very well," Loor said. "You do not need to convince me."

"Let it go, all right?" I said.

Loor looked up at the looming skyscraper. "He is in there somewhere," she said.

"Right," I added. "Let's go find him."

The two of us then walked together toward the small door that would lead us inside the strange, fantasy world of Dr. Zetlin, genius.

The creator of Lifelight.

VEELOX

We stepped into a jungle.

I'm not kidding. It was a tropical rain forest full of palm trees, dense foliage, and mosquitoes. The ground beneath us was soft, dark dirt. The temperature had to be at least ninety degrees. It was so humid, my jumpsuit was already sticking to me. I swear I even heard the sound of a distant waterfall.

"How can this be, Pendragon?" Loor asked.

I turned back and saw the black door we had just entered through. We were definitely inside the strange building called the Barbican, but it sure as heck didn't feel like we were indoors. I looked up expecting to see a ceiling, but all I saw was blackness. I half expected to see stars, but that would have been impossible. Then again, when you were inside the fantasy of a genius inventor, maybe nothing was impossible.

"This is Zetlin's world," I answered. "I think we have to be ready for anything."

A narrow path cut through the thick foliage. It was the only way to go. Loor took the lead, pushing past me and walking boldly down the path to somewhere. It reminded me of the way she took the lead down in the dark mine tunnels of

Denduron. Only this time, neither of us had any idea where we were going.

Loor walked quickly, pushing away the leafy branches that hung over the trail. I had to hang back a few feet or I would have gotten whacked by the branches as they swung back after she passed.

"What was that?" she asked, stopping short.

I heard it too. It sounded as if something were scurrying around in the underbrush, but it was so dense, it was impossible to see anything. Whatever was in there, I sure hoped it was just as hard for it to see us, too. We stood there for a second, listening, but the only sound we heard was the drip of moisture falling from the large, leafy plants.

"Keep going," I suggested.

Loor continued on. "What are we looking for?" she asked over her shoulder.

"I don't know, but I bet we'll know it when we see it."

A minute later the path led us to a clearing in the jungle. It was a wide open, circular space that looked as if it had been cleared for a jungle campground. All the plant life had been neatly cut away in a circle. I could see the sliced-off ends of branches all around, as if somebody had come through with a monster weed whacker. We walked to the center of the clearing, and stopped when we both heard more rustling in the bushes. We shot each other a look. Something was definitely out there.

"Dr. Zetlin?" I called out.

No answer. No more rustling, either.

"What kind of place is this, Pendragon?" Loor asked.

"There are jungles like this on Second Earth," I answered. "But Zetlin isn't from Second Earth so I have no clue what to expect."

At that exact instant, something shot out of the bushes. It was a long vine. But it was like it had been shot from a gun, because the vine flew right for us. Loor and I ducked back and the vine barely missed us. The end flew into the bushes on the far side and attached to something so that it stretched across the clearing like a rope.

Before we had the chance to react, another vine shot out the same way. Only this one flew behind us before attaching to a tree on the far side. Loor and I now stood between the two ropelike vines.

"Does this happen on Second Earth?" Loor asked.

"No, and I don't like it. C'mon," I said.

We ducked under the vine and ran for the far end of the clearing, where the path continued. As we ran, more vines shot from the bushes. They were coming fast now, shooting every which way—in front of us, over our heads, behind us. In seconds Loor and I were surrounded by a tangle of taut vines. They built up quickly in front of the trail, blocking our passage. There was only one way to describe what it looked like.

"Spiderweb," I said.

As if on cue, we heard more rustling in the bushes. The sound was much louder now. Whatever was making it was coming our way. Loor and I both looked back to see movement at the far edge of the clearing. There were a bunch of places where the foliage moved, making way for whatever was coming.

I was dying to know what it was. On the other hand, I didn't *really* want to die just to know what it was. If we were about to get attacked by a giant spider, I'd just as soon be someplace else. Loor didn't waste time thinking. She lunged for the side of the clearing and grabbed a five-foot-long branch. It looked strong enough that in the right hands, it could do some damage.

Loor had the right hands.

"Whatever it is," she announced, "if it charges, stay behind me."

I think we were both expecting to see a wild animal come out of the underbrush. Instead, what pushed its way out, slithering along the ground, looked more like a big cactus. Seriously. It was some kind of plant. It actually looked kind of pretty. It had a tubular body that was green and covered with thorns. The head was actually a violet-colored flower. The bud was pretty big too, about the size of a beach ball. It had large petals that opened and closed, like it was breathing.

Loor and I stood and watched in wonder as more of these strange plants pushed their way into the clearing. The flower blossoms, or whatever they were, were all different colors. Bright pink, purple, deep blue, and brilliant yellow. I counted eight in all. It was like they were creeping into the clearing, taking a curious look at who their visitors were.

"They're kind of pretty," I said.

Wrong. On cue, all eight blossoms opened up and spit out vines that shot right at us! Whoa! One of the vines latched on to my arm, cutting into my jumpsuit. The thing had razor-sharp barbs on it! I quickly pulled it off, just as another wrapped around my ankle and yanked me to the ground. It then started pulling me toward it! One quick look at the plant showed me all I needed to know. Inside the blossoms were sharp, gnashing, fanglike growths. These beautiful plants were hungry, and we had wandered into their house for a bite . . . of us.

"Loor!" I shouted.

I didn't need to. Loor had already gone to work with her whupping stick. She hacked like a lumberjack at the vine that had my leg. Two quick whacks and I was free, but the plant screamed. I swear, it actually screamed in pain. I jumped to my feet to see Loor was swinging her stick like crazy, batting away more vines that were shooting out of the plants at us.

"The trail!" I shouted.

I got behind her, grabbed the back of her jumpsuit and pulled her back toward the safety of the trail. As I pulled her back, she kept swinging away at the incoming missiles like she was in hyper batting-practice mode. She nailed most of them too, knocking them off course.

I kicked at the spiderweb of vines that was blocking the path. They may have been dense, but they weren't very strong because I could tear them down pretty easily. While I desperately tried to make an opening, Loor valiantly batted away the attacking vines. But there were too many of them. There was no way she could keep this up. I took a quick look back to see the toothy cactus plants were crawling closer, moving in for the kill.

"Just run!" I shouted.

Loor took one last swipe at an incoming vine, then turned with me and ran. We ducked through the opening in the web and sprinted along the narrow path. More vines zinged by our heads, trying to grab us and pull us back. As we got farther from the clearing, the vine attack tapered off. But we didn't stop running. Still, I feared we could easily be heading toward another nest of those nasty barb-shooting cactus plants.

After a few minutes of frantic chase, we both felt safe enough to take a rest. Good thing, too. My lungs were bursting out of my chest, that's how hard we were running. I think being terrified had something to do with it too. I stood there with my hands on my knees, gulping for air. Loor, on the other hand, barely looked winded. She scanned the jungle for any more signs of movement.

"There!" she announced.

"Please don't tell me it's another hungry vegetable," I gasped.

As strange as this sounds, rising up from the middle of the jungle was a spiral staircase. It led up and out of the foliage and disappeared into the dark. At first my brain couldn't compute why a spiral staircase would be in a dark jungle full of hungry predators. But then it hit me.

"We're inside a building," I said. "That must lead up to the next floor."

"Do we climb?" Loor asked.

"Do we have a choice?" I asked back.

Loor took the lead and continued along the path until it brought us to the foot of the stairs. They were made of metal, and a quick tug told us they were solid enough. The whole structure was overgrown with vines, like the ones that had been shooting at us. I touched them to see if they might suddenly spring to life and start attacking, but nothing happened. I took a step back and looked up to where the stairs led, but all I saw was black.

Loor gave me a quick look, then started to climb. I was right after her. The higher we got, the better view we had of the jungle below. The place was vast. But because it was so dense and dark, I couldn't see all the way to the far walls of the building. At least I thought we were still in a building. None of this really made sense, but then again, if it was a fantasy, was it supposed to make sense? It probably did to Dr. Zetlin.

After climbing for a few minutes, we found ourselves in darkness. Looking down below we saw the jungle, and to be honest, it was making my palms sweat. We were pretty high up. I was trying to figure how we would make our way back through the jungle to get out of here, when Loor stopped suddenly.

"Trouble," she said calmly.

"What is it?" I asked, though I wasn't sure I really wanted to know.

I looked up to see we had reached the next level. The circular staircase continued up through a large round hole in the black ceiling. Loor reached her hand up through that hole, but when she pulled it back down, I felt drops of water on my head. Huh? She showed me her hand. It was wet.

"I don't get it," I said, and climbed up past her. I put my hand up to the hole to find that it was actually a circle of water. As soon as I touched it, ripples spread out from my fingers, as if I were looking at an upside down pond. I had no idea how the liquid could be suspended like that and not gush down through the large opening. But it was and it didn't.

Loor said, "I am beginning to believe Dr. Zetlin does not like visitors."

"You think?" I said sarcastically. "We gotta go through this."

"Pendragon," Loor said with a firm voice. "I cannot swim."

Oh, man, I'd forgotten. As incredible an athlete as Loor was, she was like a rock in the water. This was bad. I knew what had to happen next, and it made my stomach twist.

"We gotta keep going," I said, trying to sound confident. "I'll check it out."

I really, *really* didn't want to, but what else could I do? I could tell that Loor wanted to argue, but she knew there was no other way. So before I could chicken out, I took another step up so that my head was just below the ceiling of water. I took a couple of deep breaths to expand my lungs, then held the last breath and pushed my head up into the wet.

The water was warm. That was one good thing. I only went in up to my shoulders and did my best to get a look around. There wasn't a whole lot to see, but I think that was mostly because my vision was blurred by the water. What I wouldn't have given at that moment for an air globe from Cloral! As it was, there was nothing to see when I looked around but wet blackness.

Yet when I looked straight up, I saw light coming from above. I took a step back down and dropped out of the water. My head and shoulders were wet, but very little water spilled out from above. Unbelievable.

"It's a big pool," I said. "This is the bottom, but I can't tell how far it is to the surface."

Loor and I looked at each other. We both knew what had to happen next. Loor started yanking vines off the railing of the stairs.

"I will tie one end to your ankle," she explained.

She was a few steps ahead of me. I was still trying to get my mind around the fact that I had to swim up into the unknown. Loor was already making sure I would get back to safety. She quickly tore off a length of vine that was plenty long enough for this adventure. If I swam upward for the full length of this vine and still hadn't found the surface, there would be no way I'd have enough air in my lungs to make it back to the hole.

Loor tied one end around my ankle, then stood and faced me.

"I will hold on to your waist," she said. "Please do not lose me."

"Whoa, you're not coming!"

"It is better that we stay together and make the trip only once," she explained.

She didn't show a touch of fear, though she had to be terrified. Man, this girl was brave. I wasn't sure which was worse, taking her with me, or risking the trip by myself and having to do it twice. I decided that as long as Loor was game, we'd go together.

"Okay," I said. "But if we don't find the surface right away, we're coming right back."

Loor nodded. She tied the other end of the vine around the railing of the stairs. With a quick tug, she made sure it was secure. The rest of the vine she placed in a coil on one of the stairs. Loor then stood behind me, and wrapped her arms around my waist. I could feel the strength in those arms. I sure hoped she didn't get too scared, or she'd break me in half.

"If you start running out of breath, give me two quick squeezes," I instructed. "I'll turn us around and get right back here."

"I understand," she said.

Loor was focused, battling her fear. There was no way I was going to let anything happen to her. We stood together with my head just below the water.

"Take some deep breaths," I said. "You'll be able to hold your breath longer."

We both took three deep breaths, holding the third. With a quick nod, we both walked *up* into the water.

We had to move fast. Every second counted. It was a strange feeling. A second before, we were standing on stairs with gravity pulling us down. Now the water took over, and we were pulled the other way, up. I started doing the breast-stroke, spearing my hands up, then pulling a downward stroke with as much power as I had. Loor held tight and her weight was a huge drag. It didn't matter. All I could focus on was getting to the surface as fast as possible. There was no way of knowing how far it was. After about five strokes, I started thinking about turning back, because it was going to be a lot harder to swim down than up. I made a quick decision. Five more strokes and we'd turn around.

That's when I heard a strange sound. It was high-pitched, like an engine. Of course, it was hard to know where it was coming from because we were underwater. But there was one thing for sure: Whatever it was, it was getting louder. That meant it was getting closer.

I took a quick look straight ahead and saw lights in the distance. There were five of them at our level, underwater. They looked like flashlight beams, headed our way. Fast. Whatever they were, they were definitely making the whining sound.

I didn't know what to do. Were these lights a threat? Should I turn around and get us back down to the hole? Should I pull even harder and hope we would reach the surface? Should we stay where we were and defend ourselves?

I didn't have time to decide because in seconds they were on us. All five lights dipped down and passed underneath us so fast that I couldn't get a good look at what they were. They didn't hit us, but as soon as they shot beneath, I felt a hard tug that forced me to stop swimming. I knew instantly what had happened. A quick look down confirmed it.

Whatever those speeding lights were, they severed the vine that was our lifeline to the bottom. The cut end drifted up next to me. We were floating free.

That's when Loor gave me two quick squeezes. She was running out of air.

We were trapped in a watery limbo.

VEELOX

I had to keep swimming for the surface.

We were too far away from the hole at the bottom to get back down. Besides, without the vine to guide us there was no guarantee I would even find it. No, the choice was clear. Swim up like crazy, or drown.

I kept doing the breaststroke as hard as I could. I really wished I could have kicked my legs, too, but Loor was wrapped around my lower body. My lungs were starting to ache. I think I was swimming so hard that it burned up whatever oxygen I had left.

An idea hit me: Press the button on my control bracelet and end the jump. If we didn't reach the surface in a few seconds it would be our only hope. But it was the last resort and there was no guarantee it would even work. Keep swimming.

A few agonizing seconds passed and we were still underwater. I was starting to black out. We had to get air, now. Time to abort. I reached for my control bracelet, but at the exact moment before I bailed us out, something splashed down into the water only a few yards away. Whatever it was, it was pretty big and moving fast because it made a dramatic *boom* when it hit the water. But I didn't care what it was. All I knew was that if something made a splash like that, we had to be near the surface. So I didn't hit the button, and made two more desperate strokes for air.

A moment later I broke the surface, followed right behind by Loor, both gasping for air. We had made it! But there wasn't time to celebrate because we now faced another danger. Loor couldn't swim. I had to change gears fast, and take care of her. She was already starting to flail in the water. If she clocked me by accident, I'd be out cold, and we'd both be sunk. Literally.

"Relax," I commanded. "Float on your back, Loor. I got you."

Loor rolled onto her back. She was breathing hard and her eyes were wild, but she tried to relax. I held her head above the surface and started to tread water.

"We're okay," I said, trying to sound soothing. "Let's just catch our breath and we'll get out of here."

I took the chance to look around to get my bearings. The cavernous space we were floating in was pitch black, and like the jungle below, I couldn't see the far walls of this incredible fantasy building. Again the ceiling disappeared into black. But there was something odd in the air above us. Floating midair all over this huge space were colorful, brightly lit globes. They looked to be about two feet in diameter, with each glowing a different neon color. Orange, red, green, yellow. There must have been a hundred of them, all floating in the air above us at different levels.

"They are like colorful stars," Loor said. "What could they be?"

This was good. She was calming down.

"I have no idea," I said. "They don't look dangerous—"

Suddenly there was an eruption in the water a few feet from

us. Exploding up from below came the lights that had severed our line. But now we saw them for what they really were.

They were vehicles.

All five shot up from underwater and flew into the air. They looked to me like bright, colorful motorcycles without wheels. Each had a rider wearing a helmet. They were crouched down low like jockeys behind a conelike wind-shield. They were hauling, too. The vehicles flew out of the water and continued up toward the floating globes. These things not only traveled underwater, they could fly! All five riders charged in a pack toward a bright orange globe. They sped past it, turned sharply around it, and shot ahead toward the next one.

"They're racing!" I exclaimed. "Those globes mark the racecourse!"

The five racers flew away from us, speeding from globe to globe. They all then turned together and dove back toward the water. A second later all five hit the surface and disappeared below like a pack of hungry seagulls hunting for fish.

"How cool is that!" I exclaimed. "This is a racecourse!"

"Pendragon," Loor said calmly, "I still can't swim."

Oh, right. We had to get out of the water. I took another look around and was relieved to see another spiral staircase rising out of the water only a few yards away. A few quick strokes and I had towed Loor to the stairs. We both clung to them, happy to have solid footing again. While we sat catching our breaths, we watched as the racers erupted from the water once again, shot into the sky, and charged far off into the distance. Whoever these racers were, they were good, and they had the coolest vehicles I had ever seen.

"Are you okay?" I asked Loor.

Loor nodded and said, "We must continue up."

I gazed up the staircase to see that it disappeared into blackness.

"Man," I said. "This guy Zetlin is a piece of work."

This time I took the lead and hurried up the stairs. As we rose up, we kept watching the racers zip around the globes, plunge into the water, then fly up again and back onto the airborne course. It looked like a lot of fun.

When we arrived at the ceiling, I was relieved to see this next opening wasn't water. Instead, the staircase rose up through a large, white circle.

Loor said, "How can this be? We are no longer wet."

Sure enough, our jumpsuits and our hair were completely dry. I was beyond questioning anything that happened. If we were suddenly, magically dry, so be it. Whatever. As it turned out, it was a good thing because when I reached out to the edge of the circle to touch the white band, I was surprised to feel that it was cold.

"It's snow!" I announced.

Sure enough, I was able to dig my hand into the white edge of the circle and come back with a handful of ice crystals.

"Now what?" was all I could say.

I continued up the last few steps and arrived at a small, snow cave. It was like standing up inside an igloo. It was chilly, too. Good thing we were dry.

"I guess that's the way," I said, pointing to the opening to the cave.

Neither of us had any idea what to expect outside, but we had to brave it. So the two of us walked toward the light and out of the cave. The small cavern took a turn, and as soon as we both rounded it, we were blinded by an incredibly intense, white light. After having been in the dark of the jungle and the watery racecourse, all we could do was cover our eyes and wait until they adjusted to this new environment. It took a few seconds, but when we lowered our hands, we were met with yet another incredible sight.

It looked like Antarctica.

Not that I've ever been to Antarctica, but if I had, I'm sure it would look like this. Everything was white, which explained why we were having trouble seeing. The sky was bright white too. Again, we may have been inside a building, but this time we were enveloped in such blindingly bright light that we couldn't see walls or a ceiling.

As my eyes grew more accustomed to the light, I began to make out more detail. It seemed like we were standing on a vast field of ice. It wasn't all flat, though. There were huge mounds of craggy ice that formed hills and valleys all around us.

"This Dr. Zetlin has a very strange imagination," Loor said.

Before I could agree, we heard excited shouting.

"Whooo! Yeah! Eehaaaaa!"

It sounded like a bunch of guys having an adrenaline rush. A second later five figures appeared on top of one of the icy mounds. They shot over the top, got some serious air, and then landed on the slope and slid down on what looked like snowboards. They weren't like Second Earth snowboards though. These things were round and black. They were about the size of a garbage can lid and curved up at the rim. The riders' feet were attached in the middle somehow. Man, they were good. As they sped down the slope, they did three-sixties and dodged around one another and basically looked like a stunt team. They all wore the familiar green jumpsuits, but with black helmets that covered most of their heads and faces.

Loor and I watched in awe as the five riders sped toward us. I wasn't sure if we should run, or hold our ground. I started to back away, but Loor stopped me.

"No," she said. "We cannot show fear."

Easy for her to say. But I stayed where I was.

A second later Loor and I were hit with a spray of snow as the snow riders dug in and stopped directly in front of us. It was a totally awkward moment. The five helmeted riders stood shoulder to shoulder, staring at us through dark, tinted goggles. Nobody said anything. Finally I figured it was time to cut to the chase.

"We're looking for Dr. Zetlin," I said.

The five riders looked to one another and started to laugh. I didn't expect that. Then again, I'm not sure what I expected. Finally one of them got control of himself enough to step forward.

"You can't just show up and see the Z," he said.

"It's very important," I said, feeling kind of lame. "He'll want to see us."

I had no idea how to sum up quickly why we had to see Dr. Zetlin. They didn't seem like the kind of guys who would stand still for a long-winded explanation. Or care.

"Do you know where he is?" Loor asked.

Another rider walked up to her and said, "Sure, but if you want to see him, you've got to play first."

"Play?" I asked. "Play what?"

"Slickshot!" another rider shouted.

"Yeah! Slickshot!" the others chimed in.

The riders then quickly released their boots from their snow disks, tossed them aside, and started to skate across the ice. It seemed impossible because they moved like they had ice skates on, but they didn't. They were sliding along with only their boot bottoms touching the surface. The first rider then skated back to us and stopped right in front of me.

"Here's the deal," he said. "One of you races slickshot with us. You don't have to win, just finish."

"What kind of race is it?" I asked.

The guy pointed out across the ice to the other racers who were skating along.

"It's a skating race," he explained. "There's a course over the ice marked by red arrows. We all skate the course together, first one back here wins."

"And all we have to do is finish?" I asked.

"It's not that easy," the rider explained. "There are five checkpoints. The first one has a tower with six red balls in it. One for each racer. You have to pick up a ball, then skate forward and drop it in a basket before skating to the next checkpoint. That one has six balls too. But the third checkpoint has only five balls. If you're the last one there, you're done. The next one has five balls too, but the final checkpoint has only four."

"So six start the race and only four finish," I said.

"Exactly," the guy said. "Finish the race and you can meet the Z."

"We are not here to play games," Loor said firmly.

"Too bad," the rider said with a shrug. "We are."

With that he turned and started to skate away.

"Wait!" I shouted. "I'll give it a shot. But I don't get how you guys are skating without skates."

The racer skated over to the mouth of the cave. Next to the opening was something we hadn't seen when we arrived. It was a rack full of the same black helmets like the racers wore. Next to it was a wire bin with close to forty red balls about the size of a grapefruit. I guessed those were the kind of balls that would be at the checkpoints. The guy picked up one of the helmets and skated back to us.

"Attach these to your shoes," he said while reaching into the helmet. He pulled out two wire frames that looked as if they would fit onto the sole of a shoe. Each one had two yellow pads, one for the front of the foot, one for the back. He then added, "Get used to them. We'll go set up the course."

He skated away to join the other racers.

"Maybe I should be the one to race," Loor said.

"Do you know how to skate?" I asked.

Loor looked down. She didn't like to admit defeat.

"I do," I said. "Let me try these things out."

The wires attached easily to the soles of my boots. One end clamped over my toe, the other attached over my heel. But I didn't understand how they could work like ice skates, until I put my feet down and pushed off.

"Whoa!" I shouted as I slid across the ice.

The pads must have been made of a superslick material, because I glided over the ice as easily as if I had on hockey skates. It took me all of thirty seconds to get the feel of these things and found they were even easier to control than skates. I played a couple of years of junior hockey, so I was pretty confident on the ice. With these slick pads, I found that I could turn, stop, cut, and skate backward better than at home. My confidence was building.

But we faced a tough decision. Between the two of us, Loor was the athlete. But if she couldn't skate like me, it didn't matter how strong she was. She'd never make it to the first checkpoint.

"I think I should be the one to race," I said to Loor.

Loor nodded. She knew I was right. "Why must we play

games?" she snapped. "We are on a serious mission. It should not be decided by a childish competition."

"I know," I said. "But let's do it their way. If I finish, then we'll get to Zetlin."

"And if you don't?" she asked.

I didn't have an answer to that.

The five racers then skated right up to us and stopped in a group. "Ready?" the one who gave me the helmet asked.

"Sure," I said, trying to sound like a winner. "Any other rules I should know about?"

The racers laughed again. I hated that.

"Absolutely," the first racer said. "The main rule is: Anything goes. Finish any way you can."

I didn't like the sound of that. But this was their game; I wasn't going to start arguing the finer points of slickshot. The five racers pushed off toward the starting line. I was about to follow when Loor touched my shoulder. She didn't say anything; she simply looked into my eyes. I think she was trying to give me some of her strength and confidence. My knees went weak. In that moment I was more worried about letting her down than finding Dr. Zetlin. She gave me a wink and let me go.

I pushed off while putting on my helmet and fitting the goggles over my eyes. I never wanted to win anything more in my life. For her, for me, and even for Aja. I realized that the fate of Veelox might very well be decided on this icy racecourse.

How wrong was that?

VEELOX

The five racers stood shoulder to shoulder at a tall, red post. "This is the start and finish," the first racer explained. He then pointed out the course. "The first checkpoint is dead ahead."

I looked across the flat expanse to a wall of ice that rose up in the distance. There I saw a red arrow painted on the face, pointing left.

"Just follow the arrows," the rider said. "You can't miss them. Get to the checkpoint, pick up a ball and drop it in the basket. If you miss one ball, you're out. Got it?"

"Yeah," I said.

My heart started to pump faster. This was suddenly looking like a bad idea. I had no clue as to how good these guys were. It's not like they looked like pro speed skaters or anything. Just the opposite. They were all my size. But this was their home ice. I'll bet they raced this course all the time. This was insane. But I was in it now. All I could hope was that I'd hold on long enough to stay in the race.

"On my go," the first racer said.

All six of us crouched down, ready to spring forward.

"One, two, *go!*"

What happened to three? This was a bad start. I was already a second behind and the race had barely begun. All I could do was push off and try to catch up, pumping my legs and swinging my arms for momentum. I was surprised to see that these guys didn't leave me in the dust. Or maybe I should say leave me in the frost. Not only did I keep up with them, I quickly made up the ground I had lost with the bad start. I was still last, but my confidence zoomed. Maybe I had a chance after all.

We quickly arrived at the first arrow and made the turn toward the checkpoint. I made the turn easily, crossing my feet over and trying not to lose too much speed. Up ahead I saw a rack with six of the grapefruit-size red balls. The five other racers quickly snatched one apiece while barely slowing down. I was last, but right there with them.

That is, until the fifth racer knocked the last ball off the rack. The red ball hit the ice and rolled away. I had to come to a full stop to pick it up. No way that was an accident. I guess when they said that "anything goes," they meant it. I realized there was more to worry about than just keeping pace. These guys cheated.

I snatched up the ball and took off again. A few yards ahead was a steel basket with the first five balls that the other racers had already dumped. I dropped mine off and dug in to catch up.

The other racers were skating easily. None of them looked as if they wanted the lead. That was fine with me. As long as they all were being cautious, I could keep up. This part of the course was a wide-open expanse of ice. I didn't even look for any red arrows, all I did was follow the guys in front of me.

But it got frustrating because they were all skating in one line, shoulder to shoulder. I had no hope of getting around them. I skated up behind the group, but when I put on some speed to go around, the whole group moved in front of me, blocking the way. I'd try to skate the other way, and they'd all move as one in the other direction to block me again. I was beginning to think this wasn't so much about somebody winning, as about making sure I would lose. As long as they kept me back like this, I would always be the last one to reach the rack of balls.

That would be bad news at checkpoint #3.

We quickly approached the second checkpoint. Like precision pilots the five racers smoothly moved into a single line, with me last, again. But this time I made sure to be close enough behind the fifth racer so he couldn't try anything cute with the sixth ball.

He didn't try. All six of us picked up a red ball and dumped it into the steel basket beyond the rack. This time, I was right there with them. But I was still in sixth place. Not good enough. I had to make a move.

The course then slid into a narrow canyon of ice. The walls rose up steeply on either side. There was maybe five feet between the walls where we were skating. It was so narrow, we had to skate single file. There was no way I could make up any ground.

I was in trouble. The next checkpoint only had five balls. If we stayed this way, I'd be gone. I tried to move up on the fifth racer, but it was like these guys had eyes in their butts. The whole line slid over in front of me. It was so frustrating! I was fast enough to keep up with them, but didn't have the experience to do anything else.

We were closing in on the third checkpoint. I had to make some kind of move or the race would be over. An idea came to me that was either brilliant or totally whacked. Chances were good if I tried it, I'd crash and burn. But I didn't see any other way. I looked ahead at the ice walls to either side of us. I needed a little luck, and got it. Ahead to my right I saw a spot that was a little less steep than the rest. There wasn't time to think. I had to go for it.

I made a quick move to my left and sure enough, the whole line of racers slid in that direction to block me. But then I shot to my right and skated toward the wall of ice. The slope was forgiving enough that I didn't slam into it. Instead I skated a few feet up onto the wall, forcing my chattering legs to hold firm. I then pivoted my body back left and shot for the center. The momentum from being up on the wall gave me just enough extra speed for a slingshot between the fourth and fifth skater. It was a NASCAR move all the way, and it worked.

The fifth guy couldn't believe it. My surprise move threw off his rhythm and he nearly fell. By then we were at the checkpoint rack of balls. The fifth, and last, was mine. I scooped it up and jammed it into the basket. I was still alive.

The next section of the race was hairy. We shot out of the ice canyon and the course again moved left. I now realized we were moving in a big loop, counterclockwise, back to the starting line. The racers ahead of me broke out of formation. A second later, I saw why.

The expanse of ice before us was littered with boulder-size chunks of ice. There was no straight path through. It was an obstacle course. Blasting through at full speed would be suicide. We had to back off the speed, get more control, and dodge the boulders. For me it was a relief, because I was getting tired. I'd bet anything that these guys were in better shape than I was. My only advantage was that I had so much at stake, I couldn't lose. I was racing on adrenaline.

All five of us took a different route. It was tricky, not only because I had to get through as fast as possible, but now that

I wasn't following anybody, I had to keep an eye out for the red arrows that marked the course.

I have to admit, I was doing pretty well. I can't take all the credit though. These skate pad things were incredible. They made it so easy to shift direction, I started pouring on the speed and cutting it very close to the boulders. I saw that I was actually pulling ahead of the others. It was awesome! By the time we got to the end of the boulder field, I was out in front. The checkpoint was just past the final obstacle, and the first ball was mine. Yes! But I didn't care about winning. All that mattered was the next checkpoint. I had to get one of the next balls to make sure I'd finish. I was feeling pretty confident, though, which in my experience is the kiss of death. This time was no different.

I had just grabbed the red ball and dumped it into the steel basket, ready for the final push, when something hit me on the back of the foot. At first I didn't know what it was. But I wasn't worried . . . until I put that foot down and tried to push off. Before I knew it, I lost my balance and fell to the ice. Something had happened to my skate pad.

On the ice next to me, I saw the culprit. A red ball was lying at my feet. The first racer shot up, scooped up the ball, and dumped it into the basket.

"Sorry," he said. "It got away from me."

Yeah, right. He had thrown it at me. The ball must have knocked off my skate pad and when I put my foot down, my boot caught the ice and sent me tumbling. Sure enough, I saw the wire frame of the skate pad a few feet away. I scrambled for it, desperately pulling it back over my shoe.

I quickly looked up to see the four other skaters leaving me behind. I was done. There was no way I could catch up and pass anybody before the next checkpoint. But I didn't know what else to do. So I strapped the skate pad back on and skated after them, praying for a miracle.

The racecourse again veered left and into another canyon. This one wasn't as narrow as the first, and the walls weren't quite as steep. I pushed as hard as I could, trying to catch up, but it was useless. These guys weren't taking any more chances. They were skating hard and moving faster than they had the whole race. The sad truth hit me that up until then, they had been playing with me. They knew I wasn't a threat and barely put out any effort. But now, they had their heads down and pumped their arms powerfully. I didn't stand a chance.

That's when I got the miracle I needed.

The four remaining racers were so focused, they didn't see it coming. But I did. At first I wasn't sure what it was. It didn't make sense. But nothing about this fantasy building made any sense, so I shouldn't have been surprised. A few seconds later I saw exactly what it was and it suddenly made all sorts of sense.

High up the slope on one side of the canyon, an avalanche was starting. But it wasn't about snow and ice. It was an avalanche of red balls. There must have been forty of them, all rolling down the hill, headed for the skaters. There was only one explanation.

Loor.

I looked up to the top of the rise to see her standing there with the empty wire basket that had once held all the balls. Excellent.

I glanced down to the racers. They had no clue about what was bouncing down toward them from above. The only question now was whether Loor had timed it right. There was a chance the tumbling balls would miss them entirely.

They didn't.

The balls rained down on top of the unsuspecting racers, making them scatter. One took a header and beefed it into the canyon wall. Another spun out, lost control, and came to a dead stop. A third kept going, but had to pinwheel his arms to keep his balance. One racer dodged the balls completely and kept going. I didn't care. Fourth place was all I needed.

I flashed past the three skaters who were trying to get their balance back. They didn't know what had hit them. When I got to the checkpoint, I had my choice of three balls. I felt like taking one and dumping the other two over, just to put an exclamation point on the moment. But I figured we had already cheated enough. So I picked up one of the balls, and spiked it into the steel basket with a vengeance.

I coasted home on the last leg. By then the two other racers caught up and passed me, but I didn't care. I skated across the finish line with my hands in the air chanting, "We're number four! We're number four!"

Loor jogged up and patted me on the back. I could tell she was holding back a smile.

"Good race, Pendragon," she said.

"Good thinking, Loor," I shot back.

"You cheated!" one of the racers yelled. It was the last guy who dropped out. He skated up to the finish line looking all sorts of angry. "I call foul!"

"Excuse me," I said calmly. "I thought the first rule was: Anything goes."

"But she interfered," he protested.

"But it was okay to throw a ball at me and knock my skate pad off?" I shot back. "I don't think so."

By then the sixth skater had returned. "I want another race," he demanded.

"Tough," I said.

"There won't be another race," said the first racer firmly. It was the guy who explained the race to us and who was the ultimate winner. "He competed in the same spirit as we did. The race was fair."

The guy walked up to me and held out his hand to shake. "Congratulations," he said. "Nicely done."

I took his hand and shook.

"Now it's your turn," I said. "We had a deal."

"Indeed," the guy said.

He pulled down his goggles and took off his helmet. He was a handsome guy, I'm guessing around sixteen years old. He had short, blond hair and an intense look in his eye. The second I saw him, I knew I had met him somewhere before, but couldn't figure out where.

"I always honor my wagers," he added.

That's when it hit me. I knew this guy. Sort of. I had seen him in a painting. A portrait. He was younger in the portrait, but there was no mistake. It was him.

"I'm Dr. Zetlin," he said with a wry smile. "Welcome to my fantasy."

VEELO·X

"You can't be Zetlin," I said. "Dr. Zetlin is seventy years old."

"Seventy-nine, to be exact," the kid-racer answered.

Loor and I shot each other a confused look.

"This is my fantasy," Zetlin continued. "Why would I live it as an old man?"

I asked, "So, the guy lying in the Alpha Core—"

"That would be my physical body that's seventy-nine years old," Zetlin answered. "But in here I'm a strapping sixteen. The more interesting question is, who are you two?"

After all we had been through to get here, I had to force my brain to shift gears and remember the message Aja had for him.

"We're here because Lifelight is in trouble," I said. "A virus has corrupted the processing code. We need the origin code to clean the string."

I was pretty sure that was the right message. For a second I feared it made no sense to him because Zetlin gave me a strange look. But then he turned to the other racers and said brightly, "Good race, guys! Later, all right?"

The other racers all said, "Yeah. Later! See ya, Z!" and skated off.

Zetlin then turned to us and said sternly, "Come with me."

He pulled the skate pads from his boots and stalked off. Loor and I followed right behind. It was weird. When Zetlin spoke to us, he sounded like a serious adult. But when he talked to the racers, he sounded like an excited kid. I guess his fantasy was all about reliving his youth. Whatever. All we needed was the origin code. His fantasies were his business.

"I must say, I'm impressed you two made it this far," Zetlin said. "Usually phaders don't make it past the jungle. What are your names?"

"I'm Pendragon," I answered. "This is Loor."

"Why are you hiding in this building?" Loor asked.

Uh-oh. I wasn't sure if challenging the guy was a good idea. We needed him on our side. But since the question was pure Loor, I figured I didn't have a choice.

"The Barbican is my refuge from a world I want nothing to do with," Zetlin answered. He then stopped and faced us. "And I don't like being disturbed. But you two were willing to play on my terms. You've earned the right to an audience. This way."

Who did he think he was? Some kind of king? I figured it wasn't my place to question him either, so I let it go. There were bigger problems to deal with.

Zetlin walked toward a wall of ice. I wasn't exactly sure where he was going until I saw a small black disk sticking out of the wall at waist level. Zetlin pulled on the disk and opened a door made of ice. Beyond was a small room with light blue, metallic walls. He motioned for us to enter. I figured we had come this far, we couldn't chicken out now. So Loor and I stepped inside. The room was no bigger than an elevator, and that's what it turned out to be. An elevator. Zetlin joined us inside, closed the door, touched a control button on the wall and we started up.

"I'm confused," I said. "I thought Lifelight had to follow the rules of reality. This Barbican thing is about as far from reality as I can imagine."

"That's because you don't have my imagination," Zetlin answered with a chuckle.

Good answer. Zetlin definitely had an exceptional mind. I suppose it followed that his fantasy could be just as exceptional.

"The people of Veelox haven't even begun to tap Lifelight's capabilities," Zetlin continued. "But they will."

"No, they won't," I countered. "Veelox is falling apart because everybody is living inside their own fantasy worlds."

If this news bothered Zetlin, he didn't show it. The elevator slowed to a stop and the door opened. Zetlin stepped out first, and we followed him into a space that I can best describe as the dream home for a fifteen-year-old guy. I should know. I'm a fifteen-year-old guy and I thought the place was awesome.

The space was huge, but divided up into smaller sections so it didn't feel like an airplane hangar or anything. The ceiling was made of clear glass, so we could see the sky and the last of the storm clouds passing through. That meant we were now on the top floor of the Barbican.

We first walked through a wood-floored arena that reminded me of a basketball court. But this was Veelox. Their version of basketball had soccer-style nets on each of the four walls, and green balls that looked twice the size of a basketball.

Zetlin led us across the empty court, through a door, and into another space that had the Veelox version of a game I remembered playing as a kid. You know that game where you have to knock over wooden pegs set up on a table by swinging a ball on the end of a string? I think it was called Skittles.

Well, this was like Skittles, only life-size. There were five giant balls, all hanging from ropes in the center of a round court. Instead of pegs, the idea was to knock over people. I'm serious. There was a game under way with ten kids in the center of the big court, and another ten around the circle. The kids around the outside would grab the ball and swing it into the center to try and hit one of the kids inside. Some of the kids inside really got clocked, too. It was like nasty dodgeball. I wasn't sure if it was fun or torture.

"Hey, guys," Zetlin called out. "Game's over. Let's play tomorrow, okay?"

Zetlin even used kid slang that sounded like Second Earth, but I guess that was because my Traveler brain interpreted it from whatever was the kid slang version of the language they spoke on Veelox.

"Yeah. Okay! See ya later, Z!" the players all shouted as they jogged off the court, headed for the elevator.

"You enjoy playing child games," Loor said.

"Indeed," Zetlin answered. "It relaxes me to play simple games of skill and chance."

He led us next into what looked more like living space. It was modern, with a lot of big, comfortable couches of all colors. There were giant screens on the wall that I'd bet anything were for video games. It looked like we had just missed a big party. Plates and cups were scattered everywhere. All had half eaten leftovers of I don't know what. The only thing I knew for sure was that it wasn't gloid. There were a couple of older guys wearing green jumpsuits who were cleaning the place up.

One of them saw us and said, "We'll have the place tidy in no time, Z."

"Take your time," Zetlin responded. "I don't think we'll have anybody over again today."

Wow. He had servants cleaning up after him too. Could this place get any better?

It could.

We stepped into a modern kitchen that was full of incredible smells. A dozen chefs were scurrying around, busily cooking and frying and baking and . . . man, my stomach rumbled. I had only been eating gloid for the last few days. The idea of real food sounded pretty good right about now.

A woman chef hurried up to Zetlin with a tray of freshly baked cookies. "Can I tempt you, Z?" she asked.

Zetlin nodded for us to try the cookies. I didn't want to be rude, so I took one. Who am I kidding? They smelled great. I wanted ten. But I only took one and it was delicious. It was sweet and gooey and tasted like chocolate. Loor ate one too. I could tell by the look on her face that she liked it as much as I did. As if reading my mind, another chef appeared with two glasses that I really hoped had the Veelox version of milk. What is it about milk that tastes so good with chocolate? The liquid was creamy colored, and I'm not sure if it was milk, but it sure tasted great.

"Thank you," I said to the chefs.

"Yes, thank you," Loor added.

Zetlin smiled and led us on. As soon as we stepped through the door into the next section, I knew this was our ultimate destination. One whole wall was made of glass, which meant we could look out onto the strange city of black buildings. The opposite wall held a computer console that looked very much like the Alpha Core in the Lifelight pyramid. This place wasn't about fun and games. This was where Dr. Zetlin worked. This was where we needed to be.

"First things first," Zetlin said. He walked to the control

chair and hit a few buttons on the arm controller. The building rumbled. It felt like an earthquake.

"What is happening?" Loor asked, crouching down and ready for trouble.

"Don't worry," Zetlin answered. "I'm returning the Barbican to position number one."

The walls began to move. I realized that the massive building was turning back onto its side! We heard the grinding sound of metal wheels activating and straining under the massive load. Loor and I both looked around for something to grab on to for balance.

Zetlin laughed, "Please, don't panic. The floors rotate inside the structure. We'll remain level."

Sure enough, as the wall moved, what had been the glass ceiling became the wall. A new glass ceiling appeared which was previously the far wall. Even though we weren't actually moving, all this rotating made me dizzy. The only way I could keep from falling over was to look out at the city. The city didn't move. That proved the building was rotating around us while the floor stayed level. Amazing. A few seconds later, the building shuddered and it was over. A quick look around told me that nothing seemed to have changed.

"The building is on its side again?" I asked.

"Yes," Zetlin answered. "All the floors are perfect cubes. That's how they can rotate within the frame of the Barbican. The only thing different now is that each floor is side by side with the next. In position one, there is no need to climb between floors. Everything is on one level."

"Why do you make this building turn like it does?" Loor asked.

"To keep out the uninvited, of course," Zetlin answered.

That meant us, but I wasn't going to start apologizing now. I walked over to the glass wall and gazed out at the dreary, black city.

"I don't get it," I said. "Why do you have that city out there? You could create any world you want. I'm sorry for saying this, but this whole setup is totally strange."

Zetlin joined me at the window and looked out. "This city is a reminder," he said softly.

"Of what?" I asked.

"Of life before Lifelight."

"I don't understand," I said. "Is this where you lived?"

"In a manner of speaking," Zetlin answered. "I was born and raised in Rubic City. It was a busy, thriving community, but I was never a part of it. I was too—what was the word they used?—I was too *special* to be part of the life everyone else knew."

It was strange listening to Zetlin. He looked like a sixteen-year-old kid, but his words were that of a sad old man. It was kind of creepy.

"The directors recognized my genius from the time I was an infant," he continued. "They predicted my superior intellect could change the future of Veelox." He looked at me and chuckled. "They were right."

"Then you did not live an ordinary life?" Loor asked.

"Oh, no!" Zetlin answered quickly. "I lived an extraordinary life. I was surrounded by the greatest scientific minds available. They were my teachers, but soon became my pupils. They marveled at my theories of neural-electric compatibility. It was the theory that broke down the artificial wall between thought and reality. By the time I was eight, we created the first prototype of Lifelight. It was crude, but we were able to generate visual images driven solely by brain function. That was the moment. The breakthrough. From then on, it was simply about growth."

"But what was your life like?" I asked. "I mean, yeah, you were a genius and all, but it sounds a little . . . I don't know . . . not fun."

Zetlin didn't answer. He simply looked out the window. It was slowly coming clear to me. Aja told me what it was like to grow up as a phader. Every minute was spent learning and being trained. There was no time for warmth or friendship. My guess was that Dr. Zetlin's life had been like that, times about a thousand. This horrible, black city was the image Zetlin had of his life. His real life.

I had been wrong to think Zetlin's fantasy was about reliving his youth. It was about having the childhood he was denied. This building he called the Barbican was his second chance at being a kid.

"I had a goal," he finally said. "I worked on Lifelight for sixty years. It consumed me morning and night. But I kept going because I knew it would be my only chance to escape." He pointed out through the glass. "That city. That dark, rainy cold city is there as a reminder of what life once was, and of why I will never leave the Barbican."

I felt bad for the guy. His life was a fantasy. He had no memories of real live friends or loved ones. Everything important to him was made up in his head. Worse than that, I was going to have to tell him that it wouldn't last.

"We need your help, Dr. Zetlin," I said.

Zetlin pulled himself away from the window. He was suddenly a young boy again, full of energy. He hurried to the control chair and plopped down in it.

"Right," he said. "You said something about a virus corrupting the processing code. That, I'm afraid, is impossible."

He hit a few keys on his controller and a stream of data appeared on the large monitor overhead.

"It's not impossible," I insisted. "The virus has totally infected Lifelight. It mutates people's thoughts. Instead of giving them the ideal experience, it finds what they're afraid of and hurts them. The phaders had to suspend the grid or a lot of people would—"

"They suspended the grid?" Zetlin asked in surprise.

"Yes! All over Veelox, people are in limbo waiting—"

"I know what it means," Zetlin snapped at me. He hit a few more keys and examined more data. He then stood up and announced, "I see no evidence of anything wrong."

"That's because your jump is isolated," I said. "Look, I'm on shaky ground here. I don't really know how this works."

"Then what are you doing here?" he demanded. "What kind of phader are you?"

"We're not phaders," I answered nervously. "We're here to tell you that unless we get the origin code, millions of people across Veelox are going to die."

Zetlin looked me square in the eye. "You have not convinced me," he said. "I believe this virus does not exist; therefore I will not give you the origin code. Good-bye."

Our mission was about to fail miserably. I had no idea of what to say or do to turn it around. But then we heard a familiar voice come from across the room.

"The virus is real," it said.

We all spun to see Aja. "I know it's real, because I created it. I'm a phader, and I may be responsible for the deaths of millions of people across Veelox."

VEELOX

"I know you!" Zetlin said to Aja. "You're one of the phaders from Rubic City. What is going on here? Why have these people invaded my privacy?"

Aja looked nervous. She was facing the big boss and didn't have good things to tell him.

"My name is Aja Killian," she said, her voice cracking. "I apologize, Dr. Zetlin. I would never think of entering your jump if it weren't a dire emergency. I sent my friends to find you because I need to be in the Alpha Core to hold back the Reality Bug."

"Reality Bug?" Zetlin shouted angrily. He looked like his head was about to explode. For a second I thought he was going to really tee off on Aja, but he got his emotions under control and spoke calmly. "Please explain," he demanded.

Aja hesitated. I'm sure the idea of telling the most important man in the history of Veelox that his invention was on the verge of blowing a major fuse was pretty tough. Aja's rock-solid self-confidence was looking pretty shaky.

"It's okay, Aja," I said, trying to give her encouragement. "Tell him what's going on."

"Veelox is in danger," she said nervously. "Dr. Zetlin, since you jumped into Lifelight, the people of Veelox have abandoned reality. They prefer to live in the fantasy of Lifelight than in their own lives."

"I don't blame them," Zetlin said.

"But you should!" Aja said with passion. "Your invention was supposed to give people a break from reality, not replace it. Our cities are abandoned. Food is disappearing. People don't communicate with real people anymore, they're too busy living inside their own heads and creating characters to act in their own personal dramas. Nothing is happening. Nothing is moving forward. Nothing is real. Veelox is dead."

Zetlin dismissed this and asked, "What is this Reality Bug?"

Now came the really tough part for Aja. I hoped she wouldn't get into the whole story about Travelers and Saint Dane, because right now, it didn't matter.

"I couldn't stand to let Veelox die," she said. "So I wrote a program. The idea was to make the jumps less than perfect. The program attached to the data stream of each jumper to alter the experience slightly. I thought that if the jumps became less than perfect, people wouldn't spend so much time in them and would choose to return to their real lives."

Zetlin nodded. His jaw muscles clenched. He had just heard that somebody had sabotaged his life's work. I had to give him credit, he kept his head on straight and didn't go nuts on Aja. At least not yet.

"But this . . . *program* . . . didn't work the way you planned?" he asked calmly, though he said the word "program" with total disdain.

Aja swallowed hard and said, "No. The Reality Bug was far more powerful than I thought. It acted like a wild virus that spread through the grid. Not only did it alter the jumps, it made them hyperrealistic. The jumps became dangerous. We couldn't stop it and had to suspend the grid. Now most everyone on Veelox is in limbo, waiting for me to purge the Reality Bug."

"And for that you need the origin code," Zetlin concluded.

Aja nodded. "There's one more thing," she said. "Since my friends entered your jump, I've been desperately programming firewalls into the alpha grid to keep the Reality Bug out of your jump. It's coming after you, sir. Every time I throw one up, the virus mutates and finds a way around my block. I don't know how much longer I can keep fooling it. Sooner or later, the Reality Bug is going to find its way into your jump, and you'll be in danger too."

Oh, great. That was a fairly crappy piece of news.

Zetlin stared at Aja's image for a moment, weighing what she had said. He then turned and sat back down in his control chair. "I won't give you the code," he said with finality.

Uh-oh.

"You must!" Loor demanded. "Holding it back is suicide. No, it is genocide."

"I told you before," he snapped. "I won't go back. If Lifelight is destroyed, so be it. Whoever survives will rebuild Veelox. I don't care one way or the other. This is my reality now. I'll deal with whatever it throws at me."

"But I can stop it from happening," Aja shouted. "I can save Lifelight."

"From what you tell me," Zetlin said, "Lifelight shouldn't be saved."

"But at what cost?" I asked. "The deaths of millions?"

"I have accepted Lifelight as my reality," Zetlin explained

calmly. "To me, Veelox doesn't exist. I will only deal with the reality of my life here. I belong here in the Barbican, with these people, in this body, with this life."

"But it's a life you don't deserve," I said.

Zetlin shot me a look. I didn't know where I was going with this, but I had to do something to get him to give up that code.

"How can you say that?" he asked defensively, jumping to his feet. "I *built* Lifelight."

"So what?" I continued. "From what I can see, it's all just math. Being good at math doesn't earn you a perfect life. What about the people around here? These are the only people in your life. Your only friends. Do you think they really care about you?"

"Of course they do," Zetlin answered quickly.

"Why? Because you're the Z? The guy who races with them and plays games and throws parties? Is that why they care?"

"That's exactly why," Zetlin said with confidence. "They love me."

"But they aren't real," I said. "You created them. They're puppets who do what you say. You could be a monster and they'd still love you. You took the easy way out, Zetlin. Instead of repairing your real life, you lost yourself in a fantasy. Don't you get lonely?"

Zetlin's eyes darted around the room. I was getting to him. To be honest, I think part of it was the Traveler in me at work.

"Lonely?" he said, sounding shaky. "I am surrounded by friends. We have tournaments and games. I'm the champion slickshot racer!"

"Sure you are!" I shot back. "I'll bet you're the champion at everything. It's easy when all you have to do is imagine it. I'll bet nobody ever says no to you, do they?"

This question really threw Zetlin. He didn't have to answer it.

"There's nobody to challenge you," I said softly. "Nobody to argue with. Nobody to push you and help you find new ideas. For a guy like you, that sounds like death."

Zetlin shot me a look. I had definitely hit a chord.

"You know what reality is for you?" I added. "You're lying in a tube being fed by machines. You're a living corpse. And you know the worst part? Your invention is doing the same thing to the rest of Veelox. Aja's Reality Bug may have backfired, but at least she was doing something to try and save Veelox. The whole world is on life support, barely breathing. Veelox is going to die, just like you. If that happens, your life wasn't miserable, it was tragic."

Zetlin staggered back and fell into his control chair. I had slammed him pretty hard.

Aja's image walked over to Zetlin. She stood over him and spoke reassuringly.

"Please, Dr. Zetlin," she said. "You are a great man. I would love to meet you as you are, not as a memory of yourself. I want to shake your hand and say how much I admire you."

Aja put out her hand. Zetlin looked up at her. His eyes were red, as if on the verge of tears. He reached out to touch Aja, but his hand went right through hers. Aja was only an image created by Lifelight. There was no human contact.

"Come back, Dr. Zetlin," she added. "Help rebuild Veelox."

Zetlin slowly turned and faced his computer array. Aja glanced over at me with a hopeful look. Had we gotten through to him?

"Zero," Zetlin said softly, as if he didn't have the energy to fight anymore.

"Excuse me?" Aja asked.

"I said zero. That's the origin code."

"Zero?" I repeated. "That's it? Just . . . zero?"

Zetlin gave a sly smile. "The phaders are a clever bunch. I knew they would try to crack the code, and I knew they would expect it to be a complex string of commands."

Aja smiled and said, "You really are brilliant."

"Am I?" Zetlin asked.

"I'm going to purge the Reality Bug," Aja said. An instant later, her image disappeared.

"And then what happens?" Zetlin asked. "If Veelox is in such bad shape, all this will do is clear the way for its continued decline."

"That's the next problem," I said. "There has to be a way to use Lifelight without letting it control people's lives."

"If I may say so," Loor added. "If you could help Veelox find that balance, you would truly go down in history as a great man."

"Perhaps," Zetlin said, then looked at me. "Real life is so much more difficult than fantasy."

"Yeah," I answered. "But fantasy doesn't last."

Zetlin stood up and walked over to the big glass wall to look out onto his dreary city. I couldn't begin to guess what was going through his mind.

Suddenly the monitor jumped to life with an image of Aja. She was sitting in her control chair in the Alpha Core.

"We've got trouble," she said, all business.

"With the origin code?" I asked.

"No, that worked perfectly," she answered. "I went right to the processing code and cleaned the string. I totally purged the Reality Bug from Lifelight."

"Then what is the problem?" Loor asked.

"The grid went back online by itself," she explained. "I didn't do a thing. It just happened."

"So everyone on Veelox is back in their jumps?" I asked.

"Yes." Aja's voice started to crack. She sounded scared. "But something else is happening. As soon as everyone went back online, huge amounts of data began flowing from all the Lifelight pyramids to the Alpha Core."

"Data? What does that mean, Aja?" I asked, trying not to get too freaked out.

"I . . . I'm not sure."

We watched as Aja quickly input a series of commands and then checked her control monitor. There was tension in her eyes. Whatever was happening, it wasn't good.

"This is impossible," she said, her panic growing. "Data from all over Veelox is streaming directly toward the alpha grid."

"Alpha grid," Loor repeated. "What is this alpha grid?"

"The alpha grid is where we are," Zetlin answered, stepping up behind us.

Uh-oh.

"Killian," Zetlin said, "the firewalls you created to repel this Reality Bug, are they still in place?"

"Yes, but it's like . . . it's like the data is swarming. No, it's attacking the alpha grid and dismantling the firewalls. I can't reprogram them fast enough."

While she spoke, Aja kept making rapid-fire keystrokes on her control panel.

"Could it be the Reality Bug?" I asked.

"No!" Aja screamed back from the monitor. "I cleaned the string. It should be gone. The Reality Bug is—"

The image on the monitor began to crumble. The picture

flipped and twisted and changed until another face appeared on screen. It was the last face I wanted to see.

It was Saint Dane.

"Who is that?" demanded Zetlin.

"You don't want to know" was all I could answer.

"Hello, all you desperate little Travelers," Saint Dane chuckled. "If you're seeing this recording, it means you've tried to purge the virus from Lifelight. Congratulations for getting so close! There's just one little problem. The virus cannot be deleted. I made sure of that. In fact, trying to delete it, only multiplies its strength. Right about now, every jumper on Veelox is feeding the virus. Imagine having to battle the fears of everyone on the territory? Well, come to think of it, you won't have to imagine it at all. You're going to get the chance! I can't wait to return to Veelox and see what damage my last little surprise has wrought. Until then, sweet dreams!"

Saint Dane's image on the monitor was replaced by the sight of a zillion different numbers flashing by at lightning speed. Then every light on the control console began to glow brighter. Dr. Zetlin furiously input commands on his control column. Whatever he was doing, it wasn't working.

"Nothing is responding," he announced.

"It's like an overload," I suggested. "There's too much data for the computers to handle."

The lights on the control console intensified, blinding us. We all covered our eyes and it was a good thing we did, because a second later, the large monitor over the control chair exploded. *Boom!* Loor grabbed Zetlin by the back of his jump-suit and pulled him out of his chair as a wave of shattered glass hit the seat.

All three of us cowered, afraid that something else explosive might happen. Smoke filled the room, along with the smell of burning plastic. We huddled together and cautiously peered through the smoke to see an eerie sight.

The control console had gone dark. Every light was out. The monitor was nothing more than a jagged, smoking hole in the wall. We all stood, stunned, staring at the destroyed console.

But there was more.

"What is that?" Loor asked curiously, pointing down.

On the floor, covered in bits of glass from the destroyed monitor, was a black pile of goo about the size of a softball. It was as if a soft piece of tar had been spit out of the control panel when it exploded.

"Is that a piece from the console?" I asked.

"No," Zetlin answered. "I've never seen anything like it."

I took a step forward to get a closer look. But as soon as I approached it, the odd substance began to move. It was alive! I jumped back, as if it were diseased. For all I knew, it was.

"Tell me this is part of your fantasy," I said to Zetlin.

"I have no idea what it could be," Zetlin answered.

Bad answer.

The writhing black goo began to take on different shapes. A chunk grew out from the top, pushed toward the ceiling like a growing plant. It rose up a few inches, then formed what looked like a snarling mouth on the end of a black stalk! The mouth opened, revealing a set of sharp black teeth. The teeth snapped shut and the mouth sank back down into the black ooze to become part of the glob once more.

"That was . . . gross," I croaked.

The goo continued to writhe and squirm. We saw an eyeball peek out of one side, wink, then sink back into the muck. A tiny black fist then poked its way out, flexed its fingers, then pulled back into the mass. Then a sharp, spike-looking thing poked out of the side and retracted.

The three of us stood watching in awe. It was hideous and fascinating at the same time.

"It's like living clay," I said. "It's molding itself."

As I said that, the entire black form changed into what looked like an animal. In seconds, lying before us, no more than six inches high, was a cat-looking beast with two large heads, each of which had huge fangs. The form lay on its side, writhing like a newborn. It was solid black, but as it moved, the surface subtly changed texture. For a moment it looked like fur, but it quickly changed back into black goo. It even croaked out a ratty sound.

The instant the cat image was revealed, I felt Loor stiffen beside me.

"What's the matter?" I asked her.

"It is a zhou beast," she exclaimed. "From Zadaa."

"Uh-oh," I said. "Dr. Zetlin, have you ever seen something like that?"

"Never," was his emphatic reply.

"Then it came out of your head, Loor," I said. "You know what that means?"

"It means it's here," came a sober voice near us.

We all turned to see Aja's image standing there. "It broke through the firewall," she said, sounding as if she were in shock. "I couldn't hold it back."

The black cat beast then mutated. It folded in on itself, once again becoming a formless mass. But there was a difference. It was subtle, and I wasn't sure if I was seeing it at first, but once the goo started to squirm again, there was no mistake.

The thing was growing.

"The firewalls have collapsed," Aja said. "Huge amounts

of data are streaming into the alpha grid. It's feeding that thing."

The growing black clay then squirmed and grew, and took on the form of another animal. It was now the size of a small dog. The creature was still solid black, but when it turned toward us, its eyes flashed yellow and my knees went weak.

It was a quig from Denduron.

"I know what this is," I said, barely able to get the words out.

"It is a quig," Loor said.

"No," I said soberly. "It's the Reality Bug. It's taken physical form."

And then it attacked.

VEELOX

The black little beast sprang.

We scattered. The odd creature missed everybody, and when it hit the ground, its legs collapsed. It reminded me of Bambi when he didn't have the strength to stand on his own legs. But this little demon was no cute Disney deer. My guess was, it was going to get the strength to stand up pretty quick, and when it did, we'd be in trouble. Already the black skin was transforming into the dirty-brown fur of a quig. And it was still growing. In just a few seconds it was the size of my golden retriever.

"You're done, Pendragon," Aja demanded. "Get out of the jump."

There was nothing I wanted to do more than press the bailout button on my wrist controller and kiss this fantasy good-bye, but we couldn't leave yet.

"You first, Dr. Zetlin," I said. "Time to abandon ship."

Zetlin looked like he was in shock. He stared at the groggy quig, not believing what he was seeing.

"This can't be happening," he said, stunned. "The jumps don't allow it."

"They do now!" I shouted. "You've got to get out."

"You go," he said. "I'll be right after you."

I didn't believe him. I was afraid he would stay here and try to do damage control.

"Come on, Doctor, let's go!" I shouted.

"It doesn't work that way, Pendragon," Aja corrected. "When he leaves, the jump is over. You and Loor have to go first."

I looked at the mutant quig. Its body shivered as hair grew from the oozy black mass.

"Promise me you'll leave the jump, Doctor," I begged. "You can fight this thing from the Alpha Core."

"I will," he assured me. "Get going."

The quig slowly rose to its feet. It was now twice the size of my dog, Marley, and getting stronger. I looked to Loor. She had moved behind the control chair and was holding tight to the back of it. She was ready to move if the quig attacked again.

"We should go," she said to me without taking her eyes off the quig.

"With pleasure," I said, and hit the right button on my control bracelet. "We are outta here."

It didn't work.

"Why are we still here?" Loor asked.

"Aja?" I screamed.

"I don't know," Aja's image answered. "Loor, try yours!"

Loor poked the right button on her control bracelet, but nothing happened. No! I tried hitting the button on mine rapid-fire, like one of those idiots who keep hitting the elevator button, thinking it will make the elevator come faster. That never works, and hitting my wrist controller didn't work either.

The quig stood on shaky legs, reared back and pounced.

Loor pulled the control chair right out of the floor and heaved it at the charging beast. The black chair nailed the quig, knocking it back to the floor. It lay there, breathing hard, still growing.

"Aja!" I shouted. "Get us outta here!"

"Hang on," she called back. "I'm going back to the Alpha Core."

Her image disappeared.

"C'mon!" I shouted at the others.

Until Aja figured a way to yank us out of this jump, we had to stay alive. Hanging around with this mutating, growing monster wasn't the best way to do that. Loor grabbed Zetlin by the arm and the three of us ran across the floor and through the doorway that led to the big kitchen. When we entered, the first thing I noticed was that the chefs were gone. Can't say I blame them. They may have been fantasy creations, but they were smart enough to beat feet when there was trouble.

Loor saw the empty kitchen and had a different thought. "Weapons," she exclaimed.

She vaulted over a stainless-steel counter and ran to a table that held several nasty-looking kitchen knives. She quickly tested the weight of a few and picked two that she liked.

"If that quig gets any bigger," I said, "those knives won't do squat."

"You doubt me, Pendragon?" she asked, pretending to be insulted.

She flipped a knife into the air, spun it a few times, then plucked it in midspin with the blade ready to go. She looked like a gunslinger. Or knifeslinger. Loor had been off balance ever since she arrived on Veelox. She had to deal with technology and events that were impossible for her to understand.

But now we were in a battle. Now we were in Loor land.

The mutant quig leaped into the kitchen. It had become the size of the quig from my fantasy of Davis Gregory High. Worse, it had gotten stronger. It stood in the doorway and let out a grisly bellow. The mutant quig was officially ready for action.

So was Loor. She quickly threw a knife, then another while the first was still in the air. I never should have doubted her. Both knives found their mark. The first hit the quig in the shoulder, the second in the neck. It was kind of gruesome, but I didn't care. Better him than us. The beast reared up on its back legs, bellowing in agony. I thought this fight was over before it could get started.

I was wrong.

The quig reached for the knife in its neck with a paw, and brushed it away. It didn't pull the blade out, it *pushed* it out of its body, as if its flesh were made of Jell-O. It did the same with the knife in its shoulder. Both knives clattered to the floor. No blood. No wounds. Whatever damage the knives had done to the beast's body, it had regenerated.

We were in serious trouble.

"That cannot be," Loor said, stunned.

"Yeah, it can," I said. "That's not a quig, it's the Reality Bug."

As if to prove my point, the mutant quig growled, shuddered, and grew bigger. This thing was now getting close to the size of the quigs on Denduron.

"Outta here!" I yelled, and grabbed Dr. Zetlin.

The three of us ran for the doorway that led to the video game room and charged through. This room was empty too. The cleanup crew had fled.

"Perhaps it will grow too large to follow," Zetlin said hopefully.

Crash!

The quig smashed through the doorway behind us, taking out a piece of wall as it forced its way through.

"Let's not count on that," I said, and kept running.

We made it through to the giant Skittles game. Standing in the center of the court was Aja's image. We all ran up to her.

"What's going on?" I demanded.

"I can't stop it," she said nervously. "Data is flooding in from everywhere on Veelox. It's feeding the Reality Bug and making it stronger."

"Yeah, we see that," I said. "Can you get us out of the jump?"

"Everything is frozen," she complained. "The grid is totally overloaded and I can't take control."

"So we are trapped in here?" Loor asked.

"I'll alter the jump," Zetlin offered. He lifted his arm to reveal his control bracelet and pressed the center button.

I winced. But nothing happened. Good news, bad news.

"We have no control," Zetlin said softly. He then looked at Aja and said, "You must try to isolate the alpha grid. Perhaps you can fool the virus by creating a duplicate program."

"Duplicate program?" I asked.

"Back up the alpha software," Zetlin explained. "Then make that back-up the default. The virus may recognize it and attack both."

"Divide and conquer," I said.

"Exactly," Zetlin added. "Can you do that?"

"I can try," Aja said, and disappeared.

"And all we have to do is stay alive," I added.

"I do not know how to fight this beast," Loor said.

"I do," I offered. "Quigs hate loud, piercing sounds. Their ears can't take it. We gotta find something to make a sharp sound, like a whistle. If this thing is just like a quig, it'll send it reeling."

"I know something!" Zetlin announced, and continued running across the court.

We followed him through the next doorway into the odd basketball court with the four nets. Zetlin ran right for a metal equipment locker. "We use whistles for the games," he announced.

I could have hugged the guy. We joined him at the locker and flipped it open. As he searched for the whistles, we heard the sound of the quig tearing through the doorway to get into the Skittles room.

"Not much time," I cautioned.

Zetlin found two whistles that looked like kazoos. He gave me one.

"We'll take turns," I said. "I'll blow until I run out of air, then you blow. The louder the better."

"What then?" Loor asked.

"We've got to get out of the Barbican," I said. "We've got a better chance of hiding from this thing out in that city than in this building."

We then heard a horrifying roar. All three of us looked to the doorway of the Skittles room to see . . .

The beast had grown. It was now way bigger than a normal quig. Its head was almost as wide as the doorway. I hoped these whistles would be loud enough to do a number on something that big.

"Please use the whistle," Loor said calmly.

I took a deep breath and blew into the kazoo thing. The sound it made was awful and perfect. It was a totally annoying, loud shriek—exactly what quigs hate. The beast lifted its head and bellowed in agony. It was working! We had power over the monster. My mind raced ahead, already calculating how we would take turns blowing our whistles to keep the quig away from us long enough to escape.

Our victory didn't last long.

I had run out of breath and Zetlin was about to take over, when the quig stopped hollering. That's because it was changing. Through the doorway we watched in horror as the quig's head began to grow and squirm and change shape. The fur disappeared and it once again became the slick, black color it began with. Zetlin took a deep breath, but I put a hand on his shoulder.

"Don't bother," I said. "It's not a quig anymore."

The shape of the head flattened out. The black, oily skin took on a new texture that looked like scales. The eyes changed from having the round pupils of a quig, to the vertical pupils of a snake. I hate snakes. Suddenly a pink tongue flicked into the room. It had to be three feet long.

The Reality Bug had changed itself into a snake, and snakes weren't bothered by whistles.

"The elevator!" Loor exclaimed.

We all ran to the door that led to the blue elevator. Zetlin pulled, but it didn't open. "It's not here," he announced with dread. "The players must have taken it."

I glanced over my shoulder and immediately wished I hadn't. What I saw made my stomach dance. The snake's head was too wide to fit through the doorway, but that didn't stop it. It simply turned sideways and slipped through. I stared in awe as this giant black snake slithered onto the court. Its eyes were focused on us as the rest of its long body slid in.

"Can we get the elevator here? Like soon?" I asked, trying not to sound like I was about to panic, which I was.

"It's coming," Zetlin answered.

"So is the snake," Loor said.

The mutant snake slid to the center of the court and stopped. At least its head stopped. The rest of its snaky body kept coming.

"It is coiling," Loor announced.

As the long body slid through the door, its head rose as it formed a coil. That was bad. When snakes coil, they strike.

"How much longer?" I asked.

"Almost here," Zetlin answered.

"Almost might be too late."

The snake must have been twenty feet long, the body four feet thick. It was now in a perfect coil. Perfect for striking. It dropped its jaw and hissed, revealing a couple of nasty-looking fangs that had to be a foot long.

"Dr. Zetlin?" I urged.

"It's here!" he exclaimed, and pulled the door open.

That's when the snake pulled its head back, opened its jaws, and struck.

VEELOX

We dove into the small, blue elevator and I quickly pulled the door behind us. At that exact instant the snake hit with such a force that it slammed the door shut the rest of the way, knocking me into Loor and Zetlin.

"Look!" Zetlin shouted.

Imbedded in the door, having cut clean through, were two snake fangs. A second later a stream of liquid shot from each of the huge teeth.

Venom.

We all scrambled to the side of the elevator to get out of the way. Zetlin's hand was splashed with the poison and he screamed in pain.

"Get us out of here!" I shouted at Loor.

She reached for the control buttons. I don't think she knew which was the right one, but it didn't matter so long as we got moving. The elevator lurched and we were on our way. The fangs didn't move, though. The snake was hitching a ride. Luckily the flow of venom had stopped. It must have shot out all that it had.

"We're moving sideways," I announced. "Why aren't we going down?"

"Because the Barbican is horizontal," Zetlin winced through his pain. "All the floors are on the same level."

Oh, right. I'd forgotten.

Loor took Zetlin's hand and wiped away the venom with her sleeve. I saw that the poison had left a nasty-looking red slash on the back of his hand.

"I'm fine," Zetlin said.

"How do we get out of here?" I asked, deciding to save my sympathy until after we were safe.

"We'll take the elevator across to the jungle where you first entered," Zetlin answered. "I can right the Barbican into a vertical position from there, and we can walk out the door."

"That's fine," I said, then pointed to the fangs that were still imbedded in the door. "But as long as that thing's got its jaws in us, we won't even get out of the elevator."

Suddenly, the car shuddered and stopped.

"Is that normal?" I asked.

"No," answered Zetlin. "It must be——" Before he could finish, the elevator began to shake. I looked at the fangs of our hitchhiker and saw them moving. The snake had decided to take control. A second later the fangs pulled out, leaving two holes in the door.

"Now what?" I asked.

The elevator began to rock. It felt like we were inside a small ship in rough seas. Zetlin looked at the control panel and announced, "We're in the weight room."

Weight room? Did Zetlin have a personal gym? He threw open a panel below the elevator controls to reveal a compartment with a series of odd-looking devices like the slippery skate pads we used to race across the ice. They had the same kind of wire frames that fit over shoes, but there was only one pad on the heel. It was a thicker pad, with a hole in the center.

Zetlin pulled out three pairs quickly and handed them to us.

"Put these on your shoes," he commanded.

We did as we were told. The elevator was now rocking so hard, we couldn't stand up anymore. The Reality Bug was trying to pull the car off its track. He was doing a good job. The three of us were being tossed around like kids in a carnival bounce. Only it wasn't soft and fun. It hurt.

"What are these?" I managed to ask while struggling to pull the wire over my shoes.

"It's the only way to get around in the weight room," Zetlin answered.

That didn't explain anything. He then handed us each a small controller and showed us how to slip it over our middle finger like a ring. There was a button attached to the ring that rested in the palm of your hand.

"Once we're out," Zetlin instructed, "press the button. It'll activate the inertia jets."

"Inertia jets?" Loor questioned.

She never got an answer because the elevator toppled and started spinning. The Reality Bug had pulled it from its track and tossed it. It felt like we were inside a washing machine as the little car rolled over and over on its side. I braced myself as best I could, waiting for an impact. But it didn't come. We just kept spinning. It seemed impossible, but the rotating elevator didn't slow down.

Zetlin went for the door handle. "Follow me!" he ordered.

"Don't!" I yelled. I thought he'd kill himself for sure. But he had no fear. He pushed open the door and heaved himself out. Loor followed right after him. I figured if we were going to go down, we should do it together, so I dove for the door and launched myself out.

"Launch" was the perfect word to describe it. As soon as

I cleared the door I covered my head and curled up, ready to land hard. But I didn't. I realized after a few seconds that I wasn't going to, either. That's because I was floating. I took a cautious peek out from between my arms to see it was pitch black, with stars everywhere. I was drifting in outer space! This wasn't a weight room, it was a weight*less* room. Far off to my right, the elevator car was still spinning out of control. I watched it in wonder for a second, then felt something touch me on the shoulder.

"Ahhh!" I spun around fast, expecting to see the fangs of the black snake about to close on my head. But it was Dr. Zetlin. He was hanging next to me with Loor. He held her hand. They were both upside down. Or maybe I was the one upside down.

"The inertia jets shoot from your heels," he explained. "Point your body where you want to go, and touch the button in your palm. You can maneuver by adjusting the direction your heels face."

I touched the button in my palm . . . and rocketed up. Whoa! These things were powerful!

"Easy!" Zetlin ordered. "Just touch it."

I spun around and touched the button tentatively. Sure enough, I was able to control it. When I took my finger off the button, I slowed down pretty quick. It was easy to get used to. Under other circumstances, this would be the most totally amazing, fun experience possible. It was like we were floating in outer space without space suits. But these weren't other circumstances. Somewhere out there among the stars was a giant, poisonous snake trying to kill us.

"Follow me," Zetlin announced. "I know the way to the far side."

"How?" I asked, looking around at nothing but nothing.

"I know the star formations," Zetlin answered.

I had to take his word for it. If it were up to Loor or me, we'd be floating around here forever.

That's when the snake came into view. It was far below us, floating free. At least I think it was below us. It was impossible to tell up from down.

"We're in luck," Zetlin said. "There's no way it can maneuver in here."

Excellent. The Reality Bug had chosen the absolute worst place to pull the elevator off its track. I figured it would float helplessly in here with no way to escape. That would give us enough time to get out of the Barbican and for Aja to untangle the software. Suddenly there was hope.

And just as suddenly it came crashing down.

The snake had no way of fighting the weightlessness, so it began to change. We watched in horror as huge, human-like arms sprouted from the snake body. The hands were massive and strong. They groped around as if trying to grab on to something.

"What is it doing?" Loor asked.

A second later we had our answer. The massive hands found what they were looking for.

"The elevator track," Zetlin said soberly.

The elevator track was the only solid thing in this world of weightlessness. The huge hands grabbed on to the dark track and the creature had control. It moved, hand over hand, in the exact direction we needed to go.

"Hurry," Zetlin said, and took off flying, his inertia jets making a soft whooshing sound as he moved.

Loor went next. She started in the wrong direction, but shifted her legs and soon had enough control so she could follow Zetlin. I then hit my button . . . and spun in a tight circle.

Oops. I realized I had only one foot in the right position. The other was floating free. Idiot! I backed off on the button, twisted my body into the right position, made sure my heels were together, and took off. After a few seconds I had it figured out. It really was easy. Just a slight movement of my heel altered my direction and I learned how to make midcourse corrections. In no time, I was sailing along next to Loor, with Zetlin in the lead.

I glanced back and down over my shoulder to see that the Reality Bug was moving quickly along the track, hand over huge hand. But with the help of the inertia jets, we were moving faster.

Zetlin then changed direction and shot down at a steep angle. Loor and I were able to follow right behind. I looked forward and saw a small, glowing red rectangle that seemed to be hovering in space. This is where Zetlin was headed. He stopped at the door-shaped rectangle and gave it a push. It was the door out.

I looked back to see the huge black snake with the human arms gaining ground. It opened its jaws and hissed angrily.

"Hurry, please," I said to Zetlin.

Loor and I followed him and stepped through the doorway. I instantly felt the pull of gravity as we were back on solid ground. I quickly pushed the door shut behind me. It was a heavy door, much heavier than anything we had come across in this wacky building so far. It was more like a hatch than a door. When I closed it, I saw there was a heavy latch. I slammed it home. Anything we could do to slow down the Reality Bug was a good thing.

"Keep moving!" Zetlin ordered.

We were in a short, dark chamber about ten feet long. On the far end was another door that Zetlin pushed open. When we stepped through, we entered another space that I can best describe as being like the inside of a giant clock. It was a huge room full of gigantic, heavy gears. All around us and high above were massive, interlocking cogs and flywheels and I don't know what else.

"This is the center of the Barbican," Zetlin explained as he closed the door behind us. "This machinery rotates the building. I think we're safe in here."

"How do you figure that?" I asked.

Zetlin slapped the wall next to the door we had just come through. "This wall is the structural core of the Barbican. It's five feet thick. That monster is too big to come through the doors, and there's no possibility of it crashing through this wall, I don't care how strong it gets.

"I hope you're right," I said.

He wasn't.

The proof appeared at the bottom of the door that Zetlin had just closed.

"It doesn't need to break down the wall," I said, pointing to the door.

An ink-black liquid was leaking its way into the room through the edges around the door. Like oily poison it oozed through the seams, poured onto the floor, and continued to move across it.

The Reality Bug had gone liquid.

"This way, hurry," Zetlin said, and ran off.

He didn't need to add the "hurry." We were right after him. There was no telling how long it would take the Reality Bug to ooze into the room and reform as something nasty. We had to keep moving.

"We'll take the zips," he said.

"Zips?" I asked.

We followed Zetlin through the giant machinery. I felt like an ant running through a monstrous engine, that's how big the mechanism was. He led us to a row of vehicles that I recognized from when we first arrived. They were the motorcycle-looking speeders that we saw racing underwater and in the air. Zetlin grabbed a helmet from the seat of one and jumped on.

"Whoa, we don't know how to drive these!" I complained.

"Not a problem," Zetlin answered. "A child could drive them. Watch." He grabbed the handlebars and said, "Right grip is speed, left grip is brake." He then pointed down. His right foot was resting on a pedal. "Heel back gives you nose up. Toes down, you dive. Keep your foot flat for level flight. Steering is obvious."

We then heard a gruesome scream coming from back in the machinery. It was a loud, metallic, tearing sound. The Reality Bug had reformed. Loor and I gave each other a nervous look. We then each grabbed a helmet and jumped onto a zip. We were going to have to learn how to drive these babies, fast.

"Buckle in," Zetlin said while pulling a bar around his waist. "If you're not locked in when you hit the water, you'll be thrown."

"Hit the water?" Loor asked nervously.

Zetlin then flipped a switch under the handlebars and his zip whined to life. Loor and I did the same. I could feel the hum of power coming from the zip. It felt like being on a motorcycle, like Uncle Press's. But I had never driven one myself. The closest I had come was one of those kiddie rides at the mall that you put a quarter in and it bucks around a little bit. Something told me this was going to be a little bit different. I glanced at Zetlin and he pushed his heel down. The nose cone of the zip tilted up into the air like a missile getting ready to fly.

"Let's go," he shouted, and hit the throttle. Instantly his zip launched. He shot into the air, turned sharply, and stopped, hovering over us. "C'mon!" he yelled.

I looked to Loor. Loor shrugged and followed Zetlin's lead. She pushed her heel down, the nose lifted up, and she took off. She shot past Zetlin, nearly hitting him.

Note to self: Avoid hitting things.

Zetlin turned his zip and chased after her. I had to go too, or I'd lose them. I dropped my heel and felt the front of the zip lift up. I was now pointed to the ceiling.

"Hobey-ho," I said under my breath, and twisted the throttle. The zip bucked forward and I shot into the air. The ride was incredible. It turned easily and I quickly got used to the throttle and brake. The foot pedal was a little trickier. I couldn't keep the zip level at first, and it was making me seasick. But after playing with it for a while, I was able to level out. Man, I would love to have one of these for real. Too bad it was just a fantasy vehicle.

I saw Zetlin and Loor hovering together ahead of me and quickly joined them. The three of us floated there among the giant gears, fifty feet in the air.

"Are you two all right?" Zetlin asked.

"I'm good," I said.

"I am as well," Loor said.

"Then let's keep moving."

He was about to throttle up when Loor said, "But I cannot swim."

"You won't have to," Zetlin answered.

We then heard another roar coming from deeper in the machine room. We all looked down to where we had come from, but saw nothing. The Reality Bug wasn't down there.

It was up with us.

"There it is!" Zetlin shouted.

From far back among the gears and cogs, I saw a shadow swoop up from below. I only got a glimpse of it, but what I saw I won't forget. It had the head of a bird, with a long, sharp beak. Its body looked human, with a wide, strong chest. Its legs were birdlike as well. And it had wings. Huge, black wings, like a bat.

The Reality Bug was airborne.

We all turned and pushed the zip vehicles forward. We flew in formation, with Zetlin in the lead and Loor and me together behind him. Zetlin led us on a wild ride through the incredible machinery. I guess he wanted to lose the flying Reality Bug, but Loor and I had a heck of a time trying to keep up. He flew low to the ground, under some steel beams. He then took a sharp right and led us through a narrow corridor. We had to fly single file because it wasn't wide enough for two across. We then shot out of the corridor and climbed steeply until we were near the ceiling. From up there, the round gears below us looked like curved, steel mountains.

It was amazing that we were able to keep up with him, but the zips were easy to handle. I think part of it was because these were fantasy vehicles, and in our minds we knew we had to fly them, so we did.

We were fast approaching the far wall of the machine room. There was a square opening that glowed with bright, white light.

"We're going to the glacier!" Zetlin called back.

I figured the next room in this incredible building was going to be the snowy ice field where we raced Zetlin in slick-shot. That was good; we were getting closer to the jungle.

But then a shadow appeared far off to our left and in front of us. All of our crazy stunt flying was a waste. The

Reality Bug had found its own route and was racing us to the opening. We were on a collision course. We were headed straight for the opening; the bird was coming from far to our left. We had to beat it. All three of us throttled up. The freakish, giant bird sped closer. I tried to calculate who would get to the opening first. Either way, it would be close. The three of us were side by side going flat out. I squeezed the throttle, hoping it would make the zip go faster. This was totally dangerous. There was no way we could pull out going this fast. We were either going to escape, or crash right into the Reality Bug. It all depended on who got to the opening first.

A second later the three of us flashed into the white light. We had made it. The bird flew right past the opening. There was no way it could have made the sharp turn going that fast. It was going to have to circle around and hit it square on. We were going to need those few seconds to gain some ground.

We now found ourselves speeding high over the icy race-course. Zetlin didn't try any hot, evasive maneuvers this time. I think he simply wanted speed. That was cool by me. Speed was good. I didn't even look around to see if the Reality Bug–bird had made it into the ice world. This was all about getting across this frozen wasteland as fast as possible. It was a flat-out race.

After a minute Zetlin motioned that he was going down. He dipped his nose and shot for what looked like a sheer wall of ice. We had reached the far side of the ice room. But I didn't see any openings. We had to trust that Zetlin knew where he was going. I didn't think he wanted to splat against the ice like a bug on a windshield.

On the snow below, I saw a winged shadow. The bug was behind us and moving up fast.

"There!" Loor shouted.

I saw it too. There was an opening cut into the ice. It was our doorway to the next room.

"We've got to go underwater!" Zetlin shouted back to us. "I doubt the bird can follow us."

What made him think that? From what I'd seen, the Reality Bug could do anything it wanted. Still, maybe the extra few seconds it took to transform into something else would give us the edge we needed.

But Loor couldn't swim.

"Loor?" I shouted.

"Do not worry," she said. "I will make it."

She was going to have to be incredibly brave. I knew she would be. Zetlin shot into the ice tunnel with us right behind. We sped through the short tunnel, blasted out the far side and entered pitch black. There was nothing to see but the series of colorful globes hanging in the air that marked the racecourse.

"Crouch down low before you hit the water," Zetlin ordered. "Don't slow down. Keep breathing." He then dropped the nose of his zip and shot for the water.

We followed him blindly. Man, I was scared. For Loor, and for me, too. I didn't know what to expect when we hit the water. Was it going to be so jarring that I'd get ripped off the zip? Should I really keep breathing? Should I wet my pants? I crouched down low inside the clear nose cone and gritted my teeth. The water came up fast. Zetlin hit with a splash. Two seconds later Loor and I hit too.

It was a jolt, but nothing I couldn't handle. The pointed nose cone must have absorbed most of the shock. Better still,

I could breathe. The helmet must have had something to do with that.

I glanced to Loor to see she was charging along right next to me. She was incredible.

It was easy to see Zetlin because the moment we hit the water, our headlights came on. The water rippled over the top of my nose cone, making the whole vehicle shiver. Turning was only slightly tougher than in the air. That must have had something to do with the water resistance. Still, we were moving fast.

I heard a huge splash in the water behind us. There was only one thing that could have made that sound. The Reality Bug was now wet. I wondered if the bird creature also went underwater, or had the bug mutated itself into something sharklike. I had to shake that image out of my head.

Our trip underwater didn't last long. Up ahead I saw the vague outline of another square opening. Zetlin aimed his zip toward it and we steered for Zetlin. Seconds later we blasted through the opening . . .

And out into the air high over the jungle. I glanced back at the opening to see it was a square of water. Nothing poured out, just like the strange round opening Loor and I had gone through when we first arrived. It was impossible, yet there it was. I noticed that my clothes weren't even wet. Unbelievable.

Zetlin gunned his zip and beat it for the jungle floor. I didn't want to run into any more of those vine-shooting plants, but it was better to get lost in the jungle than to be flying wide open for the Reality Bug to see us.

Zetlin flew his zip right for the deck. He leveled out a few feet above the jungle floor, speeding along a path. Loor was right behind him and I was right behind Loor. We were moving fast. I kept my eye on her back, looking for any movement that would warn me when the next turn was coming. We were on the home stretch. Soon we'd be at the entrance to the Barbican and home free.

After a few minutes of jungle jumping, Zetlin slowed down as he approached the far wall of the building. We had been racing for a while now, and my heart was thumping like crazy. Zetlin stopped his zip, jumped off, and ran up to a control panel that was built into the wall. He opened up the cover and started hitting buttons.

"Why don't we fly the zips out of here?" I asked.

"They don't work outside the Barbican," Zetlin answered. "We've got to go to position two so we can walk out."

He hit a few more buttons, and the building started to shake. I heard the far-off sound of screeching metal and could imagine the massive gears starting to turn. I could only hope they'd turn fast enough so we could get down and out of here before the bug found us. The building rumbled and started to move.

"It won't be long," Zetlin assured us.

We heard a tortured squealing sound, as if metal were being torn apart. A second later the building stopped moving.

"What happened?" Loor asked.

Zetlin went right back to the controls. He furiously hit a few keys, but nothing changed.

"I don't understand," he announced nervously. "All the indicators say we should be moving."

"When we were back in the machine room," I said, "there was a horrible sound. Could the Reality Bug have messed with the machinery?"

We then heard a piercing shriek come from deep within the jungle. We all looked up.

"I don't know," Zetlin said. "But the Barbican isn't moving. If it doesn't go vertical, we can't get out."

VEELOX

Another shrill squeal echoed through the jungle.

It was so loud that it felt like needles to the brain. A flock of colorful birds took flight not far behind us. We then heard the sound of crashing, crunching trees. Whatever the Reality Bug had changed into, it was big.

And it was coming.

"This can't be the only way out of here!" I complained.

"There is one other way," Zetlin said. "It is an emergency corridor, but I have never used it."

"I think now would be a good time to give it a shot," I said quickly.

More crashing trees. Closer this time. I could hear the tearing and crunching of plants as the Reality Bug moved through the jungle, looking for us. Hunting for us.

"Where is this exit?" Loor asked.

"Back in the machine room," was Zetlin's answer.

"Machine room?" I shouted. "Why didn't we use it when we were there?"

"Because I didn't know the Reality Bug was capable of sabotaging the Barbican" was Zetlin's logical answer.

"Okay, no problem," I said, trying to keep calm. "We gotta get back there."

That's when we saw it. Crashing through the tropical trees only yards away came a terrifying sight. The Reality Bug had transformed itself into, well, into some kind of green bug. It had multiple, tarantula-style legs, a long scaly body, and a massive head with pincers that snapped in front of its red, fleshy mouth. And it had grown. This beast now towered over us like we were in some kind of Japanese monster movie.

When it appeared through the trees it stopped, reared its head and let out another one of those painful shrieks.

"We are in the wrong place," Loor announced, and gunned her zip. She shot into the air, making sure to keep out of reach of the monster bug.

But she didn't get far. No sooner had she taken off than the bug turned its head toward her and shot out a clear, ropelike cord from its mouth.

"Loor!" I shouted, but it was too late. The thread caught the back of her zip in midflight and held her there like a kite at the end of a string. Loor gunned the throttle, trying to shake it, but the filament held firm. I saw that it was reeling Loor in like a fish on the line. The pincers around its mouth snapped in anticipation. The spider had caught its prey and was ready to feed.

"I'm gonna bail her out," I shouted, and was about to fly up and get her off her zip and onto mine. But Zetlin was quicker. He shot off the ground and throttled up to full speed. I thought he was going way too fast to stop right next to Loor, but that wasn't his plan. He aimed his zip halfway between the struggling Loor and the giant bug, blasting into the taut filament, snapping it in half. Totally smart move. Loor sped forward as if propelled from a slingshot.

"Yes!" I shouted, and instantly wished I hadn't. I was now alone, with the Reality Bug looming over me. Oops. I might as well have shouted: "Here I am! Come and get me!" It was time to go. I turned hard, to my left to stay as far away from the beast as possible, and throttled up. Out of the corner of my eye I saw it turn toward me and shoot out another cord. I quickly pushed my toe down, making the zip dive. The cord shot right over my shoulder, barely missing me. By the time the big bug reloaded, I was gone. A quick look over my shoulder showed me that it was scrambling back the way it had come, following the wide trail it had already cut through the jungle.

The race was back on.

I retreated in the direction of the water portal and soon caught up with Loor and Zetlin.

"Nice move," I shouted at Zetlin.

"I am very good," he answered.

He *was* good. Not modest, but good.

"Follow me back to the machine room," he announced, and throttled up. Loor and I gunned our zips and settled in behind him. I was confident we would make it. The Reality Bug was getting bigger and that meant it was slower. If we kept the pedal to the metal, we'd beat it to the machine room and get out of there with no problem.

Or so I thought.

The big liquid square that was the portal to the water room appeared in the distance. The three of us were flying toward it at full speed. In a few seconds we'd hit the water and be on our way. Zetlin turned back to us and shouted, "You two okay?"

We both nodded.

"Don't slow down. We can beat this thing," he added with confidence.

Because Zetlin was turned back toward us, he didn't see that something had appeared ahead. We were on a direct course for the big square of water, moving as fast as ever. But in that quick moment, I saw that there was something covering the opening. It took an instant for my brain to compute, but I realized what was stretched across the square.

It was a web. The Reality Bug must have spun a web after it came through, and it was about to catch a couple of speedy flies.

"Look out!" I screamed.

Too late. Loor and I turned hard and pulled out, but Zetlin didn't have a chance. He barely had time to look forward when he slammed right into the web. I had a fleeting hope that it would snap like the cord Zetlin severed before, but it didn't. This wasn't just one cord, it was an interlocking web.

Loor and I circled back quickly to see that Zetlin was stuck in the sticky cords. His zip had crashed to the ground, leaving him tangled and helpless like, well, like a fly caught in a spiderweb. I wasn't even sure if he was conscious. Or alive.

Loor pulled her zip right up to Zetlin and hovered next to him.

"Are you all right?" she asked.

Zetlin nodded. Whew. He was shaken, but alive and awake. He was also trapped in a spiderweb. I looked down to the jungle below to see the giant bug in the distance, scurrying toward us. Its eight legs were thrashing hard to speed it along to see if anything tasty was caught in its trap. We had to get Zetlin out of there fast. But how?

Loor had the answer. She reached into her jumpsuit and pulled out a vicious-looking kitchen knife. I didn't know she had kept one, but I was glad she had.

"Help me, Pendragon," she ordered. "Go below him."

I eased my zip down and underneath Zetlin. Loor went to work cutting away the web. I grabbed hold of Zetlin's legs, ready for him to drop down onto my zip. While Loor sliced away, I snuck a look back down. The Reality Bug was getting closer. If it decided to change into a bird, it could fly right up and have us. But it didn't. The giant bug just kept charging through the jungle.

A few seconds later Zetlin fell loose from the web and Loor eased him onto the zip in front of me.

"Are you with us?" I asked him.

"Yes," he said, but sounded loopy. We didn't have time to rescue his zip, so Zetlin leaned forward into the nose cone of my zip, giving me a clear view forward.

"I suggest you hurry," Zetlin said.

I looked up to Loor and asked, "Is the web clear?"

"Clear enough," she answered.

The two of us then pulled away from the web, made a wide circle back, and gunned the vehicles toward the hole she had cut. Loor was first and sailed through with room to spare. I was right behind her and shot through the tendrils and into the water.

Speed was everything now. Loor and I drove our zips side by side, squeezing the throttles, coaxing every last bit of power out of the strange but cool fantasy machines. Loor made the first move to surface. Zetlin and I were right behind. We both launched up and out of the water, headed for the icy opening that would lead us to the slickshot course.

Minutes later we blasted through the ice tunnel and shot out over the bright, frozen glacier. We kept pushing the zips forward, not even taking a second to turn and see if the Reality Bug was on our butts.

Zetlin never looked up from inside his position in the nose

of my zip. Just as well. Both Loor and I knew where we had to go, and a short few minutes later we were sailing over the giant gears of the machine room.

"There's the trouble," I said while pointing down.

Sure enough, two massive metal bars had been jammed between a set of gear wheels. When the Barbican started to move, it jammed up the works. Not only was the Reality Bug vicious, it was smart.

I motioned to Loor for us to land, and the two of us guided our zips down to the floor.

"Dr. Zetlin," I said. "We're in the machine room. How do we get out of here?"

Zetlin pulled himself up from the nose of the zip. He looked groggy.

"Are you hurt?" Loor asked.

"Just rattled," Zetlin answered. He looked around, scanning the vast machine room. "There!" he announced. He pointed to a round, vertical tube not far from us that stretched from the floor to the ceiling. It was made of the same light blue aluminum as the inside of the elevator.

"That's the dead center of the Barbican," he said. "And our way out."

"We should leave these vehicles and travel on foot," Loor said. "We do not want the monster knowing where we are."

Excellent idea.

"Let's go," I said and the three of us hurried across the floor of the machine room, headed for this blue cylinder. We kept looking back, expecting the Reality Bug to appear. But it didn't. I was beginning to think it had run out of tricks and was trapped back in that jungle. Good. I hoped the vine-shooting cactus plants were gnawing away on it.

It only took us a few minutes to get to the cylinder. It was about four feet wide and shot straight up. Zetlin directed us to a square hatch that had a wheel built into it.

"This leads down into the arch that braces the Barbican," he explained while spinning the wheel. "We can climb all the way to the ground inside the arch."

He pulled open the hatch and entered first. Loor went next and I followed last. It was dark inside the round tube, especially after I closed the hatch and spun the wheel that locked it. Our eyes adjusted in a few seconds and I saw a metal ladder that ran the length of the tube. Zetlin got on the ladder and climbed down. Loor and I followed quickly. The ladder went down several feet to a platform.

"This platform is the very top of the arch," Zetlin explained. "There are metal stairs on either end that will take us down."

Yikes. I thought back to seeing this arch from outside. It was huge, which meant it was a long way down. I was beginning to realize why this wasn't Zetlin's first choice of escape route.

Loor was thinking the same thing. "If the Reality Bug follows us in here . . ."

She didn't have to finish the sentence. We knew we'd be trapped.

"I know," Zetlin said. "But it's the only way down."

I didn't want to waste any more time, so I started walking toward the end of the platform. I must have gone about thirty yards when I came upon a set of metal stairs with metal handrails. The stairs curved down and away into the dark. Gulp.

"Be careful," Zetlin said. "It's a long way down."

I didn't need that reminder. I turned around and went down the stairs backward, with a death grip on the handrails to either side. Loor followed me and Zetlin was last. It was tough at first because the stairs weren't very steep. It was like walking on my hands and feet. I thought back to the shape of the arch to remember it curved at the top. I figured that the farther down we got, the steeper it would get and that is exactly what happened. Soon I was climbing nearly straight down, as if on a ladder. I moved as fast as it felt safe to go. Speed was good, but if I tripped . . . *splat*. I didn't know what scared me more: falling into this dark hole, or having the Reality Bug attack from above. Either way, it was good motivation to keep moving.

None of us spoke on the way down. There wasn't a whole lot to talk about. But I knew we were all thinking the same thing. Keep moving, get down and out of here before the bug finds us.

Suddenly the entire structure shook. It was so fast and hard, it nearly pulled me off the stairs. We all stopped, clutching the handrails for safety.

"What was that?" I called out.

"I don't know," answered Zetlin. "Keep going, but use caution."

I started down again. Another minute went by and the structure shook again. We all held tight and didn't move.

"It's gotta be the bug," I said. "Maybe it's trying to break through one of the walls."

We started moving again, but now with the fear that at any moment we could get thrown off the stairs by these mysterious jolts. It happened three more times, and each time we held tight. Then, finally, after what seemed like a lifetime, we made it to the ground. Nobody stopped to celebrate. We were now at the base of one side of the arch, in the widest part of the structure.

"There is the way out," Loor said, pointing to a door not far from us. We all ran to it and Loor pulled it open.

It was pouring rain outside, but I didn't care. We were out! We hurried away from the arch, trying to get as much distance between us and the Reality Bug as possible. We must have run at least a half mile down the wide street before we felt safe enough to stop. The three of us found refuge in the entryway of one of the black buildings.

As we stood there, catching our breath, I looked back at the incredible structure that was the Barbican. What an impossible, amazing, breathtaking building. It hung in the air, on its side, offering no clue as to the wonders inside. It seemed both spectacular, and sad.

I glanced to Dr. Zetlin and saw he wasn't looking at the building. He was actually looking down the rainy street of his dreary fantasy city. It was a place that was here to remind him of a life he had fled. Now it was his refuge.

"Dr. Zetlin?" I said softly.

"I swore I would never return," he said, his voice cracking.

I looked out at the city to try and see it through his eyes. Rain bounced off the gray streets. It was a pretty depressing place. It struck me that there were no people. From the time the Reality Bug started to wreak havoc, I hadn't seen a single soul. I didn't know if everybody had fled, or the fantasy had somehow altered and wiped out everybody but the real people. Us. I guess it didn't matter. We didn't belong here. None of us did.

"This isn't reality either," Loor reminded him.

"It is to me," he said.

We then heard a sound that at first I thought was thunder. It was a deep, violent booming sound that came from the direction of the Barbican. We looked at the building, but there was nothing unusual to see. We heard two more loud booms.

"Whatever it is," Loor said, "it is what made the arch shake when we were climbing down."

But what was it?

The answer came quickly. We heard another huge booming sound. Zetlin gasped.

Something was attacking the Barbican . . . from inside. Chunks of the building were tearing away and crashing to the ground below. I think we all knew what it was, but didn't want to believe it.

"It wasn't trying to break down a wall," I gasped. "It was trying to break out."

Then a huge black shape erupted from the far end of the building. It was the end that held the jungle. We watched in awe as a massive fist pushed its way up and out of the building. The sound of wrenching metal and breaking glass cut through the pounding rain. The fist pulled back into the building and another shape pushed up. It looked like a monster was being hatched from the horizontal structure. The black mass pushed up and out of the hole, tearing it wider, sending chunks of wrecked building to the pavement. The mass writhed and twisted, and then opened its eyes.

It was the head of the beast and it was a creature from hell. It looked like an animal, but no animal I had ever seen. The shape was like a boar's head, with a snout and long, curling teeth. The eyes were snake eyes with vertical slits. The beast had gigantic horns that curled up and around like a ram. The whole head was covered with black, oily fur.

The beast forced its head up through the hole and opened its mouth to bellow as it struggled to push out of the building. The gaping mouth was bloodred and full of multiple rows of yellow teeth.

We watched, mesmerized, as the beast punched out another hole. Its fist blasted out, making the escape hole even bigger. It then punched its other fist through so both arms were free. Now it could lift its colossal chest out of the structure. Its chest and arms were almost human, with massive muscles. The thing was still growing as we watched. It was now too big to fit inside the end of the building. We could hear the sound of wrenching metal as the beast's weight pushed down on the one end. If it grew any bigger, the building would collapse.

The beast howled again and smashed its fist down on top of the building. It blasted open another huge hole and water came flooding out. It had broken open the room that held the underwater racecourse. Tons of water spewed from the building like a waterfall and crashed onto the street. There was so much water that, in just a few seconds, the surge made it all the way to us, and we stood knee-deep in a river. But we didn't move. We were already soaking wet from the rain. A foot more of water wasn't going to make things any worse.

The beast pushed against the top of the building and lifted one leg out, then the other. We saw that the bottom half of the monster was furry, with hooves for feet. It heaved itself out of the hole and stood on top of the horizontal building. Last out was the creature's tail. It was long and bone white, like a rat's tail. The monster stood on its two hoofed feet, with its tail wrapped around one leg, and howled. It was a horrible, angry sound that made my blood freeze. We were staring at the physical being of the Reality Bug. All the fears of the people of Veelox had fed this thing, made it real, and let it grow.

The three of us were absolutely powerless against it.

The monster then climbed off the building and slid down one side of the arch. Now it was on the ground. The question was, would it start looking for us? It stood tall, looked around, and sniffed the air. I saw its piggy snout moving as it searched for smells. I really hoped we were downwind. Any second I expected the beast to catch our scent and start coming.

But it didn't. It gave one last look around, then fell to its knees.

"What is it doing?" Loor asked.

The beast balled up its monster hand into a fist, raised it into the air, brought it down hard, and punched the ground. The force was so strong it shook the street as if it had been slammed with an earthquake. The monster did it again. Its muscles rippled with strength as it punched the ground again. And again. And again. He kept punching at the same area, eventually blasting a crater in the cement.

The look on Zetlin's face told me he didn't have any better idea than we did about why the beast was punching the street.

"What's happening?" came a frightened voice from behind us.

The three of us jumped in surprise, and turned to see . . .

Aja. She walked past us with her eyes fixed on the beast.

"What's happening?" I asked back. "You tell us! We've been running from that thing since we saw you. Are you gonna get us out of here or what?"

Aja didn't answer me. She just kept staring at the Reality Bug.

As the beast pummeled the ground, its head changed. It went from the strange, piglike creature, to the head of a bird with a long, curved beak. The beak opened to reveal huge, pointed teeth. Its body then changed to something like a reptile. Its head then changed again. It became a gruesome, fleshless skull with dead eyes and fanged teeth.

"It's feeding on the fear of the whole territory," Aja gasped.

"Aja," Loor asked calmly. "Do you know why it is punching the ground?"

Aja turned to us. Her face was totally blank. "I think it's trying to escape," she said.

"It already escaped," I said. "Look at that building. It's destroyed."

Aja shook her head. It was creepy to see her like this. Aja was brilliant and she showed it in her eyes. But those normally sharp eyes now looked vacant, as if her mind wouldn't accept what was happening.

"No," she said. "It's trying to escape from the fantasy."

Zetlin shot her a look. "What do you mean?" he demanded.

"The Alpha Core," she continued as if in a trance. "It's being torn apart. Every time it pounds the ground, I can feel it in the core."

"That's impossible," Zetlin said. "The Alpha Core is reality."

"That's what I'm trying to tell you," Aja said with finality. "The Reality Bug has gotten more powerful than Lifelight itself. It's trying to escape from this fantasy . . . and break into reality."

VEELOX

Was it possible? Could the Reality Bug rip a seam in Zetlin's fantasy and escape into the real world? If this monster got into the pyramid through the Alpha Core, it would tear the place apart. The people in the pyramid would be doomed, not to mention the rest of Veelox. Could that really happen?

Of course it could. Why would I doubt it? None of the rules of reality applied to anything I'd seen on Veelox, what made me think they would start to kick in now? No way. If this thing got loose, it would lay waste all of Veelox.

And Saint Dane would have his first territory.

"Why is this happening?" Loor asked with a firm voice. She sounded a lot more in control than I was feeling.

I had no idea how to answer that question, until I saw that she was holding up her wrist controller. The square button to the far right was glowing white. I quickly lifted up my wrist to see the button on my controller was glowing as well. A glance to Zetlin showed that his was glowing too.

"Aja?" I yelled. "What does this mean?"

I held up my wrist controller for her to see, but she kept staring at the monster beast as it crashed its fist into the pavement over and over. This nightmare was her creation. I think she was in shock. I jumped in front of her, getting right in her face.

"Aja!" I screamed, and held my controller up to her face. "Why is it doing this?"

Aja slowly focused on the controller. She looked at it strangely for a second, as if not knowing what it was. Then I saw her eyes focus. An idea was forming. Aja was coming back. "Just before the Alpha Core began to shake," she said slowly, "the alpha grid opened up."

"What does that mean?" Loor demanded.

"I think the Reality Bug is focusing all of its strength to fight its way out," Aja said. "That might give us control of the jump, at least for a little while."

I quickly spun to the others. "We're getting out, now! Loor! Hit the button."

Loor didn't question. She immediately hit the glowing button . . . and disappeared.

"Yes!" I ran to Dr. Zetlin, who was staring vacantly at the monster. "Dr. Zetlin, I'm getting out of the jump. You've got to follow me."

Zetlin didn't take his eyes from the monster. I grabbed the guy by the shoulders and forced him to look at me.

"Listen!" I screamed. "We've got to end this jump. Maybe that'll stop the Reality Bug."

"And if it doesn't?" he asked slowly.

"We've got a better chance of you fighting it from the Alpha Core than running away from it in here. My faith is in you, and Aja. You gotta end this."

Zetlin glanced back at the beast. I saw something change in his eyes. He became focused and alert. He looked back to me and nodded.

"Go," he said. "I'll be right behind you."

This time I believed him. I looked to Aja's image. "I'll see you in the Alpha Core, all right?"

"Hurry," she said, and disappeared.

"I'm gone!" I said to Zetlin, and hit the right button.

The world went black.

I had enough sense not to move right away. The last time I did that, I slammed my head on the inside of the jump tube. But was I back? Had I finally returned to reality?

My answer came quickly. Light crept into my jump tube as the silver disk slipped sideways into the wall. The table slid out of the tube, and all I saw was Loor. She stood over me, looking like an angel that had been sent to my rescue.

"Are we back?" I asked. "For real this time?"

"I believe so," Loor answered.

I hopped off the table and ran out of the cubicle, headed for the Alpha Core. Seated in the control chair was Aja. When she saw me, she jumped out of her chair and threw her arms around me in a huge hug. I half expected her to fly right through me like a ghostly image. But she didn't. She was solid. It was her. The real deal. We were back.

"I never thought you'd get out of there," she said.

I hadn't expected this big welcome, but I wasn't complaining. "What's happening?" I asked.

Aja pulled away from me and sat back in the control chair. I was happy to see she was focused again.

"As soon as Dr. Zetlin left his jump, everything stopped," she explained while pointing to the monitor, which was black. "The pounding stopped too. I think when he ended his jump, the Reality Bug ended with it."

Loor had joined us. "Could it be that easy?" she asked.

Aja hit a few buttons on her console. A data stream appeared on the monitor. She scanned it, then announced, "I think so. Lifelight is back to normal." She turned to me and giggled. "It's over."

"So where is Zetlin?" I asked.

Aja leaped out of her chair and ran into the jump cubicle. The center disk was still closed. Aja hit a few buttons above it, but then hesitated. I could guess what was going through her mind, because I was thinking the same thing. Opening up this jump tube felt like we were unsealing a tomb. Zetlin hadn't been out of there in years. It was exciting and creepy at the same time.

"It's okay," I said, trying to be reassuring. "It's time for him to come out."

Aja nodded, then hit the last button. The silver disk slid back from the center tube, and with a soft hum, the table emerged. The three of us stood together, nervously waiting to get our first view of Dr. Zetlin. The *real* Dr. Zetlin.

Lying on the jump table was an elderly man with closed eyes. He wore the familiar green jumpsuit and had his hands folded in front of him. His skin was pasty white for lack of sun. His head was bald, and he had a scraggly beard. That made sense. He hadn't shaved in three years. There was a definite Rip Van Winkle vibe going on. He even had his round glasses on. I wasn't sure why he needed those in the jump tube, but who am I to judge? It was incredible to think this was the same guy we had just been racing through a fantasy with . . . when he was sixteen years old. The only proof was the red slash mark on the back of his hand, where he had been splashed with venom. This was Dr. Zetlin all right. In the flesh.

For a second I feared he was dead. He sure looked dead. But then he slowly opened his eyes and squinted from the light. After all, his eyes had been closed for a long time.

"My head hurts," he whispered.

I guess he was still hurting from his collision with the web. He began to sit up, so the three of us quickly helped him. The guy felt frail. No big surprise. He was seventy-nine years old and hadn't had any exercise in a while.

"I'm as weak as a kitten," he announced.

We got him up straight, and he took a deep breath. He felt his beard as if it were an alien attachment. He took off his glasses and rubbed his eyes. He then took his first look at all of us. I now recognized the guy we knew from inside the fantasy. He may have been in an old body, but his eyes were the same. He looked at each of us in turn, then asked, "What is the status?"

Aja took a step forward and reported, "We think that when you ended the jump, it destroyed the Reality Bug. There's no sign of it anywhere. And may I add, it's an honor to meet you in person, Dr. Zetlin."

Zetlin looked Aja up and down, then said, "Yeah, whatever."

He slid off the table onto wobbly legs. We all rushed to keep him from toppling over, but he pushed us away.

"I'm a little rusty," he said gruffly. "Not feeble."

We backed off.

Zetlin took a couple of unsteady steps, then stopped, and stood up straight. "I'd forgotten what it was like to be in this body," he explained. With every step he took, he got more sure of himself. He made his way out of the jump cubicle and headed for the Alpha Core. By the time he made it to the control chair, he was looking pretty steady. Suddenly, seventy-nine didn't seem so old anymore.

Zetlin dropped himself into the chair as if he owned it.

Actually, he did. He glanced up at the data on the monitor, looking for something. I'm glad it made sense to him, because to me it was nothing but a jumble of numbers and symbols.

"Killian!" he barked.

Aja ran up to him and stood at attention. "Yes, Doctor?" she said professionally. She was now working for the master.

"You've examined the entire alpha grid, and the main grid?" Zetlin asked.

"Yes," she said. "Lifelight is back online. The jumps are performing normally. I don't see any sign of the Reality Bug. Anywhere."

Slam!

The entire room rocked. It was such a strong, sudden impact, I lost my balance. Loor had to catch me and hold me up.

Slam!

The room was jolted again. I heard something crash to the floor in the jump cubicle. What I saw through the door was impossible, yet there it was. A hole had been blasted into the ceiling beyond. Debris covered the floor. But it wasn't the damage that rocked me. It was what I saw peering down from the hole above.

It was the hollow socket of a giant skeleton head. The bug wasn't dead. It had just broken through to reality.

None of us could move. We were frozen in shock. The head moved away and a second later a massive, black fist slammed into the hole again, smashing it open wider.

I looked back to the control console where the monitor was suddenly going haywire. Numbers flashed by incredibly fast. Aja and Zetlin were furiously hitting buttons, trying to get control.

"Where did it come from?" Aja screamed.

"It must have fled to another part of the grid when my

jump ended," Zetlin said quickly. "But it found its way back."

Oh, yeah, it found its way back, all right.

The pounding continued. The ceiling was collapsing and the hole was growing wider. The monster now started grabbing at the damaged area, ripping up pieces to make its entryway into our world bigger.

Loor glanced around the room, searching for a weapon. But it was futile. There was no weapon any of us could use to stop this thing.

Another crash. I looked into the cubicle to see its fist had broken all the way through. It wasn't going to take this beast very long to tear apart the entire pyramid.

"Look," Aja said, pointing to the data on the monitor. "It's drawing data from all over Veelox. That's how it got so powerful. It's still feeding on the fears of all the jumpers."

"Then stop feeding it!" I shouted.

Aja and Zetlin shot me a look like I was crazy.

"It's feeding itself, Pendragon," Aja answered impatiently. "We don't have a whole lot of say in the matter."

I heard a guttural growl and turned toward the cubicle. What I saw made me forget to breathe. The giant skull had pushed its way down through the hole and was peering at us. Being so close, I could smell its decay. We all watched in stunned fear as flesh began to grow on the skeletal head. Eyes grew from the sockets and oily skin spread out over the face to form features. In seconds, the beast had become a hideous baboon-looking head with white, pupil-less eyes. The monster grunted, and pulled back up into the ceiling. It was about to start its final assault.

If we were going to do something, it had to be now.

"There's gotta be a way!" I argued. "Can't you cut off the power supply?"

"Didn't you hear me? It's coming from every jumper on Veelox," Aja answered.

"So what!" I shouted back. "Shut it down! Shut it all down. If people aren't jumping, the Reality Bug can't feed on their fears!"

"I told you, we can't do that!" Aja shot back. "It's too dangerous!"

"More dangerous than this?" Loor asked calmly.

Boom!

A foot crashed through the ceiling. It was birdlike, with huge saber claws.

"That's why we suspended the grid before," Aja argued. "We can't shut Lifelight down."

"But if we don't stop it, it's going to destroy the pyramid and turn on the rest of Veelox," I yelled. "If it's getting strength from the jumpers, we've got to cut it off!"

"The grid cannot be shut down, Pendragon!" Aja shouted back.

Crash!

The huge bird leg was now kicking at the doorway into the Alpha Core, smashing it wider, opening the portal between fantasy and reality.

"Dr. Zetlin," I screamed. "It's a machine! There's gotta be a way to shut it down."

Zetlin didn't answer. He didn't even look at me. He was hiding something.

"Dr. Zetlin!" I screamed. "Can we shut this down?"

The beast kept kicking at the doorway, cracking it open. Chunks of material flew across the room. Zetlin was hit by a flying particle. It jolted him and made him look up at the horror that was fighting to get at us. To get at Veelox.

"My whole life has been about Lifelight," he said in a daze.

"If I shut it down, my life will have been worthless."

"That means it *can* be shut down?" Aja asked with surprise.

"Dr. Zetlin," Loor said calmly, "your life has not been worthless, and it is not yet over. But unless you do all you can to stop this horror, it *will* be over and you will forever be known as the man who let Veelox die."

Zetlin winced. Loor's words had gotten through to him. But he continued to stare at the beast that was nearly on us.

"Doctor," I said, trying to will him to listen to reason. "If you can do something, you have to do it now."

Zetlin gave me a quick look, then spun back to the control console. He had made a decision. He was shutting down Lifelight.

"What can I do?" Aja asked.

"Nothing," Zetlin said with sadness as he made some rapid-fire entries on the console.

"Will this cut off the data feeding the Reality Bug?" I asked.

"Theoretically," Zetlin shrugged. "But I truly don't know. I've never encountered this situation before."

Yeah, no kidding.

The Reality Bug began mutating again. The giant birdlike leg began to twist and mold until the foot transformed into a repulsive insect head. Most of the head was made up of a round mouth that was ringed with multiple rows of gnashing, pointed teeth. The leg itself grew into a snakelike body.

In this form, the hole from Lifelight was now big enough for the Reality Bug to slither into Veelox.

"Hurry!" I shouted at Zetlin.

Zetlin was calm. He reached around his neck and pulled out a red plastic card on a chain, like the green one Aja had used to suspend the grid.

The Reality Bug dropped farther into the jump chamber.

Its snaky body made wet, squishing sounds as it hit the floor.

Aja, Loor, and I huddled together near the control console as the nasty-looking creature slithered into the Alpha Core, its teeth making a revolting sucking sound as it sought its prey. Us.

Zetlin stayed focused. He jammed the red card into the slot and made quick keystrokes on the control pad.

"Do you need verification?" Aja asked, without taking her eyes off the bug that was slipping closer.

"No," he said sadly. "I have control."

He then reached up to a clear plastic cover that protected a red toggle switch. He flipped the cover up to reveal the switch, and glanced back at the Reality Bug.

The bug opened its round, evil mouth, ready to descend on us.

Zetlin closed his eyes . . . and threw the switch.

The Reality Bug froze. In that single second, it went from a living entity to an immobile statue. It was like a freeze-frame in a movie.

Every light on the control console went dark. It was as simple as that. Lifelight had been turned off.

The four of us stared in wonder at the frozen Reality Bug, waiting for the next move. It stayed in that same, rock-solid position for a moment, then its skin began to change. The entire surface of the beast became a vast series of numbers. It was as if we were looking at the raw data that had been gathered to create the monster. The shape of the creature remained, but every bit of detail was replaced by numbers. Billions of green, glowing computer numbers.

The numbers then began to count down. Each set of digits sped on a freefall to zero. As each numeral reached zero, it disappeared, taking a small chunk of the monster with it. It was like the beast was decaying, bit by bit, number by number. The Reality Bug was being deleted before our eyes. The whole process took no more than thirty seconds. But when it was done, there was nothing left. The only sign that it had ever been there was the gaping hole left in the ceiling of the jump cubicle.

The Reality Bug had been starved to death.

And Lifelight was dead.

VEELOX

The next few days were spent in a blur of activity. Because Lifelight had been shut down, thousands of jumpers had no choice but to leave the pyramid and return to their lives in Rubic City. It was a strange thing to see.

People wandered out of the pyramid, hiding their eyes from the bright sun. Most seemed dazed, as if they weren't sure what they should be doing or where they should go. I saw a few people arguing with phaders, demanding to be put back into their jumps. But the phaders could only shrug helplessly. Lifelight was dead. Whether the people of Veelox liked it or not, they had to deal with real life once again.

While the jumpers had to come to grips with the reality of reality, there were big doings among the people who ran Lifelight. Bottom line was, Lifelight had been shut down and the directors wanted to know why. Most of what happened over the next few days I couldn't take part in, because, well, I didn't belong. But there was a major inquiry and poor Aja was at the center of it. Luckily for her, she had a pretty good ally . . . Dr. Zetlin. Together the two of them faced the directors to answer the tough questions about why Lifelight was no more.

There was nothing Loor or I could do to help, so we went to stay with Evangeline and wait for news. But rather than sit in the quiet old mansion, wondering what was going on at the pyramid, Loor and I took a pedal vehicle and toured Rubic City to watch it come back to life.

It was pretty cool.

The streets were now full of people. Stores reopened for business. Once-grimy windows were washed sparkling clean. People even began to change out of their green jumpsuits to wear normal clothes again.

As we rode through the streets we listened in on people's conversations. Of course the number one topic was Lifelight. People wanted to know what went wrong. But as the hours passed, we began hearing other conversations. People spoke about normal things like wanting to repaint their houses, or when they might expect fresh vegetables at the market, or about how much they missed seeing each other. I could only imagine that the same things were happening all over Veelox.

It was all good. The territory wouldn't be reborn overnight, but it was definitely on its way. As happy as I was for the people of Veelox, this news had much bigger meaning for Loor and me. It meant that Saint Dane had been turned back once again. He thought he was in a no-lose situation. He wasn't.

I have to admit, I was feeling pretty good about myself. Yeah, it was great and important to beat Saint Dane. That's the main thing. But after having been embarrassed on First Earth, I felt that on Veelox I was able to pull the Travelers together and get the best from all of us. Aja was certain she had beaten Saint Dane before I even showed up, and make no mistake, she played a huge part in our victory. Maybe the most important part. But without the help of Loor and myself, it would have been a disaster.

As Loor and I pedaled around the reawakening city, I was actually beginning to accept the idea that maybe I *was* the lead Traveler. I still had no idea why I was chosen for the job, or who did the choosing, but my confidence was starting to grow. I went so far as to think that if I could continue to lead the Travelers the way I did on Veelox, then the ultimate victory over Saint Dane was possible.

I had come a very long way from that night when Uncle Press first brought me to the flume.

Aja didn't return to her house for a couple of days. Evangeline was a wonderful host. She fed us gloid (we avoided the blue like the plague), and made up comfortable rooms for us. It was the first time I had spent with Loor when we weren't in the middle of some crisis.

I didn't hate it.

She told me about her life growing up as a warrior-in-training, and I told her about Stony Brook. Okay, my life wasn't exactly as exciting as hers, but she listened and pretended to be interested. It was a great time. Loor and I had been through some hairy adventures, but we were now connecting on a whole new level. I think they call it "normal." I always had a ton of respect for her. Now I felt as if I had found a friend.

I could have gone on like this forever, but it wasn't meant to be. For on the afternoon of the third day, while the two of us pedaled through a new neighborhood, Loor made an announcement.

"There is nothing more for me to do here, Pendragon," she said. "I need to return to Zadaa."

This hit me out of left field and my thoughts were jumbled. "But, I thought . . . I was hoping . . ."

"What were you hoping?" Loor asked.

I took a breath to get my head together, then said, "I don't see why we should split up. Saint Dane is going to show up again, I guarantee it. It would be better if we were together to deal with whatever he throws at us. Right?"

Loor gave this some thought, then answered, "You are right. We do not know where Saint Dane will surface. But I do know there is trouble on Zadaa. I want to be there and ready."

"Okay, I get that," I said. "But Saint Dane went to a territory called Eelong and Gunny followed him. I think we should go to Eelong."

"I agree," Loor said. "But we do not know for certain where Saint Dane plans to strike next. Yes, he went to Eelong, but Zadaa is on the verge of a civil war. How are we to know which he plans to attack first?"

I couldn't argue with that.

"Go to Eelong," she continued. "I will return to Zadaa. When events come clear, we can always find each other."

I racked my brain trying to come up with reasons for us to stay together, but couldn't undo her logic. What I had to admit to myself was that the real reason I wanted us together was because I didn't want to be alone. Uncle Press was gone, Spader had issues, and Gunny was on Eelong. Even Aja had her hands full here on Veelox. The truth was that if Loor went back to Zadaa, I would be on my own. That scared me.

"Maybe I should go to Zadaa with you," I offered.

"Then what of Eelong?" Loor asked. "Gunny has not returned. I believe you should find him."

Gunny was only supposed to be on Eelong a short time. The plan was for him to get a quick look around and then return to Veelox. He didn't. I got so caught up in Lifelight that I couldn't go looking for him. Loor was right. What had to happen now was obvious. Saint Dane went to Eelong. Gunny followed him. Gunny didn't come back.

I had to go to Eelong.

Without another word of argument, I turned the pedal vehicle and headed for the flume. It was a little trickier dropping into the manhole this time because the street was no longer deserted. We had to wait until nobody was watching, then quickly lift the metal lid and drop into the derelict subway below. A few minutes later the two of us stood at the mouth of the flume. This day had not turned out the way I had expected.

"Say good-bye to Aja for me," Loor said. "And Evangeline."

I nodded. I didn't want to say good-bye to anybody. Especially Loor.

"Thank you for coming to Veelox," I said.

"Gratitude is unnecessary," she declared. "I am a Traveler."

"But I threw you into a pretty nasty situation without a whole lot of warning and . . . you are an amazing person, Loor."

I wanted to hug her, but she wasn't the sentimental type. So I was surprised when she reached forward and touched my cheek. It was a tender gesture. Something I never thought she was capable of.

"I feel the same about you, Pendragon," she said sincerely. "I am glad you are our leader . . . and my friend."

I felt a swell of pride and emotion. I hate to admit this, but my eyes started to tear up. There was no way I was going to let her see that, so I willed myself to get a grip. She backed away and stepped into the flume.

"Zadaa!" she called into the dark tunnel. The flume came alive with light and sound. The far off musical notes were on their way to grab her and take her home. I had to fight the urge to jump in after her. That wouldn't have been cool.

"Find me," was all I said.

"I will," Loor answered.

The gray stone walls melted into crystal as the light grew so bright I had to squint. The last image I saw of Loor was her silhouette. A moment later she was gone.

And I was alone.

I didn't leave for Eelong right away. I needed to know how the Lifelight investigation went. Our mission on Veelox wouldn't be over until all the loose ends were tied up. So rather than jump into the flume, I went back to Evangeline's house.

When I arrived, I was surprised to find Aja sitting at the kitchen table with Evangeline, eating gloid.

"Where's Loor?" was the first thing she asked.

"She went back to Zadaa," I answered. "She asked me to say good-bye to both of you."

Aja nodded and continued eating. She looked tired as she sat there enjoying her gloid, not saying a word. I was dying to know what had happened, but I didn't jump all over her. I knew she would tell me when she was ready.

Evangeline said, "I'll leave you two to talk," and left the room. Uh-oh. I had the feeling that Aja had news, and it wasn't necessarily good.

"There's a public meeting tomorrow," Aja finally said. "The directors are going to announce the findings of their investigation to all of Veelox."

"What did you tell them?" I asked.

"Basically, I lied," Aja admitted. "I said there was a software problem that corrupted the jump data and threatened the safety of the jumpers."

"That wasn't a lie," I said.

Aja sniffed. "No, but it wasn't exactly the whole truth."

"They believed you?" I asked.

"They had to. I had Dr. Zetlin on my side. The directors may be powerful, but they don't mess with the Z."

"So he backed up your story?"

"Every word," Aja quickly answered. "He didn't say anything about the Reality Bug and took full responsibility for shutting down Lifelight."

"And they bought it?" I asked.

"Remember, Pendragon, we were the only ones who saw the Reality Bug, but there were thousands of people all over Veelox whose jumps had gone sour. People were scared. They knew there was trouble."

"What about the damage to the Alpha Core? How did you explain that?"

"We played dumb. To be honest, neither of us could come up with a logical explanation so we told them we didn't know how it happened. They had to believe us because there was no way we could have done the damage ourselves."

"You've been gone three days," I said. "Were they questioning you the whole time?"

"No. Most of the time we spent troubleshooting the grid, checking every possible bit of data to make sure nothing else was corrupted," she answered. "Of course, I was also looking for any sign of the Reality Bug."

"And?"

"It's gone," she said with confidence. "Totally."

"So you're a hero," I said with a smile. "The people of Veelox see you as the coolheaded phader who averted disaster."

"Maybe," she said. She then put her spoon down and sat back in her chair. She didn't take her eyes off me. "What do *you* see me as?"

This was a loaded question. I knew how important this was to her.

"I see you as the Traveler who beat Saint Dane and saved her territory," I answered with authority.

Aja smiled. "With a little help," she said coyly.

"None of us can do it on our own," I reminded her.

Aja nodded. "Did we really do it, Pendragon?" she asked tentatively. "Did we save the territory from Saint Dane?"

"You gotta take a look around Rubic City," I said. "The place is coming alive. You've given them a second chance."

The look on Aja's face said it all. She felt as if her entire life had been about preparing for this challenge. It may not have played out exactly as she'd imagined, but the result was the same. She had succeeded. The look on her face was one of pure relief, and satisfaction.

"So what is the public meeting about?" I asked.

"I think they want to explain to the people what happened," she answered. "People all over Veelox will be watching. Who knows? Maybe they're going to give me a medal."

The big meeting was held early the next morning.

It was all very exciting. Thousands upon thousands of people streamed into the pyramid to gather on the central floor. After getting used to Rubic City as a ghost town, it was amazing to see so many people flowing through the streets, all headed for one place.

I went with Aja and Evangeline. With the huge crowd flooding into the pyramid, it felt like we were going to the Super Bowl. As we walked along the glass corridor of the core, it was eerie to see all of the control stations dark. Not a single monitor or indicator light was lit. We entered the main chamber of the pyramid. It was even more breathtaking now because it was loaded with people. Not only was the main floor packed, but there were people standing on every level above us, looking down at the floor. Everyone was orderly, but there was electricity in the air.

As in the core, all the Lifelight indicator lights were out. The thousands of lights that had marked the jump cubicles were all dark. Seeing this made me believe that Lifelight was truly dead.

Aja led us through the crowd to the center of the pyramid floor, where there was a round stage. It was raised just enough so that everyone could see it. On the stage were fifteen chairs. Aja didn't need to explain. This was where the directors would sit.

"We can go down front," Aja explained. "I'm sort of part of this."

"This is so exciting!" Evangeline exclaimed.

No sooner did we arrive at the platform, than the general buzzing of voices stopped. The show was about to begin. A section of crowd parted for a line of people who were walking to the stage. These people wore yellow jumpsuits and walked in single file. I looked at Aja. She nodded. These were the directors. They were all adults, some with gray hair. They climbed a few steps to the platform and marched in front of the seats.

I saw that the last person in line was Dr. Zetlin. I had to do a double-take because his beard was gone and he didn't look as ghostly white as when he first came out of his jump. He looked almost human, and definitely more like the young guy we raced through the Barbican with . . . plus about sixty years. He glanced down, saw us standing in front, and winked.

All fifteen people sat down, except for one woman who walked to the front of the stage. She looked to be the oldest person of the group, except for Dr. Zetlin, that is. She had short, sandy-colored hair and sharp eyes. The woman surveyed the crowd, making sure to look up to the heights of the pyramid. It was like she was trying to make eye contact with each and every person there. The crowd of thousands went eerily quiet.

"That's Dr. Kree Sever," Aja whispered, "the prime director."

"Is she, like, the boss?" I asked.

"Yes," Aja answered. "You're staying in her house."

Right. I knew that name sounded familiar. This was the woman who was nice enough to let Aja and Evangeline live in her mansion. Now that she was out of Lifelight, I wondered if Aja and Evangeline would have to find a new place to live.

"Welcome to all those who have come here today," Dr. Sever began in a strong voice. "And to those who are watching from distant parts of Veelox."

Her voice was amplified throughout the pyramid. I guessed she had a microphone, which is also how they heard her at remote locations.

"After three days of exhaustive research," she continued, "we, the directors of Lifelight, have come before you in order to explain recent events, and to present the decision we have made regarding the future."

The woman sounded kind of like a politician running for office, rather than a scientist. I think she liked being in front of a crowd.

"We are honored," she continued, "to have with us a man whom we all know, but few have had the privilege to see in person, until today. I'm speaking about none other than the creator of Lifelight himself, the esteemed Dr. Zetlin."

The pyramid broke out in wild applause. It was deafening. Zetlin didn't move. In fact, he looked embarrassed. After five minutes of this standing O, Dr. Sever quieted the crowd and continued, "What better person to explain the confusing events of the last few days, than the one man who knows more about Lifelight than any other? It is my great pleasure to present to you the legendary Dr. Zetlin."

The crowd erupted again. I was betting this kind of applause was happening all over Veelox. Dr. Zetlin slowly rose to his feet, nodded to Dr. Sever, and walked to the front of the stage. He raised his hands to quiet the crowd. Nobody wanted to stop. It took another five minutes before the place finally quieted down.

"My friends," Dr. Zetlin began, "I stand before you today a humbled man. Never, in my wildest imagination, could I have foreseen the events that happened here and across Veelox."

I looked around to see that every eye was focused on Dr. Zetlin. He was a legend. No, he was a superstar. For these people to see him in person must have been pretty awesome.

"I'm not speaking of the problems that were encountered with Lifelight that prompted me to shut it down," he continued. "I am speaking of the state my beloved Veelox has fallen into because of my invention. For that, I am ashamed."

A slight nervous murmur went through the crowd. I don't think they were expecting to hear bad news.

"I designed Lifelight to be a celebration of life, not a substitute," he continued. "Living an ideal existence is difficult to resist. I know. I am just as guilty as any of you. My intent was to stay inside the perfect world of my choosing, never to be bothered with the challenges of reality again. But it is a fool's paradise. We have become a society of individuals whose only concern is our own comfort, pleasure, and amusement. By embracing Lifelight, we have turned our backs on our cities, on our neighbors, and worst of all, on our loved ones."

There were thousands of people in the pyramid, but they

were as silent as a painting. It was kind of creepy.

"I believe the problems we encountered a few days ago may very well prove to be our salvation," Zetlin said. "Corrupt data had infected the grid, disrupting many of the jumps."

Corrupt data? That was a nice way of describing Aja's Reality Bug.

"Thanks to the quick and fearless actions taken by Aja Killian, the senior phader in Rubic City, the problem was contained."

Dr. Zetlin pointed to Aja. The crowd applauded. Aja stepped forward and raised her hand in acknowledgment. When the applause died down, Zetlin continued, "But in order to purge the grid of this corrupt data, I made the difficult decision to shut down Lifelight entirely. We were doubly successful. The grid was cleared, and Veelox was given a second chance."

Dr. Zetlin was doing an excellent job. He was not only explaining to the people of Veelox why Lifelight had been shut down, he was telling them why it was a good thing.

"It is my wish that until we can learn how best to utilize Lifelight for the good of all of Veelox, that we not even consider bringing it back online."

Another concerned murmur went through the crowd. That last statement surprised them.

"And I pledge to work with the directors, and with all of you, to find a balance that will bring as much joy from living in the reality of Veelox, as we found in the fantasy of Lifelight. Thank you."

The people all applauded, but not with the same enthusiasm as when Zetlin was first introduced. I don't think they liked the idea of not being able to jump back into Lifelight. But I figured they didn't have a choice. They were going to have to learn how to deal with reality again, whether they liked it or not.

Dr. Zetlin sat down at his place and gave us another look, and a nod. I smiled at him. It must have been tough to stand in front of the entire population of Veelox and announce that his life's work was flawed. But I truly believed that with his help, the people of Veelox would one day figure out how to get the best from Lifelight, without giving up their real lives.

Dr. Sever then stood and addressed the crowd, saying, "We have much to thank Dr. Zetlin for. His genius and vision not only created the wonder that is Lifelight, but he rescued Veelox from a potentially disastrous incident by making the hard decision to shut down the grid. Moreover, he and his colleague, Aja Killian, have worked tirelessly to ensure that the problem that nearly destroyed Lifelight is no more."

That was followed by a round of applause.

Sever continued, "We respect Dr. Zetlin's considered opinions as to the future of Veelox and of Lifelight. We, the directors agree that we must work to find the proper use of Lifelight in our ever changing society. However . . ."

However? She let the word hang. I had the feeling that something was coming, and it wasn't going to be good.

"We disagree with Dr. Zetlin in how to go about that. We feel that the only possible way to best understand how to utilize Lifelight is to explore those options . . . while it is fully operational."

Uh-oh. An excited buzz went through the crowd. Zetlin jumped to his feet in anger.

"No!" he shouted. "That defeats the purpose! If people go back into their jumps, we'll be right back where we were!"

"With all due respect, Doctor, we don't think so," Sever said with a superior attitude. "Lessons have been learned. It is the decision of the directors to bring Lifelight back into operation immediately."

Sever waved her hand. It was a signal. Suddenly the Lifelight pyramid sprang back to life. People looked around in wonder as the operational lights came back on. It was like Christmas had come to Veelox as the pyramid was once again alive with the multiple lights of Lifelight. Once the people realized what was happening, they cheered. They actually cheered. It was like their team had just pulled out a surprise victory in sudden death.

"What is happening?" Evangeline asked, confused.

"Did you know about this?" I screamed at Aja to be heard over the crowd.

"No!" she answered. "When they wanted us to troubleshoot the grid, I didn't think they wanted to go back online!"

People started pushing to get off the floor. The once orderly crowd had been charged with energy. None of them wanted to be left out. They were all hurrying to get back to a jump cubicle and reenter their fantasies.

"We've gotta stop them!" I pleaded.

Aja jumped up on to the stage and ran to Dr. Zetlin.

"Do something!" she begged.

Zetlin said, "If we can get to the Alpha Core before the jumps begin, I can take control."

Aja grabbed him by the hand and pulled him off the stage.

"Hurry!" Evangeline shouted.

We left her by the stage and the three of us pushed our way through the surging crowd, back to the Alpha Core.

"What are you going to do?" I asked Zetlin as we fought our way through.

"They know the origin code now, so they have control," he panted. "I can override the phaders, but only if they haven't gotten the grid back online yet. Once that happens, I won't be able to control anything from the Alpha Core. We'll be at the mercy of whatever the directors want."

"Stop those people!" Dr. Sever ordered from the stage, pointing at us.

A group of phaders started after us, but they were having just as much trouble getting through the massive crowd as we were. I looked up into the pyramid and saw jump cubicle doors opening up all over. Some people pushed others out of the way to get in first. Young people took advantage of the weak and pulled them out of the cubicles to take it for themselves. It was a musical chairs, nightmare riot. Nobody wanted to be left out. They didn't care what Zetlin had said. They didn't care about the future of Veelox. They were addicted to their own fantasies and would do anything to get back in.

We had to take control and shut down Lifelight, for good.

We finally made it back into the core. Down the long corridor of glass I saw phaders taking their places in the control chairs, preparing to begin the jumps. But there was still time. The control stations were still dark.

Aja ran to the door leading to the Alpha Core and inserted her green card. The door didn't open. She tried it again; it stayed closed.

"Your card has been disallowed," came a voice from behind us. It was Dr. Sever. She walked up to us with several strong-arm-looking phaders.

"Your actions over the last few days are still suspect, Aja," Sever said. "Until we complete a full investigation, we can't allow you access to Lifelight."

"Dr. Sever," Zetlin said calmly, "please, give it some time. You hold the future of Veelox in your hands. Won't you please wait?"

"I'm sorry Dr. Zetlin," she said with a smile. "I'm afraid it's too late. Every pyramid on Veelox is moments away from going back online."

As if on cue, the core came to life. The millions of indicator lights flashed once again as images appeared on the thousands of monitors. The jumpers were back in their fantasies. Dr. Zetlin closed his eyes and dropped his head in defeat.

I was stunned. Moments before, I felt sure we had pulled Veelox back from the brink of collapse. But now the territory was in as much danger as the moment I first arrived. No, it was worse. Aja's Reality Bug had failed. Veelox had reached a critical turning point, and was pushed the wrong way.

There was no other way to say it:

Saint Dane had won.

"This is all thanks to you, Dr. Zetlin," Sever said. "You got rid of that nasty little bug quite nicely. Now we can return to normal."

Bug? Did she say bug? Nobody knew about the bug except . . .

Dr. Sever then leaned down to me and whispered in my ear. There was a subtle change in her voice. To everyone else she still sounded like Dr. Kree Sever, prime director of Lifelight. But the cold tone of her voice said something very different to me.

"How does it feel, Pendragon?" she said with an iciness that made me shiver. "The first territory of Halla is mine."

☻ SECOND EARTH ☻

Bobby's image disappeared abruptly.

Mark and Courtney were left staring at nothing. They had left the Sherwood house and returned to the privacy of Courtney's father's basement workshop to watch the journal.

"That's it?" Courtney asked, upset. "He stopped recording his journal right there? That's not fair!"

Before Mark could offer an opinion, another image flickered to life. The recording wasn't yet complete. Courtney and Mark watched in wonder as the 3-D projection formed in front of them.

"There's more!" Mark exclaimed.

But the image that appeared before them wasn't Bobby's. It was Aja Killian's.

"Hello to you, Mark Dimond and Courtney Chetwynde," Aja began. "My name is Aja Killian, the Traveler from Veelox. Pendragon has told me all about you two, and that he trusts you both very much. This is why I am completing his journal for him."

Aja took off her small yellow glasses and rubbed her eyes. She looked tired.

"Pendragon is gone," she continued. "He left Veelox shortly after Lifelight was brought back online. His destination was the territory of Eelong to search for the Traveler named Gunny. I feel as if my duty is to stay here to do all I can to keep Veelox from falling further into decay. I have the help of Dr. Zetlin, but I'm afraid we are fighting a losing battle. The directors have all returned to Lifelight. Most of the phaders and vedders have also left on their own jumps. There aren't enough people left in reality to monitor the jumps, let alone care for their real lives. The pull of fantasy was just too strong. Saint Dane has won. Veelox is near dead."

Aja was holding back tears.

"Pendragon asked me to finish his journal so you would know the state of Veelox, and to send it on to you. It is the least I can do. I feel as if I have failed the territory, failed the Travelers, and failed Pendragon. My only hope is that we can stop Saint Dane on the other territories, so that the only casualty of this evil war will be Veelox. My home."

She swallowed hard and then said, "In my heart, I know this is not the way it was meant to be. This is the end of Bobby Pendragon's Journal Number Fifteen. Good-bye."

Aja's image disappeared. The journal, and Bobby's adventure on Veelox, was now complete. Mark picked up the small silver projector and stared at it, as if hoping there were one last bit of news that would leap from it to give this story a happy ending.

There wasn't.

"So what does this mean?" Courtney asked nervously. "Saint Dane always said that as soon as the first domino fell, the others would fall easily."

"I-I really don't know," Mark said somberly.

Courtney jumped to her feet and paced. "I hate this!" she

exclaimed. "I feel totally helpless. All this stuff is going on and all we can do is sit around and hear about it like a couple of nimrods."

This made Mark smile. "I thought you only wanted to worry about school and soccer and normal life?" he asked.

Courtney stopped and looked straight at Mark. "The hell with soccer," she declared. "I thought we were supposed to be acolytes?"

"Now you're talking!" declared Mark.

Early the next morning the two were back sitting on the couch in the apartment of Tom Dorney. Together they watched all three of Bobby's journals from Veelox. Afterward they described to Dorney what happened at the Sherwood house with the quigs and the stunning appearance of a flume.

"If that doesn't say we're ready to be acolytes," Courtney concluded, "then tell us what will."

Dorney scratched his chin. He then hoisted himself up out of his easy chair, grumbled, and shuffled into the kitchen.

"Does this mean he's pulling our chain again?" Courtney asked.

Mark shrugged. "Give him a chance."

Dorney shuffled back into the living room with a glass of water. He didn't offer any to Mark or Courtney. The guy wasn't exactly a great host. He sat back down in his chair, spilling some water on his lap.

Courtney rolled her eyes, but neither said anything. The ball was still in Dorney's court.

"You're going to get messages," he said calmly. "Sometimes from Travelers, other times from acolytes on other territories."

Mark and Courtney sat up straight. Things had just gotten very interesting.

Courtney asked, "What kind of—"

"Let me speak," Dorney snapped.

Courtney shut up.

"They'll come to you through the ring," Dorney continued. "Like the message I sent to you. They may tell you that a Traveler will be arriving and that you need to provide Second Earth clothing. That's usually the case. But Pendragon may need something specific."

"Like when you had to take care of Press's motorcycle," Mark jumped in. He couldn't resist. He was getting excited.

"Yes," Dorney answered, then took a sip of water.

"What about the quigs?" Courtney asked.

"Protect yourself," Dorney answered. "There's no magic wand you can wave to make them go away. They aren't always around, but you have to be prepared when they are. I'll tell you one thing, they're afraid of the flumes. Don't ask me why. When a flume activates, you won't see any quigs around."

"Can we contact other acolytes?" Mark asked.

"Look at your ring," Dorney ordered.

Mark held up his hand so he and Courtney could see the heavy ring with the dark gray stone surrounded by the odd, carved symbols.

"Each of those symbols represents a territory," Dorney explained. "There are ten in all."

"Ten territories," Mark repeated softly, as if he had just been given the secret of the ages.

"If you know the name of an acolyte," Dorney continued, "take the ring off and call out that name. The symbol from their territory will activate the ring and you can send a message."

"So if I took off the ring and said: 'Evangeline,' the symbol for Veelox would open up the ring and I could send a note to her?"

"That's right."

"Is that how we should get in touch with you?" Mark asked.

"You could," Dorney answered. "Or you could pick up the telephone."

"Oh. Right," Mark said, feeling dumb.

"Can we contact Bobby through the ring?" Courtney asked.

"No," was Dorney's quick answer. "Only the acolytes. Travelers don't need to be bothered with our problems."

"Is there anything else?" Mark asked.

Dorney took some time to think about that answer. He looked out the window, his mind seeming to fly a million miles away. Courtney and Mark looked at each other. They weren't sure if Dorney had tuned them out, or was having deep thoughts.

"You are the acolytes from Second Earth now," Dorney finally said. "With Press gone, I'm no longer needed. It may be an easy job compared to what the Travelers do, but I think you'll agree it's an important one."

"We do. Absolutely. Yessir," they assured him.

Dorney looked back out the window with a frown on his face.

"Is there something you're not telling us?" Courtney asked.

Dorney sighed and said, "It's just a feeling."

"What?" demanded Courtney.

"I don't know," Dorney said anxiously. "I didn't like what I heard about Veelox."

"Yeah, no kidding," Courtney said.

Dorney looked at them. For the first time since they'd met him, Mark and Courtney actually felt as if he were softening up a bit.

"What I mean to say is," Dorney continued, "be careful. Saint Dane has finally had a victory, and there's no telling what's next. From this point on, I can't guarantee that the old rules still apply."

◆　　　◆　　　◆

Mark and Courtney took the train back to Stony Brook with that ominous warning still on their minds. Neither said much. They both had to get their minds around the fact that they now were officially acolytes. The only question was, what next?

"I want to go to the flume," Mark announced.

"Why?" Courtney asked.

"We'll bring some of our clothes to leave there."

"But nobody told us they needed clothes," Courtney countered.

"I know. Just thinking ahead."

The two fell silent for a moment, then Courtney said, "That's just an excuse to go there, isn't it?"

Mark was ready to argue, but decided not to. He nodded. "I guess I just want to see it again. To prove it's real."

"I hear you," Courtney said. "I do too."

When they got off the train in Connecticut, they both went home and gathered up a bunch of clothes they thought a Traveler from some distant territory might need to blend in on Second Earth. Courtney picked out a bunch of simple, functional things like jeans, T-shirts, a sweater, socks, hiking boots, and underwear. She debated about bringing one of her bras, but figured that was overkill.

Mark gathered up a bunch of clothes that were totally out of style. It wasn't like he had a choice. That's all Mark had. He found sweatshirts with logos that meant nothing, no-name jeans, and generic sneakers. Style was not something Mark concerned himself with. He hoped the Travelers wouldn't either.

Mark brought one other thing from his house that he hoped he wouldn't need. He borrowed the sharp poker from his parents' fireplace toolset. It was woefully inadequate to deal with an attacking quig-dog, but it was all he could find.

Mark and Courtney met in front of the gates to the Sherwood

house, each with a loaded backpack. They didn't say a word to each other as they walked around the side of the property to the tree that would give them access to the yard. Once over the wall, Mark held the fireplace poker, ready to defend them against a rampaging quig. Courtney saw that Mark's hand was shaking like Jell-O, so she gently took the poker from him. If either of them had a chance of fighting off a charging quig, it would be Courtney.

But they didn't run into any of the yellow-eyed beasts. They made it through the house, down to the basement, and into the root cellar that held the flume. No problem. They emptied their backpacks and neatly folded the clothes in a pile. Courtney looked at some of the geek clothes Mark brought, and chuckled.

"Oh, yeah, Bobby's gonna blend right in wearing a bright yellow hooded sweatshirt with a red logo that says, *Cool Dude!*

"Give me a break," Mark said defensively. "It's my favorite sweatshirt."

Courtney shook her head in disbelief. When they were finished, they both gazed into the dark tunnel to the territories. They stood together silently, each with their own thoughts as to what the future might hold.

"I'm scared and excited at the same time," Mark finally said.

"Really," Courtney added. "I want to be part of this, but it's scary not knowing what to expect."

"Can you imagine being a Traveler?" Mark asked while stepping into the mouth of the tunnel.

"Well, no," Courtney answered, "to be honest."

"Well, I've thought about it a lot!" Mark declared. "It would be awesome, stepping into a flume and announcing the next amazing place you'd like to go."

"It's pretty unbelievable," Courtney agreed.

"Look at this thing!" Mark said, scanning the flume. "It's kinda like having a jet fighter."

"It is?" Courtney asked with a chuckle.

"Yeah. You know what it's capable of, but have no idea what to do to make it go."

"It's not all that hard," Courtney said, "if you're a Traveler."

Mark smiled, turned to face the dark tunnel, and shouted out: *"Eelong!"*

He looked back to Courtney and said, "Could you imagine if—"

"Mark!" Courtney shouted.

Mark saw the terrified look on Courtney's face. She was looking deeper into the flume. What was back there? Mark spun quickly to see the impossible.

The flume was coming to life!

Mark jumped out of the tunnel and ran to Courtney. The two backed away toward the far wall of the root cellar, hugging each other in fear.

"D-Did I do that?" Mark asked.

"Or is somebody coming?" Courtney added.

The light appeared from the depths of the tunnel. The musical notes were faint at first but quickly grew louder. The rocky walls began to crackle and groan. Mark and Courtney could only stare in awe.

"I-I don't really want to go to Eelong," Mark cried. Courtney held him tighter, ready to hold him back if she felt him getting pulled into the flume.

The gray walls melted into glorious crystal as the bright light and sound arrived at the mouth. Mark and Courtney had to squint. They didn't dare put their hands in front of their eyes, though. They were too busy hanging on to each other.

They soon realized they weren't about to be pulled into the tunnel. Something else was headed their way. Through the bright light they saw a tall, dark silhouette walk out of the flume. Oddly, unlike everything they had ever heard about how the flumes worked, once the passenger arrived, the sparkling light didn't go away. The jangle of music stayed too. Whatever was happening now, it was out of the ordinary. Mark and Courtney opened their eyes. What they saw made them want to close them again, because standing in the mouth of the flume was Saint Dane.

He had arrived on Second Earth.

The two had never seen him before, but there was no mistaking the tall demon with the long gray hair, piercing blue eyes, and dark clothes. The light behind him continued to burn and the walls remained crystal. This had never happened before, at least not that Mark or Courtney knew.

"And so it begins," Saint Dane cackled. "The walls are beginning to crack. The power that once was, will no longer be. It is a whole new game, with new rules."

Saint Dane roared out a laugh. With a sudden burst of light from deep inside the flume, his hair caught fire! His long gray mane exploded in dancing flames, burning right down to his skull. Mark and Courtney watched in horror as the flames reflected in his demonic eyes. Saint Dane laughed the whole while, as if he were enjoying it.

Mark and Courtney didn't move. If Courtney had her wits about her, she would have felt that Mark was trembling.

The fire burned away all of Saint Dane's hair, leaving him bald, with angry red streaks that looked like inflamed veins running from the back of his head to his forehead. His eyes had changed too. The steely blue color had gone nearly white. He fixed those intense eyes on the two new acolytes and smiled. He then tossed a dirty, cloth bag at their feet.

"A present for Pendragon," Saint Dane hissed. "Be sure he gets it, won't you?" Saint Dane took a step back into the light of the flume. "What was meant to be, is no longer," he announced.

Saint Dane then began to transform. His body turned liquid and he leaned over to put his hands on the ground. At the same time his body mutated into that of a huge, jungle cat. It was the size of a lion, but speckled with black spots. The big cat then snarled at Mark and Courtney, and leaped into the flume. An instant later the light swept him up and disappeared into the depths. The music faded away, the crystal walls turned back to stone, and the light shrank to a pin spot.

But it didn't disappear entirely.

Before Mark and Courtney could get their heads back together, the light began to grow again. The music became louder and the walls went crystal again.

"My brain is exploding," Mark uttered.

A second later the bright light flashed at the mouth of the tunnel and deposited another passenger.

"Bobby!" Mark and Courtney shouted, and ran to him. They threw their arms around him in fear and relief. The tunnel then returned to its normal, quiet state.

But Bobby wasn't there to give them comfort. "What happened?" he demanded.

Mark and Courtney pulled away. Both of them were supercharged with adrenaline. "It was Saint Dane!" Courtney shouted. "His hair burned! It was horrible!"

"He said the rules have ch-changed, Bobby," Mark stuttered. "What did he m-mean?"

Bobby took a step back from the others. Mark and Courtney felt him tense up.

"What did you do?" Bobby demanded. It sounded like he was scolding them.

"Do?" Courtney said. "We didn't do anything!"

Both Mark and Courtney focused on Bobby. He was wearing rags. His feet were bare, his hair was a mess and he had a coating of dirt all over his body. He didn't smell so hot either.

"What happened to you?" Mark asked.

"It doesn't matter!" Bobby shouted back. He was just as charged up as they were. "Did you activate the flume?"

Mark and Courtney looked to each other. It took a while for them to register what Bobby was asking. Finally Mark said, "Uh, I g-guess so. I said 'Eelong'—"

"No!" Bobby shouted in frustration.

"What's the matter?" Courtney asked. "We're not Travelers. We can't control the flume."

"Things have changed," Bobby shouted out. "Saint Dane's power is growing. He's got his first territory. It's all about changing the nature of things."

"So . . . that means we can use the flumes?" Courtney asked.

"Don't!" Bobby demanded. "It'll just make things worse."

Mark then remembered something. He ran back to the door of the root cellar and picked up the bag Saint Dane had thrown at them.

"He said this was for you," Mark said, handing the bag to Bobby.

Bobby took it like it was the last thing in the world he wanted. He turned the rotten bag upside down, and something fell onto the floor.

Courtney screamed. Mark took a step back, not believing his eyes. Bobby stood firm, staring at the floor, his jaw muscles clenching.

Lying at his feet was a human hand. It was large and dark skinned. As gruesome as this was, there was something else about it that made it nearly unbearable to look at. On its finger, was a Traveler ring.

"Gunny," Bobby whispered in agony.

The three stood there, unable to move. Finally Bobby took a brave breath, picked up the hand and jammed it into the bag.

"Bobby, what's happening?" Courtney asked.

"You'll know when I send my journal," he said. He then turned back and ran into the mouth of the flume, clutching the bag with Gunny's hand. "*Eelong!*" he called out. The flume sprang back to life. The light and music started on their way back for him.

Mark was nearly in tears.

"Is Gunny all right?" he asked.

"He's alive," Bobby said. "But I don't know for how long."

"Tell us what to do!" Courtney pleaded.

"Nothing," Bobby answered. "Wait for my journal. And whatever you do, do *not* activate the flume. That's exactly what Saint Dane wants, and it is not the way things were meant to be."

With a final flash of light and jumble of notes, Bobby was swept up and into the flume, leaving his two friends alone.

Mark Dimond was ready for an adventure.

He was about to get one.

to be continued

Where will Bobby Pendragon's adventures take him next? Here is a look at Pendragon: Book Five: BLACK WATER

EELONG

I looked to the base of the tree and saw the small opening that I had crawled out of. It was so small compared to this monster tree that if I didn't know it was there, I'd have missed it. Sure enough, carved in the bark just above the opening was the star symbol that marked it as a gate to the flume. Unbelievable. Now the hanging vines in the cavern below made sense. They were the root system of this immense tree. I walked along the base, running my hand across the rough bark. You could live in this tree . . . with all of your friends and their families, and still have room for a Keebler cookie factory. I took a step back, looked up, and laughed. The impossible kept proving itself to be possible. What was I going to see next?

The answer came quickly, and it wasn't a good one.

I felt something hit the back of my leg. I looked down and instantly wished I hadn't because lying in the ground next to my leg was an arm. A bloody, human arm. I quickly looked up in the direction it came from and felt like the wind was knocked out of me. If the big tree hadn't been there to catch me, I would have fallen back on my butt.

Standing ten yards away from me was a beast. It was like nothing I had ever seen before. The first thing I thought of was . . . dinosaur. It stood upright on two legs, with a long, thick tail that whipped back and forth angrily. It looked to be around seven feet tall, with powerful arms, and hands and feet that were three-finger talons. Its entire body was bright green, like a lizard, with scales covering it. But what I couldn't take my eyes off of was its head: It was reptilian with a snoutlike nose. It had bright green hair that swept back from its forehead and fell halfway down its back. But most hideous of all was its mouth. It looked like a shark mouth, with multiple rows of sharp teeth that were all about tearing flesh.

And that's exactly what it was doing, because clasped in its jaws was another human arm. Blood ran into the beast's mouth and down its chin. If I hadn't been so scared, I would have gotten sick. We held eye contact. I could feel this monster sizing me up. Its eyes were red and angry. Without looking away, it closed its jaws, crunching the arm like a dry twig. The sound made my stomach turn. The monster flipped out a green tongue and sucked the shattered arm into its mouth. One gulp later, the arm was gone. Swallowed. Bone and all. Gross. It turned back to me and broke out into a bloody grin.

I was next on the menu.

Welcome to Eelong.

It was a quig. It had to be. Every territory had its own

quigs that prowled the flumes. They were somehow put there by Saint Dane, but I haven't figured out how that happened, yet. On Denduron they were prehistoric-looking bears. On Cloral they were killer sharks. Zadaa had snakes and the Earth territories had vicious dogs. Veelox was strangely quig-free, but I think that's because Saint Dane was already done with that territory by the time I showed up. Now it was looking like the quigs on Eelong were mutant, dinosaur-like reptiles. One thing was certain, it was a meat eater. Human meat. The bloody arm at my feet was proof of that. I didn't want to know where the rest of the body might be.

The beast locked its red eyes on me and drew back its lips, revealing yet another row of pointed teeth. Swell. Its long green hair spiked out, like an angry cat. It hissed, and I got a whiff of something nasty. It was sending out a disgusting scent that smelled like rotten fish. This thing was going to pounce, and it was going to hurt. I was totally defenseless. Worse, the giant tree was behind me. It was like being trapped in a dead end. I took a tentative step to my right. The beast mirrored my move. I took a step back. So did the beast. It felt like I was playing basketball and this monster was playing defense. Only, it didn't want to steal the ball. It wanted to steal my head.

That's when I saw a flicker of movement to my left. I looked quickly, afraid that another quig might be circling in. But what I saw was my salvation. Poking his head out from the hole at the base of the tree was a person! At least I thought it was a person. The guy had straggly hair and a long beard. I only saw him for an instant, because he popped his head back into the hole like a scared turtle. He must have poked his nose out, seen the quig, and changed his mind about coming out. Good thinking. I wished I had done the same. But seeing him reminded me that I had an escape route. The trick would be to get to it before the quig got to me.

The two of us stood facing each other like gunslingers. I hoped it didn't realize that I didn't have a gun and wasn't prepared to sling anything. I knew that if I bolted for the hole, the quig would leap at me, and it would all be over except for the chewing. All I needed was a couple of seconds for a head start. But how?

An idea came to me. A hideous idea. If I hadn't been so desperate, there was no way I would have been able to pull it off. But if there was one thing I learned since becoming a Traveler it was that self-preservation is a pretty strong motivator. Without taking another second to talk myself out of it, I slowly bent my knees and reached for the ground. I saw the hair on the back of the beast grow higher. It was waiting to see what I was going to do. I cautiously picked up the bloody arm that lay at my feet. I know, how gross can you get? I grabbed the arm at the elbow trying not to think about what it was. When I touched it, I almost gagged because it was still warm. Whoever it belonged to had been using it not long before. I had to push that thought away or I'd have lost my lunch . . . and probably my life along with it. As soon as I picked up the arm, the rotten smell from the beast grew stronger. I think the sight of the bloody arm was getting it psyched, like blood in the water does to a shark. That was okay. It meant I had a chance. I slowly stood back up and held the dismembered arm out to my side. The beast's red eyes followed it like it was some tasty morsel. Gross.

The next few seconds were critical. They meant the difference between buying myself the time I'd need to get to safety and experiencing total failure, which meant the quig would eat me and then get the arm anyway. It all depended on how stupid this quig was. I waved the arm, tantalizing the beast, which stayed focused on it. The horrible smell grew stronger. Oh yeah, the quig wanted the arm, all right. I reared back and flung the arm off to my right.

The beast went for it. The instant it moved I bolted for the hole like a base runner stealing second when the pitcher goes into his windup. I could only hope the quig would keep going for the arm and not decide I was more interesting. I didn't stop to look back, because every second counted. I ran for the hole and dove inside, headfirst. I hit the ground and scrambled to crawl inside. I thought I had made it, when I heard a bellowing howl from outside and a burning sensation in my leg. The beast was back and it had me by the ankle! It was too big to follow me inside, but that wouldn't matter if it pulled me back out. I kicked for all I was worth and felt its sharp talons rake across my skin. No way was I giving up. The beast was going to have to work for its supper. With one hard kick, I yanked my leg free of its grip. I was loose! I tried to bend my leg and get it inside, but couldn't. A quick look back showed me that one of its talons had caught in the braided twine that held my cloth boot on. It still had me!

I frantically wriggled my foot, trying to pull it out of the boot. I actually cursed myself for doing such a good job tying the twine with half hitches and square knots I had learned in Boy Scouts. Why did I have to do such a good job? I expected to feel the pain from the monster's jaws clamping down on my leg, biting me like some giant Buffalo wing, but that didn't stop me from squirming to get away. Then suddenly I felt something snap. It wasn't my leg, I'm glad to say. The beast's claw must have severed the twine, because my foot slipped out of the cloth shoe. I quickly tucked my knees up to my chest to keep my feet out of reach. Looking back, I saw the long, green, scaly arm of the monster reaching inside the hole, groping to get at me. Its sharp talons whipped back and forth blindly, finding nothing but air and a few dangling vines. It was pretty charged up, and the rotten-fish smell got so bad, it made me gag. But the beast had lost. With a final bellow of frustration, it pulled its arm out and gave up. I suppose it went back and got the arm as a consolation prize.

I lay inside the dark space, breathing hard, trying to get my head back together. Now that I was safe, the reality of what had happened finally hit me. I had picked up a human arm and used it as bait to save myself from getting eaten. How disgusting was that? I looked down at my leg and saw three long scrapes that ran from my knee to my ankle. I gingerly touched them and found, luckily, that they weren't very deep. They would just sting for a while. Eelong was shaping up to be a nasty place.

I had to find another way out of this tree. I wasn't about to stick my head out of that hole. For all I knew, Little Godzilla was waiting outside, savoring its arm-snack and waiting me out. As much as I wanted to flume out of there, it wasn't an option. I had to get away from this tree, away from the quigs, and find Gunny. So I got on my hands and knees and started to crawl around, pushing my way through the dangling vines, looking for another escape route. I figured there had to be one. If not, where did the guy come from who poked his head out of the hole? He sure wasn't down in the flume-cavern when I was there. And for that matter, who *was* that guy?

I passed by the hole that led down to the flume and continued crawling with one hand out in front in case I hit a dead end. But that dead end never came. I kept crawling deeper and deeper into the tree. What I first thought was a small space was actually a tunnel that brought me into the very core of this behemoth tree. As I crawled along I saw that it was actually getting lighter. Of course that didn't make sense, but when did something silly like "making sense" matter? I soon felt confidant enough that I no longer held my hand out in front of me. Up ahead, I saw light at the end of the tunnel. Literally. I hadn't been crawling for that long, so there was no way I had gone all the way through to the other side of the tree. It was way too big for that. But I didn't stop to wonder what to expect, I'd see for myself soon enough.

When I reached the mouth of the tunnel, I crawled out and stood up to view an incredible sight. The tree was hollow. Or at least, this part of it was. I found myself in a huge space that had been carved out of the core of the immense tree. I was kidding before about being able to live in this tree along with cookie-making elves, but this room proved it was possible. The walls were made of, well, wood. Duh. Light came in through cracks that ran up and down and all around, like veins. I'm not sure if the hollowing-out was natural or done by hand. If it was by hand, then it had to have been done a long time ago because everything looked aged, with bits of green moss growing everywhere. Looking straight up was like looking into the mouth of the flume. It disappeared into blackness. There was no ceiling. For all I knew, this tree was hollow all the way to the top. I saw multiple levels and ledges that led to other tunnels, like the one I just crawled out of. I wasn't sure how you got from one level to the next. I suppose you could climb the vines that clung to the walls, but that would be tough for anybody but Spiderman.

Now that I was safe from the quig outside, I began to wonder who the people of Eelong were. By the look of that hairy guy who poked his head out of the hole, they didn't exactly seem to be a race of advanced mathematicians. I figured they were a primitive, tribal society who lived in these incredible trees. If they were more advanced than that, they certainly didn't prove it with the clothes they made. Besides, I had yet to see any sign of tools or buildings or anything else you'd expect to see from a society that had advanced beyond the stone age. I was beginning to think I would have to deal with cavemen. Or tree-men.

"Hello?" I called out, my voice echoing. "Anybody here?" All I got back was the gentle groaning of the tree. I glanced around, trying to figure out which tunnel I'd take to find another way out . . . when I was shoved from behind with such force, it nearly knocked me off my feet.

I spun around quickly and came face-to-face with the guy who had peeked out of the hole before. He was short, probably no more than five feet tall. His hair was long and tangled. So was his beard. In fact, I think his head hair was tangled up in his beard hair—not a good look. His skin was white and filthy, and he wore the same kind of rags that I did. The guy was crouched down low and breathing heavily. A line of drool ran from his mouth and down his

gnarly beard. He may have looked human, but he was acting more like a wild animal.

"H-hello," I said, trying to calm him. I held my hand
out the way you hold your hand out to a dog when you
want to show you're not a threat. "My name is . . ."

Before I could say another word, my arm was grabbed
and yanked to the side. I looked in surprise to see that a
vine had been thrown around my arm like a lasso.
Holding the other end was another person, looking just as
hairy and gnarly as the first. I opened my mouth to say
something, when another lasso of vine was thrown
around my shoulders from behind. It pulled snug around
me, locking my arms into my sides. I looked back to see a
third guy yanking it tight. Another vine whipped around
my ankles. This one was pulled so hard, it yanked my feet
out from under me. I hit the ground, the wind knocked
out of me.

"Wait . . . wait . . ." I gasped, trying to get air. I wanted
to use my powers of Traveler mind-persuasion, but things
were happening so fast, I couldn't think straight. "I'm a
friend!" was all I could get out. I know, not exactly convincing, but what else could I say? A second later it didn't
matter because one of the guys leapt at me and jammed a
fistful of cloth into my mouth, making me gag. Not good.
I didn't think any of these dudes knew the Heimlich
maneuver. I figured they must have seen me as a threat. An
invader. I needed to show them I meant no harm, because
they seemed ready to put some serious hurt on me.

The guy who jammed the cloth in my mouth sat on my
chest, staring down at me. I was pinned, unable to move.
I looked up into his eyes, and saw something that made
any hope I had of reasoning with these people fly out the

window. I don't know why I didn't realize it before, but I didn't. Now it was too late. The lizard-beast that attacked me outside may have been deadly. It may have been trying to eat me. But there was one thing that it wasn't. Its eyes should have told me. Its eyes were red. Quigs didn't have red eyes. Quigs had yellow eyes. And as I looked up at the guy who was sitting on my chest, I saw that his eyes were yellow. And vicious. He opened his mouth into a grotesque smile to reveal rows of sharp, bloodstained teeth. A thin line of drool ran down his lips and fell onto my cheek.

In that one instant, the horrible truth hit me: the quigs on Eelong were human.

PENDRAGON

Journal of an Adventure Through Time and Space

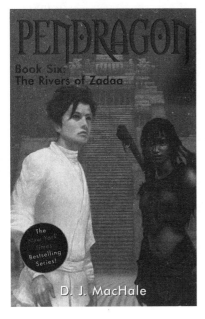

Bobby Pendragon continues his pursuit of Saint Dane in **The Rivers of Zadaa**

Bobby Pendragon has followed Saint Dane to the territory of Zadaa, where Saint Dane's influence has fueled the fire of discontent between two warring tribes: the Rokador and the Batu. This is also the territory where the Traveler Loor lives, and together she and Bobby work to thwart Saint Dane's efforts to destroy Zadaa.

D. J. MacHale is a writer, director, and producer of several popular television series and movies, including *29 Down*; *Are You Afraid of the Dark?*; *Encyclopedia Brown, Boy Detective*; *Tower of Terror*; and *Ghostwriter*. Pendragon, his first book series, became an instant hit that included a *New York Times* bestseller. He lives in Southern California with his wife, Evangeline; his daughter, Keaton; a golden retriever, Maggie; and a kitten, Kaboodle.